For Joan

There is a tide in the affairs of men,
Which, taken at the flood, leads on to fortune;
Omitted, all the voyage of their lives
Is bound in shallows and in miseries.

Shakespeare - Julius Caesar, Act IV scene III

Chapter 1 – 1590

It was a warm September day, the kind of day Hugh O'Neill loved most. He stood at the open window of his castle and looked at the surrounding countryside, O'Neill country since time immemorial. Seven miles distant, he could just make out the great lake glistening in the sunlight and the meandering line of the Blackwater that flowed into it. The dark green of the vast wood encircling it stood out and between there and the castle, the sun reflected up at him from the many small lochs. Yellow fields of ripe corn nestled lazily in the valleys between the small, scrubby hills and the heavy boglands. His ancestors had chosen the site well, being strategically located at the intersection of ten roads.

The sight, this day, did not evoke in him the usual sense of contentment. He was glad, however, to see that along all the routes people were making their way towards his castle. His summons to the leaders of the O'Neill clan and all his subsidiary clans, the O'Hagans, Quinns, O'Hanlons, MacMahons, O'Cahans, Devlins, Magennis and O'Donnellys, had not gone unheeded. It would be a difficult day, a day that would involve great personal loss, but to loss he was no stranger. It would also be a day when he would deal with one of the great obstacles of his life once and for all.

Of all the people whom he had summoned, there was one couple, the O'Hagans, whose arrival he most anxiously awaited. They were the foster parents of his two sons, Hugh Óg and Henry. He had sent for the O'Hagans and his sons the previous night, on learning from the physician that his wife, Siobhán, wouldn't recover. They should be here by now, he thought. His sons were only four and six, very young to be separated from their natural parents, but it was the Irish way.

He, himself, had been fostered by the O'Hagans for five years at the same age and it had done him no harm, indeed, it had done him much good and he had loved the O'Hagans ever since. He remembered how, in later years, he had cried when the then English Lord Deputy, Sir Henry Sidney, had recommended to his father that an English family foster him so that he would learn their language and ways. Yet, right from the first day with the Hovendens, who farmed some of his grandparents' land in County Offaly, just inside the English Pale, he had felt totally at home with these people. His foster father, Giles, he had learnt to respect but not love because of his intense reserve. However, he had come to love his foster mother, Ellen, a large hearted, gentle English woman and his foster brothers, Henry, Piers,

Richard and Walter. Indeed, he trusted them as much as his natural brothers and was indebted to them for the help they had given him over the years. No, all things considered, fostering made perfect sense; it cultivated life long friendships, which could be called upon in times of need. It had been hard on Siobhán though, she hadn't wanted to see her babies leave but she knew it had to be done.

Where were they, he thought. They must get here soon. Siobhán was fading fast. He wondered if he should cancel the gathering that he had called, but then dismissed the notion. He had to deal with the matter and the sooner the better. People would have travelled a long way to answer his summons. The Queen's letters, demanding that he turn over Hugh McShane, were becoming more impatient and angry. He was not going to acquiesce. He finally had his enemy at his mercy and he was not going to let him escape.

He heard someone enter the room behind him and he turned to see Rose, his daughter by his first wife, Aoife. She looked drawn and tired and yet that very tiredness gave her beauty an extra dimension, evoking a feeling of protection in Hugh. She was tall and thin, with long blonde hair, which she wore up in the Irish fashion, plaited and wrapped in a rolled linen headcloth. Her eyes were blue and her skin fair, the very cast of her mother. She was dressed in the Irish fashion, the traditional women's léine that reached to her ankles, over which she wore a long, red tunic with laced bodice and a string of amber beads around her neck. Her husband would not allow her or any of his people imitate the English in any manner, and even if he was incarcerated in Dublin Castle for the last three years, she still obeyed his wishes. O'Neill, however, was dressed like an English Earl, bearded and coifed in a manner that would have befitted the court of the Queen herself. He was on the Queen's Council of Ireland, the only Irishman so honoured. He had visited Elizabeth's court, met the queen and had impressed her greatly.

Looking at Rose, O'Neill thought that there was none of him in her. He was of medium height, dark haired, brown eyed and powerfully built. He was just in his fortieth year, but in the absolute peak of physical condition. If the need arose, for weeks on end he could spend all his hours on horseback, and the need had arisen much in the last few months. He then smiled to himself, recognising his error; there might well be no physical trace of him in Rose, but in temperament, she and he were very alike, slow to anger, with a keen government over impatience and impetuous action. She was a good daughter, all a father could ask for, kind, obedient, helpful and loving. She had stayed at her stepmother's side every night for the last week, a companion in her lonely sickness.

He found himself wondering, not for the first time, how such a child as Rose could have resulted from the tempestuous marriage that he and Aoife had endured. He had been fortunate that Aoife had rejected Rose when she left him, just as she had rejected everything else to do with him. If she had taken their daughter with her, he would never have come to know her. It was Aoife's loss that she never maintained contact with her. In spite of the situation, he smiled at his daughter. He wanted to lighten her sadness. "Well," he asked, "how is she?"

"Not good father. The physician said that I must fetch you. It won't be long now." At this she began to cry.

Hugh went and put his arm around her frail shoulders, "Come daughter. We must go to her."

They both walked in silence from the chamber and mounted the turret stairs to the bedchamber where Siobhán lay. They entered the darkened place and saw her, pale and thin after her long illness. She was dark haired with enormous green eyes which, because of her extreme gauntness, dominated the rest of her face. Her visage was haggard, the cheek and chin bones very pronounced. She had been an attractive woman but now was so reduced in appearance, that her present form mocked grimly at what had once been. The physician, who had been sitting beside the bed, removed himself to a settle at the casement. Hugh struggled to control the internal turmoil that he was feeling.

Siobhán turned in the bed to see him and with a huge effort raised herself onto her elbow. Beads of perspiration stippled her forehead. Rose took a cloth and wiped them away.

"Have they come, Henry and Hugh Óg?"

Hugh shook his head, "Not yet, but they can't be long now."

"Oh, Hugh," she cried, "I don't think I can last much longer. I'm so tired. I'd like to have seen them one more time."

"Now, don't be foolish. You'll recover. You'll see the boys grow into men," Hugh said.

Siobhán shook her head. "I'm so tired Hugh. So very tired. I know that if I allow myself sleep, I'll never wake up again. Promise me you'll look after them. If you marry again, you'll not forget them."

"How could I do that?" Hugh asked with barely concealed agitation.

Rose, upset at Siobhán's torment, took her hand. "Whist," she said softly, "you know that could never happen. See how he's looked after me. Could any girl have a better father?"

"Yes, yes you're right, I'm being foolish," Siobhán murmured as she feebly squeezed Rose's hand. "And you've been a good daughter to him and a good friend to me." She turned her attention again to Hugh. "There is something else that I want you to promise, Hugh, not just for me but for your daughter, Rose. Hugh Roe, you must get him out of Dublin Castle. I cannot endure the thought of his being locked away there."

"Yes, I promise, but you know of all my endeavours on his account. I've written to the Privy Council and the Queen about him often enough," Hugh replied.

Summoning all her remaining power, Siobhán raised herself up even further. "You've done the Queen and the English many favours and this is the way they repay you, by locking up your wife's brother, your daughter's husband! Rose might as well be a widow. And you know Hugh Roe has committed no crime other than being an O'Donnell!" Siobhán shook her head weakly. "It's been three years, Hugh! Three years that he has rotted away in that prison. And what do the English do in his absence? They set a sheriff in O'Donnell lands. And because my father is old and weak, they encourage strife and rebellion against him. Donnell O'Donnell is, even now, trying to take the O'Donnell Chieftainship from him. And the only person left to stop him is my mother."

Hugh observed without a trace of irony, "But what a mother. I'd rather face ten Donnells than Ineen Dubh."

Siobhán continued in greater agitation. "My mother says you cannot reason with the English. They only understand one thing, the sword and God forgive me, but as I lie here on my death bed, I think she's right."

Alarmed at her mounting disquiet, Rose tried to quell her, but Siobhán struggled on. "What about the hostages from the Spanish Armada? My father handed them over to the Lord Deputy for Hugh Roe's release. He reneged then and again after the inducement of £2,000 my mother later paid him."

She was suddenly convulsed by a bout of coughing and fell back onto the bed. Just then, there was a gentle knock on the door and a tall, handsome man opened it and looked into the sombre interior. It was Hugh's English foster brother, Henry Hovendon. He looked at Hugh, a question in his eyes. Hugh nodded that he should wait outside. Henry withdrew silently.

The bout of coughing passed, yet Siobhán still gasped for breath. When she had regained it, she looked into Hugh's eyes. "It is my dying wish. You've to promise me to do whatever it takes to have him released. Do you promise?"

"Yes, yes I do," Hugh answered.

Siobhán sighed, "Very well. I'm going to rest now. I'm tired, very tired." She sank low onto the bed and within seconds had fallen into a fitful sleep. Hugh signalled to Rose to join him outside. The physician returned to his place beside the bed. They quietly left, closing the door gently behind them.

Henry Hovendon, who had been sitting on a settle in the passageway, rose as they emerged. He waited as Hugh talked to his daughter. "Rose, I must deal with some business that cannot wait. Will you stay with her?"

"Of course I will, Father."

"Make sure the keening women are on hand. She must have a proper wake. Send for the priest again, he might comfort her. It's for times like these that I hide him here. Go back to her now. I must go."

"Yes, Father."

Hugh turned to Henry and the two of them started down the turret staircase.

"Well, Henry, have they all come?"

"Most of them."

"And any word from Hugh McShane's brother, Conn?"

"No, no word. It looks like he's prepared to desert him rather than deal with you."

"So be it."

"And you're still ready to go through with what you've planned?"

Hugh sighed and shrugged his shoulders. "There is no other way. It must be done. Otherwise, the McShanes will thwart every step I'll ever take. They'll never be happy to live under my rule, believing that one of them should be Chief as their father, Shane, was. Now that the useless drunkard who holds the title recognises Conn as his successor, the people might go over to them. There have already been too many defections."

Henry couldn't understand Hugh's obsession with the hereditary Chieftainship of the O'Neill clan, which Turlough, his cousin, now held. To Henry, it represented the past, a time and a way of life that was gone. This was the brave, new world. Elizabethan soldiers and sailors were carving out names and fortunes for themselves all over. Yes, Turlough O'Neill held the title of The O'Neill, the elected leader of the O'Neill clan, but he was old and sick and couldn't live much longer. Hugh already had undermined his support and had more adherents than him. More importantly, it was Hugh whom the Queen had recognised as the leader of the O'Neills, raising him to the title of Earl of Tyrone, a title that Turlough had sought for many years. The Gaelic title should be ignored, Henry thought. Hugh had a much more prestigious one now. Henry voiced his thoughts. "Why do you still value that Gaelic title? You know the Queen has forbidden it. You're the Earl of Tyrone, a much nobler and greater honour."

"You're still an ignorant Englishman, Henry. Here in Ulster, an Earldom means nothing. It has no history. The O'Neill title dates back to before Christ. That's what matters here and when Turlough finally dies, I'm going to make sure that I take it."

"The Queen won't tolerate it."

"I'll tell her that if I don't take it, someone else will and create mischief."

The two had, by now, left the dim recesses of the castle and entered into the mellow September sun. The castle was a typical Irish one, consisting of a four storied stone keep, surrounded by a courtyard and a collection of miscellaneous buildings. It was protected by an outside wall of stone, through which the gates opened into the surrounding countryside. The buildings were mainly made of earth, with thatched roofs, housing the stables and stores. As they passed into the courtyard, they noticed Richard Hovendon approaching. He bore a striking resemblance to his brother, Henry, having the same good looks, blond hair and beard. Henry had just time enough to warn Hugh before Richard reached them. "Richard is not too happy about your plans."

Hugh beamed at Richard. "I'm glad to see you, brother, and I am indebted for what you did for me against Hugh McShane and his Scot mercenaries."

Hugh had been attacked by Hugh McShane, who had returned to Ulster after one and a half years of banishment in Scotland, fortified with an army of 2000 native mercenaries. He had recruited them from his mother's clan, the MacLeans, and he and Turlough O'Neill had defeated Hugh in battle. Just as the situation was in extremity, Richard Hovendon had mounted a counter attack on western Tyrone, the power base of the McShanes. At his disposal was a large force of Scot mercenaries and English soldiers from the Pale. This force had burned a number of fortifications, including Dunnalong Castle, and wreaked havoc in Hugh McShane's countryside, luring him back to defend his territory. Then, luck favoured O'Neill when McShane fell into the hands of his ally, Maguire, who delivered him up.

Richard nodded. "You're welcome brother. You know that you can count on my support when I can justify my actions to Her Majesty. However, I'm worried about what you plan on doing here today. Will you not reconsider? As well as upsetting the Queen, it will make it much more difficult to raise mercenaries again in Scotland. McShane's mother, Catherine McLean, is a powerful woman. She could deny you access to your traditional source of troops."

"I cannot reconsider, Richard," O'Neill said simply.

Richard sighed. "Well, then I would prefer not to stay and witness the proceedings. May I go with your blessing?"

O'Neill smiled. "Of course you may. I won't forget your services these last few weeks."

Richard nodded and smiled wanly. "What are brothers for if not to help each other?" He turned and walked swiftly towards the stables, nodding to his men to follow him. O'Neill turned to Henry. "Perhaps you should leave too?"

"No, Hugh, I'll stay," Hovendon replied without hesitation.

They walked together, out through the gates of the castle, to the large field, located in a hollow just beyond the walls. There, tables were set out in the sunshine, bearing the ample food and drink, which Hugh had provided. All around the castle were scattered the dwellings of his workers. Not being freemen, these were not invited to partake in the proceedings, so they stood at their doorways and watched. O'Neill and Hovendon ignored them as they walked briskly down the hill. "Are they bringing Hugh McShane out?" Hugh asked.

"Yes. I told them to have him ready. See, they are now bringing him forth."

Hugh looked back towards the gate of the castle and saw the tall, proud figure, which he recognised immediately, standing on the back of a cart that was being escorted by fifty of his best men. He turned back towards the crowd of summoned clients who were standing in loose knots around the trestle tables. He could sense their mood. Normally the plentiful victuals would have engendered a cheery humour, but there was an air of tension and apprehension in them today. Some of them resented the tone of his summons. They were all free men, not like the landless labourers or churls. They knew of O'Neill's defeat by Turlough and Hugh McShane, and some of them now doubted the wisdom of adhering to Hugh's cause. The rest were firmly in his camp and would never desert him. They were his own people, the people around Dungannon who had supported his father and brother, before their murder by Shane, Hugh McShane's father. Both Hugh O'Neill and the McShanes had been too young to take the prized Gaelic title on Shane's death and Turlough O'Neill, a distant cousin, had been elected The O'Neill. Now, at last, Hugh could smell the title for himself. If he proceeded boldly, he could finally achieve the goal that he had worked towards all his life.

Hugh stood on a little hill, under a thorn bush and looked at the assembled crowd. Henry stood behind him. In raiment, they stood apart from all the others who were dressed and wore their hair in the Irish style - long, with a glib combed down over their foreheads to eyebrow length. The cart with the prisoner and its escort pulled up beside O'Neill. Just then, Richard Hovendon and his retinue galloped out of the castle gates and headed south. O'Neill waited until the noise of the galloping soldiers died away. He observed the reaction of the crowd as they recognised the prisoner who stood proudly gazing at them from the cart. Both his arms and legs were bound and one of O'Neill's captains, Pedro Blanco, a Spaniard from the Great Armada who had remained with him after being shipwrecked in Ireland, stood by his side.

There was a noose around McShane's neck and the rope was coiled on the bottom of the cart. A murmur ran through the crowd. Some of those present smiled in satisfaction, but others looked disquieted. When the sound of the departing horses had finally receded, O'Neill held up his hand for silence.

"I have called you here today to witness my dealings with Hugh Gaveloch McShane. As you all know, he has been, for many a year, causing murder and destruction in this province. He has brought with him to Ulster many thousands of Scottish mercenaries, to spoil our country and ravish our women, refusing to recognise our laws."

At this, McShane angrily interrupted, "I will never recognise your law! Why should anyone recognise a blacksmith's grandson as..."

O'Neill nodded to Blanco who tightened the noose and stopped McShane's speech in mid flow. O'Neill stared at the assembled crowd who looked back at him unflinchingly. Hugh had guessed that his prisoner would allude to that worn theme. It was one of the taunts he had come to terms with over the years and it no longer had any power to wound him. It had been different when he was younger, but he was not going to give McShane an opportunity to speak of it now. In any case, everyone present knew how O'Neill's grandmother, Alison Kelly, had married a blacksmith and borne a son, Mathew, whom her lover, Conn O'Neill, The O'Neill and First Earl of Tyrone, had recognised as his own. Conn had nominated Mathew as his heir to the Earldom. His eldest, legitimate son, Shane, not accepting his disinheritance, waged war on Mathew, inheriting The O'Neill title through the popular wish of the people. But the Queen never granted him the Earldom. Hugh knew that Shane's five sons were regarded as the legitimate heirs by many of the people and were popular because of their hatred of the English. Of the five, the Queen's men held Henry and Art, he would now deal with Hugh and was at peace with Brian. So that only left Conn.

O'Neill continued, "We cannot continue warring constantly with one another. What about all the widows and orphans, the cost to the countryside, the famine that stalks our land as the crops are burned in the fields? I see an Ulster that is at peace with itself, where from one end to the other, people can leave their doors open without any risk of thieves stealing the little they have."

At these sentiments, some of O'Neill's closest allies in the crowd nodded their heads in agreement. The majority, however, remained motionless, wondering where all this was leading.

"I want it to be possible for people to leave their cattle out over night, once again, as it was in my grandfather's time. We need unwavering, central authority to make ourselves strong, strong enough to protect our homesteads and way of life."

At this, a murmur of approval arose from O'Neill's allies.

"There is only one way to achieve this. Murderers and those who breach the peace must be dealt with. Those who murder, must pay for their crimes. Those who kill and kill persistently, must in turn be killed if they will not desist."

This time, a rumble of disquiet ran through the crowd. Under Brehon Law, which was the Irish system of law for thousands of years, murderers were not killed but instead were made pay a fine of blood money to the family of the murdered victim. What use was there in killing another person, when by allowing him live, he could do something useful for the injured family by paying money to the widow or orphans of the victim? The same treatment was true for thieves. They were made repay the value of what they had stolen. There were no jails in Ulster, there was no need of them. Jails were an English custom and one despised by the Irish.

O'Neill had expected this reaction and continued, ignoring their disapproval. "I have made peace with McShane's brother, Brian. He has accepted my leadership and in return, I have guaranteed him my protection. I have written to Conn Mac Shane and offered to spare this man's life, if both he and Conn submit to my government. I gave Conn fourteen days to ratify the agreement and those fourteen days ran out two days ago. He said that he'd rather see his brother hang, than submit to me."

An ugly murmur ran through the crowd.

Hugh held up his hand for silence. "I will give Hugh McShane one more chance to reconsider his position and pledge his allegiance to my rule."

He motioned to Blanco to release the noose, which was tight around the prisoner's throat. He removed it and McShane took a number of deep breaths. When he had regained his equanimity, he looked around at the gathered crowd. Slowly, he looked into the faces of the people that he recognised. He then addressed them. "I will never recognise this impostor, this usurper, this English loving toady as anything other than the low born bastard that he is. What is more, I know that there is not one Ulster man that would dare hang a McShane in cold blood. An act like that would be recorded for all of history, as one of the vilest ever perpetrated by an Irishman and I know that you would not stand here and see a Spanish outcast or an English mercenary carry out such a crime before your eyes."

O'Neill bounded onto the cart beside him and took the noose in his hands. Again, he addressed the crowd who had quietened on seeing him act thus. "I would not ask anyone to do that which I would not be prepared to do myself," he said. He attempted to put the noose over McShane who began to struggle. Up until this point, the latter had not believed that he was in any danger. He had thought that O'Neill had wished only to shame him in front of the assembled freemen. A deadly hush fell over the crowd, no one moved and the air was still. Suddenly, the silence was rent by the keening of mourners from the castle. Siobhán was dead.

Loss, though expected, hardened Hugh's heart. McShane's movements were restricted by the ropes binding his arms and feet, but he jerked his head from side to side, evading the noose. Blanco caught him by the shoulders and kept him still while O'Neill slipped the loop over his head and tightened the knot. Then, he took the rope and threw it over a thick branch high up on the thorn tree. Hugh jumped from the cart, pulled the rope tightly and secured it to one of the branches near the bottom of the tree. He worked fast, wrapping it around the branch several times, ensuring that it was secure. McShane could no longer talk as the rope was so strained that he had to stand on tiptoe in an effort to breathe. The only sound that could be heard was the keening, which echoed across the fields, lending the proceedings a macabre eeriness at odds with the warm sunshine.

O'Neill walked around to the horse, which was tethered to the cart. He hit its rump and it moved forwards, pulling the vehicle from under the prisoner who stumbled off its end. The fall was not enough to break his neck, but he hung motionless and for a few seconds, swayed gently in the light breeze. Slowly, his face suffused with redness and his mouth opened and shut, unable to draw any air into his lungs, like a fish cast from water. His eyes protruded from their sockets, staring wildly. His body became a paroxysm of reflexes, gyrating, flexing and unflexing as he desperately tried to inhale. In the stillness of the crowd, the keening of the women from the castle seemed to become louder, dominating the countryside. The birds stopped singing. McShane lost control of his bladder and his innards voided themselves.

His frantic, grotesque dance with death continued another two minutes, in total, just over five, which seemed like five long hours to the assembled multitude. Finally, the body reached limp inertia and swayed in the breeze again, as before. His face had now turned the blue of death and O'Neill motioned to Pedro to cut him down. Blanco reversed the cart underneath the swaying body and the toes grated along its boards. He climbed its side and, taking out his knife, cut through the rope. The lifeless form collapsed into the cart with a sickening thud. O'Neill addressed Pedro. "See that you dispose of it where no one will find it." Pedro nodded and, taking the reins of the horse, spurred it into movement.

The cart trundled off in the same direction that Richard Hovendon had taken. The crowd was still, quiet and sullen. O'Neill turned away from them and headed back to the castle. He had rid himself of one of his most dangerous enemies and, at the same time, had made a point to all of them that would make them think before they might desert him in the future. Now, he had to see about burying his wife.

In Monaghan Castle, three of the most important Irish officials of Queen Elizabeth's administration had come together for a meeting to discuss the future of Ulster. Sir Henry Bagenal, Chief Commissioner of Ulster and Marshal of the Queen's army in Ireland, at thirty-eight, was the youngest man of those present. He had ridden from his home in Newry to be at the gathering. His title as Chief Commissioner of Ulster was mainly honorary, as the Queen's writ did not run in the vast majority of that province, which still held to its Gaelic ways and customs.

Bagenal had been born in Ulster. His father, Nicholas Bagenal, had fled from Newcastle-upon-Lyme in Staffordshire in 1542, his name defamed because of his part in a manslaughter there. Though he had been of humble origins, he had, through loyal service to the Queen in subduing the natives, managed to build up a reasonable estate in Newry, located on the eastern coast of Ulster. There, he evicted the monks from their Cistercian Abbey and converted their fine buildings into his own abode.

On the death of Shane O'Neill, Nicholas managed to extend his influence over the neighbouring Irish lords of Magennis and O'Hanlon. He thus removed them from the orbit of The O'Neill Chieftaincy and brought them under his protection, ensuring that they paid their protection money to him and not to The O'Neill. The Queen appointed him Marshal of her forces in Ireland, a post that he held until his declining health had forced him to hand over the title to his son, Henry. Nicholas had died shortly afterwards and Henry had taken charge of the family's fortunes. Now, McMahon's lands in Monaghan were to be confiscated and Henry was determined to have his share.

Sir William Fitzwilliam, Lord Deputy of Ireland, had called the meeting. He sat at the head of the table. He was now in his sixty-fourth year and in his second term as Lord Deputy. His previous term had been in the 1570s, for a period of four years. He had been reinstated in 1588, the year of the Great Armada, even though his military experience had been limited to what little action he had seen in Ireland. His greatest boast was that he had been governor of Fotheringay at the time of the execution of Mary Queen of Scots. He had known keen financial trouble and the second appointment as Lord Deputy couldn't have come at a better time.

After the wrecking of the Spanish Armada on the coast of Ireland, he had travelled the country's length and breadth to get his hands on some of the treasure that the boats were said to have carried. But the only profit he made from the shipwrecks, was the sale of hostages back to Spain. Nevertheless, he soon found other sources of income. As head of the Commission of Leases, Wards and Liveries, he was able to retain most of the fines for himself. Crown rents and payments for pardons could also be pocketed and he could also sell sheriffs' offices for a tidy sum. He had arrived in Monaghan with three hundred troops earlier in the week to carry out the trial of Hugh Roe McMahon, Chief of the McMahons, and ruler of the county of Monaghan. He knew that there was profit to be a made out of this business, before this matter was concluded.

From the west, the Governor of Connaught, Sir Richard Bingham, had made the journey to guarantee his share of the spoils. Bingham had been born in Dorset and from his youth, had been trained in military service. He had served in Scotland, assisted at the Battle of Lepanto against the Turks, saw service in France, the Netherlands and in Ireland, before being rewarded by the Queen when appointed to his present position, some six years previously. He was of very small stature, barely five foot in height, with a narrow face, accentuated by a pointed, neatly trimmed beard. Now, in his sixty-second year, he had lost none of his zeal for taming the Irish with the sword. In the six years since his appointment, he had earned for himself the title, "Flail of Connaught" owing to the brutal methods he had used to quell that province. Now, he wished to spread his influence into Ulster and to conquer O'Donnell's Donegal and Maguire's Monaghan.

When Bagenal was seated, Fitzwilliam opened the meeting. "I have called you here because I have decided that it is time that we went about civilising Ulster and winning it for the Queen. It has been too long left in its unruly state and all fugitives from our rule can fly thither and receive sanctuary from Her Majesty's justice. It is also the fount of all rebellion in the country. I intend making a start with Monaghan and to use this settlement as a model for the reduction of all of Ulster."

Bingham and Bagenal smiled. They smelt blood and profit.

"And how do you intend going about that laudable task?" Bingham asked.

"First we hang McMahon." Fitzwilliam paused to see what effect his words would have on his two guests.

"The trial hasn't taken place yet. How can you be sure of its outcome?" Bagenal asked.

Fitzwilliam smiled. "Why, what other verdict can the jury ordain? Is he not guilty? Did he not surrender his lands to Her Majesty and did she not regrant them to him, on the understanding that he follow English law? And yet what does he do? He seeks to continue collecting his customary dues from his old under-lord, Ever Mac Conn MacMahon. And what does he do when Ever tells him that he's now the Queen's loyal subject, paying her rent and under her protection? He attacks him and wastes his country."

Bingham concurred. "Yes. They are all happy to secure their titles from the crown and to guarantee the inheritance for their offspring, but they still want to keep their traditional rents."

"But we have promised their sublords protection against regional overlords. We must render that protection. We must break the power of each and every Chief in Ulster and we will start with McMahon. Once we destroy the Chiefs and their hold over the people, we can then introduce English law and language," Fitzwilliam answered.

Still, Bagenal wasn't convinced. He had lived among the Irish all his life and he reckoned that he understood them better than either of the other two men. "How can you be sure of the result of the trial? Is he not being tried in his own country?" he queried.

Fitzwilliam responded, "Firstly, the jury, which drew up the indictment, was composed of soldiers rather than freeholders of the country and secondly, the jury is made up of four soldiers and nine gentlemen. The soldiers, naturally, are allowed come and go as they please. McMahon's countrymen, however, are my guests, well hardly guests, as I have kept them without food for the last twenty-four hours. They have all been chosen with great care. McMahon has wronged each of them in the past. Yet, they are slow to condemn him to death, fearing the odium of their fellow countrymen. Still, I have made it very clear to them that they will not be freed until they are prepared to find him guilty."

Bingham interjected, "This arrangement serves our cause well."

Fitzwilliam continued in satisfaction. "Yes, and the best part of it is that I received eight hundred cattle from McMahon, in return for making him Chief a few months ago." All three broke into laughter.

When the merriment subsided, Bagenal cleared his throat and asked the one question that interested him above all others.

"And how are his lands to be divided?"

"I have given that a lot of thought," Fitzwilliam replied. "Gaelic society draws its strength from the overlordship of the Chief, his military power coming from sublords who supply him with soldiers. The Chieftainship goes to the strongest candidate, which of course leads to wars of succession. We must make a major assault on the class structure of Gaelic society. I propose to divide the territory amongst the chief Lords of the country and to give freeholders the land they farm, as their own, eradicating the necessity for supplying military support to the Chief."

Neither Bingham nor Bagenal relished aspects of this proposal. "But what about our soldiers? Are they not deserving of some reward for their many years' service? Why, Henry is entitled to his share!" Bingham argued.

Bagenal appreciated Bingham's intervention on his behalf. They had an informal understanding; Bingham's area of influence would be western Ulster, whereas eastern Ulster was to be his.

"And Henry shall have his share," Fitzwilliam answered. "But there is no point in taking too much. Henry must enjoy what he acquires and hold it in peace and profit. We must raise up some of the Irish, make them hold what they have from Her Majesty, recognising that it is theirs and their descendants for all time, provided that they remain loyal to their benevolent Queen. They shall, of course, pay her rent for her protection. We shall have them fighting her wars yet!"

Bagenal was now content that he was extending his territory. He had found his progress in eastern Tyrone stymied at every turn by O'Neill who replaced Bagenal's client Chiefs with his own. The McMahon Chieftain was one of O'Neill's underlords. He would not be happy with developments.

"And what about Tyrone? He will want a share at the very least," he added.

Fitzwilliam laughed. "He has become far too powerful in the last few years. It is time that we brought his inordinate pride down to size. He shall get nothing. We shall gradually undermine his strength. Then, when we have stripped away the branches, we shall lay the axe to the base of the tree itself and bring the whole crashing to the ground."

Bingham enquired, "And what of me? I have conquered Mayo and Leitrim for the Queen, taken Sligo Castle and driven O'Reilly out of Cavan. All Connaught is now at peace, except for those Connaught men who have fled into western Ulster and who are a destabilising influence on their home province. They receive help and encouragement from the O'Donnells and Maguires. Do I have a free hand to deal with the problem as I see fit?"

Bagenal chuckled. He knew Bingham's free hand, goad the Irish into rebellion and then proclaim them traitors and confiscate their lands. Once the land was in the Queen's possession, she usually didn't worry about the means that got it there. It was best to make sure that there were no survivors, if possible. It led to less record keeping and less likelihood of complaints to the Privy Council in London.

Fitzwilliam nodded. He also knew Bingham's free hand and how he would operate. "Be patient. The O'Donnells fight among themselves and weaken their strength. If Donnell O'Donnell wins the Chieftainship, then we will have a man with whom we can do business. You continue to aid him?"

"Yes. I have installed the sheriff, Captain Willis, in Donegal and sent Captain Connill to help him," Bingham responded.

"Good. Concentrate on Maguire for now," Fitzwilliam replied.

Bingham nodded contentedly. The meeting had gone as he had hoped. The previous Deputy, Perrot, had not approved of his methods. He had thought that the Irish should have equal rights before the law, as had all Englishmen. Fitzwilliam, Bagenal and he had engineered Perrot's downfall and now he was lodged in the Tower of London, under sentence of death. Yes, the final subjugation of this God forsaken country could now happen. The Irish would be taught their place. A question came to his mind. "And you Sir William? What will your reward be for all the good work that you have done here?"

Fitzwilliam replied, "There are a lot of freeholders and chief Lords in McMahon's country. Let us just say, that the division of the property will be dependant on the inducements, which I get from each. There is nothing wrong with a little private enterprise, once Her Majesty also gains from the transactions."

Bingham concurred. "Quite right, Sir William. Well, is our business finished?"

Fitzwilliam rose from the table. "Yes, what about a stoup of wine? Will you join me in my chamber? "

Bingham and Bagenal both rose. "Certainly," Bagenal replied, while Bingham nodded his assent. He would flail the Ulster men into obedience as he had the men of Connaught. This was what he was destined to do. They both followed Fitzwilliam to the door where he paused and turned back to face them.

"I do hope that you will stay for the hanging, tomorrow," he said.

Bagenal nodded and Bingham answered, "I never miss a good hanging myself and any day one of those Irish Chiefs hang, is a very good day indeed."

The O'Donnell's land of Tirconnell was situated on the north western seaboard of Ireland, the second most powerful Lordship in Ulster, after O'Neill's Tyrone. The Laggan district, on the River Foyle, contained some of the best land in Ireland and the long Donegal coastline, more than compensated for the rest of the area that was mostly mountainous, unproductive terrain. Tirconnell had always fostered strong trading links with England, Scotland and the Continent, the main export being fish. In times of peace, the Donegal men prospered, but this was not one of those times. On the eastern side of Teelin Bay, two rival armies faced each other to contest the O'Donnell Chieftainship

Donough Mac Sweeney, the leader of O'Donnell's Gallowglasses cursed his bad luck. His Chief, The O'Donnell, had not ordered him to war; rather it had been his Chief's wife, Ineen Dubh. What was shameful for a Gallowglass to admit was that he had been afraid to ignore her summons.

Ineen Dubh, the Black Daughter, was the nickname of Finola, daughter of James McDonald of the Isles in Scotland. She had been brought up at the Court of the Stuarts of Scotland and had come to Ireland in 1569 to marry Hugh O'Donnell, the O'Donnell Chieftain. The ties between the Scottish Highlands and Ireland were deep and strong. They both spoke the same language as a result of a fifth century Irish invasion of, and settlement in Argyll and the Scottish highlands. There was still constant travel back and forth across the narrow seas, which separated the two countries and Scottish mercenaries were hired by the Irish to help carry out their wars. Another factor uniting the Scots and the Irish was a hatred of the English and the recent kidnapping and imprisonment of her son, Hugh Roe, augmented Ineen Dubh's loathing.

She had married a much older man and now, when she needed his help, his health failed. In her forty-seventh year, she found herself on the side of a hill, surrounded by her personal bodyguard of Scot mercenaries. She had assembled a host of soldiers to fight Donnell O'Donnell's army in order to retain the Chieftainship for her husband, Hugh. Hugh had been married previously and Donnell O'Donnell was the eldest son of his first marriage. Donnell, an excellent soldier and leader in battle, saw his chance, with his half brother in jail and his father in decline. He decided to depose him and take the Chieftainship for himself. He had already brought under his power and jurisdiction that part of Donegal westward from Bearnas to the Drowes and also the people of Boghaine and Boylagh.

Ineen Dubh had to keep her husband hidden away at home as he had fallen into senility. She knew that if his weakness was ever made public, he would be deposed, Gaelic law ordaining that one could not rule if not in full health. Truth to tell, it wasn't for her husband that she wanted the Chieftainship, but for her first born son, Hugh Roe and she was not going to let her stepson steal it from him. She had sent to Scotland and procured an army there and was not only reliant on the two thousand Scot mercenaries who had answered her call, but had also drawn upon the O'Donnell Gallowglasses, the Mac Sweeneys and the Irish Lords, still obedient to her husband.

The Gallowglasses were originally mercenary soldiers who had crossed from Scotland to fight in Irish wars. Over the years, they had settled in Ireland, different families, supporting individual Irish lords. The MacSweeney Gallowglasses had settled in Donegal in the fourteenth century, where The O'Donnell had given them land in return for the supply of trained fighting men to assist in his wars. The MacSweeneys had to supply three hundred Gallowglasses who spent their time training for war. They, no more than the Irish freemen, did not work on the land. Such labour was beneath them. They were of great strength and stature, were dressed from neck to heel in chain mail and conical iron helmets, and armed with their great two-handed swords and battle-axes.

Donough Mac Sweeney hastened up the hill to where Ineen Dubh stood, watching both armies. He walked through her bodyguard who kept a close eye on him. Being outsiders, they didn't trust any of the natives, which he was, as far as they were concerned. Their one duty was to make sure that Ineen Dubh was protected. Mac Sweeney didn't like the new Scot mercenaries. They came from different clans to his, usually staying for just a season, before returning back over the seas to their native land. They kept themselves cut off from the rest of the army. They served the highest bidder and Donough was too well aware that maybe next year, he might have to face the same men on the battlefield if they got better terms from a rival Lord. Ineen Dubh had always insisted on having her own mercenaries to protect her, and that had rankled with him. His men should have been good enough.

He reached Ineen Dubh, removed his helmet and addressed her. "We're ready. My men have worked around behind Donnell's army and the archers are positioned on their flanks."

Ineen Dubh nodded. "Well then, let us begin. Your men know that Donnell's life is not to be spared. The man who brings me his head, will be well rewarded."

Donough assented, turned and hastened back to the army, positioned on the hill. There, fifteen hundred of the Scot mercenaries awaited his return. The other five hundred had been divided into two companies of archers, who had worked around both flanks of the enemy's army. They were hidden in the woods, where they would be protected from Donnell's horse.

Donnell's army was made up mainly of Irish kerne or infantry. They were lightly armed with bow and arrows, javelins, swords and spears. As well as his own followers, Turlough O'Neill had sent him some of his own men and three hundred of his Gallowglasses. In number, the armies were roughly equal in size, but Ineen Dubh had the superior troops.

Once Donough had rejoined his ranks, he ordered the bagpiper to strike up the clan song. This was the signal for attack. Immediately, the remaining five hundred archers, with Ineen Dubh's troops, advanced to the front of their army and loosed their arrows at the enemy. At the same time, two flights of arrows were launched from the two other flanks into Donnell's army. The hail of arrows flew true and, coming simultaneously from three directions, confused their enemy. Within three minutes, each archer had launched five arrows apiece and great gaps had appeared in the enemy's ranks.

The archers on the flank, nearest Donnell's horse, had been ordered to concentrate on that area and had cut down riders and horses in great swathes. Ineen Dubh's cavalry charged Donnell's, while the Scots and the Gallowglasses attacked the main body of infantry, from front and rear.

Donnell's horse was shot out from under him and he was wounded in the shoulder and leg. He raised himself to his feet and noticed his horsemen, those that were still unscathed, riding away in utter confusion. He was in no man's land, surrounded by dying men and animals. He looked around and saw his enemy's horse charging towards him, while the archers had drawn their swords and were charging from his left. There was no possibility of retreating as the MacSweeney Gallowglasses were charging from that direction.

His main army still stood and had reformed itself to face the overwhelming odds. He decided that with it lay his best hope of shelter and he began limping towards it. His men, most of them too petrified to move, watched him and the advancing enemy. Then five of them rushed out to help and others followed their example. Their formation was broken just at the wrong moment, as the shock of the mass attack hit it from front and rear. The attackers broke through, like a powerful wave through a castle of sand.

Donnell never reached his rescuing party. One of the horsemen reached him first and sliced his sword hand off, with a single swipe of his weapon. Donnell sank to his knees. The horseman dismounted and walked over to him, as his companions destroyed the rescuing party. Donnell knelt and watched him approach, while his blood pumped out in rhythmic spurts onto the damp grass. The horseman raised his sword and, in one fell swoop, parted Donnell's head from his shoulders. The head bounced across the grass and for a moment, Donnell's body remained in its kneeling position before it slowly collapsed, blood erupting now from the neck. The horseman picked up the head and rode around the fighting mass of men, hollering aloud in Gaelic, "Look, look at your leader now, the great Donnell"

At first no one could hear him. The din of battle was so loud that men could only think of killing or being killed. The fighting was now hand to hand and both sides battled blow for blow. It was one vast, confusing, mass of men who struck, mangled, slaughtered and cut down one another. Every minute, more men were being laid low and Donnell's lightly armed soldiers were suffering terribly at the hands and axes of the Scots and Gallowglasses.

Ineen Dubh's horse could do no more. If they attacked the fighting mass, they could just as easily kill their own, as Donnell's men. So they took off after Donnell's retreating horse, all except the one horseman holding Donnell's head that continued circling the bloodied, fermenting mass of men. No quarter was to be given and none was expected. Donnell's men, who by now had seen their leader's head, lost heart and were now only interested in escaping with their lives. They tried to fight their way out in ones and twos, but there was no means of evasion. The fighting lasted another hour, until none of Donnell's men remained standing. Then the Gallowglasses and Scots claimed the victors' spoils. They went through the battlefield, robbing the corpses of anything worth taking, weapons, armour, clothes, but particularly money. Any of the soldiers not already dead, they quickly dispatched by slitting their throats.

As Donough McSweeney went through the bodies, collecting his share, his previous misgivings totally evaporated. He felt ebullient, a craftsman who had performed as he was expected to and had done the best job he could. What was even better, the casualties among his own men had been light and every man of his knew and shared with him the knowledge that this was what they were born to. It was their heritage. And this was just the start. They would follow up their victory by raiding Donnell's defenceless country, pillaging everything that was of value. Donnell had gambled and lost. Ineen Dubh had gambled and won.

Back on the hill, Ineen Dubh stood watching the aftermath of the battle. At her feet, lay Donnell's head, his face buried in the clay. She enjoyed seeing the final acts of the fight, the total annihilation of the enemy. It was one threat removed forever. Dusk was setting in and the white, naked bodies of Donnell's dead soldiers gleamed in the fading light, like some spectral beings caught between this world and the next. Somewhere far off in the forest, a wolf howled at the newly rising moon. The wolves will eat well tonight, she thought.

Chapter 2

Henry Hovendon stood at the edge of Woodquay while he watched the boat from England tie up at the harbour. He was perished from standing around as the boat was late and he had arrived early. An east wind blew up along the Liffey and, from time to time, fierce showers of hail lashed the capital. He had been forced to take shelter in the porch of St. Audoen's church; there were no taverns near enough the docks to retreat into while he awaited O'Neill's arrival from London. To the rear of St Audeon's, Dublin town was perched on top of a humpbacked hill, the houses and buildings crowded together, cleaving to the hillside, like moss to a wall. Circling the town was its stone rampart, as if supporting it and arresting its descent into the river Poddle and the plain below.

The quay was bustling with activity, one freight boat being unloaded by the city crane, while three more were waiting their turn. The importers' wagons were backed up as far as the port entrance and labourers and travellers milled around, ebbing and flowing like the tide of the river. Henry anxiously watched the gangplank as the travellers disembarked and then finally noticed Hugh descending. When he had seen him off eight weeks previously, he had not expected him to be gone so long. He pushed his way through the throng and met him at the bottom of the gangplank. O'Neill embraced him. "Henry, it's great to see you."

Henry replied joyfully, "It's good to see you, Hugh. You gave me a right surprise when you were not on the boat last week. I didn't know what had gone awry."

"Did you bring a coach?"

Henry nodded. "Yes. It's just outside the port gates."

"Good. We'll wait until we're safely inside it to discuss matters."

They both pushed their way through the crowd. "Where do you want to go first?" Henry asked.

"Is Bagenal in town?"

"Yes. He's down for the Council meeting that is called for tomorrow. He is staying in his usual lodgings," Henry answered.

"Right. Well, I might as well get my business over first."

They had reached the coach and Hugh climbed inside out of the raw, cold wind, which whistled piercingly around him. Henry gave directions to the driver and climbed in beside him. The coach pulled off, making its way slowly through the thronged streets, which teemed with life

Within the city's walls, land was at a premium and every spare inch was built upon. The timbered and wattle houses were squeezed together, line upon line, facing opposite one another, only a narrow distance between them, so that the streets were constantly thrust into cold shadow. The streets themselves were unpaved and strewn with domestic refuse and offal pitched out from the houses. There, it was trampled underfoot by the inhabitants. All along the streetsides, hawkers had set up their stalls, selling everything from bread to ale to farm produce. The surprising thing about the city was that it was full of live animals. Horses and their stables were everywhere; hens, chickens, cattle and even pigs were in transit through the capital on their way to the butchers who fed the populace.

What Hugh liked least about cities were the noise and smell and Dublin, though smaller, was no better than London. Everywhere there was din; from the hawkers shouting their wares, to the craftsmen at their work, to the rowdy customers of the many taverns, to the noise generated by all the animals. The smell was even more repugnant. It came from the open sewers that ran down the side of the streets, from the dunghills and the animal waste on the thoroughfare, from the stables, from the pigsties and from the people themselves.

Being on the Queen's Council of Ireland, Hugh was acutely aware of the three major problems from which Dublin suffered, poverty, pestilence and pigs. Like all cities, this capital suffered many times from disease. The city fathers blamed the swine and the beggars for spreading it. The nomadic habits of the beggars, their unclean habits and their power of carrying infection from place to place, made them very unwelcome. And yet, it proved nearly impossible to exclude them from the city. Famine in country areas sent swarms of starving people here and at other times, plentiful harvests, greeted by depressed prices, had almost the same effect.

The city was, essentially, English. Its English settlers controlled the entry to the guilds and no Irish were allowed to earn their living as merchants or tradesmen. The Irish inhabitants were relegated to the most menial and unskilled of labour, and were at best tolerated, but were always objects of suspicion. The pigs ran wild through the city and no matter how the city elders tried to eradicate them, they could not get rid of them. It was no wonder that Hugh, when he had to visit any city, always longed for Ulster and its wide open, under populated countryside.

Now that they were underway, Hugh began his account of his progress in London. "Initially, all went well. While I awaited my appointment with the Queen and her Privy Council, I was invited to stay at Sir Henry Wallop's London residence." Hugh grew animate at the memory. " I never before beheld such a splendid house, Henry. He advised me about furnishings for my castle and had a retainer take me all over the city to pick out the very best household stuffs. I've a whole ship chartered to bring it home."

Henry smiled. "Why, Hugh. If I did not know better, I'd say that you might be out to impress a lady, an English lady."

Hugh guffawed, enjoying these sallies at his romantic plans. "We'll come to that later. I got the lead export license for re-roofing Dungannon Castle. The supplier accepted my word about the castle's dimensions, so I got enough to do it five times over. Then I went to a further two dealers. There's plenty should we ever have need of it."

Henry was pleased. The English administration kept a very tight rein on the supply of gunpowder, bullets and arms to the Irish and even though Hugh had fought for the English, they never allowed him free access to supplies. The lead would be melted down to make bullets and Henry himself had been on trips to Scotland to buy powder. It was vital to be able to wage war, if Hugh's ambitions were ever to be realised

Henry pressed on, "But tell me what went amiss? Did the letters from Fitzwilliam and Bishop Loftus not help?"

"If I hadn't had them, I'd have been in direst need. They attested that I'd done the English administration in Ireland a favour in executing Hugh McShane and, as both men are on the Council, their opinion was valued. When I eventually got an audience with the Privy Council, the letters helped sway them. They may have cost a bit, but they were well worth it. Essex and Ormonde also put in a good word for me. Finally, they agreed that I could return home."

"That's when you wrote telling me that you were coming? So what happened?"

"Yes and would have done so, were it not for Conn McShane." Hugh flushed red with anger at the memory. "I was at Beaumaris awaiting ship. I was feeling well satisfied with myself. I thought that I had successfully handled affairs before the Privy Council. But, just as I was about to board ship, a detachment of the Queen's soldiers arrived at the port, arrested me and escorted me back to London. Conn McShane had arrived there just after I had departed for the coast. He had letters with him from Turlough, the Earl of Kildare and the Lord Devlin, supporting his claims. He presented a long list of accusations. Most damaging of those, were that I had a reciprocal alliance with Angus McDonald, that I had given assistance to the survivors of the Spanish Armada, and that I had planned the escape of Hugh Roe O'Donnell."

"Well, it's impossible to prove the alliance, or your part in Hugh

Roe's escape. Regarding the Armada, did you not remind them of my work on your behalf?" Henry asked.

"I did," Hugh replied, casting his mind back to when the Armada had been shipwrecked on the Irish coastline and Hovendon, appointed as captain in his forces, had massacred three hundred from one of the wrecks. He, himself, had aided the survivors of another Spanish shipwreck. Thus, he managed to maintain good relations with the English and Spanish.

O'Neill continued. "Conn is wily, too wily. He cited my marriage alliances and fosterings as proof of my ambitions to make myself great in Ulster. He also recounted how, some years ago, I hanged another of his brothers, Edmond."

"And what happened?" Henry asked.

"I argued that I was innocent, that I had done a service for Her Majesty by removing an arch traitor from her Realm as vouched for in the letters from the Irish Council. I also maintained that those accusations could only be examined at home, where witnesses could be called to vouch for my actions. Conn argued strongly that if I was tried in Ireland, my friends were so many there, and my forces so great, that no one would dare accuse me. In the end, my plea won out and they were persuaded to allow me return."

"Heavens be praised. Conn can never compete with your connections in Dublin," Henry rejoined.

"Yes. And he knows it. It was a great advantage that he could not address them in English. It was just one more barrier that he had to overcome. He also undermined his case by asking that his arrears in rent be written off. But enough of these matters. Tell me, what news is there of O'Donnell?" Hugh asked. He had been frustrated to learn, while in London, that his scheme for O'Donnell's escape had been foiled.

"He's bearing up. They have leg and arm irons on him now. He was bitterly disappointed when O'Toole's men handed him over."

"And O'Toole? Did you deal with him?" Hugh enquired.

"Yes, I met him. He had a fanciful story that he had only arrested O'Donnell as the English had surrounded the wood, in which he was hiding. He claimed it was only a matter of time before they found him. I let him know of your extreme displeasure and what would happen to him if he ever let you down again. I wager he got the message."

"Good. And did you talk to Fitzwilliam?"

"Yes, Hugh. He said that he was blameless in O'Donnell's recapture, that he had kept his part of the bargain. The gates were open and he successfully delayed mounting the posse. He told me, though, that he has a problem with the jail Constable, Seagar, one of those highly principled officials. He is not averse to making a profit out of his prisoners, but would not commit what could be judged a treasonous act. He regards it as a personal affront that O'Donnell escaped. He's determined that he will not escape again."

Hugh shook his head. "We have to get O'Donnell out. I need him. As long as there is no one in charge in Donegal, Turlough and the McShanes can do as they like."

Henry nodded. "I have made a deal with Fitzwilliam, which I hope you'll approve."

"Yes, you know I trust you."

"He wants four times what you paid him for the first escape."

O'Neill sneered. "He's nothing but a highway man. It's robbery, pure and simple. He's making himself rich at my expense."

"He argues that he will have to replace Seagar with someone more amenable to our requirements. He will then have to pay him a share and another one or two of the guards will have to be brought into the plan. It is a dangerous business. They could lose their heads if the Queen ever found out."

"He has got away with far more in the past. How are you to pay him?"

"Half up front and the rest when O'Donnell is back in Donegal."

Hugh growled. "That should make him concentrate on making sure that he isn't caught." Then a question came to him. "And what about the McShanes, Art and Henry? I'd prefer them to be in my hands than in the Queen's power. I do not wish her setting them up against me in the future."

"That is looked after. They will be moved into the same cell as O'Donnell and when he breaks free, they will be able to go with him."

Hugh was thoughtful for a moment. "What happens if they become friends and, when they do break out, O'Donnell favours them, against me?"

Henry allayed his disquiet. "We had better ensure that they do not have too much time to become well acquainted. Still, there is very bad blood there, on account of Hugh Roe's father defeating theirs. Do not worry unduly."

The coach pulled to a halt and Henry looked out the window. "Well, we have arrived."

Hugh was suddenly reminded of the task that he had set himself for today. After his detention in London, there were times when he thought that he might not get to carry out his intentions. Now that the moment was finally upon him, he still was uncertain what formula of words he should use. He hated having to ask Bagenal for anything. He was a pompous, boastful man and yet he would have to deal with him, as he was a presence in Ulster and one that couldn't be ignored. If Bagenal's father were still alive, it would have been easier. It didn't help that Bagenal was two years his junior. It was demeaning that he had to ask him for his sister, Mabel, in marriage.

He looked at Henry. "Did you tell him why I wanted to meet him?"

Henry grinned. "No, I left that honour to yourself."

"And do you think he has any idea of the purpose of my visit? Do you think Mabel said anything?"

"No. He was very surprised. At first he pretended to be too busy to meet you, but then his curiosity got the better of him. I think he expects you want to see him about Monaghan and the division of McMahon's land."

O'Neill was glad. He had been afraid that Mabel might have said something to him. It was better this way. They could sort it out, man to man. Logically, Bagenal should be gratified. There were not many richer men in Ireland than him. Bagenal should see the advantages to a link with his family and, provided he was satisfied with what he held already in Ulster and was prepared to hold it under him, then it could be a very advantageous alliance. He would gain a beautiful English wife and, in the process, he would transform one of his enemies into a relation, and in the longer term they'd combine for each other's mutual benefit. The division of Monaghan was an example. Bagenal could get some small share once his own rights were recognised. "And McMahon. Then it's true that they hanged him?"

Henry nodded. "Yes, outside his own door. And what of O'Reilly?"

Hugh shook his head. "After the Scots yielded him up, he was brought to the Tower and tried. He was always a brave man and died one too. He refused to recognise the English court's right to try him, or the Queen as his monarch. She had heard that he had made an effigy of her and used it for his archers' target practice. That and his help for the survivors of the Spanish Armada were enough to damn him beyond any hope of redemption. He was hanged, drawn and quartered on Tyburn Hill. Two good men gone. It's a mad country altogether over there. Perrot has been sentenced to death, even though he was probably the fairest Lord Deputy that we ever had and had worked hard in the English interest all his life. The fact that he's supposed to be Henry VIII's bastard brother, does little to aid him."

"I am as glad not to be moving in such lofty circles, the higher you climb, the further you may fall."

Hugh turned to him. "I'm very aware of it and if you're Irish, the supports are even more likely to be undermined. Still Henry, let us stop being so morbid and go and tell Bagenal the good news. He's going to have a wedding in the family."

Henry smiled and they both alighted from the coach and made for the door of the inn.

Dublin Castle was built on the orders of King John in 1213 as the strong point for his administration in Ireland. Since its construction, it had functioned as a military fortress, a prison, treasury, court of law and the seat of English administration in Ireland. The area within the walls was enormous, more like a small town than a castle. Every possible type of building had sprung up there; the customary stables, barracks for the soldiers, kitchens, bakeries, prisons, storehouses for arms, gunpowder and food, the official residence of the Lord Deputy, offices and the Great Hall itself.

The Lord Deputy, Sir William Fitzwilliam, sat in his chamber behind his table that was overflowing with parchments, dealing with matters of state. He had divided them into two bundles, those that were urgent and those that need not be attended to. His sole rationale for the division of the work was whether or not he could make a profit from it. He was in extremely good temper. He had a number of spiritual livings, for which he would get a good price and also a number of lucrative export licences that he knew would be in great demand.

He was always very careful how he conducted his business. He never accepted money himself. All illicit moneys or property were channelled through proxies, either relatives, such as his daughter, Lady Dyer, or some minor officials whom he could trust. He had a large family and too many relatives, all of whom had to be provided for. He also had a position to maintain in society and the Queen did not pay enough for him to live in the style that the Queen's first official ought. There was only one person with whom he dealt openly regarding the granting of favours, and that was the Earl of Tyrone. He could earn a year's salary in one deal with him and now he was undertaking the most dangerous and lucrative intrigue so far. He decided that it was time to deal with Philip Seagar, the Constable of Dublin Castle. He had kept him waiting long enough. He summoned his clerk, John Marshall, who entered the chamber. "Yes, my lord?"

"Show Seagar in."

Marshall withdrew silently. He always reminded Fitzwilliam of a cat, he moved so quietly and with such feline grace. As he waited for Seagar, he reorganised his papers. Seagar had been appointed by his predecessor, Sir John Perrot, and was firmly in Perrot's camp. Fitzwilliam had replaced most of Perrot's appointments when the chance presented, but the removal of Seagar would have been difficult to justify. Up until this, he'd been a model gaoler, but now Fitzwilliam's opportunity had finally arrived. What was more, he'd profit out of it as well.

The door opened, Marshall showed Seagar in and then withdrew. Seagar stood in front of the table and stared sullenly at Fitzwilliam. The latter left him standing for a few minutes as he leafed through his papers. He then put them down and composing his features into a look of stern disapproval, addressed him. "I'm very disappointed in your discharge of the Queen's office. It is unacceptable that the most dangerous rebel in the country was allowed to escape from what should be the most secure prison in the land. It makes a mockery of the Queen's honour and gives her enemies comfort."

Seagar squirmed. He had been ill at ease at the prospect of this interview. He avoided the Lord Deputy's presence as much as possible and when they did meet, they tended to ignore each other. The only contact they had was over the running of the Castle gaol and that was always business like and brief. He cleared his throat. "I grant you that it was unfortunate that the prisoner should have escaped but I can promise you that there will never be another escape while the castle is under my command. O'Donnell is under twenty four-hour guard, in solitary confinement and in irons."

Fitzwilliam replied. "There will never be another escape from the Castle during your appointment, because I'm relieving you of your command as of this minute. You may return and collect your belongings. I want you and your family out of there before night."

Seagar waxed purple. He had expected Fitzwilliam to use the escape as a means of undermining him, but had never foreseen this. He spluttered, almost incoherent with rage. "You overstep your authority, Sir. I hold the office from the Queen. You cannot replace me. I have given good service to Her Majesty over the years and..."

Fitzwilliam raised his hand. "Enough," he growled. "I have already written to the Queen and told her of my decision and the reasons for it. She is not pleased that O'Donnell escaped. It was no thanks to you that he was recaptured. I have the power, as the Queen's representative, to make such decisions and I would be in breach of my duty, if I did not replace you."

Seagar found it difficult to believe what he was hearing. He would be ruined. With Perrot in the tower, he could no longer use his connections to procure some other office. Patronage was everything, not only in Ireland but also in England. The possibility that he might no longer be able to provide for his wife and family, filled him with rage against the man who planned to replace him. He found himself shouting. "This is a travesty. I shall contact the Queen myself. I will not be ruined by the likes of you."

Fitzwilliam smiled cynically. "Perhaps you should contact your patron in the Tower. Maybe he could get you a position there. I'm sure that he would be glad to have you as his gaoler."

"And who will replace me? Which one of your cronies?"

"I have found a good man for the job, John Maplesden."

"Maplesden! That rogue! You fill Her Majesty's service with the lowest and basest of creatures. I know how you run the country, how you misuse your office, how you profit at Her Majesty's expense."

Fitzwilliam rose. "I must warn you to mind your tongue. If you dare repeat such falsehoods, I will make sure that you regret it. It will also gain you nothing, for the Queen will recognise your motives as revenge against me for carrying out my duty in replacing you."

"I'm sure that she's heard the rumours already. Even the dogs on the streets know about you."

"Marshall," Fitzwilliam roared loudly, before addressing Seagar again. "Always remember what I did to your former patron. You might very well find yourself keeping him company." The door opened and Marshall entered. "Show Mr. Seagar out and have Mr. Maplesden come in."

Marshall held the door open and Seagar stood for a few moments as he considered what his next step should be. Fitzwilliam sat again at his table, turning his attention back to the work upon it. Finally, deciding that there was no point in saying anything further, Seagar turned and stormed out. Marshall followed him and closed the door behind them both.

Fitzwilliam put down his documents. It had gone much as he had anticipated. He wasn't worried about Seagar. He had no proof and without it, he would never be believed. There was a knock on the door and Marshall showed in John Maplesden. He was a man in his late fifties, so overweight and unkempt, that he resembled a walking haystack. Fitzwilliam had used him as a go between in the past when he needed someone trustworthy to carry out delicate matters.

Maplesden had come to Ireland some thirty years previously and had spent that time living on his wits. Perrot had not approved of his methods, which at times bordered on the illegal, and Maplesden had not thrived under his appointment. Things had improved considerably since the arrival of Fitzwilliam and he wondered, ever since he had received the summons from him, what it could possibly mean. He hoped that Fitzwilliam needed him to carry out some sensitive business. He was in debt again and his creditors were pressing him for payment.

Fitzwilliam waited until Marshall had withdrawn, before commencing. "Well John, I have a proposition for you, from which we both may make a very tidy sum. Are you agreeable?"

Maplesden smiled. "Of course. You know me; reliable, discreet and always anxious to make a few groats. What do I have to do?"

Fitzwilliam opened a coffer and took out a corked jug of whiskey. It was one thing that the Irish really knew how to make. He took two goblets and poured two large measures. Maplesden's eyes lit up with delight. He hadn't had a drink yet today and it would be very welcome. Fitzwilliam handed it to him and in a quiet, confidential tone continued. "It is a very delicate matter and as I said, we both will profit handsomely from it. I will have to appoint you Constable of the Castle as, in that appointment, you will be able to carry out a certain task, which will ensure our reward. It will require the utmost secrecy on your behalf, for if we are discovered, we shall both end up on the gallows. But one cannot make great profit without great peril."

Maplesden now understood why Seagar had almost knocked him over as he rushed from the Deputy's office and had shot him a glance of pure hatred. There had never been cordial feelings between them as Seagar was, in Maplesden's eyes, a religious, over scrupulous fool. He had rejoiced when he had heard of O'Donnell's escape as it had made Seagar the butt of tavern jests. He smiled to himself. The idea of his taking up another profession at his age amused him. Still, he had been a soldier in his younger days and in his mind, that would qualify him sufficiently for the post.

"A great profit, you say?" he asked as he wondered what he was expected to do. He knew that there was a profit to be made out of the running of Her Majesty's jails, but that would be a small one, taking many years to accrue to him, especially if he had to give Fitzwilliam a share.

"Yes," Fitzwilliam answered, "A great profit for a short period of work. Your appointment will be of short duration. You are not going to be a success in your new position and I am going to have to remove you from your office as a result of an incompetence that you will perpetrate. It must be seen as an incompetence like Seagar's, not a treachery."

Suddenly Maplesden knew what was expected of him "Is it O'Donnell, you wish him to escape?"

Fitzwilliam nodded. "That is how we shall make our profit. There are also two others who must go with him. The sons of Shane O'Neill, Art and Henry. You must move all three into the one cell."

Maplesden could now deduce who was behind the whole scheme. It could only be the Earl of Tyrone. He whistled. The stakes were indeed high.

"One must never be able to prove that you or I had any part in the escape. Once they are out of the Castle, it's up to their patron to make sure that they make it safely back home. We will have to be seen to mount a search, of course."

Maplesden nodded. "Of course."

"O'Donnell is in irons. Don't remove them. You cannot be seen to do anything that will make his escape easier. Put the McShanes in irons also. I'll leave it to you to decide how they will contrive it. Leave it for some time, but not too long. Christmas might be a good time with the laxity that it brings."

Maplesden, rejoicing in his good fortune, replied, "Never fear, My Lord, I shall see to it."

Fitzwilliam nodded. "Good man. Now here is your letter of appointment and something on account. There's treble that amount when the task is completed." He took a letter and a bag of coins from a chest and handed them to Maplesden. The latter read the document through, folded it and put it away safely. He then allowed the bag of coin weigh in his hand, before opening it and looking inside. On seeing the warm yellow glow of the coin, contentment spread throughout his bloated body. He put the bag safely inside his jerkin and smiled. He'd be able to pay off his debtors and have money left over from the amount that he'd already got. Fate was definitely favouring him. Fitzwilliam took the whiskey jug again and poured. Maplesden watched the gold coloured liquid glide into his goblet and thought of all the pleasure that yellow coloured things had brought him.

"A drink to seal our deal, John," Fitzwilliam continued, "and then I want you to get over to the prison and turn Seagar out."

Maplesden drained the whiskey in one draught. "That would give me great pleasure. Your trust in me will not be disappointed." He set down his goblet, rose and took his leave. Fitzwilliam watched him go, amused at the sight of the wobbling mass of fat that was John Maplesden on a mission. He was secure in the knowledge that he could never be implicated as there were no witnesses to their meeting and, whereas there would be talk, talk without proof, as he knew only too well, was worthless.

Henry Hovendon and Hugh O'Neill were shown into a parlour of the inn frequented by Marshal Bagenal when on business in Dublin. They were left waiting for half an hour and, just as they were about to despair of his arrival, the door opened and Bagenal and Sir Thomas Maria Wingfield entered.

Sir Thomas had recently arrived from England and was a captain in the Queen's army. He was a tall, angular man with little in his physiognomy to elicit curiosity or admiration. A thirst for adventure and desire for financial reward had made him ambitious to serve in

Ireland, where he knew the pickings were rich. He was descended from a well-connected family, was in his twenty-fifth year, and already knighted. Bagenal had taken him under his wing since his arrival. He had stayed with him and his family and a steady mutual regard had drawn them into fellowship. Indeed, so strong was the resemblance in the cast of their personalities, that it would not have been difficult to mistake them as siblings. Bagenal strode into the middle of the chamber and stood by the table, looking at the two visitors.

He was disappointed to see O'Neill. He had encouraged Conn McShane in his journey to England and had coached him on what to say. He was annoyed that his plan hadn't worked. He recognised the Earl as his greatest rival in Ulster and it would have been agreeable if McShane had neutralised him. It irritated him more than anything else that O'Neill had been raised to the status of Earl, especially as O'Neill did not really have any great appreciation for the honour. "Well, I see you were allowed home. I wouldn't have wagered much on your chances of ever being allowed back. Your luck still holds," he said.

O'Neill smiled. "Your wager would have been safe. I only carried out a service for Her Majesty. You know how much trouble Hugh McShane fermented in Ulster."

"That may well be, but all executions must be carried out only on the Queen's orders. We cannot have people taking the law into their own hands. Those days are gone, thank God."

O'Neill replied evenly, "Sometimes desperate problems call for desperate measures, as you well know."

Bagenal refused to be drawn. He was eager to bring the meeting to a head and have done with it. He had been in good spirits beforehand. He had accepted Wingfield's application to him for his sister Mabel's hand in marriage. Both men had some celebrating to do. Also, he didn't want to be drawn on the division of MacMahon's land, on which theme he felt sure O'Neill had come to debate. Time enough for that when it would be too late for O'Neill to interfere. He resented having to see the Earl at all but, as they served on the Council together, it would have been unwise not to grant him this meeting. "Well, I have another appointment to go to, for which I'm already late so, if you could get to the point as quickly as possible, I'd appreciate it."

O'Neill cleared his throat. He disliked Bagenal for his arrogant gracelessness and uncouth manner. He always tried to bully his way both inside and outside the Council. He lacked a keen mind, relying instead on bluster and thinly veiled intimidation, to achieve his ends. Still, somehow or other, they would have to come to an agreement over Ulster. "I would like to talk to you in private," Hugh said.

"And is that why you brought Hovendon with you? You brought your witness. I need one too. I wish Sir Thomas to stay. I have no secrets that a captain in Her Majesty's army cannot hear."

Bagenal stood waiting for O'Neill to continue. He saw his discomfort and delighted at it. After a pause, O'Neill proceeded. "I have come today to appeal for an end to the division that exists between our families. There is no real reason why we cannot coexist as brothers and manage Ulster in peace and contentment so that we can both gain the most profit from our lands, and the people of Ulster can live in peace and harmony."

Bagenal snorted in spite of himself. The idea of him ever calling O'Neill "brother" was so ludicrous, that it didn't bear considering. As far as he was concerned, the Irish were an inferior race and he would never trust any of them. He believed in his heart that no Irishman could ever be a legitimate Earl. It was a title given to them for a short time, until the English would be in a better position to pull them down. In addition, he had no time at all for the Hovendens, whom he regarded as traitors to the English cause, because of the loyalty they showed O'Neill. "I hold what I have from Her Majesty and I serve only her," he said.

Bagenal knew that O'Neill was trying his diplomatic best and that it had served him well over the years with many Englishmen, more influential than himself. He also knew that O'Neill could count on some of Her Majesty's most important men as his friends. The Earl of Leicester and he had been particularly close and Leicester's death had robbed O'Neill of a very loyal ally. That had been a happy day for Bagenal, even though it had not left O'Neill totally devoid of influence in England. He had served with, among others, the First Earl of Essex and they also had been close during the Earl's lifetime. His son, the second Earl of Essex had, to Bagenal's great disappointment, kept that friendship alive. Bagenal, however, prided himself on being a man not given to being deceived by traitors like O'Neill.

O'Neill continued. "I serve only her as well. Have I not spilt my blood on her behalf? Have I not protected the Pale for many years now? Have I not campaigned in Munster to her benefit? We both wish the same outcome, a strong peaceful country for Her Majesty."

"And she shall have it," Bagenal answered dourly.

O'Neill nodded. "That she will, because men like you and I shall make sure that she gets it. Our two families fight for the same end. I think that there should be a formal alliance between us."

Bagenal was now totally bewildered. What could he mean? An alliance? What sort of alliance? "I am totally at a loss as to what you are proposing. There cannot be a military alliance between us. As I already told you, I owe allegiance to no one but the Queen and God, and in that order too."

"No, it is a different form of alliance, of which I speak. I refer to a marriage alliance between our two houses."

Bagenal wondered whether or not he was hearing correctly. The meeting was taking on a nightmarish quality. What were they thinking of, of whom were they thinking, he wondered. He did not even know how many sisters O'Neill had. If O'Neill thought for one moment that he would marry some Irish savage, he would need to think again. Maybe O'Neill thought that he could buy him, just like he seemed to think that he could buy everything else in this country. Well, there was no dowry large enough to entice him even to consider the matter for a single second. He looked from O'Neill to Hovenden and then to Sir Thomas who was half smiling at O'Neill's temerity.

"Marriage alliance," he managed to say at last. "What are you saying, man? Are you mad?

"I wish to ask for the hand of your sister, Mabel, in marriage," Hugh answered.

Bagenal looked at him incredulously. Had he gone mad? Mabel! He looked at Sir Thomas whose smile had waned. Bagenal was Mabel's guardian since their father's death some years previously. His father had married late in life and Mabel was now barely twenty, less than half O'Neill's age. She had been left £2,000 in his will as a dowry, a very generous amount that would help ensure that she would get a suitable husband. She was also very beautiful, but coupled with that beauty and physical delicacy was an impassionate, rebellious mind, which vigorously opposed any of her brother's attempts to tame it. Now that she had acquired her twentieth year, he had set about procuring a husband for her, with a certain amount of trepidation. Few men would wish to have a wife so devoid of docility. He had set his heart on having Sir Thomas as his brother-in-law and had arranged to have them together as much as possible over the last few months. The stratagem had worked and Bagenal rejoiced that his scheming had paid off. His prospects, coupled and bolstered by those of Wingfield, would surely increase.

Now the spectre of O'Neill as his brother-in-law had made his blood run cold and all his earlier gratification vanished. The contemplation of mixing his blood with that of Irish rebels appalled him. He was furious at O'Neill for having the boldness to consider such a request, let alone putting it in words. Could he be so blind and stupid not to realise that he'd rather see Mabel dead than married to an Irish heathen?

O'Neill, taking Bagenal's silence as encouragement, continued. "I have already met Mistress Mabel a number of times and I am most impressed by her. I think we could be happy together."

Bagenal finally found his voice. "It cannot be. It could never be. It is just impossible."

O'Neill looked at him warily, but continued. "You need not concern yourself about her dowry. I shall be quite happy with the £2,000 left her in her father's will. You will not be called on to add anything to it. I am renovating my castle with all the best furniture and fittings from London. She shall want for nothing."

Wingfield, who had remained silent throughout the meeting, now found himself compelled to speak. "Sir Henry has already told you that it is impossible. If you are a gentleman, you will accept his word, as Mistress Mabel's guardian, that it is so."

His tone was sullen and O'Neill felt puzzled at his interjection. "I do not think, Sir Thomas, that this matter is any of your affair. It only concerns Sir Henry and myself."

Wingfield snarled, "It does concern me, as Mistress Mabel is to be my wife."

O'Neill fell silent and Bagenal revelled at his look of undisguised surprise. Still angry, Bagenal added. "What Sir Thomas says is true. We have just concluded our negotiations on the matter. They are to be married and that's an end to the issue."

"Has your sister agreed?" O'Neill asked.

The question seemed too bold for Bagenal. Did O'Neill not know that Mabel would have to do as he, her guardian, dictated? Was he casting aspersions on his manliness, implying that he would have to consult with Mabel regarding her future husband? O'Neill knew very well that this was the way things were done, marriages were arranged as the head of the household saw fit. "My sister will do as she is told," he answered abruptly.

"I think that I can say, if she were given the choice, she would disagree," O'Neill ventured.

Wingfield laughed scornfully. "And do you think that she would pick you, a man twice her age and a native? Talk sense, man."

"Let Mistress Mabel choose. I will abide by her choice. If you are so sure, what have you to lose?" O'Neill retorted with asperity.

Bagenal could endure no more. "You do not comprehend. I've made the choice for her and I've chosen Sir Thomas. What's more, even if there were no Sir Thomas, I would still not consider you a suitable mate. I don't think that I can be any plainer than that, Sir, so let that be an end to the matter."

He paused, breathing heavily, attempting to regain control of his feelings. He was acutely aware that they would be facing each other across the Council chambers probably for a long time to come, and did not wish to antagonise O'Neill completely.

"Sir Thomas and I have an engagement to attend. We must leave now. We shall not talk about this matter again. You may show yourselves out." He turned to Wingfield.

"Come, Sir Thomas."

He and Wingfield left the chamber and as he did, he noticed that O'Neill remained sitting, his face impassive. Hovenden's face, however, he could read like an book, and in that face he read undisguised hatred.

Hugh Roe O'Donnell was finding his reincarceration in Dublin Castle very difficult to support. To have escaped and to have tasted freedom again, only to have it snatched from his grasp, had almost destroyed him. He had trusted O'Toole and his betrayal by him had been a total shock.

Three years previously, he had been kidnapped and brought to Dublin. His father had offended the English by expelling from his land of Donegal, an English sheriff, Captain Willis, and some other officials whose object had been to plunder from O'Donnell's people. The Lord Deputy of the time, Sir John Perrot, had known that the English were not strong enough to invade Donegal, as many of the Queen's troops had gone to the wars in Flanders. Owing to depleted numbers, he used guile instead to force The O'Donnell's return to obedience. He commissioned a ship to sail to Donegal and its captain to pose as a dealer in fine wines. Perrot had also put fifty soldiers aboard. On reaching Donegal, the captain invited the sons of the local lords to join him in sampling the cargo. Once aboard and drunk, these lords were locked in a cabin and the ship set sail for Dublin. Hugh Roe had awoken to find himself sailing for the capital.

Since then, Hugh Roe had been lodged in Dublin Castle as Her Majesty's prisoner. The English didn't feed their hostages out of the public purse. Their relations were expected to pay for their upkeep. Those not paid for, were left in cages to beg for alms and lived off that which the populace deemed fit to give them. Hugh Roe did not have to beg for charity, like many of the other hostages, his family in Donegal ensuring that he had enough money to keep himself. The Castle's Chief Constable, William Seagar, however, overcharged him for all that was supplied to him, only allowing him the bare necessities for survival.

His three years among the English had convinced him that Ineen Dubh was right in her hatred of them. They had treated him despicably. He was allowed visitors from time to time, provided the guards were well bribed, and from those visitors he heard the news of home. These communications caused him great anxiety and he longed to be back to defend his claim to the Chieftainship.

The Castle consisted of a walled enclosure with four towers at its corners. The gate was located in the middle of the northern wall and was made up of a strong barrier and portcullis. On either side of this, were a further two towers, which lent it protection. Hugh Roe's cell was located on the second floor of its southeastern tower.

The Castle Constable, Seagar, had been extremely angry with him on his return, clapping him in irons and leaving him on a diet of bread and water for the first week after his recapture. After his anger subsided, Seagar allowed himself be bribed once again into supplying the prisoner with better food. Hugh Roe was once again allowed exercise in the castle compound, but now he did so in irons, with two guards in constant attendance. He was forbidden any communication with the other inmates and during the hour, which was allotted to him for his exercise, all other prisoners were kept within. For the rest of the time, he was kept in solitary confinement and as none of the guards assigned to his cell spoke any Irish, he was denied any conversation.

Nevertheless, after the first week, he began to recover his spirits. He reasoned that if he had escaped once, he could always do so again. He trusted O'Neill to use his influence to devise another plan and hoped that he would come and visit him in person. He had always assured him that he would one day regain his freedom. Hugh Roe was certain that he had, by now, dealt with O'Toole regarding his treachery, and that he would pick a better facilitator next time.

Henry Hovendon had visited him and kept him informed of O'Neill's stay in England. Now that O'Neill had returned from London, Hugh Roe felt more confident, having feared that O'Neill might have been imprisoned on the word of Conn McShane. That would have left him totally without an ally who understood the workings of the English administration.

He was surprised to hear the bolt on his cell door being drawn, and the key in the lock being turned. His gaolers only called on him at meal or exercise time. It could only mean one thing, a visitor. He leaped to his feet and waited anxiously to see who it might be. He had not talked to anyone since Henry Hovendon had been to visit and that had not been very satisfactory because a guard had been present.

The door opened and one of the fattest men that Hugh Roe had ever seen, walked into his cell. Tom Nolan, an Irishman, who was used as an interpreter by the English, followed him. Next came two prisoners, also in irons. Hugh Roe recognised them as he had seen them in the castle yard before his last escape. They were Shane O'Neill's sons, Henry and Art.

Henry was tall, thin and well built. He was known for his prowess in battle, his courage and recklessness, but also for the darker side of his soul, his cruelty and arrogance. People said that he, probably more than any of his brothers, most resembled his father. Art, however, was short and stocky and had never gone into battle, as a matter of principle. He liked his comfort and his food and his term in jail had done nothing to lessen his girth. He had a keen interest in books and learning, which he had inherited from his mother and had been fostered in the household of Tadhg Dall Ó Huiginn, the foremost poet of the O'Neills.

Both brothers had never talked to O'Donnell. Being his enemies in their native Ulster, they did not have any reason to befriend him in prison. Hugh Roe was perplexed about their arrival in his cell. For a moment, he wondered if they were going to execute them all. It had happened in the past. A previous Lord Deputy, the Earl of Sussex, had called all the Chiefs of Leinster together and had hanged the lot of them. Two hundred of the leading men in Leinster dead in one evening! Leinster had never recovered from that awful evening's work. And that had happened barely seven years previously. He always knew that if he were no longer of any use to the English, they wouldn't hesitate to be rid of him. The need for him as hostage, guaranteeing his father's good behaviour, would be eliminated. Without doubt, Hugh Roe would lose his life. He had not heard of any further threats to his father's Chieftainship but he was very aware that his hold on the title was extremely tenuous. The news he received from home was bad and getting worse. The English soldiers were once again installed in Donegal and roamed where they willed, plundering and pillaging with impunity. All his old feelings of powerlessness swept over him. Maybe already it was too late, maybe his chance was gone.

Nolan stood in the centre of the cell and addressed Hugh Roe. "This is the new Constable of the Castle, Mr. John Maplesden, whom you see before you."

Maplesden, hearing his own name, nodded at Hugh Roe. Hugh Roe looked at him impassively. Nolan continued, "He has decided to reorganise the prisoners under his care. The high category prisoners, whose escape would cause him the most damage, are to be put in irons. He has deemed that you and the McShanes fall into that classification and that you three shall be imprisoned together to ensure a better watch over you."

Hugh Roe, relieved that he was not to be executed, nonetheless did not wish to be locked up with the McShanes. He protested. "I do not wish to share a cell with the McShanes, it is barely big enough for one."

Henry O'Neill interjected angrily, "And do you think that we want to share a cell with an O'Donnell, a supporter of that usurper, the Earl of Tyrone? I'd rather sleep in the open, than share a cell with one of the English loving O'Donnells."

The injustice of being called an English lover cut deeply into Hugh Roe. "How can you say that of me? If I were an English lover, would I be here?"

Henry laughed sarcastically. "Isn't it how they always treat their friends? Traitors finish having no friends on either side. Both races despise them. I'm looking forward to the day you and the rest of your family get your just deserts."

O'Donnell's temper flared. "And do you think that you'll live to see such a day? If I had a sword, we'd finish this here and now."

Art had been impatiently watching the two of them. When he got the opportunity to interrupt, he seized it. "Will the two of you consider your position. You're both in gaol, put here by the English. For now, we've a common enemy. It is foolish that we fight among ourselves. It is exactly what the English would want."

He paused and looked at both men. O'Donnell considered what he had said. Nolan was busy translating for Maplesden. O'Donnell looked at the Constable whose smug look infuriated him. Maplesden addressed the prisoners and they waited for Nolan to translate. "The Constable tells me to inform you that you have no choice in your accommodation, so you must suffer one another's company."

When Nolan had finished, Maplesden nodded to him and left the cell. Nolan followed and locked the door behind him. The three prisoners stood in silence, watching each other as the key was turned in the lock and the bolt was drawn back. They remained unmoving as the footsteps of their two gaolers receded into the distance. Then, when the sound had finally died away, Art crossed to Hugh Roe, his hand outstretched. "Any enemy of the English is a friend of mine. We must declare a truce and unite together against them. Any other course of action would be absolute folly."

Hugh Roe looked at the outstretched hand and considered Art's words. He was right. If they pulled together, then they might escape. Could he trust them? Could they be in league with the English? Well, if they were, he'd never escape. Still, if the opportunity arose, he'd take it and then he'd find out on which side they really were. He took Art's hand. "I'd deal with the Devil to get out of here, so I suppose I can risk co-operating with the McShanes"

Art shook the hand vigorously. "Good man, Hugh Roe." Art turned to Henry. "Well, Henry? What do you say? "

Henry shook his head. "Once an O'Donnell, always an O'Donnell. If there's an opportunity to escape and it demands that we co-operate, well then, I'll co-operate. Once we're out of here though, he can go his way and I'll go mine."

Hugh Roe replied, "I can readily agree with that."

Art rejoined. "Good. Let us hope we will not be obliged to share such cramped conditions for too long."

Chapter 3

The kitchen staff at Sir Patrick Barnewall's house was busy preparing a special banquet for their master, mistress and their expected guests. Sir Patrick's house lay in Turvey, just nine miles from Dublin City and his wife, Mary, and her sister, Mabel Bagenal, were upstairs, putting the final touches to what raiment they would wear. Mary was twenty-eight, whereas Mabel, the youngest of the family, was only twenty years of age.

The latter was unable to contain her excitement as she prepared. Her love, the object of all her desires, the one who filled her mind during every waking moment and her dreams at night, was coming to dine. Her feelings had swung from deepest despair one short week before, to the heights of unimaginable optimism. When her brother had told her that she was to marry Sir Thomas Wingfield, she had been crushed, bewildered, and then wildly angry. When she had refused, telling him of her love for Hugh O'Neill, he had become apoplectic with rage. He had always been tyrannical and, since their father's death the previous year, there was no one to rein in his inclination to despotism. He had locked her in her chamber and denied her any food until she agreed to marry Wingfield. She had pleaded with him, but he would not be moved. In duplicity, she consented to the marriage, asking that she be allowed come to Dublin to her brother-in-law's house to purchase cloth for her marriage clothes, to which proposal he had agreed. She and her sister, Mary, had always loved each other dearly. Their mother had died when they were both young and as the only women in the house, their mutual devotion and affection had deepened. She knew that Mary's husband, Sir Patrick, relied greatly on Hugh O'Neill, as he was the largest client in Sir Patrick's wine importing business.

On her arrival in Dublin, Mabel secretly conveyed a message to Hugh, informing him of her whereabouts. Hugh had done the rest and managed to obtain an invitation to dine with them. She had guessed that Sir Patrick could not deny him such a request and had been proved right.

She turned to her sister who was trying to decide which robe to wear. "Mary," she exclaimed excitedly, "do I look presentable?"

Mary laughed as she looked at Mabel's face. "For the hundredth time, Mabel, yes. You are most becoming. Do I need to repeat myself?"

Mabel blushed. "Forgive me, Mary. It is just that I am nervous. I have not seen him in two months. I can hardly believe that he is to come here tonight."

Mabel noticed a worried frown pass over Mary's face. "It had better be beyond belief, as far as our brother is concerned. If he knew, he would be very angry and never speak to me again. I can only hope and pray that I am acting sagely. I confess, I do not know how you and Sir Patrick persuaded me to this course."

Mabel ran to Mary, taking both her hands in hers. "Oh, Mary, of course you have acted prudently. You have never been cruel or unfeeling to any one. You must, at least, allow me the consolation of being on speaking terms with him, to let him know that Henry's rejection of his suit is not my doing. I'm sure Sir Patrick would wish us to remain cordial. His business so depends upon it."

Mary privately acknowledged that it would be foolish to jeopardise the amity of such a client as O'Neill and that they must seek to retain friendly relations with him. The task for Mabel would be more difficult. She would have to quell this foolish infatuation. Since her mother's death and Mary's removal to the capital these past seven years, Mabel had been allowed to indulge her undisciplined spirit. Her father had been much occupied with affairs of state and allowed Mabel go unchecked. Mary saw the dangers of such licence and too late, regretted her father's oversight.

Mabel dropped Mary's hands and returned to the looking glass. She rearranged her hair, drawing it back from her face and placing it high on her head in the form of a loosely coiled chignon. She measured the effect, unsure which way to wear it. She saw Mary in the reflection, watching her and smiling once again.

Mary was curious. Henry and Mabel held such disparate views about O'Neill. She wished to know more. "Tell me something about the Earl of Tyrone. One hears such different reports..."

Mabel swung around, the released hair cascading down about her illuminated face. "Where do I start, Mary?" She reached for her sister's hands and drew her onto the bed beside her, before continuing. "I remember so clearly the first time I ever saw him. I was only a girl, no more than eleven years of age. He had come to Newry to see Father and I was walking through the main street. He was on horseback and it was late afternoon. He had approached from the west and the sun was setting behind him. When I looked up, the dazzling reflections from his armour made it painful to behold him. He wore his hair short, in the English fashion. To me, he was more like one of the ancient knights of King Arthur than a modern man, and I stood there transfixed."

Stirred by the memory and its associations, Mabel rose from the bed. She went to the casement and looking out, continued. "He saw me and reined in his horse, asking me who I was. I just stood there, mute, and felt all the blood rush to my cheeks. Then I ran away in confusion. He met me later at our house and afterwards, always brought me tokens when he came visiting. Since his wife's death, he started bringing me different kinds of gifts, gold chains, rings, jewels, as if his intent had deepened and that he was bent on wooing me. I never let Henry know."

Mary nodded, "That was wise. Had Henry known, he would have prohibited you from seeing him. You know they say that he was cruel to his first wife. I have heard it said that..."

"No, stop, Mary, " Mabel cut in vigorously. "I do not wish to hear gossip about him. I met him and his wife, Siobhán, in Dublin Castle and they seemed content. He treated her well. I will not listen to false-hood." Mabel had heard plenty of vile stories from Henry and had believed none of them. She knew that jealousy blinded folk, making them say all manner of things. She smiled at her sister. "He has exhib-ited nothing but kindness to me."

"Yes, Mabel. That may very well be, but he is not one of us, he is one of them, Irish. You remember how we used to laugh at them because of their savage customs and laws?"

Mabel interrupted vehemently. "But you do not understand, Mary. He is not one of them, or at least, he is unique for an Irishman. He speaks perfect English, granted with an accent, but I would prefer his to father's coarse Staffordshire one, which always shamed me when we were in company. His family held the Kingship of Ireland for over six hundred unbroken years. He is no savage. He was brought up in the Pale. He is a friend of all the most important men in Ireland and England. Which of our families has the greater pedigree?"

Mary gravely replied. "It is as well our father didn't live to hear one of his daughters speak so. If Henry heard you, he would cut you off. Do you know what he said to me about your proposed liaison? That he would rather see you burn, than see you married to an Irish savage. When he called on me, he swore to high heaven that it would never come to pass that his honest blood, which had so often been spilt in repressing the Irish rabble, would ever be mingled with that of a pack of traitors like the O'Neills."

Mabel sighed. "It grieves me to hear him speak so. Hugh has never committed any treacherous act and it is jealousy and bigotry on Henry's part that makes him speak so. Henry seeks to control and ruin my life and I will not have it!"

Mary shook her head. "Fie Mabel. You must never say such a thing to Henry. We women must do as our guardians tell us. I did not know Sir Patrick before I was betrothed to him and look how well we have made out. I have grown to love him and he returns that sentiment. It might be so for you and your English captain."

Mabel suddenly felt trapped again. "No, Mary! I do not love him. I could never love him! I will never marry unless it is for love and I love only one man."

A perturbed shadow crossed Mary's face. "Mabel, you would never actually consider marrying him? You must never consider it! Even if he is an educated Irishman and an Earl, he is still Irish. I could never see you living among them."

Mabel turned to the looking glass and began rearranging the fallen tresses. She could see Mary looking at her in the reflection as she awaited a reply. When one was not forthcoming, Mary exclaimed angrily. "Mabel, you must give me your word that you will not consider such an outlandish proposition. Your brother would never, ever countenance it!"

Still Mabel did not reply, continuing with her hair. She stole a glance at her sister's worried face and playfully stuck her tongue out. Mary shook her head. "I knew," she said, "that this was a grave error! I said so to Sir Patrick, but he dismissed my fears as imagined folly. This is the one and only time that I will betray my brother's trust. After this, you shall be obliged to do your duty."

Mary once again awaited Mabel's response. The latter, however, contented herself with the private thought that she would make the best of her opportunity. Rebuffed, Mary exclaimed, "I must go and check on the preparations. Our guests are arriving soon and when they do, you are to behave as a lady, betrothed to another. I will be watching you. Do not spend much longer on your attire."

Mary turned and left the chamber in agitation. When she had closed the door, Mabel hurried over to it and listened to Mary's footsteps receding in the distance. Then, when she was sure that her sister was not about to return, she went to the chest and opened it. There, hidden amongst the linen shifts, was a bunch of letters. Mabel had spoken true when she said she had not seen Hugh in two months. She had, however, been in correspondence with him. A friend from the Irish Council, William Warren, had been their messenger. Mabel rummaged through the bundle and extracted the most recent communication. Her hands trembled as she opened it and reread its contents for the thousandth time. Her girlish heart swelled with delight. She carefully refolded it, putting it back with the rest of the bundle and returned them to the chest. Finally, she took one last look in the glass, adjusted a loosened tendril of hair and, with an almost unbearable sense of anticipation, left the bedchamber and hurried downstairs.

The regime in Dublin Castle had improved for Hugh Roe, Henry and Art since the appointment of the new Constable. They were still in chains, but they were now allowed have their dinner in the refectory, with the rest of the prisoners. Henry still chose to sit apart from Hugh Roe but Art continually accompanied him. They were allowed an hour, after which they had to return to their cell where they had another hour before they were finally locked up for the night. Henry usually returned to his cell on his own, but when, after a half an hour, he saw Hugh Roe and Art leave, he quietly put some bread in the pocket of his mantle and rose to follow them. As he did so, one of his companions grabbed him. "You're not leaving already, Henry? Stay and talk. Surely you're not that anxious to be in O'Donnell's company. Don't you see enough of him?"

Henry laughed. "Indeed, you speak true. No, I must go to the privy. Whatever the English are feeding us, gives me the gripes. I wouldn't be surprised if they're trying to poison us."

His companions agreed. "Bloody bastards," one of them shouted. Henry left and he saw his brother and Hugh Roe disappear into the tower, where their cell was located. He quickened his step to catch up with them but made sure that he didn't break into a run, careful not to incur his gaoler's suspicion. When he got to the tower, he bounded up the two flights of steps to their cell. There was no one there so he raced up the third flight to the privy, which was located on the outer wall of the tower where the floor of the chamber cantilevered out over the moat that encircled the castle. In the floor was a hole, which was used as the lavatory, the human wastes falling down into the moat.

On entering, he saw O'Donnell on the floor, filing at his leg irons. Art stood watching him. Hugh Roe commented sarcastically to him. "So, you're going to join us after all."

Henry nodded. "I do not like it. Maplesden leaves a file and rope in our cell. He allows Neill O'Hagan visit us and help arrange your escape. They're probably going to kill us, once we attempt to leave."

"I've already told you, Henry, O'Neill has bribed Maplesden. We've naught to fear. If you wish to come, you are welcome, but the decision is yours," Art answered.

"I will not take the risk that you are wrong. Being locked up here is hellish. But I would not wish to be beholden to O'Neill for anything."

Art cut in anxiously. "You will not be. He has paid to get Hugh Roe free. The fact that we escape too, is nothing to do with him. We must take the opportunity now that it has presented itself. He would probably prefer if you stayed here where you cannot cause any problems for him."

Hugh Roe removed the last leg iron, threw it into the corner and handed the file to Art. "Here, Art, make haste."

Henry walked over to the opening in the floor of the privy and looked down. "You really think that we will get through that?"

Hugh Roe replied, " I did it once before."

Henry scratched his head. "What about Art? He is not going first. He'll probably get stuck like a cork in a cask and then none of us will escape."

Art looked up from his filing. "I am getting through that hole, come what may. Ten years here is long enough for me. My only comfort was eating. There was naught else to do?"

Henry laughed. "You were always fat, brother. You resemble our benefactor, Maplesden, now."

Art removed the last chain and threw it into the corner, beside Hugh Roe's. He angrily cast the file at Henry, saying, "I should not even give you this!"

Henry laughed mirthlessly, took the implement and started filing vigorously at his chains. Hugh Roe took the rope and tied it to the bars on the door of the privy. He pulled on it with all his weight. It held. "I will go first," he said.

He was concerned about what Henry had said. Art was indeed very heavy but he himself was getting out whatever about the others. He removed his mantle so that he would be able to climb more easily. He lay on his stomach and let his legs dangle through the opening. He caught hold of the rope and eased himself through the aperture and found himself hanging free in the night air.

It was almost Christmas and it had grown dark early. A cold north wind blew sharply and Hugh Roe felt its icy edge go through him like a blade. He swung the rope in towards the castle wall, using his legs to help take some of the weight. Eventually, he reached the ground and released the rope. He gave it a quick whip like shake and sent a ripple running up it to the two brothers waiting above. He looked up and saw two legs appear in the opening. He noticed the sky and grew anxious. It was grey and leaden. It is definitely cold enough for snow, he thought. Then he saw Henry making his decent. He held the bottom of the rope tightly against the wall to aid him. Within a few minutes, he arrived safely below beside Hugh Roe. They were standing on a narrow ledge of earth, the moat separating them from dry land and freedom on the other side. "I hope he remembers to throw down our cloaks," Hugh Roe said. "I am frozen already."

They looked up and saw the third pair of legs appear through the opening. Hugh Roe swore to himself. Art had forgotten the mantles and he could not risk calling out to remind him. O'Donnell and Henry held onto the rope. Next, they saw the hips and rump appear in the aperture and then nothing more. They waited for a few moments and still nothing happened.

"What did I tell you! He's stuck!" Henry said. "What must we do now?"

Hugh Roe looked up. "Give him a little time. He should manage to squeeze through somehow."

They watched the legs squirming as Art attempted to extricate himself from his predicament. Henry, in desperation, grabbed the rope tightly and started to pull on it in short sharp tugs. They watched and then, with a surge, Art came free. It happened suddenly and it was obvious that he had been caught by surprise, as he fell through the air for a few feet before clutching the rope and arresting his descent. He remained dangling in mid air for a few moments and then he began to manoeuvre downwards, very slowly. Hugh Roe and Henry held the rope tightly so that Art could use the wall to help him lower himself. All went well until Art was about ten feet from the ground. His burned, chafed hands lost their command of the rope and letting go, he fell on top of the his two waiting companions. All three collapsed in a heap, Hugh Roe and Henry barely managing to stop Art and themselves from rolling into the moat. They slowly got to their feet. "My ankle, I think I've damaged it." Art moaned.

"You nearly killed us, you great big oaf," hissed Henry.

Hugh Roe shushed the two of them. "Come. We must follow the wall around until we get to the drawbridge. We'll have to cross there, unless you want to swim the moat."

"I can't swim," Art confessed.

"Very well, that's decided then," Hugh Roe concluded.

Slowly and carefully, they made their way around the walls of the castle until they reached its drawbridge. On gaining it, they noticed the gates still open and a soldier standing guard. "See, I told you it was all too simple," Henry muttered.

"We'll just have to cross underneath it. We can hang off it from the planks that support the bridge and swing across from arm to arm. He won't be able to see us. As long as we stay silent, we'll gain safety," Hugh Roe whispered.

Art looked unsure. "It's a long way."

"You can do it. Just keep thinking of what failure will mean. Once we get to the other side, we'll have to work our way around the water line of the moat until we reach our tower again. O'Hagan should be waiting there with another rope so that we can climb up the ditch and then we're free."

Henry grimaced. "We still have to get out of the city and home."

"That will be easy in comparison. I'll go first," O'Donnell responded.

He quickly passed the remaining few feet to the drawbridge, hugging the castle wall. The sentry would not see him unless he left the doorway, in which he was sheltering, came to the edge of the bridge and looked down into the moat. Hugh Roe knew that he wouldn't do that, unless he heard some noise that made him suspicious. He grabbed the timber under-structure of the bridge and swung himself easily across the moat. On reaching the other side, he dropped silently onto the mud wall of the ditch. He was totally masked by the bridge. He was pleased at how easy he had found the crossing.

He looked back to see Henry, already half way across the bridge. He's a tough bastard all the same, Hugh Roe thought, as Henry swung competently over the murky water to join him. He landed with a gentle thud beside him. They then both turned to watch Art. He was still on the other side, looking at the underbelly of the bridge. They saw him rock over and back as he willed himself into leaping onto the timber decking. Henry whispered, "He probably won't even get half way before he falls into the moat and drowns, the useless tub of lard."

They watched as Art leaped and grabbed hold of the wooden structure. He swung there for a number of seconds without advancing and then released one arm and moved it forward. He then did the same with the other hand and once again, he stopped and swung in mid air. "What delays him?" Henry asked. "The faster he does it, the less it will take out of him."

Hugh Roe didn't answer but continued watching Art's slow progress. Many times it looked like he'd fall but, from somewhere, tenacity came to him and he hung on. After what seemed an eternity, he reached the other side. Hugh Roe and Henry leaned out over the moat and pulled him in. Art collapsed on the mud in a heap, unable to get up. Hugh Roe leaned over him. "You must get up. They could discover our escape any moment. We have been far too slow as it is."

Hugh Roe and Henry helped him to his feet and half dragged, half carried him along the fringe of the moat. On reaching the southeastern tower, Hugh Roe whistled softly. Suddenly, a rope was thrown down the side of the moat.

"Not more bloody climbing," Art cursed.

"You go first, this time. I'll follow right behind you. Use the rope to help you climb up. Take your time. Bit by bit and you'll make it."

Art started climbing and Hugh Roe followed him. Henry remained at the bottom, watching their progress.

"If he falls on you, Hugh, you're carrion meat," Henry whispered.

Both climbers ignored him. They slowly made their way up the side of the moat, the gravel of which ran from under their feet as they entrusted their weight to it. Finally, Art reached the top and Neill O'Hagan bent over to pull him to safety. On reaching the top, Hugh Roe greeted Neill. "It's good to see you, friend."

"And you too, Hugh Roe," Neill answered. "And what about Henry? Did he come with you?"

"Yes I did," a voice answered from the moat, as Henry's face appeared above the embankment. Hugh Roe went to haul him up. He talked to Neill from over his shoulder. "What is the plan now? O'Neill told me that you would look after us from here."

"You won't look after me," Henry cut in. "I'd prefer to take my chances on my own than trust a friend of O'Neill's."

"Talk sense, man. Where will you go on your own? You've no money. How will you get home?" Neill asked.

"I'll manage. Well Art, are you coming with me?"

Art looked from Hugh Roe to his brother and back again. "It makes no sense not to stay with Hugh Roe and Neill. They got us this far, didn't they? We stand a better chance by sticking together."

"Suit yourself," Henry replied. "You'd only slow me down." And with that he was gone, melting into the darkness.

"Henry, come back. Don't be foolish," Art whispered loudly after him but it was to no avail. Hugh Roe turned back to Neill. "Well, where to now?" he asked.

"There's been a problem. Edward Eustace, an English, Protestant friend of O'Neill's, was to meet me with horses, but he never appeared. I don't know what happened to him. Maybe he grew wary of this venture."

"Can we wait any longer?" Hugh Roe asked.

"No. The gates will be locked soon for the night. We must not be trapped in Dublin. If we are, they will find you once the alarm is raised. O'Neill has proposed that we head for Glenmalure, Fiach Mac Hugh O'Byrne's stronghold. Fiach's always at war with the English. He's broken out into rebellion again, so you'll be safe there."

"How will we get there?" Hugh Roe asked, afraid of the answer that he knew was imminent.

"We'll have to cross Sliabh Ruaidh. Then, we can make our way to his castle."

"A curse on that," Hugh Roe replied. "I was afraid you would say so."

"It will be safer that way. We won't run into any of Her Majesty's troops up there," Neill said.

"You don't have any mantles with you?" Hugh Roe asked.

"No, and it's too late to get any now," Neill answered.

"We'll just have to manage. Let us get underway," Hugh Roe said. Neill untied the rope from the tree, to which it had been secured and threw it down into the moat. With that the three fugitives hurried away.

The dinner at Sir Patrick's house had passed off excellently. O'Neill and his three English companions, Sir Garret Moore, Sir William Warren and Sir Lucas Bellow, had arrived punctually and the banquet had been served promptly. Mabel was too excited to know the contentment, which true happiness conveys. Mary could not but be impressed by the well-built and handsome man that was her love, she thought.

Hugh was dressed in the most fashionable of courtier's costumes. His crimson, gold studded doublet and hose were resplendent and his manners and deportment were indistinguishable from those of the highest born English nobles. His charm was limitless and Mabel could discern Mary's surprise. She listened attentively as Hugh recounted story after story of the English court, its customs, its latest gossip, of the fall from grace of his great supporter, the Earl of Leicester and his subsequent lonely death. Mabel was proud to see how Hugh took command of the table, scarcely glancing in her direction. But she was content in the knowledge that she looked well. She was garbed in a robe of deep green velvet and silk, heavily embroidered at the bodice, and falling away in a graceful sweep from her tiny waist. Minute seed pearls studded the hem and neckline, the latter, deeply scooped revealing the milky richness of her bosom. Only one thought resided there, Hugh wanted her for his wife.

When the meal was finished, Sir Patrick rose and addressed his guests. "Would you, gentlemen, like to withdraw to my chamber to sample a very fine French claret that I recently imported and maybe indulge me in a game of cards?"

Hugh, Garett and Lucas all nodded but Sir William Warren ruefully shook his head. "I regret that I must beg to be excused. I am obliged to return home as my wife has not been feeling well of late. She is heavy with child and is ill at ease when I am absent overnight. I must, however, thank you, Sir Patrick, for a most enjoyable repast."

Sir Patrick nodded and smiled. "You are very welcome, Sir William. Come, we will see you out."

"No there is no need. I must just bid farewell to the ladies before I leave."

Sir Garrett chuckled. "You're a wily fox, Sir William. Now that we must take our leave of the ladies, you decide to return home. You have no time for us men."

Warren chivalrously agreed. "I must confess that you have found me out. Goodnight ladies. It has been a pleasure."

Warren bowed and left the chamber. After his departure Sir Patrick turned to his guests. "Come, gentlemen, to my chamber. We'll leave these ladies to their female employments." He went to Mary and kissed her lightly on the cheek. "Good night, my dear."

"Good night," she replied, and then turned to the rest of the men. "Good night, gentlemen."

The three men bowed and Hugh approached, taking Mary's hand. "It has been my pleasure to make your acquaintance. You and Sir Patrick must come north and visit me, where I will return your hospitality."

Mary smiled. "That will be for Sir Patrick to decide."

Hugh returned her smile. "Why then, I must convince him over cards." He then turned to Mabel and bowed. "I must also wish Mistress Mabel goodnight. Graced by such loveliness, it is indeed a trial to take our leave."

Mabel flushed, privately delighting in such reckless gallantry on her lover's part.

Sir Patrick added. "You must dine with us again. But come, I intend to lighten your purses before you return home. You shall pay for your dinner."

The men then withdrew, leaving the women to their own company. Mabel turned to Mary. "Well, sister. What did you think of him?" she asked excitedly.

Mary didn't answer directly. O'Neill's comment to Mabel had offended her norms of propriety. Her face assumed a look of disapproval. Mabel apprehensively awaited her sister's response and she, unwilling to hurt her, sought a reply.

"I can see why you admire him. I must confess that he surprised me. I had expected something quite different. He is indeed polished."

Mabel was gratified. "Did I not tell you so? You see, he does not resemble the ordinary Irishman. He's so refined and cultivated."

Mary grimaced. "That may well be Mabel, but it changes nothing. It still can never be. I know he has proposed honourable marriage, but your brother and guardian has said no and that must be an end of it. You can always be acquainted. When you're a married woman, you can convince your husband to include him in your circle."

Mabel shook her head passionately. "You comprehend these matters so ill, Mary. Wingfield is as much a bigot as Henry. Do you think that he could be on friendly terms with a rival, especially an Irish one? He is incensed that Hugh should even have thought of marrying me. I will not marry Wingfield. If I cannot marry Hugh, well then, I'll not marry at all!"

Mary replied anxiously. "Fie, fie Mabel. Do not say such things. I dread to think what Henry would do if he heard you speak so. You must promise me that you'll never speak thus to him. For your own sake, Mabel, you must promise me."

Mabel seethed with angry disappointment. She had hoped that once Mary had met Hugh that she would reconsider her disapproval and become her confidante. They had always been close and now she felt betrayed. Rebellion and anger welled up inside her and in her disenchantment, she retorted.

"I will not promise. I will never promise you. I tell you, I'll marry Hugh or I'll marry no one. I will not deviate from that. And now, I am going to bed where, at least, I can dream of him, where you and Henry cannot come between us."

Mabel turned and hastened away to her chamber. On reaching it, her heart was pounding so loudly, that she feared she would faint. She stood inside the door, her ear close pressed to it, listening for the sound of footsteps following. When she was sure that Mary was not in pursuit, she turned, raced to the chest and removed Hugh's letters. A feeling of release flooded her. At last, the time had come for action. She grabbed her warmest cloak, wrapping it tightly around her slim, shivering body, before slowly opening the door. She stood motionless and listened, but all that was to be heard were the distant muffled voices and laughter of the men drinking in Sir Patrick's chamber. In the quiet of the upstairs she could hear her own heart hammering against her ribs.

Slowly, she entered the passage and closed the door behind her. Carefully, she descended the stairs, and on reaching the last step, she hurried past the doors of Sir Patrick's chamber and the banqueting hall. Just then, the door to the buttery swung open and Thomas, the head butler, appeared, carrying a flagon of Rhenish. Both of them stood frozen to the spot, as if a sudden frost had rendered them immobile. Thomas's gaze went through her and beyond. Then, to Mabel's utter perplexity, he simply walked past. Mabel ran for the door, which led out onto the grounds, to the rear of the house. She opened it and hastened into the garden towards the old derelict church and graveyard, part of a monastery that had been suppressed in the time of Henry VIII.

The countryside was wrapped in a mantle of snow, which had fallen since the moon had risen. It gave the countryside a crisp, clean air and as the snowflakes were still billowing down, she threw her hood over her head. It would be another cold, snowy Christmastide, she thought to herself and hurried towards the church. Every now and again, she cast an anxious glance back over her shoulder to see if she was being followed. She expected that, at any moment, she would see her brother-in-law and some of his servants spilling out of the house. What would Hugh do then, she wondered.

On reaching the church, there was still no sign of any posse in pursuit. Perhaps Thomas had not said anything after all. It was almost too much to hope for. She took shelter in the derelict doorway and stood breathlessly looking both at the house and graveyard. Perhaps there had been a fight. Hugh would not tolerate being thwarted. She looked around again. Where was William, she thought. The eerie surroundings heightened her sense of isolation and terror.

"Psst, psst, Mistress Mabel?" a man's voice hissed.

"Yes," she replied in relief. "Is that you, William?"

Sir William Warren stood up from behind one of the snow-covered tombstones. With the moonlight shining on his snowy cloak and his face ashen from the cold, he resembled a ghostly spectre, more than a living being. Mabel, whose nerves were overwrought, emitted a shrill scream. Sir William ran quickly to her.

"Hush, Mistress Mabel, hush for God's sake! Come, my horse is around the back of the church, just out of sight."

He grasped Mabel's arm and pulled her gently but firmly to the rear of the church.

Mabel, still breathless, stammered. "William, Thomas saw me. I'm afraid that he'll tell my brother-in-law."

Warren replied. "All is well. I have talked with Thomas and paid him to leave the rear entrance open. I could not chance its being locked. Thomas will not talk."

Relief flooded Mabel. They had managed the difficult part. She was in the protection of one of Hugh's friends. The rest would be easier. They reached the horse, which neighed on seeing them. William went to him and gently rubbed his face. The horse too, was covered in snow and his owner quickly cleared the saddle. He untethered the animal and with one bound, was astride. He bent down and caught Mabel around the waist and with one easy movement, lifted her up and placed her in front of him. Mabel found herself sitting sidesaddle. She was supple and slender and this new sensation of having a man's arms around her body, made her alert to an exquisite tension in every fibre of her being. In her short twenty years, she had never experienced anything like this night. God protect me, she prayed silently, but I have no choice. I will have Hugh as my husband. William interrupted her reflections. "I could not risk taking another horse from the stable. I regret such a mode of transport for a lady of your delicacy. I trust you will not find the journey too distressing."

William spurred his horse and they set off at a gallop across the frozen countryside. Mabel could feel his warm breath on her neck. She turned to him and asked. "Where are we going, William?"

"To an inn, three miles distant, where Hugh has arranged for us to take shelter. It is located very near the Bishop of Meath's house. You are to be married there, tonight."

"Tonight," Mabel echoed. "William. Are you certain? But what of the Bishop of Meath? How did Hugh persuade him?"

William laughed. "He does not know yet, but have no fear, Hugh will be able to convince him. I think he could convince the Devil to be a good Christian."

Mabel smiled. She delighted in hearing reports of Hugh's cleverness. She thought of him and of the fact that before this night would be over, she'd be a married woman. She'd know the secret of the marriage bed. She imagined William's arms were Hugh's, his breath, Hugh's passionate breathing, his warmth, Hugh's ardour and in spite of herself, she blushed, glad that her face was hidden by her cloak.

The three fugitives were battling their way up the eastside of Sliabh Ruaidh. The snow had started falling on the mountain before it had spread into the plains below. It was bitterly cold and Hugh Roe and Art had good reason to regret leaving behind their warm mantles. The climb had been hard enough before the snow had started falling, but now, as they fought their way through the blizzard, they also had to contend with what had settled on the ground. Hugh Roe was worried that they would lose their way, as the drifts that were blanketing the countryside were obliterating the goat tracks they were following. Art had been finding the climb particularly difficult and they had to stop many times to allow him catch up with them. They were now almost at the top and suddenly Art stopped dead.

"I can go no further. I'm sorry, I just can't. I'm too cold and tired." He sat down in the snow. "You go on ahead. I'll stay here. At least I'll die a freeman."

Hugh Roe and Neill halted. Hugh Roe answered, "We'll not leave you behind. Come, Art. We haven't that far to go to the top and it will be easier going downhill. I know, because I've climbed this devil mountain before."

"No, I cannot, Hugh. I'd prefer to die here than take another step. I can't will my legs on any further."

Hugh Roe walked over to him and dragged him to his feet. "Come Neill, aid me." He threw Art's arm over his shoulder and Neill did likewise with Art's second arm. They started walking again, supporting Art's weight between the two of them. They stumbled and floundered through the snow, bent double under Art's weight. It took them another half an hour to reach the summit. When they reached it, they stopped again.

"I don't know how much farther I'll be able to drag him. He's one heavy bastard," Hugh Roe confided to Neill when they were out of earshot of Art.

"We could leave him here. No one would blame us. I'm sure of that. The conditions are atrocious. It wouldn't be the worst sort of death. He'd just fall asleep and never wake up again," Neill replied.

"No, as long as I have any strength left in my body, I'll not leave him behind," Hugh Roe answered.

"It strikes me, that Henry knew what he was doing when he left Art with us. You have to think of yourself, O'Donnell. You cannot expend all your energy in carrying him down the mountain," Neill replied.

"No. I won't leave him. Come, let's go another bit." Hugh Roe walked back to Art and dragged him to his feet, despite his vehement protestations. Neill shrugged and went to join them.

Three hours later, they were over half way down the other side of Sliabh Ruaidh. For the last hour, Art's legs had dragged uselessly behind him, leaving two continuous trails in the snow behind. Their stops for rest had become more frequent as the night wore on. Hugh Roe could no longer feel his feet. His shoes had been wet thoroughly by the snow and they were now struggling through over two feet of it. He was tired, and his tiredness seemed to be measured in proportion to Art's apparently increasing weight. Hugh Roe looked up and could see the dim sliver of dawn creasing the sky. There still was no sign of the snow ceasing. Suddenly, Hugh Roe stumbled and fell. His legs gave way and Art and Neill fell on top of him. Neill struggled to his feet and rolled Art off Hugh Roe's body.

O'Donnell shook his head. "It's no good, Neill," he said. "I can't go on any further. That last hour was almost unbearable. I forced myself to continue. I told myself I had to, every time I felt like giving up, but I've reached the end of my strength. I must rest, I must sleep before I'll be able to take another step."

"You can't sleep here. Leave Art. We haven't that much further to go. If you're not burdened by him, you can make it," Neill replied.

"No, I said I wouldn't leave him and I've used up all my strength in trying to bring him with us. Leave the two of us here. Go and get help. It's our only hope now," Hugh Roe answered.

Neill looked around at the snow-covered terrain. There was no sign of a break in the weather. He turned back to Hugh Roe imploringly. "It's not that far now. Three miles and I know where I can get some horses. Then a short ride and we'll be safe in O'Byrne's castle. I'll help you, like we've been helping Art. We can do it. If you stay here you risk certain death. O'Neill will kill me, if I leave you."

"No, Neill. I cannot and I won't leave Art. The quicker you go, the quicker you'll be back."

Neill knew that there was no changing O'Donnell's mind. "We must try and find you some shelter," he conceded, looking around the bleak landscape. He worried at what O'Neill would have to say if he left O'Donnell to die on the mountainside. His own father, who had been a foster brother to O'Neill, would be angrier still with him for failing O'Neill. Still, there was nothing more he could do. He doubted even whether he could have got O'Donnell down the mountain, on his own. He himself was very tired.

"If you're to stay here, you must remain in a sheltered spot. Over there, see the over hanging rock formation. That will give you some protection from the wind. The tree beside it should give you some protection from the falling snow. Come, you must have some shelter."

Neill aided Hugh Roe to his feet and helped him to the cliff face. He sat him down and returned for Art, dragging him across the snow and setting him down beside Hugh Roe. Neill pulled out his sword and cut some branches from the tree, shaking as much of the snow off them as he could. Next, he placed them on the ground in the shelter of the cliff. He then removed his mantle and laid it on the branches. He turned to Hugh Roe. "Here, help with Art."

"You must keep it yourself. We will be relying on you to get help. We cannot have you freezing to death," Hugh Roe argued.

"No. I'll be moving."

They lifted Art and laid him on the makeshift mattress. "Now, you must lie beside him. I will wrap the mantle around both of you. Your bodies' heat should keep you both warm for awhile." Hugh Roe lay down beside Art and Neill wrapped them both tightly together. He then addressed Hugh Roe. "You must keep awake. Whatever you do, do not fall asleep."

Hugh Roe nodded. Neill gave Art a kick. He grunted. "I'm relying on you, Art to stay awake as well. You're both to keep each other from sleeping."

"Very well, Neill. I just want to rest. I'm too cold to sleep anyway."

Neill returned to the tree and cut more branches. He then piled them up on top of the two men and stood back to appraise his work. "That's all I can do for you. I will be as fast as I can. May God keep you safe until I return with help."

Hugh Roe added, "And may He guide your steps and bring you back here soon."

With that, Neill was gone, melting instantly into the blizzard. Anxiety steeped Hugh Roe's mind as he wondered if Neill would reach safety and return before Art and he froze to death. With a colossal effort, he tried to root out doubt from his mind. What would be, would be. It was in the hands of God now and there was no more that he could do. He turned to Art and wrapped his arms around him, brushing the snow from his beard.

"Art," he said. "We must take it in turns to recount stories so that we both stay awake. Let us talk about what we'll do once we reach home. The first thing I will do is drive all the English from Donegal, every last one of them. I will repay them for all the torment that they have inflicted on me. Then I'm going to claim the Chieftainship. And you, Art?"

Hugh Roe paused to hear Art's plans, but got no reply. He listened and all he discerned was the steady breathing of one in deep sleep. Curse it, he thought and began to thump Art on the back. "Wake up, Art, damn you, wake up," he shouted and shook him vigorously. There was no reaction, except for a groan that escaped from Art's lips and then he fell asleep again. Hugh gave up the effort. Art had endured as much as he could. He should survive, he thought. As Neill had said, they'd keep each other warm.

His first night's sleep as a free man in over three years, he thought. Somehow, he had imagined a better bed and a more comfortable abode. He would survive this. He'd see his native Donegal again, his mother, father and all his family. He looked forward to being surrounded once again by the sound of the Irish language and not that horrible guttural tongue the English spoke. O'Donnell felt his eyelids closing, in spite of himself. Tired, so very tired, and now the cold was beginning to gnaw right into his bones. It was as if the marrow itself was turning to ice. Hugh Roe once again brushed the snow off his beard and hair. Already there was a blanket of it on top of the branches that Neill had arranged so carefully over them. He thought of how luckless it would be to have escaped from Dublin Castle only to freeze to death on this God forsaken mountain. No, it could not happen, it must not happen. He had so much to achieve. He had a mission, a destiny and he promised God that if he brought him alive through this travail, he would not rest until he drove every last Englishman out of Ireland.

It was so cold, though, and he was feeling deeply exhausted. He thought of his childhood when he and his brothers used go with their father on his visitations to his client Chieftains. He remembered how, in the summertime, they would sleep out in the open, under the stars. He used to bury his head under his mantle and create his own little tent. Now, he buried down under this mantle. He began thinking, warm, warm, I am feeling warm. He tried to imagine the warmth spreading out from deep within his chest, radiating throughout his whole body. After some time, he thought he felt warmer and he became drowsier and drowsier until, eventually, he fell asleep, dreaming of his triumphal return to Donegal.

Mabel paced up and down the dining chamber of the inn, in which she and William awaited Hugh's arrival. A large fire blazed in the hearth and they had been served with warm punch on their arrival, some three hours previously. She was now physically comfortable but her mind was in torment. What was keeping Hugh? Had Mary gone to her bedchamber and found her missing? If she had, what would have happened? Every time she addressed herself to that question, different responses presented themselves, all of them distressing. William had done his best to reassure her and at times, had been successful, but then the doubts would once again insinuate themselves into her mind and hold sway. William said Hugh could not leave too early without raising suspicions. But three hours! That was too long. How could he bear to be parted from her for such a length? Surely he would wish to be with her as soon as possible. He could have used the falling snow as an excuse for his leaving early, before the drifts would make travel impossible. But then, maybe, he was not aware that it was snowing. She had not been either until she had left the house. Maybe he was already cut off from her or worse still maybe, God forbid, he had got lost on the way. She turned to William. "You don't think that they could have got lost? It's still snowing very heavily," she asked nervously.

"Of course not. Bellow knows the countryside like the back of his hand. They'll be here soon," William replied. Mabel thought she detected an abatement in his usual sense of certainty. A wave of agitation coursed through her body. She was just about to cross-examine him when she heard voices in the hallway and recognised Hugh's. She ran to the door, but before she could reach it, it was flung open and Hugh strode into the chamber, closely followed by Moore and Bellow. They still wore their cloaks, which were snow covered, their boots leaving wet marks on the floor.

Mabel threw herself into Hugh's arms and he lifted her from the ground. "Oh, Hugh. I never thought you'd come. What detained you?"

Hugh smiled. "We couldn't get away from your brother-in-law. Luck was favouring his hand and he didn't want us to leave. Then, when he finally consented to our leave taking, he accompanied us to the door and on seeing the snow, insisted that we stay the night. I thought that we would never get away."

Mabel ran her hand through his beard. " Come and warm yourself by the fire and take off that cloak. I'll order some hot punch for you."

Hugh disengaged himself from Mabel's embrace and gently set her down. "Mabel, we have no time to waste," he said softly. "For all we know, they might have already discovered that you are missing. We must make one more short journey, but this time, it shall be together and on foot. After that, we will be safe and no one will ever be able to part us again. Are you strong enough to come with me?"

Mabel smiled. "I would follow you to the very gates of hell, my love."

Hugh turned to William. "And you, William?"

"I really should be getting home. My wife will be worrying. If you can do without my services, I would prefer to try and make my way there."

Hugh smiled and nodded. "But of course, William. Moore and Bellow have agreed to be my witnesses." He went to William and took his hand in his. "I won't forget the service that you have rendered me tonight, William. God speed you home."

William replied, "And God bless you and Mistress Mabel upon the path that you are embarking tonight."

With that, William turned and was gone. Hugh addressed Mabel. "Put on your cloak, my love. It's still snowing outside."

Mabel went to the fireplace and removed the mantle from the back of a chair, where it had been drying, and threw it over her shoulders.

"Come," Hugh said and the four of them passed quickly through the house and out into the street.

Mabel was surprised at the amount of snow that had fallen while she had been inside. It was now over eight inches deep on the pathway and had drifted up against the side of the inn to a depth of a few feet. Hugh's strong arm encircled her waist, lending her support. Gratefully, she leaned against him, her giddiness making it difficult to negotiate safely the slippery surface underfoot. She felt the strong, muscular torso beneath the coarse mantle and marvelled at the disparity of their forms.

After a short walk, they arrived at the Bishop's palace and passed quickly through the gates, striding up the driveway to the house. Mabel had been brought up in the reformed church and it was in this same church that she would be wed. As they proceeded, she noticed that the Bishop's abode was in darkness and her spirits sank. She had set her heart on being married tonight and she did not wish it deferred any longer. Hugh was practically lifting her along, in his haste to reach their destination, and she was too breathless to question him.

When they reached the door, Hugh, using the hilt of his sword, hammered loudly. The noise reverberated within and when there was no reply, he hammered again. Finally, they heard movement inside and after a few moments, the door creaked open a fraction and a servant peered around the doorframe. He held a candle, and in its light, they could make out a middle-aged man, dressed in night attire, a cloak hastily thrown around his shoulders. He hissed at them, "Is this any hour to come calling at a Christian's house and that of the Bishop's too? Be off with you now and don't wake His Grace from his slumbers."

Hugh answered autocratically. "We must see His Grace tonight. It is a matter of great urgency."

The servant stuck his head fully around the door and eyed the visitors He looked long and hard at Mabel and then at the others, taking in the costliness of their raiment. It was evident that he had realised that these were men of substance for, on addressing them again, his voice was modulated with politeness and restraint. He shook his head. "It is very late. Perhaps if you came back in the morning..." he began when he was interrupted by O'Neill.

"We cannot wait until the morning. It is a matter of great importance. His Grace will see me. Tell him the Earl of Tyrone must see him on an urgent matter."

Still, the servant hesitated. O'Neill raised his voice and ordered, "Go, man."

At this, the servant lost all indecisiveness and held the door open. "Come," he said and they followed him into the house.

Mabel's hopes rose. At least they were within. Now, all that remained to be done was to convince the Bishop. Still, if anyone could do that, it was Hugh. She was in awe of his authority, how he could take control of a situation to his own purpose. The servant showed them into a narrow chamber and lit the candles before retiring. The place was cold even though there were embers of a fire in the grate. Sir Garret went to it and prodded the smouldering coals with the fire iron, which lay beside it. He exposed the embers that had been hidden under the ash and then, finding some small logs, threw them upon it. "I'm sure that His Grace won't begrudge us a bit of heat," he said.

He didn't receive any answer. Hugh was pacing up and down, obviously impatient to get his business over. Bellow had collapsed into an armchair, the lateness of the hour and the amount he had drunk, finally catching up on him. Mabel too, was beginning to feel weary. She hadn't slept well these last few nights, ever since she had received Hugh's letter telling her of his plans for their elopement. Now that they were finally together, she relaxed for the first time in days. After a short interval, the servant returned and said, "His Grace will see you now." He then turned and left the chamber. O'Neill took Mabel's hand and followed him.

They walked through the darkened passageways, the guttering candle throwing grotesque shadows on the walls. Finally, they came to a door, upon which the servant knocked. A voice from within bade them enter. They followed their guide and found themselves in an oak-panelled chamber. At a table, sat a grey haired, middle aged man. He was unkempt and had evidently dressed in a hurry. On seeing Mabel, he unconsciously smoothed his hair.

The servant announced. "The Earl of Tyrone and..." He paused, looking at Hugh to supply the missing name.

"Lady Mabel Bagenal," Hugh answered.

The servant withdrew. The Bishop rose and came around from behind the table. He stretched out his hand, which O'Neill took, bending low to kiss his ring. They had met from time to time at official functions and were acquainted with each other.

"Well, Hugh, what brings you to my house at this hour of the night?" He then cast a disapproving glance at Mabel. "And what is the Marshal's sister doing in your company?"

Hugh was well aware of the Bishop's worldliness. He had bought the office and was fond of gaming and women. In the past, he had borrowed money from him to cover gambling debts, money for which Hugh had not sought repayment. He had regarded it as an investment and now he would reap the interest.

"I won't delay you or waste your time, Your Grace. Mabel and I wish to be married and we wish you to perform the service."

The Bishop paled. Mabel could see that the prospect held little joy for him.

"But of course, I should be happy to do so, once the banns are read and we have Sir Henry's permission. Why then, we'll have a very good day's celebration."

"We wish to be married tonight. If we had Sir Henry's blessing, we would not be calling on you at this late hour," Hugh retorted.

The Bishop slumped slightly, finding support from the heavy oak table.

"Hugh, what you request is well nigh impossible."

O'Neill continued, undeterred. "We are both old enough to know our own minds. We love each other and wish to be married."

Mabel could see discomfort etched on the Bishop's features. Again, he attempted to speak, choosing his words with deliberate delicacy. "Mistress Mabel is still the sister of the Queen's Marshal. Marriages, such as you propose, are within the Royal benefice to allow or disallow. I imagine that I would need the Privy Council's permission before I could carry out such a marriage. You know that the Queen dislikes Irish and English intermarriage."

"Are Mabel and I not both the Queen's loyal subjects? What is the possible harm that could come to the Queen from our union? Would it not be a boon to the country if more English and native Irish married and begot children? In any event, Mabel was born in Newry, so she is Irish born."

The Bishop shook his head apologetically. "I agree with you, but Mistress Mabel is the daughter of an English man and as such will always be regarded as English. I must have the permission of the Irish Council, at the very least."

Hugh spoke slowly and deliberately. "As you know, I am a member of Her Majesty's Council of Ireland and an Earl of the Realm. I have two more members of the Council outside, Sir Garret Moore and Sir Lucas Bellow, who are willing to act as witnesses to the marriage. Sir William Warren, another member, was with me until half an hour since and he also gives us his blessing. So, you need not concern yourself regarding permission from the Irish Council."

The Bishop nodded. "That is well. I know Sir Garrett and Sir Lucas Bellow. But there is still Sir Henry to think of. He has a violent temper and is not a man to cultivate as an enemy."

Mabel saw Hugh grimace. She knew he was struggling to rein in his mounting impatience. "And do you think that he will thank you for not marrying her? Think of her reputation. By coming with me tonight from her sister's house, she is thoroughly compromised. If you do not marry her now, there will always be a stain on her reputation. You cannot let the poor girl suffer that."

The Bishop nodded slowly. Mabel saw him looking at her, his gaze lingering on her person in a manner, which repulsed her. She had seen that type of look before and did not think it proper in a man of God. "I would not like to see her suffer," he said.

O'Neill smiled. "Good," he said. "There is just one other matter. I understand that you do great work among the sick and needy. I would like to be allowed help you with such honourable endeavour." Hugh reached into the folds of his cloak and withdrew a small purse, which he handed to him.

The Bishop took it and opened it, pouring the gold coins out into his dimpled hand. Mabel noted his smile of delight. He then placed them in a large teak chest. "You are very generous, Hugh. I will put it to work where it can do most good." He paused for a moment, before continuing. "I will carry out the marriage for the sake of Mistress

Mabel's reputation. It would be unchristian to send you away without doing so. Will my chamber suffice for the ceremony?"

Hugh smiled." It will be perfect."

The Bishop opened the door and summoned his servant who appeared instantly. Mabel wondered if he had been eavesdropping. "Fetch the two other gentlemen please, Gerard." The servant bowed and left.

Mabel now felt relief surge through her. Hugh had arranged everything, just like he had said. He was hers. She could rely on him. She would never again be threatened or forced into doing anything against her will by Henry. She would be Countess of Tyrone, wife of its Earl, one of the richest men in Ireland, united in Holy Matrimony to him, by the Bishop of Meath.

She looked about the chamber and thought how strange life was. She had always thought that she would be married in a church, to an Englishman and yet, life had not taken her upon that path. The future and all its hopeful prospects filled her with delight. Hugh and she would have many children. Her first born son would be an Earl. Yes, he had two sons from his previous marriage but Siobhán was dead and she would live long and be a mother many times. Her sons would truly be more suited to the inheritance, as she would ensure that they were brought up to know and value their English ancestry. Her thoughts were interrupted by a knock at the door and both Sir Garret and Sir Lucas entered.

The Bishop addressed both men. "Are you prepared to act as witnesses to the marriage of the Earl of Tyrone and Lady Mabel Bagenal?" he asked.

"We are," both men answered in unison.

"Well then, let us begin," the Bishop replied.

He stood before Hugh and Mabel. Hugh took Mabel's hand in his, and the witnesses each stood on opposite sides of the couple. The Bishop began reading from the yellowed pages of his prayer book and Hugh's thoughts turned to the two other marriage ceremonies that he had undertaken. They had turned out so differently. His marriage to Aoife had been stormy and passionate, a union of extremes, in its better moments, a union of desire and fulfilment, in its darker times, a union of acrimony, rancour and despair. On the whole, marriage to Siobhán had been more even, leading him to something like contentment. He mused about the kind of experience he and Mabel would enjoy. One thing, of which he was assured, it would be entirely different from the other two. He was eager that this union should take place. He was marrying an English bride because he had no doubt, in spite of what he had said to the Bishop, that Mabel was English. He loved the way she talked, her manners, the decorum and ways that stamped her as different. She was like an exotic plant or animal. He wondered how she would take to Ulster. He felt that his title of Earl of Tyrone would take on extra significance once he had taken an English bride. She would be useful as a hostess when he had English guests to stay at his castle in Dungannon. In time, her brother would come to accept this marriage and that too would be expedient.

But politics aside, there were other feelings lurking in his mind and heart. He longed to know her carnally, to feel her English flesh beneath his loins, to enter her, to know her difference, to subdue and own her. She was a virgin, rendering her innocent and exotic, unconquered and maddeningly desirable. Neither of his previous wives had been virgins, when he married. Irish marriage was based on trial unions, allowing the couple a period of time during which both could determine the suitability of the match. Often couples didn't marry until they had children together. Even then, if the union did not thrive, either partner could divorce the other. Aoife had divorced him, but he could understand her motive.

Hugh was suddenly brought back to the ceremony as the Bishop asked, "And who is to give the bride away?"

Hugh looked at Garret who answered, "I am." Garret took Mabel's hand and placed it in Hugh's.

"Do you, Hugh O'Neill, Earl of Tyrone, willingly marry the Lady Mabel Bagenal, and take her for your only betrothed wife and plight her thy troth?"

In an unwavering voice, Hugh answered, "I do."

Turning to Mabel, he asked. "Do you, Mabel Bagenal, willingly marry Hugh O'Neill, Earl of Tyrone, and take him for your betrothed husband and plight him your troth?"

Mabel, now overcome with emotion, tried to steady her voice but it escaped tremulously. "I do," she answered.

The Bishop asked hopefully, "The ring?"

Sir Lucas stepped forward and handed the ring to Hugh who slipped it onto Mabel's finger.

"Those whom God has joined together, let no man pull asunder," the Bishop concluded.

Hugh took Mabel in his arms and kissed her on the mouth. The vigour of his passion forced open her lips and she yielded to his bruising ardour. She felt herself sinking, melting and dissolving into him. Hugh's arms held her in savage possession and all swirled into a blissful, heady confusion, a delicious, disorientating chaos. When sense returned, she found herself confused, embarrassed. Hugh had never before kissed her, indeed, she had never been kissed by any man. Her first kiss and so many strangers present. Her cheeks glowed with emotion as she tried to marshal her riotous thoughts. She was a married woman. Countess O'Neill. Hugh relaxed his iron hold as Garret and Lucas crowded around them, offering their congratulations.

"Mabel," Moore said, "I have already importuned Hugh to spend a number of nights with me on your journey to your new home. I promise you a sumptuous wedding feast, to make up for the one you missed tonight." Moore's house was in Dundalk, which would be on their journey home to Ulster. It was beautiful with manicured gardens, a former Cistercian monastery.

Mabel smiled. "I would be delighted. Whatever gratifies my Lord, gratifies me."

Hugh laughed. "Thank you, Garret. I can't imagine anywhere I would rather celebrate it. But now, we must return to the inn. I'm sorry, wife, but we must spend our first night there. It's too late and dangerous to travel onward."

Mabel blushed becomingly. "Once I'm with you, husband, I do not mind where I stay."

Hugh urged, "Well, let us away and allow His Grace return to his bed." He took the Bishop's hand in his, "Many thanks, Your Grace. I'll not forget what you have done for me tonight." And with that, he turned and left. The Bishop silently watched them go.

It was almost midday when Neill and six other men, clambering back up the snow covered mountain, returned to that part where Hugh Roe and Art were sheltering. On reaching their plateau, Neill searched anxiously for some landmarks. Having at last identified the proper course, he set off anxiously through the snowy depths.

Mercifully, the snow had ceased falling but the sky held promise of more. Neill spotted the recess in the cliff's face and quickened his pace on recognising the tree, under which he had left the two fugitives sheltering. As he approached, he searched anxiously for a sign of life but could discern none. He recognised a mound where he had left the two men and calling out their names, he dived on it, digging away with his bare hands.

The other men joined in and soon they came to the branches that covered the fugitives. They dragged the branches off quickly and exposed the mantle. There was no movement from underneath. Neill gently raised it from the two men. The sight that greeted him made him call out in horror. Both men's eyebrows and beards were covered with frozen snow and when Neill went to roll back Hugh Roe's shirt-sleeve to take his pulse, he found that the thin material was frozen to his skin. He noticed that even his shoes and the leather thongs that bound them to his feet, were also frozen solid to his flesh. Neill shook him but there was no reaction. He looked at Art. He seemed to be in an even worse condition.

"Pass me the looking glass," he ordered one of the men. He took it and held it to O'Donnell's lips. Slowly, the mirror clouded over and he let out a triumphant shout. "O'Donnell's still alive. Fetch me the beer," he ordered. Lifting Hugh Roe into a sitting position, he took the beer from one of the men and poured some of it into Hugh Roe's mouth. It dribbled out the sides, as Hugh Roe made no attempt to swallow it. He motioned to one of the men to hold his head at an angle so that the liquid would flow down his throat. He did as he was directed and this time, O'Donnell imbibed. He coughed and spewed the drink back up. Hugh Roe's eyes opened and he focused on the people around him.

"All is well, Hugh Roe. I've come back," Neill said gently. "We're going to bring you down out of here. I want you to try and drink something. Here, try some more beer."

He held the flagon to Hugh Roe's lips and slowly poured some into his mouth. Hugh Roe swallowed but within a few moments, was sick again.

"It's fine," Neill said gently. "We'll get you off this mountain to somewhere warmer." He turned to the others. "Cut some branches and lash them together. We'll have to make some stretchers. Neither of these two will walk down from here."

He then turned his attention to Art, positioning the looking glass near his mouth. A slight mist frosted over the surface. Glancing quickly at his helper, he noted that his attention was distracted by O'Donnell's condition. Furtively, Neill cleared the glass. "You'll only need the one stretcher," he shouted to the men who were busy cutting branches. "McShane is dead. We'll leave him here. Cover him with some branches and stones. Nothing fancy, though. We must hurry and get O'Donnell home."

"Neill," Hugh Roe mumbled, "are you sure he's dead?"

"Yes," Neill answered. "There's nothing more we can do for him, God rest his soul. And you, how do you feel?"

"My legs, they have no feeling. I cannot move them," Hugh Roe answered.

"Don't fret. Everything will be well. It's just the cold. We'll have you down out of here in no time. Fiach has his personal physician waiting for you."

The helpers returned with the makeshift stretcher and they gently lifted Hugh Roe onto it. Neill carefully wrapped him in some warm clothes that he had brought with him. They then started slowly down the mountain. Hugh Roe rose on his elbow and looked back at the last resting-place of Art McShane. A wave of sorrow for a lost friend passed over him. He remembered his pact with God, and now he silently repeated it. He would not rest until there wasn't an Englishman left in Ireland.

Chapter 4

The day was mild and balmy, coiling around the Dungannon landscape like a warm embrace. Summer had taken Ireland by surprise, arriving early in April after a hard winter and a cruel, cold spring. As Mabel returned from a long walk to her new home, Dungannon Castle, she wondered how such loveliness could come so suddenly out of the grey and cheerless skies that had seemed tethered to the Tyrone hills for months on end.

The day, however, did not lift her spirits. They were too far sunk for a simple variation in weather to effect that change. Her first six months of marriage had not been as she had imagined and hoped. She had never thought that life in Gaelic society would be so absolutely different from everything that she had experienced before her marriage. Nothing had prepared her for the loneliness, which had assailed her right from the start of her entry into this new world.

Somewhere in the recesses of her mind, she had known that she would have to cope with another language, but it had never fully registered with her that the first language of her new home would be Irish. On her arrival, she could not utter a single word. She could not have been expected to. The only Irish people that she had dealt with in the past had all spoken English, even the Irish servants in her brother's house knew enough English to understand their orders. Now, with the exception of Hugh, Rose and Henry Hovendon, she found herself surrounded by people who spoke only the native idiom.

That, in itself, would not have been an insurmountable barrier, were it not for the fact that she knew that Hugh's people did not approve of his choice of her, an English woman, as his wife. They made it very plain to her in many different ways. Because she and they were divided by language, they did not have to make any pretence of politeness in their dealings with her. They ignored her totally and any effort that she made to communicate with them, they slighted and belittled. Even the children in the fields ran away from her when they saw her approach. Hugh's soldiers appeared to resent her very presence and whenever she passed a gathering of them, she would hear them commenting, mocking and laughing until she was out of earshot. It had done no real good when she had complained to Hugh. They had simply denied the whole business and said that they had not been talking about her. Her complaints had in fact worsened the situation. They resented her now more than ever.

This made her rely even more on her husband, Hovendon and Rose as the only amicable presences in the castle. Henry Hovendon, however, wasn't always available, as he was often away on Hugh's account. Mabel missed him during those absences as she had found him a good companion and agreeable conversationalist. She saw that he was Hugh's closest confidant and fulfilled many important roles in the administration of her husband's affairs. He was Hugh's private secretary and dealt with all his correspondence. He also oversaw the accounts. Henry had explained the Gaelic system of government to her. At first, she had found it all impenetrable but now she began to comprehend its intricacies and how totally it differed from the English model.

The Chieftain was elected by members of the ruling Sept or family within the clan and did not inherit by feudal primogeniture. Under Gaelic law, a brother could succeed a brother, a nephew, an uncle, or a younger son, a father. Besides the ruling class, Gaelic society was composed of freemen and landless labourers or churls. The churls were the backbone of Gaelic society. They worked from dawn till dusk for their Chieftain and received few privileges in return. They were tied to the land where they were born and were, to all intents and purposes, slaves to it. They were denied the right to bear arms. That right was only granted to the nobles and freemen. The nobles fought on horseback and the freemen on foot.

Henry had explained how Gaelic war was a very class-conscious phenomenon and how Hugh had dared break that tradition by training his churls in the use of arms. They delighted in what they saw as an elevation in status. After their long days in the fields, they spent most of their free time practising with the weapons that he had supplied to them. Mabel could see how they loved her husband, tirelessly trying to please him in their prowess with a gun. Sometimes, he even made a present of the weapon to one of them, who showed a particular aptitude in its use.

This innovation in arming the churls had not been popular with his nobles and freemen but he had eventually persuaded them to accept it. Gaelic Society had other divisions, which Mabel had come to know and respect. These divisions embraced the learned classes, which included the poets or filí, the dispensers of the law or brehons and the most revered of all casts, the bards or the story-tellers - custodians of the clan's history.

She had also learned from Henry the origin of the Chieftain's power. Hugh's authority was based on a system of clientship, in which the more sublords he had under his control, the more powerful he became. In addition to having to supply an agreed number of soldiers to assist him in times of war, the sublords had to provide other dues and tributes. These included an annual payment of cattle, sheep, grain, flour, honey and candles and the provision of lodgings for him and his retinue. Henry had explained how he was responsible for the recording of all these obligations and for ensuring that they were delivered on time.

As well as the wealth that the Chieftain derived from his sublords, Mabel learned that he also amassed wealth from the Gaelic system of tenure of land, which differed radically from the feudal system. On being elected to the Chieftainship, the Chieftain acquired a life long interest in the extensive lands pertaining to the position. On his death, the lands were passed to the new Chieftain. Even though Turlough O'Neill was still the Chief of the O'Neills, Hugh had succeeded in taking most of the Chieftain's lands from him by force. When Turlough had complained to Lord Deputy, Fitzwilliam, the Lord Deputy had recommended that Hugh pay Turlough rent. Henry had laughed when he recounted Hugh's boldness in ignoring the edict. He had built up a demesne agricultural system on those lands and on the monastery lands, over which he had control, further enhancing his wealth. Mabel had been very surprised to learn just how rich Hugh really was. Henry had explained everything to her and she had felt grateful for the way in which he had taken time in instructing her in the day to day affairs of the Earldom.

In addition, she was also extremely appreciative of the manner in which Rose had welcomed and befriended her since her arrival in Dungannon. Their ages were similar, even if their backgrounds were totally different. Yet, she had felt totally at ease with Rose from their first meeting, being drawn to the girl's obvious refinement of mind and gentility of manner.

She had been delighted to discover that she spoke English. Rose's command of it stemmed from an English tutor whom Hugh had engaged to teach all his children. He believed that they would be at a severe disadvantage if they could not speak English in the modern world in which they would grow up.

Initially, Rose's fluency had been hesitant and unsure but gradually she had improved and now the two women were able to communicate with little difficulty. Rose had even proposed teaching Mabel Gaelic but Mabel was finding the language very difficult to master. There was no common root to the two tongues and the structure and rules of grammar rendered the language well nigh inaccessible. Still, she was determined to learn even if her motivation was simply to shock the soldiers when she would answer them back in their own tongue. Until then, it would be Rose's and her secret. Even Hugh didn't even know that she had started to learn. He would be happy that she was making the effort.

Well he would have been happy, Mabel thought ruefully, if it hadn't been for what had happened so recently. She had fully expected that her brother would be angered by their marriage, but she had never thought that he would summon Hugh to Monaghan for an enquiry regarding its validity. When Hugh had ignored the summons, Henry had turned up in Dungannon at the head of an army of horse and foot and arrested Hugh, bringing him by force to Monaghan. When Mabel had attempted to talk to Henry, he had denied her as his sister, refusing to have anything to do with her. He had then detained Hugh for twenty days while he investigated the legality of their marriage. He had insisted that Hugh had never divorced his first wife and it had taken all that time to convince him that this was not the case.

Hugh had arrived back to Dungannon Castle the previous day, irate in the extreme and Mabel felt impotent in her ability to cheer her husband. In addition, she had been finding the intimacy of the marriage bed very difficult. It had not been as she had imagined. She found the rawness of his approach to love making, intimidating and found herself retreating into herself in fear and something bordering on disgust. She knew that she didn't please him but she did not know what she should do to improve matters. There was no one to whom she could talk. She couldn't converse with Henry and she could hardly confide in Rose, her husband's daughter. Still, her youth and girlish fancy rendered her sanguine that things would get better. Hugh was busy preparing for some important visitor whom he was expecting later in the day. She hoped the visitor would dissipate the cloud of brooding ire, which she sensed in her husband.

Mabel passed into the courtyard and her heart sank. Sitting in the sunshine, near the entrance to the keep, were three women whom she had found particularly obnoxious. Of all the inhabitants of Dungannon, these were the worst in their treatment of her. Mabel couldn't understand their antagonism. They were not that much older than her, were pleasant enough looking but their behaviour to her showed them to be cruel and callous. She wondered what their function in the castle was because every time she had come upon them, they seemed remarkable for their slovenly idleness. She had noticed Rose's detachment from them and had meant to enquire about their function, but then had determined that she would have to fight her own battles if she was ever to get any respect in her new home.

As Mabel went to pass the three, the prettiest one, a girl of about twenty with hazel eyes and a shock of unruly red hair, stood up and barred her way. She addressed her in Gaelic and from her stance, hands on hips, her facial expression one of disdainful hauteur, Mabel knew that what the girl was saying was insulting and demeaning. Her thoughts were confirmed when the two listening women dissolved into mocking laughter and the girl who had confronted her, smiled sarcastically. Mabel flushed with embarrassed anger. "Get out of my way," she said as she attempted to pass, but the girl stepped forward again to block her path. Her tormentor put out her hand and felt the top of Mabel's dress. She pulled the bodice forward and looked down Mabel's bosom, commenting in savage spleen. The other two women screamed in malevolent delight. Mabel guessed at what she had said and felt tears of mortification forming in her eyes. She determined to push her way past her torturer and just as she was about to do so, she heard a voice shout in anger.

Looking up, she saw Rose at the door of the keep, white with rage. Never before had Mabel seen her in such baleful extremity. Her tormentor stopped, moved out of Mabel's path and returned Rose's glance with a sullen scowl. She made some reply but its mocking defiance had all but disappeared.

As Rose replied, Mabel noticed the two other women rise from their seats and hasten away from the keep. When Rose ceased speaking, the girl looked around and on seeing her supporters hurry across the courtyard, she turned on her heel and followed them. Mabel turned to Rose. "Thank you Rose. I was unsure how to cast her off."

Rose replied. "Those three are trouble. Do not heed them. If I had my way, they would not be allowed into the castle."

"Why, Rose? Why do they hate me so much? I never did anything to them," Mabel asked.

"I know you didn't. They're just jealous. They would resent any new wife that father would bring here but they can show it more openly to you because you're an outsider and an English one at that. The fact that you don't speak Gaelic, aids their boldness."

Mabel was puzzled. " Why should those women scorn me so? Are they related to you?"

Rose shook her head. "No, they're not!" she answered emphatically.

"What do they do? Are they servants?" Mabel asked.

"Of a type," Rose answered cryptically.

"But they never seem to do anything. They just loiter around the courtyard all day. They don't deserve to be employed here. I'm going to ask Hugh to get rid of them," Mabel said.

"I would not do that, Mabel," Rose counselled.

"But why not? When he hears of how they have treated me, he cannot allow them stay. You can vouch to him that what I say is true. What were they saying to me anyway?" Mabel asked.

"It doesn't really matter what the likes of them say," Rose answered falteringly.

Mabel noticed hesitation stamped on Rose's thoughtful brow. "What, Rose?" she asked, "why shouldn't I talk to Hugh about removing them? I know you would not advise me against it, unless there was a very good reason not to do so. I'd like to know your mind upon this matter, though."

"I'm not sure how the English manage their marriage affairs. My father didn't tell you about them, their position in the castle?" Rose asked doubtfully.

"No. He never mentioned them," Mabel answered.

Rose demurred before embarking upon a halting explanation. "Well, he never told me not to tell you and seeing that everyone else in the castle knows, I don't see why you should be kept in ignorance. First of all, you should know that it's a very common arrangement in Gaelic society. It's nothing unusual and it's no reflection on you."

Mabel was mystified. "What, Rose? What's not a reflection on me?" she asked.

"I didn't know the English word for what they are, for what they do, so I asked Henry Hovendon and he told me that in English, women like them are called concubines or courtesans," Rose answered and paused to see what reaction her words would have on Mabel. Henry had warned her that Mabel might not be aware of such Gaelic customs. Nor did it seem as if her father had told her anything about it. Rose's gentle heart rebuked her for the pain she knew she had inflicted on this young and almost friendless English girl.

Mabel listened aghast, trying to make sense of Rose's words. Paramours, courtesans. Rose could not mean what she thought she meant. It was just impossible. She must have misunderstood Henry's translation. She asked in disbelief. "Whose concubines? Not Hugh's. No Rose, it could not be. Tell me that it's not so."

Rose bowed her head apologetically. "I'm sorry that it should cause you pain. As I said, it is nothing to do with you, it's no reflection on you. It means nothing. It is an old custom and Gaelic wives accept it. You are still his wife. You have the position and status that any of those harlots would sell their souls to possess. It's your children that will be able to contest the Chieftainship."

Mabel regarded her in disbelief. Her heart raced and a cold sweat broke out over her body. Hugh kept mistresses, not even mistresses but paid women who serviced him, she thought. They were no more than glorified prostitutes and he frequented them. Her mind anxiously reviewed their short married life together. How long after their wedding day did he betray her with one of them, she wondered. A week, a month? She flushed with embarrassment and shame. No wonder the soldiers made fun of her. To think that she had never even suspected it. All those times, when he had been absent from her on business matters, was he with one of them then, she wondered. She turned away from the thought. She couldn't believe that he could betray her like that. He would have to get rid of them. What were people to think? She felt anger displace her embarrassment and confusion.

"I must talk to him. If what you say is true..." Mabel paused, considering what she had said. "I'm sorry, Rose, I know you would not tell me a lie and I am glad that you told me what has happened in the past. Now that he is married, he can have no need of such women. I'm sure that he would not have frequented them since our union." She stopped and looked pleadingly at Rose for verification of her thesis. Rose was silent. Mabel continued agitatedly. "Nevertheless, I will not suffer this..." she paused, struggling to find a suitable word, " this arrangement to continue any longer now that I know of it. I will go to Hugh and insist that they leave the castle and never return. If I thought they still served him, I could not stay here."

Rose became distraught. "No. Mabel. You must not speak so. You must turn a blind eye to it."

"Where is he?" Mabel demanded.

"He's putting the final touches to the preparations for his guest. He's in the Great Hall with Hovendon and the castle servants. It would be unwise to confront him when he is in company," Rose answered.

Mabel shook her head vehemently. "I will not suffer those women to be on the castle grounds for another minute. I will go to him and demand that they be banished."

Rose pleaded, "Talk to him, by all means, but choose your time. Wait until you're alone together."

Mabel's resolve had strengthened. She would not wait. She would deal with this matter right away.

She hurried into the keep and made straight for the turret stairs and climbed the two flights until she reached the Great Hall, on the second floor. She strode in. The place was a riot of colour and confusion as servants, bards, minstrels and kitchen staff busied themselves for some lavish entertainment. She spied Hugh conversing with Hovendon in the enormous glazed embrasure of the window, which looked out with unimpeded view over the western plain. The immense banqueting table was set for a formal meal and a roaring log fire blazed in the chimney.

Mabel accosted her husband. "I must talk with you," she demanded. The imperiousness of her tone and the challenge in it stilled the room. Everyone turned to stare at Hugh's English wife.

Hugh's gaze fell on her and he asked impatiently. "Can you not see that I am busy?"

Mabel answered defiantly. "That may well be, but I demand that you make time to talk to your wife." She spat out the words "your wife" and Hugh looked at her for a few moments, before replying. Mabel noticed the coldness of his demeanour and it made her more determined to deal with this issue immediately.

Finally, he answered curtly, "You forget yourself, Madam and the status to which I have elevated you. I have important business to finish. I must make sure that all is properly prepared for our guest. We will talk later," he said.

"And who is this guest that you would put his needs before those of your wife's? I demand that you come and talk with me in private," Mabel answered.

"I have had enough demands from your family to last me a lifetime. I will never again answer any ultimatum that your brother delivers and I am not about to answer those of a mere woman," Hugh answered angrily.

Mabel's eyes flashed fire. "Well then, you force me to speak in front of strangers. I want ... no, I insist that the three doxies that you have kept in the past be banished from this castle immediately and that their like never again cross the my path," she cried with unalloyed passion.

Hugh snarled. "You must know your place, Madam. Your are my wife and you will not embarrass me in public by attempting to lay down the law to me. Your brother tries that and I don't appreciate it."

Mabel flushed scarlet at such untoward resistance to what was surely a legitimate demand. Too late, she realised that her approach to the problem was wrong but she had not been able to help herself. She was acutely aware of the audience and its rapt attention to her parley with Hugh. She now wished that she had taken Rose's advice and waited for a more opportune time to confront her husband. Nevertheless, she was in the right and she would not be cowed. There was no reason that those women should remain in the castle. She could not allow him treat her like this in public. She was already the laughing stock of the area. She would have to stand up for herself. "And I will not have those women in the castle. Either they go or I will," she threatened.

Hugh snorted in derision. "And where would you go? Back to that brother of yours? The brother who came into my country and had me arrested like a common criminal? Do you have any idea what that did to my prestige among my own people? It took all my powers of persuasion to stop my countrymen from attacking him. I allowed myself be humiliated by him, for your sake, because he was your brother."

Mabel answered. "I admit that he was wrong in what he did, but he had the Queen's summons. You are obliged to obey Her Majesty's command, even if it means doing Henry's bidding." Mabel saw the sinews of Hugh's face tighten in ill concealed anger.

"I should have been allowed make my own way to Monaghan. And when I arrived there, he made me camp outside the town for twenty days, in the foulest of weather, while he investigated every aspect of our marriage. He insisted that I had never been divorced from Aoife, stating that he would not allow me go until I produced the actual sentence of divorce, confirmed under its seal, proving beyond doubt that both the legal divorce and the church annulment were in order. This I eventually managed to do. And did he then apologise for his libellous claims that I had seduced you and entered into a bigamous marriage? Of course not!" Hugh paused for breath.

Mabel had never seen him this angry before but she was determined not to be intimidated. "As I have already said, his behaviour was wrong. That he should treat his sister and her husband in such a manner, is an error. However, I think your tolerance of those vile creatures whom I have seen, does me grave injury. Will you or will you not banish them?"

"I have told you already I will not be lead by a Bagenal again."

Mabel's temper flared. "I am not a Bagenal! I am your wife, Countess of Tyrone. I deserve some respect! What do you intend doing with those women?"

"Nothing!" he thundered in response. "Now go and get ready. One of your duties is that you act as hostess and help entertain our guests."

Mabel was temporarily lost for words. She looked about her. Rose had entered, silent as a shadow and Hovendon looked on in discomfiture. All the rest had shrunk into the dim margins of the hall, ignorant of this foreign tongue but all too certain of the tenor of its tone. Mabel sensed that she had gone too far to back down now. "If they do not go, then I will. Make your choice," she demanded.

Hugh looked at her for a few moments, before replying. His face frightened her. She could see that he was trying to control his retort and she wondered if she had finally pushed the matter too far.

Finally, he spoke. "And where would you go? To your precious brother? Do you know how much he thinks of you now? He says that you will never see a penny of the £2,000 dowry that your father left you. He would rather see you starve to death than give you what would buy one crust of bread to keep you alive. If you want to go to him, off with you. I will not stand in your way. If you are going to stay here, then you do so on my terms. I will not be ruled by any woman."

Mabel was crushed. She felt tears of mortification bead her eyelashes. She had never felt so humiliated in all her life, even during the worst excesses of her brother's tyranny. Yet, she could not resist one last jibe. "I do hope you have told Her Majesty that. I'm sure that she would be most interested to hear of your opinion on women. I think the proper term is treason, is that not so?" With that she turned on her heel and departed.

Once she had left the Great Hall, the tears came. She felt helpless. She had left her brother's house to escape his tyranny and now she found herself hostage to more. She wanted to be out of the castle. Blindly, she ran down the turret stairs and out into the sunshine. She had to get away. Mary would probably take her in, even though she was, undoubtedly, still irate over the elopement. Mabel had heard that Henry had blamed her sister. And what would her brother-in-law, Patrick, think? He did much business with Hugh. Would that make him wary of offering her refuge from her husband?

Mabel heard footsteps running after her and Hovendon's voice calling out. She hastened her own step. She did not wish to talk to him, let alone have him see her like this.

"Madam, wait," he shouted, but she ran stumblingly forward. She had reached the castle gates and raced through them into the open countryside beyond. She noticed the guard looking at her in surprise. Finally, Henry drew abreast of her.

"Wait, Madam. Don't run away. He does not mean to be so short with you. He is upset at his treatment at the hands of your brother," he said. Mabel did not reply. Henry walked beside her silently.

Finally, they arrived at a stream and Mabel slumped onto a tree stump and gazed into the limpid water. Henry stood beside her. Mabel's feelings were now in full sway. The tears fell freely. On seeing them, Henry knelt in front of her and looked sympathetically into her face. "Don't cry, Countess," he said gently. "He is a proud man who has been humiliated and treated very badly. He cannot be seen to be ruled by his wife. This is all a wretched misunderstanding. He asked me to follow you. He did not mean to hurt you so."

Henry's sympathy only made Mabel feel more miserable. She sobbed, "Oh Henry, I'm finding all this so difficult. It's not what I imagined. They're so different from us. How do you put up with them?"

Henry smiled, "Put up with whom?" he asked.

"The Irish!" she answered vehemently.

Henry's smile broadened. "When you get to know them, they're the best in the world. Once you're fluent in the language, you'll see how warm they can be. When they accept you, they'll go to the ends of the earth to do your bidding."

Mabel grimaced. "When will I ever master that language? It's tortuous!"

"I mastered it. It's as hard for them to learn English," Henry answered.

"It's not just the language, it's my husband. I have been totally mortified by him. He has wounded me to the quick. You know what those women are."

Henry sighed. "Yes, but they have always been here. All his previous wives accepted them. If you wish to change him, you must be gentler with him. It's not that unusual. All the ruling classes of Europe have courtesans. People would think less of him if he did not have them. Neither you nor I know if has frequented them since your marriage to him. I doubt he has. I know that he loves you very much"

"But I feel that his love has been totally undermined. I don't know if I can trust him any more," Mabel answered. " I loved him. I loved him so much, I gave away my world and surrendered my life to him and now how does he repay that sacrifice? By humiliating and crushing me. No, he cannot do this. He will not do this."

"You must not throw everything away over a misunderstanding. Give it time. Come to the feast. Learn to understand his ways and know his love of you," Henry added.

"But Henry, how can I ever raise my head again, knowing what I do?" she asked.

Henry observed Mabel's strained, blanched face. "Give him time, Countess. Look at how your anger wounds and damages him. He must be seen to be master in this Gaelic world as well as Earl in the English one. Put away your fears about these paramours. They are trappings only. Would they mock you if they owned his affection? Your hold on him excites their spleen. See the truth of his situation and if you love him, as you say, well for his sake, do his bidding and lend him your support."

He paused, wondering if his words would effect some change in her. Glimpsing some decontraction in Mabel's knitted brow, Hovendon ventured gently.

"Come to the feast. Are you not curious to see who the expected guest is?" he asked.

"I do not care if it is the Queen herself. I cannot attend," Mabel answered.

"Rose will be disappointed if you are not there," Henry added, sensing an abatement in Mabel's agitation. "Hugh did not want to tell you because he felt that you might not have been able to keep the news from her. Hugh Roe is coming home. He'll be here tonight. I know Rose has almost given up hope. She will be delirious with joy. He's to spend one night here and then he and Rose will travel on to Donegal. He has some business there that he is eager to finish," Henry confided.

Mabel, even in her own misery, felt better for this communication. She knew how Rose had agonised over the delay in seeing Hugh Roe and been agitated lest he be caught on his journey northwards. It was almost five months since his escape and now, finally, they would be reunited. It had been doubtful that he would survive his ordeal on the mountain. It had been over a month before he had recovered from the fever that he had contracted that same night. His feet had been frost bitten and it had been necessary to amputate two of his toes. This had further delayed him and when he had finally recovered, he had to make the dangerous journey north through the Pale, a price on his head. Rose had received some letters from him, yet she had no idea that he had begun his journey home.

"Why did not my husband tell Rose that he was on his way? Is this more of his damnable selfishness and politicking? Rose has been mewed up with worry every day about his safety," Mabel queried with spirit.

"There were many risks. Your husband didn't want to fill her with hopes lest they'd be dashed again. Out of love and consideration for her interest, he employed Neill O'Hagan to escort Hugh Roe. He knew that Neill's command of English would be vital. He also arranged safe houses along the way for him. Hugh Roe spent three days with Garrett Moore, you remember him?"

Mabel did remember. She had spent the first week of her married life in his house and had nothing but the warmest of memories of her sojourn there. What alchemy was there in Hugh that he had contrived to persuade an Englishman and a member of the Queen's Council to shelter an escapee from Her Majesty's prison? Not for the first time, did Mabel inwardly marvel at her husband's power and influence over people. He commanded with such authority and in a manner most smooth and polished. Indeed, it was this very power that had first drawn her to him. In girlish admiration, she had luxuriated in the notion of what it would be to hold sway over such a mind and heart as his. If only Hugh and her brother, Henry, could have agreed, then much of this trouble could have been avoided.

A welter of doubt and conflicting emotion overcame her. She sensed Hugh's love for her and bore witness daily to the tenderness, with which he dealt with Rose. And was there not tenderness in his careful solicitude of her physical comforts, she wondered. She recalled the elegant furnishing and tapestries, which Hugh had ordered for her apartment, the rich brocades and velvets he had bought to be made up into her splendid bridal trousseau. Memory pushed open the door of tenderness and she thought of the magnificent gold necklace he placed about her throat the night they became secretly betrothed. These, and a thousand other kindnesses, clamoured for vindication of his love for her. Mabel looked into the clear, honest eyes of Henry Hovendon. Maybe he was right. Maybe she should go to the feast. She wished to see Hugh Roe. She had heard much about him from Rose and it was evident that Hugh admired him greatly. He had risked much to free him and spent considerable sums of money in aiding his escape.

She said slowly, "I will attend this feast, Henry, but I will not be duped. I am his wife. If I am to support him, why then, he must abide by me and do his duty by me, as a husband"

"God bless you, Countess," Henry answered. "Hugh will be pleased, but remember, not a word to Rose. It must be a surprise. Come, we must away."

With that, they both arose and turned their faces in the direction of the castle.

Henry Bagenal and Sir Maria Wingfield sat in Bagenal's chamber in his large home in Newry. Surprisingly, Mabel's marriage had drawn both men even closer than before. Wingfield felt every bit as much cheated as Bagenal. He regarded O'Neill as a purloiner of his property and hated him for it. Foolishly, he had spoken of his engagement to his fellow officers and they had teased him mercilessly that an Irish native should have bested him. He acknowledged the pain, which the incident had caused Bagenal and he knew that his friend greatly regretted that liaison. They had both devised the plan that had led to O'Neill's arrest and summons to Monaghan. They knew, however, that for now, they could do no more. O'Neill had influential friends. They had, nonetheless, a long-term stratagem, which would enable them get their revenge eventually.

"So, who's next?" Wingfield asked.

"Pheilim O'Neill," Bagenal answered.

"And who is he?" Wingfield enquired.

"Pheilim was the Chief Lord of Killetra. In the past, I attempted to bring him under my and Her Majesty's government. He refused. I waged war on him, but could not defeat him. He was considerably weakened, though. Hugh O'Neill, spying an opportunity to serve his own ends, installed his foster brother, O'Hagan, in Pheilim's lands and with the help of O'Neill's soldiers, O'Hagan now rules in Killetra and Pheilim is reduced to the status of bush kerne in his own domain."

"I see. And is he important?" Wingfield asked.

"No, but his territory is. Both O'Neill and I have been trying to take control of it these last eleven years. Pheilim's land is strategically located between my zone of influence and O'Neill's. If I control it, then I will command the main crossing point into Tyrone. That will make O'Neill sleep less soundly in his bed at night."

Wingfield laughed. "I'll show him in."

He went to the door and opened it, motioning Pheilim to enter. Bagenal watched his entry. He was delighted to see that the pride and arrogance that he had displayed in previous meetings had vanished. Bagenal had sent for him on a promise of safe conduct but he had not been sure that he would come. He noticed that he had his interpreter with him. The latter opened the meeting.

"Pheilim wants it to be known that he wishes to submit to Her Majesty, the great Queen Elizabeth. He now realises the error of his ways. He is sorry for his rebellion and he knows that he now comes with nothing to offer her, as O'Hagan and O'Neill have stolen his lands. He regrets that he did not submit to Her Majesty when he was asked to do so and that he did not accept her protection, wishing now that he had been wiser. He would sue for a pardon from Her Majesty and it would give him great happiness were she to grant him one."

Bagenal tried to disguise the delight he felt on hearing the interpreter's words. This would be easier than he had hoped. He paused for a number of minutes as if considering the request. "Her Majesty is just and good to all her subjects. This rebellion causes her much pain, but she is not a vindictive monarch. If a subject is truly sorry and repents his former way of life, she can be merciful." He paused again and allowed the interpreter translate. He saw hope flood Pheilim's face. When the interpreter had finished he continued. "Her Majesty has, in her great wisdom, seen fit to grant me the power of issuing pardons on her behalf. Those that I forgive in her name, she also forgives." Bagenal decided to embellish the truth. "Her Majesty was pained when she heard of your rebellion, but she was even more pained when she heard of your dispossession by her enemies."

Again Bagenal paused to allow the translation take place. He could see that his falsehood had gone down well. He continued. "Do you renounce your rebellious ways and do you swear to be a loyal subject to Her Majesty?"

When the question was conveyed to him, Pheilim nodded and took a crucifix from around his neck, hysterically assenting in Gaelic. Bagenal watched him, not allowing the distaste that he felt for the man or his crucifix to show. The Irish were such a superstitious, bar-barous race. He smiled encouragingly at Pheilim but his eyes remained cold.

Bagenal continued, "Her most noble and kind Royal Highness is willing to reinstate you in your lands. I and her army in Ulster, will achieve that goal. You will then recognise Her Majesty as your Sovereign, you will pay her rents to be agreed, you will allow one of her sheriffs on your land and you will allow a garrison to be based at Toome, the main crossing point from Tyrone into Clandeboye."

Bagenal waited while his speech was translated. Pheilim fell on his knees before him and kissed his hand. Bagenal noticed that there were tears in his eyes. Such an outpouring of emotion embarrassed him. He motioned him to rise. Then he addressed the interpreter. "You must tell him if he ever goes back on our agreement, there will be no mercy shown him. I will follow him to the ends of the earth if he ever betrays my mistress, her most Royal Highness. Ask him does he accept all my terms."

As soon as the request was translated, Pheilim gave the necessary acceptance. Bagenal nodded. "You may tell him that he is now free to leave. He is to return here in a week's time and we will enter his lands and restore him to his rightful inheritance. Furthermore, Her Majesty will guarantee that the lands will be handed down from father to first-born son from now on. You may translate for him outside. We are fin-ished for now."

Wingfield opened the door for them. They left, Pheilim bowing eagerly as he exited. When the door was closed, Wingfield laughed heartily. "You are indeed expert at this practice. How many more must we see?" he asked.

"That is all for today. We have three more tomorrow. We shall hem O'Neill in yet. He'll rue the day he crossed me. Next week, we'll start with Pheilim's territory. Come, let us to dinner. I'm famished," Bagenal answered.

"There is something I must tell you," Wingfield interrupted. "I have been considering requesting a transfer to the war in Flanders. I want to see some real action."

Bagenal was dismayed. He had imagined that he and Wingfield would work closely in the reduction and ultimate destruction of O'Neill. He felt Wingfield's change of heart as a betrayal of his own, dearest purpose. He wondered what he could do or say to change his mind. "We will see some action, next week. We'll hunt the O'Hagans out of Pheilim's territory," he said.

"Yes. That's exactly what you will do, because when they'll see that they are up against a superior force, they'll run away like all Irish rebels. O'Neill won't go to war over Pheilim's land. He has too much to lose. I want to fight a brave enemy, one that doesn't flee before us. I wish to fight for the Protestant cause in Flanders. I wish to help teach the Spanish a lesson!" Wingfield exclaimed.

"But what of O'Neill and the Irish? They're Catholic also," Bagenal ventured.

Wingfield smiled. "If you are ever really to go to war with O'Neill, head to head, be sure and send for me. I would not miss such an opportunity. In the meantime, I'll get all the experience I can."

Bagenal nodded. He'd make sure that day came, the day when O'Neill would finally be goaded into showing his hand and then, it would be well to have people like Wingfield to call on. He said tersely, "I'll remember your words."

Mabel and Rose walked through the assembled crowd that packed the courtyard of Dungannon Castle and spilled beyond into the surrounding countryside. The multitude had begun to arrive in the late afternoon, from as far away as Hugh Roe's Donegal as well as from the four corners of O'Neill's own territory. Mabel had pledged to keep Rose ignorant of the identity of the expected guest and she had done her best to mitigate her companion's curiosity by accompanying her all evening. Finally, Rose had tired of being inside and had asked to go out to see what was happening.

Hugh had organised his minstrels to provide music for the waiting crowd and had laid on plenty of oatcakes, buttermilk, meats and beer. All the Irish who could play instruments had brought them along and the sound of the revelry outside had been too much to ignore. Hugh also had ordered large bonfires to be lit in the courtyard, a traditional way of welcoming returning heroes and in the descending darkness, the flames cast flickering shadows on the assembled, celebrating crowd.

Mabel and Rose stopped to watch a troupe of dancers who were engaged in a country dance, the Baludry, accompanied by five pipers and three bodhrán players. Rose twined Mabel's arm around her waist and both watched the chains of dancers as they executed the intricate movements, coiling and uncoiling around each other in large, undulating circles. Without warning, the pace of the music quickened and the male and female dancers came together in pairs, gyrating about one another, rotating faster and faster, in pace with the music. The women's skirts billowed out, revealing their upper legs and Mabel averted her gaze but not before recognising something primeval, urgent and earthy in the pulsating rhythm of the music and the throbbing drum of feet on flagstone. Initially, her mind revolted against such a spectacle, her English sense of propriety and decorum appalled at this licence and flagrant exhibition. Yet the abandon and energy of the dance ensnared her spirit, drawing her deeper and deeper into its world of anarchic liberation and wild release.

All around them, the spectators were joining in, old and young, men and women until the courtyard seemed to be a heaving, revolving mass of people. Finally, the music came to a halt and a tumult of voice replaced that of the wild melody. Mabel was glad of its cessation. She needed calm, space and quiet to organise the channels of her thought. Beside her, Rose suddenly turned to listen to some voices. "There are people from Donegal here. I recognise the accent," she said excitedly. "Come, I must see if they have any news of Hugh Roe."

"How can you possibly tell that?" Mabel asked. "When you speak Gaelic, you all sound the same."

"No, Mabel. The Donegal tongue has a much softer melody. Come. Let's find these people and talk to them." She caught Mabel's hand and wound her way through the crowd. They reached a group on the outskirts of the keep and Rose hailed them excitedly in Gaelic. They turned around to look at the two women and Mabel saw the face of one of them, a youth in his late teens, break into a smile of recognition. Rose whooped in joy and threw her arms around him, while her companion stood watching them, curious as to the vehemence of their embrace.

Rose turned back to Mabel and took both her hands, drawing her forward. "This is Hugh Roe's brother, Rory," she said excitedly. "He will not tell me why he is here, other than that he has arrived to welcome home a great hero. Tell me Mabel, or do you know? I hardly dare hope. Is it Hugh Roe who is expected?"

Mabel could deny the truth no longer. She had wished to tell Rose all evening and now had her excuse. "Yes," she said, "it is Hugh Roe."

Rose's face radiated delight. Barely able to contain her excitement, she gripped Mabel's wrist. "Come," she said. "Let's go up on the battlements."

She began to push her way through the swarming multitudes, forcing a path in the direction of the parapet. They climbed the uneven stone steps and joined the throng who were already aloft, some of whom were watching the approaching guests and others of whom were watching the festivities below. The crowd parted, allowing the two women pass to the front of the wall. Away in the distance, bonfires lit up the night time landscape. Mabel could make out a body of approaching horsemen.

"You love him very much?" she asked Rose.

Rose turned to her, smiling warmly, "Yes. I do, with all my heart.

We married when we were only fifteen. It was a political union. Father wanted it, as did Hugh Roe's father. I hadn't wished to be married, but I did as I was told," Rose answered.

"But it all turned out well?" Mabel asked.

"Yes," Rose answered. "I liked Hugh Roe from the beginning. Even though he was very young, he mixed freely with all classes of people from soldiers to nobles and seemed to draw respect from all. At thirteen, he even had commanded the O'Donnell horse against Turlough O'Neill."

Mabel smiled. "So, you still love him?" she enquired delicately.

"Yes," Rose replied shyly. But at that moment her attention was distracted by a particular hubbub in the midst of the general commotion.

"Look!" she exclaimed excitedly.

Mabel's gaze followed her extended arm and saw that a group of Hugh's bagpipers were marching to meet the approaching horsemen with Hugh at their head. She observed one of the men from the approaching troop alight from his horse, go to Hugh and embrace him. The older man enveloped him in his broad arms. The bagpipes struck up the O'Donnell clan song and the crowd on the ramparts shouted to one another excitedly, "Tá sé tagtha."

News of Hugh Roe's arrival spread rapidly as the call was taken up by the assembled mass in the courtyard who flowed out through the gates of the castle and into the surrounding fields. The shouts of exultation rose to the listening women. Rose was torn between delight at the welcome for her husband and relief that Mabel couldn't understand the crowd's expressions of hatred for the English who had dared imprison him. She saw her husband being lifted onto the shoulders of the multitude and carried towards the castle through the ranks of peasantry who had gathered to salute him. As Hugh Roe was swept into the courtyard, Rose turned to Mabel and said, "Come, we must join him."

They forced their way down through the throng on the battlements who now too, wanted to descend and greet the hero. As they alighted from the steps, they saw members of the crowd grasping Hugh Roe's hands and kissing his feet. Rose shouted, "Hugh Roe!" but her voice was drowned in the sound of the music and the tumult of the people. He was carried over to the castle keep and set down at its entrance. This was at a higher level than the watching crowd and he stood and looked into the sea of faces. He saw Hugh below and bent to draw him up alongside him. He then held up his hands for silence and waited for the crowd to become still.

Addressing them in Gaelic, he said, "It gives me great solace and pride to be back among Irishmen, the salt of the earth and to be on Ulster soil again." At this, he knelt on the ground and kissed the dark scree, which bordered the entrance to the keep. A huge cheer ripped through the assembled throng. As he got to his feet, he heard Rose's voice calling to him from the multitude. He searched the faces anxiously and saw her at a distance, vainly trying to reach him. "Let her through," he shouted. "Let my wife, whom I haven't seen for three long years, join me."

The crowd attempted to accommodate Rose but found it was well nigh impossible to separate, so densely was it packed. With a surge, Rose felt the ground being withdrawn from beneath her feet. Countless arms and bodies supported her as she moved upwards and forwards in the direction of her husband. O'Donnell leaned down and with one quick movement, lifted her up beside him and kissed her. The crowd cheered. Flushed and dizzy with excitement, Rose clung tremblingly to her husband. From the depths of the throng, Mabel observed the proceedings. She was glad of her friend's joy. Yet, as an outsider, part of the world held accountable for his suppression and incarceration, divided by the cultural barrier of language and habit, Mabel felt removed from the heaving, sweating mass of bodies, which surrounded her. She observed Hugh Roe's greeting of his wife and noticed Rose's blushing acknowledgement of their bond. The marked lonesomeness of Rose's plight, which Mabel had always sensed, seemed to dissolve before her very eyes. Here she was, before her and this crowd, united, welcomed and embraced by the returning hero.

Mabel shifted her attention to Hugh Roe and with something like surprise, saw before her a handsome, strong limbed youth with flaming hair and chiselled features. In age, Mabel reckoned him only a year or two her junior but there was something about him, which suggested the maturity and tenor of one twice his years. His rich base voice rang out over the assembled crowd.

"I would like to thank you all for coming to meet me here today. I have long dreamed of this day and I have promised God that if he delivered me safely from the English, that I would not rest until I had driven them first from Donegal and then from the rest of Ireland. I now promise you that I will honour that pledge."

The crowd erupted again. This is what they wanted to hear.

Mabel wondered at what message had been imparted and could only dimly speculate at its content. She saw her husband step forward and hold up his hands for silence. "Hugh Roe has travelled far and through many dangers, to be with us here. I must bring him into the castle and do him honour. You are free to celebrate here. There's plenty more food and wine. We will join you again," he said.

Mabel gathered from his gestures that he was urging the crowd to continue with their celebrations. She noticed Henry Hovendon anxiously waiting to guide Hugh Roe into the privacy of the keep. With a jolt of memory, she recalled that she had pledged to attend. Slowly and with difficulty, Mabel edged her way through the throng before reaching the steep wooden steps, which lead into the dim interior of the keep.

Within, the sweet melody of harp and lute mingled with the heightened babble of Irish voices. On arriving at the top of the turret steps, Mabel stood at the entrance to the Great Hall and gazed at the spectacle. Over two hundred people had milled inside. The banqueting table, which ran the length of the interior, was laden with victuals. Enormous mounds of mutton, veal, poultry and pork rested on huge wooden platters. Large vessels filled to overflowing with beer, buttermilk, whiskey and mead, stood at each end of the table. Copious fruits and sweetmeats adorned huge vessels at the centre of the display and all along the table's massive oaken surface, were tall piles of oaten cakes and dishes of fresh unsalted butter, cabbage, onions, wild garlic, watercress and leeks. Leathern gourds of Spanish and French wines stood at the ready; whole roasted salmon and trout from the Blackwater River sat in massive dishes, garnished with sprigs of wild rosemary and in the enormous recess of the chimney, over the blazing wood fire, a whole cow turned slowly on a spit.

Mabel scanned the crowd in search of Rose and Hugh Roe. Finally, her eyes alighted on them, flanked by her husband, on the elevated dais at the southern end of the hall. She had hoped to greet her guest on her own, to be able to afford him her exclusive attention. But the memory of her recent encounter with Hugh blunted her inclination and for a moment, she felt the impetus to turn. Just then, Henry Hovendon appeared at her side and with smiling countenance, gently guided her through the throng. From his elevated position, at the far end of the hall, Hugh observed her progress. Mabel, unable to avoid his gaze, looked with what command she could into his strong, resolute face. He and I have matters to resolve but our moment is not now, Mabel thought inwardly. I must conduct myself with what dignity I can to greet this guest.

However much or little of her mediation Hugh silently decoded, Mabel could not gauge, as she had, by this, come to where Rose and Hugh Roe were standing. The former, seeing her approach, reached out in generous embrace, then placed Mabel's hand into that of her newly returned husband. Hugh Roe, observing her silently for a few seconds, bent low and kissed her fingertips but Mabel, at once, sensed some reserve in the young man's response. She heard Rose utter her name and tried vainly to understand Hugh Roe's Gaelic utterance of reply. She detected a minute disquiet in Rose, who hesitated slightly before translating, "My husband is honoured to know you and adds that it is seldom such loveliness is found this far north."

Mabel struggled to reconcile the gracious words with what seemed a coolness and restraint in her guest's general bearing. Just then, she felt her husband's shadow cut across the stream of light, in which she stood. He addressed her in English. "Our honoured guest and I need to speak privately before the feast. We will withdraw upstairs to my chamber. Go fetch some goblets and a gourd of wine and see that our other guests are well provided." With that, he took Hugh Roe by the elbow and steered him to the opening of the stairway, which led to the private chambers high above the Great Hall. Mabel started involuntarily, incensed by the curtness of his command but Rose, ever watchful, gently laid a restraining hand upon her.

"Mabel, do not follow. Now is not the time to resolve your disagreement," she said.

Mabel stopped, looking beleaguredly into her companion's face, reading therein gentleness and compassion and yet a storm of anger tossed within her. "He treats me as a servant and I will not endure such insult. For your sake, I will do as you ask and not mar your husband's homecoming, but know that I will not be held to silence," she said.

Dismayed, Rose knew for certain that other storm clouds were gathering upon her father's horizon and secretly worried if even one as strong as he could withstand assaults from both within and out. Mabel detached herself from Rose's grip and turning her back, departed.

Overhead the Great Hall lay two apartments, O'Neill's bed chamber and the solar. The latter was a chamber of ample proportion. In each corner, four stone corbels supported the massive weight of the dark roof timbers. Light streamed in through the trefoil windows on three of the four sides. Brocaded tapestries hung on the fourth wall, flanking the O'Neill banner with its proud emblem - a bold red hand held aloft by twin lions and underneath it the motto, "Lámh dhearg abú". Hugh ushered O'Donnell into the chamber, motioning him to be seated in the oak armchair beside the chimney piece.

O'Donnell turned to Hugh and addressed him. "May God and all his saints reward you, Hugh, for what you have done for me," he said.

"No need for thanks, Hugh replied. "We are kin."

"What has become of Henry McShane?" Hugh Roe asked.

"Never fear. I have him safe where he can do us no injury. I reckon he would prefer to have remained in Dublin Castle, than to be lodged where I have him," Hugh replied. "But enough of him. I only wish that you would stay longer with us before you journey homeward."

"No, I've been away too long already. My people need me. I must drive these English upstarts from Donegal before they start to feel at home in my domain. That done, I will reclaim the O'Donnell Lordship of Connaught and drive Bingham from his lair," O'Donnell replied.

Hugh was surprised. He had thought that Hugh Roe would be content to reclaim his own lands, avenging the wrongs done his tribe. "You must be careful and not undertake more than is wise," he cautioned. "It is one thing to run them out of your own territory where you have many friends and know the region, but another altogether to invade a new area."

O'Donnell smiled. "We must not be always on the defensive," he answered. "The O'Donnells were rulers of Connaught in the past and will be again."

Inwardly, Hugh worried at the scope of his ambition. "There is much to do in Ulster before you can think of that. You have yet to obtain The O'Donnell title."

Undeterred, Hugh Roe replied. "It is clear that my father can no longer hold that. My mother and I will convince him to make it over to me. Then, you and I will divide Ulster between us. You're welcome to the entire province, outside Donegal. As for Connaught, of course, that I claim as my own. Agreed?"

Hugh appraised O'Donnell for a few seconds, silently taking stock of the young man's determination, before holding out his hand. "Agreed," he said. He wondered privately what sort of an influence he had just unleashed in Ulster and what command he would require to channel that force. He would have to do his utmost to marshal him, no simple task. He thought of Rose and could understand what fascination this young man exerted over her.

Hugh Roe continued urgently, "First, I must wipe out all opposition to my rule and you must depose Turlough. I pledge my support to you and expect your support in equal measure. Together we will rule Ulster and drive these English usurpers from our shores."

Doubt weighed heavy on O'Neill. Did Hugh Roe know what he was saying? Had he not himself borne witness to the power of the English? It would be well nigh impossible to shift them. Gently, Hugh remonstrated with the younger man. "Do not underestimate them. They are more powerful than you think. I have seen, at first hand, the reserves of strength that they command in England. You must know how far you can push them. Yes, take the Chieftainship and remove the English from your lands, but after that, proceed with caution. The

Queen has now her attention turned elsewhere, but should she be goaded into engaging with us, there could only be one victor and it would not be us. Their reserves of strength far outweigh ours. We would need an Ireland, united behind us, and that we will never achieve as long as these inter clan rivalries persist."

O'Donnell waxed impatient. "O'Neill, where is your fighting spirit, man? Have you grown soft and not considered an external backer? The English support the Dutch against the Spanish. Why should not the Spanish support us against the English? I'm going to appeal to them for aid in ridding this country of them. They're bound to come to our help," O'Donnell concluded with unwavering sureness.

O'Neill paused momentarily before deciding not to disclose the fact, that over the last five years, he had maintained an agent at the Spanish court. He still doubted O'Donnell's discretion. To dabble in such a stratagem required total trust in one's agent. He'd found this in his kinsman, Edmund Óg McDonnell, who worked in Spain on his behalf. So far, the only outcome from such an enterprise had been the return of several Irish captains from the Spanish army whom O'Neill had employed as instructors in the military training of his churls. He had gleaned enough evidence from McDonnell's sensitive and discreet overtures, to know that there was no likelihood of imminent military help from the Spanish monarch. "There is nothing in this world that one can count on with certainty," Hugh rebutted. "If you manage to win their support, why then, that alters everything. But you must know, with certainty, that such support is vouchsafed. If you are determined to persist on this dangerous course, you should ensure that your messengers are reliable and discreet. Should the English get proof of your plans, you will be proclaimed a traitor. And you know the penalty that carries."

"I am prepared to run that risk," Hugh Roe answered unhesitatingly.

"Then you must build up a modern army, one that can meet the English on the field and defeat them in open battle. You must increase the number of men who carry guns. The day of the Gallowglass is past and their way of warfaring outmoded, so they must do service as pikemen. You must increase your ranks and the only way to do so is to allow the churls bear arms."

O'Donnell stopped short. "The Gallowglasses will not change and it would never be accepted that the churls bear arms."

"I have already started the process," O'Neill countered. "An army must be properly trained. Already, I'm using captains who have seen service in the English or Spanish armies. I will allow you have some to assist in training your men."

O'Donnell nodded. "I accept, but will not this strategy require much time, time which strengthens the English grip on our lands?" he asked.

O'Neill sensed the young man's impatience. His nature lacked not in courage, but the measured thinking and reflective cast of mind that came with older years, was sadly absent. He had seen such natures before and knew too well, that men such as O'Donnell could easily destroy themselves in wanton impetuousness.

O'Neill continued tactfully, resolved to win the young man to the wiser course. "You know I've been granted an army of five hundred men for the defence of the Pale, soldiers paid for and trained by the English. For the past number of years, I've rotated that number, so I have far more than five hundred trained men to call on, if and when the need arises. I have a core but I must build on it. And even then, the only means of attack I will entertain, is defence."

"We will see what alliances we can build, but I am determined to enforce my rule on Connaught," O'Donnell answered.

Again O'Neill persisted. "We must consult on all our strategies with due caution and consideration. If we are to be allies, I must know that I can trust you not to do anything rash. I've many connections who will furnish me with much useful intelligence on English plans. I have experience in dealing with them and I want your troth, that you will follow my guidance."

O'Donnell paused as he considered Hugh's condition. His whole nature yearned for immediate action, yet he could not ignore all that the older man had done so skilfully to devise his escape. "Agreed," he answered slowly.

"Good," Hugh returned and grasped the younger man's hand warmly.

"But now we have talked enough business. We are ignoring our womenfolk and there are many waiting to meet you, including that wild brother of yours with a party from Donegal. Come let us join them. We have much celebrating to do and the night is yet young."

Chapter 5

Mabel was busy supervising the meal being prepared for the guests who were due to arrive at any moment. She was looking forward to the gathering. It had been nine months since she had seen Rose and they would have much to discuss. Hugh had summoned Hugh Roe and Hugh Maguire for an urgent meeting. There was trouble in Maguire's land and he had been appealing to O'Neill for aid. Maguire was Chieftain of the neighbouring county of Fermanagh and was Hugh's strongest sublord. He was twenty-one, of an age with Hugh Roe, also married to another of Hugh's daughters, Sarah. Maguire was to bring Sarah with him and Mabel was curious to see how much she resembled either Hugh or Rose. It would be agreeable too to have some women around the castle with whom she could talk.

Mabel's command of Gaelic had improved enormously. Hugh had employed a tutor for her and she had spent four hours a day studying it. She now found that she had enough to get by and was able to supervise the servants and ensure that the soldiers no longer belittled her.

Her fluency allowed her ably to oversee the running of the castle. Initially she had turned her attention to the kitchens. When she had first arrived, the custom had been to half cook meat in its own hide while suspended over a fire. She had insisted that proper ovens be installed and had instructed the cook in how to bake the meats thoroughly and how to prepare sauces to complement each dish. Proper bread, not the disgusting oak cakes that they were so accustomed to, was baked each morning. She had been unsuccessful in weaning them off their foul buttermilk, but she made sure that there was an adequate supply of ordinary, fresh milk available, for her own consumption. She prided herself that the fare in Hugh's castle would now compare favourably with that in her brother's house in Newry.

Another one of her culinary innovations had been the purchase of a complete set of cutlery for the table. The native Irish had greeted this with amazement. Up until then, they had just used knifes to cut their food and ate with their fingers. Of course some of Hugh's native friends complained, saying that they preferred to eat good plain food in the traditional manner, refusing to use the forks provided, but Mabel had ignored them. Hugh and Hovendon, however, seemed greatly to appreciate the improvement in the general standard and presentation of the fare.

When she was satisfied with the quality and preparation of the food, she turned her attention to the castle and its furnishing. Hugh had purchased well in London but the castle still lacked a woman's touch. They had made trips together to master craftsmen and merchants in Dublin and she had enjoyed seeking household stuffs that would modernise the castle, making it a home to be proud of. In that matter, she had found Hugh a joy. He did not mind extravagance, and she had indulged in that generosity, purchasing large collections of silver and gilt plate, cups, bowls, ewers, jugs, salts and candlesticks, heavily gilded in precious materials.

At first she had been cautious when she identified expensive items like the heavily brocaded fabrics for wall and bed hangings, which she desired, but soon realised that she was not dealing with a parsimonious miser like her brother, Henry. As a result, she was now very proud of the transformation that she had worked on Dungannon Castle, and eager to know what Rose would think. Hugh need never be ashamed of having any of his English friends to visit any more, she thought.

Sir Garrett Moore and his wife had come and stayed for ten days and had derived great pleasure from their sojourn. Hugh had brought them all fishing on the Blackwater and they had enjoyed the country air together. Every night they had delighted in the music of Hugh's harpists and minstrels, savoured the very best of meats, wines and fishes before playing Primero or Gleek into the early hours.

Hugh had many other influential Englishmen stay with him and Mabel derived some solace in acting as hostess. This lessened somewhat her sense of isolation and inferiority among the natives. It renewed in her the vestiges of a belief that she was of some worth, giving her respite from the mounting belief that she was simply a token wife, abandoned in a backwater of native insolence and barbarism.

Of all the visits, that which had most gratified her, was Sir Patrick's and her sister's. Mabel had rejoiced to have the opportunity of being reconciled with Mary. She had grieved at how Hugh and she had abused her sister's trust and hospitality. Mary, on the other hand, disliked family disputes, having had to endure Henry's wrath for nearly six months, making her feel permanently estranged from all her blood relations. She was glad to see Mabel again and had been very impressed at the enormity of the territory over which Hugh held sway and the splendour of Mabel's lifestyle. She saw, at first hand, how valuable Hugh's patronage of Sir Patrick's business really was. During their visit, Mabel, at times, had been tempted to confide in her sister, unburdening herself of the difficulties and misgivings which she had battled to overcome in the long, solitary months since her wedding, but she sensed that Mary might not be sympathetic.

Now that Mabel was sure that all the preparations were in hand, she decided to leave the heat of the kitchen and go out to her favourite spot by the stream and there, await the visitors' arrival. On leaving the castle, she noticed that a cool wind had blown up. April weather could be so unpredictable, she thought. She was suddenly aware that this was her second spring at Dungannon. As she walked through the courtyard, deep in her own thoughts, Fr. Mac Donald, Hugh's private chaplain who was returning to the castle from some business or other, hailed her. "Dia dhuit," he said.

Mabel smiled and returned the customary reply in Gaelic. "God and Mary be with you."

She kept walking, knowing that if she stopped, he would undoubtedly detain her. It always amazed her how the Irish never tired of talking. She liked Fr. Mac Donald but her tolerance of him was limited. She had, on Hugh's urging, converted to Catholicism. She wondered what Henry would say about her conversion but, in his hatred of Catholics, he always seemed to overlook the fact that her father had been one, before the Reformation had forced him and many other English people to abandon the ancient faith.

She was also beginning to come to grips with the dual nature of Hugh's life. In the first months of her marriage, she had wondered at the dichotomy of his existence - Gaelic tribal Chieftain in Ulster, English speaking Earl in Dublin. Whenever they visited the capital, they went to St. Patrick's Cathedral and attended the Protestant services. Hugh's attendance was very unusual, as few other Irishmen participated in such services, for fear of their mortal souls. Slowly, Mabel found herself slipping into the same mind set, Catholic in Ulster, Protestant in Dublin, Irish speaking wife of a Gaelic Chieftain in Dungannon, English countess in the Pale.

The change to Catholicism had been a relatively easy one. There was practically no difference in the basic beliefs, the main one being the dispute regarding the head of the church, which to Mabel, was a purely political question. That question, however, was becoming more important as, of late, a new breed of priest had begun to appear in Ulster, who, in her eyes, was fermenting unnecessary trouble.

These priests had been taught in seminaries in Spain and Rome and regarded themselves as soldiers of the Counter Reformation. They were sent to Protestant countries to ferment revolution and bring about the return to the one true faith. They found fertile ground in Ulster and travelled far and wide, preaching to all that would listen, that it was their duty to rise up and depose the heretic Elizabeth from the English throne.

Mabel had met some of those preachers and bishops and had found their zealousness disturbing. Maguire, on his last visit, had brought the newly appointed Archbishop of Armagh with him, Primate McGauran. Mabel instantly disliked the man who had ignored her completely. She abhorred his appetite for war. He was too easy with his promises of aid from Spain and the Pope and in his talk of a Holy War and indulgences for all who fought and died serving such a glorious cause. She was glad that she saw no inclination in Hugh towards mounting a holy crusade against Protestantism. To her, politics and religion should be separate and people should be free to worship as they saw fit. Had not the Queen herself said that she did not wish to have a window into men's souls?

Mabel's thoughts were interrupted by the sound of approaching horses. She looked up and saw four figures riding through the castle gates. She was disappointed to see the crow like figure of the Archbishop astride one of the stallions. He was a tall, lean man in his early thirties with a sharp unsympathetic face who always dressed in black. Then she saw Rose and immediately dismissed all thoughts of the Primate.

"Rose," she shouted. "Rose, over here."

Rose looked in her direction and on seeing Mabel, rode over to her. She dismounted agilely and embraced her mother-in-law. "Mabel, it's good to see you," she said in English.

The other three horsemen came towards them. Mabel acknowledged Hugh Roe and Hugh Maguire with a slight bow. They both saluted her. Mabel addressed Hugh Roe in Gaelic. "I believe congratulations are appropriate. You are now The O'Donnell."

"Yes," Hugh Roe answered, "It is good to have what is lawfully mine."

Mabel still perceived something of a reserve in his bearing towards her, as if intercourse with her was a struggle, something that did not come naturally but had to be attained through careful cultivation.

Mabel then turned to Hugh Maguire. He cut a very impressive figure, over six feet tall and built on a large scale. Like Hugh Roe, he had red hair but had, in addition, a thick, long beard. In temperament he also resembled O'Donnell, passionate, impulsive, brave and popular with his people. She admired him greatly and felt at ease with him, sensing inclusiveness and welcome in his presence.

"You promised me that you would bring Sarah this time. I hope you have not let me down," she said to him.

"I am very sorry to have to disappoint you, Mabel," he replied. "Sarah is with child these last three months and has been feeling unwell from time to time. Unfortunately, she did not feel able to travel on this occasion."

Mabel nodded. "I do hope that it is nothing serious?" she enquired.

Maguire smiled and shook his head. "No, nothing but the normal feelings of a woman in her condition. It will pass," he said.

"God grant her and the baby good health," Mabel answered, then added. "Hugh wishes you to go to him in his chamber. He desires to have the meeting before dinner. Leave Rose with me and we will see you anon."

Maguire nodded. "Until later then," he said and the three men took their leave of the women. As they left, Mabel looked at the departing figure of the Archbishop. She felt that she had gained the victory this time, having ignored him completely. She couldn't help her antagonism towards him and regretted that he would be joining them for dinner. He seemed to be drawing Maguire under his influence. That would be a great pity, she thought.

She turned to her companion. "Well, Rose. This is indeed good news that Hugh Roe had driven Willis from Donegal."

"Yes," Rose replied, "if only that would make others content, but I fear success brings strange rewards."

Mabel noted the anxiety in Rose's reply and how her spirits were not as buoyant as she had expected. Disquiet seemed to stamp her youthful brow. "Why say you that Rose?" Mabel queried. "How could not all be well, given Hugh Roe's recent successes?"

Rose hesitated slightly before replying. "Yes, yes. My husband's successes are indeed most welcome but there are those who would have been happier if he had failed in his endeavours. I fear for him, but he scorns such sentiments."

"Of whom do you speak?" Mabel asked perplexed.

"Niall Garve O'Donnell," Rose replied, "a cousin to Hugh Roe and another claimant to the O'Donnellship. He is a man of coarse manner whom I dislike greatly."

Mabel interjected, "But you need not allow one such as him, ruin your happiness. He wields no power."

Rose listened attentively to Mabel's words but anxiety still beset her. " I wish I could agree with you, Mabel, yet I fear him. But there are other matters which oppress me, not least of which is Ineen Dubh."

"Ineen Dubh," Mabel queried. " But why? Has she not been instrumental in achieving the O'Donnellship for Hugh Roe?"

"Oh yes. She organised the whole affair," Rose hastily rejoined. "She forced Hugh Roe's father to resign from the Chieftainship, then managed Hugh Roe's inauguration very carefully, timing it so that Niall Garve O'Donnell was in Dublin, seeking English support."

"She truly is a wily creature," Mabel commented.

"I know of no woman like her," Rose observed. "As head of the O'Donnell Council she summoned those supportive of Hugh Roe to Kilmacrenan, surrounded it with her Scottish mercenary army and had him inaugurated in the traditional fashion."

"And what did Niall Garve make of all this, when he returned from Dublin?" Mabel asked with curiosity.

"When he was presented with the news, he submitted, knowing how inferior his own support was. Still, I do not trust him. I fear his coarseness masks a dangerously shrewd mind. Hugh Roe has pledged to give his sister, Nuala, to him in marriage, in an effort to bind him to his own cause. I am glad that it is not I. I do not think I would be able to endure him." Rose answered.

Mabel, who had often considered, with perplexity, the requirements placed on Chieftains' daughters, asked, " Must all Irish women marry for duty?"

Rose shook her head. "The churls are free to do as they like, but we may not. Love may come with time and children. And we can always divorce our husbands if they do not treat us as they should, reclaiming our entire dowry. But these are dark thoughts indeed."

"I will have nothing to bring with me, if ever I leave Hugh," Mabel added, "Henry never released my dowry."

Rose heard the darkness in Mabel's voice and feared that her father's marriage had not brought either him or Mabel comfort. In an attempt to dispel the thought she said, "Father does not have need of that money."

Mabel smiled. "I am not so certain. I have spent so much on the castle that, perhaps, he would have been glad to have it. It rankles deeply with him that my brother keeps from him, that which is his by right. But enough of such matters. Come, you must look at what we have done since you left. I've been longing for you to see."

The two women began walking towards the keep when Mabel remembered Rose's earlier remark. "You said that there was some trouble with Ineen Dubh?" she asked.

Rose smiled wanly. "Oh yes. Ineen Dubh desires an heir for Hugh Roe."

Mabel, immediately comprehending her anxiety, said reassuringly. "But you have plenty of time for that. You are yet but one and twenty."

"Yes," Rose answered. "But she is a demanding woman. She delights in having Hugh Roe back, and spends an inordinate amount of time counselling him. I fear Hugh Roe yields too readily to her influence"

"And you, would you wish to have a child?" Mabel asked.

Rose nodded, "Yes. But I would not wish to have a babe of mine fostered. I was, and found that I had no natural mother to return home to."

"What happened between your mother and Hugh?" Mabel enquired, curious about that early marriage, which Hugh seemed so reluctant to discuss.

"I am not certain. I've heard stories but I never asked him directly," Rose answered.

"And your mother? What has become of her?" Mabel enquired.

"I have not seen her since I was seven years old. It seems that she found happiness in another marriage and other children," Rose answered.

Mabel detected a tremulousness in her companion's voice. "I am sorry, Rose," she said.

"Do not be," Rose replied. " We were never really known to one another." The theme was painful. Rose wished to cease speaking of herself "And you? Do you desire children?"

"Yes, yes, sometime," Mabel replied, censoring from that spoken desire, the knowledge that Hugh hardly ever frequented her bed.

The women had arrived at the keep and entered it out of the cool wind that had continued to strengthen. As they ascended the stairs, Mabel wondered silently if ever she would have a child to ease her isolation and fill her life, a life that seemed increasingly barren and bereft.

Hugh O'Neill was carefully considering a letter, which he had just received from Dublin. It was from the Lord Deputy, Fitzwilliam, demanding that Hugh give aid to the newly appointed Fermanagh sheriff, Captain Humphrey Willis. Hugh recognised the appointment as more of Fitzwilliam's private enterprising. He had heard the rumours of how Willis had managed to procure his previous position as sheriff in O'Donnell's Donegal. It was said that he had bribed Fitzwilliam with gold that he had acquired from one of the ships from the Spanish Armada. He had proven totally unfit for the job, being nothing other than a freebooter and thief. His sojourn in Donegal had been a disaster for English interests in the region and yet, here was Fitzwilliam rewarding him with an appointment to another sensitive posting. As long as the English preferred the likes of Willis, they'd never win the Irish over and get them to embrace English rule.

Hugh sighed at the thought of the impending meeting. O'Donnell and Maguire, being both so young, had all the enthusiasm and recklessness of youth and all the dearth of wisdom that age and experience brings. He had been trying to rein in Maguire for the last few months by complaining to Dublin about Willis' behaviour, but he was making no advance. Suddenly the door was thrown open and O'Donnell entered. Hugh quickly concealed the letter, groaning inwardly when he saw the Archbishop in tow. Why couldn't Maguire have left him at home, he wondered. He rose to greet the men.

O'Donnell embraced him warmly. "Well Hugh," he said. "It's good to see you."

"And you also," Hugh replied, then shook hands vigorously with Maguire. Hugh then turned to the Archbishop who proffered his hand. Hugh took it and masking his feeling of reluctance, kissed the sacred ring. He did not hold with the pomp and circumstance with which both churches in Ireland adorned themselves. He turned his attention back to the general gathering.

"Well gentleman, Your Grace, you are very welcome. Can I offer you some wine?" he asked.

Maguire and O'Donnell nodded but the Archbishop answered disapprovingly. "Not for me. Alcohol is the root of many of the problems that dog this land. If people drank less, the country might be in a far better state," he replied.

O'Donnell laughed. "That may be, but it would be a much more boring place," he said

Hugh ignored the Archbishop's comment and poured three large goblets of wine. O'Donnell took his and having drained it, said, "I bring you good news, Hugh. Turlough has finally agreed to resign from the Chieftainship and make it over to you. He asked to meet me yesterday and he's prepared to acknowledge you as the next Chieftain, provided that you agree to pay him a yearly pension, the amount to be decided by both of you."

Hugh rejoiced. He had worked towards this goal for most of his life. So, finally, he's prepared to acknowledge me as his successor, Hugh thought. He privately acknowledged Hugh Roe's part in bringing Turlough to that decision. He had raided Turlough's land ceaselessly from the west while Hugh had raided it from the east. Between the two of them, Turlough had known little peace. Hugh knew the magnitude of his debt to O'Donnell but voiced a doubt. "But will he step down immediately?" he asked.

"He says he will if you agree to pay him his pension directly," Hugh Roe answered.

This was better than Hugh had hoped for. It would mean that he could forget about Turlough and turn his attention to more important matters. "And do you think that he is sincere?" he asked.

Hugh Roe nodded. "Yes. He looks worn out, every one of his seventy odd years. His excessive life style has finally been his undoing. It's said that he still drinks two pints of whiskey every day."

Hugh laughed. "It seems to preserve the useless article. Still, it's great news. My blessing on you, Hugh Roe."

Hugh Roe replied. "Soon, we will both have what we want."

Maguire interrupted, "Yes, but how long will you have it to retain?" Hugh looked at him. Maguire's lands bordered his and controlled the entrance to Tyrone from the south. Hugh was, as were the English, very aware of the strategic importance of Maguire's kingdom.

"We will hold it," O'Donnell answered.

Maguire laughed bitterly. "Do you not see what's happening under your noses?" he asked. "They are picking us off, one by one. McMahon was one of your Lords, Hugh. He relied on you for protection and you relied on him for your hereditary rents, and where is he now? Gone, totally disappeared and strangers rule in his place. O'Reilly's Cavan is no more either. I say, shame on us for standing by, and allowing the destruction of our neighbours occur, without even raising our armies to aid them. And now my lands are next in line in the English march northwards, and they are ever eager to steal more territory from us. I am your sublord and I turn to you for protection. I have kept my side of our bargain. I want you to keep yours because, make no mistake, if I fall, then it's only a matter of time until you and O'Donnell follow me into oblivion. It had been the same all over the country. One by one, the Gaelic rulers in Leinster fell. The great Earls of Desmond are no more. The Earls of Kildare are wiped from the face of the earth. You both must fight with me now or, as surely as night follows day, you will fight later on your own."

Hugh nodded sympathetically. "I understand that you are angry but we must carefully consider our position. We must not do anything rash."

Maguire flared into an anger, born of and nurtured by frustration. "And while you are considering your position, Fermanagh burns. I need help and I need it now. Willis has brought over three hundred trained troops with him from the Pale. They are, even now as you procrastinate, laying waste my lands. Just as you, Hugh, owe me protection, I, in turn, owe my people protection. If I cannot give them that, they will have to turn to someone who can. If you do not aid me, all your other sublords will see that your protection is of no practical use when it really matters. They will come to an agreement with the English before the English take their lands by force."

O'Donnell interrupted forcibly, "Anyone who makes an agreement with the English, will be betrayed in the end. I'd rather attempt to deal with the Devil than deal with them."

Maguire continued, "Yes, that may be, but deal with them I must. And it's not only with Willis that I must do battle. There is also Bingham who raids my lands from Connaught. Three times in the last five months he has pillaged and destroyed my people. Even now, as we speak, he is in western Fermanagh and my men are attempting to turn him out. And that is not the end of my problems. The crown garrisons in the neighbouring counties of Monaghan and Cavan, raid my territory at will, counties that up until this would have been friendly to our way of life." Maguire sighed and then appealed to both Chiefs. "I am not exaggerating when I say if I do not get help now, I won't be around to receive it later."

The Archbishop intervened. "His Catholic Majesty of Spain is very interested in your cause. He sent me to report on the situation here. I have written to him and requested that he send eight to ten thousand soldiers to drive the English heretics from your country. The Pope is also in favour of your cause and has excommunicated the heretic Elizabeth and removes you from your allegiance to her. It would help your cause if you were to write to King Philip of Spain and promise to support his army when it arrives here."

Hugh replied, "That is all very well, but when will those soldiers come? If we rise and are destroyed before they land, what good will that do the Spanish army? They will need friends in good stead who will be able to aid them. We must await their arrival, before we show our hand."

Maguire cut in urgently. "I do not have the luxury of time!"

O'Donnell felt that it was his turn to speak. "You asked me when I arrived home in Ulster, to be careful and not to do anything that would precipitate an all out war. I took your advice and I did as you wished. When you requested that I come to Dundalk and to submit to Fitzwilliam last August, I did it, even though it stuck in my craw to kneel before that bodach who incarcerated me for over three years. I accepted your reasoning that, as the English had been driven out of Donegal, my submission would, in fact, mean nothing. That it would be even beneficial, in removing from the English the absolute need to assemble an army to invade my country. But that does not mean that the English have been totally inactive in my lands either. Bingham has also invaded Donegal three times and has caused much damage and loss of life. I agree with Maguire that they will not rest until we are all destroyed."

Hugh knew that Maguire and O'Donnell were speaking the truth but he also knew that there could be only one victor in an all out war, unless they received aid from outside and he was far from sure that such help would be forthcoming. The King of Spain would use his soldiers in whatever way was likely to be of most benefit to Spain. Hugh found it difficult to believe that Philip II was overly concerned about the Irish Catholics unless their needs coincided with his. It would be very easy for Philip to encourage them into rebellion for his own benefit, without ever intending to give any practical aid. Elizabeth would have to bring one of her armies home from Flanders to put the rebellion down and that would aid the Spanish there.

Hugh was still hopeful that they could strike a favourable deal with the English but they were not in a position to do so yet. They would have to negotiate from a position of strength and they had quite a path to travel before they'd be at that vantage point. He chose his words carefully. "We are still not strong enough for a general rebellion. If eight thousand Spanish troops were to land in Ulster tomorrow morning, then everything would be changed totally. Somehow, I do not think that is going to happen."

O'Donnell answered. "No, maybe not tomorrow, but there's no reason to assume that it cannot happen in the future. I have decided to request that aid. We need it and if we do not seek it, we cannot expect it."

"And who will you trust with such a letter? Were it to fall into the wrong hands, you would be declared a traitor and Elizabeth would not rest until you'd be hung drawn and quartered on Tyburn Hill, like many a good Irishman before you." O'Neill answered, shuddering with the certain knowledge that such a fate could not be avoided.

The Archbishop interjected. "The Archbishop of Tuam is to travel to Spain next week. You can trust him to guard your letters with his life. He would never allow them fall into your enemies' hands."

"I have written two letters," O'Donnell continued, "one is to the Irish lords in the service of Spain. I have told them of our persecution by the English. I have asked them to intercede with the Spanish King on our behalf. I have also written directly to King Philip, asking him for his help and promised that I shall fight to the death against the English. I have told him of how I have driven them from my territory. Maguire and O'Rourke have signed the letter as well. I'd like for you to do so too."

Hugh shook his head decisively. He had always had a deep distrust of committing anything to paper, even being hesitant to speak of delicate matters if more than two persons were present.

"I will not do so," Hugh answered.

"But why?" Maguire asked. "You cannot fail to see why the letters must be dispatched."

"I will not put myself into a position where treason can be proved against me. I must be in the position where I can deal with the English and act as an honest broker between you, should you need it."

"So, I am to be destroyed? I am to be thrown to the wolves," Maguire retorted in mounting ire.

"I did not say that I will not help you. I will send my brother, Cormac, with three hundred of my best troops to aid you. If the English find out that they are with you, I will say that I could not control them. I'm sure that Hugh Roe will send you some more troops as well."

"Yes, I will send you another two hundred. I cannot spare any more because I must counter the threat posed by Bingham," O'Donnell replied.

"Good. That will suffice. I'll run Willis out of Fermanagh and then I'll follow Bingham into Connaught and kill the bastard," Maguire said.

"No, you must not leave your own territory. As long as you are simply defending yourself, you can always plead self-defence. If you go on the offensive, you will play into their hands," O'Neill cautioned.

"It is hard not to strike back at Bingham. He claims the right to enter O'Donnell's and my territory when he is, as he says, in hot pursuit of rebels or to arrest Catholic clergymen. Why can I not follow his murderers when they retreat with my cattle back to his land?" Maguire asked querulously.

O'Neill sighed. " I know it is very alluring but for all our sakes, you must avoid that temptation. Patience is everything in this matter. Bagenal sorely tempts mine. He has replaced many of my men in eastern Ulster with his own. My own son-in-law, Henry Óg, has gone over to him. Pheilim O'Neill is to allow him install a garrison on my borders. I cannot permit that. I must make an example of him to frighten the others back into obedience."

The Archbishop interrupted again. "If you will not sign the letters, can the Archbishop of Tuam inform his Majesty of Spain that you would support a Spanish army, should one land in Ulster?"

Hugh considered the request. He could not see any harm in that. "Yes," he replied, "he can."

"The Lord be praised," the Archbishop rejoined.

They had set out while it was still dark so that they would be in position before dawn. Sir Richard Bingham had chosen his guide well; one of Connor Roe Maguire's most trusted men, who knew the area intimately. Connor Roe was Hugh Maguire's half brother and rival for the Chieftainship of Fermanagh. Because Connor Roe's powerbase was the smaller, he had no choice but to look for aid outside Fermanagh to help him in his attempt to wrest the title from Hugh Maguire. Connor

Roe had been seized upon by the English as a means of fermenting trouble in Fermanagh and was now so identified with them, that he had well earned his nickname, 'the Queen's Maguire.'

It had been a cold, frosty night and a chilly April morning dawned. Spiders' webs glistened on the trees and bushes in the early morning sunshine, like pieces of exquisite lace hung out to dry. Bingham disliked campaigning so early in the year. It was always cold at night and the days could still be very miserable. It had been easier when he was younger but he still believed fervently in the enrichment of his family's fortune and in the destruction of the Irish way of life.

He could make out the small church in the clearing beneath him and the small settlement of houses around it. Good, we're in the right place, let's hope our information is accurate, he thought. He looked down and noted that all was quiet. He turned to his men, picking out two of them to send ahead on foot.

"There may be a sentry or some dogs. Bring your bow and arrows and silence them. We do not want to give them any warning."

He had not brought all his men with him on this operation. He had chosen his detachment carefully, taking with him his very best and most ruthless fighters. He had brought fifty mounted soldiers and fifty infantry. The rest he had left back at the camp, which they had established just inside the western borders of Fermanagh. They would guard the cattle and other valuables that they had pillaged from the area.

This was their fourth week in the field and his army was beginning to become quarrelsome at the amount of time spent living in camps and away from the comforts of home. Nevertheless, he wanted to carry out this last operation before he left. Then, he would be happy to leave and he would return again when the crops were in the fields and destroy them. He knew that it was very unlikely that they would have deposed of Maguire before then, but he was confident that it was only a matter of time before they would eradicate him. Then, they would have no further need of Connor Roe Maguire either. He would be destroyed also.

Bingham had already chosen who would rule in Fermanagh - his good friend and relation, Sir Ralph Lane. He and Lane had campaigned together for many years in Connaught and Lane would rule Fermanagh as his client. Bingham knew he could trust him totally. He, himself, would have enough to do in holding onto all he had in Connaught and in winning Donegal for himself. His two men returned.

"There was one sentry, a young boy fast asleep. They evidently didn't think that we would come this way. He won't be raising any alarm. We slit his throat," the younger of the men said.

"Good," Bingham replied, "I want half of you to work your way around to the other side of the settlement and wait for my signal. Sir Ralph, you take the guide and your choice of men."

Sir Ralph, a man in his late fifties, nodded. He was dressed in full armour and was eager for action. He was finally to be rewarded for all his loyalty and was excited at the prospect of gaining command in Fermanagh. He quickly chose his men and they silently disappeared into the mist, which was now rising from the ground in the early morning sunshine.

Bingham watched them go. He wasn't worried about this engagement. His guide was right. It was just a churl's settlement around a simple church. There would be no fighting men here. He noticed twelve to fifteen thatched wooden buildings, some with small pigsties and vegetable gardens. He noted the blacksmith's forge at the edge of the cluster of houses and he smiled to himself. He had made inventive use of forges in the past and he was glad to see it. He had brought his best men with him because he had heard that one of those accursed foreign papist priests was based at this church and he was determined that he would not escape. It incensed him that the priest was free to spew out his falsehoods and superstition to the gullible Irish, fermenting rebellion against their lawful Queen. Bingham did not allow his thoughts run to religion too often. He attended the reformed church but, in his heart, he denied its message. He only believed in the here and now. He would live on in the legacy that he would leave his family, and in history, as the conqueror of the Irish, a deed that no English man would ever forget or fail to regard with gratitude.

He saw a figure dressed in black leave one of the houses and head for the small church. Bingham guessed that it was the priest and that he was going to call his congregation to Mass by ringing the small bell that was visible on the side of the church. Bingham felt a surge of exhilaration. Their march through the night would have been worthwhile after all. He turned to his men. "Light the torches," he said.

Immediately they did his bidding and he leaned over to one of the soldiers. "Here, give me that", he said. "The footmen can begin their approach."

Mounting his horse, he took the torch from the soldier and waved it over and back in view of the mountain opposite. He watched and after a few moments, he saw a light answer, returning the signal. He turned to his men. "Mount up," he ordered.

He could now see many more lights on the slope opposite. He drew his pistol and discharged it into the air. The loud report reverberated around the mountains and the birds, cackling loudly with fear, rose from the trees. "Charge", he shouted and they rode as hard as they could down through the thicket towards the settlement.

Bingham was exhilarated. He galloped towards the houses, carrying the torch high over his head, aware of his men following behind him. He could see the moving lights on the other hillside also approach. The priest, on hearing the shot, had frozen and looked up at the hill. When he beheld the approaching soldiers, he rang the bell furiously, to alert the villagers. A brave man, Bingham thought, but a foolish one. He had not even tried to escape. Now, it would be too late.

He rode at the nearest house. A low door opened and a bleary eyed man looked out. The Irish peasants usually slept naked, their mantles thrown over them for warmth. Their houses consisted of one single low circular room walled in wood. The houses had no windows or chimneys, a small hole in the roof letting out the smoke from the fire. On the floor, were strewn rushes on which the inhabitants slept. Bingham's Puritanism revolted at the idea of the whole family sleeping naked together in the one space, especially when he considered the number of children they had and what they had to do to make them.

He looked at the man who stood, rubbing the sleep from his eyes, still unaware of exactly what was going on. Bingham could see other forms stirring in the house behind him and he saw a naked woman coming to the door to join her man. He threw the burning torch over their heads. It landed on the rushes behind them immediately catching fire. Bingham gave a whoop of triumph and rode past. The man, woman and their family ran out of the burning house straight into Bingham's troops that were following him at full gallop. One of the troops hacked at the man with his sword and he fell, an ugly wound gaping open in his stomach, out of which his intestines spilled onto the ground. Two of the man's young children were trampled underfoot by the large horses that carried the armoured fighting men and his wife and the remaining children tried to run for the cover of the surrounding woods. Three of the soldiers peeled off the attacking mob and followed the woman. They reached her before she could escape, knocking her to the ground. They then dismounted and dragged her screaming and kicking into the nearby bushes.

The rest of Bingham's men charged through the village, yelling and throwing their torches at the thatched roofs. All the doors opened and the terrified men, women and children poured out, screaming in terror, trying to evade the treacherous foe. They tried to escape to the surrounding woods, but the English were attacking them from all sides, trampling them underfoot or hacking them down with their weapons.

Bingham reined in his horse to see where the priest had gone. He looked around anxiously. The domestic animals had become loose, and a frantic pig charged around blindly, driven mad by the flames and smoke. Bingham saw the bloodlust in his men and was excited by the sight of them following the naked people, like avenging angels, putting them to the sword. He saw that they were sparing the comeliest women for later, binding their arms and feet. The men would deserve to relieve their frustrations after this day's work. The churls had no fight in them, he thought contemptuously. Dawn was definitely the best time for this type of work. There was something about being only half-awake and naked, that erased people's aggression.

Then he saw what he was looking for. The priest was attempting to escape. He saw him run behind the forge, making for the hill. He spurred his horse and followed him. With that, he observed a large, well built man with a thick mop of dark hair and beard, emerge from the forge. He was dressed only in a shirt and Bingham could see his bulging arm and leg muscles. He carried an axe in his right hand. He raised it, gripping it in both hands and stood, protecting the priest's escape.

Bingham realised that the smith was going to fight. He laughed. He would easily kill him. He charged the man. The smith saw him coming and Bingham expected that he would turn aside and run. Instead, he stood his ground and lifted his axe. At the last minute, Bingham realised that the axe would be used on his horse, and the smith could cripple it, before he would be able to strike him down. He cursed himself. He had been too confident. He should have brought his lance, then he could have picked off the smith before he could do him any damage. Bingham pulled on the reins desperately and the horse skidded to a halt, rearing up and turning its head away from the smith. The blow fell on the horse's neck, and the blade of the axe bit deeply into the powerful muscles. Blood spurted like a fountain and the horse fell. Bingham, in spite of his age, was off its back before it hit the ground.

He was enraged. The war-horse had cost him a fortune and had served him through the wars in Connaught. It was maddening to lose the magnificent beast to the axe of a lowly blacksmith. He rounded its body and lunged furiously with his sword. The smith, however, was no soft victim. He easily parried Bingham's sword with the stout handle of the axe, which he held in both hands. Bingham struck harder and harder but the smith was unwavering, Bingham's blows hardly jarring him at all. Then the smith started to counter-attack, putting Bingham on the defensive. He took his sword in both hands and parried the blows with great difficulty. The blacksmith was much stronger than he was, and without the advantage of being on horseback, Bingham was in danger of being overcome.

Suddenly, he was in fear of his life. He was been forced backwards but his feet connected with the body of his dead horse. He stumbled and fell, landing in a puddle of warm blood. His sword fell from his hand. The smith stood over him and raised his axe. Bingham could see nothing but the tall figure and over him the sun rising from the east behind. He prepared himself for the blow. To die like this, at the hands of a smith, appalled him. With that, he saw the smith suddenly writhe and twist and the point of a sword appear in the middle of his chest. He dropped his axe. Over his face there spread an expression that Bingham knew well and had seen often. His eyes showed surprise and shock, his mouth opened as if to scream, but no sound issued forth and his skin suddenly looked grey. It was the look of a man mortally wounded. The blade came further forward and then disappeared back into the wound. The smith's eyes rolled up into his head and a bright red stain appeared on his shirtfront, instantly growing large. He collapsed and Bingham only just avoided the falling body.

Bingham was in a state of shock. His legs felt weak and now that he was no longer in danger, he realised how near he had come to total disaster. He took a number of deep breaths before focusing on the figure in front of him.

Standing over him was Sir Ralph, holding out his hand to him. He stooped slightly. "Well, Sir Richard. It's just as well I came along."

Bingham took the hand and pulled himself upright. "I was too confident," he said. He spun around and scanned the whole scene.

The village was now a burning inferno. There were dead bodies gleaming in the flames and women screaming in the bushes. He saw one of his soldiers grab a newborn baby and throw it into the middle of the fire. The hideous screams reached him. He turned to Sir Ralph. "And the priest? Did he get away?" he asked anxiously.

Sir Ralph shook his head. "We got him," he answered.

"And is he still alive?" Bingham enquired.

"Yes. We knew you wanted him preserved," he replied.

Bingham was relieved. The day was not ruined. He began to recover from the shock.

"Good, bring him to me," he commanded. He then turned to another of his men.

"Get the fire started in the forge." It was the only building that was not on fire as the soldiers had concentrated on the inhabited ones.

"You want me to burn it down?" the soldier asked.

"No, you imbecile. Get the bellows working and start the fire. We have work to do," he answered.

He noticed some of his soldiers returning with some men and women whom they had captured. They brought them over to where he was standing. He looked at them carefully. The women were weeping and both sexes were trying to cover their nakedness. Everything that they had owned had been burnt. He wondered how many of the women had been raped by his men.

"Separate the men from the women," he ordered.

His men rushed to do his bidding. Soon, there were two distinct groups, the men standing warily together, while the women huddled closer for warmth and protection. They watched the heavily armed invaders, unable to understand anything they were saying. They had heard of the English devils that lived to the south, but as they had never been off the land that they were born on, they had never expected to meet them here. The priest had warned them that the English were in league with the Devil and he had been right.

"Kill the men," Bingham ordered.

On his command, his soldiers drew their swords and fell on the defenceless wretches. They panicked but that only made matters worse as, in their attempts to avoid the swords and pikes of the English, they tripped and trampled upon each other. They had to watch as their neighbours were impaled on pikes or were driven through by swords, knowing that it was only a matter of seconds before they would suffer the same fate. Their cries of horror and fear rang around the hillside and the screams of the women who had to watch the butchering of their menfolk, mingled with theirs in terror, despair and disbelief. The soldiers continued with their task until not one of the Irishmen remained alive.

The priest was dragged over to Bingham and thrown to the ground. He was bound hand and foot.

"For God's sake man, what are you doing? Those people are poor harmless folk. This is the worst form of savagery imaginable," he said.

Bingham looked at him and saw that he was a young man in his early thirties. He kicked him into the face. The priest doubled over in pain. It had taken an enormous effort on Bingham's part not to draw his sword right then and run him through. Purple in the face and spewing saliva, he shouted at the priest. "You dare address a loyal subject of the Queen, whom you violate with your lies and deeds. It is you who have brought them to this. You, and the people that have sent you."

He turned back to the women. "Hang them," he ordered.

His men began to carry out his orders immediately. They took four ropes and threw them over the stout, sturdy branch of a large tree, which grew in front of the forge. They expertly judged the height of the nooses and fastened the ropes tightly to another branch of the tree. The women could now see what their fate was to be and a terrible howl rose from them. There were seven women in all and the soldiers grabbed four at random. They fought to get free of their grip and tried to clutch the other three women, but their struggles were in vain. They were dragged screaming to the ropes and the soldiers quickly tied their hands behind their backs. Two of them lifted each of the women, while a third slipped the noose around their necks. They then released them. The soldiers laughed as the naked women twisted and turned, frantically trying to breathe. They gradually turned blue and as each woman lost control of her bodily functions, the soldiers let out a cheer. Finally, their struggles ceased and Bingham ordered. "Remove them and hang the others."

A soldier loosened the nooses and the dead women were taken down and thrown to one side. The remaining women were dragged, screaming hysterically towards the nooses that swung in the breeze. Witnessing the death agonies of their unfortunate companions had increased their delirious terror. The soldiers, however, worked with great efficiency and soon they had the women strung up, watching them with less interest this time. It was surprising how quickly the horrific became mundane. The priest prayed silently. Finally, the women's struggle with death was over and they swung lifelessly in the air.

One of Bingham's captains came up to him. "Will we cut them down?" he asked.

"No. Leave them there as a warning to others," he answered. He looked at the dead bodies that littered the field, which his men were gathering and laying out side by side on the grass in front of him. It was a good day's work he thought to himself. They had harboured a papist priest and had suffered the consequences.

Bingham turned to face the priest who had struggled to his feet, his face a bloody pulp. "The blood of all those people is on your hands," he said. "You accursed papist priests are responsible for so much evil in the world. You dare incite rebellion against lawfully appointed monarchs. Now you must pay for your crime." He turned to his men. "Bring him to the forge," he said.

Two of the soldiers grabbed the priest's arms and dragged him after Bingham's retreating figure. They entered the deserted forge in which the fire burned brightly. Bingham picked up a sledgehammer, which lay in the corner. "Is there anyone here who can use this hammer?" he asked.

One of his men stepped forward. "My father was a blacksmith," he answered.

Bingham looked at him. He was well built and should be up to the task. "I want each of his arms and legs broken in three places," he said.

"Yes, Sir," he replied. He turned to two of his fellow soldiers. "Bring him to the vice," he said.

They dragged him over and the soldier caught his hand and tightened it in the implement. Then the soldier raised the hammer and brought it down with all his force on the priest's arm just above the wrist. The crack of the breaking bone could be heard quite clearly, followed by a howl of anguish from the priest, who then fainted. The soldier released his hand from the vice and he and two other soldiers dragged him over to the water trough immersing his head in it. After a few moments, the priest revived and the soldiers dragged him back.

Bingham waited until they had placed his hand back in the vice. Just as the soldier had the hammer raised over his head, Bingham held up his hand and the soldier paused.

"If you tell me where your Archbishop is hiding, I can finish this off quickly. The choice is yours," he said.

The priest shook his head. "I'll never tell you anything. You can only hurt my mortal body. My soul will be saved, whereas yours will rot in eternal damnation," he replied.

Bingham smiled sadistically. "I'll be outside. If he changes his mind let me know," he said.

He left the forge and passed out into the sunshine. He heard another howl of anguish from the priest. He walked over and surveyed the dead bodies. One of his men approached him.

"Will we bury them?" he asked.

"No, leave them for the wolfs," he replied.

He heard more screams from the priest and smiled. He did not really care whether or not he disclosed any information. He would find the Archbishop eventually and when he did, he would deal with him. No, he enjoyed the quandary into which he had put this miserable priest. He could get relief from his pain if he betrayed the Archbishop. He would have to make that choice. He sat down to wait. Fifteen minutes later the soldiers dragged the priest out and threw him on the ground in front of Bingham. His body fell awkwardly on the ground, his limbs making grotesque shapes as they lay in unnatural angles.

"Well?" he asked.

"Nothing," the soldier, who had carried out the torture, answered. "I broke both his arms at the wrist, the elbow and the shoulder and his legs at the ankle, knee and thigh but he wouldn't talk. I held his arm in the fire but that did not loosen his tongue either."

Bingham nodded. "Tie him to the steeple of the church and then burn it," he said.

The priest, racked in pain, could only manage, "Mercy, for God's sake mercy."

Bingham walked away and his men quickly put a noose over the priest's head and under his shoulders. He screamed in pain as they roughly lifted the broken arms and allowed them drop back over the rope again. Two of the soldiers had climbed up onto the roof and they hauled him up and tied him to the steeple. They then quickly descended and joined the other soldiers who were busily stacking the church with straw and rushes. One of the soldiers lit a torch from the fire in the forge. He brought it to the church and threw it in.

Bingham watched approvingly. He would have a slow, painful death, he thought. Another one of those vermin hunted down and destroyed. Also, another good step taken in his plan to goad Maguire into rebellion. He saw the inside of the church catch fire.

"Let us head back to camp," he said to his captain. "There will be double rations and beer allowance for everyone tonight,"

His men cheered, mounted their horses and prepared to leave.

Chapter 6

Hugh O'Neill, Mabel and his troupe of personal bodyguards had travelled up the Bann River to Toome. There, they were to meet Art O'Hagan, Hugh's nominee for the Lordship of Sir Phelim O'Neill's lands, and Sir Pheilim O'Neill, his adversary. Fortune had not favoured Art since Bagenal had taken Sir Pheilim's part in the internal power struggle for that Lordship. Art had been driven back across the Bann by the combined forces of Sir Pheilim and Bagenal. O'Neill wished to broker a peaceful solution between both claimants. Hugh Maguire, anxious to confer with O'Neill, was expected also.

Of all his sons-in-law, Hugh Maguire was probably his favourite. He was a giant of a man, not only in physique but also in nature, full of fun and devilment, always the first to initiate a celebration and the last to leave the drinking table at night. He ruled his territory well, constant in his dealings with his people, continually willing to lend a helping hand or postpone the payments of rents due in cases of genuine misfortune or want.

O'Neill was concerned that Maguire might not continue to fight a defensive war against the English, as he talked more and more of invading Bingham's lands in Connaught. Maguire was becoming desperate to find a solution. He had even tried to placate Bingham through bribery, but Bingham had simply taken the money and continued raiding as before.

O'Neill, himself, had also tried to dissuade Bingham, but to no avail. Both men knew that it was in Maguire's Fermanagh that the Great Lakes narrowed at Enniskillen, forming the Gap of the Erne. Whoever held that Gap held the key to the North and O'Neill's country. As a consequence, O'Neill could not afford to let Maguire fall.

O'Neill had appealed to the Privy Council on Maguire's part and it had listened to his complaints, ordering Bingham to desist from harassing his neighbour. Bingham had, as always, simply ignored the command. So, Maguire's Fermanagh continued to be raided by Bingham from the west and Henshaw, the Queen's ruler in Monaghan, from the east.

Hugh had set up their tent on a crannóg in the middle of the river. The flap of his tent parted and Patrick, the captain of his bodyguard, entered. "Sir Pheilim O'Neill has arrived. He requests an audience with you. He would like to get his business over with and depart," he said.

O'Neill sighed. Sir Pheilim was a problem and he was still unsure how to deal with him. It was every bit as important to him that he control Sir Pheilim's land and the crossing at Toome, as it was that the Gap of the Erne should not fall into English hands. O'Neill had been gradually spreading his authority far beyond the areas, which he had agreed with the English would constitute O'Neill territory. He had pushed his personal influence beyond his borders, east beyond Lough Neagh, south below the Great Lakes and south west into Monaghan, in an attempt to undermine the English settlement there, establishing trustworthy sublords willing to acknowledge his sovereignty. Bagenal still tried to halt the spread of his influence, either by establishing his own man or by sending in the army with its officials to impose the Queen's writ. Nevertheless, O'Neill had been successful in besting him.

"Tell him to wait," he said

"I think that he dislikes waiting outside there with the O'Hagans. You could cut the tension with a sword," Patrick replied.

"Good. Did he come alone?" Hugh asked.

"No, he brought his son with him," Patrick answered.

"Tell him that I must talk with Maguire before I can see him. Has he arrived?" Hugh asked.

"I saw a boat approaching and there's no mistaking him, standing up in the prow," Patrick answered.

"Very well," Hugh replied. "Show him in when he arrives. Let Sir Pheilim stew."

Patrick withdrew silently and Hugh heard Mabel clear her throat. She had been sitting at a makeshift table, writing some letters. "Hugh, I think that you should see him. You have the time before Maguire arrives. He's the Queen's man. I don't think that it's wise setting up your own men in opposition to..." she began.

O'Neill laughed derisively. "You think! You think! Do you think that you might not be totally impartial in this matter? Sir Pheilim is not Her Majesty's man, he is your brother's. Henry has no right to interfere in the running of the North. The North has always selected its own rulers without any interference from outsiders. We must be allowed to have the freedom that we've always enjoyed."

"But Her Majesty has recognised Sir Pheilim as..." Mabel attempted to argue.

"Her Majesty has been led astray by your brother. I will not have you take his part against me," Hugh interjected abruptly.

Mabel's lip trembled and tears came to her eyes. She turned back to her letters and O'Neill returned to his thoughts. For the thousandth time Mabel wondered how this marriage had gone so wrong, what had become of all the ardour and excitement of their initial courtship. She could, by now, manage somewhat better the isolation and loneliness that she felt in Dungannon. Her acquisition of Gaelic had helped in the day to day requirements of the castle, but she had not found herself any more accepted by Hugh's people than she had first been.

She found it difficult to accept the Irish native without disgust. They so totally lacked finesse and were unashamedly bawdy. But, undoubtedly, the biggest blow to her self-esteem had been her discovery that Hugh continued to keep his mistresses at another castle. She had considered leaving him and had made enquiries of her sister if she and her husband, Sir Patrick, would offer her refuge. Sir Patrick had refused and Mabel had not been able to countenance asking Henry to allow her return home. She had chosen to stay, but relations between Hugh and her had deteriorated to the point of constant argument.

The oppressive silence was broken when Patrick returned and announced, "The Maguire has arrived."

Maguire swept into the tent, catching his head in the flap and very nearly knocking the whole structure over. "You could have made it a bit higher," he muttered. He stood beside O'Neill, over a foot taller than him. His clothes were mud splattered and his red beard and hair were covered in dust. His eyes were dimmed, their usual warmth and friendship not as discernible to Mabel's eye. He strode over to Hugh, his hand outstretched. "Hugh, it's good to see you again," he said.

Hugh smiled and nodded. "And you also," he replied.

Maguire released Hugh's hand and turned towards Mabel. She enjoyed his sense of humour and how he had never made her feel excluded or worthless.

"Well, Mabel," he said, "as ever, you are in much health and beauty."

Mabel answered, "You have not lost your talent for charming, but tell me, any news of Sarah? Are you a father yet?" she asked.

Maguire's eyes were briefly illuminated. "A baby son. Fine wee healthy lad, last Friday. You know what that makes you, Hugh? A grandfather!"

Hugh smiled. "That's great news. My first grandson! Come we must drink to celebrate." He went to the table, took a jug of whiskey and poured measures for the three of them.

Mabel asked, "And what about Sarah?"

"The finest," Maguire answered. "It didn't knock a bother out of her."

Hugh handed the three goblets around. "To the new arrival, a future Chief of Fermanagh," he said.

Hugh and Maguire emptied their vessels, Mabel only taking a sip from hers. When Maguire lowered his, she noted how his face had lost its sense of animation.

"How can you talk of a future Chief of Fermanagh when I might not be here, come the summer. This is a bad business, Hugh. I must know if I can count on your help. If you and O'Donnell join with me, we can defeat them and drive them out of Ulster," he said.

O'Neill hesitated a few moments, before answering. "I have been trying to arrange a parley with the Lord Deputy, so you can put your case directly to him. He has agreed to meet you. We must bring about a cessation to hostilities."

Maguire's loud, disbelieving laugh boomed around the tent. "Hugh, it was not I who started this fight. I never wanted it. As you well know, I had no other option but to fight or lose all. O'Rourke and McMahon did not want to do battle either and look what happened to them! It all started like this for them too. The Lord Deputy will insist that I allow sheriffs into my country, sheriffs like Wallis. I would have to permit English justice decide all quarrels. Once they're in, they look for more and more concessions and then Bingham will return to his old tricks. No, it is already too far-gone. If I do not fight now, my people will depose me and find someone else to lead them. I cannot have two masters, Hugh. It just does not work. I will live and rule as I have always done, or if I am not allowed that, I will fight, even if I fight alone."

Maguire stopped to draw breath. He inhaled deeply, his forehead corrugated with barely repressed anger. Hugh remained silent, wanting Maguire to have his say before he talked. After a few moments, Maguire continued. "There is one thing that I want you to consider, Hugh and be sure to give it due thought. Do you honestly think that the English monster will be satisfied when it has consumed me? Do you think that it will leave the rest of you to live in peace? Any man with eyes in his head must see the inevitability of their march north. They will destroy us, one by one, not because they are braver or better fighters than us. No, but because we choose to fight in isolation. Did not O'Rourke put up a brilliant fight over three long years and, yet, he is gone, an English upstart ruling in his place? Either you fight with me now, while I am still around to help you, or you fight later, on your own, when they have picked off all your friends, one by one, and then they will finally turn their attention on you."

O'Neill mused deeply. This would be more difficult than he had imagined. Maguire was making sense and yet O'Neill had seen the English state at first hand on his visits to court and he knew that while Maguire was recommending that they fight, such a fight would be lost before it would be properly begun. He also had seen war at close quarters when he had campaigned with the English, both in Munster, against the Earl of Desmond and with Essex, in Ulster. The reality and butchery of that war had never left his mind. He had done things, of which he had never dreamt himself capable. He remembered the widespread famine that they had induced in Munster and the thousands of innocents who died from starvation. His whole inclination shrank from entering such a war again, especially when, this time, he would be on the opposite side.

And yet, he had been worried of late. Bagenal was right, he could never rule as an English Earl would in England. He had been impressed by the examples of Earldom that he had seen there, the likes of Essex and Leicester. It had taken him over half his lifetime to realise that their greatness came from the greatness of England, that they were an embodiment of the English tradition. They were loved and respected, as much for the continuity they represented, as for themselves. An Irish Earl, however, was an anomaly and would always invite suspicion from his own people and from his English masters. The alternative was to continue in his own Gaelic tradition, King by ancient law and, of course, his own prowess, admired and respected by his own people, praised by his poets, part of an ancient continuity, with a real sense of dignity. Hugh struggled with the thought of having to choose between either. He still had not dared have himself inaugurated as The O'Neill. Somehow or other, he would have to try to reconcile both traditions.

He turned towards Maguire, aware that Mabel apprehensively awaited his reply. "You don't understand fully the forces that you propose fighting. The war will be fought here and not in England. It will be our people who will suffer. The English forces that you see in Ireland are but a faint shadow of the beast that sleeps in England and it would be better for all of us, if we let it slumber. I am sure that the Lord Deputy is willing to grant you a pardon. All you have to do is ask," he said.

Maguire shook his head. "Why would I need a pardon? For defending myself and my people against a robber and murderer? You cannot make a deal with the Devil. Even if the Lord Deputy wished to keep faith with me, Bingham would ignore any agreement that we would reach. I realise that we may not be able to defeat the English on our own, but if we receive help from the Spanish, then we could drive them from our shores. They, at least, share our religion and we could be equal partners with them. The English won't rest as long as there is a single native freeman left in the country," he said.

Hugh began to loose patience with his son-in-law. "I have heard of the Spanish and all the aid that they will shower on us. The Earl of Desmond heard the same thing and what happened him when he believed it and rebelled? He ended up a fugitive in his own land and died a traitor. He was hounded from place to place and was finally betrayed by one of his own, for a few pieces of silver." Hugh stopped and reined in his emotions. He had to win Maguire over to his point of view. He continued in a more conciliatory tone, "O'Donnell never stops talking about all the men and aid that he is about to receive from Spain, but he has had the sense not to show his hand yet. Wait until the Spanish arrive. What's wrong with gaining some time? Postpone your fight. I guarantee you that I will do everything in my power to make sure that you get a fair hearing. I will do my utmost to have Bingham removed. If the English can be brought to recognise our right to rule, like we always have, and to allow us a Palatine status like Ormonde enjoys, then all might yet turn out right, " he said.

Maguire erupted, "All I here from you is wait, wait, wait. You are not listening to me. I cannot afford to wait. You and O'Donnell cannot afford to wait either. You just don't know that yet! So, you will not join me?"

Hugh reluctantly shook his head, "It would be the wrong move at this moment."

"And O'Donnell?" Maguire asked.

"I cannot talk for him, but I strongly advised him to await help from Spain," he answered. His voice dropped as he pleaded with Maguire, "I am asking you to reconsider. Give me time to try to help you, or time for O'Donnell's Spanish troops to arrive. O'Donnell and I will continue to give you what aid we can to protect your territory. You must not, on any account, operate outside your own jurisdiction. Trust me on this and follow my advice."

Maguire shook his head vehemently. "I will not stand idly by and allow my people be butchered by the likes of Bingham and Henshaw. If they interfere in my lands again, I'll follow them to England itself, to make them pay. There is no point in my going to the Lord Deputy, just like with hindsight, there was no point in my coming here. I have squandered my time. I should have stayed at home to defend my people. Just remember, when I am gone and it comes to your time to fight, you could have had me by your side."

He stormed from the tent and Hugh watched him go, with a heavy heart. He called after him, "Wait, Hugh. Don't leave. We must talk some more." But it was in vain. Hugh cursed inwardly. This was a bad outcome and he feared worse was to come. He would also have to contend with Hugh Roe and his impetuous foolishness. Why was he cursed with such rash sons-in-law?

O'Donnell had allowed the monks and priests back into his lands, and they overran them, preaching sedition and rebellion to his people, who were only too anxious to drink it all in. He had managed to keep them from rebellion, which was no mean feat, as Hugh well knew from dealing with his own clansmen. Hugh had always controlled the type and number of priests who roamed Tyrone. Now, the priests, committed to the Counter Reformation, who spilled over the border from Donegal into his lands, had begun to incite his own people to rebellion. All Hugh's carefully assembled world was in danger of being ripped apart by his impulsive sons-in-law. He was angry, angry with O'Donnell, angry with Maguire, angry with the priests but especially angry at the English administration in Ireland. They did not seem to realise the trouble that they were storing up for all of them.

Mabel sat silently, not daring to talk. She had never seen Maguire so enraged. She felt Hugh's advice to him had been good. She had always disliked Bingham, who was, in her eyes, a ruthless, bloodthirsty man lacking any refinement or social graces. Just as she was about to make comment, the flap of the tent opened and Patrick entered. "Sir Pheilim wishes to know if you will meet him now? he asked.

Hugh shrugged his shoulders in exasperation. This was just another problem that he could have done without. "Yes, I will see him now," he answered. "But, Patrick, I will not meet him in here, in private. I will come out and we will talk where the O'Hagans can witness our conversation."

Patrick withdrew and Hugh stood up to put on his sword. There was no need to take chances. Mabel watched him, deciding to make one more appeal. "Hugh, please reconsider. What difference can it make whether it is an O'Hagan or Pheilim who rules here? Let the Queen's will be done."

Hugh turned to Mabel and was about to reply, but thought better of it. What was the point? She just didn't understand. Instead, he strode to the flap of the tent and out into the grey dawn. Seated at the makeshift table, were Sir Pheilim and his eldest son, while the O'Hagans were seated some distance away, in the shadow of some trees. Mabel followed Hugh out and stood at the tent, observing the gathering.

On seeing Hugh, Sir Pheilim and his son got to their feet and the O'Hagans drifted towards the table, to overhear what developments might ensue. Hugh noticed Pheilim's nervousness as he shifted awkwardly from foot to foot, clenching and unclenching his fists. The tension in the air was palpable as Pheilim proffered his hand.

"Your Grace, I trust you are well," he said.

Hugh ignored the hand and replied, "I cannot complain about my health."

Both men stood staring at each other and Hugh noticed the beads of perspiration on Pheilim's forehead. The latter broke the silence. "I have come here today as there seems to be some misunderstanding. I have been appointed the Lord of the Mournes. See, here is the grant with Her Majesty's seal." Sir Pheilim searched about his person and produced a scroll, which he held out to O'Neill. Hugh kept his hands by his side, making no effort to take it from him. Eventually, Sir Pheilim dropped his outstretched hand, cleared his throat and continued, "I have been led to believe that you, as an Earl of the Realm, would honour Her Majesty's order. Since my appointment, I have had to deal with the O'Hagans who raid my lands and claim that you have made a grant of the Mournes to them. They kill my people and destroy my crops. I appeal to you, if you have any control over them, to call them off."

At this, the O'Hagans broke into laughter. There was then a silence as they all awaited O'Neill's comments. Hugh stood mute and unmoving. Finally, he spoke in anger. "The O'Hagans have the prior claim and my support. Her Majesty has no right to appoint the Lord of the Mournes. It has never been a title that the English monarchy has had a right to bestow. You must relinquish the title and then, you and your supporters will be left to live in peace. Otherwise, the matter must be settled as these matters always are, by the sword."

At this, a loud cheer rose from the ranks of the O'Hagans and their faces broke into wide satisfied grins. They strained forward to see how Sir Pheilim would take this communication. He paled visibly and his son, Connor, nervously placed his hand on his sword. "I am surprised and shocked at your answer. Did you not promise at the last Council meeting, in Dublin, that you would abide by Her Majesty's ruling in this case?" he asked.

"The Council in Dublin cannot decide what goes on here in the North. You heard my judgement. It had always been the prerogative of The O'Neill to nominate the Lord of the Mournes. Do you accept my ruling?" he asked.

Sir Pheilim shook his head in disbelief. "I cannot. I must ask you to keep your word. The O'Hagans have no right to my lands. What you propose is not just," he added limply.

"I have spoken," Hugh answered. He turned to Mabel. "Come, wife. It is time that we returned to Dungannon."

"Surely that is not your final word?" Sir Pheilim asked.

Hugh ignored the pleading face and took Mabel by the elbow. He began walking towards his boat, which his bodyguards had started to make ready. Sir Pheilim and his son followed Hugh, the O'Hagans following them, at a slight distance. Sir Pheilim was obviously distressed but Hugh paid no further heed to him. On reaching the boat, O'Neill handed Mabel into it. Sir Pheilim, realising that his visit had been a wasted, foolhardy one, said piteously, "May God be with you, my Lord."

O'Neill looked into his eyes and replied, "May God be at defiance with you until nightfall."

He then turned away, nodded at the oarsmen and the boat pulled out from the bank. His bodyguards had also returned to their boats and they followed O'Neill's vessel, leaving Sir Pheilim, his son and the O'Hagans on the crannóg. The O'Hagans surrounded the two desolate figures. Mabel sat opposite her husband in the boat, looking back at the scene that was developing on the island. She saw two of the O'Hagans put their arms around Sir Pheilim, evidently trying to coax him back to the camp. The other O'Hagans also surrounded him and it seemed as if Sir Pheilim was going peacefully with them. Then, when they were no more than thirty paces from the river, she saw the sunlight glinting as it reflected off a sword, which flashed through the air, cutting into the shoulder of Sir Pheilim's sword arm. He never got a chance to draw his weapon, as the others drew their swords and hacked at his body, which fell in a bloody mess to the ground. Horrified, Mabel stood up in the boat and shouted at Hugh, "Murder, Hugh, murder!"

The horror in her voice was unmistakable and the rowers, who could not understand English, paused in their stroke and glanced at Hugh, who with a look, indicated that they should continue rowing. The boat moved on again and Mabel stood transfixed, watching the figures on the beach. Hugh did not move, continuing to look in the opposite direction. Sir Pheilim's son, Connor, taking advantage of the confusion that surrounded his father's murder, broke free and ran for the river. The O'Hagans, once sated with their butchery, noticed Connor's escape. They turned and followed him to a man, baying like hungry wolfs. Connor reached his boat and hurriedly fumbled with the rope, trying to untie it.

Mabel saw the bloodthirsty crowd running towards him, their swords unsheathed. She screamed at Hugh, "For God's sake, Hugh, do something or they'll murder his son also."

Hugh still sat impassively, not answering her. She looked at him desperately, realising that he was not going to intervene. For one mad moment, she considered diving into the water and swimming back to the island.

Connor had managed to get the rope untied and to push the boat out into the current just as the leading O'Hagan reached him. The latter leaped into the water and caught the side of the boat, capsizing it, causing Connor to fall into the river. Both men struggled to their feet.

Connor made to splash through the shallows towards the boat, but the other man dived at him, grabbed him around the waist, submerging him again. The two men wrestled, thrashing and churning up the water until four more of the O'Hagans reached the bank and jumped in. They made for the struggling men and on reaching them, they drew them asunder. By now, the rest of the O'Hagans had reached the shore and stood watching.

Two of the O'Hagans took Connor by the arms, another caught hold of his legs, lifting him out of the water, while a fourth plunged his head underneath. Mabel could see the contortions that Connor's body underwent as he struggled vainly for breath.

Beside herself with horror, she looked down at Hugh and screamed at him, "Hugh, please, for God's sake, do something! They have murdered Sir Pheilim and now they are drowning his son before my very eyes. For pity's sake, do something! You are the only one who can stop this. They are under the Queen's protection! For that, and no other reason, you must intervene to save the son, at least. He has no part in your quarrel with Pheilim."

By now, Mabel was weeping, her eyes wild with fear and repulsion. The oarsmen looked at her with curiosity, wondering what exactly she was saying to Hugh.

O'Neill looked contemptuously at her and snarled, "Sit down and be quiet. It does not concern you."

Mabel drew in her breath sharply and hissed, "God damn you to hell, O'Neill! Do you have no humanity? A man is being murdered and you refuse to help!"

Hugh ignored her. Mabel felt an ungovernable anger well up in her and was overcome by an urge to lash out at him, at his unsympathetic, measured calm. "You bastard! I was warned about you and I would not listen. I was too much in love to believe any of the awful things that were said about you. I should have listened to Henry. He told me that under the superficial charm lurked a cruel savage every bit as bad as any other wild Irish barbarian. Is this how you repay Her Majesty, after all that she has done for you? She raised you up from nothing and made you an Earl of the Realm."

Mabel's tears had ceased and her cheeks were flushed in anger. Hugh laughed sardonically. "Oh yes, that is all I ever hear. How much Her Majesty has done for me. But do you know what the truth of the matter is? She has never given me anything that I did not already possess. When I received the Earldom, I already controlled the lands which went with it. I had won it for myself. It should have been mine by birth and given to me on my brother, Brian's death. She has, if anything, treated me abominably. For over twenty years, I have remained loyal to her and what thanks do I get?" he asked.

He paused as if he expected an answer, but Mabel's gaze was on the fast receding shoreline where the O'Hagans were bringing the dead body of Cormac back up the beach. Hugh continued, "All I have received from her is suspicion at every turn. Your brother implicates me in every ludicrous plot that his feverish imagination conjures up. How anyone could be so gullible as to believe that I would risk all on some of the stupid schemes, of which he accuses me, is beyond belief. I have to prove my innocence over and over again."

"So this is an innocent act?" Mabel asked wrathfully.

"I have always expended my own wealth and even my own blood, on her behalf. I have carried out shameful acts to further her interests in Ireland. And what reward do I receive in return? None! Instead, she allows her officers constantly to undermine me. Is that any reward for loyal service?" he asked.

Mabel was taken aback at the vehemence of her husband's outburst. She had never imagined that he harboured such feelings of embitterment against the Queen and her officials. He had kept it well hidden, even from her. She wondered at how he could mingle so freely and easily in the English world, making friends and connections, while all the time nursing such resentment. She, like many others, had been completely deceived. She realised, with a start, that she had never really known him at all. She had never imagined that he could be a cold-blooded murderer. She wondered if he had ever loved her or what it was that had driven him to woo her. A sense of intense despair and sadness engulfed her. She could not, would not stay in his company one day longer. No matter what it took, no matter how she would have to crawl to her brother, begging his forgiveness and a roof over her head, she would leave him.

"Hugh," she said, "I must tell you that we are finished. Tomorrow I will return to Newry, to my brother's house."

Hugh laughed bitterly. "I'm sure that he will be delighted to see you," he said.

Mabel ignored the interruption. In spite of her best efforts to control them, she felt tears coursing down her cheeks. "When I married you, I envisioned a very different life. I gave up everything for you, my home, my family, my friends. I made all those sacrifices. I put up with the loneliness and the slights, which I have had to endure. I even put up with your aloofness and coldness, but I cannot live with a murderer, which is what you are because you incited those people to carry out those acts. I only wish that I had believed my brother's reports of you. I could have saved myself much heartbreak."

Hugh spoke icily, "And you think that you were the only one that made an error? I actually thought that I was marrying a woman of tremendous character and intelligence. Instead, I married an ignorant, prudish daughter of a tradesman, no more fitted to be a Countess than to be one of the whores in Southwark."

Mabel reddened. His words hurt her to the quick. Their intimate life had never been a source of contentment or fulfilment. He knew well where and how to wound.

"You would know much about whores, seeing how you keep so many of them," she replied. "Well, you can have them and they are welcome to you. I won't share you with them ever again. A pox upon you all."

Hugh laughed humourlessly. "You know your departure will not be a source of sorrow to anyone at Dungannon. The atmosphere should improve enormously, though I couldn't say the same for Newry," he added.

Mabel was outraged that he would not acknowledge the sacrifices she had made for him and that he should align himself with her detractors in Dungannon. She spat at him, "I hate you, your people and your stinking country. You are a barbarous man living among barbarous people."

"And are your people so much better?" he asked gruffly. He then stopped and went on in a disarmingly quiet tone, "Mabel, you call me a murderer but what do you think your father was or your brother is? Their hands are covered in blood. This is my country, not yours nor the Queen's. Is she not guilty of murder on the grandest scale of all? She has attempted to annex our land, with disastrous results. How many tens of thousands have died in Munster as a result of her actions, people who would be alive today, but for her? We are two different, distinct peoples, with different languages and cultures, each as valid as the other. She pushes too hard, too fast. She does not appear to realise the different world that she is dealing in. She wants to take our language, our laws, our religion from us. People do not change in a generation, not even in a few generations. She can rule, but only through Irishmen, strong Irishman who give her their allegiance while they rule over a Gaelic speaking, Catholic Ireland. I must assert my authority and at times I, as all rulers, must set an example for those who would flout my law. The people must be given time to come to terms with the idea of one ruler to whom they owe allegiance. Otherwise, if the Queen keeps importing men like your father, brother and Bingham, deposing Irishmen to give them land, it will end in greater bloodshed. Together as peoples, we have much to offer each other, once it is not presumed that we have to be identical. You English must respect us and our ways or, otherwise, God help us all."

Mabel made no answer. The only sound that could be heard was the oars dipping into and out of the water. The oarsmen themselves looked straight ahead as if unaware of the argument. O'Neill gazed at the passing shoreline and a wave of sadness descended on him. How had it come to this? He had been so sure that they would be happy. If he had known that it would end in this manner, he would never have started the whole sorry business. Now, his brother-in-law would be proven right and how he would gloat over that.

He anxiously scanned his thought to ascertain how much Mabel could tell him about his affairs in Tyrone. She could implicate him in Pheilim's murder. He felt demoralised. His marriage had achieved the very opposite end to what he had hoped. He and Henry Bagenal would be even more estranged. He wondered if their thwarted marriage was an omen for the wider relationship between the two countries. Was that fated to end in heartbreak for both peoples as well? Hugh allowed his mind wander to the fate of Pheilim and his son. If he were ever to fulfil his ambitions, there would have to be casualties. He had learnt that from the English. They had to realise that Ulster was Irish and more importantly, the Irish had to realise that he, Hugh, was the power in Ulster.

Another leave-taking, three marriages over and still he had not found what he sought - someone he could love, a soul mate, someone whom he could trust with his secret thoughts and ambitions. He found it difficult to be sure of people. He had few confidants. Henry Hovendon was probably the closest person to him. O'Neill had come to love the Englishman who knew how to keep his own counsel. Hovendon, he was sure, would never betray him for money or any other inducement.

He wondered was it ever possible to find and hold that elusive quality, contentment. His marriages, alike, had all teasingly held out the prospect, but just as he had been about to reach out and grasp it, it vanished, disappearing before him like the mist off Lough Swilly on a summer morning. Sadness and dissatisfaction stirred in his heart. He was impotent to dispel such sentiments, knowing well that the past was a weight that left its print on the present and possibly too, might mark the future.

He recalled his past and how he had returned to the North after his nine years exile in the Pale. He could remember how, in his youthful naivety, he had held up English rule as the ideal form of government. The thought now amused him and the flat, white face, reflected in the calm water of the river, gave him back a ghost of a smile.

Of course, part of his attraction to the English cause was that they had supported his father and his brother, Brian, against their enemies,

Shane and Turlough O'Neill. He had a selfish interest in the English cause, expecting them to nominate him to his rightful inheritance as The O'Neill. When they had failed to do so, he had been bitterly disappointed, but he had continued to aid them in the hope that they would eventually grant him what was his by right.

He could never separate the rendering of that aid from the ultimate destruction of his first marriage to Aoife. She was the daughter of Sir Brian O'Neill, Chief of the O'Neills of Clanaboy. She had been Hugh's first love, a beautiful girl, comely figured with long red hair, blue eyes and delicate features. In temperament, she was wild and passionate. He had never since met anyone like her. But Aoife held very definite views on most matters and such tenacious single mindness led to many disputes. In the early months such arguments were inevitably resolved in the ardour of their love-making but as time went by, the one barrier that they had at first ignored, became insurmountable - her implacable hostility towards the English and her husband's co-operation with them.

She constantly berated him for "toadying up to the English" as she called it and when he went to campaign with the Queen's army in Munster, she had been outraged. If she had known of the atrocities that army had perpetrated, she would have left him even sooner. She had come to learn later, however, of the part he had played with the English army in Ulster and his support of Essex who massacred her own family. That had been the ultimate blow to their union. Her loathing of him had been so intense that she could not suffer even to take their children with her. Too much of O'Neill base blood flowed through their veins.

Hugh's reverie was interrupted by the sound of the boat running up onto the sand. Mabel didn't wait for assistance but leaped out and waded through the shallows to dry land. She ran to the waiting horses, mounted hers and rode off. With heavy heart, Hugh mounted his steed and turned in the direction of Dungannon.

Chapter 7

Hugh Roe had spent the summer brooding over his troubles. He had given his word to O'Neill that he would not rebel against the Queen, but he was finding it increasingly difficult to honour that pledge. It was easier for Hugh to remain loyal. O'Neill's lands were insulated on all sides from the tyranny and brutality of Bingham's activities. Hugh Roe had always known that Bingham would try and goad him into rebellion and time had proven him right. For the moment, it was difficult not to strike back at the heartland of his enemy.

On returning to Donegal, Hugh Roe had been shocked at the deterioration in his Lordship. Three years had passed without any strong central authority. It had been a time of great uncertainty and insecurity for his people when they could not plan with any confidence for the future, where everything that they built up could be destroyed overnight, when even their lives were not safe. Each claimant to the Chieftainship raided, pillaged and murdered the supporters of the others, except for the English, who, in the interests of fair play, raided everyone. Finally, a large number of peasants had done the unthinkable. They had left the land on which they had lived for generations, turning their backs on Donegal, and had gone to find more peaceful territories where they might live in tranquillity.

This had been a major upset to Hugh Roe who relied on the churls to carry out the farm work and without whom, the wealth of his lordship was much diminished. There was a ready market for them elsewhere, as the wars in Munster and Leinster had depleted the number of available labourers. It was a very worrying innovation. If the churls were free to move to better work and safer lands, then one of the central foundations of Gaelic society would be undermined. Hugh Roe had his churls followed into the provinces to where they had fled. They were informed of his election to The O'Donnell Chieftainship and of the change for the better in Donegal. But few had returned. Although they rebuilt their dwellings, tilled the lands and sowed their crops again, they had no confidence in the future. Whatever they built, whatever they sowed, could be wiped out in a day again by the likes of Bingham and Willis. The further south Hugh Roe journeyed, the more he sensed uncertainty in the air. Bingham's constant raids too ensured that that sense of insecurity was not allowed to ebb.

Hugh Roe retaliated as best he could but it was difficult to catch Bingham during any of his escapades. Bingham was immensely aided

in being able to pay for guides into Donegal, men who had supported Donnell against Ineen Dubh. Hugh Roe could only call on his
Gallowglasses and horse to repel the English. It was all very well for
O'Neill to recommend that he train his churls in the art of warfare, but
the reality was that he had not even enough churls to plant his lands
and look after his herds of cattle.

Now the situation had worsened. A force of English soldiers had
invaded Fermanagh some weeks previously, accompanied by his
father-in-law, in his capacity as Earl of Tyrone. O'Neill had found it
necessary to adopt such a stratagem in the interest of maintaining the
Queen's trust in him. The invasion had stirred Hugh Roe's people.
They had demanded that he join with Maguire and turn on the
invaders. O'Donnell had called his Council to a meeting at Donegal
Castle and now was on his way to attend it.

O'Donnell's castle at Donegal was the strongest and largest of all
his properties. As he rode in through the gates, the sentries saluted
him. He looked up at the roof of the Tower House and saw other sentries alert and at their posts. He dismounted quickly and one of the
grooms led his horse away to the stables at the western wall. From the
amount of horses present, he gauged that most of those summoned
had already arrived. Ineen Dubh was undoubtedly present. He noticed
her personal bodyguard of sullen Scottish mercenaries sitting and
talking with one another in the courtyard. They glanced at him, only
to dismiss him, returning instead to their desultory conversation.
Hugh Roe resented having armed troops not answering to him in his
territory.

He entered the keep and raced up the turreted stairs to the Great
Hall. He would have to defend a course of action with which he did
not fully agree. He would not have called the meeting if it had been
left to him, but Ineen Dubh, in her role as head of the O'Donnell
Council, had insisted upon it. Her husband had granted her that position as his strength declined and she had been loath to surrender it.
Hugh Roe knew that if he were ever to take the reins himself, he
would have to remove her. She was too definite in her opinions and
where the English were concerned, she could only see continuous
warfare, without mercy or quarter. He had come to accept that far
more caution, delicacy and dissembling would have to be employed if
they were to succeed. Hugh O'Neill was right. They would have to
plan carefully. The English had been a presence in the country for
over four hundred years and would not be removed overnight.

Mentally, he checked through the members of the Council. Niall
Garve would back Ineen Dubh. He would do so, not out of any love
or respect for her, but to undermine Hugh Roe. His marriage to Nuala

had gone ahead but Hugh Roe was still not confident of his brother-in-law's allegiance. Next, The O'Doherty, the Chieftain of Inishowen in northern Donegal, was a man difficult to predict. He had fought with Ineen Dubh against Donnell but had, at first, refused to acknowledge Hugh Roe's election. Hugh Roe could not be sure of him. Thirdly, there was Hugh Dubh O'Donnell, whose lands were located beside The O'Doherty's. He had also considered himself as a likely successor to the title and would probably vote against him. So, he conjectured, there would most likely be four opposing votes.

He could be absolutely sure of four supporting votes. His two foster parents, The O'Cahan Chieftain and the Gallowglass leader, Mac Sweeney na dTuadh would vote with him. As would The O'Friel and Eoin O'Gallagher, a wise man who had been his father's adviser before Ineen Dubh had replaced him in that capacity. That left his own vote and the votes of the two other Gallowglass leaders, Mac Sweeney Fanad and Mac Sweeney Banagh.

As he reached the top step, he paused momentarily to collect his thoughts. He could hear conversation from within, Ineen Dubh's loud argumentative voice carrying through the thick, oak door, to where he stood. He breathed deeply, opened the door and strode inside. A large fire blazed in the chimney piece and the table was amply provided with victuals. The guests were arranged around the hall in little groups, deep in conversation. He saw Ineen Dubh conversing with Niall Garve, Hugh Dubh and O'Doherty. He was right, he thought, they were obviously planning their approach to this parley. He saw Rose and his sister, Nuala, circulating amongst the guests with refreshments. Nuala looks unhappy, he thought. He was very fond of her. He had felt badly about telling her that she was to marry Niall Garve, but he had felt that such an alliance was imperative. She looked over, saw him and smiled warmly. He returned her smile, feeling both remorse and guilt. He hoped that in time she would learn to be happy with her husband and perhaps even exert a civilising influence over him. A silence fell and all eyes turned on him.

Ineen Dubh broke into a harangue, "So, you've come at last! Let us get started. We have much to discuss."

Rose, carrying a pitcher and goblet, walked over to Hugh Roe. "Would you like some wine, husband?" she asked, smiling warmly at him.

Hugh Roe nodded. He would take it. He must appear totally at ease.

"Thank you, Rose," he answered. Ineen Dubh visibly stiffened, incensed that her daughter-in-law should in any way delay the proceedings.

The council members drifted to the table and were seated. Hugh

Roe noticed that Ineen Dubh and her three conspirators sat down beside each other. The three Gallowglass leaders also sat next to one another. Rose and Nuala circled the table refilling the guests' goblets. Rose approached Ineen Dubh with her pitcher.

"Leave it," Ineen Dubh ordered splenetically, "we can help ourselves. It's time we got down to work."

Rose left the pitcher and she and Nuala withdrew to a nook in the chimney piece at the other end of the hall. Hugh Roe noted Ineen Dubh's tone and resented it. Rose had always been dutiful and courteous to her and Ineen Dubh treated her with ill-disguised contempt. He struggled to ignore the insult and start the business of parley.

"We have come here today to discuss the situation in Fermanagh and to decide what is the best course for us to take. As you know, The Maguire's lands are invaded by the English and he is sorely pressed."

Niall Garve interrupted, "Don't forget your great friend, the Earl of Tyrone, is marching with them once again. He shows his true colours, always the lap dog to the English. Do we want Donegal to follow the same route?"

Hugh Roe answered, "You have a short memory, Niall Garve. Where were you when I was inaugurated? In Dublin, seeking the aid of those very same English! They are in Fermanagh because they have been invited in by Connor Roe Maguire. He will not accept that the people have spoken and chosen Hugh Maguire as their leader. It is wrong that rejected candidates then try to thwart the wishes of the people and have themselves installed through the interference of outside forces."

He saw Niall Garve's face flush and a look of unguarded hatred spread across it. Hugh Roe realised that already he had done what he had sworn he would not, allow the meeting dwindle to a personal vendetta. He would have to be wilier. He had to try and win the majority over. He continued in a more equitable tone, "For over seven hundred years there has been enmity between the O'Neills and the O'Donnells. Historically, it has been the O'Donnells who have been the supporters of the English in Ulster and the O'Neills have been allied with the now vanished great House of Kildare. Times have changed. We have changed with them. The treachery of the present generation of English has made us turn our backs on them. We have established friendly relations with the O'Neills for the first time in centuries. We must take a course that will preserve our freedom and rights and we must be careful to follow the right paths in all our dealings."

Niall Garve snarled, "But how can you say that we have turned our backs on the English, on the one hand, and that we have made a pact with O'Neill on the other? They are one and the same animal."

"That is not so," Hugh Roe answered. "O'Neill must tread a careful course. He has already delayed the English invasion by convincing them that Maguire would seek a pardon. That gave Maguire time to harvest his crops and move his herds to safety in our lands. If the English had come earlier, they would have burnt the crops in the fields and taken all his cattle. Famine and death would have ravished his territory."

"If he is such a friend of Maguire's, then why does he campaign with the English and waste his country?" Niall Garve asked contemptuously.

"Because he promised that if he could not bring Maguire in, he would join with them in putting him down," Hugh Roe answered. "He goes with them to slow them down. His first act was to strip Connor Roe's lands bare and to waste them, until the Lord Deputy ordered him to cease. All that plunder has made its way to Tyrone and Connor Roe will never see any of it again, no matter what the Deputy demands."

Ineen Dubh could stay silent no longer. A torrent of words issued from her. "I cannot listen to such nonsense, Hugh Roe. You have much to learn in the ways of the world. We all know the record of the Earl of Tyrone. I know what he did to my family on Ratlin Island. He accompanied the English there and no doubt joined in the slaughter. We know of his action in Munster and how he supported Essex against Brian O'Neill and his family. I have warned you about him and all his treacherous clan." With that, she cast a look of disdain in the direction of Rose.

"You did not refuse his help when you needed it against Turlough, though," her son countered.

"He never helped us except when his needs coincided with ours. Do not be a fool for the likes of him and do not think that just because you're married to his precious daughter, that he wouldn't attack you, just as easily as he attacks his other son-in-law! He was to do such great things to gain your freedom from Dublin Castle. I was tired of hearing of all the friends in high places that he had among the English, but in the end what could he do for you? Nothing! You'd still be rotting there if you were waiting on him to gain your release."

Neill Garve and O'Doherty snickered. Hugh Roe was almost goaded into declaring O'Neill's part in his rescue but struggled to resist the temptation. O'Neill had never wished his involvement to be known.

"I would never be influenced by O'Neill to forget my distrust of the English," Hugh Roe answered.

"Well, stand up for yourself and your people and prove that you are not their lackey. Bingham raids your lands and kills your people. The dead cry out for vengeance. Now Bagenal and O'Neill raid

Maguire. You must join with him and drive those usurpers from Ulster once and for all. Any one not prepared to fight does not deserve the name of Ulsterman," Ineen Dubh declared with spirit.

A murmur of assent went around the table.

"But with what shall I fight?" Hugh Roe asked. "Our power is diminished because we have chosen to fight among ourselves for so long. We need time to regroup and rearm. Then we will be in a position to do battle, with a hope of winning. When we get help from Spain..."

Niall Garve interrupted disdainfully, "Not that old dream again. You use it to justify your inaction. We must help Maguire. Call a general hosting and join him in his battle."

Ineen Dubh smiled victoriously. "Niall Garve is right. Now is the time for revenge," she added in delighted alliance.

O'Donnell was outraged. He struggled to keep a rein on his feelings. They did not want to comprehend. "The campaigning season is nearly over. Winter is not far away and when the weather breaks, the English will have to return to winter quarters. They will not be able to exploit what gains they make in this campaign. We will have gained another year for our preparations," he argued.

"So, we should attack them now. They will not be able to retaliate until next spring at the earliest," Ineen Dubh answered.

"Yes, but they will spend the winter planning next year's campaign. They will bring armies over from England and Flanders. We must not bring that upon ourselves yet," Hugh Roe answered. He felt as if the meeting was drifting away from him. He looked around the table seeking some support from those who had not already spoken. His eyes alighted on Eoin O'Gallagher. "And what do the rest of you think?" he asked. "Eoin?"

Eoin slowly nodded his head. "I can see both sides of the argument," he began. "It is true that our power is much diminished. It is also true that we should give aid to Maguire. I think that there is a way that we can do that without bringing the whole might of the English down on our heads."

Hugh Roe nodded, "I would be very eager to hear your suggestion."

Eoin continued, "The Scottish mercenaries whom you took on for the fighting season to help protect your lands, they are not yet gone home?" he asked.

"No, not yet," Hugh Roe answered.

"And how much fighting did you get out of them for your outlay?" Eoin enquired.

"None. We could not catch Bingham on any of his raids. Still, they were a deterrent," Hugh Roe returned.

"And how many have you and where are they now?" Eoin asked.

"In Ballyshannon, on the border with Connaught, protecting Donegal from Bingham. There are three hundred of them in total," Hugh Roe replied.

"So, they are on the borders of Fermanagh also. Send them to Maguire. One set of Scot mercenaries looks much like any other. Who's to say that they were sent to him by you and in your pay? You aid Maguire and yet the English cannot accuse you of rebellion," Eoin said with calm and measured logic.

The wily old fox, Hugh Roe thought. Of course, it would be an admirable compromise. He would hold faith with both O'Neill and Maguire. No wonder his father had valued O'Gallagher so much, making him his chief adviser. Ineen Dubh and Niall Garve would have to agree to it, he thought. He was wrong.

"It is not enough, " Ineen Dubh said. "It will not tilt the balance in Maguire's favour."

"I agree, " Niall Garve added. "The O'Donnell must be seen in the field side by side with Maguire. Only then will the people get the leadership that they deserve."

Eoin interrupted them, "Hugh Roe will have done his share. He will have aided Maguire. There is nothing to stop Ineen Dubh from sending her personal bodyguard to aid Maguire, and you, Niall Garve, can always send your people to help him also. Hugh Roe need only claim that you do so, without his knowledge. The English would easily believe that you, Ineen Dubh, would be ungovernable."

This evoked a laugh from the gathering around the table. Ineen Dubh, however, remained impassive. After the merriment had subsided, Eoin continued, "And as for Niall Garve, the English know of his past ambitions in regard to The O'Donnell title and would easily believe that he was combining with Maguire to gain his aid in an attempt to wrest the title from Hugh Roe. That way, they would have no reason to attack Hugh Roe or Donegal."

Hugh Roe felt the thrill of triumph. Eoin's argument was masterful. Ineen Dubh and Niall Garve were stuck for words. Hugh Roe knew that his mother would never part with her bodyguard. She had too many important and powerful people murdered in the past, ever to sleep soundly in her bed at night. And as for Niall Garve, for all his words, he would never support Maguire on his own, being unwilling to risk the annihilation of his power base. Neither commented and both looked uncomfortable.

Hugh Roe opened up the discussion to some of the others that had sat silently until now. He first addressed his supporters. "How says

Mac Sweeney na dTuadh?" he asked.

"As you know, I and my men will fight whenever The O'Donnell calls on our service. I think, however, that in this case, your council is the wise one. Why deplete our strength, when we have paid mercenaries to do the fighting for us?" he replied.

"And the other Mac Sweeneys? Are they in agreement with those sentiments?" Hugh Roe asked.

They both nodded their assent. Hugh Roe was pleased. "And The O'Cahan?" he asked.

"I'm in agreement with you," The O'Cahan answered. Hugh Roe had expected no less from his foster father.

It was all over now. Victory was with Hugh Roe, but he would ask The O'Doherty and Hugh Dubh their opinions, for the sake of completeness. "And The O'Doherty and Hugh Dubh?"

"Maguire's lands are far distant from mine. I owe him nothing and I will be guided by The O'Donnell in such matters," O'Doherty answered.

"My feelings are similar," Hugh Dubh replied.

Hugh Roe was surprised and glanced at the faces of Ineen Dubh and Niall Garve. Ineen Dubh pushed back her chair angrily and got to her feet. "It is a sad day for Donegal," she spat in spleen.

"The meeting is not over yet," said Hugh Roe in a steely voice. There was one more issue that he had to resolve in this session. "Sit down!" he ordered.

A deadly hush fell over the assembled Council and Rose and Nuala, who had been talking quietly to each other at the other end of the hall, looked around in startled surprise. No one had ever heard anyone speak to Ineen Dubh like this before. She paused, shocked at the tone taken by her son. Hugh Roe waited for her next move. She collected herself and answered in an imperious voice, "I have wasted enough time here already. My journey was a vain one. I am returning home. "

"I will not waste your time any more, Mother. The new O'Donnell always selects a new Council. I have waited till today to do so, to allow some continuity from the old regime. Now I think the time is right. I am replacing you with Eoin. I will not be needing your service on the Council any more, but I would like to thank you for all you have done for Donegal and me," Hugh Roe announced with finality. His blood pounded in his temples as he saw the ire leap into his mother's eyes. But he would not be cowed.

Ineen Dubh stood absolutely still. She had miscalculated. It was now Hugh Roe who held the reins of power. She glanced around the table, realising that there was no one there who would not be glad to see the back of her. Even Niall Garve would relish her discomfiture. Finally, she spoke. "You need me. If it were not for me, Donnell would now rule in Donegal and you would have been executed long ago. Who arranged your inauguration? You are beholden to me."

"And I'm grateful for all you've done," Hugh Roe replied, "but it is time that I took control." He looked around the table. "There can only be one ruler." He held Niall Garve's gaze before turning back to his mother. "You may go," he finished.

Ineen Dubh stood at the table, unable to believe that she had been humiliated in such a public fashion. Hugh Roe turned back to the others. He addressed Mac Sweeney na dTuadh. "You go to Ballyshannon. Take charge of the mercenaries, bring them to Maguire and have them join with his forces," he ordered.

"Yes, and will I stay and command them in the battle?" Mac Sweeney asked.

"Yes," replied Hugh Roe "But now we must talk about preparing our country for war. We will have to consider training the churls."

"My men would not be happy about such an innovation," Mac Sweeney Fanad answered.

Ineen Dubh, who had all this while been ignored, turned and imperiously swept out of the hall. Hugh Roe recognised the look of absolute ire on her face. He had seen it before and was glad that she had not allowed her temper best her. He knew how savagely destructive she could be. He rejoiced privately that he had held his own, and bitter as might his relationship with his mother be, he now was in command - both he and she knew it in their deepest core. Once she had left, Hugh Roe relaxed, a sudden weariness overcoming him. "We have done enough for today. Mac Sweeney na dTuadh should make for Ballyshannon. We'll meet again after we see how Maguire fares. We will have a better idea of what we're facing then," he said.

It had been an eventful meeting. Hugh Roe looked over at Rose and beckoned to her to join him. She hurried over to him, her tender face radiant and smiling at this new strength in her ever-surprising lord.

Hugh O'Neill left his tent and stepped out into the early morning drizzle. He stretched his back. It had been another broken night's sleep. This campaigning is getting more difficult the older I get, he thought. He looked across the valley and could still make out the campfires of Maguire's men in the early morning gloom. Damn, he thought. He had told Maguire that he was not to stand and fight. Why was he always so stubborn? First, his son-in-law raided Bingham's Sligo and Roscommon and then, when Hugh had procured a truce for him,

Maguire had broken it by raiding Monaghan. Hugh had been left with no choice but to join the English on this campaign. They were already deeply suspicious of him and had he refused, they would have declared him a traitor as well. Bagenal would have made sure of that.

The previous spring he had been summoned to Dublin to answer three charges of treason; firstly, of foreign conspiracy with an unfriendly ruler, secondly, being party to Maguire's rebellion and finally, being party to the murder of Pheilim O'Neill. He had refused to go to Dublin, fearing arrest, so the Council travelled to Dundalk instead. There, he had intimidated them by arriving escorted by his army of over five thousand. The English lacked sufficient information to succeed in indicting him. Pheilim's murder had been the most awkward to explain but O'Neill had passed it off as revenge by the O'Hagans. Eventually, Hugh's friends on the Council won the day and he was released with a commission to bring Maguire in. He had promised that if he could not do so, he would join with the English, reduce Maguire's country and bring him to justice.

Now, he was fulfilling that promise. He looked around and saw that during the night, most of his men had left. Henry Hovendon, who had been up before him and had added fresh timber to the fire, huddled over it in an attempt to induce some warmth into his weary bones. Hugh joined him. "Why are they not all gone?" he asked.

"Your Irish troops were only too delighted when I suggested to them that they should abscond. Your English born troops, however, refused to desert you or the English cause, unless expressly ordered to do so by you. Captains Marshall and Lee are to be commended for their duty and loyalty to you."

O'Neill groaned. He had been afraid of that. He knew that his Irish troops would know that Hovendon would never have proposed such a course, unless he had Hugh's prior agreement. He also knew that their hearts weren't in this fight against fellow Irishmen. His forty-four English soldiers, however, did not share such reluctance to fight.

His plan was now in tatters. He had instructed his cavalry to remain with him and once morning arrived, he had planned to use the desertion of his infantry, as an excuse for leaving himself in pursuit of them. He had tried to absent himself the previous day, once it seemed likely that Maguire would stand and fight. His pretext had been lack of supplies for his troops but Bagenal resisted the ploy.

"Look who's coming," Hovendon said in a tired voice.

Hugh turned and saw Bagenal riding across the open ground that separated the English camp from his own. Both sets of troops had kept separate, their leaders' dislike for one another being so obvious, that even Hugh's English soldiers had not felt that it would be proper to fraternise with fellow countrymen.

Bagenal rode over to the campfire where Hugh and Hovendon awaited him. He seemed disappointed to see Hugh. He'd probably be delighted if I had turned and run, Hugh thought. It would have given him something more to complain about in his report to the Privy Council. Hugh still sat on the Irish Council and his friends and supporters on it outnumbered Bagenal's, frustrating him greatly. Relations between both men had declined to their lowest level on Mabel's return to her brother's house in Newry.

Bagenal reined his horse in just in front of both men. "Where are your men?" he asked belligerently.

"Some must have slipped away in the night. I told you that we were running short of food and that they had close links with Maguire's people."

Bagenal snorted derisively, "Any man who cannot control his men is no soldier. I trust that such cowards will pay for their treachery. If they were English soldiers, they would be hanged, for such an act."

Hugh answered through gritted teeth, "I will deal with them after our own custom and law."

"It is a great treachery, we have need of greater numbers," Bagenal answered. "It seems the rebels will stand and fight. I sent scouts to ascertain how many men they have and it appears that we are evenly matched. God willing, we will attack and destroy them today."

"They are still all present?" Hugh asked.

"Yes, it seems so. Let's march forward for a better look at their deployment," Bagenal suggested.

Bagenal dismounted and both men walked through the trees until they reached the edge of the wood. This overlooked the valley below them, through which a broad stream, swollen with the autumnal rains, flowed. They were right on the most western tip of Maguire's country. If he had retreated any further from them, he would have found himself in Connaught.

Hugh was deeply angered by him. There was no point in such a course. They had already wasted his country. The prior warning that Maguire had received from Hugh of the English plans had guaranteed that his losses had been low. There was no point in Maguire's engaging the enemy, he risked disaster by so doing but there was no talking to this headstrong son-in-law.

O'Neill turned his attention back to the scene in front of him. From the wood's edge where they stood, lay a vast plain that would have to be traversed before they could attack Maguire's men, who held the ford. Hugh could make out perhaps four or five hundred men guarding it. The rest of Maguire's men would be held in reserve, probably on the top of the opposite hill. Maguire himself and his horse would be stationed there.

"Well," Bagenal asked, "what do you make of his position? We will have to cross the open plain to attack him. There will be no cover for us. I think we should send our infantrymen in first to confront them. Then, when they have softened them up, we should commit our horse."

Hugh looked for a few minutes. Maguire's forces occupied a large salient, created by a bend in the river. He recognised that such a position gave the English forces the advantage. "See how the river winds around his position. We must station our best musketeers on both flanks. The trees and water will protect them and from both Maguire flanks, they can sweep his men with fire. That will help weaken their resolve. We will allow them do their work for some time before we make our approach, attacking from the front. It they do not fall back from their position, they will suffer much loss."

Bagenal nodded. "Yes," he said begrudgingly, "that makes sense."

Two returning scouts recognised O'Neill and Bagenal and hurried over to them.

"The rebels have somewhere between a thousand and fifteen hundred troops. Maguire has many musketeers and Gallowglasses. We also saw the approach of another body of Gallowglasses who were welcomed with great cheers and rejoicing," one of them volunteered.

"And O'Donnell, any sign of him?" Bagenal asked.

"No. If he were there, we would have spied his standards," the guide answered.

Hugh was relieved at this intelligence. It was enough that he would be fighting one son-in-law. Perhaps Maguire would withdraw yet. He would make sure that his own standards were displayed prominently and perhaps that might encourage him to leave the field.

"How wide is the ford?" he asked the guide.

"Over seventy paces," he replied.

"So our horse and infantry could cross at the same time?" Hugh asked.

"Yes," the guide answered.

"Very well," said O'Neill. "I and my men will take the left flank of the attacking infantrymen. You and your men shall take the right. Agreed?"

Bagenal delayed before replying. He resented O'Neill taking charge, and yet what he proposed made sense. He would be able to keep an eye on him and make sure that he didn't slip away. O'Neill would have to take part in the battle and maybe, with some good fortune, he might get killed.

"Agreed," he finally replied. "Come, we must put our plans into action. We will not receive any more reinforcements, but Maguire might. We must not delay. O'Donnell is not that far distant and might yet decide to join him."

"O'Donnell will remain loyal," O'Neill answered with a conviction that he did not possess. They turned back up the hill to rejoin their men.

Maguire watched the opposite hill fill with enemy soldiers. A mass of infantrymen was crossing the northern end of the low ridge and marching down into the plain towards the ford. Their uniforms were the dark green of the English army but he also saw the red colours of O'Neill's English troops among them. The English horse appeared on top of the ridge. Again, he could make out O'Neill's men on the right, whereas Bagenal's men took up the left position. All the flags above them were English, except for the red hand of Ulster, which was proudly unfurled in the stiff breeze. Even at this distance, Maguire could make out O'Neill's figure. Damn it, he thought. He and his men should be long gone. More and more soldiers appeared until he found it hard to estimate the number.

"We must order our men to hold their fire until they are nearer. The main body must square up tightly to face the enemy," Mac Sweeney na dTuadh suggested.

Maguire nodded. "Let it be done," he said

Mac Sweeney gave the order to one of his men and he hurried away to relay it to O'Donnell's and Maguire's Scottish Gallowglasses. The enemy infantry was two hundred yards away and advancing steadily to the beat of their drums and the wail of O'Neill's bagpipes. The English guns, aimed at Maguire's flanks, were firing into his men and causing great havoc. Maguire could hear the instructions being shouted in Gaelic to his men. They quickly regrouped to face the enemy's main body.

The advancing enemy looks steady, Maguire thought. Their leading troops had momentarily paused to allow the horse behind, catch up, but now, reformed with the infantry in the middle and the horse on either side, they were ready to advance again. The rank and file were ramrod straight. Their officers wore bright uniforms and carried their swords in their hands. The English on Maguire's flanks continued to pour shot into the side of his defensive formation, but his men stoically endured the punishment as their officers made sure that their column was tightly packed and ready to repel the charge when it came.

Maguire licked his dry lips. So this was what it was like to face the dreaded English in open battle. Impressive looking bastards, he thought, and so disciplined. The enemy now filled the landscape ahead. They came in a solid column, marching at a steady pace. As they advanced, they held their fire, just as Maguire's men were holding theirs. He heard one of his officers give the order to fire, and a volley rang out across the valley. Dense gunpowder smoke rose from his men's weapons. The leading ranks of the English thinned and fell, but the order had come too soon and the effect had not been all that he had hoped for.

He heard his officer ordering his men to reload as the English forces broke into a run. It was now a race against time for his musketeers. They had to remove their muskets from their stands, load the powder and shot, thrusting it home with ramrods. After that, the flashpan had to be primed and the match affixed. The English stopped when they were fifty paces nearer the river and discharged their weapons. Huge gaps appeared in Maguire's men and the English horse and pikemen charged. It was all happening too fast. Maguire's own men were still in the process of reloading when he saw the enemy infantry and horse cross the ford.

The musket fire from the woods on both his flanks, was dense, an unending crackle of shots, each flash momentarily illuminating the fog of powder smoke that spread through the trees on either side of his army. It was hellish, flash after flash of fire blooming in the dark of the woods, the blood curdling roars of the charging enemy, echoing through the trees and from every side, the moans of dying men coupled with shrieks of pain. He heard the leader of the Gallowglasses shout at his men to close up, another shouting desperately for reinforcements, and at the same time cheering his men forward to meet the English. However, too many of his ranks were being pinned backwards against the trees to their rear, in real danger of being overwhelmed.

Maguire knew that he had manoeuvred wrongly. He had chosen his defensive position badly. His men had to fight on three fronts, as the shot poured into them from their right and left flanks. He took pride in these soldiers and had paid a lot to obtain his Gallowglasses, but if he could not pick the right location for them to fight in, then it was he who was at fault and not his men. He thought about spurring his horse down the slope and into the battle to aid his soldiers or even to cross the ford and into the woods, to root out the musketeers who had caused such damage, but he knew that was now impossible. He would have to pass his own men and even as he watched, they broke in front of the English charge and scattered into forlorn groups, which were soon surrounded and attacked.

"Come," Mac Sweeney Fanad said. "We must away or else we too will die on this field. This day is lost. We must live to fight another."

Maguire looked at the mayhem and destruction below him and tears came to his eyes. "We must aid them," he said.

"There is nothing you can do for them now. They are mercenaries. They knew the risks. You paid them well in employing them. They broke in the face of the enemy, that is their fault. They did not give you time to aid them. Come, or all is lost," Mac Sweeney added urgently.

Maguire saw that some of the English horse had ignored the battle below and were riding up the hill. Down below, the Gallowglasses were courageously fighting the enemy who had them pinned into small, desperate groups. Mac Sweeney was right, Maguire thought. He turned away from the scene. "Imeoidhmid," he said and rode off.

O'Neill had been among the first of the horse across the ford. He ignored the musket balls, which whipped around him. Henry Hovendon and Dudley Loftus, the son of a fellow Council member, were at his side. They charged at the Gallowglasses who broke and fled under the combined assault of the English forces. Hugh rode at one of them and drove his spear through the man's chain mail and into his stomach. The momentum of his charge drove the spear point deep, so deep that Hugh was certain that he felt its razor sharp tip, lodge against the man's backbone. The Gallowglass fell to the ground and his body jerked like a gaffed and landed fish. His mouth opened and closed but no words issued forth.

Out of the corner of his eye, Hugh saw another Gallowglass charge towards him. He gave the spear a savage twist, in an effort to free it. It became dislodged and as he turned to face his assailant, he saw that he was too late. The man was on top of him, lunging at him with the long spear, which he carried. O'Neill pulled on the reins of his horse, which reared onto its hind legs. The spear missed its target, driving deep into his leg instead. He felt a sharp pain in his thigh and was relieved to see Henry Hovendon ride up behind the Gallowglass and strike him down. Hugh's blood flowed freely as he wrenched the weapon from his thigh and threw it at the fleeing body of men.

Henry Hovendon rode over to him. He saw the blood that ran down the side of his horse and leggings. "Come," Henry said. "We must stop that bleeding." He grasped Hugh's horse and led him back over the river. When they reached the other side, Henry brought Hugh to a sheltered area among the trees and helped him dismount. He sat him down and then proceeded to cut off some of his cloak. Hurrying to the river, he washed it, returned and tied it tightly around Hugh's thigh. "It doesn't seem too deep. We must get you back to the camp and have the physician look at it. He will have to singe the wound to purify it and to stop the bleeding," Henry suggested.

Hovendon helped Hugh remount, before riding back to the camp. Hugh felt weak. The thought that he could have been killed upset him far more than the wound, which he had received.

Bagenal was jubilant. He had killed seven rebels with his own hands. It had been so easy. Once they had broken and run, it had been a simple matter for one on horseback to run them through. Now, there were no more to be followed in the open, the survivors disappearing into the dense wood where the horses could not pursue them.

Bagenal dismounted and followed his infantrymen into the dark of the trees. All around him, he could hear the sounds of battle and the cries of the injured and dying. He saw the dead bodies, which lay where they had fallen and delighted to see that they were, for the most part, those of the enemy. He lost contact with his men as he pushed his way deeper into the undergrowth. He paused, a snaphaunce pistol in his hand, attempting to get his bearings.

Deep in the wood, he could see muskets flashing, their garish flames momentarily illuminating the gloom. He could hear men shouting, but he had no idea where the enemy and his men had gone. Suddenly he heard a terrible war cry close to him and wheeling around, he saw a large Gallowglass appear from behind a tree and charge towards him. He panicked and fired his pistol single-handedly, missing the fast approaching enemy. Dropping the pistol, he drew his sword as the Gallowglass brought his large battleaxe down on him, from above his head. The axe became snared on an overhanging branch and in slicing through it, the blade turned in his attacker's hand, flat side out. It connected with the side of Bagenal's helmet and its force thrust him violently back against a tree trunk.

He was badly winded, hot pain coursing through his brain. In terror, he saw the Gallowglass raise his axe again, but he summoned all his strength and with an enormous effort, leaped forward, lunging at the big man's bearded face. He drove his sword-point into his neck, thrusting it home hard. The man's eyes closed. Bagenal felt relief. He pulled the sword out and raised his arm to deflect the axe, which now fell from the dead man's hand. In pulling the sword from the Gallowglass, he dragged him forward and the dead body fell in a heap on top of him. Bagenal could feel the Gallowglass's warm blood running down his face. He pushed the body away and unsteadily got to his feet. His head throbbed violently, the shock of the encounter unsettling him greatly. He slowly and carefully retraced his steps, not wishing to meet any more hostile soldiers.

Four hours later, the battlefield was quiet again, the victorious soldiers having picked the bodies clean. O'Neill and Bagenal sat around the campfire. Bagenal's face was a swollen pulp of bruised and livid flesh but the pain had eased and he was now feeling victorious. This victory would be turned into a mighty and glorious feat when he reported it to Her Majesty. Over four hundred rebels lay dead on the field. English casualties had been light and Maguire's power was destroyed. He must, however, make sure that O'Neill's report on this day would concur with his.

"We have done a good day's work for the Queen," he commenced.

"That we have," O'Neill answered. "I hope that you no longer doubt my loyalty. I risked my life for her and spilled my blood, here today, in her cause. You will mention that in your report on this day's doing."

"Indeed, provided that you mention my service in leading the attack and killing seven rebels by my own hand," Bagenal replied.

O'Neill had not seen Bagenal kill anyone, but if that was what he wanted him to say, say it he would. Maybe at last there could be some easing of the enmity between them. At the very least, this day should have gained him some breathing space. "I shall," he said. "I must return to Dungannon. My leg pains me, but I think we have done well here. There is not much more we can achieve."

"Agreed. I intend returning home also. I will leave three hundred men with Connor Maguire. I will set him the task of taking Maguire's Castle at Enniskillen," Bagenal replied.

"And what of Hugh Maguire?" Hugh asked.

"Escaped," Bagenal answered.

"A pity," Hugh said, though the news relieved him greatly. "I and my men will break camp and head for Tyrone. I trust that you will report this day fairly, giving me due praise, as I shall give you yours?"

"Undoubtedly," Bagenal answered.

He watched O'Neill as he limped away towards his men. He'd give him his due, certainly. He would report how O'Neill tried to be off before the fight and how his men took little part in the battle. He would also report how he had found a letter on the Gallowglass captain, stating the terms under which Hugh Roe O'Donnell had employed him for the fighting season. Bagenal would prove them all traitors yet.

Chapter 8

The fields around Dungannon were shrouded in crisp, white snow. As far as the eye could see, the landscape was bleak and cheerless, a searing north wind howling across the open countryside. Hugh O'Neill stood on the battlements of his castle and surveyed the scene despondently. The sky was a deep, leaden grey. There's a lot more snow to fall yet, he thought. It was becoming another dismal winter.

In the far distance, he spied a body of horsemen, approaching from the west. It could only be one party. No one else would travel in weather like this, unless they had extremely urgent business. He watched closely, until he recognised the leading horseman's large frame and red beard, visible under his cloak. Good, he thought, Maguire has answered my summons. Maguire had need of him now, more than ever, but he too had need of him.

He turned from the battlements and strode quickly to the turret. On entering, he shook the snow from his cloak and hair, but the white did not leave his sideburns, middle age having gained a hold there. He hurried down the stairs to his chamber where a large log fire blazed in the hearth. Bracketed reed torches lit the room, the narrow windows, insufficient to provide adequate light. It would be the first meeting between them since their battle. He was glad that his son-in-law had swallowed his pride and finally agreed to this parley.

Hugh went to the chest in which he kept his official documents and removed a letter from it. It bore the large, heavy wax seal of the Queen, herself. It was unusual to get a commission directly from Her Majesty, but this was one honour that he could have done without.

After Maguire's rebellion, the Irish Council had concluded that O'Donnell had also been implicated. It was not only on the evidence of the dead Gallowglass's letter, but their spies in Donegal had also confirmed their suspicions. They had written to the Queen and asked her resolution to the problem. She had instructed that O'Neill should deal with O'Donnell because of the marriage alliances between their respective families and O'Donnell's dependence on him. If O'Donnell proved impervious to influence, Hugh was to use force to get his submission.

Hugh had decided not to co-operate with the Queen. This decision had caused him much soul searching and sleeplessness. He knew he was embarking upon a very dangerous path. He was outraged that he had received no acknowledgement for his service with Her Majesty's forces against Maguire, even though he was aware that this was occasioned by Bagenal's maliciousness. That still rankled with him. He had kept his part of the bargain. He had praised his brother-in-law's part in the action, but Bagenal had not reciprocated, as agreed. His report to Her Majesty implied that O'Neill had been in league with Maguire and that he had done his utmost to avoid being present at the battle. As a consequence, Hugh was more determined than ever that Bagenal would have to be removed.

His thoughts were interrupted by a knock on the door. "Come in," he shouted. The door opened and Hovendon and Maguire entered. Maguire's face was set in a scowl of angry impatience. Hugh noticed how much thinner he had become and how the lines around his eyes and on his forehead had deepened. The six months, during which he had been living rough, had left their mark. Maguire immediately launched forth. "Well it's good to see that you live in such comfort and warmth, while I and your daughter live the life of bush kerne in our own lands."

Hugh sighed. He would have to try and calm Maguire. "Come and make yourself warm in front of the fire. You have travelled far and must be tired and hungry." He turned to Hovendon, "Whiskey for all of us," he ordered.

"Not for me," Maguire answered. "I've come to hear what you have to say and then I'll take my leave."

Hugh knew that this was going to be difficult. "Very well," he said. "I regret that things have come to this pass..."

Maguire interrupted, "And what about your part in all of this?" he asked angrily.

"You know you should not have given battle. I told you that there was nothing to be gained from it. You wasted your forces and, in the process, gave Bagenal the upper hand," Hugh replied.

Maguire snorted, "It is easy to lie on another man's wounds. You have not had to witness the desolation of your lands, yet. You have not had to stand idly by, while your people are slaughtered and your women raped. We'll see how you react when you are in that position and believe me, that day is not far off. I asked you, I begged both you and O'Donnell to join with me while I was still strong, but you would not. Shortly, it will be your turn. Enniskillen has fallen. The gateway to your lands is now in English hands and they can raid your territory, as they see fit."

Hugh was dismayed. He had not expected this development. Enniskillen Castle had been built in an eminently defensible position, owing to its island location on the River Erne, divided on all sides from the mainland by wide stretches of water. It had the reputation of being impregnable. Its fall was an absolute disaster. Such news would send a wave of panic throughout the whole of the North. The Irish lacked the heavy guns for retaking such a stronghold. The only option was siege. But starving the defenders into surrender would be a lengthy process and give the English ample time to mobilise a force to resist such a strategy. "But how? When?" he asked in alarm.

"It fell last Wednesday. It only took them ten days in all. I had left a garrison of thirty-six fighting men, which should have been ample for the job. Captain Dowdall led the English. His artillery blazed away at the castle for a number of days, doing little damage to the walls. At that point, I was confident that it could hold out almost indefinitely," he replied.

"As long as it had ample food, water and munitions, there should not have been a problem. So, what went amiss?" Hugh asked.

"Connor O'Cassidy, that's what!" Maguire answered angrily. "When I think of all I did for that man and his family..." He regained control before continuing. "Dowdall put one hundred of his men into his largest boat. He protected them from our missiles with a roof, reinforced with hide-covered hurdles. O Cassidy steered the vessel so that it avoided the stakes that we had driven into the bed of the lake and brought it to rest under the wall of the barbican, where eventually the bastards made a breach. My men retreated into the keep, but the English quickly succeeded in mining it. The men had no choice but to surrender or be blown to pieces."

"It's a bad business," Hugh said.

"That it is! And what is worse, many of my followers have deserted me. Did you know that the English have made that bodach, Connor Roe Maguire, Sheriff of Fermanagh?"

Hugh nodded. "It was at Bagenal's suggestion," he replied.

"Connor has been in contact with most of my sublords and I am afraid that they will defect to him," Maguire continued wrathfully. "The English offer them the lands that they use, as their own, to pass on to their first born sons. The English and their greed are the ruin of this country. The land is not theirs to bestow. It belongs to the clan."

Hugh nodded, though not fully in agreement with such an opinion. He realised how much of an attraction it was to the freemen and the lesser nobles, to hold their land as their own. He, himself, wished that his son, Hugh, would inherit both the Earldom and The O'Neill title directly from him, and that he would be the founder of a great house to rival the Earldoms of England. "They attempt to force English ways on the country," he commented, without disclosing his true sentiments.

"I have always said that they would!" Maguire answered stridently. "There is nothing stopping them from dealing with my country now, as they did with McMahon's Monaghan. You need not feel too secure either. I, at least, rebelled. McMahon was executed because some of his clan rebelled against the English, though he himself remained loyal. Never forget, the English say the Lord is responsible for all the members of his clan, and it would be very easy for them to implicate you in some outbreak of violence or other."

O'Neill privately acknowledged that Maguire was right. Bagenal had wasted no time after their battle in rushing to Dublin, where he had proposed the settlement of Fermanagh along the lines of that achieved in Monaghan. The Queen had cited it as an exemplary achievement now that it was yielding good rent to the crown. The Irish churls were flocking to the English courts of justice, which had been installed there. Monaghan freeholders were now serving willingly in the royal forces, preferring this new regime to the older one.

He looked at Maguire who stood in the centre of the chamber. There was no easy way to tell him. He said gently. "Your fears are well founded. Most of your sublords have already submitted. They and Connor have agreed to maintain one hundred and twenty English troops for four months, at their own expense, and to assist the crown in hunting you down."

Maguire paled. This was much worse than he had imagined. "And we know what their justice will entail. Hanged at the door of my own castle, like McMahon! What can I do now? It is all over. If my own people turn against me, then I'm finished," he said.

You still have a lot of your wealth intact. Your cattle have been held safely for you by O'Donnell and me," Hugh said.

"Yes, but even that resource is finite. I can sell them to purchase more Gallowglasses from Scotland, but they fight for money, not pride. I saw what they did for me against the English. They hadn't the stomach for the fight when it came to it. You need men who are fighting to the death to defend their territory, men with a long-term interest in the outcome. I cannot achieve victory with only foreigners to back me," Maguire said despairingly.

"I know your people have not deserted you, they love you. It is only the sublords and that is for their own selfish gain. O'Donnell and I will back you, O'Donnell openly, I through my brother, Cormac, and others of my sublords," Hugh said soothingly.

"But is it not too late? Why are you prepared to change now?" Maguire asked.

"The Queen has ordered me to bring O'Donnell in, one way or the other. I am not prepared to do that. The English seem to think that they can rule Ulster through the likes of Bagenal. They must be shown that they are mistaken. I will not co-operate with them. Bagenal has set up his own men in opposition to mine in the lands bordering his territory. He has displaced my men from South Clandeboye, Killultagh, Kilwarlin, Kinelarty, Orior and Oriel. I will supply the displaced with fighting men and release them against his supporters. Furthermore, I will encourage my people to turn on the English and raid their lands, down into the Pale itself," he answered with determination.

"But why not join in openly? If you were to declare yourself in opposition to their presence and interference in our country, the people would flock to you," Maguire urged.

"The people don't make an army. What we need are fully trained, professional soldiers who can meet the English in battle and defeat them, not skirmish and retreat into the bogs. I'm finding it well nigh impossible to hire Gallowglasses in Scotland. The McShanes' mother uses all her power to stop me, now that I hold her precious Henry and Conn. The Queen has demanded that I turn them over to her, but I do not trust her not to set them up against me at the first suitable opportunity," Hugh replied.

"You are wise in that distrust. Look how she uses Connor Roe. But where will you get the men that you need?" Maguire asked.

"By remodelling my forces. I have dismissed all the English soldiers who served in my army, as I cannot risk having a spy in my midst. Over the years, I have rotated the five hundred Irish soldiers whom the Queen allowed me keep. I have called up all my trained people and they form the core of my new force. I have also had a proclamation read in all the churches in Tyrone, last Sunday, seeking two thousand men to volunteer to serve in the defence of Tyrone. Already, we have had over five times that amount, coming forward."

Maguire looked amazed at the temerity of his father-in-law. "And where did you get that number?" he asked.

"The churls," Hugh answered. He saw disapproval seep into Maguire's face. "I have already tried them and they make excellent foot soldiers. They are pleased to serve, all their life having been bred to obey our orders. They are loyal to a fault and can suffer immense hardship. They are eager to learn and are much cheaper than the Gallowglasses," he continued.

Maguire refused to be convinced that this type of compromise was strategically sound. "So, what do you intend doing with this army of yours, if you refuse to use it openly against the English?" he asked.

"I will use my strength to make the English think again and will no longer co-operate. I will stir up as much trouble as I can. They will fear that, should I join the rebellion, all will be lost. When they realise how much they need us then, and only then, will I talk with them, but under two preconditions. Firstly, I will not meet with any delegation that includes Bagenal and also, there must be a postponement of any military action against Ulster," Hugh replied.

"And what do I do in the meantime?" Maguire asked.

"O'Donnell and I will give you men to aid you in your fight. Cormac, with three hundred men, will join you and O'Donnell will give you as many more. I suggest that you make haste back home and force each of your Lords to return to their proper obedience to you. When you have achieved that, you must besiege Enniskillen Castle," Hugh replied.

Maguire laughed, in spite of himself. "If only it were that simple. Still, I am willing to try. Perhaps O'Donnell's Spanish with their big guns will come and aid us." He paused and held his hand out to Hugh. "My thanks to you, Hugh," he said, grateful for the older man's support.

Hugh took the hand and shook it. "Perhaps you will have that drink now," he said.

Maguire nodded. Henry poured three measures of whiskey.

"To success," Hugh said.

"Success," both men echoed.

The Lord Deputy, Fitzwilliam, was being jolted from side to side in his coach, which travelled slowly over the snow-covered tracks of eastern Ulster. He had travelled north in a series of litters and coaches, escorted by a troop of one hundred heavily armed horsemen. The trip had been an unpleasant one, and his sick bones had felt every inch of the journey. His health, which had been in decline for a number of years, had deteriorated sharply over this severe winter. His gout had become almost unbearable, and the kidney stone that he suffered from, was causing him even more pain than usual. He could no longer ride, indeed, he could not even rise from his seat, unaided. Inwardly, he cursed this land and his appointment. I'm too old for this position, he thought, as a rut caused the coach to lurch forward and throw him heavily against its side. I should be at home, enjoying the delights of my garden. Yet, he was afraid to vacate his post. O'Neill was complaining loudly and often about Bagenal and him. He knew what had happened the previous Lord Deputy, Perrot, after his retirement to England. He, himself, had played a large part in his downfall. That piece of work had gained him enemies at home and he was aware that there were men there, who would be only too glad to be revenged upon him, in turn.

He pulled the blankets tightly around his body. It was cold and the coach offered little protection from the elements. I can't be too far away now, he thought. The coach pulled to a halt and Fitzwilliam stuck his head out the window. He was relieved to see Henry Bagenal's house at last, having feared that they would be delayed by another snowdrift or fallen tree. He saw Henry and a female standing on the steps to the house. Both hurried down to meet him. The captain of the horse leaned into the coach, aided Fitzwilliam to his feet and helped him out. Henry was beside him in an instant. "This is a great honour," he began.

Fitzwilliam held up his hand to quieten him. "Let us get in out of this accursed cold and then we can have the pleasantries," he said impatiently.

"But of course," Bagenal said accommodatingly. "Come, follow me."

Bagenal walked briskly towards the house and Fitzwilliam turned his attention for the first time to the woman who was with him. She bowed and it took him a few seconds to recognise her. "Lady Mabel," he said in surprise.

"My Lord," she replied before turning and following Henry back up the steps.

Fitzwilliam's captain took his master's arm and helped him slowly mount the steps. He watched Mabel's retreating figure. He was shocked at her appearance. She had become so thin and pale. He remembered her from festivities she had attended at Dublin Castle. Then, she had been a beautiful, radiant young woman. But now, her face had become gaunt and strained and the lines around her eyes and forehead were deep. On reaching the top of the steps, Fitzwilliam removed his arm roughly from his helper and dismissed him with a wave of his hand. He followed the Bagenals into the large banqueting hall, where a fire burned brightly in the grate. Fitzwilliam limped over to it and placed himself in front of the flames, allowing his back absorb the heat. It eased some of the pain and stiffness. Henry took a chair and carried it over to him. Fitzwilliam sat into it with a sigh of relief.

"Mabel, fetch the Lord Deputy some wine," Henry barked.

Mabel rushed to do her brother's bidding.

"We missed you at the last Council meeting," Fitzwilliam said.

"Yes, I was sorry that I could not attend, but I dared not leave Ulster. The whole province has broken out into disorder. My appointments in the neighbouring domains have come under attack. Even my own tenants are riotous. I have no doubt who is behind all the trouble," Bagenal said angrily, "that demon O'Neill and his lieutenants!"

Mabel handed Fitzwilliam a goblet of wine and then served her brother. Neither man acknowledged her. "The Council received a communication from him. He complains about the two of us, about my government and your treatment of him. He will only meet with a delegation from them, if you and I are not members of such a party," Fitzwilliam said with a snort.

Bagenal listened with incredulity. "Why that is unacceptable, My Lord! No rebel can set down terms with Her Majesty's Council. He must meet with whomsoever Her Majesty or the Council decides to send to him," he said.

"He says that he will not meet us as he does not trust us. He quoted the example of Sir John Perrot and blames our machinations for his languishing in the Tower. He says he will not receive a fair hearing from us. The Council accepted his demands and from its members, chose to send Archbishop Loftus, Sir Robert Gardiner and Sir Anthony Leger as commissioners to investigate the matter," Fitzwilliam said curtly.

Bagenal became fearful. "But they are all friends of his. This does not augur well," he said, shaking his head in disapproval. Both men remained silent a few moments, caught in their innermost thoughts. At length, Bagenal spoke. "What about sending some soldiers with them and secretly ordering them to arrest O'Neill when he comes to treat and bring him to Dublin? Then we can have him confined in Dublin Castle. That will soon make him rue his treachery," he added eagerly.

Fitzwilliam shook his head. "He has demanded a letter of protection before meeting with the councillors. It has been dispatched to him," he said.

Bagenal was appalled. "But this is unheard of. How can a member of the Queen's Irish Council demand such a guarantee to meet with its other members? It proves his guilt," he said bitterly.

Reluctantly, Fitzwilliam disagreed. "Unfortunately not," he replied. "The councillors' task is to meet with O'Neill, discover what his thinking is in respect of Her Majesty, and what designs he has to trouble the tranquillity of the country. They must determine whether he will adhere to the rebels or not. In short, they are to do all within law, reason and discretion to stay and pacify these present broils."

Bagenal sneered. "He will lead them astray with his talk and palaver. Give me an army and I will solve these problems the only way they can ever be resolved, by the sword!"

Fitzwilliam shook his head in a mixture of weariness and impatience. "If we had the army for the job, do you think that we would have let things get so out of hand?" he asked. "We would have moved against O'Donnell long since. We don't have the strength, so for now, all we can do is to send the commissioners and hope that they will bring him to heel."

He was every bit as much worried by the present turn of events as Bagenal, if not more so. Bagenal, at least, had always been consistent in his treatment of O'Neill, never entering into any clandestine dealings with him, unlike Fitzwilliam, who had accepted numerous bribes over the years. Now, he worried that such covert dealings might become known. He bitterly regretted such arrangements. He had compromised himself utterly. As Lord Deputy, he should have been above reproach. O'Neill knew that too. Fitzwilliam dared not push too hard against him. Yet, he recognised that O'Neill was dangerous and that something had to be done to destroy him. He would have to use Bagenal and his hatred of O'Neill to achieve his own goal.

He chose his words carefully. "We have not sufficient proof to damn him in the Queen's eyes. We need to have irrefutable evidence." He paused and looked at Mabel. She had removed herself from their company and sat at the casement, looking out at the surrounding country, apparently not listening to their conversation. Fitzwilliam doubted that she could be so disinterested in news of her husband. "What we need is the testimony of one who was in his company for a considerable amount of time, one who lived in his castle, under his roof and shared his life. Such a person would surely be able to tell us much that would be of use to us now, in our time of need," he said with feigned gentleness.

He noticed Mabel start involuntarily. She shot him a quick, nervous glance. He saw fear on her face and terror gathering in her eyes. It was obvious that she did not relish the turn the conversation had taken. Before she could say anything, Henry angrily burst into speech. "You need not expect to learn anything that would be of advantage to us from my sister. I have tried and she has steadfastly refused to supply me with any intelligence that would be of use to us. I ask you, Lord Deputy, is that any way to repay me for taking her back, after the shame she has brought on the Bagenal name? Shame that could have been avoided had followed my guidance and not allowed her own stubbornness lead her astray. She has paid for that wantonness. He made a fool of her by keeping his whores in the same castle as her, and yet she refuses to help me in plotting his downfall. What make you of such a woman, my Lord Deputy?"

Mabel spoke in a hesitant, trembling voice. "But I cannot supply that which I have no knowledge of. I have told my brother all that I know."

Bagenal regarded her bitterly. "And she expects me to believe that in all her time with him, she did not see some signs of his present traitorous behaviour? You know what has been my most grievous fault, my Lord? It is that of softness. I should have left her find her own way in the world because she has sinned most deplorably against God and me. But no! I could not do so, for our mother's sake and because I would not have a Bagenal tramp the roads as a common beggar. And yet, I had expected more thanks than this for my generosity," he said savagely.

Fitzwilliam nodded in agreement but spoke in a conciliatory tone. "Perhaps she is not aware of what might be of use to us," he said to Bagenal, before returning his attention to Mabel. "Did he ever receive any messengers from foreign princes, especially from the Queen's most mortal enemy, the King of Spain?" he asked.

Mabel raised her tear-stained face to the Lord Deputy. "No, my Lord. I am quite definite on that matter," she answered, struggling to control her feelings.

Fitzwilliam pressed further. "And what of foreign priests? I hear they overrun the North, preaching their message of hate and blasphemy."

"No, he didn't hold with them. He regarded them as an undesirable influence on his people. He did his utmost to keep them off his lands," Mabel answered.

"But he does allow the Popish religion to be practised openly?" Fitzwilliam queried.

Mabel leaned forward in her chair, eager to persuade the Lord Deputy. "That is so, but it is also practised in Dublin by the majority of the English settlers. He has no choice in the matter. His people would disown him, if he were not to allow them worship as they saw fit. He chooses the priests himself, and makes sure that they follow his guidance in political matters and do not ferment trouble among his churls," she answered.

Fitzwilliam sighed, before continuing. "But think, Mistress Mabel. There must be something that you can tell us that can be of use. Surely you must want to see him repaid for the way he treated you. Did he incite others to rebel? What about Maguire? O'Donnell?"

Mabel paused and looked at the Lord Deputy's eager face. She knew that she would disappoint him too. She had wrestled with herself on this score countless times. As much as she had been harshly treated by O'Neill, she could never find bitterness deep enough in her heart to betray him. Live with him she could not, but nor could she endure the notion of destroying him. Her woman's feelings were still too tender for such a course. Hugh's treatment of Pheilim and his son was no worse than conduct she had witnessed by her late father and brother. She had learned something of history's lessons from Hugh and could not distance herself from the fact that her own family's holding at Newry, had been achieved at the cost of much bloodshed. She struggled to frame a response. "No, he always seemed most anxious to avoid a war with Her Majesty's forces. You must realize that I was not present at all his meetings. I helped keep his house. He didn't tell me everything," she answered limply.

Bagenal interrupted angrily. "You are wasting your time, my Lord. She is of no use to us and would have been better off dead, than returning home to me."

Mabel, stung by the savagery of her brother's words, was unable to deny that death would indeed be preferable to her present lot. How had it all gone so very wrong, she wondered? She had been so certain that she had made the right decision in marrying Hugh. Coming home and throwing herself on Henry's mercy had been the most difficult and demeaning action she had ever undertaken. Her feelings then had been a riot of uncertainty and sadness. Henry had demanded much from her, in return for his taking her in, repentance, servility, and intelligence about Hugh. All she had wanted to do was allow the wounds to heal without picking at them and opening them afresh each day. In the beginning, she had hoped that Hugh would turn up and demand that she return, but as time went on, she realised that he would never undertake such a course. She thought about him constantly, wondering if perhaps she had not been too judgmental. Did not all rulers of men have to execute people, at times, if their power was threatened?

Later, she had recognised that she would never have another chance at happiness. She had ruined her life entirely. What English man would want to marry The O'Neill's cast-off, even if divorced? Neither would any Irishman wish to take her as his wife. The future troubled her greatly. She had wished to be married and have children, to be domestically content, like Mary. She could not see herself spending the rest of her life living in her brother's house. And yet, she had no place else to turn. Sir Patrick and Mary withheld refuge from her. The future looked bleak indeed. Overcome with despair, she wept, her thin, frail body racked with grief.

Bagenal raised his goblet and threw it violently into the grate where it shattered into many pieces. "Confound it! Is a man not to have any peace in his own house? If you cannot control yourself, get to your chamber, Madam and do not let us see you at dinner," he shouted.

Mabel jumped to her feet in terror and rushed, sobbing, from the chamber. She raced to her bedchamber. It was cold, no fire having been lit in the empty grate. She climbed under the bed coverings, without removing any of her clothes. At least I shall not have to attend dinner, she thought. She had lost all desire for food and drink and found it well nigh impossible to be in her brother's company, at table. She glanced out through the casement at the leaden clouds. Still no brightness. She closed her eyes and her heaviness of heart deepened. She craved sleep, blessed sleep, but even that was to be denied her. For several nights she had woken up at midnight and been unable to find elusive slumber again. The aching darkness stretched out in front of her as she tossed and turned, unable to silence her wretched mind or soothe herself with pleasing thoughts. Her ideas turned inward, chasing one another in incessant frenzy till she cried out in terror and despair, "Blessed Mary and all the saints, have pity upon me and leave me not so alone." But the chamber only gave back her words in dull echo and after many hours of anguish, she would eventually sink into the fractured sleep of hopelessness.

The Lord Chancellor, Archbishop Loftus, Sir Robert Gardiner, Chief Justice of the King's Bench, and Sir Anthony Leger, Master of the Rolls sat in the conference chamber of the Civic Hall in Dundalk. They were weary of their task, as in the seven days that they had been stationed there, they had not yet succeeded in meeting with the rebels or with the Earl of Tyrone. Sir Robert Gardiner had ridden out into the countryside to meet with O'Neill and O'Donnell, but until this evening, neither had agreed to enter Dundalk and negotiate with the councillors. They now anxiously awaited their arrival. At the sound of approaching horsemen, Loftus rose from his seat and went to the casement overlooking the courtyard. "It is them. I cannot see O'Donnell. It seems to be just O'Neill and Hovendon," he said.

Ledger nodded. "I am not surprised. O'Donnell is probably staying with the army that they have positioned between Dublin and here. They are not taking any chances. To be frank, I am offended. O'Neill is acquainted with us long enough to know that we are men of honour and would not break our word," he said.

The Archbishop nodded. "He rather overestimates our strength, if our intelligence is correct, regarding the number of his men. Two thousand is quite a muster. They must know that we do not have that many to call on in the whole of the country," he said.

"We must listen to his grievances carefully. I do not believe that we three will be able to address them here and now. We will promise to send them to the Queen. That is why I wished him to draw them up himself. They are too serious for us to misrepresent or be accused of misrepresenting," Gardiner said, before being interrupted by a knock on the door, which he then opened.

O'Neill and Henry Hovendon strode in. The Archbishop beckoned to them to sit, whereupon they drew up two empty chairs. Both men's clothes were dusty from the ride and all present sensed the chill of their reserve.

"A drink, some refreshment?" Gardiner enquired.

"No thank you," Hugh answered abruptly. "We should get down to business. I have no liking to prolong my visit here."

"Very well," Loftus said. "I believe that you have a document to present to us."

"Yes," Hugh answered and motioned to Hovendon to hand it to him. He took it and opened it before them. "I will go through the principal arguments," he continued. "Firstly, on my visit here last year, when I was called before the Council, Bagenal bribed Fitzwilliam in an effort to have me destroyed."

Loftus interrupted vehemently. "But you cannot include such an allegation. You must have proof. We cannot allow such an assertion be passed onto Her Majesty."

Hugh grimaced. "The proof is obvious for any who will see it. In any event, you do not comprehend me. This is my submission and I have Sir Robert's word that it will be passed on in its entirety. If that is not so, then I am wasting my time and I will take my leave of you," he replied.

There was silence for a few moments as the councillors considered what he had said.

"These are not our views, so I do not see the difficulty in passing them on, but I would ask you to reconsider, for your own sake," Gardiner replied in supplication.

Hugh summoned all the residual patience at his command, before replying. "I considered long and hard ere I put ink to parchment. This is the final document," he said.

"Very well," Loftus said resignedly. "Proceed."

Hugh had much time to marshal his thoughts on his journey from Dungannon. He knew precisely what tone to adopt and what words to use to carry his message in a way that could not be misconstrued. "Fitzwilliam and Bagenal seek to destroy my name in court and as they are in Burleigh's faction, I fear for my future. Bagenal has, through such influence, unbeknownst to the Queen, obtained a commission to determine all disputes in the Kingdom of Ulster. I will not allow such a man hold sway over me," he continued.

"We know not of such a commission that extends over your lands," Loftus answered.

Undeterred, Hugh continued. "He claims it, nevertheless. That man has continually tried to undermine my position, by attacking my supporters. He is so jealous and covetous of my position, that he would not even give to my wife, Mabel, the dowry that was left to her by her father in his will," he said with undisguised bitterness.

St. Ledger interrupted. "Such a matter is between the two of you and is not worthy of the Queen's attention."

O'Neill would not be deflected by this line of argument. "Yet, he received £400 for his recent service against Maguire and I got not one penny, even though the same campaign had cost me £3,000 and injury to my person. My foster brothers, Richard Hovendon and Henry served most valiantly when the Great Armada threatened our shores. They handed over many captured Spanish captains to the Lord Deputy who, in spite of the ransoms which he received, never gave them either thanks or reward."

Loftus noticed an angry flush mount and overspread O'Neill's countenance. "Such a matter is now far in the past. Perhaps it may have been simply overlooked. We are, as is the Queen, most grateful for the services rendered," Loftus answered.

O'Neill was not to be mollified and continued in trenchant manner. "These are not the only complaints of ingratitude, which I must level. Hugh Roe McMahon, Lord of Monaghan, attended the Lord Deputy on his word of protection and yet, was executed as a traitor, contrary to all natural justice. To compound matters, what happened with the division of his lands? Who was the main benefactor? Bagenal! Fitzwilliam became a rich man from the numerous bribes, which he pocketed. The rest of the lands went to men of no account. Again, my services were ignored, even though I had obtained a letter from the Privy Council, to settle my outstanding claims on the estate of the late Sir Ross McMahon."

The councillors looked from one to the other. O'Neill's reasoning was faultless. It did indeed appear as if wrong had been perpetrated upon him. Gardiner commented. "If that were indeed so, it was not acceptable."

O'Neill sensed the beginnings of a sympathy. "I and the people of Monaghan, want the Sheriff of Monaghan, Henshaw, and Vice-Constable, Moate of the Blackwater Fort, removed from their offices. They are but interested in personal gain and are totally in the service of Bagenal. I demand that they be replaced by upright gentlemen who can stand impartially between me and my adversaries," he stipulated.

"And is that all?" Loftus asked.

"There is more in the deposition, but those are its salient arguments. I cannot emphasise enough, the fractured state of relations between the Irish Lords of the North and the Lord Deputy and Bagenal," Hugh said bitterly. He then paused and continued in a more conciliatory tone. "I have no complaints about you, gentlemen. I know that you are all honourable men and would happily serve under any of you, were you to be appointed Lord Deputy. In essence, what I am demanding is that there must be change if there is not to be a total rift between Dublin and Ulster."

Loftus nodded his head slowly. "Our thanks for your frank discussion and the document, which you have prepared for us. I wonder if you could withdraw for a few minutes while we discuss your proposals?" he asked.

"Very well," Hugh answered. "I shall wait outside."

Hugh and Hovendon rose and left the chamber. The three councillors waited until they had withdrawn before speaking.

"Well, gentlemen," Loftus said, "what are we to make of this?"

"I think the precedent of Monaghan and what is planned for Fermanagh is the cause of the present trouble with all the Ulster Lords," Gardiner said. "O'Donnell and O'Neill fear a similar fate for their lands, and we must not forget the part which malice plays between the Earl and the Marshal in this whole sorry tale. I think that we should try pacification. The situation, thus far, has been handled most inexpertly. It is my opinion that Maguire be pardoned, Bagenal's commission revoked and Henshaw be removed from government in Monaghan. We all know that Fitzwilliam should be replaced. The Earl's ruffled feathers must be smoothed and if he is pacified, then I believe that O'Donnell and Maguire will fall into line, as they are both O'Neill's creatures and will be lead by him."

St Ledger saw the benefit of such a method. "I am inclined to agree with Sir Robert," he said. "We all have seen how Fitzwilliam governs and know his faults."

Loftus nodded. "There is only one other alternative. If the remedy you propose is not to Her Majesty's liking, then she must, forthwith, send over a good and sufficient number of soldiers, under the direction of some man of action, and so chastise the rebels."

Gardiner concurred, but spied an impediment. "Agreed, but it must be pointed out to her, that this will not be accomplished without great toil and charge, especially in this time of great scarcity of corn and victuals."

All the men assented. There was nothing left to do but invite O'Neill and Hovendon to return.

"Very well. Show them back in," Loftus ordered.

Gardiner went to the door and invited both men to enter. When they were seated, Loftus took up the theme. "We are prepared to send your submission to the Queen. We ask, in return, that you do your best to discourage raids on Her Majesty's subjects, that you keep O'Donnell and his people in obedience, and you prevent the ingress of Scot mercenaries. If O'Donnell leads any rebellion against the crown, you must promise to suppress it."

O'Neill, too well versed in the art of dissimulation to show relief, replied. "I will do so, if, for your part, you, as Her Majesty's councillors, do promise that no violence be perpetrated by Her Majesty's subjects or soldiers on either myself, O'Donnell or our countries, until my grievances have been made known to the Queen and her resolution given," he answered.

Loftus looked at the other two councillors. "Agreed?" he asked. The two others nodded. "Agreed," they said in unison.

Hugh got to his feet and shook hands with all three. "Have the papers drawn up," he said. "I will return on the morrow to sign them. I bid you all good night."

Without any further formalities, he left the chamber, Hovendon following after him. They hurried down the stairs, hands on their swords. Once outside, they mounted their horses and rode, without speaking, through the gates of the town. When they had covered a quarter of a mile, Hugh slowed his horse to a gentle trot and waited for Hovendon to catch up.

"Well," Hovendon asked, "are you pleased with your night's work?"

"Tolerably," Hugh answered. "At the very least, we have gained some time. I have been thinking, though. I need to gain access to Scottish mercenaries. My only hope is Sorley Bwee."

Hovendon's thoughts immediately flew to the massacre on Ratlin Island. "But he has never forgiven you for your part in the destruction of his people," he answered.

O'Neill had already anticipated the thought. "Times have moved on. The English have tried to remove him from Ireland many times in the past, and will do so again. If he has any cunning, he will recognise the good that would come from an alliance between the two of us. I want you to go to him and propose such an arrangement."

"And what will I offer him to bind the relationship?" Hovendon asked.

"He has a number of daughters. Tell him that I will marry one of them. How much stronger an alliance can two men make?" Hugh asked.

Hovendon was saddened. Hugh's marriage to Mabel had irrevocably failed. He had liked and pitied the beautiful English girl, well understanding O'Neill's restless passion for her. That such sentiment had so completely disappeared, dismayed him. "And what of Mabel?" he asked.

"She has deserted me. Under Brehon law, that is reason enough to seek a divorce. Tell him that it will be a trial marriage, until the divorce is settled. That is nothing unusual," Hugh answered.

"I will leave tomorrow," Hovendon said and thought of Mabel. As they rode in silence back to their camp, he pondered her fate at her brother's hands.

Chapter 9

It was the first of August, the first day of autumn, one of the four traditional quarter days of the Gaelic calendar. It was also the festival of Lug, the Celtic God and the tradition of celebrating this day, Lughnasa, had survived in Gaelic Ireland despite the arrival of Christianity, over a thousand years previously. It was drawing to a close and the peasants, who had gathered in Dungannon Castle were, by now, replete with food and drink.

The Lord of each region had to honour this day by providing a feast for all his people. There were copious amounts of food and drink to celebrate the harvest, which would be gathered and safely stored for the long winter. O'Neill had ordered that three whole oxen, numerous sheep and pigs be roasted in the castle courtyard. Tables had been piled high with oaten cakes, while the guests drank the castle cellar dry of beer, wine and whiskey. By nightfall, the celebrations were at their height and the sound of music and dancing spilled out from the castle and across the open countryside. As Hugh looked around him, he could see young men and women disappearing into the shadows. It was a day that would have its own tangible results among his churls, he thought, as the free drink loosened inhibitions. The following April there would be many Lughnasa babies. He watched the bonfires being lit and once they had taken hold, he retreated from the courtyard into the castle, his trial bride following behind him.

Her father, Sorley Bwee, had left some hours previously. Hugh had been surprised when he saw his daughter, Ciara, who had been brought to seal the new alliance between them. She was barely thirteen and Hugh had found her eagerness to please him, grating. He had received the thousand Gallowglass soldiers whom Sorley Bwee had engaged for him, some weeks previously, and had just paid him the arrangement fee that they had agreed. As the marriage between himself and Ciara was not yet formalised, there was no dowry due him. Mabel and he would have to be divorced before this new union could be solemnised, and he had not applied for the divorce yet, knowing full well that Bagenal would strongly contest the granting of it. Apart from that, he had far more serious problems to worry about, as the slide towards all out war in Ulster was gaining pace.

Financial worries were beginning to beset him too. Everywhere he turned, he was met by constant demands for money. Even this day, which he would normally finance without a second thought, amounted to an unwelcome burden. Yet, he could not economise on such a festival. To do so would damage his standing with his people.

For the thousandth time, he thought about his expenditure. The nineteen hundred volunteer soldiers were a new expense. Luckily, it would be a good harvest, he thought. That would lessen his outlay of cash, which he sorely needed, at present. If he had not the current problem with the English, his financial worries would not have been so pressing. He would have relied on the traditional support of his freemen for the defence of his Lordship.

In addition, there was the matter of equipping his men. The new recruits had to be supplied with arms. Over the years, he had gathered weapons, imported lead and powder whenever and however he could get his hands on it. He had been able to buy powder in all the major Irish towns from merchants eager to make a handsome profit. He could import it too from the lowland Scottish burghs, even, at times, from as far away as Danzig. He, himself, had started to experiment in its manufacture and whereas charcoal was plentiful in Ulster, he still had the trouble of importing sulphur from abroad. He had also established good relations with merchants in Manchester, Liverpool and Birmingham; they were willing to sell him weapons and to send them concealed in hogsheads and dryfats.

He had no doubt that these diverse sources would continue to supply him, provided he had could pay them, but it all came back to finances. If he was to win this fight, he had to organise his lands and the rest of Ulster into an economy dedicated to all out war. It would put an enormous strain on the province, but he would have to ensure that Ulster could live with that pressure.

As he passed through the Great Hall, he heard Hovendon call after him. He swung around and collided with Ciara, who had been running to keep up with him. She fell to the ground. He leaned down and helped her to her feet, noticing her lip tremble and tears form in her eyes.

"I'm sorry, Master," she said, cringing as if expecting to be struck. Not for the first time did Hugh wonder if Sorley Bwee had played an elaborate joke on him. This girl was so young and lacking in spirit. He had not yet been able to decide if she was desperately shy and anxious to please him, or just a half-wit. She had sat beside him at dinner and talked to him childishly about her puppy and kittens, her brothers and sisters. He turned away from her to Hovendon. "Yes," he answered gruffly.

Hovendon mistook the impatience in his manner for annoyance at the delay he was causing in Hugh's retirement to his bridal chamber. "A messenger has arrived from Maguire and O'Donnell. They have learned of the approach of Duke and his relieving force. They want you to join them or, at the very least, to send them reinforcements," he said. "Their man is waiting outside."

Hugh felt a wave of anger surge through him. O'Donnell had shown his hand two months previously and joined Maguire in his siege of Enniskillen. He had brought with him two thousand Scottish Gallowglasses. They had set up their camps on either side of the castle and were attempting to starve the garrison out. Hugh had sent them his newly acquired thousand Scots, as soon as he had intelligence from Dublin of Duke's approach. Maguire and O'Donnell now had a combined force of over four thousand men, more than enough to deal with the English.

"What more do they want of me?" he asked in English, not wishing Ciara to understand their conversation. She had been standing, awaiting his instruction and now withdrew to the table and waited uncomfortably for the conclusion of the men's exchange.

Hugh continued, "They have no need of more men."

"They want the prestige of having you and your men in their midst. Neither of them have total confidence in the Scots. They do not yet understand fully the politics in which you are engaged," Hovendon answered.

Hugh sighed. "I will not change my stance now. I will not join with them openly. It is in none of our interest," he said.

"They then asked, if you answered thus, that you would send your brother, Cormac and some five hundred of your best troops to them. They are in dire need of accomplished musketeers. The Scots have but few guns, relying on their bowmen. They make excellent shock troops, but not against an enemy rich in weapons who can cut them down before they get to close quarters," Hovendon answered.

"Must they always pull out of me so?" Hugh asked angrily. "It seems an excessive demand."

"That may be so, but this is their first test. Maguire has the memory of his last engagement fresh in his mind. O'Donnell has not had time to train his own men yet. What our cause now most needs is a victory. I think it would aid them greatly if you do as they have requested," Hovendon said.

Hugh felt his anger melt away. He could not really blame them for being anxious. They were in the field while he was safe in his castle, enjoying peace and security. "Send Cormac and three hundred of my best men. Have them remove their uniforms. I do not want them being identified as mine," he said.

Hovendon bowed and turned to leave.

"Henry," Hugh said, "I must talk to you further. I wish you to travel to Scotland. We are in need of more guns and powder. See if you can lure some Scottish gunsmiths to Dungannon to make our weapons here."

"Such men are expensive to employ and the King of Scotland will not wish to lose them," Hovendon answered.

"I am aware of that. You are free to offer whatever it will take to entice them to come. Leave tomorrow, after you organise the men for Enniskillen," Hugh said.

Hovendon groaned inwardly, anticipating the men's response. "I will give the orders to their constables to remove them from the celebrations. They will be unhappy at missing the rest of the festivities," he answered

"That is what is expected of them, to be ready at all times," Hugh answered in vexation.

Hovendon bowed and withdrew without further comment. Hugh turned and made for the staircase in the corner of the chamber. Ciara sprang to her feet and asked nervously, "Will I come with you, my Lord?"

Hugh turned to her and gruffly agreed, before mounting the steps. Ciara followed quickly behind him. On reaching his bedchamber, Hugh threw the door open. He was greatly angered at the decisions daily being forced upon him. Ciara followed him and stood meekly waiting.

"Close the door," Hugh ordered.

Ciara hurried to do as she was bid.

"Take off your clothes," Hugh commanded.

Ciara took off her tunic and shoes and stood beside the bed in her linen shirt, blushing scarlet in confusion and embarrassment.

"I do not know what to do," she said shyly. "You will have to tell me."

This was not how Hugh was used to proceeding. He went to her. She lifted up her face to him and he could read the fear in it. He leaned over and kissed her on the mouth. Her lips were rigid and unmoving. His anger surged. "Take off your shirt and lie on the bed," he ordered.

She pulled the undershirt over her head. She was very thin and her breasts were only beginning to bud. A light brown fuzz of hair covered the triangle between her legs. Obediently, she walked to the bed and lay down on it.

Hugh kicked off his shoes and sat beside her. He ran his hand over her body. Her skin was soft. He felt her shiver at his touch and he knew that it was not from passion but from fear, perhaps even loathing. She smiled nervously up at him but he could see tears in her eyes. He knew that to her, he appeared an old man, and he could not deny that in his eyes, she was nothing but a child.

He remembered Rose's departure from Dungannon on the occasion of her marriage to O'Donnell. He had thought that she was too young, even then, and had to steel himself not to delay the match. She had been fifteen, already a woman and marrying a man her own age. This was not how he had imagined his first night with his new bride. He needed his woman to be in the grip of passion, moaning and sweating beneath him. He felt cheated and his mood darkened further. He wondered for a moment if there was anything that he could do to awaken desire in himself and passion in her, but knew in his heart that it was in vain. She was but a child and he could not blind himself to that. She was still smiling but the tears had overfilled her eyes and trickled down her cheeks. He got his shoes and put them on again.

"Do I not please you, my Lord?" she asked nervously.

He was about to answer angrily, but gained control of his disappointment and frustration. It was not her fault. He had to remember that she was but a pawn in the whole business between her father and himself. He would have to be careful how he dealt with the matter. He had need of Sorley Bwee. He would visit his favourite courtesan, Máire, to get relief from his frustration. "You can go to sleep," he said gently. "I will not force you to do anything that you do not wish to do. You can get dressed again. I will arrange a different sleeping chamber for you, tomorrow night."

He turned and left the chamber. Ciara grabbed her undershirt, quickly drawing it over her head and sank back gratefully into the bed.

A lone horseman rode through the bleak countryside of the North, as the winter's icy wind cut though it, like a sharpened sword. Hugh O'Neill was riding out of his territory and into Maguire's Fermanagh for a meeting with the principal members in the confederacy of Irish nobles that he had built up. O'Donnell, Maguire, Hugh's brother, Cormac and Hugh himself had wooed many lesser Lords to their cause but, knowing how easily those same Lords could desert and return to the English side, they had taken hostages from them to guarantee their loyalty.

Enniskillen was still in English hands. It had been on the point of surrender some five months previously, when the new Lord Deputy, Sir William Russell, had managed to re-provision it with the help of a large force. Hugh was still hopeful, however, that this new Lord Deputy might prove more amenable to their demands, than Fitzwilliam had been. Once he returned south, the Irish had once again besieged Enniskillen and he was aware that now the supplies of the defenders would again be running low.

Hugh wondered how long more he could keep his part in the rebellion secret. His inaction against the rebels had cast deep suspicion upon him. He spurred his horse as he saw Enniskillen Castle and the Irish camp in the distance. As he approached, two men appeared from the forest at the side of the track and blocked his path, training their guns on him. When he got nearer, they recognised him, lowered their weapons and moved off the track. As he passed, they stood to attention and saluted. He rode into the camp through the gate set in the earthen embankments that had been erected around it.

It now resembled a village, rather than a temporary camp. All around him were the timber and wattle structures that had grown up over the previous summer, so that the army might face the onslaught of winter. They were the typical chimneyless constructions, which the Irish built when they periodically moved their cattle to different pastures. Smoke from fires that were lit within, spilled out the doors and into the cold winter air. Most of the men, except for those on sentry duty, were keeping warm inside, out of the icy weather.

Hugh rode on until he came to the building that housed the three leaders. It was located in the centre of the compound and there, the carpenters had built them a wooden structure with a stone chimney. Hugh dismounted and strode inside. He was pleased to see Maguire and Cormac sitting at the fire, but immediately noted O'Donnell's absence. Maguire rose to his feet on seeing him. "Hugh," he said, "come in and join us. It's good to see you. It's great to have someone break the monotony."

He fetched a goblet, filled it with whiskey and passed it to Hugh who took it and drank deeply. Both Cormac and Maguire looked the worst for wear. Living as they did, away from the luxuries of home, it was inevitable that they would find their present life unappealing, nothing to do from one day till the next, except wait until either the garrison surrendered or the English made another attempt to relieve it. It was important that Enniskillen be taken and this time, its relief could not be allowed.

He nodded at Cormac who acknowledged him in like manner. "Any sign of weakening in their resolve?" he asked.

Maguire shook his head. "No, but they are not as cocky as they were. They no longer hurl insults at our men when they call on them to surrender."

"And where is O'Donnell?" Hugh asked.

"Hunting. This inaction drives him mad," Maguire answered.

"And I bring bad tidings to upset him further," Hugh said. "The English army from Brittany will soon sail. We must take Enniskillen before they arrive." He had learned, with dismay, that two thousand of the Queen's best troops were being redeployed to Ireland.

Maguire whistled. "That's easier said than done. If we try and storm it, there's no guarantee that we will take it, and we could lose a lot of men in the attempt. Look at the height of the walls," he urged.

Cormac nodded. "It would be courting disaster. The men will not do it and I could not ask them to. The only way is to starve them out."

Hugh nodded. "It is difficult, but perhaps we can bribe the captain. Seek a parley with him. See what you can do."

Cormac shrugged. "You do not know the captain. He's one of those men that would rather die than betray his cause," he said. "If we had thought there was any chance of striking a deal with him, we'd have already made overtures to him."

"Hugh, do you have any idea how hard our lot here is?" Maguire interjected with more than a touch of asperity. "We'd be delighted to be shut of this business."

"I fully appreciate your predicament here," Hugh answered, "But war is never easy and what is more the Blackwater Fort must also be taken. I cannot leave that in English hands, in the present climate. It will give them too easy a route into my lands."

Both men looked at him with incredulity, his relentlessness was staggering, obliterating everyone else's personal needs, as long as his own were served. Yet, they could not but acknowledge, that it was this very characteristic, which was needed if ever they were to claim victory.

"And when are you going to join us openly?" Maguire asked provocatively.

"Not yet," Hugh answered. "I must keep up the subterfuge a little longer, in case we win a diplomatic victory."

Cormac snorted, unable to contain himself any longer. "So I must put myself in the line of danger, yet again!"

Hugh looked at his brother. He had realised for some while that Cormac was unhappy, acting as his stalking horse. He was a good soldier and commander and he had been taking advantage of him. Still, it was necessary. He had come to ask Cormac to lead the attack, but now thought better of it. "No, you should remain here with our allies. We must take Enniskillen and if the garrison hear that you have withdrawn, it will only give them reassurance. I have asked Art to carry out the attack," he said.

This was a falsehood. He had not even considered offering Art the position but, now that he thought of it, it was probably not a bad notion. Art was his half brother, the son of one of his father's concubines. He had grown up in Dungannon and stayed loyal to Hugh and

Cormac over the years. Hugh had given him the command of a detachment of horse and he had never found him wanting in bravery or loyalty. He would be pleased at the chance of controlling an operation and do everything possible to ensure its success. "I want some of O'Donnell's Gallowglasses to join him. Art will need twenty of their best archers. They should join him the night after next, at the ruins of Benburb Castle. From there, it's only a two mile march to the fort," Hugh said.

"I will see to it," Maguire said, somewhat mollified that the war was being extended. "The more of those garrisons we remove, the better. You'll stay for something to eat?"

"Yes, and then I must get back. The fewer people that know of my absence from Dungannon, the better. I travelled without an escort so that I might not be noticed," Hugh answered.

" Not a wise move," Maguire replied, "you can never tell what knaves are about the woods these days."

"Never fear, I can look after myself," Hugh answered. "I must be back in Dungannon before nightfall."

Newry was a hive of activity as Mabel wandered aimlessly through its bustling streets. She longed to be outside its walls, away from the smell of the damp wooden buildings, the thatched roofs, thick with grime from years of cooking fires, the foul, ancient stables and the fetid, old dungheaps. She decided that she would leave the safety of the town and find solace in the green fields beyond, where the river ran swiftly.

She pushed her way through the milling crowds. There was an air of industry about the townsfolk who were busy repairing the walls or laying in stores. The smiths worked tirelessly, manufacturing weapons for the war. She stood out of the way of a squadron of horse, which forced its way through the narrow streets with little thought for the townspeople whom it had come to protect. Those same townspeople seemed more cohesive than Mabel had ever known them to be. They had joined together, united in opposition against the common enemy, the Irish rebels who had burned the surrounding countryside and murdered what settlers they could. The Irish, who normally lived in the town, had left as they were regarded with suspicion and hostility. Mabel wished that she could share the town's communal spirit. She passed out through the gates and down to the river but only felt an increased sense of isolation and desolation.

When she reached the water's edge, she sat down and spent a long time staring at the town walls and the men working diligently upon them. She had no enthusiasm for anything. Even when Henry had held the harvest fair and celebrations, she had been unable to join in the festivities and had simply wandered listlessly from table to table, unable to eat or join in the merriment. Oftentimes, she would recall the hopes she had nurtured for her future, the effort she had put into the furnishing of her home in Dungannon and how quickly and completely those hopes had been dashed.

Despite her lassitude, she knew that the war in Ulster threw a long shadow and she could sense, beneath the facade of confidence, a deep undercurrent of fear. The townsfolk feared that what they had built might not last the threatened backlash from the natives whom they had dispossessed. They had already seen what revenge they were capable of meeting out.

While she sat looking vacantly at the moving water, her brother came into view. He led his horse across the bridge from the forest that surrounded the town. He had been away for a number of weeks in Dublin where he had attended the Council meetings to argue his opinion. He would be astonished at the destruction that had been wreaked on his lands in his absence.

"What the devil happened here?" he asked when he came within speaking distance of his sister. "All the farm dwellings have been burned down. There's neither man nor livestock for miles!"

"The Irish came the week before last with a troop of mounted horse. They burned and looted the surrounding countryside, right up to the gates of the town," Mabel answered.

Henry paled with shock and the scar on his forehead showed livid. "O'Neill," he breathed. "That devil is behind this!"

"Most of the people escaped to the town," Mabel said expressionlessly. "You were fortunate to make it home safely. They could still be in the area."

"I had an escort as far as Dundalk. They wanted to remain overnight and rest their horses but I was eager to return home so I pressed on. I've been away too long already. Did you ensure that our tenants delivered up our share of the harvest and did you store it away, as I directed you?" he asked querulously.

Suddenly, her old fears returned. He would be furious with her and she didn't have the strength to resist him. "I didn't manage to do it," she said fearfully, "our tenants were too preoccupied with defending their farms."

"You waste your time and mine. I feed and look after you and this is how you repay me by not carrying out a simple request," he said angrily.

"Do not be angry," she said, trembling.

"Why should I not be? My tenants are butchered and my sister does not look after my interests. Why do you not aid me?" he shouted in fury. His horse pricked up its ears and neighed uneasily.

"I did not know how to do so," Mabel answered tearfully.

"O'Neill is responsible for all this," Henry said through gritted teeth. "One of these days, I'm going to butcher him like a fat pig, I swear it by all the saints."

"But they say that he has remained loyal and that it is other, lesser men that work this evil in our midst," Mabel said hesitantly, unsure whether her words might sooth or further anger her brother.

Henry grew red. "Do you know what he has done now?" he asked viciously. "They are all so afraid that they constantly attempt to appease that ingrate. I have been ordered not to interfere with his lands or attack him. Why can't anyone else see that the example we are setting with that bastard, will be our ruin? Everyday more and more of the Irish stir themselves and become less amenable to our rule. The disturbances have even spread into Leinster with Fiach MacHugh and the O'Byrnes burning the countryside right up to the very walls of Dublin. Last week they burned the village of Crumlin and got clean away. It's a bad business when the Lord Deputy is not even able to protect people who live within sight of Dublin's walls." He spluttered to a halt. Mabel looked at him and felt a wave of anxiety pass over her. She feared her brother's dark moods and longed to be away from him.

Bagenal stood looking into the distance. "And to add to these ill tidings, I am to be removed from my position," he said in a voice, which trembled with suppressed emotion. He paused to regain control and continued contemptuously. "The Queen, seemingly, has some doubt about my capacity as a military commander so she is to send a military leader with foreign experience to take charge in Ulster. The Bagenals have held that charge for the last forty odd years and now we are about to be replaced. We, who have had such a stake in the future of this colony, are to be replaced by blow-ins who know nothing about this country."

Here he paused again, not trusting himself to go on further for the moment. Mabel knew how her brother prided himself on his appointment as Marshal of the Queen's army, succeeding their father. And now he was not to be left even in control of Ulster. It would indeed be a sorry blow to his pride.

"And who is she to send?" she asked.

"She is to send Sir John Norris," Bagenal answered, "who does not meet with Russell's approval."

"But why should Russell not welcome him? Is he not a good soldier?" Mabel asked in puzzlement.

"No, it is not that. He has served with distinction in Flanders. There are two factions at court; Essex's to which Russell, Loftus and O'Neill belong, whereas Sir John and I support the Cecils. The Queen attempts to keep some balance in these matters," he said with the air of one who was explaining to a simpleton, some perfectly obvious matter. "Ever wily, she splits the command, ensuring that neither faction grows too strong."

Mabel found it difficult to keep up with all the intrigues of court. She guessed that the Queen would not have replaced her brother, unless she doubted Henry's military ability, but kept her thoughts to herself.

"Also," he continued, "he arrives with a special patent from the Queen that makes him independent of the Lord Deputy in matters concerning Ulster." He paused momentarily, a worried frown passing over his face. "It is not good for English power in Ireland. Mark my words, such a division of responsibility will bode ill for this province. The Queen tried such an arrangement in the past when she gave the first Earl of Essex such power and the then Lord Deputy, Fitzwilliam, did not aid him in his campaigning in Ulster. I can see a similar disaster looming here, as the jealousies between the two men may cause a similar breach," he said somberly.

"And what of you? What position shall you hold?" she asked.

"I know not," he answered gruffly. "Until Sir John arrives with his army of veterans, I am simply to hold the line in Ulster. The Deputy has given me all the soldiers who can be spared from garrison duties in the rest of Ireland. He cannot risk running down the numbers in any of the other provinces. I'm to have fifteen hundred men and am to ensure that all the garrisons are provisioned."

"It is a noble task," Mabel said in an effort to appease her brother and dissolve his anger.

"It is important, yes, and when the army from Flanders arrives, it will defeat all the traitors in Ulster and bring O'Neill before the Council. I will then bear witness against him and have him executed. O'Neill is being lulled into a false sense of security by the appointment of his patron's nominee. I am told that Essex has finally seen through him. O'Neill will be unprepared for the onslaught that is to be mounted against him. At least, I shall have the consolation of seeing your husband brought low. He spat out the word "husband". Mabel turned away. "The man that you should have married is returning with the army from Flanders," he continued. "I wrote to him and he requested that he be allowed back. And have no illusion that he is returning on your account," he said contemptuously. "You are damaged goods. No decent Englishman would have anything to do with you. He must avenge the slight O'Neill did to his honour. You, lady, will never again know a man's company."

Mabel felt her eyes fill with tears. It was callous of Henry to persist in wounding her. She got to her feet and left disconsolately. He watched her go and took his horse by the reins, then started for the town. Mabel went in the opposite direction, not caring that she could be putting her life in danger. She crossed the bridge and followed the path, deep in her own thoughts.

Four years ago, she thought, my brother arranged a perfectly reasonable match for me. Wingfield wasn't old, repulsive or poor. He would have been accepted by any other girl in my position, but I refused him, because I thought Hugh loved me. All the trouble that followed has been brought about by my own blindness. She wished that she had been blessed with a child before leaving Tyrone. She was profoundly aware of her own mortality. She had seen too many people die recently and a child would have given her a stake in the future. A child would have been a companion in her loneliness, someone to love, raise and cherish. She sat on the grassy roadside and sobbed in desperation and grief.

Donegal Castle had been quite since Hugh Roe and his men had left for the siege at Enniskillen. Rose had found the time extremely long and lonely. When Hugh Roe was absent, she missed him greatly. Donegal became a foreign place in his absence and her thoughts turned to the familiar, in the form of her father's castle at Dungannon. She tried to pass the time as best she could, but the interests, which she could develop were limited.

The last week had not been too difficult as Nuala had come home to Donegal. She had confided in Rose about her unhappiness at the hands of her husband. Niall Garve had treated her badly, ignoring and belittling her as the mood took him, visiting her bed only when he was inebriated, and flaunting his kept women in front of her, for all to see. Yet, he did not dare to set her aside as that would be to risk directly insulting Hugh Roe. But Nuala knew that her brother needed his loyalty and was afraid to press for a divorce from him. Rose had offered to talk to Hugh Roe about her unhappiness but Nuala had implored her not to.

Rose had retired to her chamber as usual, after the evening meal. Hugh Roe's bard and musicians had accompanied him to Enniskillen, so the customary entertainment after eating had been discontinued. Nuala had gone to visit her foster parents, who lived some miles distant, leaving Rose to dine on her own. It was cold outside and a large fire burned in the grate. She quickly removed her outer clothes and slipped into bed, dressed in her shift. The bed was big and lonely without Hugh Roe but Nuala had joined her there during the last week and they had talked into the early morning before falling off to sleep. It was there that Nuala confided to Rose that she was pregnant and Rose had been unsure if congratulations were what Nuala wished to hear. Rose had enjoyed the companionship and would miss Nuala when she returned to Niall Garve. Suddenly, she heard the sound of horses clattering into the courtyard outside and guessed that it was Nuala returning for the night.

She burrowed deep under the bedclothes and waited for her. She heard footsteps on the turret stairs and was surprised at their speed and weight. The door swung open and Hugh Roe strode in. Rose gasped in surprise and delight.

"Hugh Roe!" she exclaimed. "I didn't expect you. Are you home for good? Have you taken Enniskillen?" she asked excitedly.

"No," Hugh Roe answered wearily.

"But all is still well there?" she asked anxiously. "There has been no change for the worse?"

Hugh Roe shook his head as he walked over to the fire and stood in front of it. "All is as it was," he said. "No change. I've grown weary of the siege and now we have just learned that your father's forces, under Art, managed to take the Blackwater Fort in but one day. It was only a wooden structure, but it still makes our efforts at Enniskillen appear feeble."

"You cannot compare one with the other," she said, eager to reassure him. "Time will yet resolve everything in your favour. Patience will get its just reward, you'll see."

Hugh Roe looked at her without speaking and Rose could read unhappiness on the face she knew and loved so much. She saw the tiny lines beginning to form on his forehead and around his eyes and a spring of love and warmth rose within her. He was not yet twenty-four and already he was involved on a course that would bring him into conflict with one of the strongest kingdoms in Europe and one of its most difficult monarchs. Yet, she knew that he never doubted his mission and that certainty and confidence made her love him even more. "What is it, my love? What troubles you?" she asked.

"Have you any news for me?" he asked and Rose guessed immediately from the gentle emphasis on the word "you", for what he yearned. She flushed in embarrassment at the disappointment that she felt in being unable to give him what he so desired. Her womanhood was undermined. Everywhere she went, she saw pregnant women. The servants in the castle seemed to be with child endlessly and now Nuala, in spite of her distaste for Niall Garve, was also pregnant. "No," she said simply. "I have not." She bowed her head apologetically. Hugh Roe turned away from her and looked into the fire. She threw the covers back and crossed over the wooden floor to him. She lay her hand on his shoulder, but he did not turn around. "Be patient. Time will solve that problem also, my love," she said gently.

She turned him around to face her and saw tears in his eyes. He brushed them away furiously. Rose tried to embrace him but he removed himself from her touch.

"What is it, my love?" she asked in panic. She had never before seen him upset like this.

"It's nothing. Nothing," he said.

Rose took his hand and looked into his eyes. "Hugh Roe?" she asked.

"Do not mind me. I'm being foolish," he said.

"Please tell me what troubles you, Hugh Roe. Otherwise, I will think that it is I who cause you such grief," she said.

"No, wife. It is not you," he said. After a few moments struggle with some inner turmoil, he continued. "As I returned, I got to thinking of a time in the past when I made the same journey with my father and now he is gone for ever from us. The night on Sliabh Ruaidh came to mind and I thought of Art McShane and began thinking of how uncertain and transient life is. I know the course that I'm taking is a dangerous one, and I thought, if the worst should happen..."

"Do not think like that," Rose interrupted. "I could not bear it if anything happened you."

"It does not weaken my resolve to follow the path that I have set myself, but it is just that... I would like to have a child. Our child. Someone to live on after me," he said falteringly, seeing the hurt that was unmistakably gathering in Rose's eyes.

"I would not want to deny you anything that you wish," she said in barely concealed distress. "If you desire a child, I will release you from your bond with me. I will not stand in your way, should you wish to divorce me."

At the thought of parting from him, tears flowed down her face. She could hardly believe that she was offering him the choice of putting her away and of taking another. She awaited his reply with dread.

He regarded her with great tenderness. "I said, I wished to have a child with you, someone that would remind you of me, if I was gone. Someone that would personify our love."

Rose smiled and placed her arms around his neck.

He enfolded her in his embrace. "I could not put you away," he said softly, "not even if we could never have children. In all the time

I spent away, I thought of you every day and longed to be back again with you. Now that we have been given the chance to be together, I will never allow us be apart. If we are fated not to have children, then we will live with that."

Rose felt a wave of gladness overcome her. Never before had she felt so much in love with him. She pulled his mouth to hers and kissed him on the lips. His lips met hers and he responded passionately.

Later, too exhausted to speak or move, she lay beside Hugh Roe, her soft breasts crushed against him, her mouth close to his ear and her fingers entwined in his hair. She felt content and her mind thought vaguely, this is what life is about, man and woman together, closeness and love, and if ever an act deserved to be blessed with children, then this one does. Her thoughts were interrupted by the sound of horses arriving in the courtyard below. Reluctantly, she stirred and said urgently to Hugh Roe, "Nuala, she's here on a visit and has been sleeping with me. That must be her now. We must get dressed."

She quickly picked up her nightshift and slipped it over her head. She took Hugh Roe's clothes from the ground and turned to see him, still lying on the bed. She tossed the clothes to him. "Make haste, put something on," she urged softly. He smiled at her, rose from the bed and drew his trews on slowly. He threw his shirt over his head just as the door swung open and Nuala raced into the chamber. "Hugh Roe," she exclaimed. "They told me that you'd returned."

Hugh Roe smiled and held his arms out to his sister who ran to him and embraced him. "I'm delighted to see you home, brother. I hope that it is for good," she said.

Hugh Roe took both her hands and held her at arm's length. "I must return to war again. I have a favour to ask of you. I want Niall Garve to join with me and campaign in Connaught on my behalf. So, I want you to do without him for awhile," he said.

Rose watched Nuala's face as she considered Hugh Roe's request. She knew what turmoil she must be feeling. It would no longer be possible for her to consider leaving Niall Garve. That would give him reason to deny Hugh Roe's over-lordship. Sympathy for her beleaguered sister-in-law welled within her, as she saw how Nuala wrestled with her own feelings and then denied them, on her brother's account.

"For you, brother, I would, willingly," she said.

"Good," Hugh Roe said. "We will travel to Castle Finn tomorrow and I will make him the offer."

"Hugh Roe!" Rose exclaimed in dismay. "You must stay longer!"

"Alas, I have promised Maguire that I will rejoin him at Enniskillen as soon as possible. When that business is resolved, we will be together again. But come, we must make the most of our time now. I asked the servants to ready some food and drink. We have much to discuss."

He grasped Rose's hand and the three of them left the chamber together.

Chapter 10

Mabel sat in the casement of her brother's house and, with a heavy heart, looked out at the approaching horsemen. She saw the Queen's colours fluttering in the breeze as they thundered across the open fields towards the house. The figures were still too far distant to recognise any of them, but she watched closely to see if she could recognise Wingfield. It has been over four years, she thought in surprise. Could that really be all it was? She felt like she had aged greatly in the interim. What would the new Lord Deputy be like? She had not seen him yet and her brother's opinion of him hadn't been very flattering. Still, she often found that their opinions differed. His disapproval of Russell need not mean that she would dislike him. They have brought a large escort with them, she thought. A sign of the troubled times we live in, when Her Majesty's subjects are not safe to travel the Queen's highways.

Her thoughts were rudely interrupted as the chamber door crashed open and her brother stood impatiently before her. "Come, make haste, women. Our guests are almost upon us," he said angrily.

Mabel sighed inwardly. Why did he always have to become so agitated? She had often noticed how strained he became in the company of nobility, adopting a servile manner that embarrassed her. "I have made sure that all is well in the kitchen. The food is ready and I've checked that the table is set out," she said wearily.

Henry flushed with annoyance. "You must act as hostess at my table. Our guests will be famished after their long ride. That is your function, indeed, it is all that you are good for. You will not show me up by absenting yourself. Do as you are bid and do not dare test my temper any more by drawing any further attention to yourself."

Mabel digested the implication of his words. She knew that she had become a curiosity, someone at whom people pointed in the street. She suspected that Russell would be curious to see what sort of a woman would have married the arch traitor, O'Neill. She rose meekly. "I will go to the kitchens and get them to ready the food for serving. When you bring your guests to the dining chamber, I will be there to serve you," she said.

"See that you do," Henry responded abruptly. "Do not make me come searching for you."

He turned and hastened towards the main entrance to greet his guests. Mabel walked listlessly in the opposite direction. She reached a stairs and descended its cold stone steps, which led to the door of the kitchen. She opened it and entered. The atmosphere struck her like a blow. The air was hot and heavy with the smell of cooking and there was a raucous din of clattering pans and shouted orders. The head cook, all red with heat and hurry, was preparing the food with the aid of seven young kitchen hands.

The kitchen was a large, open chamber with two large fireplaces at either end, both blazing fiercely. In each chimneypiece, joints of meat were cooking on spits. Vegetables were being boiled in great iron pots, which overhung the flames. Two men stood at a chopping block, cutting large loaves of freshly baked white bread. Other servants were rushing about and all seemed to be utter pandemonium. Mabel looked around anxiously for the head steward, Thomas, and saw him at the other end of the kitchen. She signalled to him, managing to catch his eye. He hurried over to her. "Yes, Madam," he asked respectfully. "May I be of service?"

"Is everything ready, Thomas?" she asked nervously, knowing if there was a problem, she would be held responsible.

Thomas nodded. "But of course, Madam. All is as it should be," he replied.

"Very well," Mabel answered looking all around her. "You may start serving the meal." Thomas nodded, turned from her and clapped his hands. "It is time," he said, and the kitchen became even busier.

Mabel watched as servants plucked stones that had been heating among the embers of the fire and dropped them into the soup pots to keep the liquid hot, while being transported from the kitchen to the dining hall. It was an excessive amount of food to prepare, she thought. Henry had been determined to make an impression upon the Lord Deputy, wishing to prove that things were just as civilised in Newry as in London.

She turned and left the kitchen as Thomas hurriedly organised the food onto platters and designated specific servants to carry each dish. She slowly retraced her steps until she came to the door of the dining hall. She paused outside, listening to the low, indistinct murmur of voices from within. She longed to leave the house but knew that she had not the energy for such a course. She grasped the handle, turned it, and walked in.

An immediate hush fell over the hall and the three men turned to look at her. She saw Wingfield standing by the casement. He gave her the slightest of bows before turning his gaze back on the vista outside. The Lord Deputy scrutinised her from head to toe and she found his gaze disturbing. It was haughty and penetrating, as if he was observing something distasteful.

"My sister, Mabel, my Lord," Henry said by way of introduction.

Russell bowed a hint of something approaching a sneer, playing momentarily on his thin lips. "Madam," he said.

"You are very welcome to our house, my Lord," Mabel ventured.

"Thank you," he replied. Mabel turned towards Wingfield and addressed him. "And you, Sir Thomas. It is good to see you home safe from the wars."

Wingfield turned and again nodded at her coldly.

"Well, where is the dinner?" Henry demanded. "Our guests are famished."

With that, Mabel opened the door to allow the steward and servants enter. "We may take our places at table," Mabel said and she motioned where each should sit. The procession of servants seemed endless, as one after the other placed the contents of their trays in front of the guests. In addition to serving the normal range of meats, Henry's English cook had prepared his specialities, dishes of boar's head and peacock pie. He had also sculpted and gilded an elaborate model of the house in spun sugar and marzipan, which was placed at the centre of the table. Copious amounts of mead and Rhenish stood in leathern gourds. The servants, having done their duty, retired to the kitchens.

The men took their knives and began cutting portions from their favoured meats. Mabel, having no appetite, took some bread and a little mutton so that her platter would not appear empty.

"Now that we are alone, my Lord, I beg to know what news have you from Dublin or the Queen," her brother asked.

Russell paused in his eating, wiped his hands, and then pulled from underneath his doublet, a parchment, which he handed to Henry. "Read," he said, "you will be pleased."

Henry took the parchment and unrolled it. Mabel could see the Queen's seal affixed to it. She saw Henry's face gradually change as first, a hint of a smile appeared on the corner of his mouth, which then spread until his whole face was suffused with pleasure. When he had finished reading, he looked up and asked urgently. "My Lord, has this been issued yet?"

Russell shook his head. "It is being printed secretly at this very moment in Dublin in both Gaelic and English. The Queen is very definite about the timing of its release. It must not be proclaimed publicly until Norris arrives in Ireland and takes up his command in Ulster. It will then justify his campaign against Tyrone," he answered.

"This is, indeed, a fortunate day," Henry answered joyfully. "All my past misfortunes, I do readily forget, now that I have lived to see this." He took the parchment and passed it to Mabel. "Here, sister," he said, " read this, that you may be enlightened."

Mabel took the document and looked at the heading. Her blood froze as she read, "Proclamation of the Earl of Tyrone as Traitor." She hurriedly read through the document. In spite of the exemplification, which Hugh had received from the Queen in 1567, his father, Mathew, was now deemed a bastard. In amazement, she saw that Turlough O'Neill was now officially "a very loyal, noble subject." She read on and saw that Hugh was accused of murdering Hugh Gavelock McShane and of imprisoning two of his brothers. Furthermore, he was also deemed responsible for seducing O'Donnell and other Ulster lords from their allegiance to the Royal Sovereign, and had used his brothers and bastard sons to support the traitor Maguire.

Her spirits fell when she saw that he was being cited as a known practiser with Spain. This, indeed, was as serious a crime as one could be charged with. His real object, she read, was to usurp sovereign power and be, in effect, "a Prince of Ulster." No wonder Henry was exultant. He had promoted such a line of thinking for a long time and was patently delighted that his opinion had, at last, become official state thinking. He would claim that he was the first to recognise Hugh's treachery and thus regard himself as the Queen's shrewdest official in Ireland.

She noted the proclamation's conclusion in a promise of pardon for the lives and restoration of lands to those who were willing to desert O'Neill's cause. She gazed abstractedly at the document, no longer reading it. Anxiety steeped both her mind and heart. Did Hugh know of this? Was it too late for him to sue for a pardon? She was surprised to find that she still cared about what happened to him. Unlike Henry, she did not feel the need for revenge or desire to gloat over his misfortune. She remembered Dungannon and her time there. She was aghast at the notion of its being destroyed.

Her attention returned to the men who had continued talking while she read the document. When would they move north, she wondered? She listened again to their conversation. It was the Lord Deputy who was speaking. "Norris has been delayed in London and is not expected for another month or so. We cannot lose that time. Already the Blackwater forts have fallen to the rebels. If we wait any longer, Monaghan and Enniskillen might also fall to them as they are almost totally devoid of food and supplies."

Henry nodded. "They cannot be allowed fall. It would be disastrous for us all. So what do you plan, my Lord?" he asked.

"I have come," Russell replied, "to offer you the command of a force that will provision both centres. Wingfield will act as your second in command. He has garnered much experience on the Continent and would be of great use to you."

Mabel noted her brother's expression of delight. Hugh declared a traitor and he was to have command again in Ulster. Of course, it would never occur to him to ask why the Lord Deputy, himself, did not undertake such an important task. No, if she knew him, he would be blinded by the perceived honour of the offer and not see it possibly as a poisoned cup.

"And what troops shall I have for such a task?" he asked.

"You have well over two thousand men, a fair proportion of whom are from the Brittany contingent of veterans," Russell answered.

"That may be so, but a thousand of them are newly arrived recruits from England, who have had little training. And we will be obliged to leave a garrison behind to protect Newry," Wingfield interrupted.

"Even so, you will still have adequate forces to carry out your mission. You are no longer on the Continent, Sir Thomas, and you do not oppose well trained and armed Spanish troops, rather a disorganised, badly armed rabble of rebels and cut throats who would never dare face Her Majesty's army in open battle," Russell replied.

"We are still short of certain provisions. Powder is in scant supply. If we are to re-provision the garrisons, we will have little enough to distribute among the relieving army. Such dearth must surely compromise our task," Wingfield countered.

"As I have already said, the Irish will not dare contest our passage," Russell answered with more than a hint of ire in his voice. He was not used to being questioned and the temerity of Wingfield's opinion angered him.

"Why then do we need to take the field with such a large force, simply to guard a supply wagon convoy? I do not relish the prospect of sending men out who have not enough powder to defend themselves adequately," Wingfield commented, a thread of insubordination lacing his voice.

"Because your mission will have two aims; firstly, the re-provisioning of the outposts and secondly, to cow the Irish when they see what forces we can put in the field," Russell answered impatiently. He turned to Bagenal, effecting a very deliberate snub of Wingfield. "Well, Bagenal, are you up to the challenge?"

Henry face creased into a smile. "Of course I am. And, God willing, I hope that I get to cross swords with O'Neill," he replied.

Russell nodded. "Good, but remember, your orders are specific. You are to deliver supplies, change the garrison and that is all. You are not to follow or seek out O'Neill. We must wait on all our forces, before we will undertake that operation. Agreed?"

Henry gave his agreement.

"Good," Russell said. "So hopefully, before long, we shall be as successful in Ulster as we have been in Leinster."

"Have there been developments there?" Bagenal asked with interest.

"Yes indeed," Russell answered. "I have mounted a number of campaigns against Fiach McHugh but the Wicklow Mountains made operations difficult and he continues to elude my grasp. However, I met with some success on my last journey thither. We arrested his best general, Walter Reagh Fitzgerald, brought him to Dublin and publicly hanged him in chains."

"Good," Bagenal said. "That country will be quieter for that. But McHugh is still at large?"

"Yes. I came upon his party one night and surprised them. They were sleeping in a clearing in one of their woods. McHugh escaped in his nightclothes but left behind his wife. I brought her back to Dublin and had her burned to death in front of Dublin Castle," Russell replied and laughed maliciously. " It made good entertainment for the townspeople. She was a fat old lady and burned quite well."

Henry chuckled but Mabel emitted an involuntary gasp of horror. The three men turned to look at her. "But what was her crime?" she asked.

"She was married to an arch traitor who constantly undermined Her Majesty's rule in this country," Russell said coldly.

"But that is not reason enough surely," Mabel said in consternation.

Henry interrupted angrily, mortified by his sister's interjection. "All traitors' wives should be treated in such a manner," he said viciously. "Then traitors might think more, before they rebel and their wives might exert more influence over them."

Mabel felt as if he had struck her. The blood rushed to her cheeks. So, that was what he would wish for her. She looked at Russell and saw him smile gloatingly, curious to see how she would react. Her glance fell on Wingfield and his eyes met hers, but there was no sympathy in them, only cold hostility. She considered leaving but knew that her brother would punish her for such a display of spirit and disobedience. In that moment, she realised that she could no longer remain under his roof. She lowered her eyes and looked at her platter from which she had not yet taken a morsel of food. After a few moments, the men returned to their conversation. She would sit out the remainder of the meal and, at the first opportunity, she would excuse herself, go to her chamber and think about how she might flee.

Mabel wondered whether she could warn Hugh of the danger he was under. Surely, it was not possible that outright war would erupt in Ulster? Hugh, for all his faults, was not an uneducated, bloodthirsty savage. Sense must prevail, a compromise must be reached. If he knew that he was about to be proclaimed traitor, perhaps he could sue for pardon and thus deny her brother the victory he so craved. War made no sense to her. She did not understand how decent men could ever think that battle could adjudicate matters better than reason and goodwill. She was beginning to suspect that goodwill and reason had little to do with driving mankind forward, rather greed, hatred, bigotry and passion were what impelled humanity blindly onward.

She glanced at her brother. She hated him for how he had treated her and despised him for being unable to forgive her. His cruelty and lack of humanity appalled her. Yes, she would travel to Dungannon and warn Hugh of his impending doom. They still were man and wife. Hugh had walked a narrow path between English ambition and Irish waywardness and probably had managed that path as well as anyone. He could still avert this impending disaster, able to see further than men like her brother. She thought of the dreams she nurtured when they had first married. Did they all count for nothing? She felt that if she didn't remove herself from Henry's grasp, she would not survive. There had to be something more for her. Perhaps, if she travelled to Hugh, risking her life to tell him of the danger he was in, all might be well again.

The gathering at Newry would not have been so confident had they known that, a bare fifteen miles away, the object of their discussions, Hugh O'Neill, was dining with one of Bagenal's most important and loyal sublords, Sir Hugh Magennis, Lord of Iveagh. Because of his lands' proximity to those of Bagenal's, he had come under the latter's influence, taking the side of the English in all their battles. He had refused to join the Irish Confederacy when asked to do so by O'Donnell and Maguire. Now, Hugh had travelled to meet him at his Antrim domains, in an effort to persuade him from his allegiance to the English cause, which in the past, they both had campaigned upon together. Hugh was acutely aware that the loss of Magennis's support would seriously undermine Bagenal's position and strengthen his own. He had brought Henry Hovendon with him, as Magennis and he had developed cordial relations during the many campaigns they had fought together.

The meal had passed off sociably. Hovendon and Magennis had traded stories and anecdotes but Hugh, for once, was tongue tied, barely hearing any of the conversation or tasting any of the food placed before him. At forty-five years of age, he was in thrall. It was Magennis's daughter, Catherine, who had awoken in him feelings that he never dreamt he could experience at this late age of life.

Magennis's wife had died some years previously and Catherine, the first born daughter, had joined them, taking her mother's place as hostess.

From the moment he saw her, Hugh was captivated. She had the most exquisite face that he had ever beheld and he had never imagined that a person could be as flawlessly beautiful. Her long, ebony hair was parted in the middle, and her face, beautiful as it was, possessed rarer qualities - serenity, sympathy and kindness. Even though only a tender nineteen years, her large, green eyes, reflected a wisdom and understanding that he had seen but seldom in his life. Most striking of all was her sense of grace and composure. He could never imagine her behaving in any way that would undermine such an intrinsic sense of style and equanimity. Yet, he could see that she, for all her poise, exuded human warmth. He noticed how easy she was with her father, the soft glances that passed between them, and how genuinely she laughed at his storytelling. He was captivated by her laugh, seeing the tiny laughter lines appear around her eyes. Once, during the meal, when she was pouring wine into his goblet, her hand brushed his and his whole being trembled at her touch. He realised, not without surprise, that he had not even looked at her form, being so taken by her face and manner. On observing it, he saw that it was slender and supple and most pleasing to behold.

As the meal progressed, Hugh took every opportunity to steal sidelong glances at her. Upon its conclusion their hostess arose. "Now, I must excuse myself. I am sure you have plenty to talk about. It was a pleasure to meet you both," she said and bowed to her two guests.

Hugh got to his feet. His sense of composure had deserted him and all he could manage was, "It was our pleasure, Mistress Catherine."

Catherine emitted a silvery laugh and then stopped abruptly when she saw the flush of embarrassment appear on Hugh's face. She laid her hand on his arm. "Forgive me," she said. "It's just that I have never been addressed as Mistress Catherine before."

Hugh felt the warmth of her hand through his sleeve and was unable to summon a response. He nodded dumbly.

Hovendon bowed and addressed her. "Good night, Catherine and our gracious thanks for such hospitality," he said.

She smiled at him warmly and was gone.

Hugh recognised how distracted he had become and attempted to concentrate on the purpose of his visit. Disorientated and bemused, he cut straight to the pending issue without his usual finesse. "We have come to ask you to join with us, against Bagenal and the English. We must force them to recognise our hereditary rights," he said.

Magennis hesitated before answering, confused and shocked. "But are you involved in this madness?" he asked in bewilderment. "Bagenal had always maintained that you were, but I did not believe him."

"Yes," Hugh answered. "We must stick with our countrymen on this matter. If we do not, then we will all go under, one by one."

Magennis shook his head. "I do not understand. You have always maintained the English position in Ulster. Now you change sides, but you do not do it openly and yet you expect me to?"

"Our conversation is between the three of us and shall go no further. I wish to know if I can call upon you when the need arises. I will not ask you to declare yourself, unless I do so first," Hugh replied.

"But my lands are next to Bagenal's. I shall be in the front line." Magennis replied. "You must understand, Hugh, I have no argument with him. Our family has been subordinate to the Bagenals for almost thirty years now and we have survived, even thrived. Why should I throw all that away, throw away the protection that I enjoy from the Queen's army, for your sake? I do not see how you could guarantee my safety against the English."

"If we all stand together we will be stronger than the English. We can make them bend to our will," Hugh rebutted.

"Talk sense, man. When did you ever see the Irish standing together? Never, and you never will," Magennis said without checking his rising impatience. "That is why we are in the position that we find ourselves today." He paused for a moment before continuing in a more reasonable tone. "Look, Hugh. I cannot and will not desert the Queen's side. I would recommend that you consider your own position carefully. I do not believe that this is a fight you can possibly win and I'm not going to ruin my family and supporters in following a hopeless cause."

"And if we prove to you that it is not hopeless?" Hugh asked.

"If you prove that, then we might talk again, but for now, I want no more discussion of such matters. It makes me very ill at ease. It is late and I think that we should call a halt to the proceedings. You have far to travel home," Magennis replied with finality.

Hugh acknowledged that there was no more that could be said on the matter for now. Normally, the drinking would have gone on late into the night and they would have been offered a bed. He had pushed affairs too far and too quickly. Magennis, no doubt, felt that they had abused his hospitality. He cursed himself inwardly for offending him. "Our gracious thanks for your hospitality," Hugh said. "We will take our leave and hope that we will yet come to see eye to eye on this matter."

He turned and left the chamber, hearing Hovendon offering his thanks in turn before hurrying after him. Magennis stayed in the dining chamber, making no effort to see them safely off. Hugh strode ahead of Hovendon through the torch lit passageways, out of the castle, and into the courtyard. There, he mounted his broad hoofed Ulster garron, and rode through the castle gates into the descending gloom.

His mind was in turmoil. He thought of Catherine. He could still feel the touch of her hand and her breath on his neck as she leaned over him to pour the wine. He could not accept that he would never feel that touch again. Such a possibility filled him with physical pain. It was not to be endured, he would possess her and make her love him. He would worship her, he would find in her the tranquil waters where he could shelter from the storms of his existence.

He heard Hovendon following after him but he did not slacken pace to allow him catch up until they were well clear of the castle walls. Then he turned to him. "I must have her," he said. "She must be mine."

Hovendon looked at him in amazement, "Who?"

"Catherine," Hugh answered tersely. "I must have her! I desire her to be my wife."

Hovendon was confounded. "But, you have two wives already. You are still married to Mabel and what of Sorley Bwee's daughter?" he asked.

"Mabel is long gone and it is Bagenal, alone, who denies me a divorce. As for Sorley Bwee's daughter, she was never my wife."

"That may be so," Hovendon answered, "but in his eyes, she is your wife and it will cause great damage to his reputation, if you deny her publicly. You must also consider that you need his influence in Scotland, now more than ever. If there is to be a war, you must keep open the supply of Scottish mercenaries. He is your only possible source. You have fallen foul of the rest of the Scots."

Hugh felt angry with Hovendon for being so blunt. And yet, that was what he valued so much in him. Hovendon would never agree with him if he thought that he was embarking upon the wrong path. At times, that had infuriated Hugh but, when he later and more soberly reflected upon his advice, he usually found that his judgement was sound. "I can manage without the Scots. We have built up our own forces," he said haughtily.

"Why should you risk all for an infatuation that will last but a few weeks? You know that. Look at all the women you've had and discarded. What is she, but one more?" Hovendon asked provocatively.

Hugh did not answer but rode on ahead, incensed. He was angered that Hovendon was not of his mind. But, how could he explain his feelings to him without seeming a foolish, middle aged man? He perceived that Hovendon had caught up again, but refused to acknowledge him. After a few moments, Hovendon addressed him in a more diplomatic fashion.

"What you propose is not possible. Magennis will never allow his daughter marry you, because you are husband to his patron's and lord's, sister. Bagenal would never forgive him and would do all in his power to destroy him. The Queen, herself, would learn of the match and disapprove. You must, for your own good, put such thoughts from your mind."

Hugh did not answer, but rode on silently. Hovendon allowed his horse drop back a few paces and followed behind him. Hugh reflected upon what Hovendon had said. It would be madness to antagonise Sorley Bwee. He realised that he was trapped. The notion that he might never possess Magennis' daughter filled him with a restlessness that cut him right to the soul. He would have to try and put her out of his head for now, but he vowed to himself, that one day she would be his.

The Irish camp at Enniskillen had settled down into the boredom of siege warfare, a boredom like no other in its all consuming monotony and dullness. It seemed as if it would last forever. For the participants, there was no life beyond the camp in which they resided. Their initial good humour and optimism had long ago deserted them, and now it was the month of May, and still the castle held out. The prospect of spending the summer living in the encampment, which would become vermin and fly ridden, was dispiriting.

O'Donnell was anxious for the matter to be resolved. He dared not leave the area. If he did, an English force might yet again re-provision the castle. While he was detained here and Niall Garve campaigned in Connaught, their own lands were left defenceless. Sir Richard Bingham had taken advantage of their absence by ordering his brother, George, to sail from Sligo to Lough Swilly in Donegal. George was the governor of Sligo. On arriving in Lough Swilly, he plundered the monastery of Rathmullen, stripping it bare of all its treasures, before murdering the monks and torching the buildings. This had been a sore blow to Hugh Roe's pride and reputation, an insult he burned to avenge.

Niall Garve had not been idle and had kept Hugh Roe informed of his progress. In Connaught, he had plundered the English and all their supporters, stole their cattle and burnt their houses. He sent the large herds back to Donegal, and while Hugh Roe was pleased to receive his share, he was more anxious that his brother-in-law should lay siege to Sligo, ensuring that George Bingham remained contained within its walls.

That had been some weeks since and now, Hugh Roe had been woken from his sleep with the news that a messenger from Niall Garve had arrived, demanding an immediate audience with him. He struggled into his clothing and wrapped his mantle around him before stepping out from his tent into the sharp morning air. It was just after dawn and the sun's red rays were appearing over the mountain, lighting up the lake that surrounded the castle. Hugh Roe stopped to look at the beauty of the new day before its troubles and disappointments took hold. He was weary in spirit and longed for some relief to lighten this cursed burden of waiting. Wearily, he walked over to the camp kitchen where the messenger was being fed, after his night's ride. His news must be pressing if he rode overnight, Hugh Roe thought.

He entered the tent and saw the messenger, a leg of mutton in one hand and a pitcher of beer in the other. He was tall and his long dark hair and beard were covered with dust from his journey. When he saw Hugh Roe he placed the food and drink on the table and lifted a bag that lay at his feet.

"Yes?" Hugh Roe said. "You have a message for me?"

The messenger nodded, quickly swallowing his last mouthful. "Niall Garve has sent good tidings. He has done as you requested and Sligo is now in our hands. It is only a matter of time before all of north Connaught will desert the English cause and join us in battle."

Hugh Roe looked at him in amazement. He couldn't believe what he was hearing. Sligo Castle was the key to the whole province of Connaught. If it truly was in his hands, he could enter the province without interference and bind its Chiefs to his cause. All the exiles that had fled to Donegal could now return and ferment uprisings in their own lands. Before long, he would have the whole province in revolt. It could hardly be true. He and Maguire were nearly a year besieging Enniskillen and now he was to believe that Sligo had fallen in a matter of weeks.

"But how?" he asked incredulously.

"Niall Garve had secret correspondence with Bingham's second in command, one Ulick Burke. He has ambitions to be the Earl of Clanrickard, a title that his uncle currently holds. As the Earl is firmly in the English camp, Niall Garve promised him support to unseat his uncle. In return, he slew his commanding officer, Captain George Bingham, and delivered the castle to Niall Garve. A fitting retribution for a man who would desecrate Rathmullen," the messenger said with pride.

Hugh Roe attempted to digest the communication. Elation surged through his whole being. This was excellent news for the O'Donnells, far more important than the taking of Enniskillen. The Blackwater forts and Sligo were theirs. He now realised, with a renewed surge of interest, that it was imperative to take Enniskillen and so build upon this advantage. He held his hand out to Niall Garve's messenger. "You have brought me great tidings, this morning. My thanks to you," he said.

The messenger nodded at this acknowledgement. "I have also brought you a gift from Niall Garve." He took his bag, opened it and tipped its contents out on the earthen floor. A bearded head fell out and rolled across the ground. Hugh Roe looked at it, observing that the hair and beard were trimmed in the English fashion and the man had been in his fifties. "Who is it?" he asked.

"None other than Captain George Bingham," the messenger answered.

Hugh Roe lifted the head by its hair and looked into the face. The dead man's eyes stared lifelessly back at him. "Ugly bastard, like his brother," he commented, gratified that, finally, one of the Bingham clan had got their just deserts. This would bring the war and its personal cost finally home to his brother, Richard. Some day, I will hold his head too in my hands, he thought.

"Niall Garve suggests that, as the garrison for Enniskillen was, for the most part made up of George Bingham's men, you might use this head to demoralise them," the messenger commented.

Hugh Roe considered the idea for a few moments. It would be worth a try. He turned to one of the guards present. "Go, wake Cormac and Maguire. Tell them that I must confer with them." The guard left and Hugh Roe turned to the cook. "Look after this man well," he said, "he has brought us great tidings this day." With that, he replaced the head in the bag and went back to his quarters.

Some hours later, Captain Smith, entrusted with the charge of the garrison, left the castle and walked into the open to confer with Cormac. It was the first time that Smith had agreed to meet, face to face, with any of the rebels. They met underneath the castle walls, Cormac all too aware of the guns, trained upon him from the battlements above. Earlier, one of his men had approached the walls and thrown the bag, containing the head, into the courtyard, and issued a request for parley.

He nodded at Smith, noticing how thin and sickly he looked. "It is time you surrendered. You have fought well and beyond the call of duty. Sligo and the Blackwater forts are in our hands. Monaghan will soon fall. Her Majesty has decided to abandon you. She has other more pressing matters in Connaught and the Pale to deal with. We will offer you safe passage out of our lands, provided you surrender now.

Otherwise, if you make us wait longer, every one of you will die by the sword. This is your final offer," Cormac said.

Smith stood looking at him for a few minutes as Cormac waited patiently.

"And we are to be allowed bring our weapons?" he asked.

"Yes," Cormac answered.

"And boats and some food for the journey?" he enquired.

"But of course. We want possession of the castle. A little food and some boats are a small price to pay," Cormac replied.

"Agreed," Smith answered.

"Very well, I will make the arrangements," Cormac said before withdrawing.

A couple of hours later, Cormac was back with a detachment of troops, Hugh Maguire and two boats. The gate opened and the weary, starved men marched out. They resembled a grotesque parade of skeletal marionettes, their painfully thin limbs, swinging in time to the beat of their drummer. There were only thirty of them in all.

Cormac, Maguire and their men watched as they approached the water's edge. Then, Cormac shouted in Irish, "Anois," and suddenly, musketeers appeared from the bottom of the vessels where they had been hiding under blankets. They and Cormac's men aimed and fired at close range before the English ranks had an opportunity to raise their weapons. The little band of marching men was decimated. Cormac's men charged at those who were still standing and butchered them with their swords. They were in no condition to put up much of a fight and it was all over in a matter of minutes. Every last one of them was dispatched. Revenge, at last, for all the months of waiting.

When the task was complete, Cormac stood and surveyed the scene. He looked at the dead bodies, but could feel little pity for them. They had chosen to come to a foreign country to ply the trade of a soldier and had met a soldier's death. Yet, he did not feel right about what he had done. He would not be boasting to his grandchildren about how he had dealt with this Enniskillen garrison. He checked his own men and was glad to see that they were all uninjured. He turned to one of them and ordered him to dispose of the bodies, then walked after Maguire who headed into the castle.

Maguire had ordered those chosen for garrison duty to enter with him. As he passed through its gates, he was relieved to be finally back inside again. There had been times when he had gravely doubted if he would ever regain it. Now all had changed. The three victories that they had gained, Enniskillen, Sligo Castle and the Blackwater forts, would reverberate through Ulster and draw more men to their standards. For the first time in over a year, Maguire felt confident about the future.

It was well past midnight and Mabel lay awake, listening for any noise from the now quiet house. It was over half an hour since she had heard her brother and his guests retire for the night. Her heart pounded as she considered what she was about to attempt. If she were caught, there would be no mercy shown her. Still, she was prepared to take that risk. Anything was better than the life that she had been subjected to for the last two years. Fully dressed, she pushed the covers back from her bed and rose silently. Her mind returned to that night when she had eloped with Hugh. There would be no English gentleman waiting to assist her on this occasion, however. No, she was putting her trust in an Irish stable hand.

After dinner, she had excused herself, saying that she wished to take some air outside. The men had made no comment, so she had passed into the garden and from there, had made her way to the stables, where she had met Connor, who tended her horse. She had promised him some of her jewellery in return for escorting her to Dungannon. The generosity of her inducement swayed him. She emptied the drawer where she stored her valuables, fingering each piece before dropping it into a velvet pouch. They had all been presents from Hugh, reminders of happier times. She took the necklace, which he had given her when she had agreed to be his wife. It was solid gold, a beautiful piece that had cost him the enormous sum of £500. She would never part with that. She picked out a silver bracelet and slipped it on her arm. She would offer that to Connor.

She looked around the chamber for one last time. She had suffered black loneliness and bleak despair in its confines. Then she turned and walked silently to the door, and on reaching it, she extinguished her candle and slowly turned the oak handle. She stood in the open doorway listening carefully to detect any noise, allowing her eyes get used to the darkness. The house was still and quiet. Now, she must go and see if she could find the proclamation. The last she had seen of it was when Henry had set it down on the buffet in the dining chamber.

She stepped into the passageway and slowly walked along it, careful not to make any noise. She would have to pass Henry's chamber. Normally, he was a light sleeper, but she hoped that the wine he had consumed would have induced in him a sound slumber. When she came to his door, her heart was pounding so loudly that she could scarcely believe that its beat would not awaken him. She paused, listened and heard a deep, loud snoring from within. Good, she thought, he will not wake before morn.

She descended the steps to the dining chamber and opened the door. It creaked as it swung back and she paused, unable to move, waiting to hear if she had been discovered. The house remained silent. She entered. Moonlight bathed the interior, throwing a shaft of light across its centre. It was in total disarray, empty wine pitchers littering it and the table, as yet, uncleared. The servants would set it to rights early in the morning before Henry rose.

She made her way over to the buffet and searched for the document. It wasn't there. She looked again, then searched the floor, but there was no trace of it. She searched the whole chamber, panic mounting with the realisation that she could not locate it. Finally, she concluded that Henry must have brought it with him to his bedchamber. Damn him, she thought. Even though drunk, he still had enough wit to remember it. It was a valuable trophy that he would cherish for a long time to come. She could always go without it, she reflected. No, she had pictured herself arriving in Dungannon and handing it to Hugh. He would take it, read it and when he realised how much she had risked to bring it to him, he would be grateful and they could start again. If she arrived and only told him of it, it would not be the same. She would have to have it.

She abandoned the dining chamber, leaving the door open and mounted the steps, retracing her way until she came to Henry's door. Once again, she listened and heard the reassuring sound of his snoring. She paused momentarily, turned the handle and slowly and gingerly entered. Henry's room was to the back of the house and shrouded in darkness. She stayed in the doorway, allowing her eyes adapt to the gloom. She shut them tightly, then opened them again. She could make out her brother's form, lying on top of the bed, his arms outspread. When she was certain that she could see all the obstacles of furniture that the room presented, she stealthily moved forward. Henry's snoring continued, like the ebb and flow of the tide. Finally, she reached the bed and looking down at the sleeping figure, spied her object. The parchment was under his arm. He had been reading it before falling asleep.

She looked at it for a few moments before determining that she had come too far to turn back now. She reached down and grasped it gently. Carefully, she pulled it out, inch by inch, from under the inert limb. Her heart was beating fast and then, Henry grunted in his sleep, turned over, mumbled something indistinct and the snoring stopped. Mabel stood rigid, not daring to breathe and then the snoring resumed, louder than before. Mabel took the parchment and glided noiselessly to the door. She slipped out into the passage, closing the door behind her. She paused, taking deep breaths until her heart slowed a little. When her agitation had slackened somewhat, she proceeded back along the passageway, down the stairway until she came to the back entrance of the house. She drew back the heavy bolt, swung open the door and slipped outside, closing it quietly behind her.

Now, at last, she was out in the open and she ran to the stables. Upon entering, the only sound she heard was that of the horses moving in their stalls. Her spirits fell. Where was Conor? Had she come this far only to fail now? She felt an arm on her shoulder and she jumped involuntarily. It was the groom. "Come," he said and led Mabel around to the back of the stables. There, he had two horses already saddled. He helped Mabel mount and then swiftly took charge of his own horse.

"We will follow the river until we are well distant from the house. When we are away from your brother's lands, we will take to the road. We are lucky. We have a full moon to guide us on our way. We must ride all night and come morning, we will be well out of your brother's reach," he whispered.

Mabel nodded. She would have no problem in staying awake. Anxiety would take care of that. She looked up at the full moon. What was it that the sages said? She attempted to recall, before memory finally provided her with the reply. Full moons make for madness. She hoped that this would not prove true.

Chapter 11

The news of the fall of Enniskillen and Sligo had swept across the North like a tidal wave, breaking on a confined beach, spreading into every nook and cranny of Ulster. Outside the tiny zones of English influence therein, the rest of Ulster celebrated with a vigour and exuberance not seen since the times of the Red Branch in the fourth century when, again and again, Ulster men defeated the Connaught men in battle.

Hugh O'Neill, buoyed up by the victories gained by the confederate forces, had called a meeting of their leaders to discuss the future. As he awaited the designated hour, he sat at his table re-reading correspondence from his ally on the Irish Council, Sir Robert Gardiner. He read again the proclamation that named him traitor. Even though it was before his very eyes, he found it difficult to believe that things had finally come to such a pass. The proclamation was still secret and O'Neill had decided not yet to inform the other Irish Lords of its existence. He had determined finally to take the leap his fellow conspirators so desired. He was about to declare himself openly on the Irish side and he wished them to think that he had taken this initiative rather than been coerced.

Such a prospect greatly disconcerted him. He felt angered that circumstances had conspired to bring him to this decision. He felt fear too, fear of the future and of the unknown, but his overriding sentiment was one of frustration, frustration at the stance adopted by Elizabeth and her Privy Council. His only source of consolation was his determination to make them regret their treatment of him. At least, he would have the opportunity to be revenged upon Bingham and Bagenal. With luck, he would get to cross swords with both of them, but if he had to chose to avenge himself on only one, then that would have to be Bagenal.

He was aware that all the invited leaders were awaiting him in the Great Hall. He had left them long enough. It was time to make his decision known. He replaced the parchment in the chest and locked it. He then left the chamber and descended the stairs. As he approached the hall, he heard the sounds of merriment and festivity through the thick doors. They have every reason to celebrate, he thought, and I must appear to be of like sentiment. He opened the door and walked in. Hugh Roe, Cormac, Maguire, Hovendon and Art were sitting at the oak table, each with large pitchers of whiskey in front of them. On seeing him, Maguire leaped to his feet and ran to meet him, throwing both his arms around him. "I'm no longer without a country," he said joyfully. "Enniskillen is mine again."

"It is indeed good news," Hugh answered. "Enniskillen, the Blackwater forts and Sligo Castle are all ours. You have done well, all of you."

O'Donnell poured a measure and brought it to Hugh. "Here, it has been a long time since we had so much to celebrate and since the English have had such a reduced presence in Ulster," he said with a laugh.

Hugh looked at the smiling faces before him. The years had evaporated from Maguire like mist from the hillside on a sunny day. He took the drink and asked. "The garrison?"

"Destroyed," Hugh Roe answered.

"Good," Hugh replied. "It was a major mistake letting the Blackwater contingent escape. We must now hold what we have." He continued, "I have received information that Bagenal is to attempt to re-provision Monaghan. He's to have a large force to aid him, a force that will contain many of the Brittany veterans. We must halt him."

Cormac asked with deliberate irony. "And what do you mean by 'we'? Are you finally going to join us openly?"

"Yes," Hugh answered simply.

There was a moment's silence as the news was digested. Then, Maguire whooped in delight. "Now," he said, "now we will run all the English out of Ulster."

Hugh Roe crossed to Hugh and embraced him. "It has been a long time coming, but I delight in your public support of us. It will make a difference with King Philip and encourage him to send us aid."

"Yes," Maguire interrupted excitedly. "He has been awaiting such an opportunity. By God, we might even drive the English from the whole island!"

"That may be, but until the Spanish arrive, we must plan our defence in their absence," Hugh answered patiently.

"But why defence?" Hugh Roe asked querulously. "We should take the initiative. Now that you have joined us, we have the men."

Hugh shook his head. "No, no offensive," he answered. "You must all be clear on one matter. If I join you, then more than ever, I must be in control. You have fared well under my guidance so far. Unless you all follow my tactics in the future, then I cannot risk all with you."

Maguire nodded. "You will not find me in disagreement," he said amicably.

Hugh Roe paused, considering the request. All eyes turned on him expectantly. "Agreed," he answered, not without some hesitation.

Hugh had noted O'Donnell's reluctance in consenting to this one demand and privately stored it up in his memory. He continued. "I have thought long and hard about the best way to conduct the war we are about to embark upon. We must not allow our forces be embroiled in open battle where the English will have the advantage. Their presence in Ulster is small at present. What do they hold? Newry, on the eastern coast and then nothing until they march thirty miles, mostly through forest and bog, until they reach Armagh. Then, they have to cover another thirty-eight miles to reach Monaghan Fort. As of now, they hold nothing else in all of Ulster."

"And hopefully, before long, they won't have those few strongholds either," Maguire interjected.

"The English cannot find us, unless we wish them to," Hugh continued persuasively, "however, we can always find them when they revictual their forts. The first thing we must do is to stop the garrisons from raiding outwards. We must have men ready to repulse them if they attempt to leave their station. Then, we must starve them out."

"We already do that," Cormac interrupted.

"Yes, but that is only the first step. Next, we must ambush their lines. At the moment, they are supplied from Dublin, through Dundalk and Newry. From there, the provisions are distributed to Monaghan and Armagh. It's a long supply line, needing a major allotment of resources and men to guarantee its safety. We must attack the escorting army whenever possible, demoralising them, making them hate the task, not knowing when they are about to be killed by an enemy they cannot even see."

"Yes," Maguire concurred with a wry smile.

Hugh continued. "The wind and weather will be on our side. They will be marching into hostile country. In wintertime, the journey will be even more hazardous. We will poison the wells and streams along their route. On no account, however, must they be allowed leave behind any new fort or settlement. They will no sooner have reprovisioned their fortifications, than it will be time for them to start the process again. We will make them sick and tired of the whole venture before long."

Maguire nodded in agreement but O'Donnell's forehead creased into a frown. "But Hugh, we must take the offensive. How else can we win?" he asked.

"We will fight, but on our terms," Hugh answered. "We must hold what we have and build on it. The reserves in strength that they possess far outweigh ours. We must build a larger confederacy than that which we have already established and spread rebellion into the four provinces of Ireland. We have a long, hard road before us and we will need courage and, above all, faith in our cause, if we are to succeed."

"You will not find me wanting," Maguire interjected.

Hugh nodded approvingly. "Let us start by releasing the clans and driving the settlers from their lands in Monaghan, Cavan and Louth, banishing them to their cities where they will become a burden on the English administration. It need not even be an organised campaign. We need only let our clans know that they are free to plunder the settlers. They won't be long sorting themselves and the English army is too small to protect them all."

"That will be an easy task. Once they see what is afoot, panic won't be long setting in and they'll run for shelter," Maguire added.

O'Donnell nodded but still harboured doubts. "It can be done, but what other steps should we take?"

"We must send your priests out into the country to work for us. We need their rhetoric to encourage rebellion. We will make Catholicism one of our causes and personal freedom of worship, one of our demands. The Old English should support that cause," Hugh replied.

He observed Hugh Roe to see how he would take his suggestion. He, himself, knew that he could change his allegiance between Protestantism and Catholicism, with great ease, O'Donnell, however, valued and observed the old faith, seeming to embrace everything contrary to the English. Hugh Roe's misgivings gave way and he answered, not detecting Hugh's cynicism. "Yes, I can send to Spain for more priests. There are many Irish who have travelled there to be ordained, who would revel in returning to preach against the Queen."

"But when will you let the English know of your decision?" Maguire eagerly enquired of Hugh. "When will you let the Irish know of it? As soon as it becomes known that The O'Neill is in rebellion, it will increase our support in all parts of Ireland."

"I will let them know by taking the field against Bagenal's army," Hugh answered quietly. "I have long been eager to revenge the slights that I've suffered at his hands. This is my opportunity. We shall see which of us is the better soldier."

Hugh Roe nodded. "Revenge deferred is greatly satisfying."

O'Neill agreed, recognising the truth of his words. "We do not have much time to prepare. I want all of you with me. We will assemble most of our forces, leaving enough men to protect our western borders against Bingham. I want you, O'Donnell, to return to Donegal, assemble all your sublords and have them swear allegiance to the confederacy in your presence, promising to remain in the field and refusing pardon until all our wrongs are satisfactorily addressed. The English must not be able to divide us as they have in the past."

"I will do so," O'Donnell answered.

"I want you ready to march once we have notice of Bagenal's departure," Hugh said before turning his attention to Maguire. "You Hugh, are to do the same in Fermanagh. I will call on you once I have news."

"I will be waiting," Maguire answered.

"Good," Hugh said. "Art and Cormac, you must gather all our nobles here and they must take the oath in my presence."

Art and Cormac nodded. "Henry," Hugh continued, addressing Hovendon, "Call on Magennis again and tell him that circumstances have now changed. I have now declared myself. He must be persuaded to join with us in our fight for freedom and Catholicism. Do your best to convince him."

Hovendon raised his eyebrows ironically, but Hugh chose to ignore him. "From this day on, we must work towards nothing else other than successfully prosecuting this war. We should..."

Hugh's words were arrested by a resounding knock on the door of the Great Hall. He was angered. He had posted two of his most trusted men there and had ordered them, on no account, to interrupt this meeting. Normally, they would never dare ignore his directions. He hastened impatiently towards the door but before reaching it, it opened and one of the guards entered. "I'm sorry, my Lord, but you have a visitor who insists that she must talk to you immediately on a matter of great urgency," he said, looking most ill at ease. "She has travelled far to be here and I was unsure what to do."

Hugh looked at him blankly, at a loss as to whom he could be referring. "We are not to be disturbed. I will talk with whomsoever it is later," he said sharply. Then, from the other side of the door, he heard the rounded, clear English tones of a woman he could not fail to recognise. "Forgive me, husband, but I must talk to you on matters of great import," Mabel ventured, stepping past the guard and into the hall.

Hugh could not believe his eyes. To him, she was already as one dead. He looked at her and was dumbfounded. Her person was so changed as to be almost unrecognisable. Unhappiness had imprinted itself deeply on her face, which had become lined with sorrow. Gone were the feminine contours and loveliness of her form. In its place was a figure, gaunt in extremity. Her once beautiful hair was sparse and streaked with grey. She was besmirched with the dust of the road and to all who observed her, it was apparent that she had undertaken an arduous journey.

Hugh wondered what her motive was in returning to Dungannon. Mabel's gaze wandered past her husband. She nodded acknowledgement of Hugh Roe, Maguire and Hovendon, but gave no semblance of recognising Art or Cormac. Art, she hardly knew, as he had never spoken to her, having no interest in persons or things English. Cormac, on the other hand, had never approved of the marriage and had made that fact known to her.

"I see no reason why you should return here," Hugh said icily. "I am too much occupied to squander time in conference with you." He turned to the guard who had followed Mabel into the hall. "Bring her to the kitchen and get her something to eat. I will send for her at my leisure," he ordered.

The guard put his hand on Mabel's shoulder and attempted to steer her away. She broke free. "Is this how you treat me, husband?" she asked forlornly. "Have you forgotten that I was once mistress of this castle?"

"That was a long time ago," Hugh answered stiffly. "Those days are well gone, Madam. It was you who left here and forfeited those rights. You chose your brother to whose house you should return immediately. There is no welcome for you here."

Mabel stood in the centre of the hall, her lower lip trembling, attempting to keep her sentiments under control. "I came here out of friendship. I cannot bear the thought that there will be war between our peoples. It will gain neither party anything," she said earnestly.

Hugh snorted. "Then why do they attempt to steal our lands? Let them stay out of Ulster and there will be no war," he retorted.

"That will not happen. The Queen believes that all of Ireland is part of her kingdom and that you seek too much independence," she said urgently.

"We will tolerate them once they stay out of Ulster," Cormac said coldly.

"Out of all of Ireland," Maguire added.

Mabel turned to him. "You do not comprehend what you confront. You play into the hands of people like my brother," she said, appealing to one who had shown her friendship in the past.

"Do not deign to condescend to us, Madam," Hugh interrupted cuttingly. He had little time for such histrionics. There was so much to be done and so little time. "Did your brother send you here to spy on us?" he asked contemptuously.

"No, he knows nothing of my journeying hither. When he discovers my action, he will be enraged," she answered.

"You should have stayed in Newry and spared him the annoyance," Hugh retorted abruptly.

"You still do not see," she pleaded. "I have come here to warn you of the forces being dispatched hither from England and the Continent. You must seek a pardon now before it is too late for all of you."

Hugh shook his head dismissively. "Of course we have learned of their plans. I had foreknowledge, before anyone on the Irish Council, that troops were being sent from Brittany. My sources in England informed me."

Mabel was momentarily crest-fallen, but then reached inside her cloak and produced the proclamation. "But did you know of this?" she asked as she handed it to Hugh. "The new Lord Deputy brought it with him to Newry the day before last. I stole it while the household slept and made my way here with it so that you would be warned."

Hugh took the parchment and opened it. Dismayed, he saw that it was a copy of his proclamation. His mind raced forward, pondering whether or not to admit his fore knowledge. If he were to do so, the others would then question why he had not confided in them. They might recognise that his decision to join them openly had been forced upon him.

"You see," Mabel continued. "The Queen now endeavours to crush you. You have all pushed too far. You must pull back from the brink."

"Why has not this document been issued, if it is genuine?" O'Neill asked.

"Because it is to remain secret, giving the English the advantage until the army arrives in Ulster to campaign against you all," she answered.

Hugh took the document and shredded it into a score of pieces. He would not give it to the others to read for themselves and learn of promised pardons. "This changes nothing, rather it confirms me in the course I have chosen," he said dismissively. He turned to face the men. "It appears that I am about to be declared a traitor," he said with a laugh. "I must verify that title, giving them due cause to label me thus." Rounding upon Mabel, he said, "You have had a wasted journey, Madam, and you may now return to your brother and inform him that we are willing and able to meet him in battle. We shall soon determine who is to be master in Ulster."

All colour drained from Mabel's face and her slender frame trembled pitifully. "But I cannot return to my brother's house," she said nervously. "I can never again return there, after what I've done."

"There is no welcome for you here, Madam," Hugh retorted ruthlessly. He had already one trial wife of whom he wished to be rid. The notion of Mabel's return filled him with horror. "You belong to neither side," he continued. "It would be better for you if you left Ulster altogether."

Hugh's coldness cut her to the quick. "No, Hugh," she said in panic, "do not say that. I've no place else to go. Even were I to go to my sister's house, I would not be safe. Henry would see to it that I be arrested and tried for treason. You heard what they did to Fiach McHugh's wife. Henry has already said all wives of traitors deserve such treatment."

Hugh shook his head. "You are being hysterical, Madam. He would never behave so to his own sister."

"But he would," Mabel answered in mounting panic. "You do not comprehend him fully. He abhors you all and all things Irish, but he especially hates you, Hugh. If he thought that he could damage you through me, he would not hesitate to do so," she said.

"He need not think so foolish a thought, as there is nothing between us any longer, Madam. I presumed that would have been apparent to you both," he answered coldly.

A paroxysm of terror seized Mabel. "Do not speak so, Hugh," she pleaded stridently. "I risked all to bring you news of this. For the sake of what we once had, give me sanctuary. If another had risked as much for you, you would have rewarded them with your protection."

"Take her away," Hugh ordered the guard.

The guard approached and took Mabel by the arm, attempting to guide her towards the door. Mabel struggled free. "Hugh," she shrieked, "Hugh, have pity, for God's sake." He turned his back on her, finding such a display of emotion repulsive. He wished it to be over. He signalled at Hovendon who advanced towards Mabel. "Come," he said gently and after a few moments, she allowed herself be led away.

After the door closed, an awkward silence fell on the assembled gathering. Maguire finally spoke. "You cannot send her back, Hugh."

O'Neill's brow grew cloudy. "That is my concern. We have more important things to consider. I want to know how many soldiers you can each commit to ambush Bagenal?" he asked gruffly, attempting to banish from his mind all thoughts of Mabel and her untimely return.

It was early morning and already the drummers were beating wildly while English troops rose and prepared themselves for another day's march through hostile territory. High in the surrounding hills, a party of Irish soldiers watched the activity far below in what the English called Fort Monaghan. It had been a Franciscan monastery but, after the overthrow of the McMahon Chief, the English had converted it into a military barracks. The thick, strong surrounding walls and the buildings themselves had been ideal for the purpose. It was a formidable fortification and though the deposed McMahons, with some of Maguire's men, had kept it under siege for almost six months, they had not succeeded in taking it. Down in the camp, the English commander, Sir Henry Bagenal, was waiting for his officers so that he could conduct a council of war.

One by one, the officers arrived. They were not the same confident group that had set out from Newry just two days previously. Bagenal had marched to Monaghan's aid with provisions and a force, consisting of nineteen companies of foot and six troops of horse, amounting to some 1,750 men, made up of the Brittany veterans and newly arrived raw recruits from Staffordshire.

Bagenal had only one senior company officer, Sir Edward Duke, who commanded the horse, and no field officers to lead the infantrymen. He also had no officers of intermediate rank between the company captains and his own staff. He found too that there were only three experienced captains assigned to his command, Wingfield, Wilmot and Brett, the remaining Brittany companies being led by subalterns.

Bagenal's forces had marched in the usual three divisions of vanguard, battle and rearward. He had reached Monaghan, but only after coming under unexpected, sustained skirmishing from the Irish forces. His army had been relieved to sleep within the strong, stout walls of the fortification and now, on this new morning, Bagenal's challenge was to plan their march home to safety.

He waited until all the officers were present before starting. "I have called you here so that we may plan our march and review yesterday's engagement. Captain Brett, do you have the numbers for the dead and injured?" he asked.

"At least twelve men dead and thirty wounded, including three lieutenants. Another fifty are missing. The surgeons did what they could for the wounded. We cannot leave them here and yet many of them will not survive the journey," he answered.

"God must decide that," Bagenal answered. "We must load them on the empty wagons and bring them with us. They will retard our march, but we must not leave our wounded comrades behind us. Yesterday could have been much worse, were it not for the prompt action of Captain Cuney in securing the pass at Crossdall. I must commend him and his troops, especially as they are but recently come to these wars. They acquitted themselves well under enemy fire."

Wingfield listened with growing anger. He regarded the previous day's action as unprofessional and incompetent. He could stay silent no longer, "We were lucky yesterday," he said heatedly. "Were we up against a better army, we would not have come off as easily."

Bagenal ignored the comment. "On the return march, I intend commanding the van and you, Wingfield, will be stationed with the Staffordshire men who will need the benefit of your experience to bring up the rear. Captain Cuney shall be your second in command."

Wingfield did not reply, unhappy at his new posting. He would have preferred to remain in the battle with his own men, but knew that it was pointless to complain. He looked at Cuney, wondering how he and his men would take to a stranger being placed in command over them. He had an air of quiet confidence about him, a man whom Wingfield reckoned would be useful in a tight fight. Cuney, noting that he was under observation, nodded amicably at him. Good, thought Wingfield. We will have enough to contend with, without further rivalries to cause complications.

"The main battle will be commanded by Captains Willmount and Brett," Bagenal continued. "We will return the same way as we came."

Wingfield interjected again. "I am concerned about the amount of powder, which was used up on yesterday's march. The new recruits shot their weapons at shadows. They have very little powder left. I think that we should leave only half the barrels of powder here, bringing the other half with us, to repulse the rebels should they attack us again."

"That would be folly. It would necessitate our making the journey to Monaghan soon again to deliver the balance of the powder. In any event, the Irish will never face us in a fair fight. They are content to lurk behind trees and cast their javelins at us, like the cowards that they are. They are no threat to an army such as ours," Bagenal said dismissively before turning to Duke. "And you, Sir Edward, you shall once again be in charge of the horse."

Sir Edward Duke, a large corpulent man, in his late fifties, dressed head to foot in armour, now rose to his feet. "I must disagree with you, Marshal Bagenal. I saw what they did to my army when we marched in an effort to relieve the siege of Enniskillen last year. Mark my words, they will attempt to ambush us on our return. This country gives them much cover, and my horse will be unable to get in among the trees and root them out," he said.

"You exaggerate. They are a motley collection of wood kerne and cattle herders," Bagenal answered derisively.

"With respect, Marshall, I disagree. They might not meet us in open battle, but they can cause havoc among our ranks with their gunfire. What I saw of them on the road to Enniskillen, was a revelation to me. I have never seen, in any other place in all my life, more ready or perfect shot. If the general standard of their troops can match that, then we are facing a real trial of strength," Duke continued.

"And we must not forget that the situation has worsened since then," Wingfield added. "O'Neill, with all his forces, has joined the rebels. He has served with us in the past and is aware of our tactics. His forces will have had time to fortify the pass at Crossdall. We shall not negotiate it as easily on the journey home, as we did in our coming here."

"I will be in the vanguard," Bagenal answered confidently. "I will make sure that we win through. And now to your stations. We must make haste and start our march."

"I believe that we should return by another route," Wingfield said, deliberately ignoring Bagenal's imperiousness. "Why should we give them the advantage of preparing the ground against us?"

Bagenal snorted in exasperation at the questions. He resented his authority being undermined in front of the other men. "You know full well, that an army such as ours, with wagons and ordinance, must keep to the roads, such as they are. If we do not, we will be lost. The surrounding countryside is full of bogs, forests and wetlands. It would be impossible for our army to cut through it and would invite disaster to try such a course."

"I have talked with our guide," Wingfield continued doggedly. "He says that it is possible to avoid the pass at Crossdall. Instead of returning in an easterly direction, if we head southeast towards Muckno Lake, we can avoid it altogether. The guide assures me that there is a track that we can follow."

"It would make better sense," Duke added.

Bagenal paused grudgingly, before yielding. "Tell the guide to join me in the vanguard. Now make haste. Has the garrison been changed?"

"Yes," Wingfield answered.

"Well then, let's get out of here and back to civilisation."

It was ten o'clock before they marched out in their three columns, the drums beating time and the flags proudly unfurled, blowing in the late May breeze. The day would be a sunny one and the surrounding countryside was lush and green. High in the near by hills, O'Neill and Maguire were watching the tiny figures as they emerged from the fort. O'Donnell had not answered O'Neill's summons, choosing instead to join Niall Garve in Connaught.

O'Neill and Maguire sat on their horses, twin pillars of metal as the sun glinted off their burnished armour. "They are not returning the way they came," Maguire said.

"It is of no great concern. There are as many wooded areas, hills, streams and fens on that route, as the one they abandon. We will still be able to work up close to the column while remaining under cover. You must send for the men we left at Crossdall and tell them to follow us," O'Neill answered.

"And we will have the McMahons in our company, giving us approximately three thousand men in all," Maguire replied.

"Yes, but do not forget, his men are all untrained. Still," O'Neill continued, "McMahon's knowledge of the local terrain, will aid us greatly. We must confer with him and delay the column, while we find a suitable location where we can pin it down and destroy it."

Maguire asked, "And what of our dispositions?"

"You will be in command of the horse, once again. I will keep fifty of my own horsemen as bodyguard and divide my infantry, giving half to Cormac. Wherever Bagenal chooses to station himself, is where I and my men will attack," O'Neill said, as he spurred his horse and headed back towards the rest of the army, hidden just over the neighbouring hill.

Just after eleven-o clock the English got their first glimpse in the distance of the Irish, having barely covered two miles over the rough, boggy terrain. Their wagons continually stuck in the mire and had to be hauled free before the column could advance. They were marching five abreast, in bodies of pikemen and shot. The Irish sent in skirmishers all along the length of the column, opening fire from both sides. Cuney and Wingfield, both on horseback, were riding together at the front of the rearward section. Ahead was the chain of wagons, empty now, except for the wounded who moaned in pain as the rutted track caused them to be jolted violently from side to side. The rear had to halt, their path blocked by a wagon, sunk deep into the mire. As the musket balls whistled about the English soldiers, they looked nervously around at the surrounding woods. It was not difficult to pinpoint the skirmishers' location, as the flash of guns and clouds of dark smoke were easily detected.

Wingfield looked at the men he was to command, the bulk of them conscripts. Sheriffs in various English counties were obliged to supply a designated number of recruits for the Queen's Irish army. This they did for the most part, by picking up vagabonds, the unemployed and other undesirables. If these were in short supply, the shortfall was made up by emptying the jails. The conscripts then received minimal military instruction before being dispatched to Ireland. Wingfield had seen to it that they had received intensive training once they arrived. They had been reluctant students and he was obliged to have a number of them severely flogged to instil some discipline among them. He wondered how they would behave if the Irish made a major charge against them.

He turned his horse and rode back along the length of the column until he saw the scout master. "Take fifty men and drive those skirmishers back so that they are out of range of our column," he ordered, before riding quickly back to Cuney.

"Come with me," Wingfield ordered him as he galloped forward to the stalled wagon. There, he sought out the carriage-master who was at the rear of the impeded vehicle, trying to have it freed. Wingfield glanced forward and was relieved to see that the battle section had also halted its progress to wait for the rear, closing the gap that had opened up between them. That gap is already too large, Wingfield thought.

"You must keep the wagons moving. Otherwise we will be sitting targets for the rebels," he ordered urgently, dismounting from his horse. "Here, take my horse and Cuney's and use them to help pull any wagon that gets bogged down in the mire."

He looked at Cuney who reluctantly dismounted. Wingfield drew his long petronel, and ran back towards the rear. Bullets whistled through the air, but given the distance that the Irish were from him, they flew wide and harmlessly. "Come," he shouted back over his shoulder, "we must rejoin our men."

They both reached the relative safety of the rear and paused at its head, conversing in low tones so that they would not be overhead by the rest of their force. "We are better off dismounted," Wingfield said breathlessly. "We will fight side by side with our men."

"And make less obvious targets for the Irish shot," Cuney replied wryly.

"That too," Wingfield retorted humourlessly.

Cuney surveyed the surrounding scene. "Look, they've got that wagon moving again."

"Good," Wingfield said relieved. "Let us advance too. You proceed along the right side of the column and I will take the left. Let yourself be seen by the men. Encourage them along and I will meet you at its rear."

The column continued marching for the next hour, coming under continuous fire from the surrounding forests and hills. Wingfield had to send out more skirmishers in an attempt to keep the Irish out of range. His skirmishers were suffering heavy losses, as time and time again, they were driven back to shelter with the rear, adding their wounded to the growing number already mounted on the wagons. Finally, they came to open, boggy ground, and caught sight of a substantial section of the Irish army, perched on top of a hill, overlooking the plain. It consisted of a large body of horse, seconded by a formed square of pike and shot, who looked on menacingly as the English army trooped across the plain, marching to the steady beat of their drummers.

"Why doesn't our cavalry attack them?" Cuney asked.

"Because of the ground. Our heavy horse would never manage to cross those bogs," Wingfield replied.

"So, we are safe from attack then?" Cuney enquired.

"No," Wingfield answered. "If they've picked this location, then they know a safe path through. We must be on our guard. It does not bode well to see them organised in such a perfect formation. They have never before fought in such fashion."

They looked ahead and saw the vanguard reach the other side of the plain, again entering a wooded area. All of a sudden, they heard the ominous rattle of gunfire in the distance. As the battle section approached the wood, more than three hundred Irish skirmishers advanced over the bog, from one firm tussock to another, as sure-footed and nimble as mountain goats. The English, who tried to repulse them, sank into the muddy water and bottomless ponds of marsh, unable to differentiate between the firm and yielding ground. The other soldiers watched helplessly as their companions drowned before their very eyes.

Wingfield's attention was distracted from those wretches as he noticed that the Irish army was on the move from their hillside van-tagepoint. Their horse came galloping sure-footedly over the ground and the enemy square advanced at a frightening pace. "Form square! Form square!" Wingfield shouted anxiously to his men.

The drummers immediately beat out the signal for the manoeuvre and the men began to deploy into the fighting formation. Wingfield knew that this was the most dangerous time for any army, as no mat-ter how rehearsed the movement was, a temporary disorder always occurred in establishing the square. The colours took up their position in the middle, the bright ensigns of the captains billowing in the sharpening wind. Around them, eight halberdiers were stationed, their purpose being the protection of the colours. The pikemen massed around them, the base of their fifteen-foot pikes, grounded in the earth, their points directed up and out to deflect any enemy horse. On either side of the square, the shot was stationed. The training that the men had received stood to them and the urgency of the situation made them complete the manoeuvre swiftly. Wingfield and Cuney took their place on both sides of the pikemen.

They watched as their skirmishers retreated rapidly to the newly formed square, whose pikes bristled like the spines of a hedgehog. The pikemen had left gaps in their ranks and through these, the retreating skirmishers were quickly and smoothly absorbed into the safety of the formation, before it closed ranks, just in time to face the charging horsemen. These charged straight at the square, until, at the last moment, they wheeled across in front of it, discharging their javelins. The Irish skirmishers targeted the English shot on the square's flanks, to distract fire from their horse. Meanwhile, the Irish square had marched unhindered, still in formation, and had taken up position between the rear and the battle section, protecting their men from the English cavalry.

Wingfield shouted at his soldiers. "Stand firm! Stand firm! If you break, all is lost." He saw the javelins land among his men and feared that if a gap appeared in their ranks, the Irish horse would ride in and make short work of them. All around him was smoke and noise. He heard the wild, foreign howling of the Irish and felt in a far more alien place than he had ever been on the Continent. He looked over the plain towards the battle section, but that too was shrouded in gun smoke and had also deployed. They were isolated and would have to fight on their own, he thought. Troop after troop of horsemen charged and wheeled away, only to be replaced by another, which repeated the manoeuvre. Wingfield was well aware that he was witnessing a historic day in Irish warfare. Never before had an Irish army performed as this one did, foot and horse supporting each other perfectly. Obviously O'Neill had managed to effect a total change of operations in his army.

Wingfield was alarmed at the amount of men who were being shot all around him. "Hold your fire until they are well within range!" he shouted. He raised his revolver and took aim at a skinny, bearded youth that had just shot one of his men through the temple. He steadied his arm and fired, shouting in triumph when he saw the youth fall. He hastened to reload and when he had gone through the complicated manoeuvre, the wounded youth had been rescued and carried out of range.

He turned to Ensign Hicks, who was on his right hand side. "The pikemen may be holding, but we are coming off worse than the Irish shot. They are discharging two shots, for every one of ours and they can move out of our range to reload. They are far more accurate than our men," he said in ill-concealed dismay.

Hicks, another recruit from the Brittany veterans, whom Wingfield had insisted on joining him in the rear, answered nervously. "Even allowing for the inexperience of our men, I think the Irish shot would compare with any shot that the English army can call upon. Damn the Lord Deputy and Bagenal! We might yet pay dearly for our lack of powder, if they dog us and attempt to force the issue."

As he spoke, the Irish withdrew, their horse galloping away over the bogs while their foot travelled lightly across it. The Irish disengaged right along the field. Their square had repulsed the English horse before retreating to the safety of the bogs. An eerie silence fell over the plain. The English soldiers stood still, nervously clutching their weapons, as they looked anxiously in the direction of the retreating enemy. The Irish disappeared behind the hill. The English found the sudden disengagement almost as frightening as the original howling charge of their enemy. After a few moments, Wingfield gave the order, "Marching formation," and the men broke the carefully formed square, revealing the dead and wounded in their midst. "Place the badly wounded in the wagons," Wingfield ordered. "Anyone who can, must walk. I want their comrades to aid them. Bind up their wounds. Collect any weapons and powder from the dead and bring them with us."

Minutes later Wingfield walked up and down before his men, bellowing, "Before we march, I want you to reload. You were a disgrace to the Queen's army. Most of you loosed your first volley before the Irish were even within range. Next time, take your cue from the Irish, they seem to be no mean hands at estimating the actual range. When they fire, you return fire and not before. Any man who breaks that order, I'll have horse whipped if he succeeds in returning to Newry."

When the wounded had been tended to, the column marched again, more slowly now, because of the wounded amongst them.

O'Neill looked up at the late evening sun, which was beginning to sink behind the mountains beside him. He found it difficult to contain the elation, which consumed him. For over four hours, his men had held the ford at Clontibret and neither the English horse nor foot, had been able to force a way through. What most pleased him, was the performance of his own heavy horse. On three separate occasions, they had met the English cavalry and routed them. Never before had Irish horse been able to defeat their enemy in open battle. He looked around for Cormac and hastened over to him.

"A messenger from Maguire informs me that the rear is on the point of breaking. Twice already the formation wavered, but Maguire's cavalry was too light to push home its advantage. He seeks my heavier horse to destroy it fully. I will go to him with my bodyguard. Fifty such horse will achieve much," he said

"But your place is here with our own men. We must hold this pass for victory to be ours," Cormac argued.

"If we destroy one of their sections, the rest will not stand. They are much demoralised as it is," he said.

He turned to the captain of his bodyguard. "Come," he said. "We must aid Maguire. We will skirt the battlefield. Keep to the left, near the hills and a half mile further back, we will reach the rear."

"Yes, my Lord," O'Reilly replied.

Hugh drove his horse on, the light breeze a balm as the day was still very warm. As they skirted the battle, he heard a shout. "O'Neill, O'Neill, to me, to me!"

He turned in his saddle and saw a detachment of enemy horse gallop out from the battle. Even at a distance of over a thousand paces, he recognised its leader, William Seagrave, and his good spirits deserted him. Seagrave, a giant of a man at over six foot six, was a Palesman who had long held a personal grudge against Hugh. He was known for his prowess on the tiltyard and Hugh was anxious not to cross lances with him. He saw, however, that they would meet unless he turned and retreated to his men at the ford. This, he could not do.

"What do we do, my Lord?" O'Reilly asked.

"Turn and face them," Hugh answered resignedly.

His men reined in their horses and did as they were told.

"Do we charge, my Lord?" O'Reilly questioned.

"No, use your pistols. Wait until they are within range and make your shots count."

He watched his men draw a protective cordon, a hundred paces in front of him. Hugh knew that his strategy was risky. If their aim were not true, the attacking force would have the advantage. A man, stationary upon a horse, could not hope to unseat another at full charge. The distance closed between both bodies of men and, when they were no more than eighty paces apart, he heard O'Reilly shout, "Fire!"

The revolvers spat flame and smoke and his vision of the attacking horde was momentarily obscured. Then, with dismay, he saw Seagrave burst through his men and charge straight at him. Hugh spurred his horse savagely and rode to meet him. Seagrave smiled vindictively as he aimed his lance at Hugh.

Hugh concentrated, bringing all his will to bear upon the task at hand. He must aim his lance at Seagrave's chest. He knew that on impact, Seagrave's mount would be travelling at twice his speed and that Seagrave, himself, was much larger and stronger than he. He waited until they were only paces apart and then pulled hard on his horse's reins, causing it to rear and turn sharply away from Seagrave. Hugh saw a surprised look overspread his enemy's face but, he reacted quickly, managing to catch Hugh a glancing blow, almost unseating him.

Hugh rode on, desperately trying to remain mounted. Finally, he pulled himself upright, wheeled his horse around, anxious to locate Seagrave. He was dismayed to find him almost upon him. Once again, he pulled the reins hard to the left and Seagrave's lance missed him. Seagrave quickly disposed of it and Hugh saw him lean from his saddle, intent on grasping him. Desperately, he tried to evade his clutches but Seagrave was not to be denied. Hugh fell heavily from his horse. Both men hit the ground together and, much as Hugh tried to escape Seagrave's grip, he could not. Badly winded, they both rolled across the hard, blackened turf, before finally coming to rest. Seagrave, recovering first, rolled on top of him. Quickly, he placed a knee on one of Hugh's hands, raising his sword above his head. Hugh fumbled desperately for his dagger, but knew he would be too late. Then, there was a flash of metal and he saw Seagrave's arm and sword fly upwards. His blood pumped from the wound and flowed down upon Hugh's face. Seagrave's face betrayed a look of shock as he looked at his bleeding shoulder. Hugh, grasping his dagger, drove it deep under his armour and into his groin, pushing with all his strength. Seagrave screamed in agony as Hugh twisted the knife, thrusting it upwards until he reached his stomach, which he slit. Seagrave's innards spilled out upon Hugh in a bloody, stinking mess. One of his men rolled Seagrave off him and ran him through with his sword.

His men were now all around him and Hugh found himself being helped to his feet. He stood there for a moment, his heart racing, weak and in shock, now that the danger had passed. He looked around and saw his army streaming towards him, having abandoned the pass, Cormac at their head. Bagenal, taking advantage of the confusion, was grasping his opportunity and making for it.

Cormac rode up to him. "Hugh, are you wounded?" he asked anxiously.

"Why did you leave the pass undefended?" Hugh questioned angrily. "You have allowed them escape. They were all but beaten."

"Yes, but winning the battle was but a small matter when compared to ensuring your safety," Cormac replied. "Surely, you must see how we have proved ourselves. We need never fear an English army again."

Hugh paused and considered Cormac's words. He was right. Two days earlier it would have been unthinkable that the Queen's army could suffer such a humiliation. He would see to it that more would follow. He would draw off his forces and block the Moyry Pass, cutting Newry off from Dublin, confining the remnants of the army there. He would force the English to take them to Dublin by sea. It would be the ultimate defeat - proof that the Queen's army dared not show its face in the field.

He had shown his allies how successful his tactics could be, the controlled attacks on marching columns being the correct strategy to follow. From now on, the Queen would realise that every time she attempted such an operation, she courted disaster. He was content to await her next move, knowing that, through his agents, he would have advance knowledge of her plans. He was overjoyed to have dented her and Bagenal's arrogance. He had sworn that they would pay for having forced him into rebellion, and that payment was just beginning.

Chapter 12

Sir John Norris, Commander in Chief of Her Majesty's army in Ulster and his troop of bodyguards rode up the track leading to Henry Bagenal's house, outside Newry. He rode with difficulty as his left hand, which was injured, rested on his horse's saddle. A musket ball had passed through the muscle of his upper arm, luckily avoiding the bone, but now as the journey was drawing to a close, it throbbed painfully. He allowed it lie, limp and useless, while he held the reins in his right hand. He noticed the sentries, alert and watchful, scanning the surrounding country from the safety of the wall, encircling the house and grounds. He is taking adequate precautions to ensure his own safety, even though he is doing little for anyone else's, Sir John thought disparagingly. He had scant respect for Bagenal's military ability and had been incensed when he learned, on his arrival in Ireland, of the disaster at Clontibret. If they had waited another week, he could have led the army and the disaster could have been averted.

Sir John, however, did not think so meanly of his own abilities. He had served in Ireland before and had campaigned in Ulster with the first Earl of Essex and had shared the credit for the destruction of the McDonnells on Ratlin Island. He had then been appointed President of Munster and, after a number of years in that post, had been dispatched to the wars on the Continent. There, he gained much valuable experience in the Low Countries, in France, and was one of the few to emerge with credit from the disastrous English expedition to Portugal in 1589. He would have preferred to remain on the Continent where battles were fought on a larger scale, but had no choice in the matter. He resented being back again in Ireland and having to carry out the type of warfare that Irish campaigns necessitated.

This was the second mission that he had undertaken since that return. On arriving, he and the Lord Deputy, Russell, had marched north with a large army, proclaiming O'Neill traitor, and advanced through Armagh, intending to cross into Tyrone and capture Dungannon. However, when they reached the Blackwater, they were faced with an even larger army. After a stand off of some days, they decided not to attempt a passage, and returned instead to Newry via Armagh town. O'Neill had burnt the town but had spared the large stone built cathedral that was set atop an imposing hill, dominating the surrounding countryside. The English had promptly fortified it and placed a garrison inside. It made an excellent exchange for the fort that they had lost on the Blackwater.

Norris's second mission, upon which he was currently engaged, was the victualling of that new garrison. He had managed the first half of the job, successfully delivering half of the provisions. He had been only able to carry half of the necessary materials, owing to the lack of draught horses, so he would have to make another trip. He was in black humour at the lack of organisation that he saw all around him since his return to Ireland and rode noisily into Bagenal's court-yard, before dismounting angrily from his horse.

He marched quickly up the stone steps to the door of the house and rapped on it with the hilt of his sword. After a few minutes, the door opened and a servant appeared. "Where is your master?" Norris asked impatiently.

"He is not receiving visitors," the servant answered.

Norris grabbed the man's arm. "He will see the Queen's Lord General," he shouted. "Where is he? Lead me to him!"

The servant nodded, afraid of this enraged Englishman and Norris followed him along the narrow passageways. Bagenal had not been seen in Dublin since Clontibret. He had returned to his estate and remained there, stripped of all command. This was a blessing, as he had enough to do in trying to hold onto his own lands. The Irish victory had emboldened the natives who had risen up in an effort to sweep all English from Ulster. His closeness to the garrison at Newry and the soldiers he had been allowed for his own protection had saved him from such a disaster. Norris and the servant arrived before a door, to which the servant pointed, too afraid to enter. Norris released his grip on the man's arm, and he scuttled off down the passageway.

He opened the door and entered. The sight that met him stopped him dead. Slumped in a seat, in front of an empty fireplace, sat Bagenal with a large pitcher in front of him. Even from where he stood, Norris could smell the scent of whiskey mingled with the stale, sour odour of sweat and dirt. Bagenal was unshaven. Judging from the unkempt growth on his face, it had been weeks since water had been applied to it. His hair was lank and matted to his head. He was but an ugly shadow of the man Norris had known in his time as President of Munster. Surprise and shock registered on Bagenal's face on seeing his visitor. Norris strode over to the window and threw it open, allowing some fresh air into the chamber. "This is no way to live," he said angrily to Bagenal. "You look like you have gone native, man. Pull yourself together and stop drinking this poison." He took the pitcher, carried it to the casement, emptying its contents onto the earth outside.

Bagenal bristled at the analogy. "You have no knowledge of what it is to live among the Irish, trying to hold the country for Her Majesty."

"I do know that I sent you orders, demanding that you meet with my army at Dundalk, bringing with you as many draught horses as you could muster. Did you not receive my messages?" Norris asked heatedly.

"And where was I to get such horses? My tenants are all dead, my lands burned and all my livestock stolen. Everything that my family has built up over the years has been destroyed. I thought that by remaining here, I could defend my property, but I was mistaken. I have become a prisoner in my own house, unable to venture out without a strong armed force," Bagenal answered sourly.

"Your first duty is to Her Majesty," Norris reminded him impatiently. "You should never forget that."

Bagenal nodded. "Yes, and I have always tried to serve her before any consideration for my own self. But my selflessness has gained me naught. I have now only one aim remaining and that is to be revenged upon O'Neill."

"Well then, you should have answered my summons," Norris countered balefully. "You might have had your ambition realised."

Bagenal stopped short, not fully understanding the import of Norris' words. Curiosity seized him. "Why? Did your Lordship have occasion to engage him?"

"We did as we intended. We met with no trouble on our outward journey but on returning, we were attacked by O'Neill's horse, midway between Armagh and Newry. It was an affair of small numbers only, but the cavalry fighting was brisk. I was wounded in the arm," Norris answered.

"Gravely?" Bagenal asked.

"It is but a scratch and will heal," Norris answered brusquely. "My brother, Sir Thomas, unfortunately received a more serious wound in the thigh. We drove the traitors off, but it is not a good portent that they venture to attack in such open country."

Bagenal ran his hand through his greasy hair. "The only thing that gives me comfort in my misfortune, is that finally Essex is in agreement with Cecil that O'Neill must be destroyed," he said.

Norris looked at him for a few moments, wondering if he should divulge Cecil's instructions, given to him before he left London. Finally, he decided that it was unavoidable. Bagenal would eventually get to hear of the disagreement between the two camps at court. "Things have changed. Cecil in now in favour of coming to some peace arrangement with O'Neill. He ordered me to do everything possible to bring one about."

Bagenal leaped to his feet. "You cannot mean it, Sir. After his treachery at Clontibret, the man must hang like any common criminal. Who has intervened on his behalf? Ormonde? He was ever too soft with that arch rebel!"

"Ormonde did make representations on his behalf, but Cecil would not be swayed by such pleadings. No, it is more serious than that. A letter that O'Neill and O'Donnell sent to the Spanish King has fallen into our hands. In it, they request Spanish aid in their fight against us," Norris answered.

"So, we have the proof that we need. He should be hung, drawn and quartered for such treachery. I have long dreamed of having such confirmation in my hands," Bagenal said with animation.

Norris recognised immediately Bagenal's obsession with revenging himself on O'Neill. His lack of overview would always preclude him from appreciating the broader interest. He could govern neither his temper nor enthusiasm. Such men made him uneasy. He could never trust them with matters requiring diplomacy. Still, he would have to attempt to make him comprehend the fragile situation that existed, not only in Ireland but in England itself.

"You do not comprehend the risks. In their letter, they claim to be fighting for the establishment of the Catholic religion and have made an offer of the Kingdom of Ireland to King Philip. They have said that if they receive adequate assurances of aid from him, before the feast of St. Philip and St. James next year, they will not make peace with us," Norris explained.

"But what likelihood is there that he will send help to such a collection of base rebels?" Bagenal asked in disbelief.

"You know how King Philip clings deeply to Catholicism and there are many in England itself, who practice it secretly. The Irish have chosen the perfect means to couch an appeal for aid from him. He is now old and in poor health. He longs to save more souls for the church, before he dies. What is even more worrying, is that the letter makes plain that this is not the first appeal to him," Norris answered.

"But you have the letter. Use it against him. Do not make peace. You can never trust O'Neill's oath. He will lie and lead you astray while he continues to deal with the Spanish," Bagenal urged eagerly.

"We have also learned that an English seminary priest in O'Neill's entourage, was sent through Scotland to Spain, with a copy of the letter. He slipped through our hands and made it safely there. The Queen wants us to enter into full scale negotiations as soon as possible, to stay their plans," Norris replied.

"But there is enough time to destroy them, before King Philip can aid them," Bagenal said urgently.

"Yes, if they stood and fought us in open battle," Norris answered wearily, tired of Bagenal's resistance to his explanations. Bagenal of all people should know of the difficulties involved in trying to gain a quick victory.

"Even if the Spanish do send ships, our navy will do to them what was done to the Great Armada seven years since," Bagenal said belligerently.

He has been too long stuck in this backwater and has lost sight of how times have changed, Norris thought. "Things have moved on since then," Norris countered. "King Philip has learned from that disaster and from his past failures."

"Our best men can still make cowards of any Spanish," Bagenal argued.

"Sir Francis Drake and Sir John Hawkins sailed this summer to attempt a raid on the Atlantic treasure fleets. They were beaten off by the far superior Spanish force. Hawkins died soon after. Drake did not long survive him, and died of dysentery," Norris said with genuine regret.

Bagenal paused, considering the news. "These are indeed sad tidings. The nation will rue the loss of two such brave commanders," he said at length.

"More than you can comprehend. We have learned through our spies in Spain that Philip is preparing a formidable Armada to invade England or Ireland before the end of the century. Plans are only at the initial stages, but the Queen is anxious that the Irish rebels be brought back to loyalty as soon as possible. She does not wish any invading force to receive help from renegades," Norris explained patiently.

"It would be better if she sent over an army large enough to eradicate all traitors in Ireland. Otherwise, they could change their allegiance, should such an invasion become a reality," Bagenal argued.

"If Her Majesty had the means, that would be the proper course. As you well know, the last two harvests in England have been the worst in living memory. Famine stalks the land and the people die of starvation. Men find it hard to get work. Any further taxation on her subjects to fund expensive, unpopular foreign wars, could result in rebellion," Norris continued.

"Those men who have no work, should be enlisted in the army and made serve their country," Bagenal continued doggedly.

Norris sighed wearily. "Being forced to serve in foreign wars is no longer finding favour with the populace. We are living in dangerous times. Subjects are beginning to flout the Queen's commands. Her Majesty must be aware of how much she can ask of her people, without pushing them too far."

"But the Queen must rule and subjects must obey. It is the natural law. Otherwise, all is anarchy," Bagenal shouted, forgetting himself.

Norris was losing patience. Bagenal had never gained any experience outside of this small province in which he had grown up. It would have been far better for him if he had spent a number of years in Her Majesty's service on the Continent, like his younger brother, Samuel, who appeared to be a much brighter and reliable man, he thought.

"She will lose her kingdom to the Spanish King, if she does not have the men to defend it," Bagenal continued. "From what you tell me, there is no hope. The Privy Council and the Queen seem to be content to blind themselves to the troubles that are brewing and take no steps to address them."

Norris looked at Bagenal who had slumped back into his chair. He had been advised by Cecil to bring him into his confidence. Cecil worried that the enmity between O'Neill and Bagenal might hinder the negotiation of a truce. Looking at the wreck of a man before him, Norris wondered if it had been a wise decision, but he was obliged to do as he was bid.

"There is hope. A decision has been taken and it is a brave one. For once, all are in agreement, even Cecil, who believes an attack would be cheaper and safer than waiting on events. If England is not to be taken by surprise, prompt action will have to be taken. There must be no more of the pinprick raids that we have mounted against the Spanish in the past. We will conduct a major attack on Spanish interests early next year. The plans are being drawn up and will cause a major drain on Her Majesty's finances. That is why she does not want a prolonged, expensive struggle in Ireland," Norris confided.

"And will we bring the war to Spain itself?" Bagenal asked, suddenly hopeful.

"The location of where the attack will be mounted, will remain a secret, as we must not allow the Spanish learn of our plans," Norris replied.

"And who will command the venture?" Bagenal asked.

"The command is not yet decided. Nevertheless, I hope Her Majesty organises it in better fashion than she has done here. At least the Lord Deputy stayed in Dublin this time and let me carry out my task," Norris replied with satisfaction. As long as Russell stayed out of Ulster, he would do his utmost to bring the hostilities to an end. He found Russell's overbearing arrogance impossible to support, nor had he any great regard for his military ability.

Bagenal nodded sympathetically. "I am prepared to do what I can to aid you in making war on the rebels, but I would be of no use in any peace talks that you might undertake," he said.

"Very well," Norris replied. "It would help me greatly if you could find more pack horses. O'Neill's men raid the Pale, stealing what live-stock that they can find. The support that I have received from that quarter has been scant. The Palesmen wish their own lands to be defended, but the least they could do, is supply our army with the required horses. It's to protect them, that we are waging this war."

Bagenal agreed. "For many years now, they have been unreliable in times of need. I will do my best to get you the horses."

"Good," Norris answered. "Now I must ride back to Newry and organise the wagons for the return march to Armagh. You have but a week." With that he turned and proceeded to leave the chamber.

"Wait, I shall see you out," Bagenal said and hurried after him.

It was late September, over three months since Mabel had returned to Dungannon, and she had found the time both difficult and demean-ing. Hugh had ignored her presence, avoiding her company com-pletely. Dungannon was even lonelier than before, but preferable to her brother's house. Henry Hovendon had arranged accommodation for her in one of the wooden dwellings that had sprung up outside where the castle walls had been.

All stone structures at Dungannon, including the castle and its surrounding walls, had been demolished. Initially, Hugh had started reinforcing the castle according to a design drawn up by Pedro Blanco, his Spanish captain, intending to transform it into a fortress. On discovering, however, that the English were equipped with power-ful siege guns, he had revised his plan and instead decided to dis-mantle it. He ordered all his sublords to do likewise, and now there was not one single stone building left in all of Tyrone that the English could usurp and garrison. All his valuables, furniture, weapons and powder reserves, he had consigned to secret crannógs, hidden in the most impenetrable parts of his domain. If he ever had to abandon Dungannon in the face of overwhelming odds, he could torch the town and the English would not gain anything from its capture.

Hovendon had seen to it that two servants were allocated to Mabel. She found Dungannon utterly changed from the sleepy, rustic place that she had first entered when she came north as a young bride. There was an air of industry and confidence about the place. It seemed to have become the hub of Ulster, to which regular delegations arrived from all over the province, seeking audiences with Hugh. A large encampment had sprung up to the south, where Hugh's army was gar-risoned. Every day, it undertook several hours of drill, and the sight and sounds of the marching men disturbed Mabel. In addition, the priests of the Counter Reformation were encouraged to spread their message of a just war in the name of religion, and Hugh's callous use of creed for his own ends, appalled her.

She had been horrified when he had joined the rebels and attacked the Queen's army. Never would she forget the evening that Hugh's victorious army returned to Dungannon. The celebrations had continued for a week, with an abandonment and revelry that she could never have imagined. She thought of how her brother in Newry must feel. He had failed so completely. This war was such a waste of lives, she thought. She could feel doom and death in the air and worried for the future. But other, more personal matters oppressed her.

She had learned of Hugh's trial marriage to Ciara, soon after her arrival in Dungannon and felt betrayed by him, seeing then, with absolute clarity, that he had never really loved her. At first, she had felt hatred and envy of Ciara, but she soon came to realise, that she too was even more a pawn in Hugh's politicking than she herself had ever been.

Hugh had finally decided to take the title of The O'Neill and was to be inaugurated in the traditional manner, dating back to the dawn of Irish Celtic society. Turlough had died a week earlier, and now Hugh had no longer any reason to delay assuming the title. From all over the North and as far away as Connaught, men were travelling to witness the inauguration of this latest O'Neill Chieftain. The victory at Clontibret had greatly added to his prestige among the native Irish and had given the event an added significance. Nevertheless, Mabel felt that he was compounding his original error of rebellion. Hugh had been expressly forbidden by the Queen to accept The O'Neillship and until now, good sense had persuaded him to leave it unclaimed, even though Turlough had resigned in his favour, two years previously. Now, as Mabel walked through what were once the castle grounds, observing the occupants preparing to travel to the festivities at Tullyhoe, she decided that she too would attend. She had no doubt that Hugh would see her as an unwelcome guest. Even though she would have to undertake the journey alone and on foot, the magnitude of the event persuaded her to venture forth.

She reached Tullyhoe late in the afternoon, exhausted and feverish after her exertions. It had taken much longer to complete the journey than she had expected. She had found that she had to stop and rest frequently, as her limbs were lacking the strength they once possessed. She had been ill with the ague on a number of occasions since her return to Dungannon, and her constitution had been weakened further. Inactivity and loss of appetite had contributed in rendering her thinner and feebler than before.

On the journey, none of her fellow travellers could have suspected that she was their Chieftain's English wife. Her return to Dungannon had been kept secret, on Hugh's orders, and nobody would expect her to be walking the roads like a common churl.

Now, she looked in amazement at the crowds that had gathered around Tullyhoe. The landscape was uninspiring, - a straggle of low hills, poor grass and ground, broken by much rock and stone. All around, trestle tables had been erected and piled high with food and drink. Mabel made for the nearest one, which was surrounded by a heaving throng of people, anxious to partake of the free hospitality. The sun had made her thirsty and she eagerly sought something to drink. She attempted to join the horde of revellers, but found herself being jostled by the crowd and unable to make any headway. Disappointed, she sat on a nearby rock watching the multitude.

Deep in her own thoughts, she started as someone addressed her from behind. She turned and saw one of the servants from Dungannon, holding a tankard of beer out to her. "If you are thirsty, Madam?" she said gently.

Mabel, gratified at her kindness, took the drink and thanked her.

"But you must make haste, Madam, the ceremony is all but over," she said as she hurried off to join her companions, who headed in the direction of the cheering throngs. Mabel drained the vessel thirstily and looked about her. The surrounding countryside was a sea of surging bodies. All Hugh's sub-lords were present with their families and supporters. The event was open to all and many of the churls had made the journey, along with their families. No one wished to miss one of the great events of the Gaelic world, the installation of a new O'Neill Chieftain.

Mabel felt light-headed after the beer, having had nothing to eat since the previous day. She rose unsteadily and walked towards the hill. As she approached, the crowd thickened and she found that she had to push her way through. The drink gave her courage and she commanded the churls to let her pass. Recognising the tone as that of one used to giving orders, they parted and she made her way slowly to the front, until she came to a line of soldiers. She looked up at the inaugural throne where the ceremony was taking place. Again, the crowd renewed its cheers. She observed Hugh, sumptuously dressed in black velvet, a red cloak generously draped about his shoulders, his head bare his hands raised, addressing the crowd. Once quiet had descended on the multitude, he spoke. "My people, I am proud to be elected to this great title, which many valiant men have held in the past, to be part of a tradition that stretches back in an unbroken line over the centuries."

He paused as the crowd clamoured its approval. After a few moments, he continued, "As you know, the English intend destroying our past and our traditions, reducing us to their customs and way of life, robbing us of everything that we hold dear, our language, laws and religion. We cannot allow that happen. There comes a time and place when one must fight and that time is now and the place is here."

Again, the crowd burst into a mighty roar, taking up the chant, "Fight! Fight! Fight!" Hugh held up his hands again for silence, but this time had to wait longer as the crowd had become almost ungovernable. Mabel looked around the assembled multitude and saw that everyone present was united in lust for blood and war. She felt an outsider, aghast at the way Hugh was churning up such hatred and bitterness. Finally, the crowd quietened and he continued. "I appeal to all of you to follow me and to trust me. I do not promise you an easy road, but I do promise victory in the end. The time has come to roll the English tide backwards and drive the enemy out of Ireland."

The crowd roared back its approval. Mabel knew that Hugh's people had been confused and frustrated for years by his unwillingness to fight, by his circumspection and diplomacy. Here, at last, was something they could understand and respect. He concluded. "Now it is the time for celebration. Let us eat, drink and be merry. Lámh dhearg abú!"

The crowd took up the O'Neill war cry and it rang around the hills. Hugh departed to the ceremonial hall, followed by his bishops, clansmen and invited guests. It was a structure of enormous proportions that had been recently erected. Splendid banners of rich silk, bearing the O'Neill crest, adorned the facade. Mabel perceived the wondrous handcraft of many master craftsmen who must long have laboured over the intricate Celtic carvings etched on the surface of the splendid granite walls.

She spied Rose suddenly and felt a desire to speak to her. Perhaps she could talk some sense into Hugh. She pushed her way down towards the line of soldiers who were holding back the main throng of people from the ceremonial area. She tried to attract Rose's attention, but she was not looking in her direction. Mabel reached the line of soldiers and looked in vain for a face that she could recognise. She attempted to force her way through, but the soldiers stopped her, ignoring her pleas. She shouted after Rose, but with the distance between them and the noise of the crowd, she had little hope of being heard.

Indeed, Rose herself had much to dwell upon as she followed Hugh Roe. Her emotions were confused. She knew how much her father had looked forward to this day and was happy for him, but there was part of her that felt disquiet at the speed of change in the political situation immediately about her. She paused, thinking she heard someone calling her and she turned, looking towards the mass of people upon the hill opposite. It was awash with bodies. She scanned the faces and then saw Mabel, beckoning vigorously to her. She called to Hugh Roe who turned towards her.

"Look, Hugh Roe, it's Mabel," she said excitedly.

Hugh Roe looked and his countenance changed. "What is she doing here?" he asked disapprovingly.

"But why should she not be here?" Rose asked in surprise. "Father said that she was ill, but she must have felt better. I should go to her."

"Your father will not approve of her attendance here. She should have stayed away," he answered abruptly.

"But she returned to warn Father of his proclamation as a traitor. She never betrayed him," Rose said.

"She was not invited. Your father does not need his people to be reminded that he once married an English woman. English people are not welcome any more in the North, " Hugh Roe said angrily.

"They are still married, Hugh Roe. I pity her. I think she deserves more from Father," Rose retorted, sensing that such an overt defence would anger her husband even further.

"It is but a mockery of a marriage. They do not live as man and wife. What use is such a marriage, where there is no hope of children? It would be better if it was finished and he was free to make a better union," Hugh Roe said scowlingly.

Rose blanched. She looked at her husband who did not return her gaze, turning instead to look after the other invited guests who were fast disappearing into the ceremonial hall. Rose was cut to the quick. Hugh Roe could not be so insensitive that he would not realise how hurtful his words were to her, she thought. She considered how he had been away for long periods, campaigning in Connaught and in Ulster and how, since his return, he had been aloof and distant, but she had attributed that to the concerns he had with the ongoing war. Obviously, she had been wrong. She had been keenly aware of his desire for a child and, each month, she had hoped that his wish would be granted, but so far, her prayers had not been answered. Did he wish to be free of their union, despite all his protestations of devotion only a short while previously, she wondered. Surely not. He turned back towards her, his eyes cold. "Are you coming?" he asked impatiently.

She paused, considering his question, and then, for the first time ever, disregarded his wishes. "No, I will follow you. I must talk with Mabel," she said reluctantly.

Hugh Roe turned and, without a backward glance, walked briskly away to join the others. Rose watched him go, before turning in the direction of Mabel.

Now that the formal part of the inauguration was over, Hugh had two more matters to conclude before he could enjoy the rest of the occasion. There was one guest in particular that he longed to meet. His progress to the trestle table was slow, as he continually was obliged to stop and accept the congratulations, which were offered from all present. He scanned the hall for the one he yearned to see, but could find no sight of her. His heart sank as he considered the possibility that she might not have come, but then dismissed the notion. He had not seen her father yet and he would not have dared miss this day.

He spied his three children by Siobhán, wending their way through the throng, towards him. Could that be Órla, he wondered in surprise. It was almost a year since he had last seen her, having been absent the last two times they had come to visit Dungannon. She had grown and matured in that time and the resemblance to her mother was more marked than before. She has become an attractive young woman, he thought, as he mentally calculated her present age. She must be thirteen now, he conjectured. He looked with pride at his two sons, Hugh Óg who was now ten and Henry who must be eight. They have turned into handsome young lads, he thought. He had the finest of tutors employed so that they would have the best education possible. In another few years, they would return to Dungannon and he would have to initiate them in the running of the Chieftainship.

They stopped before him, smiling shyly up at him. "Can I come home to Dungannon now that you're The O'Neill and join your army and fight the English?" Hugh Óg asked excitedly. Hugh laughed long and loudly. It was typical of the lad. He was always anxious to learn new things, impatient to grow up. He reminded him of himself at the same age and of how he longed to be with his own father, riding into battle. Hugh looked at Henry who remained in the background. He was much quieter and more serious than Hugh Óg. Henry nodded at him and Órla asked, "Can we come home to Dungannon, Father? We have learned as much as we can. It's so quiet where we stay, we never see anything and we hear of so many exciting things that are happening at home."

Hugh smiled. "Not for another while," he replied. "Dungannon is very busy and is not safe for you, at present. We do not know if the English will attempt to take it again soon. I would prefer to have you all safely away from there," he replied.

"I wouldn't mind the danger, I'd like to be there," Órla answered.

Hugh Óg added, "I'd like to help. We've heard of all the battles you've won and it's so dull and tedious just doing our lessons with our tutors."

"No, you must remain where you are. Use the time well and prepare for the responsibilities that will be yours some day. That is your duty and, when the time is right, then I'll send for you and teach you all I know," Hugh said and then lost his train of thought as he saw Hugh Magennis and his daughter, Catherine. Hugh felt his pulse quicken at the sight of her. She was as beautiful as he remembered and the white, closely fitting brocade gown she wore, became her marvellously well.

She smiled on reaching him. Her father addressed him first. "Well done, Hugh. You are the first man since your grandfather, Conn, to hold both titles and only the second man ever to do so. You have attained the greatest honours that both the English and your own people can grant you. You must be very proud."

Hugh nodded. After Bagenal's defeat, Magennis had no option but to change sides and join his confederation of Irish Chieftains, whatever his private thoughts on the matter might have been. Hugh bowed in acknowledgement, then turned to Catherine. "Well Catherine, I'm glad that you could come today," he said gently.

She smiled again and he checked an urge to reach out and smooth the wisps of dark hair that had fallen across her forehead. "I'm delighted to be here," she answered. "I will tell my grandchildren about the time I saw the great Hugh O'Neill being inaugurated at Tullyhoe," she said playfully.

Hugh felt Hugh Óg pulling at his cloak. He looked down at the small face of his son, already bored and jealous of his attention to these two strangers. "I'm hungry," he said. "Will you come and have something to eat with us, Father?"

"I will join you shortly. I have some business to discuss with our guests first," Hugh answered.

"Are they your children?" Catherine asked with interest.

"Yes, Órla, Hugh Óg and Henry. These are my children by Siobhán," Hugh explained.

"I will see that they have something to eat. You and Father can talk and we will join you afterwards," Catherine said with a smile, taking the two boys by the hand and leading them away. Órla followed, looking none too pleased that Catherine had usurped her role as guardian. Hugh watched Catherine as she disappeared into the crowd and then self-consciously turned to Magennis. To his surprise, he saw that he too was watching the retreating figures, but it was upon Órla that his attention had become fixed. Magennis turned to Hugh when she had disappeared from sight. "Well," he said. "You have business to discuss with me?" he asked.

"Yes," Hugh answered. "I want to propose an alliance. A closer one than that, which we already have. A marriage alliance."

Magennis looked uncomfortable. "If you are proposing a marriage between you and Catherine, I must say no. I have heard of the two wives you keep at Dungannon. I will not allow my daughter become part of your collection. She deserves more from a husband than that," he said.

"I agree. Catherine does deserve more and she shall have my undivided love. Sorley Bwee's daughter means nothing to me. She was never my wife and the arrangement I entered into with her father was an error. As for Mabel, she returned here against my will. As soon as these present troubles pass, our divorce can be formalised," Hugh confided earnestly.

"So, you should not talk of Catherine until such problems are resolved. Even then, how would I know that you would not turn your back on her, like you are doing now on these other two women?" Magennis asked.

"I will not. As a man gets older, he learns wisdom. I know that Catherine and I could be happy together," Hugh answered.

"There is no point in discussing the matter. You are not free and Catherine is no concubine or servant with whom you can trifle. I will not see her honour besmirched," Magennis said, with more than a hint of defiance.

"You should consider remarrying yourself. You are still a young man. You could have another family, the son that you deserve to carry on your line. It must be lonely for you since your wife died," Hugh said placatingly.

"I manage," Magennis answered abruptly.

"As part of our alliance, I am prepared to offer you my daughter, Órla, in marriage. A daughter for a daughter. Neither of us need be lonely," Hugh said, with as much persuasion as he could muster.

He watched Magennis's face closely in an effort to read it. He saw initial surprise cross it followed by, what to him seemed, a long period of reflection. Magennis turned and looked in the direction Hugh's children and his daughter had gone, before turning back to Hugh. "When you are a free man, we will talk about your proposal," he said in a neutral tone.

"And until then, you will not give Catherine's hand to any other?" Hugh asked, anxious to secure Magennis to a bargain.

"She will not remain unmarried for ever," Magennis answered equivocally, "but she will not be marrying in the immediate future either."

Just then Maguire came up behind O'Neill and thumped him energetically on the back. "Well done," he boomed. "We've made a decent Irishman of you at last. It's a great day, now that you've finally claimed your birthright. There'll be no looking back from here out. Finally, we'll deal with the English once and for all."

Hugh looked at Maguire's beaming face. He seemed even more pleased than Hugh himself. O'Neill knew that he would need to divulge his plans to him and the sooner the better. "Where's O'Donnell?" he asked.

"He's over there," Maguire answered with a laugh. "He's drinking like they'll be no tomorrow. Even I could not match him at the moment."

"Tell him I have to talk with him. Summon him, before he has too much to drink. We must talk in private. Meet me where the horses are stabled," Hugh ordered. Maguire disappeared into the throng. Hugh returned his attention to Magennis. "We will talk of these matters again, my friend," he said. "We have much to gain in agreeing with one another."

Magennis bowed low and Hugh left the swarming crowd of celebrating revellers.

The stables, to the rear of the hall, were protected by Hugh's personal bodyguard. After a few minutes, Maguire and O'Donnell appeared. "Well Hugh, you are quite an orator. You have talents, which I never suspected," O'Donnell said in mock surprise.

Hugh noted the flush of inebriation in his son-in-law's cheeks. "I must speak with you. Come, I have prepared a tent nearby where we will be able to talk without fear of being overheard," O'Neill said. He turned and walked to where one of his bodyguards stood, holding three horses. Maguire looked questioningly at O'Donnell but the latter merely shrugged his shoulders in response. Without a word or a backward glance, O'Neill leapt onto his horse and galloped away. O'Donnell and Maguire followed after him.

After a short, ten-minute ride, they came to a number of tents beside a broad, straggling brook. One of Hugh's cooks and several of his serving women were busy preparing a meal and the smell of roasting beef, lingered tantalisingly in the air. All three dismounted and followed Hugh into the largest tent, guarded by six of his bodyguards. Inside, was a low trestle table, around which were cushions made from fern and covered with cloth. The table was set with simple wooden platters and meaders and on it rested a large mound of freshly baked oatcakes and a large earthenware flagon of Spanish sack. Hugh's principal bodyguard stuck his head into the tent and asked, "Will you eat now, my Lord?"

Hugh nodded and the soldier withdrew. Within a few minutes, the servants entered to serve the beef, which was cut into joints and flavoured with wild rosemary, garlic and cress.

When they were alone again, O'Donnell fixed Hugh with a questioning glance and asked, "Well, Hugh, what is this about?"

Maguire added. "Yes. You've made me curious. It must be important to make you leave your own celebration."

"I wanted you to know as soon as possible. This morning, I dispatched Hovendon to Dublin with a letter for the Lord Deputy. I have sued for peace and a pardon," Hugh answered. He paused to see what effect his words would have on the two men. O'Donnell's mouth fell open in astonishment and Maguire, incensed, jumped to his feet, knocking over one of the leather gourds. "You cannot betray our cause. We had the upper hand over the English at Clontibret and can do even more damage, should they come into Ulster again. It is folly to talk of pardon and peace. Who wants their concord?"

O'Donnell added. "But Hugh, what of your talk of victory just now and of driving the English out of Ulster? You are either The O'Neill or the Earl of Tyrone. You must choose which. You cannot be both."

Hugh had expected such a reaction and was not surprised. "I am still determined to gain the final victory, but sometimes a circuitous route is the wisest one to follow," he said. He sensed O'Donnell's ire.

"There will be no surrender," Hugh Roe countered, "never by me, in any case. I have made an oath before God and I will never rest until I carry it out. We have promises of Spanish help, so why should we seek a pardon?"

Hugh wondered how he could make him understand? "Hugh Roe, Spanish promises are one thing, Spanish aid is quite a different matter. I have had a letter from Ormonde. He says that the English are prepared to enter into discussions, to grant us pardons and concede to some of our demands. It can do no harm to open up negotiations. While we are so engaged, there must be a truce between us. We can delay in this manner, until we see if Spanish help indeed arrives."

O'Donnell shook his head. "But if we are engaged in truce, then we cannot extend our area of influence. Niall Garve and I have done well in Connaught. All the province is in revolt, save Galway and Clare. We should continue to spread the war to other parts of the country."

Maguire nodded in agreement. "I agree with Hugh Roe. If we treat with the English now, it will be perceived as weakness. Our followers will not know how to interpret such a course and might be tempted to make their own deals with the English. The unity that we have built up could crumble into dust. What you propose is very hazardous."

Hugh sighed. "Yes, it is that, but I have to ask you to trust me. There are only two ways that we can win this war. Firstly, by getting

Spanish help or secondly, by protracting this war and inducing a continuous haemorrhage in the Queen's finances. Eventually, she may conclude that Ireland is not worth the cost. A truce will not affect our standing, but will be a serious blow to Her Majesty's. We will discuss terms, but we need not accept them. In the meantime, we gain time."

"I will not relinquish any of the gains I have made in Connaught," O'Donnell retorted.

"That will be a condition of the truce, we all hold what we have," Hugh answered in an attempt to mollify him. "It will give us more time to prepare ourselves. And we can save expenditure by standing down part of our armies. I must know now if you agree to enter into negotiations?" Hugh asked.

"Only under those conditions," O'Donnell answered.

"And you?" Hugh asked Maguire.

"I will let you two negotiate and concern myself with my own Lordship," he answered.

"Good. We must give leadership to the rest of our people, ensuring that they follow our wishes and make peace only when we instruct them," Hugh said. "But come, we will rejoin the celebrations now that we have agreed this business." Upon his suggestion, all three rose and left the tent.

Chapter 13

Mabel's accommodation was at the opposite end of Dungannon to that of Hugh's. Henry Hovendon guided Rose through the hastily constructed wooden buildings that had sprung up since the demolition of the castle. An urgent summons from him had induced her to undertake this visit. Mabel was ill and Henry had been told by Hugh's physician that she would not recover. On meeting Rose, Henry had urged that they visit Mabel directly. Any delay, he had said, might prove disastrous. Henry pointed to a small, wooden structure at the end of a row of dwellings and strode quickly in its direction.

"Is there no hope?" Rose asked.

Henry stopped and turned directly to Rose, his handsome face, corrugated in a worried frown. "There is always hope of a miracle, but it will take one if she is to recover," he replied. Rose could not fail to notice the note of sadness that darkened his voice before he turned and hurried once again towards the dwelling.

"And what ails her?" Rose asked anxiously

"Ague," Henry answered with a shudder.

"But it can be cured. Weakened whiskey and a light diet and it will pass eventually," Rose said, eager to allay Henry's obvious disquiet.

"It keeps recurring with her. When she is afflicted, she vomits continually, coupled with a loss of great quantities of blood. Her strength is all but gone. It's a sorry sight to see such a woman so reduced," Henry said despondently.

"And has everything been done?" Rose asked, her face betraying her mounting concern.

"Yes. She has requested to see you often in the last few days," he continued. "Indeed, she has asked to see others too, her sister, brother and Hugh, but you were the only one whom I could prevail upon to come. Hopefully, your visit will give her some comfort."

Rose was disquieted at what Henry had left unsaid - her father's lovelessness towards his former wife and how ruthlessly single-minded he could be in ignoring her situation. Such callousness wounded Rose, but she loyally struggled to see the dilemma from his point of view. "You know Father is with Hugh Roe at the truce parleys. Of course, I had to come on hearing such ill tidings regarding Mabel," she volunteered. "But how is it that you are back in Dungannon? Were you not advising Hugh Roe and Father at the talks? Has an agreement been reached?"

"Yes. The Queen has conceded to practically all our demands, except for liberty of conscience. Of course, there will be commissions to sort out the finer points," Henry answered as they reached Mabel's abode.

"Why, that is indeed good news. So, will Hugh Roe and Father return today?" Rose asked.

"No," Henry answered. "All the Irish Lords, even Maguire, with the sole exceptions of Hugh Roe and your father, must make personal submissions before the commissioners in the market place at Drogheda tomorrow. Hugh Roe and Hugh must stay to witness those submissions before returning home. But come, we must make our visit. I have little stomach for celebrating or even talking about that news, since I heard the sad tidings about Mabel," he said, upon entering the dwelling.

Rose followed and immediately was assaulted by the stench of decay. Henry passed quickly through the empty first chamber and knocked gently on the door to the next, before pushing it open, calling softly, "Mabel."

She lay on a narrow bed, dozing. At its foot, the physician whom Henry had summoned was sitting, half-asleep. The only window in the chamber was obscured by a large blanket draped over it, so that the light inside was murky. The room smelt of vomit, blood and excrement and Rose felt her gorge rise in her throat. Henry went to the window and violently pulled the blanket down, allowing fresh air drift in.

"It's better that she rest and the dark will help her do so," the physician protested.

"She needs some fresh air, not this foul stench," Henry answered roughly. "Go wait outside. We will send for you should we have need," he ordered.

The physician rose and withdrew silently. Mabel stirred in the bed and attempted to raise herself onto her elbow. "Is that you, Hugh? Have you come to see me at last?" she asked uncertainly.

"No, Mabel. It's me, Henry. And look, I've brought Rose with me to visit you," he answered.

Mabel sank back onto the bed. Rose was shocked at what she beheld. Mabel's face was as haggard as that of an old woman and the matted wisps of hair that hung around her head, were streaked with grey. On a stool by the head of the bed, was a pile of torn linen strips and a basin spattered with bloodied vomit. Underneath it, was a pail covered by a piece of cloth, around which, flies buzzed. Mabel held out an emaciated hand, which Rose grasped, noticing how cold and clammy it was. Henry strode over to the door, opened it and angrily shouted to the physician. "Clean up in here, and do not leave the chamber in such a fashion again."

The physician returned and speedily did as he was bid. Rose bent over and quickly kissed Mabel on the cheek. "Ah, Mabel, it is as well that I have come to nurse you. Henry says that you are on the mend. How do you feel?" she asked.

Mabel shook her head. "You are just in time to say farewell, Rose, but it was good of you to come. I have the accursed Irish ague - revenge on us for coming into this country and God's revenge on me for the path I have chosen in life," she answered in barely suppressed agitation.

"It will pass," Rose answered with forced brightness. "You have had it before and got over it. It will be no different this time."

"Nay Rose, it has weakened me too much. I am paying for my sins, sins of pride and vanity. Death and destruction are what my sins have brought to this land? It is I who am to blame for every death that has occurred because of the enmity between my brother and Hugh," Mabel said with rising distress.

"Nay, Mabel," Rose answered in concern for her friend's upset. "Those matters have naught to do with you."

"But it was my wickedness that caused this war. How many will die before it comes to an end?" Mabel asked in agitation.

"None. There is to be a peace. Now, is not that good news?" Rose asked, hoping that this communication would quell Mabel's growing restlessness.

Mabel became still, with difficulty trying to grasp the implication of Rose's words. "Can it be true?" she asked Henry, who had remained standing at the bottom of the bed.

Henry nodded. "Yes it is. All will be peaceful again, as it was. Hugh has been pardoned and there will be no more reason for war between both races."

Mabel sank back onto her befouled pallet. "Thank God. My prayers have been answered. I was so afraid that Hugh and Henry would kill one another. You have indeed brought good news," she said and closed her eyes, exhausted from the effort that speaking had required.

Rose watched her closely and after a few minutes, noted that Mabel's breathing took on the regularity of one sleeping. She turned to Henry. "She sleeps. The rest will do her good," she said.

"Yes," Henry replied. "I will take my leave. I have business to complete for your father. Come, you should have something to eat and get some rest. You must be weary after such a journey. The physician can send for us should there be any change."

Rose shook her head. "I will stay with her for awhile. I am not hungry."

Henry nodded. "As you wish. I will call again later," he said and then withdrew.

Rose sat by the window and looked out at the surrounding countryside. She found it foreign and strange. She missed the dominating presence of Dungannon Castle, its splendid edifice and bulwarks. Sadly, she recalled all Mabel's girlish enthusiasm for its decoration and finery and of her youthful energy expended on its embellishment. How things change, she thought. There is such little constancy in this life of ours. Such a train of thought drew her on to more melancholic reflection. She thought of Hugh and Mabel and their disintegrated marriage. Why had things to become so complicated, she wondered? Everything had augured so well at first, but all had changed. She thought of her own marriage and felt an icy grip clutch her heart. Despite her best endeavours, she felt Hugh Roe was drifting further and further from her. The war had not helped them. Rose's hopeful heart whispered, now that it was over perhaps things might get better. Please God, make it so, she prayed silently.

Her train of thinking was interrupted as Mabel heaved a heavy groan before waking and crying out sharply. Rose leaped from her chair and rushed to her side. "What is it, Mabel? What is the matter?"

"I had a dream," she panted in a frightened voice, " and in it, the Evil One came for me. Oh Rose, it fills me with dread. His eyes were glowing embers and his hands burned into my arm. I woke, just as the flames were engulfing me." She anxiously scanned her arm, trying to discern the Devil's imprint.

Rose laid her hand on her forehead, which was clammy and said, "It was but a dream, naught but fancy's work. You've confessed to the priest and received absolution."

"But have I really been forgiven? Have I repented sufficiently? I was so certain that my undertakings were just. But now, I know them to have been in error. Evil has come from my stubbornness. Oh Rose, I am so afraid!" Mabel cried out, her face assuming a look of absolute dread. She groaned in terror. "Help me Rose! He has followed me here from my dreams. Look, he approaches. Keep him away, Rose, do not let him take me!"

"Hush, Mabel, hush. There is no one here, but I. All this is but your imagining," Rose said, attempting to take Mabel's hand in hers. Mabel pulled her hand away and sat up. She was now staring in horror at a point over Rose's left shoulder. Rose glanced nervously behind and was relieved to see that the chamber was empty. Just then, Mabel emitted a long, agonised shriek, causing Rose to leap from the bed. "He thrusts his claws into my innards and I have such pain, such pain there," Mabel cried as tears of helplessness coursed down her cheeks.

Rose called urgently for the physician who hurried into the chamber. Mabel lay back in the bed, writhing and moaning.

"It's not good," he said, perceiving the slime on Mabel's lips and how her glistening face had taken on a greenish pallor. She began vomiting and purging. He and Rose worked anxiously trying to ease her.

Mabel retched violently into the basin. All that issued forth, was a dark, bloody mucus, but she continued, as if expelling the very stomach from her body. She paused momentarily and looked at Rose with wide, horror-stricken eyes, "The priest," she requested hoarsely. "I must have him!"

Rose turned to the physician. "Is there not any more you can do for her?" she asked desperately.

"No, it is in the hands of God now," he answered wearily. "All I can do is to help her passing."

"I can do that. Go, get the priest, but hurry, man, hurry," Rose urged anxiously.

He turned and left. Rose's inability to help frustrated her as no other thing on earth could. "Mabel," she said gently, " the physician is gone for the priest. It will not be long until he comes. Do not fret. Recall some pleasant memory, something that will give you comfort," she urged.

A few minutes later the bloody purging and vomiting eased slightly. Rose gently mopped Mabel's forehead and hair. Taking one of the linen cloths, she wet it and carefully cleaned the blood that had become encrusted around Mabel's mouth. Mabel lay on the pallet, totally spent. "I'm dying, Rose," she said, "I will never see my family or Hugh again. Death would be a relief, if I could be sure that I will not be confined to the infernal depths." She struggled onto her elbow again, looking feverishly around. "Where is the priest? I need him. I cannot die without him being present. I must make sure I am forgiven of all my trespasses," she cried with mounting agitation.

"He will be here directly. All will be well. You will not die Mabel," Rose said reassuringly. She wondered to herself at the delay. Please God, she prayed, let him get here in time. Allow her that much comfort. Suddenly, Mabel started up wildly, looking at Rose with terror filled eyes. "He is here again, awaiting me. He knows that the end is nigh. He sees my death. Can you not see him, laughing at me?" she asked in horror.

"Mabel, there is nothing there," Rose said despairingly. "See, there is no-one here but myself."

Mabel shook her head wildly. "Oh God aid me, aid me," she cried in terror. Rose put her arms around her, trying to ease her back onto the bed, but she twisted and turned to fight her, as her eyes stayed riveted to the same spot. Suddenly, she gave a shrill scream of pain and doubling over with spasm, began again to vomit. The door opened and the priest and physician rushed into the chamber. The physician took Mabel's hand and felt her pulse. It was so feeble and lagging, that he knew there was no time to be lost in the administration of the Last Rites. He shook his head, "God pity her," he said and the priest nodded and began intoning the prayers for the dying.

The physician and Rose knelt at the side of the bed and joined in the aspirations. Rose could not concentrate, so shaken was she by the events, which she had just witnessed. Everything had happened so quickly. The incantations, meanwhile, soothed Mabel and at last, she lay back quietly. She was receiving the spiritual relief she so yearned, comforting her much more than any abatement in her physical discomfort. When the priest had finished, he made the sign of the cross on her forehead. He then nodded at Rose who got up and stood beside Mabel. Mabel's eyes flickered open and she smiled up at her. She whispered weakly, "Now he is gone, he waits for me no longer. I can die in peace. God bless you Rose for all your kindness."

Rose's eyes filled as she leaned over and kissed the grey forehead. Mabel remained quiet for another few moments. Henry Hovendon slipped into the chamber, edged towards the filthy pallet and gently rested his hand on Mabel's brow. She did not open her eyes but gave a long shudder and finally, her breathing ceased. The priest crossed himself. Rose did likewise. My second mother-in-law to die, she reflected. She felt empty inside. A sense of loneliness descended on her as she thought of the past and the time she and Mabel had spent together. How could it all have culminated in this, she wondered. What sense did Mabel's existence have? The question hung limply, unanswered in her mind. The priest walked over to her and laid his hand on her shoulder. "She is gone to a far better place where she will get comfort. She has suffered enough in this life. I will make arrangements for her keening. She became a good Catholic in the last few years. We will send her off well," he said gently, bowed and left the chamber.

Henry fetched a cracked goblet from the corner, poured some whiskey into it and handed it to Rose. "Drink," he ordered.

Rose gazed one last time upon Mabel. Her mind was numb. She raised the amber liquid to her lips and drained it in one draught. It burnt her throat and stomach but it was good to feel a sensation, any sensation. Then, Henry took her by the elbow and she allowed him lead her away.

Henry Bagenal strode over the bridge that spanned the moat around Dublin Castle and walked through the open gates. Two large sentries appeared, barring his way. "Halt," the corporal in charge ordered in an English accent. "State your business and your reason for seeking entry to the Castle."

"How dare you stop me! I'd have you know that I'm on Her Majesty's Council of Ireland. Step out of my way," Bagenal replied brusquely, attempting to force his way past him.

"I don't care if you are on the Privy Council itself. My orders are not to allow anyone enter, unless they have a pass from the Lord Deputy," the corporal said, moving to bar Bagenal's passage once again. "I will ask you once more. State your name and business and we will see if we can find someone who will vouch for you."

"I will vouch for him," a voice said, and Bagenal turned to see Sir Thomas Wingfield crossing the bridge behind him. "I was in the tavern opposite and I thought it was you," he said to Bagenal, drawing abreast of him. "When did you return from England?"

Still bristling at the sentry's rebuff, Bagenal answered with little grace. "Two days ago. And a waste of time it was too. I suspect that I was summoned there, simply to remove me from my lands in Newry. I never even got to meet the Privy Council and was only finally allowed home, when I gave my word that I wouldn't cross O'Neill. If I could meet him, I'd rip his head from his body with my bare hands," he said bitterly.

"You must not be heard saying that," Wingfield said in a low, urgent voice. "Norris has just completed a peace agreement with the rebels. They are all to be pardoned, are to hold their lands and estates and to submit to the crown. The Lord Deputy does not like the arrangement, but the Queen has given it her blessing and that is all that matters."

"Damnation," Bagenal shouted. "That man is allied with the Devil, mark my words, but such an alliance shall not save him. I will make sure of that."

Bagenal's complexion waxed livid. "There is nothing that can be done," Wingfield responded. "The Queen wishes for this truce and any man who shall thwart her, shall pay most dearly for it. You must govern your anger. We are obliged to wait and see if O'Neill is true to his word and remains loyal to the crown. If he does not, only then can we plot his destruction."

"I cannot wait, I will be revenged," Bagenal said belligerently. "Do you know what he has done? My sister received a communication from him earlier this week. Mabel is dead and he is to blame, as much as if he had strangled her with his own hands. And do you know how he honoured her memory? Within two days, he married Hugh Magennis's daughter and Magennis married one of his spawn. My blood boils at the insult."

Wingfield paused, considering the news. He thought of the young woman that he had once wished to make his wife. Her refusal of him had been a turning point in his life. He had never married since. He doubted if he would ever do so now. He had chosen to return to Ireland, to this God forsaken isle, in an effort to exact vengeance on O'Neill. He had once loved Mabel and more than his pride had been damaged by the incident. He felt sadness at the news of her death. All could have been so different, he thought. "It is sad news and it shows O'Neill for the monster he is. I am sorry to hear of Mabel's passing. I pray that she might find more happiness in the next world, than she did in this one," he said gently.

"And I hope she rots in hell for the grief and shame that she has brought on my house," Bagenal spat venomously.

Wingfield was taken aback by such viciousness. "Fie, fie Henry, you must not wish ill on the dead," he said earnestly. "Such thoughts lack Christian compassion."

Bagenal shook his head angrily. "She deserves naught," he said, but stopped up suddenly as someone in the distance caught his attention. "Is that Norris?" he asked eagerly and without awaiting a reply, ran towards the figure that had just emerged from the Lord Deputy's house. "Sir John," he shouted urgently, "Sir John, a moment, I must talk with you."

Wingfield hastened after Bagenal, with a heavy heart. There would be trouble and there was no way to prevent it. Norris had stopped and on Bagenal's reaching him, the latter immediately launched into a tirade. "I hear that you are responsible for a most appalling act of cowardice and stupidity. You brokered a truce with those traitors," he shouted.

"Have a care, man," Norris ordered, his voice steely. "The Queen approves of the deal that I have made and who are you to quibble with her judgement?"

"If you executed your duty, you would have destroyed them. You have misled the Queen in your advice. They will always be traitors. You cannot trust them. I know. I have witnessed their character all my life. They have made a fool of you, Sir," Bagenal said contemptuously.

"You do not realise the handicaps under which I laboured" Norris replied angrily. "The Queen complains of the excessive charge that I put on her purse, refusing to grant the means to prosecute this war." A high colour had overspread Norris' features as his pride and dignity were nettled by such an acerbic attack. He continued. "Save your spleen. I did as I was ordered. I got Her Majesty the truce that she desired. That man in there," he said pointing at the Lord Deputy's house, "has made my job impossible. I have asked more than once to be relieved of it, but the Queen refuses, so I must do as I am told."

Norris ceased speaking, but Bagenal remained impervious to his residual ire. "No amount of complaints and excuses will hide the fact that you have made a major error in your handling of this situation," he countered doggedly. "What is to become of my lands? I will not allow O'Neill gain at my expense from this so called peace."

"It has been decided that he will retain all the land and sublords whom he currently governs," Norris answered.

"Like Magennis, his new father-in-law?" Bagenal asked. He was gratified to see that Norris at least looked uncomfortable at this allusion.

"I was saddened to learn of your sister's death, but we cannot allow our private affairs interfere with matters of state. Yes, Magennis will now be under his protection and shall answer to the Queen, through him," he answered.

"I will never accept such an arrangement," Bagenal thundered. "Magennis has been one of my family's client Lords for over thirty years. I will not surrender him."

"You will do as you are bid," Norris said with menace. "You were only allowed home, after the Queen sought my opinion on the matter. I can easily revoke it and have you sent back to London again where you might not have such a pleasant sojourn next time."

"Come away," Wingfield urged anxiously, before adding in more confidential tones to Sir John, "He is distraught at the news of his sister. I will vouch for his behaviour," he said.

"I need no man to vouch for my behaviour," Bagenal shouted angrily. "I am my own master and will do as I see fit!"

"Come, we shall talk again of the matter when you are less ruffled," Wingfield said to him. "If you are proven right, and their submission is but a ruse, then we both shall have our chance of revenge. Otherwise, we shall obey the Queen's wishes."

He turned to Norris. "We are no traitors, Sir John."

Norris nodded as Bagenal opened his mouth to reply. Wingfield caught him by the arm and pulled him away. They walked back towards the Castle gates. Norris watched them go, hoping fervently that Bagenal would be proved wrong. He himself was certain that the brokered peace would solve Ulster's troubles, and he felt confident about the good opinion in which he held O'Neill. The Irish Lords had had good reason to be unhappy and now that their grievances had been redressed fairly, they had no cause to be disloyal to the crown. I must head back north and arrange for the final part of the truce. All that finally remains to be undertaken, is the delivery of the official pardons to O'Neill and O'Donnell, he thought.

Hugh O'Neill and his new bride, Catherine, were sitting side by side as they were rowed back to the landing pier from which they had set off earlier. They had spent five wonderful hours salmon fishing on the river Bann, and now, as the sun was beginning to sink in the west, they were returning with a large catch. Hugh could not remember a time when he felt so completely happy. Everything was fresh, novel and exciting to Catherine and her joy, in even the simplest things, was unalloyed. Banished temporarily were the troubles and worries of war and in their place Hugh found a world new minted.

As they approached the pier, he saw the red cloak of one of his personal bodyguard. It could only mean one thing. He had been sent from Dungannon with pressing news. Hugh had warned Henry Hovendon that he was not to be contacted except in a case of utmost urgency. He wondered what could have gone wrong. Only a disaster would have compelled Henry to interrupt this honeymoon. "Row faster!" he ordered.

"What is it, Hugh?" Catherine asked, concerned at the tone of her husband's voice. "Hopefully nothing," he replied. "A messenger awaits us, I am anxious to hear his news."

Hugh weighed up the various possibilities. He had just agreed peace terms with the English and had felt secure that, for now at least, the prospect of war had been removed. Granted, neither he nor O'Donnell had yet personally submitted, but that was a mere formality. That would not have caused the English to break the terms of the agreement. He had been pleased at what they had managed to obtain. They had not gained everything that they had sought, but they had got more than he had ever imagined they would. He was perplexed about what the problem could possibly be. Maybe someone had broken the truce, without Her Majesty's permission. Bagenal? No, he would never have the courage for such an open display of disobedience. Bingham, on the other hand, would be only too willing and able to do so. He had warned the English about him and demanded his removal.

The boat arrived at the pier and two of the soldiers leaped onto it. They aided Hugh clamber out and then turned their attention to Catherine. Hugh walked over to the horseman who bowed graciously. "Well, what business brings you here?" Hugh asked abruptly.

"A message from Henry Hovendon. He ordered me to ride here as fast as I could and give you this," he answered. He proffered a parchment, which Hugh took from him without comment. After walking some paces away, he unrolled the document. He read and then re-read the message, allowing himself absorb its amazing contents.

"A messenger from King Philip of Spain has arrived in Donegal. We await you at Killybegs. Come immediately. It is urgent that we confer with him. Henry."

Catherine was at his elbow. "What is it, Hugh?" she asked anxiously.

Hugh passed her the parchment. She took it and read it slowly before looking at him, worry etched on her brow. "You must go to meet him," she said.

"Yes," he agreed, "I must hear what he has to say."

"We will leave tonight?" she asked.

"I will leave in the morning. I will make better time in the light and he can wait upon me. We have expected a reply from them long enough. You must return to Dungannon. I will escort you there on my way to Donegal and will join you after I learn what news there is," Hugh said.

"But can I not go with you?" Catherine asked.

"It would be better if you went to Dungannon," Hugh said decisively.

Catherine's face fell, but she nodded in agreement. Hugh was content that she did not argue with him. Such a wife, was a boon to a man. "Come, we will return to our lodgings and sample some of your catch. We can yet enjoy this night, and there will be many more," he said and looked at Catherine to see if he could read any disappointment in her face. She smiled softly at him and he deeply regretted that he was to leave her side so soon. "I'm sorry that our stay here must end prematurely. We shall travel together again before long, to London, as I promised," he said gently.

"Once you are with me in Dungannon when your business is completed, then I shall not wish for more," Catherine said easily.

Hugh took her hand in his and they walked slowly across the fields, towards the demesne that had been fitted out for their sojourn. All around him, the lush Ulster countryside rolled away into the distance, but this once, he was unmindful of it. His mind grappled with this latest development. Just a few hours earlier, he had recognised that he was more happy and content than he had ever been. He had a new wife, was finally The O'Neill and was, once again, recognised by the Queen, as Earl of Tyrone. His wager of rebellion had been won. And now, just as all seemed set to fall into easy existence, the Spanish finally chose to send an ambassador. He had used the threat of

Spanish aid to intimidate the English and wring concessions from them, never really considering intercession a likely event. He considered what O'Donnell's reaction would be if there was even a vague promise of aid; he would not accept his English pardon. As for himself, unless Spanish soldiers actually landed on Ulster shores, his natural inclination was to accept the terms already granted by Elizabeth. Yet, I am obliged to hear what the Spanish have to say, O'Neill thought, regretting that once again, all might be thrown into turmoil just as it seemed that peace was returning to Ulster.

It was two days later when Hugh reached Killybegs. An Atlantic wind carried squalls of bitter rain, drenching the narrow earthen streets that separated the simple dwellings, and pitting the waters of the fishing harbour. The weather had turned once again, as an icy wind howled through the town. Hugh looked down into the harbour and saw there, in among the small fishing boats, a large Spanish Man-o-War proudly flying its Spanish flag. The sight of the majestic ship did not fail to amaze him. He turned from the harbour and rode down through the narrow streets. Ducking his head, he passed an overhanging sign for a tavern and edged his mount past a fish cart, before alighting at a corner and tying his horse to a wooden stake. He walked stiffly, rendering it apparent to any observer who might pass him, that he had ridden a long distance.

He entered a narrow alley, searching for a dwelling indicated on the map, which had accompanied Henry's letter. He shivered, stepping aside for an old woman dressed in black that carried a basket of fish. He averted his face, looking at the ground so that his hood obscured his identity. Hugh found the dwelling and knocked on its door. He scanned the alley, but there was no one in sight. The door opened and Henry Hovendon's anxious face appeared from within. "Good," he said. "You've come at last."

Hugh nodded and passed quickly inside. He shook the rain off his cloak, removed it and placed it on a chair, just inside the door. They were in a small chamber, sparsely furnished with a table and four chairs. "The Spanish ambassador. He is here?" Hugh asked.

"Yes," Henry answered. "He's with O'Donnell in the next chamber and is anxious to be away. I will inform him that you have arrived."

"A moment. Who is he?" Hugh asked.

"Captain Alonso Cobos. Hugh Boye MacDavitt is here to act as translator. He is regarded as one of Spain's ablest commanders, and has served with distinction at Lepanto, in Tunisia, Portugal and the Low Countries. It is a mark of the King's interest in our cause, that he sends such an important ambassador to meet with us."

"And is there a letter from the King himself?" Hugh asked.

"Yes, I have it in safe keeping. It merely promises us aid and states that our cause is close to his heart. In it, he says that Cobos has been entrusted with all details and can talk in his name," Hovendon answered.

"Guard the letter well. I must send it to the Council. I have already dispatched a messenger to Dublin, telling them of the arrival of a Spanish ship in Donegal," Hugh said gravely. "We must be careful how we deal with this situation and not risk all, unless we are assured of enough aid to tip the balance in our favour."

"Agreed," Hovendon replied.

"Come," said Hugh, "let us hear what the man has to say."

Hugh followed Hovendon into the adjoining chamber and there they found Cormac, Hugh Roe, MacDavitt and Cobos seated around a table, a large fire burning in the grate before them. Hugh Roe rose quickly on seeing Hugh. "Thank God and all the saints, that you've arrived at last. Two days conversation where every word must be translated, is enough to drive one to distraction."

Hugh smiled and looked with interest at Alonso. He saw before him a stockily built man with olive skin, dark hair and a spade shaped beard, specked with grey. His face bore a deep, livid scar, running from ear to jawbone, a memento, no doubt, of some previous battle. MacDavitt addressed Cobos, who rose from his seat, bowed, and offered Hugh his hand. He spoke in Spanish and MacDavitt translated. "Alonso Cobos, the emissary of the King of Spain, is delighted finally to make your acquaintance and extends the King's best wishes for your fight with the heretic Elizabeth."

Hugh nodded. "Tell him that we return the King's best wishes and are anxious to hear what news he brings from him for us."

MacDavitt translated and Alonso looked at the man in front of him. The King was deeply interested in O'Neill; an Irish warlord, a member of the Queen's Council in Ireland, raised to the status of an English Earl and yet, now prepared to play the traitor. Such an enigmatic character fascinated him. He had Cobos spend a considerable amount of time preparing for this mission, interviewing Irish captains and bishops, resident in Spain. From everything that he had learned, it was this man who held the key to success for Spanish designs in Ireland. The Spanish were already negotiating with their old enemy, the French. If Spain could sign a peace treaty with them, then they could bring all their forces to bear on the Dutch and English. It would be opportune if the English were diverted into waging war in Ireland. It would also be most just, as it was the English who had supported and encouraged the Dutch in their rebellion against their lawful ruler,

King Philip.

He began talking in Spanish, pausing from time to time so that MacDavitt could translate. "I would like you all to remember that the links between Spain and Ireland are deep and go back a long way. We are friends, friends who share the one true faith and why should not such friends give each other aid?" he asked. He paused to see what effect his words would have and was gratified to see that they all nodded approvingly. He continued in a solemn tone. "Henry II of England received a donation of Ireland from the only Englishman ever to reign as Pope, Adrian IV. That donation carried its own responsibilities. Henry was to defend the one true church and to bring the Irish church under the rule of Rome."

Raising his voice, he continued. "Now that his successors have deviated from the one true faith and try to eradicate it from the land, they have no more right in law to rule the country of Ireland." He paused again, sensing their growing interest. "You have a right, indeed you have an obligation to rise up against such a ruler, a ruler who has lost her divine right as Queen over you."

He considered his next words. He had learned since his arrival, that a treaty was already agreed with the English Queen and that only the granting of her pardon and the swearing of O'Neill's and O'Donnell's fealty, were lacking to ratify it. Already, he had ascertained that O'Donnell and Maguire hated the English so vehemently that they might be persuaded to revoke their word. O'Donnell had not even surrendered the promised hostages, whereas the Earl had delivered up two of Cormac's sons, in place of his own. That meant Cormac would be difficult to persuade and Alonso had noted the Earl's caution. He would need to step outside the guidelines that his King had set down for him, as circumstances had changed since he had set out. In the interests of Spain, he would embroider the truth. "King Philip has already received the Pope's agreement that the crown of Ireland will be stripped from the heretic Elizabeth."

An excited murmur went around the chamber. A twinge of guilt stung his conscience, but he ignored it. Relations between Philip and the Pope were at their worst ever and Alonso knew that the Pope would never do anything that might advance Spanish power and influence. "The King is most anxious that your cause will succeed. He has already raised the soldiers necessary for another Armada, which he will launch this time against the English forces in Ireland. He shall rescue you and your countrymen from the heretic Queen and so bring many souls back to the one true church," he said

He watched their faces as they listened to MacDavitt's translation. The truth was, that the soldiers had not yet been assembled, and that there was a severe shortage of manpower and ships within the Spanish Empire. The plans for an attack on England or Ireland were in existence, but that was all. The ultimate destination of the Armada had not yet been decided, and Philip, if signs were read closely, seemed to favour launching the attack on England itself. Still, Cobos's report would be important in influencing that decision, and he now believed that the attack should come through Ireland. The local support they would receive could make the difference between the success or failure of the whole venture. Five thousand battle-hardened Spanish veterans, with weapons for the ten to twelve thousand men whom Irish Lords could put in the field, would sweep away all opposition in Ireland.

He was keenly interested in seeing a fully equipped Spanish army land here. It could be the event that might influence the whole Continental war in Spain's favour and a fitting revenge for arrogant English interference in matters that did not concern them. "I have learned," he continued, "that you have almost concluded a peace treaty with the English Queen on terms satisfactory to yourselves. I would ask you to reconsider. Firstly, you cannot trust Elizabeth, as time and time again she breaks her word. Did not Shane O'Neill sign a similar treaty with her and did she not do all in her power thereafter to destroy him, breaking her sacred word?"

Once again, he watched carefully to see what effect MacDavitt's translation would have upon his audience. He saw Maguire and O'Donnell nodding energetically. Cormac and the Earl listened impassively. He had to convince them, he thought. "Secondly," he continued, "the Queen is much advanced in years. She rules a kingdom that cannot match the Spanish Empire in its wealth or power. In a war between Spain and England, there can be only one victor, the one most richly endowed, and King Philip can count on endless treasure fleets from the New World to finance his war effort."

When MacDavitt had translated these last words, Alonso continued with mounting passion. "What have the English achieved in the last eight years since the great winds of '88 destroyed our Armada? Nothing, but a string of notable failures. The Lisbon expedition, Grenville's death and the capture of the Revenge, Howards's flight, Drake's defeat and death, like that of Hawkin's. Since the Archduke Albert took over the command of the Spanish forces in the Netherlands, he has transformed the situation there and we, once again, hold the upper hand. He has installed a Spanish garrison at Calais, a bare seven miles from Dover. There is another in Brittany. Spanish forces off the Cornish coast, landed with impunity, burning villages and Protestant churches and celebrating Mass openly once again on English soil."

He listened to MacDavitt's translation, before continuing. "Another English weakness, is the great uncertainty regarding the Queen's successor. Her court is divided into two rival factions that pull constantly in opposite directions, so that decisions can never be made in time to face any new challenge. There are still many secret Catholics in England who would welcome the restoration of the one true faith. The time is now right for Spanish intervention in England. He regards it as his divine mission in life. My appeal to you, on his behalf, is that you abandon your proposed truce, becoming instead, vassals of the most glorious King Philip II of Spain. In return, he will use his forces to win your freedom and promises you his protection. Do not throw away this chance. I appeal to you, not to settle for anything other than complete victory, anything less will ultimately lead to your overthrow and destruction."

He watched them levelly. Maguire and O'Donnell were keen. He still could not read the other two men. A long pause ensued during which all eyes were focused on the Earl, who finally spoke and addressed MacDavitt. "We must talk among ourselves. Do not translate anything that we say until I tell you to. Explain to Captain Cobos," he said. MacDavitt translated and Cobos nodded his acknowledgement of their need. He and MacDavitt withdrew.

"Well," O'Neill asked. "What is your opinion?"

"We must join with them. This is the opportunity that we have been waiting for. We asked them for this help and now that it has come, we cannot reject it," O'Donnell said eagerly.

"I agree. Let's forge ahead. How could we not?" Maguire asked.

"And how do we make sure that we don't exchange one master for another?" Cormac enquired.

"Because we will be partners in the fight. Our armies will fight side by side with theirs. We have one religion. Religious difference caused much strife between the English and us," O'Donnell answered.

"If the Pope does transfer sovereignty from Elizabeth, then the Old English, who are still Catholic, will have to join us in our war and yield up their cities to our armies," Maguire added.

"Yes, we often talked about how such an initiative from the Pope would aid us. But what is your mind, Hugh?" O'Donnell asked, aware that Hugh was still silent.

Hugh looked from one to the other. He observed Cormac's sullen demeanour. He had insisted on sending Cormac's sons as pledges, instead of his own. Conn, Cormac's eldest son had already, at only sixteen, proved himself in battle by leading a troop of thirty horse at Clontibret. Brian, Cormac's second son was still but a child, barely ten years old. Hugh mused ruefully over his speed in submitting to the demand for hostages. If they went back to war, then Conn and Brian would pay the cost. There was not much that he could do about that. He would have to make his decision for the overall and long term good of Tyrone. He knew the decision that he was about to take would have repercussions that would echo down the ages. Such a choice daunted him. He had never been a gambler at heart, he had always wanted to have certainty in everything. But there was no certainty in this.

Now he had to choose, choose between staying as they were or risking all. O'Donnell was right. Spanish aid changed everything. If they had to choose, they should choose the stronger. For once in his life, he would have to risk absolutely everything. They had invited the Spanish in and, in his heart, he knew what he had to do. He looked at Cormac. "We'll get your sons out, even if we have to raid Dublin Castle itself," he said.

Cormac did not reply but just looked sceptically at him.

"So, you're in agreement," Hugh Roe asked eagerly.

"Yes," Hugh answered.

O'Donnell whooped with joy and he and Maguire threw their arms around each other.

"Wait," Hugh cautioned. "We must set out our conditions and petition King Philip to appoint a just man to rule over us. Archduke Albert would be a suitable appointment. We have heard of his success in the Netherlands and in Portugal."

"Why have a foreigner? We should look for you as our ruler," Maguire said.

"No. Whosoever the King appoints, will have to rule through us. We must make sure of King Philip's aid. Archduke Albert is reckoned to be the strongest man in Spain. He is one of only three that forms the Junta de Noche, the council that advises the King on all matters. He is both Philip's nephew and brother-in-law, the son of Maximillian II, former ruler of Germany and Austria. He would be acceptable," Hugh answered and turned to MacDavitt. "You may translate the following," he said. "Tell him that we agree to his offer of aid and that we will turn our backs on the generous peace terms that the English Queen has granted us. Cobos must write a letter certifying that when he arrived, we had concluded a peace with the Queen on terms satisfactory to ourselves. Solely on conscientious grounds and out of affection for His Majesty, we agree to take up arms again against the Queen of England, turning our hearts to God and King Philip, in whose service as faithful vassals we will remain at His Majesty's pleasure."

On learning what Hugh had said, a smile broke over Cobos's face. He nodded eagerly. "It will be done," he said. "Praise God that has brought our two nations together again."

"We must have aid and have it quickly if we are not to be forced to make peace with the heretics. You must impress on him the urgent need to help us and by doing so, he will assist Catholic liberty and win for Christ an infinite number of souls," Hugh added.

"I guarantee you that you shall have your aid before the year's end," Cobos promised, determined to have it so. He was now eager to return to Spain and report his findings. "Now that it is decided, we must fix where our men should land and how many you will need. I wish to catch the evening's tide and we have much to discuss. MacDavitt can act as scribe and we will agree all the details."

Cobos signalled his intention to MacDavitt who approached the oaken table. Hugh observed MacDavitt prepare some parchment, ink and quills and found it difficult to believe that he had really committed them all to such an uncertain enterprise.

Chapter 14

The bellow of guns rolled, like thunder, over the sun drenched harbour at Cadiz, Spain's largest oceanic port. Instinctively, without any orders, the English soldiers had knelt to shelter from the savage artillery, in the bottom of the barges that ferried them towards the shore. Captain Conveys Clifford raised his head and looked in amazement at the sight that greeted him. He was used to land battles. He had served with distinction in the English army in Flanders, but nothing had prepared him for this. The bay was filled with ships, ships that undulated in the azure water under a clear, blue sky. It should have been a pleasant sight and would have been, except for what men were inflicting barbarously on each other. The smoke from the cannons drifted lazily across the bay and the guns flashed fire as they hurled their deadly projectiles, maiming and killing without mercy. The sea battle was not yet won, but Clifford thought, as he looked around, that victory was all but theirs. Essex, however, had disobeyed his orders to await its conclusion and commanded a premature assault on the city, regardless of the cost of lives.

He listened to the drum beats that kept time for the rowers, who powered the barges towards the shore, and thought of how fortunate they had been. A month earlier, they had sailed with a flotilla of a hundred ships, forty-eight of them being Men-o-War. They had managed to make the journey to Cadiz, undiscovered, thus ensuring total surprise. They had found only four galleons and a squadron of galleys present, protecting the large, valuable merchant fleet that had been readied to sail to the New World. Clifford was glad to see that the galleys had withdrawn into the inner harbour, unable to defend themselves from the guns of the English fleet. The four Spanish Men-o-War had put up a brave fight. They had anchored broadside on their attackers. English ship after ship took its place in the assault, driving its shot hard into the sides of the galleons. Clifford had wondered, in awe, how the ships and their sailors could take such punishment. He watched as the enemy's sails were blown off, the wood of their ships splintering, soldiers and gunners being struck down, before finally perceiving bright red blood oozing from the scuppers. Gradually the guns on the Spanish ships fell silent and after three hours of constant battering, Essex had ordered Raleigh to take the Warspite right to the galleons and to board with the soldiers. As the Warspite approached, the Spaniards finally acknowledged that they could not continue the fight. In an effort to prevent the English from capturing their ships, they cut their cables and started to drift across the bay.

It was at this point that Essex had ordered the soldiers into the barges and given the order to attack. Clifford looked at the four large ships in the distance and saw that their effort to escape had failed. They had left it too late; the turning tide had caught them and swept them aground on the sandbars, off the main beaches. The four Spanish ships were named after four of the apostles and were recently built by King Philip in an effort to win naval supremacy in the Atlantic. The other eight apostles, luckily, were on duty elsewhere. He watched as the two ships nearest the attacking fleet, the St. Mathew and the St. Andrew, were boarded by the Dutch, who had contributed a squadron under their own Admiral, Jan Van Duyvenvoord. The Dutch were allowing no quarter to the Spanish. The hatred between both races was palpable, a reminder of the ferocity and brutality of their exchanges in the Netherlands. He watched as the Low Countries' flag was hoisted over both ships and observed the Dutch throwing the armour-clad Spanish into the water, where they drowned, screaming for mercy, within sight of their own city and safety.

The St. Philip and the St. Thomas were nearer the shore so Dutch ships, with a smaller draught, made towards them. He heard an explosion, first in the St. Thomas and afterwards in the other vessel. Their captains had decided to fire them, rather than lose them to the enemy. Clifford watched in wonder as the flames leaped up the shattered rigging of the boats. He saw the Spanish sailors scrambling out of the flaming hulks, most of them wearing armour that had become blackened during the fight, their faces and clothes besmirched. He could not fail to hear the desperate screams of drowning men as they carried over the water to him. Others in the boat with him looked in the direction of the stricken ships. The Spanish were still out of their depth. The Dutch ships stopped some distance away and their crews watched as the flames mounted the enemy vessels. Some wounded, blackened and charred soldiers still clung to ropes and nets that hung from the doomed vessels. The Dutch sailors cheered as, one by one, the Spanish lost their strength and released their grip on the burning ropes. They fell screaming into the water, drowning in the clear blue seas of the bay. The Dutch, in their flyboats, followed some Spanish, who had managed to clutch onto floating spars. They hacked at them until they disappeared in a bloody swirl, beneath the water. The screams, the fire, the smell of sulphur and the thunder of the guns brought images of hell to Clifford's mind. This must be something like it, he thought.

They were now rapidly approaching the shore. He was relieved to see no Spanish soldiers gathered there to contest their landing. The spot they had chosen was two miles from the city itself. Cadiz was built a few miles north of Cape Trafalgar and Gibraltar, at the head of a spit of land that jutted out, like a huge crooked finger, for some six miles, parallel to the coast. To the west of the town, lay the open sea, but to the east, were the protected waters of a huge bay. It was on its eastern side that the English were now attempting to land.

It had annoyed him greatly to contemplate the indiscipline with which the English carried out the naval battle. In comparison, the Dutch had been a model of efficiency and professionalism. Every one of the English commanders had vied with the other to be first into battle, to be the one credited with the glory of victory. The ridiculous situation had presented where Sir Frances Vere had slipped his anchor, in an effort to be at the head of the combined assault, in direct opposition to his orders. When he was overtaken by Sir Walter Raleigh, he had ordered a rope to be fastened to Raleigh's ship to pull himself abreast again. Raleigh was busy arguing with him when the guns of the four great Spanish ships had burst into action. The Lord Admiral, Howard, then made to follow. When his flagship caught up with the fleet, he had ordered a barge take him to the Mere Honour. Then he too joined in the fray. All the other captains jockeyed with each other in similar fashion, reminding Clifford of huntsmen riding hard after their quarry, jumping every fence and taking every risk, to be in at the kill, ignoring the danger they posed to themselves and the rest of the fleet. The Due Repulse, forcing her way in, collided with the Dreadnought, and both ships were out of the fight for a critical half an hour. It was lucky for us, Clifford thought, that the Spanish had not a stronger naval force stationed at Cadiz, or we might have helped them defeat us.

His thoughts were interrupted by the grazing of the boat's keel on the shingle of the beach. The soldiers hurried to disembark and Clifford looked nervously around to see if there were any Spanish soldiers hiding in wait for them.

"Make haste," he shouted at his men as they tumbled out onto the shore and hurriedly fanned out on the beach, advancing towards the dunes. All remained quiet and Clifford began to feel a little easier. The Spanish had been unable to send a force to contest their landing, he thought gratefully. He looked around and saw Essex's tall figure, his red hair showing under his helmet. He looked elated, sword in hand, ordering his men to form up quickly. On seeing Clifford, he beckoned to him. Clifford left his men and hastened over to him. On reaching him, he bowed and waited for his commander to speak.

"I want you and Mountjoy to take half our force and travel south, away from the city, until you come to a defensible position. You are to remain there and stop the Spanish from sending any relief here," he ordered imperiously. "When I have secured Cadiz, I will send for you."

Clifford recognised what lay behind the order and resented it. This was naked revenge for publicly daring to disagree with Essex's plan of attack. It did not make sense to split their forces now.

"But it is too soon for the Spanish to send reinforcements," he said, "even if they have heard of our arrival by now, it will take them a matter of weeks to assemble such a force. You should keep your men together and do all in your power to take the city as quickly as possible."

Essex shook his head and replied cuttingly, "I am the commander of this venture and I will have enough in a thousand men to carry out the task. You take the other thousand and secure our rear. Go!" he ordered brusquely.

Clifford turned and looked for his lieutenant, Cooper. "Form up half the soldiers," he ordered before turning and looking for Mountjoy. He would not have minded being assigned this task if he thought that there was any danger of being surprised from the rear, but he knew that there was not. He saw Mountjoy wading through the surf towards him, sword in hand.

Clifford admired Charles Blount, Lord Mountjoy, who was both learned and civilised. He had often thought that Mountjoy was not cut out for the battlefield and that he should be safely ensconced at home, reading his books and managing the family's estates. Still, he was glad to have him on these campaigns. It gave him someone with whom he could talk, someone who lacked the annoying airs in which Essex cloaked himself. He hastened over to him. "Charles," he said. "We are to secure the narrow isthmus and protect Essex as he attempts to take the town."

Mountjoy's handsome face fell and he was silent for a moment. Then, he replied, "If that is what we must do, then let us get to it."

Clifford approved of his reaction. If it had been any of the other Lords, they would have refused and bitterly questioned the orders. He saw that Essex had already assembled his men and he, Sir John Wingfield and Samuel Bagenal were leading the men at the double, in perfect order, across the scorching sand, towards the walls of the town, some two miles distant. He watched them for a number of minutes and when his men were assembled, he gave the order to march and they started slowly in the opposite direction. He would not go too far before establishing his defensive line, just in case Essex would have need of him.

The summons to Cadiz arrived quicker than he had expected. The next morning, Clifford found himself in the city that was, by now, totally in the hands of the English. He forced his way slowly through the streets, which were cluttered with chairs, tables, empty wine bottles, almonds, raisins and spices, which had been thrown out of the windows and doors of the houses, as the soldiers searched for more precious and portable wealth. The streets were lined with drunken soldiers who, even in their drunken state, continued to search for the spoils of victory, which were theirs by right. Any doors that were locked against them, they smashed, dragging the occupants screaming from within. Essex had expressly ordered that no Spanish civilians were to be harmed. The Dutch soldiers and sailors resented his orders that forbade them the opportunity to continue on Spanish soil, the savage reprisals and counter reprisals of the Netherlands' war. Essex had been quite forceful on the matter and had taken action against any soldiers who dared flout his orders. The Spanish were brought to the town's central square where they were sorted into those deemed worthy of ransom and those too poor to be of any value. The latter were driven from the city. There would be no desire to feed extra mouths.

Essex had taken the city as he had promised. He had been first through the unrepaired walls, cutting down men, right and left, as he urged his own soldiers to follow him through the narrow streets. He advanced, deep into the city, until he reached the main square where the Spanish had decided to make a last stand. There, they managed to stop his advance and just as he was being pushed back, Howard arrived with the rest of the army and the town was theirs

What concerned Clifford even more than the English soldiers' lack of discipline, was the fact that the Spanish merchant fleet had not yet been secured. He rounded a corner and saw that a wagon had been pulled across the way in an attempt to halt the advancing army. He dismounted, tied up his horse and squeezed past. He could see the spire of the cathedral in the distance and knew that it was located in the main square. That was where he was heading, where the English had established their headquarters. He continued to climb the narrow streets, which opened out and at last, he found himself looking at the cathedral from across the square.

He glanced about him and spotted the tavern that the English had taken over. The square was full of soldiers who were loudly and noisily enjoying the good fortune and wealth that they had discovered. The Spanish prisoners were herded together into one corner and they nervously watched the riotous conduct of their captors. He went over and pushed open the door of the tavern, passing inside into the gloom. Within, all was quiet and he noticed a number of men, sitting at tables. He scanned the chamber for someone he knew and finally his eyes alighted on John Donne. His spirits fell and he looked around anxiously to locate someone else with whom he might talk, but it was too late.

"Sir Conyers," Donne hailed him. "Sir Conyers, over here."

Clifford walked reluctantly to him. "Ah, Sir Conyers, I must get your opinion on a poem that I have just written. Well, to tell the truth, I have written five in all since I arrived here. War gives me so much inspiration! Who would have thought it?" he observed with a self-satisfied chuckle. Clifford did not wish to waste any more time on this man. He was always so damn bleak and depressing. There was enough of that in everyday life without writing about it, he thought.

"Do you know where the Earl is?" he asked. "I must talk with him, my business is most pressing."

"Yes, but first you must listen," Donne retorted with blithe unconcern. "You recall the burning of the Spanish galleon?"

He immediately launched into the poem, declaiming loudly so that all present would hear him.

"Out of a fired ship, which by no way
But drowning could be rescued from the flame
Some men leaped forth, and ever as they came
Near the foe's ship, did by their shot decay;
So all were lost which in the ship were found:
They in the sea being burnt, they in the burnt ship drowned."

He paused and waited eagerly for Clifford's comments. Clifford nodded. "Very good, Donne, but I need to meet with the Earl. It is a matter of great importance," he said.

"But I wanted you to hear my poem about the death of Sir John Wingfield. Such a noble man and such a sad death! The Earl says it can be read at his interment in the cathedral tomorrow," Donne continued.

"Where is the Earl?" Clifford asked again.

"Oh, very well. I suppose they will keep if you are in such haste. He's through there, in the next chamber," Donne answered petulantly.

Clifford went to the door of the chamber, knocking loudly upon it. The door opened and Samuel Bagenal's face appeared around it. "Conyers," he said in greeting, as he opened the door wide, "Come in."

Clifford walked past him into the chamber. He saw that most of the leaders of the army were already there ahead of him. They all looked extremely pleased with themselves. Essex was seated in a large chair at the end and the rest were standing, like subjects in front of their monarch. Essex nodded regally at him.

"We are discussing what our next move should be," the Earl said grandly. "I am of the opinion that we should hold Cadiz. Just think," he continued eagerly, leaning forward, without rising from the chair, "we have enough supplies on our ships to keep four thousand men fed for four months. In that time, a proper system of convoys could be set up so that we could be supplied from England. Imagine what a permanent base on Spanish soil could do for our cause! We could establish a blockade on Spanish shipping. Ships operating out of Cadiz harbour would be the scourge of the Spanish. Their treasure fleets would be open to attack with much less difficulty than if we were launching our raiding parties from England. It's the very strategy that would transform our war with Spain and guarantee us victory."

Clifford could not believe that Essex was proposing such a course. He knew what their orders had been. They were to attack Cadiz, take what prizes they could and then return to England. If they came upon the Spanish treasure fleet on the way home, they were authorised to attack it. They could even go in search of it, providing the weather was suitable and that they did not risk their vessels. The whole purpose of the expedition was the generation of a profit for the shareholders, the major shareholder being the Queen herself. Establishing a garrison in Cadiz would have major financial implications for her. Neither she nor the Privy Council would approve of such a course.

"Your plan has much to recommend it, Your Grace," Clifford said diplomatically, "but our orders do not include such a venture as that which you propose. We should follow our instructions and return to England with the Spanish merchant fleet. We have enough sailors to man the most valuable ships and we can easily transport their cargoes. Has a value been put on them yet?"

Essex shook his head. "That is the Lord Admiral's job. They have not been secured yet, even though I ordered him to do so. He is confident that they cannot leave the harbour, as his ships guard the exit. He has allowed our sailors shore leave so that they can secure their share of plunder. Not to do so, would have risked a mutiny. He is attempting to extract a ransom from his old adversary, The Duke of Medina Sidonia, the leader of the Great Armada. By a strange quirk of fate, it seems that the Duke's estates are located just across the bay. He witnessed the whole battle and was, once again, powerless to stop our victory."

Clifford was appalled. The idea that the merchant fleet had not been secured filled him with alarm. He knew that The Lord Admiral would not take kindly to orders from Essex, whom he regarded as an upstart. Age had not made him any mellower and the two men barely tolerated each other. The Queen had been very clear on the matter of leadership. The Lord Admiral was to take precedence at sea and Essex was to hold it on land. "But we should secure the ships. How can one demand a ransom for what one does not possess?" Clifford asked anxiously.

"I happen to agree with the Lord Deputy, on this matter," Essex rejoined. "We will operate out of here and the ransom will be useful. I intend declaring myself Governor of Cadiz and staying here with the ships."

A disapproving murmur ran around the chamber. Clifford waited but no one would speak openly. Again, he decided to have his say. "As I already said, such a proposal would run totally counter to our orders. If you wish to hold Cadiz for a matter of weeks while some of our ships awaits the treasure fleet off the Azores, then perhaps that would be acceptable to Her Majesty, but what you propose is bound to meet with her displeasure."

Clifford saw the blood rise in Essex's cheeks as he began to lose his temper. It was an all too familiar sight.

"I will decide what is acceptable or not," he said loudly. "Her Majesty entrusted me with the command here."

"The men will not tolerate it," Clifford warned. "They signed on for a short campaign. They will have made their profit and be anxious to return home to enjoy it."

"Any man who does not obey my orders, I will have hanged," Essex promised darkly. "And that includes officers," he added icily.

Clifford surveyed the chamber and saw that all the others present averted their gaze. He knew that they could not agree with Essex but they were afraid to voice their opinions. He saw Mountjoy glance at him and shrug his shoulders. He was too reliant on Essex's faction to dare disagree publicly with him. Clifford was also aware that Mountjoy had taken Essex's sister, Penelope, as his lover. He searched for Raleigh, but could not find him. There was a man never afraid to make his thoughts known. Raleigh had smoothed disagreements between Essex and the Lord Admiral in the past. He would, doubtless-ly, be in favour of seeking out the treasure fleet and returning to England. Clifford would have to exhort Raleigh to convince the Lord Admiral to secure the merchant fleet. In addition, Raleigh would have to ensure that Howard resisted Essex's plan to leave the fleet in Cadiz. Without Howard's agreement, all Essex's scheming would come to naught.

"And where is Sir Walter?" he asked.

"He was injured in the last minutes of the fight, damn unlucky for him," Essex answered. "His leg is a sorry mess, interlaced and deformed by splinters. The surgeons have done their best but you know how these things can go. Hopefully, he will not have to lose it. He is still aboard his ship. He had to miss the excitement of the last day."

Clifford guessed that he was probably glad that Raleigh had not been around to share in the glory. Still, it gave him his excuse to leave. "I am sorry to hear such sad tidings," he said. "With your permission, I would like to visit him and see how he progresses?" Essex nodded and Clifford turned and withdrew. Essex was probably as glad to see the back of him, as he was glad to leave. He opened the door and hurried through the outer chamber. He heard Donne calling his name.

"I regret that I am unable to stop. I'm on an urgent errand on behalf of the Earl," he called over his shoulder, as he passed out into the sunlit square. He would go to Raleigh's ship, tell him what was happening and would bring him with him, even if he had to have him carried on a stretcher. Together, they would impress on Howard the urgent need to secure the Spanish merchant fleet. Then, they would talk of Essex's plans and the best way to thwart them.

"We expected an answer to our letter," Hugh said. "We did not anticipate your coming in person, so soon again."

"At least, not on your own. We had hoped that when we would see you again, it would be at the head of a Spanish army," Cormac added. "The year is moving on, the end of the summer is upon us. If you do not launch your Armada soon, the weather will deny you the opportunity."

Alonso Cobos stood once again in the very room in Killibegs where he had, just months previously, met with the same Irish nobles who were now standing before him. He had sailed from Spain with favourable wind and weather behind him, making the journey in less than twelve days. He listened to MacDavitt's translation and as he did, he noted that the nobles were more reserved than on his last visit. There was an air of palpable unease in the chamber. "King Philip ordered me to visit you in person. My news is too important to entrust to a letter, especially considering what happened to the last one, which His Majesty sent to you," he said pointedly. He needed to forestall their truculence, as McDavitt had already informed him that they were concerned over the implications of Essex's raid on Cadiz. He perceived that the Earl had the good grace to look uncomfortable.

Hugh cleared his throat and replied. "Naturally, the English were extremely anxious when they heard of your visit to our shores, not to mention the other two expeditions since then from your country that arrived bearing arms. We knew that we could not keep the news of

Spanish warships, landing in Donegal, secret for long. I had to lull the English into a false sense of security. I did not wish to engage in open hostilities with them before your armies arrived."

"I understand, but did you have to send His Majesty's letter to the Queen? It gave her proof regarding our intentions and was probably what finally persuaded her to agree to the Cadiz expedition. If she had not received it, her natural caution would, perhaps, have induced her to cancel the whole operation," Cobos responded.

"One of my close friends on the Council, Sir William Warren, was sent to me to enquire about your visit. I gave him the letter, as proof of my renewed fidelity to the Queen, and he promised that the letter would be returned or destroyed, without a copy being made. He was only to say that he had heard from one of his spies of the letter's existence. When the Council sent it to London, I was in a position to accuse Warren of abusing my friendship and the Dublin Council of acting dishonourably. It gave me the reason I sought, the reason to cease all communications with them. I regret if it occasioned unforeseen problems," O'Neill answered apologetically.

Cobos nodded sympathetically. He needed these men now more than ever and his mission was to ensure that when the Spanish army arrived, they would still be there to aid it. "That is acceptable. King Philip was concerned that your action represented a change of heart," Cobos said quietly.

"There has been no change of heart," O'Donnell said heatedly. "We gave our word and we shall honour it. We have refused to confirm the treaty with the English, as we promised."

"That is indeed good news. King Philip also wished that I inform you that help is on the way and will reach you before this year is out," Cobos continued.

"But what of the weather?" Cormac asked. "You know that if your ships are not launched soon, the opportunity will be missed for this year."

"And Essex's raid on Cadiz?" O'Donnell asked. "We have heard from the English that it was a great triumph and that it has retarded, by a number of years, any plans that you might have had for such a venture."

Good, Cobos thought. Their real misgivings are now being voiced and I can set about dealing with them. "No," he said gravely. "The English did not win a great victory. Cadiz was but poorly defended. Its walls were under repair. The garrison was depleted and there were only four galleons and a squadron of galleys to protect, what was probably, the richest merchant fleet in the world. The English fleet numbered over a hundred vessels, forty-eight of which were Men-o-

War. Galleys could not dare engage such ships. Hardly a fair fight."

"It seemed a weak force to have been entrusted to defend such a valuable fleet," Cormac observed shrewdly.

"The convoy of merchant ships was to sail to the Indies. We were taken totally by surprise. On learning of the deaths of Drake and Hawkins, we were certain that the English would not mount any expedition this year. Most of the warships that had been assigned to the protection of the merchant fleet, were away in San Lucar, being equipped for the voyage across the ocean," Cobos said.

"So, the English were just lucky?" Maguire asked.

"Yes," Cobos answered. "The English had six thousand five hundred soldiers and another six thousand sailors. How could they fail to take a city that did not even have secure walls? Fortune smiled upon them but what did they do? They stayed two weeks and then sailed away with what plunder they had stolen from the people of Cadiz. They are nothing better than pirates. They put their personal finances before those of their Sovereign. In our country, such action would be viewed as treason and their leaders would have paid the price for their treachery!"

"But we heard of the losses they inflicted on King Philip when they destroyed the merchant fleet that they found in Cadiz," Cormac said.

"They did not destroy the fleet. We fired it. The English captured Cadiz and because the fleet was trapped in the harbour, they did not bother to secure the ships. Two days they spent sacking the town, day and night, drinking and celebrating, while all the time they ignored the richest spoil of all. The Duke of Medina Sidonia offered Howard two million ducats to allow the merchant fleet go free. Howard refused, so the Duke ordered the fleet's destruction. Thirty-six vessels were destroyed, the treasure aboard, worth twelve million ducats. All of that was lost to the English as well as to ourselves. In the confusion caused by the firing of the fleet, the squadron of galleys made good their escape. The Duke ensured that our loss was not the enemy's gain. It was an enormous sacrifice, but King Philip approved of the Duke's action," Cobos said grandly.

"So, the English did not achieve the great success of which they boast?" O'Donnell asked in eager curiosity.

"They did not. They were in such haste homeward with their ill gotten gains that they sailed past Lisbon without stopping. Barely forty eight hours later, the Spanish treasure fleet, laden with gold, silver and jewels worth 20 million ducats, sailed up the River Tagus into Lisbon harbour, virtually unprotected and completely unharmed. So, once again, the English managed to miss the main prize. If they had not been so eager to rush home with their personal booty, they could have made a major profit for their Queen and hurt us even more than they did," Cobos said with disdain.

"Heavens be praised," Maguire said. "Let us hope that such a venture cost them dearly."

Cobos nodded. "Our spies at the English court tell us that the Queen is very angry with Essex. She will lose greatly as a result."

"The more discord there is between the English, the more it serves our purpose," Hugh Roe said with relish.

"There is yet another advantage for your cause, of which, you may not yet know. The raid upon Cadiz has had a most miraculous effect upon King Philip's health. He had been seriously ill since I was here last and I worried that, without his interest, the plan for our Irish Armada might not be realised. Upon learning of the assault upon Cadiz, he rose from his bed, his capacity for work renewed. He is determined to wreak revenge upon the enemy, in Ireland, and will send an Armada here before the end of the year," Cobos said.

"God be praised," O'Donnell exclaimed with much relief.

"That is indeed welcome news," Maguire replied with delight.

"I don't see what news that is. You had already promised us no less on your last visit here," Cormac said gruffly.

Cobos could see that O'Neill's brother was going to be a problem. His sons must still be in the hands of the English, he conjectured. He would have to remember that and have patience with him.

"Yes, but the English raid has transformed the whole of Spain. The people had become tired of war and longed for peace. Cadiz has galvanised and united them once again with one purpose, revenge upon the English. Money has flowed into the King's treasury. The church, the Cortes, the provincial towns, the noblemen, the peasants have all, as one, donated voluntarily what they could spare so that this slight on Spanish dignity can be avenged. The whole country is united behind one imperative. The Second Armada must sail, whatever the cost in lives and money. Cadiz must be avenged at all costs!"

"So, how far advanced are the preparations?" Cormac asked.

"The man chosen to lead the Armada is Don Martin de Padilla Manrique, Adelantado Mayor of Castille, Count of Santa Gadea and Knight of the order of Alvantra," Cobos said with a flourish.

They looked at him blankly. He could not believe that they had not heard of him. Manrique was regarded in Spain as its very greatest naval commander. Now fifty-six, he had a long and distinguished experience in war, having received his baptism as a junior officer at St Quentin at the age of twenty-six. Since then his career had been a glorious one, his name having been linked with all the great naval success achieved by the Spanish. He had even managed to avoid being associated with the great naval disaster that was the first Spanish Armada. Indeed, many had thought that he should have been its leader and if fate had determined it so, then the Armada might not have met the end that it did. If the English had Drake whom the Spanish feared, the Spanish had Manrique who was equally dreaded by the English.

"He is our best naval commander. He has never lost an engagement. You heard of the Gulf of Malaga, where our ships captured three English and twenty Dutch vessels?" Cobos asked. He paused and saw that the Irish nobles nodded when his question was translated. For a moment, he wondered if they really had heard of Manrique's renown. He wondered how much they knew about the bigger world outside their own narrow horizons. He even found himself wondering if they understood all that he was saying. Trying to communicate through an interpreter was frustrating, but he persisted.

"The man who led that raid was Don Martin de Padilla Manrique. He has been the scourge of the English and the Dutch in the Mediterranean. It was but one of many victories that he gained over them," he said proudly.

"It is very encouraging for us that King Philip should chose such a man to lead the expedition," Hugh said graciously.

Cobos nodded. "The expedition will be larger than it was to be when we discussed it last. King Philip wished that I consult with you again as to its landfall. His Majesty has taken great care in selecting the regiments, which shall sail with it. He has withdrawn the best and most experienced units from Flanders and Spain itself. It will be a battle-hardened army that will be capable of destroying an army of twice its number. There are already twelve thousand troops assembled, nine thousand Spanish and three thousand of the King's best Portuguese soldiers. It has been arranged that more men will join it from Brittany."

McDavitt stuttered as he asked Cobos incredulously in Spanish, "Twelve thousand?"

Cobos nodded. "Translate," he ordered.

He watched the effect his words had on the assembled nobles. Their faces were illuminated in undisguised delight and surprise, even the two O'Neill brothers could not conceal their feelings. They talked excitedly among themselves in Gaelic and finally, O'Neill addressed him.

"This is indeed excellent news. With such an army, we will sweep the English from the country. You are correct in assuming that we would wish to change the location for their landfall. Already Ulster is maintaining over ten thousand of its own soldiers. There would not be enough food and accommodation here for such an additional force. We do not have any cities in which they might winter. We have discussed it and we are in agreement that the army should land either in Limerick, Galway or Sligo. Sligo is already in our hands and the surrounding country will welcome your forces. The peoples of Galway and Limerick are Catholic and should deliver their towns to you. In any event, they are but poorly defended and a force such as yours would have little trouble in taking any of them."

"Very well," Cobos answered. It shall be so. But what of your preparations? Have you tried to win more people to our cause?"

"Yes," O'Neill answered. "I have prevented the Lords of Eastern Ulster from attending the commission, set up there by the English, to decide matters in that region. Hugh Roe has done the same in Connaught."

"Good," Cobos said. "You must try and win as many Lords to our side as you can. It will be important yet."

"I have started to extend my Lordship over the midlands. We have dispatched communications to all the other Irish Lords, requesting their adherence to our confederacy in this war. We have concentrated on Munster, as that is the richest province in Ireland, the grain yard of the country," Hugh answered.

Cobos was satisfied. He had worried that he might find an altered political landscape in Ireland as a consequence of the Cadiz fiasco. He had given his word to the King that these men were to be trusted. If they had been found wanting, then his credibility would have been undermined. That, however, would not have been as great a disappointment to him, as the cancellation of the Armada. He firmly believed that Spain's best hope for ultimate victory over the English and their Dutch allies lay in supporting these Irish rebels. The prize was beyond imagining. Spain was already the ruler of the most powerful empire in the world. With the English and Dutch defeated, they would rule not only the New World, but also the old one. From what he had seen of the Irish countryside, it would be a welcome addition to the Spanish Empire. The Irishmen, who had made their way to serve in the Spanish army, had proven themselves as brave and fearless soldiers. Spain had always need of manpower for its armies and navy. And the navy had need of ships, and for the building of ships, wood was sorely needed. Ireland, covered in large oak trees, would be perfect for such an enterprise.

"That is good." he replied with satisfaction. "There are a large number of Irish and English émigrés who wish to travel home with the Armada and join with us in this great venture. I have the names of those who claim to be from Ulster and to be known to you. The list is long but, with your permission, I would like to go through it with you. We do not want spies travelling with us and informing the English of our intentions."

"We would be delighted to be of assistance," O'Neill answered.

"Very well," Cobos replied as he nodded to his clerk who hurriedly unrolled a parchment and passed it to him.

"Now, let me see, the first name I have here is an Eamon O'Donnell, a Franciscan priest. He claims kinship with a branch of the O'Donnells of Raphoe."

O'Donnell nodded. "I know of him, a good man. His return would be welcomed."

"Good," Cobos said as his clerk marked off the priest's name. "We have quite a number of priests on our lists. Your lands seem to be very profitable for the church."

"As it seems that we will be here for some time, perhaps I should arrange refreshments?" Hovendon suggested to the assembled company.

O'Donnell and O'Neill nodded and Hovendon rose and withdrew, relieved that things were finally moving towards a conclusion. He felt no pangs of conscience. He had decided many years earlier that his destiny and that of his foster brother would be inextricably linked and that they would either thrive or fail together. He wondered which side his brothers would choose. They would not be the only ones who would have a difficult choice to make. Even some of the native Irish would not find that decision an easy one.

Rose entered the gates of Donegal Castle and cast a smiling glance at the sentry who nodded amiably to her. The days are drawing in, she thought, noticing the dusk already upon her and that the evening had a chill that carried with it the feel of approaching winter. She mounted the stairs to the Great Hall, intending to pass through it to the stairway that led to her chambers. In the darkening gloom, she did not perceive the shadowy presence of Eoin O'Gallagher, Hugh Roe's closest adviser on the O'Donnell Council. She started when he called her name.

"Eoin," she said breathlessly, "forgive me, I did not see you there."

Eoin bowed and smiled apologetically. "No, Rose. It is I who should apologise to you. I did not mean to startle you so," he said gently. Rose looked into his kind face and saw a sadness there, in spite of the smile. She worried immediately that he bore ill tidings about Hugh Roe. Had some misfortune happened him? She fretted about these meetings that he was conducting with the Spanish officers in Killibegs.

"What is it?" she asked. "Is it Hugh Roe?"

"Hugh Roe is well, thank God," Gallagher answered. "As well as he has been for the last few months."

Rose was relieved but looked closely at Eoin. What did he mean, she wondered? Did he know something that she did not? Could Hugh Roe be ill? He had seemed tired and irritable of late. She had grown fond of Eoin during the years that she had spent in Donegal and had come to value his opinion. She saw how he had acted as a restraining influence on her husband, preventing him from committing foolhardy excesses, which he might otherwise have undertaken.

"What do you mean, Eoin?" she asked anxiously. "Has he been ill, without my knowledge?"

Gallagher shook his head. "No, Rose, not physically ill, but his spirits have not been as they ought. Have you not noticed?" he asked gently.

"Yes, but I attributed it to all the work he undertakes. He is always planning for the war, meeting with others to secure the aid that he thinks will guarantee a successful outcome," she answered. "I encourage him to take more rest, but he is driven, nay consumed by the desire to succeed in this."

Eoin nodded. "Yes, it is of paramount importance to him that he rids this country of the English plague that besets it. He is determined that he shall rule as king over Donegal and Connaught, at the very least. How posterity will view him is very important to him. He has a sense of his place in history. I am sure that you love him and that you would not deny him that place."

Rose nodded, curious about the implication, which Eoin's words still veiled. Of course she would not deny Hugh Roe his place in history. How could she?

"What are you saying?" she asked. "You know that I would never deny Hugh Roe anything."

"Not if it was within your power, but there are some things that, even with the best will in the world, we cannot give the ones we love. We have to allow others give it to them instead," Eoin said slowly and sympathetically.

Rose instantly guessed his meaning. "Has Hugh Roe spoken to you about this?" she asked, her emotions in a whirl, considering the possibility that Hugh Roe might have discussed such an intimate matter with anyone other than her. Her cheeks flushed with embarrassment as she thought of Eoin, a man old enough to be her grandfather, and Hugh Roe, discussing her failure to produce a child

"No," Owen answered emphatically, noticing Rose's upset, "he never uttered a word to me on the matter and I must beg of you to keep our conversation secret from him. It is out of concern for Hugh Roe, that I speak thus." He paused before continuing in a gentle tone. "You must have observed how melancholy he has become. I can see that he desires greatly to father a child. He wishes to found a dynasty that will endure down the ages. When you have been together as long as you have and remain childless, then it is unlikely you will ever produce an heir. Forgive my bluntness, but you must face that fact, Rose. You must face it for both of you. The love he bears you will not allow him acknowledge that you both will never parent any sons together."

Rose's emotions were in total disarray. She had worried often that Hugh Roe might not be able to accept their childlessness and this had especially troubled her over the last few months. She had managed to turn her mind away from the subject and not dwell too profoundly upon it. Now, Eoin was putting words on her deepest anxiety.

"If you really love him, you must give him his freedom. It would be the greatest gift you could ever bestow upon him. I think that I have got to know you and would not talk to you on such a delicate matter, unless I knew the depths of your selflessness," he continued.

Rose looked dumbly into the old, benign face, unable to reply. Whatever certainties and happiness she previously held, had been erased almost in an instant. Never again would the world be as it was a minute before. Her whole body trembled. How could she give him up, she asked herself. And yet, how could she stay if that only led to unhappiness and loss for Hugh Roe? Eoin was right. She could not deny him something for which he so yearned. She would have to put his needs before her own. She had no choice. If she did not, in time, he would come to resent her. Without uttering another word, Rose turned and walked towards the turret stairs, which led to her chamber. Her heart pounded and her feelings rioted against what had become an immovable, black thought. She would have to be strong. Her father would allow her return to Dungannon. Life was not meant to be happy, she thought wistfully. Now that she had faced the truth of her situation, she must carry out what was required of her before Hugh Roe returned from his meeting with the Spanish. She must pack and leave on the morrow. Climbing the steps to her chamber, she felt more wretched than she had ever felt before in her life, but steeled herself to do what, she knew, she must.

Alonso Cobos pushed his way through the crowds and the wagons that milled and thronged about Lisbon's docks. It was already dark, but the docks were still a hive of activity, stores and provisions being unloaded on the quays from wagons, stretching into the distance. The provisions did not remain long there, as they were quickly loaded onto the Armada of ships that had been assembled in the bay. Cobos was tired and thirsty. He had ridden from King Philip's palace, the Escorial, which was located thirty-two miles from Madrid. There, he had had an audience with the King himself. It had been most successful, King Philip concurring with all his proposals. He had been extremely impatient to be back, once again, in the Portuguese capital and had ridden hard to reach it before nightfall.

On the return journey, he had thought of the Escorial and the riches assembled therein. What would the Irish Lords say if they could but see it, he wondered. If one ever needed proof of the might, power and riches of Spain, one had only to view it. Its construction had cost the King three million five hundred thousand ducats, a figure so large that it was difficult to contemplate. Cobos had felt humbled there, as he waited over a week, before finally being granted the audience he so required.

At last, he arrived at Manrique's headquarters, which overlooked the docks. He passed inside and found a chamber filled with scribes, working at tables, lit by flickering candles. They were so busy at their tasks that they did not even cast a glance in his direction. Cobos stood and looked around the chamber, searching for Manrique. It was quite and peaceful after the bedlam of the docks outside, which still could be heard faintly through the mullioned windows. He listened momentarily to the crackle of parchment and the scratch of quills, before identifying the chief scribe and approaching him.

"Where is Don Martin?" he demanded

The scribe stopped writing and raised his head. The man's face betrayed his disappointment on seeing him. "Yes," Cobos said, "I'm back again and I hope that I find that things are in a better state than when I left for Madrid. But come, man where is he? I have an urgent communication from King Philip for him."

"He is not here. He left some days since, to travel to San Lucar to check on the ships that are to assemble there. He was unhappy with the reports he received about their sea worthiness."

"And when is he to return?" Cobos asked impatiently.

"He should be back by tomorrow," the clerk answered, "but, of course, it depends on how much work he had to undertake there."

"But I must deliver these orders to him. He should be here, planning the overall mission," Cobos said in vexation. He was bitterly disappointed. He had been so looking forward to this confrontation. He had been determined not to allow it even wait until the morning and had been prepared to wake Manrique, if necessary. Now he felt cheated and the prospect of having to travel to San Lucar, filled him with anger. Just then, the door opened and Manrique strode into the chamber. His hair was covered with the dust of the road and he made straight for a pitcher of water standing on a table and poured himself a large goblet, downing it in one draught.

"Incompetence," he shouted to the scribes in general. "I am surrounded by incompetence on all sides." He turned towards the chief clerk and, on seeing Cobos, he scowled. "You have rejoined us. Another misfortune to endure," he said acidly before addressing the clerk. "How much nearer completion are we to assembling the necessary provisions?"

The clerk rummaged through the documents on his desk before handing Manrique one of them. He took it and held it in his hand, not reading it. "Well, summarise," he ordered.

"The commissariat say they have been working as hard as they can. As of tonight, we have almost ninety per cent of the supplies, delivered and loaded on the ships," he said eagerly. "Would you like me to go through the items with you?"

Manrique shook his head. "I will consider them in my own time. I am weary and shall retire to my quarters for some sleep."

"Don Martin, we must talk," Cobos said forcefully.

"It will keep until the morning," Manrique answered dismissively and turned on his heel to leave the chamber.

"No, it will not! I bring urgent orders from His Majesty and you will receive them forthwith!" Cobos commanded.

He sensed Manrique hesitate before turning to face him. Cobos could read the dislike and the frustration that the other was feeling. The dislike was mutual. Manrique had not wished for this command and had begged King Philip to bestow the honour on some other admiral, pleading fatigue and sickness. The reality was that no admiral would volunteer for such a commission. They had seen how the failure of the first Armada had ruined the reputation and career of the Duke of Medina Sidonia and none of them wished to risk the repeat of such a disaster in the cold North Atlantic seas. Cobos could not help but feel that Manrique had brought that initial reluctance in accepting the commission, to its implementation. All he had heard from him was an incessant stream of complaints and reasons why the Armada would not be ready to be launched before the winter storms. It was out of concern that the Armada might not be launched this year that had prompted Cobos to travel to the Escorial and seek an audition with His Majesty. He had given his word to the Irish Lords and he would do all in his power to fulfil his promises.

Manrique turned around to face him. "You had better come through to my chamber," he said wearily.

Cobos followed him to his chamber, which was located beside the scribes' quarters. Manrique sat in a wooden armchair, behind an untidy desk, strewn with documents and maps. Cobos remained standing. "King Philip is most anxious that the Armada sails immediately. Already, too much time has passed. He will not tolerate any postponement until the spring. Here are your orders," he said as he passed him the document, bearing the King's seal.

Manrique took the document but did not open it. "And did he receive my letters stating the inadvisability of such a course?" he asked belligerently.

"Yes, and he says that it is your job to surmount such difficulties. Read for yourself," Cobos answered.

Cobos saw Manrique's face redden in anger. "You are no friend of Spain to encourage the King in his expectation that the Armada can be successfully launched in winter time. You put the well being of your new found Irish friends before that of the Spanish sailors and soldiers who must venture forth in the treacherous North Atlantic. What angers me most about this whole, rushed venture is that your Irish allies will be safe until the spring. The English never campaign in winter time."

"We have been through all this before. Your orders are re-confirmed. Follow them," Cobos ordered.

"And how do I launch a fleet that is not fully prepared? The provisions are not even fully assembled. Do you know the amount of preparation that is involved?" He took the parchment that the clerk had given him earlier and started to read.

"12,837 barrels of biscuits, 696 skins of wine, 1,498 barrels of salt pork, 1,031 barrels of fish, 6,082 barrels of cheese, 2,858 barrels of vegetables, 2,900 barrels of oil, 2,274 barrels of water, 850 barrels of vinegar, 631 barrels of rice, 1,200 barrels of powder, 30,000 cannon balls, fifty wagons, horses..."

"Spare me all the details. You have your orders. It is your responsibility to carry them out," Cobos said, not wanting to revisit all the arguments. There were always reasons for postponing campaigns and he knew, from personal experience, that one had always to move onward, despite the difficulties.

"Those details that you dismiss, are the very details that will ordain success or failure," Manrique answered bitterly. "An army that is not properly provisioned, cannot hope to succeed. Where will it find the provisions needful for winter time in Ireland?"

"You have enough supplies already embarked. You are to sail to Ireland, deliver the soldiers and return home. During the winter, regular supplies will be ferried from Coruna and Blavet," Cobos answered.

"I still do not have enough ships. The new galleons are not completed and there is now no hope of them being ready in time," Manrique said.

"It is unlikely that you will encounter the English fleet as they will not expect an invasion so late in the year. You have the remaining eight Apostles, the very best Men-o-War available anywhere and some twenty-two lesser galleons. King Philip is convinced that the force will be adequate for the task. Our spies in England inform us that the English fleet is once again laid up in Chatham and the sailors have been discharged. The English Queen is all but bankrupt. Vere and his crack regiments have been sent back to the Netherlands. We will have the benefit of total surprise on our side," Cobos said urgently, trying, for one last time, to engender some enthusiasm for this project in the other man.

"We are inviting disaster by following such a course. I have made my reservations known and now I will do my duty for the King and Spain. I pray that God will somehow grant us unseasonably good weather. When the final transport ships arrive, we will set sail for Ireland with the first fair wind, but I will not do so before then. I will not leave part of the army behind me," Manrique said stiffly.

"That is as it should be. Set sail and we will leave the rest to God," Cobos answered.

Manrique nodded and left the chamber. Cobos watched him leave, glad that at last, they had agreed the plan of campaign. He would still have to keep vigil on developments and ensure that the ships left as quickly as possible. Delay after delay had to be contended with and now it was time to put them all behind them. Come what may, the Armada would sail and when it landed in Ireland, the whole power balance in Europe would be forever altered in Spain's favour. Suddenly, he felt weary as the last few days' travel caught up with him. He would return to his quarters and get some sleep. Tomorrow would be another busy day.

Chapter 15

If the Spanish land in Ireland, then we are all doomed. Given the soldiers we have, we would be swept before them, like straw in a gale,"
Bagenal commented despondently, then asked. "But do you really
think that they are coming to this God forsaken country?"
"Who knows? The only indisputable facts we have are that on the
twenty-fourth of October, the Spanish set sail from Lisbon. Their
Armada is not as formidable as that of 1588, but large enough to gain
a toe hold on the English mainland. Over a hundred ships and thirty
of Spain's finest galleons, packed with their best soldiers!" Wingfield
answered. He was greatly disquieted. He had seen enough on the
Continent to know what Spanish soldiers were capable of, and
realised that Bagenal wasn't wrong in his estimation of the English
garrison army's inability to defeat an invading Spanish one.

He had been assigned the task of drawing up an accurate list of
English soldiers in Ireland and the result made depressing reading.
The total muster ran to 617 horse and 5,372 foot. A year previously,
the number had stood at 657 horse and 4,040 foot. The paltry increase
in numbers, over the year, was all the more disappointing in light of
the 4,000 extra troops and 300 horse that had been dispatched across
the Irish Sea in that time. That was the problem with Irish wars, he
thought. English armies seemed to disappear into the mist in this
accursed country. Illness and desertion always accounted for more
casualties than the actual fighting. As it was, they were already facing over ten thousand trained Irish troops in the North. How would
they deal with a Spanish invasion as well? It was not as if they could
even put their full complement of soldiers in the field to oppose an
invading Spanish army. Most of his men were already taken up with
garrison duties in the many towns that dotted the island. Up until
now, they had always been safe and secure behind their towns' stout
walls. But if the Spanish arrived with their siege guns, then all that
would change.

"And what is the opinion of the Privy Council? If they think there
is a danger of their landing here, then they must reinforce our army,"
Bagenal said, interrupting Wingfield's train of thought.

Wingfield shook his head angrily. "As usual, they are divided on
the issue. Essex, Lord North and Carew expect the Spaniards, once
again, to attempt an attack on the Isle of Wight or the Margate Coast.
Lord Burgley thinks they will attack Falmouth. Sir William Knollys
says Plymouth and Raleigh thinks they will attack the Thames. Only

Willoughby reckons that we shall see their ships on Irish shores."

"Their past intelligence has been most consistently inexact; it will probably end up here," Bagenal said dispiritedly. "Can none of our spies in Spain furnish us with more specific information?"

"No," Wingfield answered. "The Spanish have spread so many rumours that it is impossible to ascertain where the truth lies. The northern Irish, however, seem to have been made a promise of aid. Our spies there all report the same intelligence. They all say the Spanish will land here before the end of the year."

"It repulses me to observe how brazen the Irish have become. Even my own tenants boldly refuse to pay any rent. I can do naught about it, as they claim O'Neill's protection and I am still forbidden to cross swords with him," Bagenal railed bitterly. "I no longer dare stay in my own abode and must live permanently in this tavern. My home is no longer safe. The Irish shoot at my men from the surrounding woods. Ten good men murdered in the last month! So now, Newry is my prison. We dare not travel outside the walls without a large, armed bodyguard. Thank God we have a strong garrison, at least."

"I have come to talk with you about the garrison. We need your men. All our towns are being stripped of soldiers, leaving the bare minimum to hold them. I'm recalling four hundred of them," Wingfield said with as much authority as he could muster. He saw Bagenal's face change, reflecting a mood that Wingfield had seen only too often, outraged hostility.

"But that will leave me with but fifty men! What can I do with fifty men?" Bagenal spluttered in choler. "We will not be able to venture outside the walls, nay, we will not be even able to look over them. It is inconceivable that Newry, our one secure town in Ulster, should be reduced to such a weak state. I will not allow it. You do not have the authority to do so!"

Wingfield had expected such a reaction. He had experienced the same frightened refusal from the majors of Galway and Limerick when he reduced their garrisons. All any of them appreciated was their own need for security and safety. They did not see the peril, under which the whole country laboured. He drew Russell's authorisation from his doublet and handed it to Bagenal.

"The Lord Deputy has appointed me to carry out the task of assembling an army that will be based in Athlone, one which will march to meet the Spanish, should they arrive," he replied. "I must gather as many men there as I can safely remove from other parts of the country. We do not know where the Spanish will land, if they do come here. My wager is that they will not land in the North. The northern Lords could not feed and shelter such an army over the winter. I think it will, either be the west or south, but we cannot be sure. Athlone, located as it is in the middle of the country, more or less equidistant from the extremities, seems the preferable position for our forces."

Bagenal had read the parchment while Wingfield had been speaking and now, slowly rolled it up and returned it to him. The latter saw Bagenal's colour slowly return to a more normal hue. "And where is Norris? He is supposed to be in charge in Ulster and has been absent from the province these last few weeks," Bagenal asked.

"He and the Lord Deputy are no longer in communication with each other. He is in Athlone. He claims that he is ill and refuses to meet with anyone, insisting that he will not return to his posting until the Queen removes Russell. He still has total faith in the loyalty of the northern Irish Lords," Wingfield answered, impatient at Norris's gullibility. He was annoyed at the two commanders, who even in this time of extreme danger, could not set aside their personal antagonism for the greater good of the Realm.

"I do hope that she will not bow to such an audacious request," Bagenal observed. "That would be giving the Irish exactly what they desire. I will never forgive Norris for his part in the recall and incarceration of Bingham. The Queen has done everything to mollify the Irish, Bingham's plight is but one example. The more she gives, the more they demand. Appeasement never works. I have always said it and I will yet be proven right. If the Spanish land, we will see just how loyal the Irish are. Mark my words, and mark them well, Bingham will be sorely missed if the Spanish do invade. He would be the first man to confront them and spill his blood to stop them. The injustice of it makes me ill!"

Wingfield shared Bagenal's sentiments on the subject. What was even worse, the Queen had not yet replaced Bingham, so there was no President of Connaught to oppose a landing there, should that be the chosen location for an invasion. He had heard that Sir Conyers Clifford was favoured for the appointment, but it would, doubtless, take months before the Queen would decide between the two nominations of the rival factions on the Privy Council. There was even worse news to come, news of which Bagenal would not yet be aware.

"The Queen has decided to recall the Lord Deputy and remove Norris from his posting. She is weary of their constant fighting. Of course, with the present situation, she cannot do so until she has replacements for them," Wingfield said.

"But what of extra troops from England?" Bagenal asked again. "Even with what you gather from around the country, you will not have a large force in Athlone."

"Not even three thousand. But there is no hope of reinforcements from England. They have not enough soldiers to defend England itself and have not the time nor ships to transport the English army from the Continent to here. The fleet has been disbanded. The Earl of Essex has been appointed head of a special Council of War to advise the Queen and has taken charge of the preparations to stay any invasion of England. The local militia has been called out and put under arms. Essex has remained in London to defend it, Raleigh has hastened to Cornwall and your brother, Samuel, has been posted to defend the Isle of Wight," Wingfield answered.

"That is good news. I'm pleased that Samuel has received such a commission," Bagenal responded, glad of some small, good tidings.

"It is good that the Queen has able men such as him to call on in her time of need," Wingfield observed. "It is a pity that we do not have more men like him here in Ireland."

"The Queen can always rely on the Bagenals. Our family has never failed to do its duty. It is no longer my wish to remain in Newry, but would rather travel with my men to Athlone and confront the Spanish with you, should they land," Bagenal said.

Wingfield had effected the change he wished for in Bagenal's mood. He would need every man he could get and even if he had no great opinion of Bagenal's skill as a commander, he could not doubt his bravery or loyalty.

"I would be honoured to have you with us," he said holding out his hand to Bagenal who grasped it eagerly. "I knew that I would not find you wanting."

Bagenal was gratified. "We will teach those Spanish a lesson, just as we have taught the Irish," he said.

"We must hope that the natives in Munster and Leinster remain peaceful. I have sent messengers to each Irish Lord, appealing for their loyalty in this time of danger. They have not yet joined with the northern Irish and we had better hope and pray that they do not," Wingfield continued.

"After the devastation wreaked on the Irish in Munster, a bare sixteen years ago, they would not dare raise their arms against us. Their lands and population still have not recovered fully from the famines that followed that war," Bagenal answered.

"But if the Spanish land, who knows what might happen," Wingfield said with more than a hint of anxiety. "If the Irish acted in unison and put aside their distrust of each other, they would not even need the Spanish and could defeat us on their own."

Bagenal growled, "And that is why we will always vanquish them, because we have that unity, which they lack. So, let us hope that the weather will come to our aid once again, as it did in '88. It is already

November, well past the time when it is safe to contemplate a venture such as theirs. Who knows, we might yet not have to fight either here or in England."

Wingfield nodded. "Let us hope so, but come. We must prepare as best we can, lest it is to here they journey. You must help me pick the best soldiers."

Bagenal nodded. " Perhaps fifty soldiers is too many to leave in Newry. Twenty and some of the townspeople should be enough. Truth to tell, if the Spanish attack the town, a thousand men would not keep them out, whereas twenty good men would safeguard it from the Irish."

Wingfield nodded. "Agreed," he said as he got to his feet. "Let us choose and we will march at dawn. We cannot afford to linger."

Bagenal rose and followed him out into the cold November day.

"So what do you think of them?" O'Neill asked the solemn faced Englishman, standing at his side, as they and Henry Hovendon watched his recruits drilling in the winter morning.

"Tolerable," Tyrell answered, not taking his eyes off the marching men who were deployed smoothly into a pike formation, the shot fringing the edges of the formed square. "How long have they been in training?" he asked.

"Four months," Hugh answered.

Tyrell nodded. Hugh observed the man in front of him. He was tall and thin with a dark beard and long hair. There was an air about him of confidence and professionalism. This was a man whom Hugh wanted on his side. Hovendon had done well, as usual, and he nodded to him, in acknowledgement of his approval.

"What proportion of shot to pike have you?" Tyrell asked.

"Four to one and one horseman for every pikeman," O'Neill answered.

Tyrell nodded approvingly. "And do they train with gunpowder?" he asked.

"Yes, no expense is spared," O'Neill answered.

"Good," Tyrell responded.

They stood watching the Spanish drill master who roared the commands in a heavily accented Gaelic and any soldier that did not perform to his satisfaction, he chastised with his baton.

"The men hate him," Hovendon said.

"That is as it should be," Tyrell commented. "Drill masters have to drive their men hard. It might save their lives some day. Was he sent to you?"

"No, God help him. He's a stray from the Great Armada," Hugh answered with a laugh. "He's from the south of Spain and is constantly moaning about our weather. He wants to return home, but he's too useful to us, to permit it."

"He knows his craft," Tyrell answered as dark clouds rolled across the sky, threatening a downpour.

"So, if you have seen enough, we will return to my quarters and discuss your terms," Hugh said.

Tyrell nodded and the three men turned and started walking back towards the town. They saw a horseman approach and as he drew near, Hugh recognised O'Donnell. "Ah, Hugh Roe," Hugh hailed, as the younger man dismounted. "You've come. This is Captain Tyrell of whom I wrote."

Hugh Roe nodded and held out his hand to the Englishman who took it and shook it firmly.

"We have been watching the drilling," Hugh explained as he turned to Hovendon. "Take Captain Tyrell back and discuss terms with him, Henry. We will join you anon. He can negotiate on my behalf," Hugh explained to Tyrell who looked surprised at such a delegation of authority.

Hovendon and Tyrell walked ahead while Hugh and O'Donnell turned to look at the army. Hugh found the sight re-assuring and it was good for his men to see that he was taking a keen interest.

"Well, what do you think of him?" Hugh Roe enquired.

"I think he will be useful to our cause," Hugh answered.

"But how can you be sure that you can trust him?" Hugh Roe asked, doubtfully.

"One can never be sure that one can trust anyone. From what I see of him, I'm willing to take the risk. He was a captain in the English army and fought with distinction on the Continent, operating successfully behind Spanish lines for months on end. His bravery is unquestionable," Hugh answered.

"I distrust a man that changes sides. If he betrays his cause once, there's nothing to stop him doing so again," Hugh Roe said cautiously.

"Tyrell could not change again. He'd be regarded as a traitor with a price on his head," Hugh countered.

"Unless he's doing this with their agreement in order to spy on us. He could even assassinate you," Hugh Roe suggested.

"That is a possibility," Hugh answered, "but Henry trusts him and I will be guided by his judgement. It was he who brought him to my notice. Tyrell has been treated despicably by the Lord Deputy. In spite of his achievements to date, he has been left without a commission or any pay since he was posted here. Russell hates him because of his low birth and the success he enjoyed against the Spanish. Tyrell is eager for revenge; eager to show Russell what a soldier he is and how grievous an oversight it was to treat him so unfairly."

"Why take the risk? The Spanish will be here soon and then we will drive the English from the country. We have no need of men like him, a foreigner. I cannot see our men following him," Hugh Roe rebutted.

O'Neill was still not prepared to invest all his hopes of success in Spanish intervention, but did not wish to draw O'Donnell's wrath on that issue. "He will have five hundred good soldiers, trained churls. They have been taught to obey orders and they will do so," Hugh answered. "He and they will operate behind enemy lines, much as he did in the Netherlands. I will send him into Leinster and his mission shall be to destroy as many of the English farms and people as he can. He will have support there from the native Irish, who will supply him with food and information. The O'Byrnes and the O'Moores will join with him in open revolt. Together, they should stir the province up and cause much havoc for the English."

"And have both Chieftains agreed to join the Confederacy?" Hugh Roe asked excitedly.

"Yes, Owney O'Moore is anxious to expel the English from the country. I hear great reports of him. And we already know Fiach's reputation and loyalty to our cause," Hugh answered.

"So, others in Leinster might be enticed, or forced to join us?" Hugh Roe asked.

"That is my design," Hugh replied. "So, you are in agreement?" he asked.

"Yes," Hugh Roe answered and the two men stood watching the drilling army a while longer.

A cold wind blew across the open plain, a harbinger of rain. Within minutes, the heavens opened and both men turned and headed back towards the town. O'Donnell untethered his horse and both he and O'Neill walked on its right flank to take shelter from the rain that the wind whipped across the open countryside.

"And how is Rose?" Hugh Roe asked awkwardly, alluding at last to the subject that had lain dormant between them ever since his arrival.

Hugh had worried greatly about his daughter since her arrival back in Dungannon. She had pined away before his very eyes, attempting to hide her unhappiness from him, never complaining, and never once blaming Hugh Roe for any fault. He recognised in her some of the symptoms that he had witnessed in Mabel during her last sickness and that worried him greatly. Her unhappiness made him feel guilty about the contentment he had found with his new wife. It was as if a ghost of Mabel had come to live with him in Dungannon. Rose had told him of Hugh Roe's need for a child and, whereas he could understand his son-in-law's wish for an heir, he grieved for Rose's sadness. "She is very unhappy," he said honestly. "I fret for her."

His summons of Hugh Roe to meet Tyrell had been but a ruse to get him to Dungannon in the hope that this impasse between them might be resolved. He had to tread a careful course with O'Donnell, letting him know of his upset regarding Rose's unhappiness but not openly exhorting him into taking her back. O'Donnell remained silent a few moments before replying. "She left me. I did not ask her to go," he answered.

"I know. She told me of that, but she also told me that she did so because she believed that you would never be happy unless you had children. She left, not because she did not love you, but because she did," Hugh said gently.

"I know," Hugh Roe answered, another awkward silence descending upon them.

"Do you have children by any other lover?" Hugh asked at length.

Hugh Roe looked with surprise at his father-in-law. "No," he answered.

"A pity," Hugh said in a detached manner and both men continued walking towards the town, their cloaks secured tightly against the wind and falling rain.

After a few moments, Hugh continued. "A son, born out of wedlock, could inherit the Chieftainship after you. Look at my father. He was not legitimate."

"I have remained loyal to your daughter," Hugh Roe said stiffly, as if the admission in some way lessened his manhood. Hugh believed him. There was something ascetic about O'Donnell that had always made him think that he could very easily have dedicated his life to the church. He had that certainty of outlook, that ability only to see issues in black and white, always ignoring the grey that was so typical in men of the cloth. He could put himself through extreme hardship, if that was required, to attain a goal.

He, himself, could not comprehend such denial. He had always wanted women, large women, slim women, red haired women, blondes, brunettes or dark, he wanted to taste, smell, possess every one of them. On his visits to London, he had frequented the whorehouses of Southwark where he delighted in the company of the more exotic, foreign women. He had so many children out of wedlock, that he found it difficult to number them. It was only now, when he was well into his middle years, that he had found happiness and contentment with one woman. He desired Hugh Roe and Rose to be reunited. He knew that Rose would never remarry or find happiness with another.

"And that is an admirable loyalty," Hugh said. "But is it right that now you should abandon Rose?" he asked. "You seemed happy once?"

"I do not deny it," Hugh Roe answered.

"And you can be again," Hugh replied. "I know how loyal Rose is and what love she bears you, though why she does is a mystery to me," he added with a half laugh, attempting to bring some levity to what was an increasingly difficult conversation. "Think long and hard about what you do," he counselled. "You can always have the son you wish for, with another. I am sure that, were you to do so, Rose would not deny that child and would raise it as her own."

Hugh Roe did not reply but looked into the distance. Hugh had done as much as he dared.

"Where is she?" Hugh Roe asked eventually.

"Probably in her chamber. She does not go out much," Hugh answered.

"I will go and talk with her," Hugh Roe said and he quickened his step as they entered the warren of dwellings that constituted Dungannon.

Rose was seated in the casement of her chamber, looking out over the Dungannon fields, when she was distracted from her thoughts by a knock on the door. Before she could answer, it had swung open and Hugh Roe stood before her. His hair was matted by rain and his cloak clung damply to his frame. Her heart ached at the sight of him. How she had longed to see him over the last few weeks and here he was before her. But what did it mean, she wondered. She had dreamed of his coming to bring her back with him to Donegal, but she could not see how that could come about. And yet, he was here.

"Rose," he said with concern. " You look poorly."

She bowed her head. "I am quite well," she answered. "And you, how have you been?"

She saw that he looked wan and tired. He is probably toiling excessively as usual, she thought.

"I've missed you," he said simply. "Come home with me."

Rose's heart lurched. She had so wanted him to request this and yet she wondered if this was the proper course.

"But, Hugh Roe, would you not be better finding yourself another wife? One that could give you a child?"

"I want you," he said earnestly. Rose looked into his eyes and read honesty and openness there. "Our families are tied together in bonds of friendship and support. We should not lightly sunder those," he continued.

Rose stopped short. She had no interest in the bonds between their families, only in what existed between the two of them.

"Has my father been speaking with you? Did he summon you here?" she asked anxiously, afraid that he might have engineered this attempted reconciliation.

"No, he did not! And do you honestly think that anyone could make me do something that I did not wish?" Hugh Roe asked, with a wry smile.

Rose agreed silently. It was true, no one, not even her father could force Hugh Roe into acting against his will.

"But I will always feel that I've failed you, that your destiny should have been with someone who could give you a child. I know that it is for the best. You ask me now to return, but later, you will come to resent me. It is bound to come to pass," she said resignedly.

"No, Rose. It will not happen. I need you. We have long been together, and have come through much trial and tribulation. Life is short, we must not squander it apart. Do not remove yourself from my life as you have done," he pleaded earnestly.

He paused, waiting for Rose to say something. Confusion reigned in Rose's heart. She yearned to rush to him and embrace him, but did not trust herself.

"As for children, I have resigned myself to God's will," Hugh Roe added. "You and I must stay together because we love each other. We can foster children. It is part of my duty as The O'Donnell, a duty that I had deferred until we had children of our own. Now I can set about that task. There will be many who would wish to have their children fostered by us. My sister, Nuala, hopes that we might take Neachtan when he is a little older."

Rose felt a warm surge of hope flood through her. "Neachtan is also Niall Garve's son," she said cautiously, knowing how Hugh Roe distrusted the child's father.

"We cannot hold that against him," Hugh Roe said, with a trace of a smile. "He is still my nephew and, who knows, he might one day be the next O'Donnell Chieftain. I want to know him and influence his upbringing. Together, you and I could do much for such children. Please Rose, if you love me, come home with me now."

Rose had decided. She would return. Her spirits soared. She could see a future for them, a future where they worked together for the good of Donegal and now that they had accepted not having children, perhaps it might happen. Life was like that sometimes. He really did love her. She would never doubt him again; she would give him all the love and support that she could muster from this day forth. He had come for her, even though it was she who had turned away.

"Yes, I will return with you," she said. "I do love you Hugh Roe. I never have ceased."

She went to him. His strong arms enveloped her and held her so securely that she felt them both as one. He stroked her hair as his warm breath caressed her cheek. Desire rose in her, desire to have him love her, to share the love that she felt for him. She lifted her head and sought his mouth.

Niall Garve O'Donnell was home from Connaught, the truce having rendered his services redundant. He had vainly attempted to settle back into a life of hunting and fishing, but he found the days dull and tedious. This period of enforced inactivity did not suit him and he was oppressed by the uncertainty that hung in the air about him. He sat drinking at his table, impatiently awaiting the arrival of The O'Doherty's servants with their important charge. Where were they, he wondered angrily. If they arrived, he could get the business over with, could saddle up his horse and along with some of his men, hunt stag. He heard the sound of footsteps on the stone flags and a servant knocked, then entered the Great Hall.

"They have arrived," he said.

Niall Garve nodded and rose from his seat. "And they have the child with them?" he asked.

"Yes," the servant answered.

"Have them wait here. Where is my son?" Niall Garve asked.

"In the solar, with the mistress," he answered.

Niall Garve was disappointed. He would have preferred to confront Nuala after the deed was executed. Being well acquainted with her determination, he knew that she would object. Still, he thought, why should he be uncomfortable at the prospect of confronting his own wife, when he faced his enemies in battle without the least hesitation? He hurried to the stairs, leading to the solar. Walking straight into the upper chamber, without knocking, he saw Nuala sitting at the casement with their son, Neachtan, on her lap. She was singing and gently rocking him over and back. Neachtan, now almost two, had already grown into a handsome boy with a winning smile. His mother doted on him, hardly ever allowing him from her sight. Niall Garve considered that being in his mother's company so much was not in the child's best interest. Both had argued bitterly on this theme and he saw already how Neachtan shrank from his touch, preferring his mother's presence to his own. That timidity in Neachtan incensed him. What sort of Chieftain would he make if he were afraid of his own father, he often wondered? Neachtan would have to become strong, he thought, if he was ever be able to hold his own. No, for the sake of the future, things would have to change.

Nuala looked at Niall Garve with hostility. "Yes," she enquired. "What do you want?

"Neachtan," he said expressionlessly. "It is time that he was fostered."

Nuala looked at him uncomprehendingly. "Fostered?" she echoed.

"I have come to a pact with The O'Doherty. We will foster his son, Rory, and he will take Neachtan. I was fostered by the same clan and it is only right that Neachtan should follow in that tradition also," Niall Garve answered. He saw the colour rise in Nuala's cheeks and recognised the signs. He was in for a consummate battle.

"Our son is too young to be fostered yet, and when that day comes, it will not be the likes of O'Doherty who will bring him up. A more crass, ignorant man, I have yet to meet and I dread what influence he would wield over Neachtan," Nuala stormed.

"There is nothing amiss with O'Doherty and he has proven himself a loyal friend to my family over the years. I have made the bargain. His son is downstairs and Neachtan must return with O'Doherty's servants to Inishowen," Niall Garve countered.

"When the time comes to foster Neachtan, then Hugh Roe and Rose will undertake the task. Hugh Roe has already offered and it is the right place for him to be raised. He would get to know his uncle, The O'Donnell, and Rose's influence on him could only be for the good. You cannot deny that?" Nuala insisted.

"Indeed I could," Niall Garve replied. Between them, they would try to steal his son away from him, he thought. Nuala would do all in her power to steer Neachtan in favour of his uncle and if the lad were fostered by Hugh Roe, that would complete Niall Garve's undermining. No, he would not allow that happen. He would nurture the alliances that his family had always enjoyed and would bring up his son to be loyal to him and him only.

"It has been decided," he repeated. "I will not revoke my word."

"But Hugh Roe is your Chieftain. He has expressed a desire to foster your son. You cannot deny him. You owe him that allegiance," Nuala said angrily.

"A man is free to choose whosoever he wishes to foster his son. I have shown my allegiance to your brother. Have I not campaigned in Connaught for him and brought large sections of it under his rule?" Niall Garve retorted balefully.

"You need not claim for yourself the glory that is rightfully Hugh Roe's," Nuala said venomously. "You were just one of his captains, nothing more. Any of a hundred others could have accomplished as much."

Niall Garve was wounded at the injustice of Nuala's words. He had been greatly instrumental in the conquest of Connaught and had ensured success there. He had also offered much sound counsel to his brother-in-law, counsel that had been ignored. It irked him greatly to see all they had achieved there, being put at risk because of Hugh Roe's arrogance. The Irish of Connaught had risen and joined with them. They wished to see a return to Brehon Law and the restoration of Gaelic Chieftainships. Hugh Roe had set aside the people's choice and imposed his own favourites as Chieftains on these Connaught clans. Trouble would brew there yet.

While Niall Garve despised Hugh O'Neill, he had to admire how he conducted his business in Eastern Ulster. He never allowed sentimentality to cloud his judgement. He was always prepared to withdraw support from a personally favoured client when any clan preferred a more powerful and popular rival.

"You underestimate my contribution," he shouted.

"No, I do not," she countered. "You overestimate your importance, an importance that will diminish even further when the Spanish land? Then Hugh Roe will rule as King over his lands, maybe over all the country."

"Do not forget his partner, O'Neill. But, no doubt, he has contributed nothing either to your brother's success!" Niall Garve commented acerbically.

"You will be naught," Nuala spat at him. "So, deny my brother our son, at your peril. If you do, you will live to regret it," she threatened.

Anger surged within Niall Garve, anger at his wife, anger at the manner in which she addressed him and in the way she disdained his status. He had a greater right to the O'Donnell Chieftainship than Hugh Roe. He was more directly descended. The Elder Hugh Roe's succession had been a travesty. He would not permit his wife to lay down the law or speak such falsehoods on this or the issue of fostering his son. Neachtan was his. Hugh Roe and Rose were unable to beget a child and he was dammed if he would allow them take his as their own. However, what Nuala had said about the Spanish had stung him. He was concerned about their possible arrival. He had worried about his position in an Ireland dominated by them. Hugh Roe would always find favour with the Spanish, while he, most probably, would be viewed as dispensable. Nuala's reasoning was, unfortunately, all too sound.

He advanced and grabbed Neachtan from behind Nuala where the little lad was sheltering, frightened by the raised, argumentative voices of his parents. Nuala tried to pull him from her husband's grasp, but he pushed her roughly, causing her to fall heavily to the ground. Neachtan began to cry and call to her. Niall Garve swung him under his left arm and made for the door as Nuala got to her feet and rushed at him, clawing and spitting like a wild cat. She tore at him and as she did, he dropped the child, lashing out at her and catching her a glancing blow across the face with his fist, which sent her reeling across the chamber. Her back connected with the stone buttress. The breath was driven from her body and she slid downwards, collapsing upon the floor. Niall Garve saw that she was unable to rise. For a moment, he feared that he had killed her. At length, she moved and opened her eyes. "Mallacht ort," she gasped. Neachtan made to run to her but Niall Garve caught him and once again, gathered him under his arm. Abruptly, he turned and left the chamber, locking the door behind him. He descended the stairs to the Great Hall. On reaching it, he thrust the screaming child into the arms of O'Doherty's servant. "Here, take him," he ordered.

The servant did as he was bid, as another servant approached. "Rory, my lord," he said.

Niall Garve looked at the proffered child, wrapped in its blanket. He took it with distaste. This should be Nuala's responsibility, he thought. "Tell your master that we will look after Rory as our own," he said. "Now go and take that crying brat with you," he ordered.

O'Doherty's servants bowed and withdrew hastily. Niall Garve stood watching them depart. He called loudly for Kathleen, Neachtan's nursemaid. She came running and followed him into the infant's quarters. "This is your new charge," he said. "He's the son of The O'Doherty. Take good care of him and see that no harm comes to him or I'll have your life."

The girl nodded quickly and took the child in her arms. Niall Garve, thoroughly sickened by the wailing of children and the screaming of his wife upstairs, determined to quit the castle with all possible haste.

"Will we stay afloat?" Cobos asked anxiously, as he studied the damage that the storm had inflicted upon the great warship. Could it only have been three days since we left Lisbon with such hopes, he wondered. He had taken immense pride in the Armada as it sailed down the Tagus, pride that Spain could assemble and launch such a force, and pride in his part in ensuring that it sailed this year. He no longer felt that way. The power and force of the storm that had assailed the mighty fleet in the Bay of Biscay had humbled him. It had been so easy for him to dismiss Manrique's concerns about the weather. It had been out of pure ignorance on his part. Many times in the last twenty-four hours he had rued that decision, as he huddled in the gallery, high above the stern. He had never before been as terrified and had done the only thing left to him, pray ceaselessly. He had endured bouts of violent sea sickness, induced by the appalling motion of the ship, as the waves raised it twenty feet high on their crests, before allowing it crash down again into their grey troughs.

"The weather will determine this race," the ship's captain said grimly, looking up at the sky where dark clouds scudded across the upper atmosphere. "If it holds, we might be able to repair it sufficiently so that we can make Santander. At least we have not too far to sail, perhaps forty miles."

"And can you repair it while at sea?" Cobos asked disbelievingly, surveying the damaged vessel.

"We can do a certain amount while still at sea. Every ship carries with it extra spars and rope, lumber for planking, bolts of canvas, oxhides and lead sheeting to cover gaping holes. We have barrels of tar and oakum to calk open seams," the sea captain answered.

"And the seamen can do such work?" Cobos asked in surprise.

"We have the necessary craftsmen on board, carpenters, sail makers, coopers and blacksmiths," he answered. "If the ship is not too damaged, we stand an even chance of saving it."

The odds did not reassure Cobos. Having endured the storm, his hopes had risen that they might survive after all. He had resigned himself to death, the previous night. It was just after dawn when the winds had begun to subside and it was only now, three hours later, that Cobos had felt sufficiently recovered from his debilitating bout of sickness, to venture forth from the gallery. Here he had his quarters, quarters fitted with an enormous window, overlooking the waves. He could not imagine how the ordinary soldiers had managed to survive the storm, packed into their tiny dark quarters, deep under the ship's deck. It must have been enough to unhinge a frail mind, he thought, not knowing when the ship would fail to rise, groaning and heaving out of the trough of a wave, terrified that it would continue on downwards until it settled on the bed of the ocean, many fathoms beneath.

He looked at the debris about him. The sails were in tatters and the foremast itself had snapped like a twig at its base and been washed overboard. This was the San Martin, one of the largest and most powerful ships in the fleet, over 112 feet long, 30 feet abeam and displacing 1,000 tons. She had been an impressive sight, having three masts with square sails on the fore and main masts, a lanteen sail on the mizzen and a spritsail on the bowsprit. He looked at a lone sailor, sawing off the jagged splinters from the foremast's stump, five feet in diameter, before noticing a group of carpenters busily working on the ship's waist deck, fashioning a new rudder and sternpost. The master carpenter was checking the replacements with a cloth pattern that he had used as a template.

The blacksmith, with the aid of two ship boys, was busy making the iron bolts, pintles and gudgeons that would be used to mount the jury rudder on to the sternpost. His anvil, equipment and forging fire were set up on deck and Cobos noted the diligence and efficiency with which the crew worked.

"The rudder, that was the noise at the height of the storm?" he asked the ship's captain.

The captain looked askance. "It is impossible to tell, there were so many," he answered.

There had been one noise above all others that had stricken fear deep into Cobos's heart. That noise had been accompanied by the dreadful sound of splintering timber, as some of the stern, to which the rudder was attached, was ripped away from the vessel.

When the storm had struck, the soldiers had been ordered below and told to keep out of the way so as not to hinder the sailors' attempts to keep the vessel afloat. Now, however, things might be different.

"Could the soldiers aid you in any way?" he asked the ship's captain.

"There is still much skilled work that only the sailors can do," he replied. "However, the soldiers could man the bilge pumps. They must be kept pumping throughout all watches. Nonetheless, you must ensure that your men do not get in the way of the work."

"I will give the orders. You can have as many as you require," Cobos replied.

Cobos turned to his second-in-command at his side. "See to it," he ordered. The man bowed and walked unsteadily away towards the soldiers' quarters.

Cobos's attention was diverted to three naked men walking towards them across the deck, each of them carrying a large sack.

"Divers," the sea captain said in explanation before addressing the men. "Check out the bottom of the ship. She's leaking badly. We have to stanch it."

The men nodded and walked to the side of the ship. There, they emptied the contents of the sacks onto the deck. Cobos watched as they tied smaller sacks to their waists.

"Lead weights," the sea captain explained. " It will help them sink and stop them from drifting away from the ship."

Cobos saw the men replace the spilled materials into the sacks, heavy wads of material, hammers and nails. After tying the end of a rope to the railing that ran around the ship, they mounted it, wrapping the rope around their left arms and then plunged into the steely grey Atlantic water. Cobos shivered violently at the thought of sub-merging himself in the icy waves, which still swelled hugely. He pulled his cloak tightly around his shoulders.

"First they will find the leaks. Then, they will surface and reboard the ship. They will cut a sheet of lead to size, descend again, stuff the hole with a heavy wad of hempen fibre and nail the sheet of lead over it. They're good men, specially trained for the job," the captain explained.

Cobos shuddered as he thought of trying to carry out repairs under water.

"I don't know how weakened the hull of the ship is," the captain said. "There's water streaming in many of the seams. If it comes under any more stress, the ship could split apart. Once the holes are patched, we will put a hawser around the weakened hull, which we will cinch. It will help keep the ship together."

Cobos was amazed at what was possible at sea. "Will you use the divers to get the hawser under the ship?" he asked, curious as to how such a task would be carried out.

"No," the captain answered. "The ship's draft is too large. From the stations on both sides of the beakhead, the sailors will play out the hawser. Then the forward drift of the ship, combined with the hauling of the men on the hawser, will bring it aft, until it's under the waist. That's where we will do the cinching, where it will have the greatest reinforcing effect."

Cobos nodded, only imperfectly understanding this technical language that the captain employed so readily. He saw sailors carrying a large spar towards the damaged stump of the foremast and set about repairing it.

Satisfied that immediate danger was averted, Cobos could finally ask the question that had been uppermost in his mind. "The rest of the fleet. How do you think it fared? Could it have outrun the storm?" he asked, dreading the answer.

The captain shook his head. "Any ship which survived the storm will be badly damaged and will be fortunate to make it back to Spain. This was one of the strongest in the fleet and our survival is miracu-lous. One thing is certain, however, no ships will journey onto Ireland."

It was the answer that Cobos had feared. His spirits sank. So, they had failed after all. The Armada would be delayed until next year, at least. "Do you think we lost many ships?" he asked, desperate for some morsel of hope.

The captain glowered at him, ill concealing his impatience. "What do you wager?" he asked. "Every sailor knew that setting forth, at this time of year, was folly. His Majesty received disastrous counsel. Our Mediterranean fleet was ill suited for Atlantic tempests. I, myself, saw two ships sink beneath the waves and was unable to aid the men on board. It sickens me to see such a waste of life, lives that were thrown away on such a fruitless enterprise."

Cobos was mute. What could he say? His counsel had been gravely wrong and others had to pay for his error. He wondered if Manrique had come safe. Privately, he hoped that he had not. Relations had deteriorated so much between them before setting forth that they were no longer on speaking terms. Cobos knew that Manrique would do everything possible to undermine any future Armada to Ireland. That would be disastrous for Spain and the Irish Lords.

"But come," the captain said, breaking the awkward silence that had become established between the two of them. "There is no good to be had in allowing ourselves become distracted from the task in hand. Let us go and see if our rudder is ready."

The captain turned and walked back to where the rudder assembly was taking place on the waist deck.

"It is ready," the chief carpenter said. "I have ordered my men to set up the blocks and tackles to lower it into place. They are launching the small boat so that it can be attached correctly."

"Good," the captain answered. "You have done well."

The chief carpenter acknowledged the praise with the barest nod. He then turned to some men who were stumbling across the deck, carrying one of the ship's small cannon.

"Make haste," he called to them. "Lay it there," he said, indicating the rudder's lower part.

Cobos watched as the carpenters lashed the cannon to the after edge of the rudder.

"It will counteract the rudder's buoyancy and make it easier for the sailors to fix it in place. Once it is attached properly, the cannon will be removed," the captain explained.

Cobos, realising that his very life depended on the successful completion of this repair work, enquired. "But how will they bind it to the ship?"

"You see the four chains attached to the sternpost?" the captain asked.

Cobos nodded and the captain continued. "They will be untied and threaded through the stern of the ship. They will then be tightened to secure the new rudder assembly to the galleon. It will be a flimsy construction but should do to steer the ship, unless another storm strikes. Once we come near shore, we will need it to keep off the rocks."

"We deserve some luck after all the misfortune which we have met with on this voyage," Cobos replied.

"That we do," the captain answered. "I must go supervise the attachment of the rudder assembly myself. I wish to ensure as good a fit as possible."

Cobos followed the captain towards the stern. For a moment, he wondered if God had forsaken their cause. This was the second time that the elements had destroyed a Spanish Armada. The English would claim that God and their Protestant wind had come to their aid, once again. It wasn't God who had betrayed their cause he suddenly realised, but themselves. The fleet had not been ready in time. The commissariat had let Spain down, denied it the revenge that should have been its due. With a stab of pain, he recognised his own guilt. He should have accepted what was plainly evident and allowed the invasion be put off until next year. Now, the whole venture was delayed indefinitely.

Still, one should never accept defeat, he thought. He had seen the virtue in perseverance too often in the past, to ignore it now. If God delivered him safely back to Spain, he would regard it as a sign that his mission was favoured by him. If not, then God would have demonstrated his will.

They had reached the stern and he leaned over it. The sight that greeted him made him gasp. The original rudder had taken a large portion of the stern timbers with it and he could see the exposed beams, on which the ship had been built. Cobos was suddenly anxious about the pact he had made with God. The ship looked very fragile. Just then, the wind started to pick up and he smelt rain. Within minutes, the heavens opened and a squally shower lashed the boat. He looked down at the little vessel heaving about in the grey sea and at the sailors attempting to manipulate the makeshift rudder into place. He was glad that he was, for now, safe on deck.

Chapter 16

"So, now that we are all present, let us begin," Captain Lopez de Soto, the newly appointed Secretary to the Adelantado, Don Martin de Padilla Manrique, said in a business like fashion. He sat behind the large table that was festooned with maps and charts, all drafted for the preparation of Spain's third Armada. On the wall behind him were two large maps, one of Ireland, the other of England. On those, a number of ports stood out in broad heavy characters. On the Irish map, Cork, Galway and Limerick were highlighted whereas on the English one Liverpool, Chester, Milford Haven, Bristol, Scarborough, Newcastle, Berwick and Falmouth were indicated as ports of importance. Earlier in the year, an expert pilot had been dispatched to make a new and full survey of the English coast. The completed report, which was now lying on the desk in front of Lopez, covered all the most useful harbours of England. That, along with the previously undertaken report on Irish ports, meant that the Spanish now, for the first time, had detailed knowledge of the coasts of both islands.

Captain Alonso Cobos looked closely at Lopez in an effort to divine the news, which he had brought back to them from the King, in far off Madrid. Lopez luxuriated in the attention of the leaders of the Armada's six squadrons who were straining anxiously to hear his words. He was garbed in black, with ebony hair and beard. None of those present trusted him. He had been sent by King Philip to report back upon their efficiency. He was in constant contact with the King, either by letter or in person, and had only to ask for an audience to have his request granted. Neither Cobos nor Manrique shared the same privileges, indeed, neither had been granted a single audience since the debacle of the second Armada, now almost a year ago. They had to make do with written submissions to King Philip. Manrique found it especially frustrating as all his dispatches had to be sent through Captain Lopez and he was well aware that Lopez attached his own opinions to his, often undermining the original.

The ultimate destination of this new Armada was not yet decided and both Manrique and Cobos had tried to convince Lopez to favour their preferred destinations, England and Ireland respectively. Lopez had listened to both without indicating which arguments most swayed him. They both suspected that whichever he favoured, His Majesty would sanction. Cobos found the uncertainty very difficult to endure as so much depended upon the outcome. He could not comprehend why there should even be the least doubt on the matter. It had to be

Ireland.

"I have called you all here together on the orders of His Majesty," Lopez began. "He is most disappointed that the Armada has not sailed by now," he said to Manrique in an accusatory tone. "Your orders were clear. His Highness is impatient at the delay."

Cobos saw Manrique flush with anger and he immediately retorted with vehemence. "My dispatches explained the delay. The problems that I encountered were listed therein. Because of the lack of capable Spanish sailors and soldiers, I have had to deal with conscripted men, impounded ships and their pressed captains. I am forced to make do with Flemish and German hulks, Italian and Ragusan supply ships, whose captains are reluctant to sail into enemy waters where many of their kin have perished before."

"The King ordains that any captain not co-operating fully with the expedition, is to be hanged from his own yard arm. That will root out any malingerers," Lopez answered unsympathetically.

A middle aged man with greying hair, stepped forward. Cobos recognised Don Diego Brochero, Knight of the Order of St John of Jerusalem, who was to lead the Armada under the direction of Manrique. He was a man recognised throughout Spain for his bravery, vigour and resourcefulness.

"And what of the English fleet?" he asked. "We know for certain that somewhere out at sea, there are ninety eight enemy ships. Such a force could destroy ours."

Lopez shook his head dismissively. "They shall not be a problem. As usual the English captains, like the pirates they are, prefer to seek out our treasure fleets, disregarding their orders to attack the Armada gathered here in Ferrol."

"But have they disobeyed their Sovereign?" Manrique asked incredulously.

"They only obey their natural instincts, robbery and thieving," Lopez answered with disdain.

"And they have left for the Azores?" Manrique asked, hardly able to credit such disloyalty.

"Yes!" Lopez answered emphatically.

Cobos understood Manrique's amazement. The English knew of the preparation that had taken place for this Armada. King Philip had accepted with fortitude the disaster of the previous November and, within a few days of receiving the melancholy tidings, had started planning another Armada that would sail within the year. Cobos's admiration of King Philip had grown when he saw how he did not allow the loss of seventy-two ships and three thousand men deter him from his purpose. Now it was the end of September, late for launching a fleet such as theirs. The King was as anxious as Cobos that the Armada should put to sea without further delay. Cobos had no wish to experience another storm like that of last year.

The ultimate destination still remained undecided. It would have to be Ireland, he thought again for the umpteenth time. Already, a year had passed beyond the deadline that he had promised the northern Irish Lords for the arrival of Spanish aid. He had received communications from them, urgently requesting that help. Both he and the King were aware that the English had sent two new generals, Burgh and Clifford and a new army to destroy the Irish rebellion before any Spanish support could reach them. They knew too of a triadic attack to be mounted on the North. Clifford had managed to defeat the Irish rebellion in Connaught, retake Sligo Castle and, in the most recent news to hand, stood on the borders of Donegal with his army. His reputation and ability was well known to Cobos, and he had achieved much in the nine months since his arrival in Ireland.

Cobos found each day that he spent in port, awaiting their departure, deeply frustrating. That frustration had led to further disagreements between Manrique and himself and it was he who had encouraged Lopez to return to Madrid to confer with the King, acquainting him with the delay in their departure. He had also asked him to intercede with His Majesty regarding the destination of the Armada and to remind him of his promise to the Irish Lords. He could wait no longer.

"And has His Majesty decided which our disembarkation port is to be?" he asked, concealing the nervousness he felt.

"Yes," Lopez answered and paused, looking around the chamber at the questioning faces surrounding him.

"So, would you be so good as to tell us our destination?" Manrique asked acerbically.

"That, I cannot do," Lopez answered, "as His Majesty has given me sealed orders, which are not to be opened until the Armada is on the high seas. Even I do not know where we are headed. We will have pilots aboard ship for all the main ports in England and Ireland."

A murmur of disapproval ran around the assembled captains. Cobos tried to guess what such a stratagem could mean. Granted, it would guarantee that no spy could forewarn the English of their destination, but that could not be the sole reason for secrecy. No, Cobos thought, it must be that, being aware of Manrique's reluctance to sail for Ireland, the King decided not to confirm it as our destination so that Manrique will not lose all interest in the preparations. That must be it, he thought, relief washing over him. The King would honour his promise.

"The fleet is to assemble in Betanzos Bay, fifteen miles from here.

The King will brook no further delay. It must sail immediately," Lopez said emphatically. "There has never been a better opportunity, there is no enemy fleet to oppose us."

Manrique shook his head. "No admiral can sail with only two thirds of his fleet. I am still awaiting the rest of the ships I was promised," he said doggedly.

"Now that the English have left for the Azores, Arumburu and his Andalusian squadron of eleven fine galleons, who dared not leave Lisbon undefended until now, are sailing for Betanzos Bay," Lopez retorted.

"And what of Prince Andrea Doria with his squadron of ships and his three whole tercios of Italian veterans?" Brochero asked.

"There, the news is not so good," Lopez admitted. "The Turks are once again in the Mediterranean. Mami Pasha and thirty-four ships have left Constantinople and are cruising in the Mediterranean. That menace, combined with an unexpected attack of French Protestants across the eastern Pyrenees into Catalonia, caused His Majesty to order the Prince and his Genoian squadrons to return to the Mediterranean."

"But that will leave our fleet too weak for the task in hand," Manrique said.

"Captain Pedro de Zubiaur, his Biscayian galleys, supply ships and two thousand veterans have sailed to Blavet. He will join with you," Lopez said.

"That is better news," Brochero answered. "We will be happy to have him with us."

Cobos shared Brochero's sentiments. Zubiaur, a man of much courage and determination, would indeed be a welcome addition to their expedition.

"So, when you add those ships to what you have assembled here, you have more than enough for the task in hand. I have checked. You have forty-eight galleons, twenty-six supply boats, ten galleyzabras and seventy pinnacles to land your twenty thousand soldiers. Get them embarked and get to sea," he ordered, handing Manrique a parchment, stamped with the King's seal. "Here are your orders."

"Twenty thousand soldiers is an exaggeration," Brochero replied doggedly. "Our problems with desertion continue even though we hang all we catch. The close concentration of sailors and soldiers has led to outbreaks of disease in their ranks, which also reduces the numbers."

"All the more reason to get to sea. The King has had a proclamation printed, which can be distributed and exhibited when you reach your destination. It promises freedom and fair treatment for Catholics and all who become Catholic and calls upon them to rally to our support," Lopez said.

"And death to all who choose not to convert," Manrique said solemnly.

"Agreed," Lopez answered. "But get back to your ships and begin the embarkation of your men. Hopefully, before long, we shall be victorious and the heretics shall be defeated."

Cobos watched as the captains began to drift out of the chamber. He considered approaching Lopez to try and glean from him any hint of what was contained within the King's orders. He saw Manrique walk over to him and both men engage in a heated discussion. He would just have to be patient for another while yet he thought. At least, things were beginning to move. He would do as he was bid, return to his ship and make arrangements for the embarkation of his soldiers the following morning.

"Make haste," Tyrell shouted. "They're gaining on us." Musket balls whipped past his ears as he crashed through the trees in headlong flight from the pursuing English army under Barnwell. His men were strung out beside and in front of him as they slashed their way through the dense undergrowth, never pausing to return fire. Tyrell, himself, was bringing up the rear and he saw his men in front, climbing over the trunk of a large fallen tree that barred their path. There was no way around it as his men found themselves in a narrow mountain pass, the sides of which were far too sheer to climb. He reached the tree trunk and turned to see how much ground their pursuers had made up. Through the dense foliage, he could see a disorganised posse following them, anxious to be in at the kill. He turned on hearing a scream from one of his men and saw him clutching his arm, bright, red blood seeping through his fingers.

"Come," he urged him, pulling him along, "you must keep going."

They reached the tree and he helped his wounded comrade over it by half lifting, half pushing him, ignoring the man's cries of pain. He then hurled himself over as the balls hit and splintered the wood behind him. It's a good job that they are not pausing to aim, he thought. "Keep down," he shouted to his men. "The tree will give us some cover."

He ran, bent at the waist, his eyes riveted to the ground, anxious not to stumble. Beyond the tree trunk, the men found themselves in an open meadow, devoid of any cover. The nearest trees were a hundred paces away. They had a number of minutes to put some distance between them and their pursuers, for the moment safe from enemy fire. Shortly afterwards, the English reached the fallen tree behind them and streamed over it. Once again, the musket balls sped past them, thudding with dull echoes into the branches and trunks of the trees, which the men before him were finally reaching. Tyrell kept running. It was every man for himself.

His breath was coming in quick, short bursts as he attempted to gulp in the air he so needed. Surely, they will have discharged all their muskets soon. They cannot have re-loaded while running after the men, he thought. At last, he reached the cover of the trees, just as he heard the signal he had been awaiting. The Irish bagpipers were playing his song, Tyrell's March, a composition that O'Neill had commissioned for him on his departure from Dungannon. Almost immediately, the sides of the valley erupted into fire and smoke, musket balls raining down on the pursuing English troops who were caught in the open without any cover. He joined his men who had stopped just inside the cover of the trees and now, he ordered them to form quickly into three lines, one behind the other.

The first line, muskets on their rests, took aim carefully and calmly awaited their orders.

"Fire," Tyrell shouted. He watched as their shot struck home. The English ranks who had come to a hesitant stop, were thinned by the accuracy of his men's aim. Most of the enemy had discharged their weapons during the chase, just as he had hoped they would. He had a high opinion of his own men's skill and was not disappointed. The English were busy, trying to reload their weapons, but it was difficult for them to concentrate while under fire from all sides. In their headlong dash after his men, they had not observed the detachment of Tyrell's soldiers, hidden in the undergrowth near the fallen tree trunk. Once the English had passed them, they had taken up position behind it. There was now no easy retreat for the English, not without fighting their way out and to do that, they would have to outshoot excellent marksmen who had the added benefit of cover.

Tyrell's second line moved smoothly forward while the first line retreated to the rear, reloading their weapons, safe from the enemy's fire.

"Fire," he shouted and once again the volley rang out and death was dispensed in cold, clinical fashion. Under the fire from all sides, the English soldiers were beginning to panic and run blindly backwards in an effort to escape, the majority not bothering to reload their weapons. One thought only governed them, to find some cover from the deadly shot that poured down on top of them. This was so easy, Tyrell thought, like shooting a herd of defenceless cattle.

Barnwell attempted to rally his men but it was too late. Tyrell's third row of soldiers stepped forward, placed their muskets in the rests and once again he shouted the order and the English ranks were further thinned. He had minutely planned this ambush and the English had fallen into the trap. O'Neill had invested heavily in winning him to his service and with this day's work, he would show him how sage a decision that had been.

O'Neill had learned, some weeks earlier, how the new Lord Deputy, Burgh, planned to destroy the northern Chiefs. An army of a thousand men under the command of Barnwell was to assemble at Mullingar and, marching north, was to join with the main English army under Lord Burgh, advance through Newry and Armagh and attack Tyrone. Clifford, with a third army, was to attack O'Donnell.

Tyrell had been ordered to watch Barnwell's force and impede his movement northwards. He and his four hundred men had hovered around Mullingar, carefully watching the enemy. The disparity in numbers had given Barnwell confidence. He had decided to attack and destroy Tyrell's small Irish force, before marching north. Now Barnwell was paying the price for under-estimating this Irish force.

Tyrell peered through the fog of musket smoke at the English soldiers. Volley after volley from his men had done its work with deadly efficiency. Not one single soldier remained standing, those who were still alive, lay cowering behind the dead bodies of their fallen comrades, too afraid to raise their heads or fire back at their attackers. O'Neill's intelligence had been correct, Tyrell thought. Barnwell's army was mainly comprised of newly arrived conscripts from England. He saw that they were attempting to surrender as they waved their hands in the air and cried out in terror to their attackers. Tyrell gave the order to cease firing. The guns fell silent.

Tyrell savoured the silence for a few moments. He wiped his face with the back of his hand and saw that it was covered with black soot. He was proud of his men. They had not let him down and four hundred had defeated more than double their number. "Stand up and drop your weapons," he called out to the mass of bodies lying on the grass before him. Slowly, the surviving English soldiers got to their feet. Tyrell relished seeing Barnwell struggle to his feet and hastily re-organise his raiment, attempting to retain what little dignity he still possessed. Tyrell had warned his men that they were not to target him and once again they had faithfully followed his orders. He nodded to one of his lieutenants, Rory O'Connor, who shouted the order in Gaelic to his men and they slowly emerged from their position among the trees, into the open plain. Tyrell made a quick calculation. Fifty-five English soldiers left unwounded.

His men advanced in pairs, seizing each Englishman by the arms. Tyrell strode over to Barnwell who had slighted him when he had been stationed in Dublin.

"I arrest you on behalf of my Lord, the Earl of Tyrone," he said with malicious gratification. "Your army shall not travel north to his domains, however, you shall have the privilege of being his prisoner there."

"You, man, are a traitor to your race, your religion and your Queen. You will die a traitor's death on the gallows and I pray God that I am there to see it. What you have done in joining with the Irish is folly. At least, have the decency to let me and my men go. They can do you no harm and the wounded would not survive the march north to Tyrone," Barnwell answered hotly.

"I said you were going north. I said nothing about your men," Tyrell answered, bristling at the man's arrogance even in the present circumstances. He turned to O'Connor, addressing him in low tones. "Kill them all, except Barnwell and this one," he said, placing his hand on the English soldier nearest to him.

"Kill them?" O'Connor queried.

"Yes. We cannot take prisoners with us and we must make it so intolerable for the English soldiers in Ireland, that none will want to serve here again. They will see such a posting as little better than a death sentence," Tyrell replied.

O'Connor turned to his men who stood waiting for his order. The English soldiers looked on anxiously.

"Kill them," O'Connor shouted. His troops obeyed, drawing their daggers and lacerating the enemy soldiers, slicing savagely into their flesh. Tyrell looked on dispassionately as blood gushed from the soldiers' throats, gory bubbles spewing upon their lips.

"This is a deed for which you shall be forever cursed by all Englishmen," Barnwell shouted in outrage before being cut short by Tyrell who drew his knife and held it menacingly to his throat.

"If you do not keep silent, I might yet reconsider my plans, lighten my load north and just take just your head with me," he said viciously. Barnwell immediately fell silent, the knife at his throat, drawing a thin trickle of bloody drops.

Tyrell turned to the English soldier whom he had spared. The latter shrank back in abject terror. Tyrell towered over him. "You are free to go. You are to bring word of what happened here, to Dublin. You are to inform them of how four hundred Irish soldiers destroyed one thousand English and you are to tell them that no English man can sleep safe in his bed as long as our army is loose in Leinster. Tell them that Richard Tyrell has joined the Irish and before long, the Spanish will be here. Now go, quickly before I change my mind!" he shouted.

The soldiers, who were holding the man, released him and he

looked around confusedly, before stumbling back the way he had come. Tyrell turned to O'Connor nodding towards Barnwell. "Tie his hands behind his back and place a noose over his head so that he can be led to Tyrone, like a beast of burden. If he slows us down, strangle the bastard. But make haste, we must away"

As Tyrell made to go, O'Connor addressed him. "But the men must have the spoils of victory."

Tyrell paused and conceded reluctantly. "Yes, and see to it that as they search the bodies, they kill any who still live. There must be no survivors, other than the two permitted to live. Have our men gather all the weapons and powder. What we cannot take with us, we will send to O'Moore. He will keep Leinster in turmoil in our absence. But come, make haste, we must get north. O'Neill can do with all the help he can muster."

O'Connor nodded and hastened away to issue the orders and secure his part of the promised booty.

"I have just received news from the Privy Council. The Spanish fleet has sailed some weeks past with a large force and we know not where it is bound," Lord Thomas Burgh, Lord Deputy of Ireland, announced to his gathered officers. A murmur of surprise ran through the tent, inside the newly erected Blackwater Fort. He waited for it to subside, mopping the sweat, which ran in rivulets from his forehead, in spite of the coldness of the day.

"As you are aware, our fleet is at present in the Azores, so there is nothing that we can do to hinder their plans to land an army in Her Majesty's kingdom," he continued gravely.

"But where is it expected to make landfall?" the Earl of Kildare asked, concerned at his absence from his lands during such a time of danger.

"We know not," the Lord Deputy replied. "And there are further bad tidings. Barnwell's army is no more. He has been taken prisoner by the rebels," the Lord Deputy said grimly. A gasp of shock ran around the tent.

"There is no army to defend the Pale," the Lord Deputy continued. "The O'Moores wreak havoc there nightly and they have burned the countryside to within twelve miles of Dublin. The Irish Council have recalled me to Dublin."

Bagenal leaped to his feet. "They have not the power to recall you. It is an affront that they should even dare to attempt to do so. They are naught but a pack of cowards and should not be obeyed. You must cut off the head of this rebellion. Without its leader, it will soon be defeated."

"Why that is slander of the worst kind. I will not have Bagenal talk so about the Irish Council," Sir Geoffrey Fenton stormed.

"Silence," the Lord Deputy ordered. "I will not have voices raised at my meetings."

An uneasy silence descended on the gathering as the Lord Deputy was convulsed by a fit of coughing He swayed on his feet, looking totally dispirited and ill. Wingfield observed him closely. His pallor was extremely unhealthy. Perhaps he was suffering from more than a simple chill. Some weeks earlier, they had assaulted the Blackwater Fort. Burgh had been first to wade across the freezing river, sword in hand, water to his neck. It had been his bravery that had carried the day. His men had no choice but to follow him and though they had suffered heavy casualties, they had gained the fort.

"To cut off the head of the rebellion is not as easy as I imagined. We are here almost a month and what have we achieved? We have regained this fort. Their main forces have stood off and refuse to engage us in battle. We have tried to penetrate Tyrone's territory but it is nearly impossible with how he has plashed the woods, together with the ambushes he launches upon our men. To speak true, I fear risking the overthrow of our whole army if we continue with our present tactics. Each day, our casualties mount. If we stay here much longer, I fear our strength will be eroded beyond the point where we can even protect ourselves. I propose that we break off and return to Dublin to prepare our defences for a possible Spanish invasion," Burgh explained at length.

"But if we leave O'Neill undefeated, he shall be able to join with them when they land. Our mission was to destroy him," Bagenal said trenchantly.

"You need not remind me of my mission," the Lord Deputy answered glacially. "Circumstances change and plans must be altered. If we get dragged deep into Tyrone, the Irish could always sweep around behind us into the Pale to join with the rebels there or even to combine with a Spanish army to our backs. No, it is too great a risk. I now see the wisdom of the plan put forward by Sir Thomas," he said, nodding approvingly at Wingfield, "and am of the opinion that implementing it would be the best we can do, at this time. If the Queen supplies us with the necessary troops, if the Scottish King prohibits his merchants selling them powder and arms and if..."

"If, if, if!" Bagenal stormed. "We must destroy O'Neill now! If we attack, he will not be able to face us. He has no military training, no ability, no..."

"Silence," Burgh shouted and once again was overcome by his racking cough. When it subsided, he continued. "If you have anything to say, Sir, say it in civil fashion! I have decided that we will set up the ring of forts around the northern rebels as proposed by Sir Thomas. They will be used to hem them in, and deny them the opportunity of joining with a Spanish army."

"That approach needs time to come to fruition and we do not have that commodity." Bagenal countered desperately. "And what of Clifford? He will be relying on us to rendezvous with him. We cannot fail him."

"I will send a scout to him, telling him to leave a garrison in O'Donnell's castle at Ballyshannon, and to return to Connaught to prepare for a possible Spanish landing there," the Lord Deputy answered.

"And how many men will you leave here?" Bagenal asked.

"Three hundred, under Captain Williams," he replied.

"And what will three hundred achieve that three thousand could not?" Bagenal snorted dismissively. "They will not be able to venture out of the fort and will have to be re-provisioned regularly. It is not the way to win a war!"

"Do not attempt to lecture me on how to manage this war. I have seen far more action in the field than you, Sir, and will not suffer such insubordination!" the Lord Deputy answered balefully. "We have completed our business here. Prepare the men to move out. You are all dismissed."

Cobos pulled his cloak tightly around him against the chill north wind. The sound of guns and cheering rang periodically in his ears. The San Pablo, one of the largest galleons in the fleet, lurched unsteadily beneath his feet. From its maintop, Manrique's personal standard, an enormous swallow-tailed flag in green silk, fluttered and dipped in the stiffening breeze. Cobos was impatient, because Manrique was not present to greet them. The ships had been assembled into six lines, each line consisting of ten galleons of varying sizes and fourteen other ships, all dressed in the flags and standards of their commanding officers. It was an impressive sight, and Cobos was glad that the fleet was finally at sea. The delays had almost driven him to distraction. Embarkation had taken two days, whereupon they had sailed to Betanzos Bay, taking them over thirty hours to cover fifteen miles in gusty, squally weather. There, Manrique had insisted on awaiting a flyboat that he had sent to the Azores in order to confirm the position of the English fleet. That had returned the previous evening with the confirmation he had needed. At the same time, a frantic letter arrived from King Philip, ordering them to sea immediately. So finally, and again in October, Cobos found himself on the open sea.

This charade is at last drawing to a close, Cobos thought. He was angered that Manrique had chosen to continue the custom, which he had initiated in Betanzos Bay, of being rowed by twenty four crimson-clad oarsman in a decorated barge to inspect the fleet. The men had to line the decks of their ships and cheer as the Supreme Commander passed, while the ships' guns were fired as a mark of respect. Cobos regarded it as a monstrous waste of good powder. He saw Lopez arrive in another barge and he walked over to the ship's rail to greet him. Leaning over, he proffered his hand to aid him aboard. Lopez took it and with a spring, landed on the deck.

"Well?" Cobos asked. "Do we finally get to discover our destination?"

Lopez nodded as he drew a sealed letter from within the folds of his cloak. "It is written here," he answered.

Cobos looked at the document, eager for its contents. "Well, what does it say? There is no need for secrecy anymore," he said.

"I do not know," Lopez answered. "The King never informed me. We must wait and open it when we are all present."

Cobos watched fretfully as Manrique's barge drew alongside and observed him quickly ascend the wooden ladder. There to meet him, were the six men in charge of each of the six divisions of the Armada, Brocherio, de Arumboru, Bertendona, Zubiaur, Oliste and Cobos himself. Manrique nodded to the assembled leaders.

"Come to my quarters," he ordered before turning and marching towards the stern and the Admiral's gallery.

They climbed the steps from the waist of the ship and entered the comfortable quarters. Dusk was setting in and the lighted lanterns emitted a warm yellow glow. Through the double leaded windows, the rest of the fleet could be seen riding at anchor in the distance. They all quickly took their seats around the conference table, which Manrique had installed in his quarters before leaving Spain.

"Finally, we get to know the great secret. The orders please," he said, addressing Lopez.

Lopez handed the document to him and he impatiently broke its seal. He read in silence and then he looked at the gathering before him. He sought Cobos's face and looked straight at him. "Falmouth," he said and allowed the ghost of a triumphant smile cross his lips. "We are to proceed to Falmouth and land our troops there."

A murmur ran around the gallery. Zubiaur eagerly searched through the reports that had been drawn up on the English ports. Cobos sat slumped in his chair, unmoving. He was devastated. He had failed the Irish Lords. There would be no aid for them this year.

Perhaps there would be no aid for them ever. England, he thought. Theirs would be the first expedition to attempt a landing on English soil since the Great Armada of '88. He looked around at the other leaders. Most of them were smiling, excited at the prospect of inflicting a blow on the English in their own country. That would be revenge for Cadiz. Only Lopez looked sympathetically at him. Cobos knew that there was nothing that he could do. There was no higher authority to which he could appeal. The King had spoken and to argue the point would be treason. He attempted to keep his expression emotionless. He would not allow Manrique see his disappointment.

"Why Falmouth?" Brocherio asked.

"The harbour has room for over two hundred ships. We have a good survey of the location, but most useful of all, we have a promise of aid from the captain of Pendennis Castle, which overlooks the bay. He is the only law enforcer in the area and his castle is but lightly defended. He has agreed to hand it over to us, in return for riches, which the King had promised him," Manrique answered.

"But can we trust him?" Oliste asked.

"It hardly matters," Zubiaur said. "We can easily take such a castle as his and there is no army stationed anywhere near that town. The people are not warlike. It seems to be an excellent choice."

"Once our troops have gained possession of Falmouth, we are to leave them to occupy the peninsula. We are then to return to the Scillies, catch the English fleet on its way home and destroy it. As we are so much more powerful than it, it should not be difficult. We will remove that threat forever," Manrique continued.

"Now a stronger murmur of approval arose from the assembled leaders. The idea of landing an invasion force and then destroying the English navy gave them great heart. They knew that they would have ample time to disembark their forces before the English ships returned from the Azores. With some good fortune, they could even be dispersed by the weather with which they would have to contend.

"The Lord be praised," Zubiaur said. "Finally, we get the chance to revenge the wrongs suffered at Cadiz."

"Everything must be done properly," Manrique said urgently. "At sunset, the image of Our Lady will be held high and the evening hymn in her honour will be sung by everyone in the fleet, without exception. Each sunrise will be greeted with a fanfare of trumpets and the ships are to come up to salute me. My ship will keep under easy sail until this is completed. Then a dry Mass will be celebrated before the Armada will proceed on its way. Is that clear?" he asked as he looked around the gallery.

All present nodded. Cobos tried to combat the feelings of disappointment and betrayal, which surged up in him. He would have to ensure that this mission was a success. If it were, it would help to relieve the mounting pressure on O'Neill and O'Donnell. If the English fleet was destroyed, it would make it more difficult for them to transport soldiers and materials to Ireland.

"So, if we are all content, I have arranged that my chaplain will say Mass for us here in my gallery. Then, you can all return to your ships and tell the captains under you, of our orders."

He rose, went to the door, and called out for his priest. Cobos found himself becoming impatient at so much religion and then, guiltily, stopped himself. He could not risk bringing bad luck to the venture. He would pray for ultimate victory as fervently as any of the rest of them. God had brought him safely through one storm so that he could partake in this venture. He was sure that there was a reason for that deliverance.

Clifford threw the gristle from his beef into the fire in which it sizzled noisily. The wind was chill but at least it was no longer raining. However, he suspected that the lull in the foul weather wouldn't last. Why had everything about campaigning in this country to be so damn disagreeable, he wondered.

Some of his men still slept, others clenched their muskets tightly, while others played dice or cards as the dawn slowly gave way to early morning. They were nervous but they took comfort from their commander's obvious confidence.

Clifford was adept at dissembling. He was as nervous as his men and regretted his support of a plan he had judged to be flawed from the start. It was not that he feared a fight, or that he wished to shirk his duty, but he had a depleted force, unequal to the task assigned. He had never believed in the division of forces that Burgh's plan had called for. It had made more sense to him to attack with united forces and smash, once and for all, the enemy's armies.

Yet, if Clifford had doubts to plague his confidence, he also had compensating encouragements. With him, were the six heavy cannons that he had transported by ship from Galway to the banks of the Erne. Their arrival had given Clifford a sense of security and carried with them a promise of victory, a promise yet to be realised. The enemy had only muskets. Nevertheless, Ballyshannon Castle still held out against them in spite of the bombardment that they had maintained on its walls for over a week. The Spanish, whom O'Donnell had in his employment, had spent the summer re-enforcing the castle and had made good the task of strengthening its defences. O'Donnell had chosen to remain inside, rather than escape into the surrounding hills. If Clifford succeeded in taking the castle, then O'Donnell's capture would be all but certain, no small step in bringing about the end of the war.

A wind stirred the smoke from the fire and it drifted lazily toward the castle, where no one was visible on its ramparts.

"Perhaps they'll surrender today," Lieutenant Marshall said as he joined Clifford.

"I doubt it. They showed enough spirit when we tried to storm the breach yesterday and they have carried out repairs on it overnight," Clifford replied, thrusting a log into the midst of the glowing embers.

"But what about the report of the harper last night? Do you think he was accurate about Maguire and O'Rourke marching to O'Donnell's relief with two thousand men and Burgh withdrawing from the Blackwater?" the lieutenant asked anxiously.

"Who knows? He might have been sent to frighten us, to encourage us to lift the siege. On the other hand, perhaps his information is true. We will have to await the return of our scouts to know for sure," Clifford replied. "Let us make haste and get the guns working again. Speed will ensure our success."

Three hours later, the first scout returned with the news that the harper had indeed been speaking true. Clifford and Marshall walked away from the booming cannons, which had kept up a steady bombardment of the castle all morning, so that they could listen to the report more carefully.

The scout, a local man who had fallen foul of O'Donnell and been obliged to leave Donegal, saluted both men. "It's true," he said in broken English. "They do come."

"And you saw them with your own eyes?" Marshall asked.

"Yes. I hear one saying that O'Neill follow after them, he and his great army, when Burgh is leaving Ulster. I moved fast but still Maguire and O'Rourke are almost catching me."

Clifford turned and walked back to the gunners. "Cease firing," he ordered. The guns fell silent and a large cheer rose from the Irish soldiers on the castle's battlements. Clifford saw them gesturing excitedly towards the hill to his right. He turned to look and saw the crown of it filling up with enemy soldiers. He looked to his left and saw that more Irish troops had managed to infiltrate that wing too.

"Get the guns ready to transport. We must withdraw," he commanded in as steady a voice as he could muster. "Break camp," he shouted to the rest of his men. "We're going back to Connaught." His men started working eagerly, as anxious as him to depart. Clifford, accompanied only by twelve hundred soldiers, could no longer hope to take Ballyshannon against such a combined force. Indeed, he must extricate himself as quickly as possible from what was rapidly becoming a very dangerous situation.

The gunners ran to the river and filled their buckets with water, which they carried back to the guns. Clifford watched as they doused the red-hot weapons, which hissed fiercely, spewing out steam. He had been expecting another delivery of powder by river today and, as a consequence, had been generous in its distribution, having kept a constant bombardment upon the castle over the last week. Now, they would not be able to wait for its arrival. They would have to march with what powder they had left, as delay would prove fatal. "How much powder have we?" he asked Marshall.

"One barrel," he answered.

"Divide it up among the men," he ordered.

Marshall went to do as he was ordered and Clifford watched his men hastily dismantle the camp, loading their packhorses and mules. They hadn't brought any wagons with them. There had been no roads in the wild countryside, which they had to traverse, to accommodate such a mode of transport. He saw his gunners attempting to tie their weapons to two horses at a time but the horses could not take the weight and buckled under it.

"What will we do with them?" the gunners' ensign-in-charge asked.

"Leave them," Clifford said reluctantly. "We will win them back another day."

He looked around at his men, who were beginning to take up a marching formation. He realised, with a jolt, that they could not return the way they had come. The main body of the Irish army lay between them and the ford they had crossed on their way north. They had only one chance of escape. Just below the castle, they would have to traverse the ford, which was known for its treacherousness, even in the middle of summer. Now, after the recent rain, the river was rising fast and already had become a raging mass of water. The ford was located just above a salmon leap. There was a narrow ledge of uneven rock, which crossed the river just above a section that fell quickly away into the rapids below. It would be a hazardous crossing but they no choice but to attempt it.

Clifford jumped upon a horse and rode into the middle of his men. Standing up in the stirrups, he shouted at them. "You have all been issued with powder. I want you to make the most of it because that is all that's left. There is to be no discharging of muskets for effect, every shot must count," he said sternly, before adding. "I won't lie to you. We are in a difficult position but if you trust me and follow my orders, I promise that I will bring you safe home. Remember we stand or fall together. Now form up, we are crossing the ford below the castle."

The soldiers hastened to do as they were bid and in a short time they were ready to march. With drums beating and colours flying, they marched towards the ford. Brooke marched behind the baggage train with the rearguard, Marshall with the battle and Clifford with the vanguard. When the Irish saw what they were attempting, their army on the hill began to march towards them in an attempt to harry their escape. Clifford saw that they also had a number of small boats and that they had begun to ferry men across to the other bank to gain the opposite side before them, thus denying them safe passage. Clifford spurred his horse into the deep water and slowly waded across the ford, trailing a rope behind him. On reaching the other side, he quickly pulled the rope tight and tied it to a large tree. A soldier did likewise on the castle side and then the men of the vanguard jumped into the shoulder high water and, holding their guns over their heads, slowly and carefully made their way across the foaming water, clutching the rope, when necessary, to steady themselves. Clifford watched the progress of the Irish soldiers from the boats, which had landed some distance downstream. They now were hurrying up the bank towards him.

"Quickly," he shouted to his men in the water, and, at last, the first of them made it to the bank and struggled out onto dry ground. "Place a defensive cordon around the ford," Clifford ordered. "We must hold them off until we get all our men safely across. They ran to take up their positions, oblivious of the cold and wet. Clifford turned back to the ford.

The van was already across and the battle was more that half way there but the main body of the enemy's troops had reached the opposite side of the ford and was attacking the rear. Clifford watched as his men formed up and began trading volleys with the Irish. He saw men on both sides falling. They know how to use their weapons, he thought. The luggage train was now in the water and he observed a horse slip on the treacherous rocks underfoot. It slid under the rope, pulling the man that was leading it over the edge of the ledge, both disappearing down the rapids in a blur of moving bodies.

He grabbed Marshall who was struggling up onto the bank. "Set up your men to give covering fire to the rear as they cross," he ordered. Marshall hastily deployed the main battle and once the last of the baggage train had been hauled out of the water, he shouted across to Brooke that it was his turn to make the crossing. Brooke stood at the water's edge and ordered his men in.

"Quickly," Clifford shouted. "Get into the water and out of our line of fire so that we can cover you."

The rest of the rear jumped into the river and the battle loosed a volley at the Irish who attempted to rush the opposite bank. They immediately fell back, leaving a number of dead and wounded behind them. They formed up some distance from the far bank, too far distant to inflict much damage.

Clifford turned to survey the western bank. The van was holding off the Irish but more and more of them were being ferried across the river and making their way upstream to join in the attack. They would have to get underway, he thought anxiously. They could not afford any more delay. He ran to the river's edge and helped to haul the last of the rear from the water. "Form up," he shouted and his men quickly reassembled into marching formation, five abreast. Clifford dismounted and placed himself with the van. "Right, quick march," he ordered and the column moved off to the muted beat of the thoroughly soaked drum.

Six hours later, the English column had managed to cover only eight miles. It came under constant attack from the Irish foot and horse but it still managed to hold together. Now, however, their powder was all but gone. They had done well, Clifford thought. The soldiers had done as he had asked and not wasted any of it. Even so, it would be all for naught. Once their powder was consumed, they would have nothing to stop the Irish musketeers from firing at point blank range into their formation. No column could stand such punishment. They would be bound to break and once that happened, the Irish horse would make short work of them. Clifford looked up at the dark clouds, which had overshadowed them all along their march. Why doesn't it rain, he wondered. It always rains in this God forsaken country and now, when we most need it, it refuses to do so. And then, as if in response to his musings, he felt a drop splash on his face, and another, and another, until the heavens opened and the rain fell in torrents upon them. A triumphant roar went up from the English ranks. He saw his soldiers' matches being extinguished but, more importantly, Irish matches were also being snuffed out, one by one. Once wet, there was no way of relighting them until they dried thoroughly. They weren't defeated yet.

For the first time in over eight hours, there was no sound of gunfire. Clifford looked into the gloom of the forest. It would have to be hand to hand fighting now, he thought. That at least gave them a chance. He looked at his men. Exhaustion was etched in every lineament of their faces. They marched on in silence through the wet and now muddy wood, rain lashing them relentlessly. Clifford saw that they were almost dead on their feet. He marched down the length of the column, ignoring the personal risk to himself, encouraging them as best he could.

"Now, we'll show those traitors some English spirit. They won't be able to stand off and shoot at us, but will have to come to close quarters. Then we will show them English might," he said in an effort to raise their morale.

On reaching the rear, he fell into step beside Brooke. "It's too quiet," he said. "It won't last."

Brooke nodded. "Will they stand up to another attack?"

"They must," Clifford answered, then brusquely signalled for silence. Both men listened and heard an ominous rustle that grew in volume from the surrounding wood.

"Form up, form up," Clifford shouted and the column ceased advancing. The pikemen held their position while the musketeers, drawing their swords, stationed themselves in between them and stood facing the trees on either side of the track.

The manoeuvre had just been completed when they heard a blood-chilling scream in Gaelic as hundreds of Gallowglasses came charging out from the trees, their large battleaxes held threateningly over their heads. Clifford stood in the front row between two pikemen, sword in hand. He had heard of the Gallowglasses but this was his first time facing them in open battle. He had learned how the northern rebels had transformed them into pikemen and musketeers and was surprised to see them fighting with their original arms.

He watched as they hacked ferociously at the raised English pikes, bludgeoning their way into the body of soldiers that sheltered behind the row of pikemen. He saw one giant of a man bring his axe down on the pike of the man beside him, both weapons becoming intermeshed as their blades locked. The pikeman raised his weapon and, for a moment, the Gallowglass stood with both his hands uplifted as he tried to free his axe. Clifford, seeing his chance, darted out and drove his sword deep into the man's chest through his exposed armpit, unprotected by his armour. He pushed as hard as he could, lifting the huge man momentarily off his feet. He turned the sword inside the wound and the Gallowglass moaned, his eyes rolling in his head. Clifford allowed him fall to the ground, then pulled tenaciously to free his sword. Blood issued from his enemy's mouth. He heard a warning shout from the pikeman to his left, turning, just in time, to parry an axe blow that another enraged Gallowglass had aimed at the back of his neck. The impact jarred his shoulder and spine and his sword split at its hilt. He looked at it in horror as the Gallowglass smiled in triumph. He raised his axe over his head, not noticing the pikeman on Clifford's left who brought the blade of his pike expertly down on the back of the man's head, just under his helmet.

Clifford gratefully resumed his position and as he did, the pikeman on his right cried out in agony. He had been attempting to fend off three Gallowglasses at once and one of them had managed to get inside his guard, hacking at his leg, the axe biting deeply into the man's femur. The pikeman collapsed to the ground, shrieking in agony and dropping his weapon. Clifford grabbed it and thrust it at the attacker's face, imprinting a bloody scar from ear to chin. The Gallowglass collapsed onto his knees and was helped back from danger by another of his countrymen.

Clifford looked along the line of the column and everywhere could read the same story. As pikemen fell, their places and weapons were taken by the musketeers in an effort to stem the screaming enemy who ceaselessly launched themselves at the pikes. The noise and turmoil was over-powering, yet somehow his men held on and finally, when it was obvious that they were not going to be bested, the Gallowglasses drew back, leaving their dead united in death with the fallen English. Clifford waited some minutes and then gave the order for them to march on again.

They moved more slowly, still burdened as they were by their wounded. Initially, they had put their dead on the packhorses but now they left them where they had fallen. The rain still fell in torrents and the path beneath them had turned into a muddy quagmire, making progress even more difficult.

Clifford could no longer see the Irish foot following them. He could, however, still make out the Irish horse shadowing them. From time to time, they approached near enough to throw their lances at the retreating army, but the soldiers' shields ensured that little damage resulted from such attacks. They now came to the hardest part of their march, the ascent of the Curlew Mountains. They struggled up the steep inclines, every step harder than the last, wind and rain assailing them mercilessly. Clifford noted with relief that the Irish horse was at last disengaging and riding off to the east. He looked over the sorry remnants of his force that had set off with such high expectations. It must be reduced by half, he thought. This was a disastrous defeat; half an army lost, defeated by, what the Queen would term, a bunch of Irish rabble, six splendid field pieces abandoned to them and all the weapons of their dead soldiers! In truth, they would be fortunate to return safely to Connaught.

The Queen's administration has not yet realised just what we confront now in Ireland, Clifford reflected. The situation was urgent. They must try again to win back the Irish Lords. If they did not, and the Spanish were to land in force, then things would indeed be grim.

Brooke approached slowly, betraying his absolute tiredness. "Can we rest? The men are dead on their feet. Those who are not wounded are endeavouring to support the maimed," he asked.

"No, we are far from safety yet. I will not rest until we are within the walls of Boyle. They could yet return and attack again," Clifford answered.

Brooke emitted a groan and returned to his men. Clifford marched back to the van, easily overtaking the slowly marching column. "The worst is over. We showed those rebels and we'll conquer these mountains too. They'll be as much beer as you can drink when we get to Boyle," he promised. The column managed an unconvincing cheer and then dug deeply into their almost spent determination as they continued on their weary way.

Those damn Protestant winds again, Cobos thought. I would not mind but the English were not forewarned of our coming, so they could not have even prayed for them! Why, he wondered, why did God forsake them like this when their cause was just and right, when they were only attempting to do his bidding. The weather had steadily worsened during the last days of the Armada's advance from the Scillies. They had managed to reach a point twenty miles from the Lizard when a violent, northeasterly storm had broken in the channel. The flagship of the squadron, the San Pedro, had been so damaged that she had to fall out of her station and run before the wind. Manrique had transferred to Cobos's ship before the San Pedro ran for Spain. The remaining ships tried to ride out the relentless storm. It had blown unabated from the worst possible quarter for three days and nights and, one by one, the Spanish galleons had to give up the unequal struggle.

Cobos struggled to his feet. He was totally exhausted. He had not been able to sleep since the tempest had struck and once again, when he had laid down in an attempt to rest, he had become sick. He found some solace when he could see the sea and horizon but once he went below, it became unbearable. He made for the door to the deck. Why had he taken Manrique on board, he wondered. If it had been left to him, he too would have given up and run before the winds to Spain. Manrique, however, would have none of it. He was relentless, fighting the elements, driving the sailors on to greater efforts, all just to keep the ship in the one position, not gaining an inch nearer England.

When he opened the door, he was met by a gale force wind, laced with rain, which stung his face. He leaned into the blast and forced himself outside. He looked about the ship. The coloured banners were reduced to tatters and the sails themselves were beginning to shred. The foresail and the spritsail were severely damaged. He saw Manrique shouting at some sailors who were clinging desperately to the rigging high above him. Cobos made his way slowly over to him.

He called to him but he was unable to hear him above the noise of the storm. He looked out over the surrounding ocean. At first, he could see no other ships, but finally he managed to make out two sets of sails far in the distance.

He reached Manrique and grasped his shoulder. "Only three ships left," he shouted.

"Four," Manrique answered, as he pointed far to the stern.

It was pointless, Cobos thought. Why could he not realise it, he wondered.

"The ship cannot take much more of this," Manrique shouted and Cobos was surprised to see tears in the older man's eyes. "The water has started to come in at the seams. If we take much more punishment, they might part altogether. The pumps are working ceaselessly and are just about able to keep constant the level in the hold."

Manrique paused and looked away into the distance in an effort to control his feelings. Cobos realised that he had finally accepted what had been obvious to everyone else for a number of days. They would not be invading England this year. Cobos had come to terms with the disappointment that he had initially felt and as the fury of the storm had intensified, his fear had grown in concert with it. His prayers were now for a safe return to Spain. "You have done more than any other man could," Cobos said to his colleague. "No blame attaches itself to you. It is now your duty to save the King's ships so that they can be used again next year against the heretics."

Cobos awaited Manrique's reply. He knew, however, that blame could be attributed to Manrique because of his tardiness in launching the Armada. If they had set sail even one day earlier, they would have made a safe landfall in Falmouth and could have sat out the storm there, safe in the security of its harbour. Manrique would have questions to answer when he returned home and his reception might not be as tolerant as it had been the previous year. Cobos knew how proud a man he was and how unused to defeat he had been.

"The ships can be repaired over the winter and we can launch an even greater Armada next spring. The wind cannot always favour the English," he said encouragingly.

Manrique looked at him with a dejected stare. "Why does God not favour our endeavours?" he asked unexpectedly. "We did everything as we should. Our goal was not personal riches, but the re-establishment of the one true faith. We have tried so hard and yet our efforts do not meet with success."

Cobos shrugged his shoulders. "It has always been so. Good men must work hard to triumph in this world. Evil will always battle for dominance. But all is lost if good men give up the fight, we must never lose sight of that."

Manrique looked unconvinced. "We will head for home. Unfortunately, there is no alternative. I will give the orders and then I will retire to my quarters. I have not slept in three days. Once the boat has come around, they will have no further need of me. The wind will do the rest. We should make Spain quickly," he said.

Cobos watched as he turned and headed towards the captain of the ship. Poor man, he thought. It had been his misfortune to have Manrique foisted upon him, losing all control over his craft. He saw a look of enormous relief pass over his face as Manrique communicated the decision to him. He ran up the deck, shouting at the crew as Manrique turned and headed for his cabin. Suddenly, there was new life and vigour in the crew as they started to bring the ship around, knowing that they were finally on the way home. The ship lurched heavily to its left as it began the manoeuvre, the sails turning to catch the wind and Cobos's spirits rose at the prospect of reaching solid ground once again. His disappointment, for the moment, was forgotten in his relief at finally being in motion once again. He must tell his soldiers, he thought. They, poor souls, had much to cope with on sea journeys, confined to the bowels of the ship for most of the day and night. The ship's sudden motion would concern them. He would put them at their ease. Then, he would start thinking about how he could influence the destination of the next Armada. Hopefully, the news from Ireland would still be favourable. He longed to know. With some good fortune, there would be news when they reached Spain.

Chapter 17

The dawn was just breaking over the Ulster countryside when the peace was shattered by a lone drummer who beat the morning drum. Immediately, the tranquil scene was destroyed as the many camps disgorged themselves of English soldiers who hurried to dress and arm themselves. The cooks built up the fires that had been damped down for the night and began the breakfast preparations for the four thousand waking soldiers. In his camp, the commander of the English army, Sir Henry Bagenal leapt eagerly out of his cot and hastily dressed himself. He lifted the flap of his tent and looked out. The early morning haze covered the surrounding countryside, a sure sign of another beautiful day. Sir Henry was in buoyant mood. At last he had obtained that which he had most wanted for many years, over-all command of the English army in Ireland.

The fact that it had come about owing to the death of the Lord Deputy, Lord Burgh, and that no one else desired the appointment, did not in any way detract from his sense of achievement. Burgh had died the previous autumn on the march back to Dublin after establishing the new fort on the Blackwater. The Queen had been slow, as usual, in naming Burgh's successor and had chosen her cousin, the elderly Earl of Ormonde, to hold the position in a temporary capacity until she appointed an English general. The Continental war had taken most of her time and thus, she had not yet made the necessary appointment. During that time, neither it nor the Irish war was any nearer resolution. In Ireland, the rebels had become stronger, gathering more adherents to their cause. On the Continent the situation was even worse. England had lost an ally as France had made peace with Spain.

Bagenal had been surprised when the Irish had broken off the truce with the Queen in June. Obviously, the removal of France from the war must have given them confidence that the long expected aid from Spain was at last guaranteed. So far, that help had not materialised and it was rumoured that the Spanish King was at long last on his deathbed. Bagenal hoped and prayed fervently that the rumours were true. At least, Bagenal thought, once he was sick, there was no one to take the reins and drive an Armada westwards to Ireland. And now, finally, he was going to have the opportunity to avenge himself on O'Neill for the insult and shame that he had brought on the Bagenal name.

He had been pleased when the Queen had not agreed to abandon the Blackwater Fort to the enemy. This had been suggested by the majority of the Irish Council who feared a humiliating defeat if they were they to attempt its re-provisioning. They had, under Wingfield's prompting, planned to build another fort at the extreme tip of Ulster on Lough Foyle, thereby forcing O'Neill to fight on two fronts. The Queen approved and ordered the levying of two thousand men, to be sent to Lough Foyle as soon as the necessary supplies and ships could be found.

O'Neill had learnt of their plans and had decided to take the initiative rather than wait on developments. He had immediately besieged the Blackwater Fort and sent reinforcements to Tyrell and O'Moore in Leinster to aid them in their successful campaign there. They had kept the province in a state of emergency, plundering and ravaging as mercilessly and often as possible. Finally, the Council had been stung into action at the losses they incurred and, at Bagenal's insistence on action, decided that the Blackwater Fort must be relieved. This had been made easier as reinforcements had arrived in July.

Bagenal had assembled a force, of which he was proud. He had built his army around proven and tried veterans. He walked down to the cooks who were preparing breakfast for the officers and one of them handed him a trencher of thick bread, some pork and a pitcher of beer. He sat on the grass, eating with relish, the country air and the marching of the previous days, having given him an appetite. He looked at the five field pieces that they had brought with them, their metal, glinting in the early morning sun.

He finished his breakfast quickly and strolled through the camp. The marching will be heavy, thirsty work again today, encumbered as we are by our armour, he reflected. At least, they would not have far to go, he thought. The fort with Captain Williams and his men lay just over six miles away. They knew, from communications that they had received from him, that they had been reduced to eating their horses and any wild greens, growing on the side of their sconce. Even though there was ample water some thirty yards from their fort, the siege was so tightly drawn that they could not replenish their water casks without fighting hard to do so. They were now reduced to drinking rainwater, when they could get it.

Bagenal had deployed his commanders the night before. His infantry was to march in six regiments, each approximately seven hundred strong, at intervals of no more than a hundred yards between them. The cavalry, the guns drawn by their teams of oxen, the convoy of packhorses laden with supplies for the fort, all marched in the intervals. It had been agreed at the Council of War the previous night, that the foot regiments should march in separate bodies until they engaged the enemy and then, they should join one with another, forming the usual fighting formation of vanguard, main battle and rearguard.

Bagenal positioned himself in the vanguard, taking command of its second regiment, while Colonel, Sir Richard Percy, the Earl of Northumberland's brother, commanded its first regiment. The battle regiments were led by Captain Cosby and Wingfield, who was also second in command to Bagenal. Colonel Cuney and Captain Billings commanded the rearguard and Sir Callisthenes Brooke commanded the horse. The artillery was with the main battle. Bagenal was satisfied that he had the experienced officers required for the job in hand.

It had also been decided that the regiments would march, ready for battle, with their pikes together in the centre and their shot in sleeves, on the flanks. They expected the Irish to attempt to ambush them and that was one of the precautions that they had taken to prepare for just such an eventuality. They had also decided not to travel on the regular road west of the bank of the River Callan, a tributary of the Blackwater, where, no doubt, an ambush had been prepared for them. Instead, they marched on the eastern bank where they could advance through open and firm countryside. There was one bog barring their way, but the army brought timber with it, which Bagenal intended using to make a passage for his artillery, horses and carriages.

Bagenal called to Sir Richard Percy. "All ready?" he asked.

Sir Percy nodded. "I have sent two wings of shot ahead as an advance guard, Captains Lee and Turner are leading them. They will warn us of any ambush," he said.

"Very well, let us march," Bagenal responded. The drums beat out the order and the army set off. The column stretched out for over a mile, and it was some time before they were all in motion as the line uncoiled under the bright Ulster sunshine.

The country, through which they marched, was full of low hills, wooded mostly with a shrubby brushwood of alder, willow and holly, interspersed, every now and again, with stretches of ash and oak. The terrain did not fall very noticeably towards the Blackwater in the north and its tributary, the River Callan, meandered slowly through the hills towards it. Bagenal's army marched over the hard and hilly ground between the wooded hills. What Bagenal did not realise as yet, was that those woods and hills hid the Irish army, consisting of more than five thousand men. O'Neill, O'Donnell and Maguire had been expecting Bagenal's assault and had joined together to repel him.

If Bagenal knew the terrain, O'Neill knew it better. When he had received information that it was to be Bagenal who was to lead the English army, he had decided that he would contest the revictualling of the Blackwater Fort, no matter how many men the English put in the field. O'Neill welcomed the opportunity for revenge every bit as much as Bagenal. Still, after all these years, he smarted from Bagenal's scornful refusal of his sister's hand. Bagenal had been the thorn in his side for as long as he could remember and he was not going to allow him reap the credit for relieving the Blackwater Fort. He had defeated him once, he would do so again, but this time there would be no escape for his adversary.

O'Neill had planned well for the battle. He knew that Bagenal would eventually have to leave the river behind him and march westward to the Blackwater Fort. There was only one route open to him on that final leg of the march. Because of that, Bagenal's army would have to cross the Callan Ford to reach that route. There, the river was coloured yellow, owing to the surrounding peat, and the ford across it was known locally as the Yellow Ford. The nature of the terrain was such that he could keep an entire army hidden from view and he intended using that feature to his advantage. The English were only half a mile from the ford and so far, things were going according to plan. The skirmishers had done their job well. His scouts informed him that they had managed to lengthen the distances between the regiments. Soon it would be O'Donnell's and Maguire's turn.

Maguire and O'Donnell lay on all fours on the summit of one of the hills. They watched the first regiment of the vanguard pass. It marched quickly by, flags flying, drums beating steadily. It was marching in good order and did not seem to have suffered too many casualties. It continued on and had passed out of sight before the second regiment of the vanguard came into view. This was not marching as quickly or as confidently. Following them, came the Irish skirmishers who shot at the them from the surrounding woods. As they passed, Brian MacArt, the skirmishers' leader, climbed up the hill to where both men lay. "All is faring well," he said excitedly, throwing himself down beside them. "We have had few casualties, just some wounded."

Maguire smiled at him, infected by the younger man's enthusiasm. "You and your men have done well, Brian," he said.

O'Donnell nodded but added gravely, "Do not become too secure. There is much killing yet to be done, make no mistake. It will not all be easy."

"Never fear, I will not be found wanting," Brian answered. "I must return to my men."

With great stealth, he crawled away from them and once back in the cover of the trees, he ran speedily to rejoin his men. The two men on the hill watched as the second regiment of the van passed on over the hill. Now, they awaited the main battle's arrival. It trailed over the incline, both regiments together, assaulted on both sides by Irish skirmishers. It marched on, anxious to re-establish contact with the vanguard, dragging their field pieces with them. The English soldiers were sweating profusely from their efforts.

They watched in silence until the main battle had passed over the summit and then they both got to their feet. They signalled down to their men, hiding on the other side of the hill who hurried to join them, Maguire's on horseback, O'Donnell's on foot. They quickly took up their position, blocking the roadway. O'Donnell drew up his men on either side of Maguire's horse and positioned others in the wood, bordering the path. They then waited as the sound of the approaching rear guard, which was trading volleys with other Irish skirmishers, came closer. Finally, the first regiment of the rear, commanded by Cuney, came over the ridge. He marched more slowly when he saw the Irish army drawn up before him, over five hundred horse and fifteen hundred men. He ordered his men to halt. His regiment stood unmoving, one hundred yards from the enemy army, as the supply wagons that were travelling between the last two regiments spilled over the crown of the hill, taking up position behind him. Over the valley, an order in English rang out and the English marching column quickly and smoothly deployed into a defensive square.

All was quiet as both armies sized each other up. The Irish skirmishers broke off their attack and streamed past O'Donnell and Maguire's men. As they passed, they shouted excited greetings to their countrymen, intoxicated by the battle and the high spirits of youth. The older, battle hardened, regular Irish soldiers, however, did not reply, instead held their gaze on the English soldiers. O'Donnell's Gallowglasses were now competent pikemen, their large girth, admirably suiting the wielding of large weapons. Now, there was no sound of gunfire in this valley, though echoes of it reverberated from the next one and the valley behind the English square. Then, the second regiment of the rear marched over the hill, pausing as Billings took in the situation that presented, before marching down the hill and taking up position beside Cuney's regiment.

Billings walked over to Cuney. "Well, what do we do now?" he asked. "Will we try and push through?"

Cuney looked at the menacing army before him. His force was

probably outnumbered by two to one. If they attacked the Irish and gained the upper hand, the Irish would simply melt away into the trees. If the Irish gained the advantage, the rear would have to retreat away from the rest of their army.

"We must hold our ground," he answered. "The rest of the army will miss us and return with aid. Let us move to within range and discharge our weapons at them. The sound should alert the rest of the army that we are under attack. They will be but lightly challenged, as most of the Irish army must be ranged against us."

"I hope that your estimation is correct," Billings said nervously. "I do not relish taking on their soldiers on our own. Already, our men have suffered from their fire and are unsettled."

"We will do nothing rash. Let us test their mettle. At all costs, we must keep our men together in formation. Once the Irish see that they cannot break us, they will withdraw as usual," Cuney said.

"God willing," Billings answered grimly.

Further on, Percy and the first regiment of the vanguard had forded the Callan and traversed the Yellow Ford, oblivious to the developments, occurring at their rear. As they were under intense fire from O'Neill's skirmishers, they stopped on the summit of the second hill and there awaited the arrival of Bagenal's regiment. Percy deployed his regiment and the horse drew up beside him. His men had suffered deeply on their march but now they were sustaining their worst battering so far. As Percy watched his casualties rise under the sustained Irish fire, he became greatly agitated. He scanned the woods in front and to the right of him, desperately trying to spot Captains Lee and Turner whom he had sent out with extra reinforcements to clear a path and drive the Irish snipers back. He had lost contact with his skirmishers who were totally lost from view in the dense growth of trees.

Evan Owens, Percy's Welsh ensign, came running over to him, bent almost in two in an effort to protect himself from the flying bullets. "We cannot remain here," he said breathlessly, his eyes wide with fright. "It is certain death! We must press on to the safety of the fort or retreat and rejoin the rest of the army. If not, the cowardly knaves will be content to stand off and kill us, one by one."

Percy nodded, acknowledging the wisdom of Owen's words. But which option was the correct one, he wondered. He looked backwards towards the last hill, across a boggy plain, but still could not see any sign of Bagenal. If he went that way, he was abandoning Lee and Turner to their fate and that, he would not do. And even if he did retreat to Bagenal, they would again have to advance as they had to complete their mission and relieve the fort. They would cover the same ground three times, giving the Irish more time to shoot at them. No, they had lost enough men already. There was only one way that they could go.

He turned back to Owen who waited expectantly. "Sound the advance. We will not stop until we reach the fort," he said decisively.

Wingfield and the fourth regiment were, meantime, stuck at the ford on the river Callan. He could hear what seemed to be a major engagement behind him. He realised that the rear was obviously in trouble. His own regiment had been delayed in its crossing of the Callan as their large guns had stuck in the mud and sunk up to their axles. That delay should have given the rear ample time to catch up with them. He was worried that they had not. He had also lost contact with the first three regiments, a fact that made him even more uneasy. His men continued to come under continuous fire from the woods and, being an experienced soldier, he knew that they were wooing disaster. No army should have allowed itself be broken up so completely. Their strength was dependant on keeping together. He called over the captain of his horse. "I want a bodyguard, I must make contact with Bagenal," he said urgently.

The captain saluted. "But Sir, it is not safe for you to ride forward," he answered. "If you leave the shelter of the formation, there is no guarantee of your safety."

"Get the bodyguard together," he barked at the captain and then turned to the lieutenant who was directing the efforts to free the guns that were still stuck in the mud. "I want that gun freed before I get back and I want you to hold this ford. Until I return, you are in charge. On no account are you to leave this spot until the rear comes up, or the van comes back, or you receive other orders that override mine."

The lieutenant nodded, saluted and returned to his task. The captain of the horse rode up with forty heavily armoured men. Wingfield addressed them.

"We must locate Marshall Bagenal. We will not stop for anything or anyone until we find him. We must ignore Cosby's regiment and continue to Bagenal's. Our best hope of surviving this mission is to ride with speed. Come, follow me."

With that, Wingfield turned and galloped up the first hill. Most of the Irish were concentrating on attacking Cosby's regiment, which Wingfield saw when he reached the top of the nearby hill. They were in the process of crossing the Yellow Ford. He could also see Bagenal with the second regiment of the vanguard struggling up a second hill, away in the distance. Wingfield and his men charged across the open plain and when they reached Cosby's regiment, they skirted it, galloping through the waters of the river and continued towards Bagenal. As the Irish were slow to respond, they managed to join up with Bagenal's regiment, just as it reached the top of the incline. Wingfield was dismayed at the number of dead soldiers he had passed on his ride, the vast majority of whom were English.

He immediately sought out Bagenal and found him looking out across a wide-open cornfield towards a third hill. His visor was up and Wingfield could see the sweat running down his forehead and into his eyes. Wingfield took stock of the situation and noticed with disappointment that there was no sign of Percy's regiment.

"Marshal Bagenal," he said loudly.

Bagenal swung around in surprise. "Wingfield!" he exclaimed, before continuing indignantly. "What in all that's holy are you doing here? Who gave you permission to leave your men?"

Wingfield answered icily. "No-one but my own better conscience. I fear a major disaster. The rear is totally tied down and there is still no sign of Percy's regiment. Unless we regroup, disaster will surely befall us. Someone must go back and bring off the rear. I fear that a great mischief might have been done to it. You must call Percy's regiment back. Then, you must return and hold the Yellow Ford while Cosby can hold the Callan crossing. My regiment and I will go back for the rear. Then we must stay together, whether we decide to advance or retreat, otherwise the Irish will overthrow us."

Bagenal breathed heavily. He greatly resented Wingfield's tone. He was the commander, not him. And yet, his previous confidence had deserted him. Events were not turning out as he had expected. "I have been trying to re-establish contact with Percy's regiment for some time. All of our present difficulties are owing to him. He should never have advanced so far without us. I have attempted to catch up with him so that I could get him to wait on the rest of the army," he answered defensively.

"That may be," Wingfield returned, "but to persist in that course is now dangerous. You will only serve to stretch the army further. Send someone to order him to return."

Bagenal considered the advice. He had to admit to himself that he preferred to be near another regiment, rather than be isolated as he was here. He turned to Captain Malbie who was listening to the exchanges between both men. "Captain, take some men and find Percy. Order him to return hither," Bagenal ordered.

Malbie saluted and hastened away to execute his orders.

"I will come with you," Bagenal said to Wingfield, "I must observe the situation for myself."

Wingfield swallowed the protestation that had risen to his lips. In his estimation, there was need for decisive orders, without further delay. "And your regiment?" he asked. "Will you send it back to the ford?"

Bagenal scowled. "I will make that decision when I have reconnoitred the situation for myself," he answered. "I must go forward to meet Percy's regiment and draw it back to us. Cosby can guard the ford and you can go and look for the rear."

Wingfield disagreed. He disapproved of another regiment advancing without the rest. Bagenal's regiment had already suffered much more than his. Allied to this, he was becoming concerned about Bagenal. There was a note of hysteria underlying his speech and so he hastily reached a decision. "I will send my regiment back under Captain Smith to find the rear," he said. "He is a dependable man, not given to taking risks. I will come with you, but we must make haste, find Percy and return to join Cosby. If we can re-establish contact with each other again, all might not yet be lost."

"There is no need for you to accompany me," Bagenal said stiffly but Wingfield ignored him, turning instead to the officer of his bodyguard. "Return to my regiment and tell Captain Smith that he is to find the rear and aid it, if the rendering of such aid does not place his own regiment in danger," he ordered. "As you pass Cosby, command him to remain where he is until he receives further orders."

The captain saluted and he and his men galloped back in the direction from whence they had come. "Make haste," Bagenal shouted to his men, "we must rejoin Percy's regiment."

Captain Malbie reached the top of the third hill, having suffered no greater injury than having the plume shot from the top of his helmet. There below him, he finally saw Percy's regiment, barely a thousand paces away. He saw William's men retreating in good order towards the Blackwater Fort, away from an attacking mass of Irish infantry. They must have attempted to join with Percy, Malbie thought. Percy's regiment, however, appeared to be in extreme difficulties, bearing the brunt of attacks from Irish horse and foot. It seemed to be outnumbered by at least three to one and the Irish were out in the open, attacking them in proper formation with pike squares and musketeers on the sleeves. Damn, Malbie thought, digging his spurs into the side of his horse and galloping down the hillside, please God keep me safe.

He raced across the open ground, making himself as small a target as possible. "Go, Bess, faster," he whispered into his mount's ear as they thundered across the grass before pulling up behind the English formation. He shouted loudly, fearing that he would be mistaken for an enemy. "Message for Sir Percy from the Marshal, message for Sir Percy."

He dismounted and Sir Percy appeared from within the ranks of his men. His face was blackened from the powder and smoke of battle. "Yes," he demanded, "where the hell is the Marshal? He should be here aiding us, long since!"

Captain Malbie saluted. "The Marshal orders that you retreat and rejoin him. The army has become separated and it is imperative that it be reunited."

"Retreat!" Percy cried indignantly. "We have gained every step of our advance at the cost of English blood. Our goal is down there, at that fort," he said, pointing down to the river. "It is the rest of the army that must advance to us."

Captain Malbie shrugged. "Those are your orders. You must retreat. The army must be reunited or the whole might fail."

Percy swore inwardly. Things must be even worse than he had imagined. The thought that the whole army might be pressed as hard as he was, filled him with apprehension. He had been relying on the rest of the army to extricate him from a situation that was getting more and more desperate every minute. His men were barely holding on, as it was. It would be much more difficult to maintain their defensive formation while retreating. He would have to conceal his feelings from his soldiers.

"Give the order to retreat," he said to his drummer who immediately beat the staccato on his instrument.

On seeing the English start the retreat, the Irish gained in confidence and attacked with greater daring. Little by little, the English retraced their steps. They managed to reach the top of the third hill safely and began to traverse the cornfield. Halfway across, Percy's musketeers ran out of powder. They had fought well and had done everything possible to protect the marching column. They now sought the protection of the pike square, which parted, allowing them into the middle of their body.

Seeing their opportunity, O'Neill's horsemen charged and launched their lances into the middle of the massed men. The Irish musketeers also continued to pour their shot into them. They now could afford to come close enough to be just out of pike reach, and their fire proved all the more deadly as a result. The square still attempted to retreat in an orderly fashion, but it was proving more and more difficult.

Finally, it was too much for some of the most recent recruits from England, who, in horror, threw down their weapons and ran for a trench, leaving gaping holes in the formation. O'Neill's horse saw their chance and charged home.

Cormac was in the thick of the attacking Irish, a revolver in one hand and his bloodied sword in the other. I will not die here, he thought, feeling deep animosity for the English invaders who would kill him if they could. His anger drove him on, his horse stumbling on the grass, made slippery from the spilled blood. There were men around him, screaming unintelligibly, and the air was thick with smoke and the smell of death. The Gallowglass leader, MacDonald, passed him, his huge axe held easily. Cormac, refusing to be second, drove himself deeper into the fleeing body of men.

The English were now running away in a muddle of defeat, but there was no place to hide. Cormac galloped up the hill after them, his sword, a live thing in his hand. A regiment was broken, a victory won and death wanted its payment. His sword chopped down on the green uniforms and he did not see men, only enemy, as he galloped, slashing every enemy soldier that came within his reach. The Irish horse and foot were now among the English, inside their formation and they were all swept along, English and Irish, one heaving, hacking body of men. The soldiers were so pressed together that the dead and wounded were dragged along with them, not even having space to fall down. Cormac snarled at these upstarts that had dared invade his territory, killing them without pity. His men hacked at the enemy, cutting and splicing them, while the axes of the Gallowglasses whirled about them, parting heads from bodies, as cleanly as ears of corn from their stalks.

A red tide of Irish soldiers surged through the green, ebbing flow of English ranks, their swords and axes red too. It made no coherent sound, just a terrifying cacophony of noise. The keening for the many past sorrows, the many deaths and the memory of those past defeats, now turned to a clamour for revenge and these Irish soldiers killed mercilessly. They destroyed all in front of them until their hands were tired, until they were soaked in their enemy's blood, until there were none left to kill.

The MacDonald reached the top of the ditch and found a soldier cowering there, pleading in his foreign tongue. But the axe dropped remorselessly and the Gallowglass's lips drew back against his teeth, venting his spleen at the invaders. There were more men ahead, jumping into the ditch and he ran at them, his axe circling over his head, terrorising the fleeing force. He must have revenge and more of the enemy's blood. There was an account to be balanced and by God, he would do it.

Cormac was now howling like a possessed thing. He stood, his sword bathed in gore, desiring more English soldiers to come to him. He stalked them, teeth bared, screaming like an avenging fury. A body moved, a green arm was lifted in supplication and his blade whirled, bit down once more, clean through to the grass beneath.

An English infantryman, a farm labourer, conscripted from the peaceful dales of Staffordshire, hid quietly behind a thorn tree. He remained still, totally still, waiting for the madness to pass, thinking of the lass he had left behind, far away, hoping that their child, would be born safely. He watched the Irish captain on his horse and prayed that he would not be noticed, but the face turned and the hard cold eyes looked into his own.

"No, Sir, please," he called out but the sword took him, disembowelling him as Cormac shouted in rage, ripping again and again, thrusting down at the soldier, mutilating the body until he was stalled by a hand on his shoulder.

"Cormac," his brother said, "he's dead."

Cormac turned and saw Hugh looking at him keenly. He breathed hard and regained control of himself. He looked down in shock at the decimated body of the soldier. He heard a scream and turned to look at where a small body of trapped Englishmen was putting up a final stand against their assailants. At the other side of the trench, another English regiment was drawing up and two officers rode up to observe the slaughter.

Hugh grimaced. He recognised his old enemy by the man's girth and armour. "Bagenal," he breathed as he leaned over on his horse and called two of his bodyguards to him. They ran over hurriedly and he pointed and whispered to them. They nodded eagerly and ran away, their muskets on their shoulders.

Percy's ensign, Evan Owens, looked around him in panic. There were only eight of them still standing. In his left hand, he carried the flagpole on which Percy's precious colours were exhibited while he parried the sword thrust of an Irish soldier, with his right. The Irish could not be allowed have the colours, the disgrace would be too much to bear. He got under his attacker's guard and thrust his sword in the man's face, entering it just under his jaw. He drove it in deep, up through the man's brain and withdrew it again, allowing the man fall forward, blood erupting from the wound. He saw another two of his men go down and he turned, anxious to see if there was a way out. He swiftly broke the flagpole over his knee and removed the pennant, quickly wrapping it around his body. He shouted to his remaining men, "cover me", and ran for the ditch. His men ran with him, surrounding him in an effort to protect him and the standard, carving a path for him to the trench. He saw Percy fall from his horse some distance in front of him after taking the full force of a shot on his breastplate. Then he noticed two of Percy's bodyguards pull him to his feet and throw him down into the ditch. One by one, the small band surrounding Owens was struck down and finally, only Owens himself was left standing. He was now completely surrounded by large Gallowglasses. He stood watching them as they closed the circle around him. One of them pointed at the colours that were draped around his body.

"Tug dom é," he said, "agus ligfidh mé tú dul saor."

Owens did not know what the fierce, blood splattered soldier had said to him, but he could see the finger pointing at the colours. "Never," he shouted fiercely. "If you want them, you must kill me first."

The Gallowglass smiled a thin, cruel smile. At his nod, they all attacked in unison. Owens felt a momentary searing pain as an axe smashed through his helmet and cleaved his brain in two. All went dark for him, but the soldiers continued to hack at the dead body with their axes, chopping his head and arms from his torso. Then, the Gallowglass unwrapped the colours, now bloodstained and held them aloft, shouting triumphantly.

Bagenal and Wingfield watched in horror at what was occurring just on the other side of the trench. They saw Percy fall from the ditch and rushed forward to aid him. They dragged him to his feet and pulled him away. In all, not much more than twenty of his regiment had made it to this location.

"Are you wounded?" Wingfield asked.

Percy, badly winded, looked down at his breastplate. There were indentations on it where the musket balls had hit him, but they had not pierced his armour.

"I appear to be," he said, disorientated by the speed and completeness of his defeat. They heard a large cheer rise from the Irish and, looking up the hill, saw a large Gallowglass, standing tall and waving Percy's standard proudly. Tears of humiliation and shame came to Percy's eyes.

"I'll get the bastard," Bagenal said as he drew his revolver. He lifted his helmet's visor and rubbed the sweat from his eyes. He took careful aim and then a shot rang out. Bagenal's face assumed an expression of surprise as a musket ball hit him directly in the centre of his forehead. A red stain marked its entry and, dropping his revolver, he fell forward. Wingfield ran to him and turned him over, but it was too late. He was already dead. A triumphant roar went up from the Irish ranks as the news of Bagenal's death spread like wildfire.

"Quick," Wingfield shouted at Percy. "Help me get him back to his regiment. We cannot leave him here."

They lifted Bagenal's body between them and hurriedly carried him back towards the waiting regiment. Wingfield saw that the Irish were not stopping at the ditch but were beginning to stream across the trench, obviously intent on doing to Bagenal's regiment what they had already done to Percy's. The sight of them and Bagenal's dead body caused a sense of panic to erupt amongst the English soldiers. Wingfield stepped forward. "Marshall Bagenal is dead and I am now in command. If you obey my orders, we will get out of here. Is that understood?" he asked.

A low, unconvinced mumble ran through the regiment.

"Very well," Wingfield said. "Now we are going to retreat in an orderly fashion and rejoin the rest of the army. Cosby's men are not far behind us, just over the hill at the ford. My regiment should have found the rear and brought them forward by now. Let us make haste."

The regiment began its laborious retreat. Wingfield was concerned. He knew that most of the powder was with the battle and that Bagenal's regiment must be running low by now. The Irish fought bravely, contesting every step and he saw his men becoming more and more unsteady. He began to doubt if they would make it and just as he reached the bottom of the second hill, he heard a fanfare of horns and on looking up saw, to his absolute relief, Cosby's regiment appear on the summit. They marched slowly down to join them, meeting half way.

Cosby hastened over to them. "I saw the rear marching up. They had been sorely pressed until your regiment came behind the attacking Irish army and forced them to break off their assault. They didn't relish being caught between both our forces. Once the rear was safe, I decided to come forward to help you return," Cosby said but then spotted the dead body of Bagenal. A gasp of dismay escaped his lips. Before he could comment, he saw Percy and looked at the remnants of his regiment. "Is this all that's left of the van?" he asked in shocked tones.

Wingfield nodded while Percy answered. "Gone, all destroyed!"

Cosby was visibly shaken. "But how?" he asked.

Wingfield ignored his question. "I'm in charge now," he said decisively. "There is only one course open to us. We must return to Armagh."

Cosby shook his head. "But there is a large army to our rear. O'Donnell and Maguire are between the town and us. We had great difficulty in bringing the rear off and they have also suffered much. I think we should press on. If we all attack together, we will push through," he said.

"O'Neill's forces are between us and the fort," Percy said, not having any desire to cross swords with them again.

"Yes," Wingfield answered. "And what if we were to break through? We would then be prisoners there, just like Williams. We must abandon him to his fate or risk losing our whole force."

"It is not right," Cosby said.

"We have no choice. We are almost out of powder. We are the only English army in this country. There is no other. It is imperative for the whole future of the Irish colony that we bring what we can of this army safely back to the Pale. And believe me, that will be no easy task," Wingfield said grimly.

"And Williams?" Cosby asked

"He must starve awhile yet," Wingfield answered. "That, or surrender. But come, enough talk. Every moment's delay costs lives and risks our eventual overthrow. I will return to my own regiment and prepare them for retreat. You follow after, as quickly as you can. We will hold the fords till you arrive."

Late that afternoon, the bedraggled remnants of the English army reached Armagh Cathedral. They laboured up the hill, sweating profusely. The small garrison threw the gates open and they crowded inside, collapsing on the floor, totally exhausted. They had been fighting on the march for over seven long continuous hours and they had come to the end of their resilience.

Wingfield looked around at the spent troops, the moans of the wounded, mingling with the triumphant shouts of the Irish outside. They had got this far, but how would they escape from here, he wondered. Their powder was all but consumed. He turned to Malbie. "Have a roll call. I want to know how many are left," he said. "I'm going to do all I can to secure our position."

Malbie saluted and Wingfield went and picked his best marksmen whom he placed on the cathedral walls. He climbed up and looked at the surrounding countryside. The Irish army now flanked them on all sides and was beginning to dig itself in for a siege. He looked down at his men as the roll was being called, wondering if there ever had been as large a congregation in the cathedral before they had converted it into a barracks. O'Neill had chosen not to destroy the building, believing that the English would never use a house of God for military purposes. The monks had cursed these English desecraters who speedily hung them from the walls. Perhaps their curse was coming to pass.

Wingfield's dark musings were interrupted by Malbie who had climbed up onto the walls. "Sir Thomas," he said.

Wingfield turned away from the scene in front of him. "Yes," he answered.

"Fifteen hundred men present, of whom over a thousand are wounded, more than half seriously so. Twenty-five officers dead, not counting Marshal Bagenal. Worst of all, eleven colours were lost to the enemy," he said.

Wingfield turned back to look at the green fields around him. This was worse than he had thought. Three thousand men lost! If they remained trapped here, disease would set in, further reducing their numbers. He looked at the Irish army that was filling the plains around the cathedral. They had not suffered like his men. Wingfield realised suddenly that everything had changed utterly. English forces had suffered their worst ever defeat in Ireland. All the assumptions about the supremacy and invulnerability of the English military had been undermined forever. This day's disaster would have far reaching consequences. The northern rebels' standing would be enhanced and they would gather adherents far beyond their borders. There was no army left to stop them. It would be many months before the Queen could mobilise a force and send it across the sea to aid them. He must do what he could to save something from the debacle.

"Captain Malbie, you and the rest of the horse must rest and, at first light, I want you to mount up and attempt to escape from here. The Irish will celebrate their victory tonight and will be at their least alert at dawn. If you succeed, you are to head for Dublin and inform the Council of this day's outcome," he said.

"But what of you? You will never be able to break out without the horse to support you," Malbie said in surprise.

"Even with the horse, we could never do it. The Council must decide if we are worth ransoming. That is the only way we will escape. You must do your best for us," he replied. "They will not be able to take the cathedral so we will be relying on you for our deliverance. The Blackwater Fort must be surrendered, as must Armagh. We could not keep either without a larger army than the one we lost today. Offer both forts to the Irish, in addition to whatever else they want. We must make a deal with them."

"So, you think we must bargain with them, those traitors who have done such damage to the Queen's army and honour?" Malbie asked in disbelief.

"They have proven today that we must take their threat to the security of this kingdom seriously. I like it as little as you but, for now, we have no choice."

Malbie saluted and went to inform his troops of their orders. Wingfield looked out again at the surrounding fields as dusk began to fall. He could see the fires that the Irish had lit, winking up at him through the gloom. They might not be able to take the cathedral but they could always starve them to death. They had left most of their provisions strewn along the road to the Blackwater so that the wounded could be brought with them. The small amount of supplies, which the regular garrison had, would not go far among so many men as now needed subsistence. He would have to do what he could to keep morale up and hope for the best. With a heavy heart, he descended the ladder to the expectant men.

Prince Philip and Archduke Albert walked slowly up the passageway to the chamber in which King Philip lay. He had lain dying for over fifty-three days, fifty-three days that had seemed like an eternity to his family. He had four suppurating sores on the fingers of his right hand, another on his foot and an abscess on his right knee from which, every day, were pressed great quantities of foul smelling matter, as thick as plaster. He could not sleep or eat and his stomach was distended with dropsy. Of late, it had become impossible to change his bedclothes or his night-robe, and following the purges given by his doctors, he had lain, for the last few days, in his own excrement, surrounded by swarms of flies.

As they drew near the door of his chamber, they both pressed their perfumed handkerchiefs to their noses in an effort to protect themselves from the overpowering stench. Archduke Albert took a deep breath through the cloth, opened the door and walked quickly into the chamber. The King lay in his bed, his eyes on the High Altar of his church, which he could see through a specially constructed window. On hearing them enter, he turned to stare at them, a look of disappointment clouding his features.

"The Infanta?" he asked weakly.

"She is not well," the Archduke answered. "She sends her apologies and her wish that you find yourself in better health."

"I trust it is nothing serious," the King asked anxiously.

"No, she should be up and about again soon," the Archduke

answered.

The Infanta was the King's thirty-year-old daughter, his greatest joy and the Archduke's fiancée. The King could not have shown him any greater honour than by bestowing his beloved daughter's hand upon him. It was his dying wish that they be married. They both had come every day to sit by the King, but his daughter had found it more and more difficult of late to witness what illness had wreaked upon her father. Her vigil had cost her dearly. She had aged visibly over the last few months and it was genuine illness that had stopped her from attending today.

"You cannot bear to look at me," the King said, now turning his attention to his son who was looking away. "Do not avert your gaze. Look at me!" he ordered.

Prince Philip looked at the King, his face ashen, trying to control the nausea he felt at the sight of the old grey man in the putrid bed and the rancid smell of death and decay that filled the chamber.

"See, my son," the King continued. "This is what the world and all its kingdoms amount to in the end. Never forget it. Always do your duty by God. In the end, that is what matters most when you lie on your deathbed, as I now do."

"You need have no fear, Father," the Prince said. "You have always done God's will."

The King's eyes misted over. "I know that I have never committed any sin against any man because all I have ever done, every action I have ever undertaken, has been dictated by God's will," he said before continuing in a more distraught tone. "However, I have failed him, I have not always carried out his will with sufficient fervour."

The Archduke shook his head vehemently. "That is not true, Your Majesty. No King could have done more!"

The King's face quivered and tears of remorse ran down his cheeks. The Archduke could not believe that he had any doubts about his life or his goodness. He was a man who had lived his life in absolute piety, accepting God's will uncomplainingly. He loved his children and when his eldest child had been struck down with the strain of insanity that ran through his family, he had also accepted that cross with fortitude. He had spent three whole days making his confession, confessing sins that no other man would acknowledge as such.

"There has been excellent news from Ireland," the Archduke said, in an effort to distract the King from his morbid thoughts. The northern Lords have defeated a large English army. The whole English force in Ireland was sent against them and they were defeated in open battle. There has never before been such a reversal for English power in

Ireland. The whole island is in revolt. They say that the victory won by O'Neill is such, that he deserves favourable comparison with Parma. The Queen's Council had to write to him, begging him to release the few survivors that remained. This he did, in return for their yielding of all their strongholds in Ulster."

The King struggled onto his side and looked at the High Altar, his eyes now shining with comfort. "Thank you, Lord, for giving me this omen and comfort in my last few hours. It is what I have prayed for, a sign that my lifelong battle against the heretics has not being in vain." Slowly, he turned back to the two men at his side. "The answer was before me all along and I did not recognise it," he said. "I used the Irish ill, choosing not to fulfil my promises to them. And yet, in spite of my neglect, what transpires? They, those Irish savages, defeat the English with what little means that have. God's will is mightier than ours. I now confess that the biggest mistake of my life was that I never supported them when I should have. Were they not Catholics like us? Did they not cleave to their religion, the one true faith, in spite of persecution and all the enticements that the English offered them?"

The Archduke and Prince Philip nodded. They were glad of the King's altered mood.

"You must promise me, my son, that you will aid them in their struggle. I promise you, that is where and how the ultimate victory will be gained over the forces that are ranged against Spain. It is my dying wish. Do you promise me?" the King demanded.

"I do, Father," the Prince answered.

"Very well. It is to you that this crusade has now fallen. You must be equal to the task. Get me my scribe. I must send O'Neill my congratulations."

Prince Philip nodded to the physician who went to fetch the State Secretary. The King sank back onto the bed, taking his crucifix into his hands. He mumbled his prayers until the scribe appeared, whereupon he started to dictate a letter of congratulations. Weakened by the exertion that signing it entailed, he fell back upon his bed, grasping his crucifix once more. A peace had descended upon him. He was no longer tormented as he had been. Then, after a few minutes, his breathing slowed and his spirit, which had long struggled, was released. The physician went and held a looking glass to his mouth and after a few moments turned to the two watching men.

"I regret, Your Highness," he said addressing Prince Philip, "His Majesty is dead."

The Archduke looked at the dead body and at the new King who was overcome with sorrow. The Spanish people too would also be greatly grieved, he thought. The old King had been much esteemed and held in warm affection by his people.   And yet, the Archduke thought, his death would not be a disaster for Spain. The old King had wanted to know everything that transpired in the armed forces, insisting upon having the final word on all decisions. Such compulsion had led to a paralysis in the system of government when speedy decisions were most needed. The Archduke had great hopes for the country under the new King Philip. He would define Spain's needs and let his generals get on with their duties. Spain's enemies would now see what they could do when no longer ruled by a King, incapable of delegation. There would be a new vigour about the prosecution of the war. Of that, he had no doubt. He was looking forward to the future.

Chapter 18

Henry Hovendon moved stiffly through the meadow that led down to the gentle brook, nestling among the tall, green trees. He had been riding for many hours and his body and limbs cried out for repose, but that would have to wait for another while yet. He spied the gathering that he sought, sheltering in the shade from the warm sun, reclining on fern cushions, around a low trestle table. This was amply furnished with meats, fruits and wine and the contented laughter of the group carried across the countryside to him. Henry saw that he had been spotted as O'Neill's bodyguards appeared suddenly at the edge of the trees, gauging his approach. When they recognised him, their leader nodded in salute, before disappearing back into the trees again.

Their alert, however, had not gone unobserved and Henry saw a youth stand and look in his direction, hand shading his eyes as he peered into the sun, which was directly behind Hovendon. Then he heard the figure shout, "Uncle Henry," and the youth raced across the meadow towards him. It was his namesake, Henry Óg. Catherine had been good to Siobhán's children, insisting that they return permanently to Dungannon to be with their father. She and Hugh recently had a daughter and they had all settled down as one contented family. Henry had never known a time when Hugh's domestic situation had been as happy and carefree as now and it gladdened him to see it.

Henry Óg reached him and threw his arms around his neck, embracing him tightly. The older man quelled his natural inclination to flinch from the embrace. Henry Óg was now thirteen, a freckle-faced, red haired youth, strongly built and of average height for his years.

"Uncle Henry," Henry Óg cried excitedly, "you've finally come back!"

Henry smiled, amused at the warmth of the boy's welcome. "Yes," he said, "I had to return to see you all."

"And the wars?" the lad asked breathlessly. "Are the English driven out of Ireland yet?"

"Not yet," Henry answered, "But it should not be long now."

"Come and join us," O'Neill shouted to him as Catherine rose from the table. She took a goblet, which she filled with wine and offered it to him. Henry received it smilingly. "My thanks to you, Catherine," he said.

"Well, Uncle Henry," Hugh Óg asked, "did you bring us anything from Dublin?"

"Yes," Henry answered jokingly, "some English books so that you may practice your reading. They're in my saddle-bag."

Father Nangle, a Franciscan priest and the boy's tutor, laughed heartily at Hugh Óg's face, which had fallen in disappointment. He was a fat, middle aged, man, his ample cheeks and jowls, undulating in merriment.

"Let Henry rest, Hugh Óg," O'Neill ordered. "He is after a long journey and must be tired from his travels. Come, Henry, sit at the table and eat. You must be hungry."

"I am too stiff," Henry answered, leaning over the table and cutting a slice of mutton from a joint that lay upon the table. "I must walk and ease out my bones. I'm not as young as I once was," he said and shot Hugh a glance, so fleeting as to be unperceived by anyone else present. Hugh, however, registered it immediately. Henry had news, news that would not even wait until after the meal. He rose to his feet, goblet in hand and addressed him. "I will join you," he said. "I am getting a little old myself for this hunkering on the ground. The exercise will do me good. Come, let me show you a new horse, which I received from Tyrell. He confiscated it in Munster from some settler," he said, laughing.

"Can I come too, Father?" Henry Óg asked hopefully.

"No," Hugh answered, "You may talk with Henry later. Now we must discuss business." With that, the two men walked away and when they were out of earshot, Hugh enquired. "The news from the south is still good?"

"Yes," Henry answered. "James Butler was defeated by Brian O'Moore. His brother, the Earl of Ormonde, was defeated by Owney O'Moore and now dares not show his face outside his castle in Kilkenny. Owney and Tyrell then swept into Munster. The English troops stayed within their towns and refused to come out and defend the settlers."

"Good," Hugh said. "Did the people rise and support them?"

"Yes," Henry answered. "They were only waiting for the opportunity. They had not forgotten their slaughtered kinsmen and stolen lands. Through the province, they rose as one, sweeping the English from the land. Those few who were not killed, were driven out, deprived of everything that they held, while the Irish repossessed themselves of the castles and lands, from which they had been evicted."

"It is only just," Hugh said. "And they lost all, even Spencer and Raleigh?"

"All, without exception. Spencer's castle at Doneraile was burnt to the ground and he was lucky to have escaped with his life. They say his son was lost in the fire. He left Ireland as poor as he came hither and it is said that he suffers great penury in London."

"It is no more than he deserves," Hugh said with satisfaction.

Henry nodded. He knew how much hatred Hugh bore Spencer, dating back to when they had served together under Grey. He, himself, found it difficult to understand how the mind, which had composed the sublime "Faerie Queen" could have conceived so warped and malicious a work as "A View of the State of Ireland". Spencer had lived off the backs of the Irish for fifteen long years and it was satisfying that, finally, justice had been done.

"And what of our new Earl of Desmond? Have the people accepted him?" Hugh asked eagerly.

Again Henry nodded. There had been a need of a rallying point for the rebellion. James Fitzgerald, the late Earl's nephew, had been set up by O'Neill as Desmond's successor.

"He is accepted but I do not rate the man. He drinks too heavily and does nothing to secure his position. I fear that he will not amount to much."

"There was no one else," Hugh answered ruefully. "But, you have more concerns than that. I know you too well."

"Yes, I've heard who is to be the next Lord Deputy. In truth, he's to have the more prestigious title of Lord Lieutenant," Henry said.

Hugh looked surprised and whistled gently. "It must be forty years since that title was last awarded and that was to the Earl of Sussex. It must be some important personage. An Earl?" he asked.

"Yes, none other than the Earl of Essex," Henry answered, noting Hugh's reaction to the news. It had greatly surprised him and he saw that Hugh was equally taken aback.

"Essex! The Queen means business if she is sending her favourite to confront us. There will be no shortage of English nobles to accompany him. These are indeed bad tidings," Hugh said in concern.

"Yes. He is to bring with him an army of sixteen thousand-foot and thirteen hundred horse to reinforce the army here. The Queen has also promised to send him 2000 extra men every three months, to keep up his numbers. He has been ordered to destroy you and your allies," Henry explained, unable to couch the news in more delicate terms.

"But are you sure? You could be deliberately misinformed?" Hugh asked, still hoping that the information might be suspect.

Henry had checked and rechecked the story, hoping that it was false but all his sources confirmed its truth. The foremost general of whom the English could boast, the embodiment of English chivalry, was to march against them, accompanied by the largest English army ever to be sent across the sea to Ireland. He was the people's favourite, a man whom both commoner and noble would hasten to serve.

"Of that, I am certain," Hovendon answered.

"Over seventeen thousand soldiers from England," Hugh said in wonder. "Perhaps the presence of the Earl of Essex in this country will raise the profile of the war here and encourage the Spanish finally to become involved in our fight."

Henry shook his head. "The Dutch have launched a fleet of seventy ships against them. We need not expect aid from that quarter. Essex will be able to transfer his army safely here without any fear of attack from them."

"Are they always to have good fortune on their side?" Hugh asked in exasperation. "We need more time to strengthen our alliances with our new allies in Munster. The arrival of such an army from England will shake their confidence."

"True," Henry said. "In the face of such odds, the southern Chieftains would have no option but to treat with them."

"We must go south and gather in hostages from the southern Lords. We must do all in our power to bind them to our cause," Hugh said anxiously, eager to do something that might help strengthen their position.

"It is too late for that. Essex has already left London. However, relations between him and the Queen have soured of late. He did not desire this appointment, but had objected so strongly to all the Queen's choices that she ordained that he should undertake the task himself. It is said that, during an argument on the issue, he turned away from her in annoyance and that she boxed his ears. He started to draw his sword but was restrained by a member of the Privy Council," Henry recounted.

Hugh whistled in amazement. Essex was certainly rash. "He will dislike being away from the court for a long absence. His enemies, who are many, can work to undermine him and further turn the Queen against him. We must see how we can play this proud Earl," Hugh said, a smile forming at the corner of his lips.

"There are yet more bad tidings. Samuel Bagenal is to return to Ireland and is to be assigned a large force to defend Newry. Worse still, Clifford is to attack O'Donnell and raise his siege at Coolooney,"

Henry continued.

"O'Donnell must deal with Clifford," Hugh said without too much concern. "It is Essex who will be the major threat to our position." He paused and looked meditatively into the distance. "So, we must survive another year before we can expect aid from Spain. At times, I doubt that we shall ever see it."

Henry nodded. "We have survived thus far. We can continue for another while yet."

"True, Henry," Hugh said, "but come, we must rejoin the others. The lads will be delighted to learn that their father is to engage with the Earl of Essex. We will talk later about what we must do to prepare for his arrival."

Henry agreed. "I must tell the boys some tales of great Essex. It will make them worship you all the more when you defeat him in battle."

Hugh smiled wryly. "Fighting him will, indeed, test our skills."

Henry nodded and they both returned in silence. Soon, very soon, they would have to plan for such an eventuality.

Hugh Roe O'Donnell waited for the final prayers in Latin to finish, blessed himself and strode up to join the priest on the makeshift altar. He stood beside him, looking out over his assembled soldiers who filled the plain before him. He could smell the promise of battle in the air. The English, under Clifford, were finally on the march towards the Curlew Mountains in an effort to raise the siege of Coolooney. There, they would attempt to relieve Sir Donough O'Connor who still remained loyal to the English. He was the last remaining Chieftain loyal to the Queen in north Connaught. Niall Garve was directing the siege and O'Donnell had no intention of allowing the English relieve the castle when it must finally be on the point of surrendering. He was content at what they had achieved thus far in Connaught. He had succeeded in driving Clifford from the province, forcing him to station himself in Athlone. Now, he was attempting to interfere in the running of Connaught again and had to be halted.

His men blessed themselves and rose from their knees, wiping the dew from their trews. The sun was rising, a red, warm reassuring disk, appearing from behind the distant mountains, bathing the countryside in a red glow. The army had fasted all the previous day and every man of them had received the sacrament of Penance and the blessed Eucharist. He cleared his throat.

"Today, we march to defend our lands and our ancient faith against the soldiers of the heretic Queen. You have all prepared well for this battle. You have honoured the true Queen, the Queen of

Heaven and she will be with you in your fight. She will protect our cause and us, of that let you have no doubt. Always remember that you are fighting for your altars and your homes. On your side are right and justice. On the side of the English, is naught but injustice and treachery," he said with rising passion, his hands held out in direct appeal to them, drawing them into his certainty.

"The choice before you is to fight and conquer or lose and be imprisoned, to be dragged in chains through the streets of English towns, objects of derision and mockery. Is that what you wish?" he questioned them.

An enormous wave of voices answered him, "No."

"I tell you now, for those of you who have never before faced the English in battle, do not be alarmed by their numbers or the strangeness of their arms, but put your confidence in God alone. We have faced them before and conquered them. Under their armour, behind their guns, are mortal men, men who do not have right on their side."

A murmur of assent ran through the army. He saw the veterans of the Yellow Ford nod in agreement, confiding to the new troops, that O'Donnell's words were true.

"I am confident that we will win," he continued passionately, his sincerity, shining through his words. "Any of us here who falls in battle, will fall gloriously, fighting for justice and liberty and his name will be mentioned as long as Irishmen draw breath. And those of you who survive, will be pointed out as the companion of O'Donnell and the defender of his country," he said, his voice undulating with emotion. "In church, the people will make way for him as he passes to the altar, murmuring respectfully, 'that hero fought at Dunaveeragh'. Are you going to be that hero?" he asked, his question ringing out over the plain.

His men answered in one voice, "Yes!"

"I now must introduce you to an important personage, one who has been sent here to us by the Pope himself, the new Archbishop of Dublin, His Grace, Oviedo," O'Donnell thundered in a great crescendo of passion.

Oviedo, dressed in the purple robes of his office, stepped forward from behind the altar where he had been waiting. A murmur of surprise ran through the gathered soldiers. He raised his hands for silence. In one of his hands he held a parchment, which he handed to O'Donnell once the crowd had become still. O'Donnell then held up the document. "The Pope has given the Archbishop the power to grant indulgences to those who fight against the heretical Queen. You must all kneel to receive it," he ordered.

All present fell to their knees. The Archbishop recited the incantation over them in his heavily accented Latin, his arms aloft, calling down the blessings of heaven upon them. O'Donnell allowed himself a brief moment of jealous thought as he recalled the plumed helmet, which the Pope had sent to O'Neill, in recognition of his right to the kingship of the country. It was unjust, O'Donnell thought. He was intent on ruling over Donegal and Connaught, the traditional position of the O'Donnells. O'Neill or the King of Spain could have the rest, but never Donegal and Connaught. The Pope had also sent 22,000 gold pieces, which O'Neill had shared with him. The new Spanish King had not forgotten them either. A ship had recently arrived in Donegal with arms for 2,000 men and he had sent half to O'Neill. O'Donnell roused himself from his reverie as the prayers finally came to an end and the Archbishop made the sign of the cross over them. His men followed suit and got to their feet. O'Donnell nodded at the Archbishop and turned to the priest. "Tell His Grace I will join him shortly, I have business to attend to first," he said before climbing down from the altar and hurriedly cleaving a path through his men. Finally, he saw the person he sought. "Brian," he shouted. "Brian McDermott!"

A large man in his late thirties, turned and saluted him. His face had been hardened by misfortune. O'Donnell guessed that his mind was focused on the upcoming battle and his chance to avenge himself on the English for his ejection from his ancient lands around Boyle.

"I want you to harass the English in their march across the Curlews. You're to take six hundred men and defend the lower pass. O'Rourke is to defend the other with three hundred. I think that they will attempt the lower one, it would be madness to do otherwise. I have sent for O'Neill, who is making his way hither by forced marches, to aid us. We will be awaiting the English when they come through the mountains. Your task is to inflict as much damage on them as possible."

McDermott replied. "No Englishman will get through that pass, you can count on that," he said decisively.

O'Donnell had prepared the route carefully, some four months previously. He had set up barricades from which the defenders could ambush the attackers, had plashed the trees together and now, four months later, their branches would have grown intertwined, making an impenetrable blanket of vegetation along the sides of the narrow paths. God willing, his careful preparations would now bear fruit.

Wingfield walked up and down the passage leading to the Great Hall within Dublin Castle. It had been a long time since the capital had witnessed such excitement. Everybody there had been anxious to see Robert Devereux, the great Earl of Essex. His bravery was legendary and there was no more romantic figure in all of England. Practically the whole town had come out and besieged Christ Church Cathedral early in the day, in an effort to get a glimpse of him when he was receiving his sword of honour from Thomas Jones, Bishop of Meath. That had been Wingfield's first glimpse of him, as they had not met each other previously. He had been surrounded by a coterie of young nobles, those who would decide the future of England. Among them was the Earl of Southampton, the great patron of the arts, himself, almost as famous as Essex. Wingfield had observed quite readily their arrogant pride and hauteur and disapproved of the abject servility, which the Irish Council was displaying in their presence.

He had been summoned by Essex to wait upon him and although he had come at the appointed time, he had been kept waiting for more than three hours. He hoped that he, because of his experience in the Irish wars, might be consulted and receive some position within Essex's army.

He saw another man enter the passageway from outside, his cloak pulled around his shoulders. He walked over to the door of the Great Hall but the guards there blocked his way.

"Sir Arthur Chichester," he said with barely suppressed self-importance. "I must see the Lord Lieutenant."

"He is busy. Many seek an audience with him, but are disappointed," one of the guards answered.

Chichester searched underneath his cloak and brought out a parchment, which he handed to the guard. "Give him this," he ordered.

The guard paused a moment, but there was something imperious about Chichester's manner that suggested that he should be obeyed. The guard turned to go and as he did, Wingfield called after him.

"Would you remind the Lord Lieutenant that I still attend upon him," he said impatiently. The guard opened the door and entered the Great Hall, without even acknowledging his request.

"Sir Thomas Maria Wingfield," he said holding out his hand to Chichester, curious about what business this man had with Essex.

"Sir Arthur Chichester, brother of Sir John," the latter said brusquely. "Did you know him or are you newly come to these wars like myself?" he asked.

"I have been here many a year and had the honour of meeting your brother on one occasion," Wingfield answered.

"I have come to Ireland to avenge him. MacDonald will pay with his blood for his death," Chichester said darkly.

Wingfield nodded. He could understand Sir Arthur's desire for revenge. His brother's honour called for no less.

"We will have to defeat the Irish rebels before you shall be free to carry out your wishes," Wingfield said. "At present, he can hide behind O'Neill and his forces."

Chichester smiled a crooked, determined smile. "O'Neill features in my plans also," he said grimly. "You, undoubtedly, heard of the desecration to my brother's body?"

Wingfield nodded again. He had heard reports of how Sir John's head had been cut from his body and sent to O'Neill's camp. There, O'Neill had given it to his churls who had kicked it about, inciting their dogs to savage it.

"I have begged Her Majesty to grant me my brother's former position in Carrickfergus and promised her that if she does, I'll eliminate MacDonald and O'Neill."

Wingfield thought it would be good to have a man such as Sir Arthur on O'Neill's flank. Before he could reply, the door of the Great Hall swung open and the guard reappeared. "The Lord Lieutenant will grant you both an audience now" he announced.

Sir Arthur nodded. When they were in position behind the guard, they followed him inside. Wingfield looked around curiously at the throng that was gathered inside. They walked between the crowded tables, towards the opposite end of the hall where a large dais was situated. There, Essex sat, surrounded by the most important members of his entourage. He noticed that none of the members of the Queen's Irish Council was sitting in their company.

The feast, that had been laid on in Essex's honour, was coming to a close and the elderly Earl of Ormonde was on his feet, finishing his speech of welcome to the new Lord Lieutenant. Wingfield and Chichester stood in front of the dais until Ormonde concluded by wishing Essex all good fortune and success in his current expedition. As he sat down, the assembled multitude burst into a long and sustained applause. Wingfield kept his hands by his side. He had expected, when he had received his summons, that he would have been invited to the reception. Instead, he had been made wait outside like a common beggar. He had worked harder on the Queen's account than many of those present who only lined their own pockets at her expense. He had risked his life on many occasions on her behalf. He resented his omission.

Essex held up his hand for silence, then nodded regally at the gathering. He stood, looking haughtily around the large hall. "Thank you for your good wishes," he began. "It has been decided, after long consultations with the Irish Council and with my own advisers, that we will shake and sway the branches of the intolerable treachery that has grown in this county, before we cut out the roots. Thus, we will travel south first and crush the rebellion there before we travel northward."

The gathered populace broke into loud, approving applause. Wingfield knew that was what most of them wished to hear. Many of those present had received lands in Munster under the plantation there and were eager now, to have those lands restored to them. All the members of the Council had ensured that they personally had benefited from that plantation and it was in their interest that Essex should march south. It was not, however, in the best interests of the Queen, Wingfield thought. There was only one way that this war could be won and that was by defeating O'Neill and O'Donnell. He felt his anger rise as he thought of how those self-same Council members chose to remain in Dublin, safe within its stout walls, while people like himself, risked their lives. He looked at the fat, self-satisfied faces of the Palesmen. In the past, they had contributed regiments from their own numbers to help hold the country but now, refused to do so. Instead, they relied on Englishmen to protect them. He could not remain silent. He had expected that his opinion would have been sought on the matter. He had been at the forefront of every effort to deny the rebels the victory that they sought.

"Your Excellency," he said, his voice strong and loud, "to go south would be an error. O'Neill will allow you waste your forces against those he values not. You will use up your advantage for no good return. Cut the root and the branches will also wither. Trim the branches and leave the root, and the tree will only grow the stronger."

Essex looked at Wingfield in disbelief. He was unused to being interrupted or having his instructions questioned in public. His colour mounted and he asked angrily.

"And who are you that would dare give the Lord Lieutenant counsel that was not requested?"

"Sir Thomas Maria Wingfield, Your Excellency," Wingfield answered steadily. "I dare offer counsel only because I care that Her Majesty's resources are not misused. My counsel is not offered out of self-interest. I doubt that those who recommend that you go south could claim as much."

A disapproving murmur ran through the Great Hall. Wingfield knew that he had insulted practically every local person present, but did not care. Essex, however, was also insulted and he glowered at him, spitting his words out contemptuously.

"I have heard of you and your part in one of the most shameful episodes that ever befell an English army. You were second in command at the Yellow Ford, were you not?"

"That I was," Wingfield answered evenly.

"Well then," Essex continued with ire, "I do not comprehend how you can dare to offer counsel on military matters."

Vindictive laughter swept the hall. All present delighted in Wingfield's public humiliation. Wingfield felt betrayed. It was unjust. He had risked all in the Queen's cause. Essex smiled, allowing the Palesmen enjoy their moment, before holding up his hand.

"There are difficulties that you, for all your experience in these wars, do not seem to have understood," he continued ironically. "Pasture will be more plentiful later in the year. The army is also short of transport and until it arrives from England, we will not be able to send our full force north. We will deal with all the traitors in time. None shall escape the Queen's justice, of that you must have no doubt."

Wingfield held his peace. These were but minor problems, which were surmountable if the desire was there. However, he now recognised that he had been foolish to talk publicly as he had. Essex was evidently not the type of man who listened to counsel that did not concur with his own opinion. He would now never tolerate him in his army. The Earl observed him distastefully for another few moments and when he saw that Wingfield remained mute, turned to Chichester.

"The Queen says that I am to give you five hundred men and the Governorship of Carickfergus. She also tells me that I am to let Samuel Bagenal have eight companies at Newry, Lord Cromwell four companies at Dundalk, Lord Audley eight companies at Kells. On and on it goes, and the defence of the Pale alone has stripped me of five thousand men. If this keeps up, I shall not have enough men left for the job in hand," Essex said with discontent.

Chichester bowed low and then replied. "If you see fit to grant me the men, my Lord, I promise you that I will keep four times that number of the enemy tied up in Ulster and away from both the Pale and your Lordship's army."

Essex eyed Chichester speculatively. "You may have them," he said at length and dismissed both men with a wave of his hand. "See the marshal of my army in the morning."

Both men bowed. Wingfield understood that there was no more that he could do. He turned and walked from the Great Hall. As he passed the tables, he ignored the taunts aimed at him. Momentarily, he considered the idea of returning to England and turning his back on the whole sorry mess that Ireland had become, but quickly rejected the prospect. No, he could not leave the country until O'Neill was defeated and in his grave. That day, he would be free to pursue the rest of his life. In the meantime, he would have to find some commander who would have need of his services. It was shameful that he had fallen this low, that he would have to beg a position when he should have been granted a command of his own. Still, he would not yield. Somehow perseverance would win through.

Clifford looked in horror at the remnants of the van, which was running in headlong flight towards the battle, over which he had taken command. He saw that the Gallowglass soldiers were striking them down from behind and that his men were making no effort to defend themselves. Their screams, mingling with the triumphant shouts of the Irish mercenary soldiers, were having an unsettling effect on the main battle, which was already very shaken by the treatment that it had received since marching into the Curlews.

He lurched towards the fleeing vanguard, "Stop!" he shouted, "Turn and fight! Turn and fight!" His words had no effect. They continued to race towards him. Clifford felt a hand on his arm and spun around to see Sergeants Norris and Cooper at his side. "Come back," Norris said urgently as he watched the fleeing vanguard and their pursuers rapidly closing the distance between them. Clifford shook off the hand and drew his sword. "Stand and fight!" he screamed at them, but the fleeing soldiers' faces were incapable of even hearing his orders. Clifford could not understand how they were panicking so completely. It was not as if they were raw recruits. They were veterans of many fights before this. The Yellow Ford must have undermined the army's confidence more than he had thought.

Norris and Cooper grabbed Clifford's arms and dragged him back towards the main battle. It advanced towards them and streamed around the three men, enveloping them in its protective embrace. Their musketeers took up their position but were unable to get a clear shot at the Gallowglasses who were protected by the fleeing vanguard. They were apprehensive and awaited the impact of the howling enemy. The fleeing soldiers ran straight towards the battle square and instead of running around it, continued straight into the middle of it, forcing it to part. Clifford found himself being pushed towards the back of the formation and shouted urgently, "Close ranks! Close ranks!" But it was too late. The Gallowglasses saw their chance and followed the fleeing soldiers into the midst of the formation, splitting it apart.

The battle now broke asunder and its men ran before the attacking Gallowglass soldiers, attempting to avoid the axes that dealt out death with horrific efficiency. Clifford found himself being dragged backward as he fought against the tide of men who battered and mauled him. He fought to steady himself and get his men to stand.

"Turn and defend yourself!" he shouted in desperation, but they did not heed him. He found that all he could manage to do was stay on his feet, being forced further back down the mountain. He saw that they were being driven towards the rear guard, which stood immobile, unable to help or intervene in the disaster. The fleeing men smashed into the rear guard and it held for a few moments before it, too, fell apart, turned and ran. Those few moments were enough for Clifford to free himself from the fleeing mass. He stood with his sword drawn, facing the fleeing army. "Turn!" he shouted as he pointed his sword at his own fleeing men. "All you have to do is turn and fight the bastards! Don't let them kill you! Fight back!"

His men ignored him as they streamed past. Clifford stood there, powerless.

"It's pointless," Sergeant Norris said. "Come, we must survive to fight again. Nothing will rally them now."

"No, we must stop this slaughter," Clifford said desperately.

"Come away," Sergeant Cooper said anxiously. He observed the fleeing men continuing to stream past them and he saw the Gallowglasses coming closer.

Norris cried in desperation. "Come with us. There will be another day. This one is lost!"

Clifford shook his head. He could not believe what was happening. He could never have imagined that they could have behaved so shamefully. Their shame was his, he was their general and was ultimately responsible. He had failed his Queen. He could not live with his honour besmirched. "Go," he said. "Save yourselves." He turned back to face his enemy. Norris and Cooper stood for a moment and then Cooper turned and hastened away after the fleeing men. Norris stood an instant longer and then, shamefacedly, headed away also.

Clifford watched as the Gallowglasses ran towards him screaming fiercely, their enormous axes held over their heads. He now stood on his own, one man facing the attacking horde. One Gallowglass brought his axe down with all his weight behind the blow, but Clifford dodged to one side, deflecting the impact with his sword. The Gallowglass leaned forward, temporarily losing his balance and

Clifford turned around quickly, hitting him on the back of his head and knocking his helmet off. Clifford speedily withdrew his sword, preparing to attack him. He felt a searing pain rip through the small of his back, causing him to stumble forward. He glanced backwards and in a suddenly blurred vision, saw an enemy soldier heaving all his weight behind his pike, which he was attempting to drive into his body. He screamed as he felt the point of it burst through his stomach, pinning him to the boggy ground. Blood and innards spilled out as the flat blade of the pike's head followed the point, boring a horrific wound right through his body. He would have his wish, he thought. The blow was fatal. There could be no recovery from it.

The Gallowglass removed Clifford's helmet and lay the blade of his axe against his neck. Slowly he lifted his weapon with both hands until it was hidden behind his body. Clifford turned away and looked at the moss next to his face. He could see a tiny ladybird, balanced with sublime expertise, on top of a long blade of straggly grass that overhung the moss, swaying in the light breeze. He thought of Cadiz and their victory, then of his family and his mother. Suddenly his brain exploded in agony as the cold, sharpened blade cut through, severing his neck. Then he was soaring over his body, looking down on it, pierced through by the pike, with the Gallowglass standing over it, holding his head aloft, howling like a savage wolf as Clifford's blood ran down the soldier's arm. He saw his army still running from their pursuers and the dead and wounded bodies, littering the mountainside. Then gradually the colour drained away from the scene and night seemed to fall, a deeper, darker night than he had ever known. The darkness was followed by silence as the sound of the battle faded and then all was still.

Two months had passed since Essex had set out on his march south. Now he was back once again in Dublin Castle. He had ordered a general muster of the English forces to convene in the capital. As Wingfield was still one of the Queen's men, he had answered the summons. Walking into the courtyard of Dublin Castle, he was taken aback to see seven gallows ominously erected. He had heard the rumours that Essex's wanderings in Munster had been fruitless, but the gallows seemed to prove otherwise. Evidently he had traitors to hang. He looked around the courtyard, which was rapidly filling up with soldiers. He saw Captain Marshall coming out of the dining chamber and walking over to him.

"John," he hailed as Marshall strolled over to him. "The march south, how was it?" he asked.

"A waste of time!" he answered. "We marched all over the country but could not bring the rebels to battle. They attacked in their normal cowardly fashion. On our return we dared not risk marching through Wicklow as, by then, our force was much reduced."

"And you achieved nothing at all? No castles taken? Not even any rebels seeking readmission to the Queen's good graces?" Wingfield asked in astonishment.

"Not one rebel sued for pardon. We did take Cahir Castle but that could have been accomplished by a much smaller force"

This was indeed news to Wingfield. He had been obliged to remain in Dublin, having been unable to find a commander under whom to serve. He had deliberately avoided seeking out news of Essex's progress, as he had little doubt that his advance would be met by surrendering rebels wherever he went, the alchemy of his name alone being enough to cow them into obedience.

The city's companies paraded in the light rain that had begun to fall. Five companies faced the gallows and a large platform that had been built beside it. Two more were arranged on either side so that the capital's nine companies filled three sides of the square courtyard, the gallows and platform taking up the fourth side. The officers stood in front of their men while Marshall and Wingfield stood beside the cavalrymen.

Some men and women peered through the company intervals, in silence and sullenness. Wingfield was surprised at the mood of the crowd. Normally, the hanging of rebels was a festive occasion.

"But there have not been any notable casualties?" he asked anxiously. Enough great men had already been lost to the Irish.

"Sir Henry Norris, the President of Munster when the rebels attacked at Lismore," Marshall said ruefully. Then he leaned forward and in a low voice, confidentially whispered to Wingfield. "News of the worst of all calamities has just reached us and it has upset the Earl most deeply. Clifford and his forces were destroyed in the Curlews. A company of two thousand men was defeated by only eight hundred rebels. Fourteen hundred men lost and all arms, ammunition, standards, baggage and military stores fell into enemy hands."

Wingfield was horrified. "Clifford?" he echoed in disbelief. Clifford was one of the best of the Queen's generals. He was respected for his fairness and honesty by all, even the Irish who had got to know him. He would indeed be a great loss to the country and to Essex.

"Yes. His head was cut off and sent to Niall Garve who was besieging Coolooney Castle. When O'Connor Sligo saw it, he knew that he need not expect any aid from us and was forced to surrender his castle and join with the rebels. If we cannot aid our friends, how can we expect them to remain loyal to us?" Marshall asked, spitting contemptuously onto the grass.

This was indeed dire news, Wingfield thought. The rebels continued to grow from strength to strength, whereas their own reputation continued to decline. His thoughts were interrupted by a fanfare of trumpets. Essex appeared and mounted the large platform beside the gallows. To his right, the Earl of Southampton stood erect and unbending, a low drum beat sounding as a procession of terrified soldiers trooped into view from the Castle gaol. They were all in chains and lined up to face the platform.

"The Earls appear unhappy," Wingfield whispered to Marshall.

Marshall nodded. "The Queen is incensed. She chides Essex for going south instead of north to confront Tyrone. She accuses the Irish Council of being in league with O'Neill, for having advised Essex to such a course. She says that Norris could have achieved as much on his own with his garrison."

Wingfield felt vindicated. He had been right and perhaps now Essex would recognise that. He looked at the shivering soldiers before him.

"Why are they here?" he asked. "They are our men and not rebels."

"They are Sir Henry Harrington's men. The O'Byrnes attacked and defeated them most comprehensively. They acquitted themselves disgracefully, running from the battle without even putting up a fight," Marshall replied, falling silent as the drums ceased and Essex stepped forward. A man in chains was pulled from the line of prisoners and thrown on his knees in front of him.

"Piers Walsh, for the crime of cowardice in the face of the enemy, I sentence you to death, by the powers granted to me by Her Majesty, Queen Elizabeth," he said majestically.

Walsh, an army lieutenant, was dragged up to the platform and pulled across a wooden block, which had been placed in front of the Earl, as he vigorously protested his innocence and begged for mercy. A soldier stepped forward and, taking his large sword in both his hands, he quickly raised it over his head and brought it down on the man, missing the neck and cutting into his skull just above the level of his ears. The pleading ceased as the stricken man roared agonisingly and then fell silent. The soldier wrestled with the sword, which had become embedded in the skull, eventually freeing it and raising it again. This time, his aim was truer and he spliced into the neck, severing the bone, but still was unsuccessful in parting the head from the body. He raised the sword a third time and, to the relief of all present, managed finally to separate it from its trunk. He caught it by its dark curls and held it up for everyone present to see. His actions were met by total silence, an air of hostility permeating the assembled witnesses.

"Harrington, himself, cannot be touched as he is a member of the Queen's Privy Council. His second-in-command, Adam Loftus, the Archbishop's son, died in the encounter. All the survivors, officers and men, have been condemned to death by Essex," Marshall whispered to Wingfield.

Essex stepped forward again. "I have chosen to commute the sentence of death on the other officers. Instead, they shall be demoted to the rank of private," he said loudly.

A relieved murmur ran through the watching men as they waited to hear what fate would befall their friends. The gallows had been prepared for the common soldiers. It was only the officers that were allowed the merciful swiftness of a beheading. Surely they would not be harsher on the common soldier than they were on the officers, Wingfield thought. That would be unjust as the soldiers could only do as they were commanded.

"I have also decided to be merciful to the privates," Essex said pompously. "I have agreed to commute the sentence of death in the case of nine out of ten of the men. Pick out the unlucky ones," he ordered one of his officers who stood below him.

Immediately, the officer walked quickly along the line of condemned men, counting out loud. On reaching each tenth man, he touched him lightly on the shoulder and immediately he was seized and dragged away to the gallows. The relief of those who had escaped was tempered with concern and guilt over the fate of the wretches to die in their place. Finally, the selection was completed and seven unlucky souls stood at the base of the gallows. They were led up the steps and the nooses were placed over their heads. They all seem to accept their fate in a different fashion, Wingfield observed. Some were so shocked that they allowed themselves be led without protesting their fate or their unfortunate luck, which had decreed that they were the ones to die. Others resisted and had to be dragged, protesting vehemently. Once they were in position, the supports under the plank, on which the seven condemned men stood, were removed and they were left hanging in mid air where they writhed in agony. Wingfield averted his gaze, choosing instead to look at Essex who unsympathetically watched the death agonies of the men. Complete silence had fallen on the assembled crowd.

Wingfield observed the faces of the spectators. He could sense their resentment. Morale was bad enough before this and the Earl's own failure in Munster would not have restored it. Essex then rose, turned and walked away, followed by his entourage. The captains turned and dismissed their men. Wingfield looked towards the gallows and saw the dead bodies being removed from the nooses.

"Well, we will have need of more experienced officers after today's work," Marshall observed. "It's a shortage of officers that most afflicts us. Cashiering some of the few we have is a foolish idea," Marshall said bitterly. He paused before looking around to see if they could be overheard, then continued confidentially. "I have no faith in Essex or the commanders whom he has brought with him. He has made Southampton, Master of the Horse, against the Queen's express orders. Much of the talk that I have heard from Essex's supporters, after they have their fill of ale, is nothing short of treasonous. They have no patience or affection for the Queen and constantly speak ill of her. Such talk in his presence shows a grave lack of judgement in Essex. His pride seems to know no bounds. He has been indulged too much and has become puffed up with his own importance."

Wingfield was surprised at Marshall's candour. "And what does he propose doing next?" he asked curiously.

"We are to march north. The Queen is insistent upon it and will hear of no excuses. Will you come with us? We can do with every man we can muster and you would be a great addition, having served there so often."

Wingfield considered the request. His pride was still damaged by Essex's behaviour. But, he had been proven right, even though Essex would never acknowledge it. He could stand on his dignity and not volunteer for the expedition but he knew Essex would never stoop to ask him to take part. In spite of his misgivings, he needed to be present in case he might influence the outcome for the good. He could not stay away.

"Yes," he said. "You can rely on me."

Marshall smiled. "Good," he replied, genuinely relieved. ""Let us get to the tavern and drink on it. I wish to wipe from my mind the memory of this day."

Essex walked briskly back to the Lord Deputy's quarters and headed straight for the fire. He was wet through. He shook with cold and the Irish ague, which he had contracted on his march south. The Earl of Southampton followed him into the chamber, closing the door behind him to exclude the rest of their entourage. They needed some peace. They were constantly surrounded by people, all of them thrusting their opinions upon them. Southampton poured a stoup of whiskey and handed it to Essex.

"Here, Robert," he said. "Drink. It is one of the few benefits to serving in this accursed country."

Essex took the drink and swallowed it in one draught. His complexion, which was normally ruddy, had become more heightened than usual. "I've had another letter, Henry," he said angrily, removing the document from his jerkin where he had hidden it. "Another diatribe from Her Majesty, even worse than the last one. God damn that woman. The only thing that she knows how to do properly is to demand. Demands, demands, demands without end!"

Southampton shrugged. He was unconcerned about any letters that the Queen might write. He was already thoroughly weary of the whole Irish venture. It had turned out to be nothing like he had anticipated.

"And what does the old hag have to say?" he asked contemptuously.

"She is intolerable! You know that in her last letter she complained that we had gone south. When in my reply I pointed out that she had sanctioned my campaign, she now writes to say that 'no man will ever win honour by obedience, where our county shall receive harm by our commandments.' Can you credit that, Henry? Only a woman would be capable of such twisted logic. If you don't carry out her wishes to the last word, you are guilty of treason, and if you do, and events do not turn out well, you are equally guilty!"

Southampton laughed cruelly. "As I have often said, we need a man as Sovereign."

Essex continued wrathfully. "Do you know what she accuses me of now, Henry? Treason, that's what. She says that the reason that I will not march north is that I cannot forget my goodwill to O'Neill. The fact that everyone in Dublin, without exception, thinks that it would be unwise to attack Tyrone now, with so many of our men ill and discouraged, fails to convince her. She says that Tyrone must be well pleased to see her fair army waste its strength far from Ulster."

"Let me guess," Southampton said. "She complains of the cost of the expedition?"

"Of course she does. When is she ever not counting her gold?" Essex railed. "She complains of how the Queen of England's fortune is being spent to make a base bush kerne be deemed a famous rebel."

"I have heard how, in her rages against Tyrone, she attacks the curtains with her rusty sword," Southampton said in an effort to lighten Essex's mood. He was unsuccessful.

"The Cecils and Raleigh have been poisoning her mind against me. I knew it would be so in our absence. I wish I had never accepted the expedition to this accursed country," he moaned.

"So, let us return home. I miss London and I have no time for the type of cowardly enemy that we fight here," Southampton urged. "Leave one of the others in charge."

"That we cannot do. She commands that we must not return without her express permission," Essex answered despondently.

"So what do you counsel?" Southampton asked.

Essex ran his hands through his hair, nervously shifting from one foot to another. "We must go north. Will you have the orders issued? We must march within the week," he said.

"But what of provisions and transport?" Southampton asked

"Do the best you can. If we have to live off the land, so be it. All I want is to get this war finished and leave this damned country," Essex answered.

Southampton stood up. "I will give the orders," he said and left the chamber.

Essex dragged an oak chair to the fire and sat heavily into it. He poured himself another measure and slumped in his seat, pondering the injustices and intrigues with which he had to contend. He looked at the document again. Its irony seethed through the parchment and insulted his pride. 'Your army is sick, so why did you not act when it was well?' she demanded. 'The winter is coming, why did you not march in July. If the spring was too soon, if the summer has been spent or rather mis-spent, if the harvest has been neglected then we must conclude that none of the four quarters of the year is satisfactory for the Earl of Essex. Does he propose to end the war at all?' she persisted. Essex took the letter, crumpled it in his hands and threw it into the fire.

"Confound that woman," he exclaimed, jumping restlessly to his feet and hastening from the chamber in choler.

As Hugh O'Neill rode up to the Bellaclinthe Ford on the Lagan River he scanned the far bank anxiously, eager to make sure that no trap had been set for him. A lone horseman awaited him on the other side and, as he approached the ford, he recognised Essex. O'Neill was surprised that he had consented to meet him with no witnesses to their discussions, a fact, which would compromise him in his Queen's eyes.

As he approached, he saw Essex's unhelmeted head, his red hair being ruffled in the light breeze, while his armour glinted in the summer sun. Hugh rode to the bank opposite where he stood. O'Neill reigned in his horse when he reached the water's edge. Seeing the distance that still remained between them, he spurred his horse on and rode into the river, stopping in the middle of it where the water reached the belly of his horse.

He hailed Essex. "You are welcome to Ireland, my Lord Essex. It only grieves me that it is under such circumstances that we finally meet."

Essex frowned and answered curtly. "I have agreed to meet you only so that I might offer you two alternatives. Firstly, you may surrender and return with me to London where you may beg the Queen's forgiveness for your treachery. Or, we may fight it out army to army or person to person."

Hugh smiled and shook his head. He knew that Essex was speaking from bravado. He could not attack a force three times his number and hope to win. Essex must know that he had over nine thousand men facing his three and that his army would fall back, dragging Essex's with them, attacking them from all sides. There would be no open battle. It would be the Yellow Ford all over again and brilliant as Essex was, he would be powerless to change the inevitable outcome.

"I would not dare fight the Earl of Essex in single combat," he answered. "Your fame has reached even to the far north of this land. Neither can I go back to London as your prisoner. Too many unfortunate Irish Chieftains have done so in the past and never got to see their country again. The final alternative, that our two armies should fight, fills me with great sadness. How has it come to this, that I now face the son of my first and dearest friend?" Hugh asked and then paused before continuing. "Ever since I heard that Her Majesty had sent you hither, my heart has been heavy with grief at the thought that one day we might have to fight. And yet, there is no one else to whom I would rather talk, no one else whom I would trust so completely, one whose honour and chivalry is an example to all." Here O'Neill paused before continuing. "Your father and I fought and won many battles together. I was at his deathbed. The simple truth is that my nature is not rebellious. I was forced into conflict by Her Majesty's representatives in Ireland and indeed, much as it pains me to say it, by Her Majesty herself. She can be a very awkward monarch."

"You must not speak so of Her Majesty. I will not stand here and listen to such treasonous talk," Essex interrupted but Hugh felt that his interruption did not carry the conviction that it might.

Changing tack, he continued. "If my good friend and yours, the Earl of Leicester, was still alive, then none of this would have occurred. He would have protected my name at court and, with such a powerful ally, I would have received redress for the wrongs, which I have suffered at the hands of the many jealous people who run this country in her name. The Earl of Leicester was always a dear friend. There was never any question of my loyalty while he was alive."

Essex nodded. "Robert did say that you were the only man that could be trusted in Ireland. He would never listen to any rumours about you. I received copies of my father's reports from Ireland and in them he talked most highly of you. But why have you perpetrated these present treasons against Her Majesty?" he asked.

Hugh replied. "Neither your father nor the Earl of Leicester would wish to see us opposed like this. They both saw how unreasonable the Queen could be. Leicester died, shamefully neglected by the Queen he served so well and what was your father's reward for having bankrupted himself in her service? The debt passed from him to you. I have also spent over thirty years in her service, spilling my blood and disposing of my wealth in her cause and to what end? None but to be called a traitor for my pains. I cannot surrender to her and place myself in her power. If it were to you and you alone, I would willingly do so, but she is a woman, and a woman with a vacillating mind. One cannot know to what her next mood will prompt her. But if you were King, a man of the world, a soldier, why then I would never have been driven into rebellion to protect my life and lands."

Essex, taken aback, again interrupted. "I cannot listen to such talk, it is perfidious and treasonous."

Hugh shook his head. "There are no witnesses to our conversation so we can talk freely. I cannot deal with you in anything other than a frank and honest fashion. The King of Spain seeks my support and James of Scotland does likewise for their claim to the English throne. But the man I should like to see King is none other than yourself," he said earnestly.

"You must not talk so," Essex replied, looking anxiously over his shoulder.

"I see myself and my country as part of England's natural hinterland and I would be content to live under an English King once that King observed our language, religious freedom and customs. What has occurred in this country during the last twenty years has been scandalous. Subjects, who were content to remain loyal to the crown, were evicted from their lands. I, myself, was finally forced to take up arms. It was either that or lose all," he said as he steadied his horse, which was becoming restless and cold from standing in the fast flowing water.

"I have always said in private, that I would not wish any man to be troubled for his religion, and even though I prefer the re-formed doctrines, I believe that toleration should be the norm," Essex answered. "I would not deny any man's customs or language, once they were loyal to the English crown," he continued magnanimously.

O'Neill was satisfied. From the moment he had met Essex, he had suspected his disinterest in fighting and that his attention might be engaged in bigger schemes. You and I are natural allies," O'Neill continued insidiously. "My record speaks for itself. Until I was most foully goaded, I was the cornerstone of English power in Ulster. I can be again if I have simple guarantees for my safety and lands. I have letters of support from King James of Scotland. My difficulty is that the transfer of power from Her Majesty to a more reasonable ruler might come too late for me, even though she is an old woman much beyond her prime. Is it right or fair that she should rule when there are younger, better men for the position? Her time is past. She holds England back. There is a bright future for England but, as long as she holds the reins of power, it is unattainable."

"What are you implying?" Essex asked, glancing again over his shoulder.

"Change," O'Neill answered simply. "I will support you in whatever you decide to do. There are two alternatives. Take the throne yourself." Essex held up his hand but Hugh, ignoring it, continued. "You have the support of the common man and your army. It is time to act. If you do not like that prospect, depose her and put James on the throne. Think of it. James could deliver Scotland, you England and Wales and I, Ireland. Consider the power of such an alliance. We could take on Spain and defeat it." He paused again as he steadied his horse, which had turned in the water and he manoeuvred it back again to face Essex who remained silent and thoughtful. "My preference would be for you to take it. Did not the Queen's grandfather do likewise, and have you not blood as noble, coursing through your veins?" he asked beguilingly.

"What you talk of cannot be," Essex answered weakly.

"Of course it can. Even in Ulster, I hear of how the young and upcoming gentlemen want change and talk of you as the only choice for the throne. I promise you my loyalty, here and now, just as I gave it to your father. I will support you in your choice, whether it is to take the throne yourself or give it to James of Scotland. I have been in communication with him and he received my ambassadors graciously, honouring them with valuable gifts. He has sent me support in this rebellion and seeks my support in the battle for succession that will follow Elizabeth's death. In secret correspondence with me, he tells me that he counts you as one of his supporters and says that he has supplied you with money to buy support among your friends. You see, we have more in common than you might conjecture."

Essex coloured in embarrassment and stammered through his reply. "I know not to what you allude," he said.

"You need not fear. I destroyed his communications and the Queen will never hear of it from me," Hugh said quickly, anxious to reassure Essex. "I must repeat, we should not fight," he continued eagerly. "If you force us to, we will. Do not underestimate our strength. It is not we who have come looking for death and destruction. We have nowhere left to run. This is our home and we must defend it. We have prepared the ground well. Maguire and O'Donnell are with me. Our army outnumbers you by three to one. But why should we kill each other? O'Donnell and Maguire see no redress but to join with the Spanish. They cannot trust the Queen. You and I cannot let her legacy be the permanent sundering of amity between our two countries. Just last month, King Philip again promised us his aid and begged us not to make peace with you. I do not wish to be forced to avail of that aid. I can turn my allies away from Spain, if I can tell them that the great Earl of Essex will intercede honourably on our side with the Queen."

Essex stood looking into the water for a number of minutes. O'Neill remained silent. Finally, Essex looked at the older man. "We will not fight," he said decisively. "You must list your grievances and I will relay them to the Queen. I will agree a truce, on the understanding that you do not seek or accept any Spanish aid. You must withdraw into your own territory and not harass any more of Her Majesty's subjects."

Hugh nodded. "I will not harass them, provided they do not harass any of my allies. We each hold what we have."

Essex nodded. "Agreed. We must bring in our generals to witness our discussions on the truce. Let us get the business over with. Return here within the hour with six persons of your choice."

Hugh smiled, they would not have to fight. "You have made the right decision. Together we can avert a tragedy."

Essex looked relieved. "Be back within the hour," he ordered. "Have a petition for Her Majesty's forgiveness and your terms for an end to this war." He turned and walked back to his horse. Hugh watched him mount and ride back towards his army. He felt well pleased. He had not lost even one man. His power was as much intact as it had been before Essex's arrival. His reputation would be further enhanced but the Queen's and Essex's were diminished by this day's work. She had spent more money than ever before in Ireland, sending the largest army ever across the Irish Sea and in conclusion, she had nothing to show for it. He was still sanguine that the Spanish help, promised for so long, would arrive soon and he had planned to husband his strength until its arrival, provided he lost none of his gains by waiting. This was a greater victory that the Yellow Ford and it had been gained without the shedding of a single drop of blood. O'Donnell would not see it that way, he thought regretfully. He would be disappointed that he could not have Essex destroyed just as Clifford had been. Hugh wondered what effect his words would have on the Earl. Maybe he would risk all. And who knows, he thought, perhaps he could even be successful. Now that would be an interesting outcome, he thought as he pulled his horse's reins and rode out of the river and headed back to his army to deliver the news that there would be no battle after all.

"The Queen refuses to accept the terms I agreed with Tyrone," Essex said bitterly, holding up her letter for Southampton and Blount to see. Essex had lost weight in the few weeks since he had agreed the truce with O'Neill. He had suffered badly from ceaseless attacks of dysentery. "All I hear is endless criticism from the Privy and Irish Councils. This is an impossible country. Men like Wingfield dare openly criticise my judgement. I should have him court marshalled."

"The Irish Council would never allow it. In any event, the problem is in England. While you rot here, your enemies poison the Queen's mind against you. It is there that most damage is being done to you. We should never have come to this accursed land," Blount said bitterly.

"The Queen shows her ingratitude, as always. I suggest that we return to London with a thousand of our best men and deal with our enemies in the Council. We should force her do as we wish. If we remain here, we will lose all," Southampton said angrily.

"But you have been expressively forbidden to return," Blount said anxiously. "If you do so and bring an army with you, it will be seen as treason. To have any hope of success, they would have to have surprise on their side and they would have to cover the distance to London without news of their approach going before them. It could not be done."

Essex's eyes sparkled with animation and enthusiasm flooded him. "A thousand men might not, but a smaller number might. If I can get access to the Queen, I can persuade her that the truce with O'Neill was the correct course."

"If you leave your post without her permission, she will be further angered with you," Blount warned.

"And should he live in fear of that old crone?" Southampton asked scathingly. "No, he should steer his own course. If he stays here, all could be lost to Cecil and his cronies. Even now, the little hunchback tries to make peace with the Spanish King. Let us return to London and not waste our energies in this backwater any longer."

"Yes," Essex said enthusiastically. "I must return to London and defend myself before Her Majesty. Are you with me?" he asked both men.

"Yes," Southampton answered.

Blount hesitated for a moment before replying, his voice low. "Yes, I will always follow wherever you lead," he answered.

"Good, well let us plan the matter and decide whom we will leave in charge here," Essex proposed.

Chapter 19

"Captain Wingfield, Sir, reporting to Lord Deputy Mountjoy, Sir, as ordered, Sir," Wingfield said, standing to attention and saluting the newly appointed Lord Deputy who had recently arrived in Dublin. He had been surprised to hear that it was to be Lord Mountjoy who would replace Essex. He and Essex were close friends and Wingfield had thought that the Queen would have entrusted the position to someone less attached to the now disgraced Earl. He had concluded that it must have been as a result of her obsession with the balancing of power between the Essex and Cecil factions that had prompted her to act thus. Essex was under house arrest for deserting his post in Ireland. His party, however, still remained strong. Sir George Carew, a strong adherent to Cecil's cause, was sent to Ireland with Mountjoy and the rumour was that he was to be President of Munster.

Wingfield had been relieved when he had learned that Essex was in custody in London. He had been disgusted when he had heard of the Earl's truce with O'Neill and had, in his anger, said more than was politic. He was determined to be more diplomatic with this new Lord Deputy, knowing that Mountjoy probably had already received damaging reports about him from his disgraced friend. He would, however, if allowed, do his best to aid Mountjoy, consumed, as he was still, with desire to bring about O'Neill's downfall.

Mountjoy nodded a greeting. "You know Sir George Carew and Sir Arthur Chichester," he said, indicating the other two men present in the chamber.

"Yes, my Lord," Wingfield said, nodding an acknowledgement to both men. Carew had served in Ireland previously and Wingfield was pleased at his return. He would not be taken in by the rebels. He was smooth, plausible, cultivated, without scruple or shame. The person he most resembled, Wingfield thought, was O'Neill. They were similar in their ability to win over any opponent by their sheer personal magnetism. With the Queen, Carew was in high favour, capable of the greatest flattery, ignoring the ravages which time had wrought on her person. Wingfield knew, however, that Carew was not insincere in his loyalty to her or England. There was nothing that he would not do to achieve victory, having used diplomacy, threats, false promises, robbery, murder, forgery and assassination in the past. He would not be found wanting.

As for Chichester, he had spent much time with him over the last few months, during which they had both been confined to Dublin.

They had often talked long into the night about how best to win this war. It was unlike any other in which they had fought and they recognised that they would have to be innovative if they were to make any headway against the rebels. Chichester had been removed from his command in Carrickfergus as a condition of the truce with O'Neill. He had found his period of inactivity in Dublin particularly difficult to bear and had become a trying companion. Now, however, he smiled warmly at Wingfield and Wingfield began to allow himself feel some optimism about the meeting.

"I have been sounding out all my officers in Ireland since I arrived," Mountjoy said quietly. "Sir Arthur tells me of your theories for the prosecution of this war. Both he and Sir George inform me that you are a man whom I should have on my staff, owing to the experience that you have gained here over the years." He paused and took stock of Wingfield for a few moments, before continuing. "They have convinced me. Your function shall be to stop me from repeating the mistakes of my predecessors. Will you accept a post as one of my advisers?" he asked.

Wingfield was both surprised and flattered. He had not expected such an honour and was also unexpectedly pleased at Mountjoy's manner. There was none of the arrogance and airs, which Essex had adopted. He had been dubious when he had first heard of his appointment. Mountjoy's reputation as a courtier and dandy was well known, even in Ireland. He had heard too how the appointment had pleased O'Neill who had commented in derision, that Mountjoy would lose every chance he had of starting a fight, owing to the length of time he took over breakfast. Wingfield had ensured that the allegation reached this new Lord Deputy. At least, Mountjoy appeared to be a man who would listen and learn from others, exactly what was needed in Ireland at the moment. "And who else will you number among your advisers?" Wingfield asked.

He saw Mountjoy start involuntarily in surprise which, as quickly, he concealed. He probably expected him to accept the post gratefully, without any questions.

"My advisers will be few and will number, only those whom I feel that I can trust totally," Mountjoy responded. "I shall listen to many, but in the end, I shall make up my own mind. That is what is expected of me."

Wingfield nodded. He agreed with Mountjoy's approach. "Have I your permission to speak plainly, Sir?" he asked.

Mountjoy nodded. "I do not wish you ever to talk in any other manner," he replied. Encouraged, Wingfield launched forth. "In the past O'Neill knew of our plans as soon as we formulated them. If you wish to keep him in the dark regarding yours, you must not inform the Irish Council of them," he said.

Mountjoy nodded. "I had already decided upon that," he said. "I shall tell the Irish Council nothing, unless I wish misleading information to reach O'Neill. Then, I might use them for that purpose."

"I should be pleased to serve with you. I promise you my loyalty and discretion in all matters," Wingfield replied.

"Good," Mountjoy answered pleased, but somewhat amused at Wingfield's pomposity of manner. "Sir George shall take up the post of President in Munster. He shall attempt to win back as many rebels as he can through whatever means he cares to employ. If they do not return to proper obedience through negotiation, then he must destroy them, one by one. He is of the opinion that some of the rebels have tired already of their northern overlords and will come back peacefully."

Carew, a large man, added. "I have just received excellent news from there. Hugh Maguire, one of the three main leaders of this damnable rebellion, is dead."

Wingfield was truly pleased. Even though O'Neill held almost all the country, he felt that, finally, there was genuine hope for a turn in the tide of this war. Maguire's death would be a great loss to the rebel cause. "This is indeed great news, but how and when?" he asked.

"As you know, O'Neill has marched through Munster, taking hostages from those whom he did not trust. Our troops stayed in their garrisons, not daring to face his army. Near Cork City, Maguire left the main body of the rebels and came upon Sir Warham St.Ledger and a party of our horse. St. Ledger discharged his pistol, mortally wounding him," Carew said.

"St. Ledger should be well rewarded for such a day's work. When I see him again, I will buy him ale enough to swim in," Wingfield said with a laugh.

"Alas, even though Maguire was mortally wounded, a musket ball through his chest, he still found strength to charge St Ledger and with one blow of his battleaxe, split St Ledger's skull in two," Carew said regretfully.

"Maguire always led from the front and his strength and courage were awesome. They have not another to take his place. O'Neill is too old for such heroics and I have never been convinced by O'Donnell. He leads from the back," Wingfield said. "But what of Munster? How secure is his rebellion there? Can it be easily overturned?"

"O'Neill has miscalculated badly in his choice of leader there. Florence Mac Carthy is a drunkard, incapable of organising anything. Give me four months and I'll have it under control again," Carew said.

"Good," Mountjoy replied and, turning to Wingfield and Chichester, said, "I have agreed with the plans that you have drafted. The landing of our troops, to O'Neill's back, will go ahead. Three thousand five hundred soldiers will sail from Chester, under Sir Henry Dowcra and land at Lough Foyle. I will march north to the Blackwater and force O'Neill to send his army to confront me. That will mean that O'Donnell will be left to confront Sir Henry. He is to land and build a fort for his men."

"And I am to be reassigned to Carrickfergus," Chichester informed Wingfield. "We will make him fight on three fronts."

Wingfield nodded. It was exactly what he had hoped for. "And you will continue building forts until you have him cut off from the rest of the country?" he asked.

"Yes," Mountjoy answered. "The other tool that we shall use is famine. Those garrisons will destroy the rebels' crops, steal their cattle, for a change, and starve them into submission. If they will not come to battle, famine shall gain us the victory that might be denied us in combat. I do not intend being made a fool of as Essex was."

"The garrisons will have the added advantage that there will be places where the dissatisfied in the rebels' lands can flee to and join with us. There are many that might be convinced, for their own selfish needs, to desert their Chieftains; Turlough's son, Sir Arthur O'Neill being one," Wingfield commented.

"The one who interests me, more than any other, is Niall Garve O'Donnell. He came to us before, seeking our help to attain the Chieftainship, but we did not back him. That was an error. It allowed Hugh Roe to attain it. Niall Garve was forced to acknowledge O'Donnell as his Lord. It was he who has been the driving force behind his expansion into Connaught. He it is who achieved most of the advances. Niall Garve is ambitious. Let us play upon that," Mountjoy suggested.

"But he would not have enough men to cause much trouble to O'Donnell," Wingfield advised.

"If there was a fort in Derry and if we gave him some men, then we could see what he could do on our behalf," Mountjoy answered.

"But how would we know if we could trust him?" Chichester asked doubtfully.

"Dowcra will have to make that judgement. We must all work to win the rebels' principal supporters from their allegiance to this treacherous uprising. Promise them whatever it takes. We can always renege once we have achieved victory," Mountjoy said.

Carew guffawed. "I'll even promise them the Lord Deputy's position, until they submit. Then I'll deal with them in the appropriate manner."

"Good. Now we must get to our respective stations. Not a word of what transpired here must leave this chamber. Sir Arthur, you will have five hundred men, which will be plenty for your task. You are not to be drawn into battle but you are to raid O'Neill's supporters as often as possible," Mountjoy commanded.

"I shall do more. When last in Carrickfergus, I ordered the construction of boats to cross the lake, which separates me from O'Neill's lands. The boats were almost finished. I shall have that job completed and will use that route into the very heart of his lands. It will be nigh impossible for him to halt me," Chichester answered.

"So far, after four years of rebellion, an English army has not managed to cross the Blackwater. We need such an achievement," Carew added.

"Sir George," Mountjoy said. "You must go to Munster and do your best there. You shall have as many troops as I can spare. I am of the opinion that, if the Spanish land, they will do so in Munster. After Ulster, Munster is the next most important province that we must subdue. You must not only put down the rebellion there, but you must make sure that it will be at least another fifteen years before another one breaks out again, even if the Pope himself, with the whole Spanish army, lands there."

Wingfield understood fully. It was only fifteen years since Munster had been decimated after the Desmond rebellion. That had been ruthlessly repressed in the most savage manner and Mountjoy was seeking the same outcome again. Carew would be capable of delivering it too, Wingfield thought.

"Connaught and Leinster shall be easy to deal with once O'Donnell and O'Neill are kept within their own borders. So, do we all know what is expected of us?" Mountjoy asked.

All three men nodded. Mountjoy turned to Wingfield. "Is there any advice that you would like to give me in your new capacity?" he asked him.

Wingfield paused for a moment, taking stock of the richly dressed courtier before him. He cleared his throat nervously. "The wars in Ireland have killed more people through sickness than through battle," he said. "If you wish to survive, you will have to dress for the weather, which can chill you to the very marrow. You must travel light. Be prepared to eat less well than usual. Essex's supply train stretched for miles and slowed down our progress. The two essentials are beer and bread. On no account are you ever to drink the water."

"Never fear," Mountjoy replied. "I've laid in a plentiful supply of heavy woollen clothing. While campaigning, I shall eat as the ordinary soldier does."

Wingfield was surprised. He would never have expected a personage of his status to have such scant regard for his own comfort.

"Set about organising our army for the march north. We must move by Wednesday and be on the Blackwater by the following week. We shall stay there until we hear that Dowcra has safely landed and has secured his position. I want you to reform the army before then. Even though I am here but a few days, the weakness of our forces is evident. It is disorganised and demoralised. Several of the officers spend their time gambling, drinking and in the whorehouses. Many of them have been appointed by favour rather than by merit. You are to rid us of the incompetent ones. Promote those whom you know to be efficient and willing to carry out their orders. Discipline must be reestablished at all costs. You will have a free hand, as you've served with most of them and know their worth. If that is not done, we cannot win," Mountjoy commanded.

"Indeed," Wingfield said, "I am honoured to do your bidding."

"You are to look after the provisioning of it for the northern campaign. They must be properly equipped and have plenty of powder and shot. We will need much beer and bread," he added. "As to my wardrobe, I shall prepare that."

Wingfield saluted, turned and left the chamber. Finally, they had a Lord Deputy who might effect a change in the fortunes of the English in Ireland, he thought. Another incompetent, another defeat and the country could be lost forever. The stakes were rising all the time.

"Mother, Mother," Neachtan shouted from on top of the battlements, "Mother, there are horsemen approaching."

Nuala O'Donnell turned to Rose, anxiety furrowing her brow. "The English from Lough Foyle?" she asked.

"No," Rose said. "They would never penetrate as far as Donegal Castle, without our having prior warning. They must be friends, some of our menfolk, home at last, please God."

"Hugh Roe, perhaps!" Nuala said eagerly. "Come, let's join Neachtan and see who it is."

Rose watched her race to the steps of the battlements and mount them, two at a time. She followed. She had been disappointed too often recently to allow her hopes build. It was over six months since she had spent time with Hugh Roe, and had seen him only twice. He had passed through Donegal town on the way to and from Derry when he had marched north to oppose Dowcra and his large force that had landed there. He had chosen not to spend the night in Donegal Castle and they had not even had a chance to talk privately. She was confused and hurt. She had thought that once she returned to Donegal Castle with him everything would be resolved between them but, almost immediately, he had withdrawn again into his world of war and butchery. He was obsessed by the campaign and its successful outcome, it mattering more to him than anything or anyone else. Still, she was unsure of his feelings for her and that uncertainty seared deeply into her soul. She clung to the slim hope that if this war ceased, all would be right again but, in her heart, she doubted that it would be so.

She joined Nuala and her young son on the battlements. Neachtan was pointing north and she saw a small body of horsemen thundering across the plain towards the castle, the O'Donnell flag flapping proudly over them. Even at this distance, she could not mistake Niall Garve. His large, athletic frame was straight in his saddle and he rode a few lengths ahead of the rest of his men. "Niall Garve," she said to Nuala.

"Shush," Nuala said, her face lined with worry, but it was too late.

"Father!" Neachtan shouted excitedly as he turned and ran for the steps down into the courtyard.

"Neachtan," Nuala shouted, but to no avail. He ran on and already was too far ahead for either woman to catch him.

"So, is it still not good between you and him?" Rose asked.

"Would I spend so much time here if it was?" Nuala asked impatiently. "Neachtan," she screamed after the young boy but he was already in the courtyard and racing for the main gate of the castle, which the guards were opening.

"He merely wants to see his father," Rose said. "He'll come to no harm. He is just excited by his arrival."

"Yes," Nuala answered bitterly. "Niall Garve spends much time with O'Doherty and has had many opportunities to be with Neachtan. He brings him on his horse, which he rides like a man possessed, jumping over rivers and ditches. Neachtan loves it. He encourages a reckless streak in him. He will not listen to me when I complain about his behaviour."

"He would not hurt him. He is his father," Rose answered.

"He will be angry with me. I took Neachtan from his foster parents. They must have informed Niall Garve and now, he has come to fetch him back," Nuala answered.

Both women hastened down the stone steps and had barely reached the courtyard when Niall Garve galloped into it. Neachtan was just running towards it. Nuala screamed, thinking it impossible for Niall Garve to avoid the tiny figure that had suddenly appeared under the legs of the great horse. Niall Garve leaned over, smoothly picked the child from the ground and with one fluid movement, sat him on the horse in front of him. He reined in the animal and they came to rest, some ten paces from the women who were racing towards them.

"Again, Father, again," Neachtan shouted excitedly.

"You could have killed him," Nuala screamed angrily at Niall Garve. "What sort of folly possesses you to ride like that into here? Hand him down to me this moment."

Niall Garve held Neachtan close to him. "The child would not have been in any danger if he had been left with his foster parents," he responded icily. "You had no right to remove him."

"I am his mother," Nuala answered angrily. "That gives me every right. And what right have you to leave your post, besieging the English army in Derry? We cannot leave those vipers to our backs. It is cowardice to desert your calling. You will have to answer to Hugh Roe for it" she spat at him angrily.

"You dare accuse me of cowardice?" he asked incredulously. "Every victory of note that we have gained, I brought about. Who took Sligo, not once, but twice? I did," he said loudly. "Who fought all the difficult battles in Connaught? I did. Where was your precious brother? Gathering plunder from the defenceless churls and English settlers! He was not even present when Clifford was defeated in the Curlews. He was protecting his useless hide."

Nuala flushed with anger. "All we have achieved has been because of my brother's bravery and planning. You are jealous of his popularity and cannot stand the fact that the populace follow him and not you," she said bitterly.

"Your mother, Ineen Dubh, bought him the Chieftainship. He could never have attained it on his own. He's not man enough," Niall Garve answered contemptuously.

"And you are?" Nuala asked with a bitter laugh. "A man that is not even master in his own bedhcamber?"

Rose, who had remained silent through the argument, now saw Niall Garve colour and observed how his right hand clenched into a fist. She saw him struggle for self-control. Finally, he replied with a sneer. "Perhaps, there was nothing in it worth the mastering. In any event, we will see just who is the better man before long. I have the greater claim to the O'Donnellship and I intend taking it."

"What are you saying, Niall Garve?" Rose asked anxiously.

"You wouldn't dare rebel against the lawful O'Donnell, chosen by the people in time honoured fashion," Nuala said.

"Hardly a free election, when your mother's Scottish mercenaries ringed the site and only allowed those favourably disposed to your brother, to attend. He used outside influences to gain the Chieftainship and I will use outside influences to take it from him," Niall Garve retorted.

"You are not about to throw in your lot with the English?" Rose asked in shock only too aware of the loss that Niall Garve would be to her husband's cause. She knew that he would be losing his most competent general. "It would be wrong, Niall Garve, we must stay united. It is our only chance of victory."

"Don't waste your breath on the traitor," Nuala said dismissively. "He'd be no loss to our cause. He'd be at home with the English, vermin with vermin."

Niall Garve responded maliciously. "The English have promised me Donegal for my own. Why should they not? Did they not support my grandfather and his father and his father before him against the O'Neills? And did not all three gain from the relationship? Tell your precious brother that his days are numbered," he jeered, wheeling his horse around and facing the gate again. His bodyguards, who had joined him, had now drawn their weapons and kept a threatening eye on the outnumbered sentries.

"Wait," Nuala shouted. "Leave me my son."

Niall Garve turned in his saddle to face her. "He's to have a new foster parent," he said with a laugh. "The Lord Deputy, Mountjoy, is eager to take him under his care. I must deliver him up to Dowcra to seal our bargain. Then, I am to have the soldiers, which I need to crush your brother. Bid him farewell. If I have my way, it will be the last time that you will ever see him."

He turned again in his saddle, then raised a hand. He and his bodyguard galloped out through the gateway. Nuala screamed long and despairingly, a scream, which echoed around the courtyard and into the fields beyond. Rose went to take her in her arms but she cast her off furiously. She saw one on the sentries raise his musket and take aim at the fleeing men. Running to him, she pushed his weapon down.

"You will kill my son," she shrieked at him. She looked after the disappearing horsemen and sobbed. Rose approached her again and Nuala collapsed into her sister-in-law's arms, weeping till it seemed that she would die of grief.

"Oh Rose, what will become of him?" she asked through her sobs. "He is so young. What will become of us all?"

"Do not fret, Nuala," Rose replied. "Hugh Roe will know what to do. Right will conquer in the end. Niall Garve will get his just reward for this treachery, you will see," she said, stroking her hair. If only I could be sure of that, she thought privately to herself, secretly dreading what the future might hold.

Chapter 20

Sir Walter Raleigh pulled his cloak tightly around him to ward off the early morning frost. It was not even seven and already a select band of courtiers had gathered in the courtyard of the Tower of London. They had been ordered by the Queen to witness the execution of the Earl of Essex, a command they dared not disobey. It was Ash Wednesday, a suitable day for him to meet his maker, Raleigh thought. He, himself, was nervous. He knew not what Essex would say in his final speech and he worried that the Earl held him responsible for the pass to which he had come.

He looked around at the others gathered alongside him. They too felt the cold as, in the dark chill February dawn, a damp wind whipped in off the Thames. Most of them had come to this bleak courtyard to witness an enemy die but now, as the appointed hour drew near, their appetite for the spectacle waned. Raleigh watched as the two executioners entered, already wearing their black hoods to disguise their identity. There were two, the Queen having expressly ordained it, stating that if one should faint there would be another to perform the deed. They mounted the stairs to the block, which was located on a raised, railed platform in the middle of the courtyard.

The Earl was not to have the customary large audience for the last event of his life. He would be the first man ever to suffer formal execution within the walls of the Tower. Essex was to be spared the jeers and taunts of the public because Her Majesty could not be sure that the people might not still be in sympathy with him, in spite of his rebellion a short three weeks previously. Had he planned the coup more carefully, it might have achieved its purpose, but luckily for them, Raleigh thought, Essex's preparation had been lacking and it had all come to naught.

He wondered about Essex's state of mind. He seemed to have embraced religion with a fanatical zeal since his arrest and had made a clean breast of his guilt, naming all those who had been involved in his dastardly undertaking. They were all now safely in prison, saving Mountjoy. In his confession, Essex had revealed Mountjoy's promise to bring over his Irish army and aid his rebellion. The Queen had yet to decide if Mountjoy should be recalled from Ireland to face the charges with the others but, as he was achieving considerable success against the rebels there, Raleigh hoped that she would permit him to remain. It would be time enough to punish him, should he not succeed. In any event, there was no other general who desired the position and it would be disastrous to leave the post empty once again, while she searched for a replacement.

A drum sounded and the door to the tower, on Raleigh's left, opened and two clerics, followed by the Earl himself, entered the courtyard. Raleigh watched as both of them walked slowly and solemnly over to the platform and mounted the stairs. He saw the tall, red haired man turn to face the waiting crowd. Essex was hunched against the cold, in a plain black velvet cloak, worn over a black satin suit, in keeping with the occasion, Raleigh thought. He was stooped and seemed to have aged, having become thinner, his face deeply furrowed. He began his final speech.

"I appeal for pardon from Her Majesty for my rebellion that turned the streets of London into a battlefield. This was my last sin, this great, this bloody, this infectious sin, whereby so many, for love of me, have ventured their lives and souls, and have been drawn to offend God, to offend their Sovereign and to offend the world. I confess that I have received an honourable trial and am justly condemned. I desire all the world to forgive me, even as I do freely and from my heart, forgive all the world."

Essex nodded to the waiting crowd. It was evident that he had said all that he was going to. Relief flooded Raleigh. He shuffled as the damp from the courtyard seeped up through his shoes. He could not but think of when Essex was at the peak of his power and popularity. How far he had fallen! He watched as he attempted to unfasten his gown and ruff. His fingers were unable to manage the task and he called without thinking, "Williams." This is one time he will have to do without his serving man, Raleigh thought and Essex, realising it too, paused for a moment before continuing at the ruff and eventually managing to unhook it. Raleigh overheard him comment to the chaplain.

"I have often been in danger of my life but never has death been so certain and inevitable. Pray for me that I may remain strong."

The chaplain began a comforting drone of prayers and Essex turned to face the block. Slowly, he knelt and repeated the Lord's Prayer, which the chaplain had begun to intone. Raleigh noticed that some of the witnesses had joined in with them, the last moment of communion that they would ever share. He stripped off his black satin doublet to reveal beneath it a scarlet waistcoat. One of the executioners stepped forward with a rope and hood. Essex angrily dismissed him, refusing to be bound or blindfolded. He leaned forward and outstretching his arms, he lay flat on the board, fitting his head to the block's notch. The chaplain began the 51st Psalm:

"Have mercy upon me, O God, according to thy loving kindness:
According to the multitude of thy tender mercies,
Blot out my transgressions,
Wash me thoroughly from mine iniquity
And cleanse me from my sin."

The executioner raised his axe and the blow fell. Raleigh shivered in spite of himself. The blow had driven deep into his shoulder. Essex cried out and Raleigh thought of how they both had witnessed such executions before and had never considered that either of them would ever be subjected to such a punishment. God forbid that I should ever come to such a pass, Raleigh prayed. The executioner raised his axe a second time. Again, he missed the neck and drove deep into the other shoulder. The assembled throng fumed silently at the incompetence of the man. He raised the axe a third time and finally, connected with Essex's neck, severing the head from his body. It fell heavily onto the wooden platform and the executioner placed his foot on it to prevent it from rolling away. He bent down, lifted it, then brandished it in the air. "God save the Queen," he shouted.

"God save the Queen," the assembled witnesses answered in leaden tones.

Raleigh looked at the head of the man who had once been his friend and a wave of sadness swept over him. The eyes of the dead man seemed to be looking directly at him. He drew his cloak around him, turned from the scene and hurried away.

It had been a wet, miserable summer, the type that occurred all too regularly in Ulster. Autumn had brought no relief from the inclement weather. Tyrone's harvest had been scant enough, without losing some of it to Chichester and his men. The latter had proved to be a huge problem, one which, Hugh had not been able to solve. Chichester's raids had become so unpredictable that O'Neill had decided to leave Dungannon, having nearly been caught during one such incursion. These raids had generated great fear among his people. Chichester proved to be totally merciless, killing every man, woman and child upon whom he could lay his hands. There was no possibility that O'Neill could patrol the whole lakeshore, as he also had to keep an eye on the other garrisons which, Mountjoy had built along the Blackwater. He had retreated to one of his island hideaways and now lived a life far removed from the luxury that he had known only a short few years before. He sat in his makeshift shelter, looking out over the wind-swept lake, the waves, foaming towards the shore. He watched the boat approaching, knowing that his men would have O'Donnell with them.

He heard the vessel draw up on the shingle outside and his body-guard greet O'Donnell. His relationship with Hugh Roe had deteriorated in the last year. O'Neill had gone so far as to allow him equal leadership in every matter but that had not satisfied the younger man. He still resented it when the Queen referred to the war as "Tyrone's rebellion" or when the Pope had sent O'Neill the Papal crown. Things had been easier when Maguire was alive. His loss had been a most grievous one. Maguire had managed to keep the three of them united against the common enemy, having the gift of smoothing over any disagreements before they became pronounced.

Hugh's thoughts were interrupted by a knock on the door. It swung open and O'Donnell entered. He is still as thin as ever, Hugh thought. His clothes were mud spattered from his journey and he was soaked from the rain, which had been falling since early dawn.

"Come and warm yourself by the fire," he said to him. "I trust your journey was not too uncomfortable?"

"It had to be undertaken," O'Donnell replied shortly. "You said it was necessary that we meet and confer." He allowed his reply hang limply between them. It was obvious that he reckoned that he had more urgent matters to attend to, than ride half way across Ulster to meet with him.

O'Neill turned to his bodyguards who had also entered. "You may leave us," he said before turning back to O'Donnell. "There are some clean, dry clothes over there and something to eat on the table yonder, when you are changed."

O'Donnell took the clothes and stripped off in front of the fire. "Well, what news?" he asked, drying his body with a linen cloth, which lay on top of the folded clothes.

"Not good. Mountjoy has proved to be a far more dangerous opponent than any we have ever met before. MacCarthy has been arrested and dispatched to London. Munster has been totally vanquished and it has taken Mountjoy a bare twenty months to achieve it," O'Neill said.

"MacCarthy will cost me no tears. He failed us badly!" O'Donnell said contemptuously.

"O'Moore is dead. He was killed in a skirmish," Hugh added despondently.

"A good man gone," Hugh Roe replied regretfully. "He will be missed. He and Tyrell kept Leinster disturbed between them. Tyrell survived?"

"Yes, but he has been driven out and is back once again in Ulster. But what of your lands? Have you dealt with Niall Garve yet?" O'Neill asked, an edge of impatience discernible in his voice.

O'Donnell reddened. O'Neill knew how difficult it was for him to admit failure on any score. Niall Garve was a problem, to which Hugh Roe should have addressed himself. Ever since Niall Garve had aligned with Dowcra, their position in the North had worsened. It could have been prevented if Hugh Roe had done as he had counselled. Now they were paying for his neglect.

"Did you hear of his latest treachery? When I was in Sligo, the black bastard took Donegal Abbey from my men!"

Hugh nodded solemnly. And what were you doing in Sligo, while you left a viper like Niall Garve in your own back yard, Hugh asked mentally. Instead, he simply said. "Yes, I heard."

"Niall Garve is causing me much grievance. I should have ridded myself of him when I had the opportunity," Hugh Roe conceded with ill-concealed impatience.

Yes, but because he was one of your most successful generals, he was indispensable. O'Neill thought privately. Since joining with the English, he had performed miracles in their name.

Hugh censored his thoughts, knowing O'Donnell's temper. He wanted to conduct this interview in a reasoned manner, without it deteriorating into a heated debate. He could lay many accusations of incompetence at O'Donnell's feet. Allowing Dowcra establish his fort in Derry without challenging him, even though he had ample warning of his plans, was the first and weightiest. Leaving Dowcra there while he went to plunder Connaught with most of his forces, was another. Bequeathing responsibility to Niall Garve and a few men to keep an eye on the enemy was almost equally as bad.

"So, Lifford, Castlederg and Donegal Abbey have now all been taken by Niall Garve. It is a great loss," Hugh said. "And Mountjoy has finally managed to breach my defences on the Blackwater. He reached Benburb before we succeeded in halting his advance. He has retreated to the Pale again but, no doubt, will return with fresh troops and provisions. In the interim, the English nominee in Fermanagh, Conor Maguire, gains ground. If Hugh were still alive, that would not have happened. It is the same all over Ulster. They punish all those who do not join with them, setting up someone in opposition to them."

O'Donnell had finished changing and took a pitcher of beer and broke off some bread. "Tell me Hugh, why did you summon me here?" he asked.

O'Neill paused and observed Hugh Roe. He knew what he had to say would anger him. He addressed him in a low, reasonable voice.

"The war has turned against us, slowly at first but now, with ever increasing speed. Mountjoy, damn the man, knows what he is about. Look at the forts, which he has painstakingly built up around us.

Twenty-one so far. Another three or four and the ring will be complete. We will be imprisoned behind a wall of fortifications. His forces have managed to destroy large parts of our crops last autumn and again this year. Next year, it will be even worse. Famine is beginning to march with him and it pains me to see our people suffer so."

"We must continue in our efforts," Hugh Roe said.

O'Neill groaned inwardly. He could prescribe hardship for his people and death for his soldiers, but only if there was a possibility of victory.

"Two years ago, when Essex returned to England, I thought that we would be successful," he said earnestly. "I fear I overestimated our allies. I offered them a destiny that was beyond them. Look at what happened since then, look at the defections. Granted, there were men among those, on whom we could never really count, men like Arthur O'Neill and O'Connor Sligo. All we ever had was their inaction. But there were others whom I thought would remain loyal. Men like my own half brother, Turlough MacHenry of the Fews, Mac Mahon of Monaghan, Maguire of Fermanagh, Ever MacCooley, Mac Mahon of Farney, O'Cahan, O'Reilly of Cavan, Henry Óge O'Neill, one of my sons-in-law, Arthur Magennis, and they are only the principal men. If I were to list the lesser ones who have deserted our cause, it would take me all evening. We cannot continue with all these defections. We cannot even expect any relief in winter time, as Mountjoy does not rest then."

He paused and gazed levelly at O'Donnell. "I have taken a decision. I intend to continue the war for another three months. If, by then, the Spanish have not arrived, I intend to offer the English terms, which I know they'll accept. I have it from Cecil, through Garrett Moore, that if we wish to return to the fold, we will get good conditions. The Queen realises that there is a lot more of her wealth to be spent, before we are finally defeated. How is it that Cecil worded it?" he said, pausing to search among his papers, before finding the one he needed and continuing, "If Tyrone, O'Donnell and their allies have any purpose to become subjects again, Her Majesty is likest to receive them with tolerable conditions as she cares not for anything they hold in comparison to their obedience."

O'Donnell snorted in derision. "Of course she values our obedience because she fears a landing by the Spanish. You cannot put a restriction of time upon their arrival, Hugh. The English might not be able to continue their effort either. Already Mountjoy has had to debase their currency. We are causing them great hardship also."

O'Neill's confidence in Spanish intervention had all but disappeared. It was delayed by over six years and still it had not arrived.

"We must face the prospect that it might never arrive," he said gently to O'Donnell who, he realised, believed in help from Spain as an absolute certainty. "It is said that Cecil and the new Spanish King are in secret negotiations about a peace treaty. The longer it continues, the less likely it is that there will be help from there."

"They will come, of that I am certain. We should not sue for peace. You know what the Queen's word is worth," O'Donnell implored. "When the Spanish arrive, all our difficulties will disappear. Those who defected will hasten to rejoin us. Dowcra can be starved out. Chichester will not dare show his ugly face outside Carrickfergus. Let us fight on, the King of Spain will not fail us. You saw his last communication."

O'Neill couldn't understand O'Donnell's blind faith, in spite of all the broken Spanish promises. "Yes, I have seen his letters and all the letters his father sent us too. Unfortunately, I think we must rely upon ourselves, and even of that, I am uncertain."

O'Donnell bristled. "What are you saying, Hugh? Damn you! For once will you speak your mind."

O'Neill looked unflinchingly at him. "All our problems started when you allowed Dowcra land and become established. If you had done as you were advised, instead of leaving to collect easy plunder in Connaught, we would not be in the state we are in today."

O'Donnell laughed bitterly. "So that is it," he replied. "All this time you resented my behaviour and not a word. I had to go and relieve Tibott Burke. Dowcra had three and a half thousand men. I hadn't that many more. When I saw that they were intent on setting up a fort, I asked myself what would you do? You would say, 'leave them to the hands of time, famine and disease. They can always be starved out later.' It's how we've always dealt with such forts," he argued.

Hugh shook his head. "Three thousand five hundred men is not a garrison. It's a full army and that is not the complete extent of your error. After Niall Garve joined with them, I asked you to watch his progress. I warned you that he was most dangerous to us and that you were to capture him. But what did you do? You went off to plunder Connaught again while he played havoc in Donegal."

O'Donnell's eyes flashed fire. "At least I held my course. It was important that I helped our allies in Connaught. As long as they are in rebellion, they keep some of the English soldiers engaged. Connaught is still in revolt, unlike Munster and that is, in no small part, due to me. Some of the blame for our present situation lies with you," he said angrily, pausing and awaiting a reaction from O'Neill, who kept silent.

O'Donnell continued. "Our allies have seen you make peace time and time again and they have followed your lead, uncertain of your intent. You have asked them to retreat too often. You have made a custom of it and now, they have not waited for you but have, under pressure, made truces of their own. You cannot blame them. Some of them were sorely pressed and you did not assist them. I am sure they mean to withdraw their submission once they have the opportunity. They may prolong their obedience to the English until the time for action is past. Now it will take a victory of the magnitude of the Yellow Ford, or the arrival of the Spanish to win them back."

O'Neill nodded. "I find it difficult to see either happening. If I am forced to make another truce, then that will be my final one. It will be under terms, with which I can live and I will honour them," he replied.

O'Donnell was incensed. "And what of the terms we agreed together? Which of them would you drop? All of them?" He reached inside his jerkin and took out a folded and badly worn piece of parchment. He started to read from it. "That the Catholic Apostolic and Roman religion be openly preached and taught throughout all Ireland as well as in the cities and.."

"I know the conditions. I agreed them too," O'Neill interrupted. "I will agree to a three month extension of our present rebellion, on one condition only," he continued, "and that is, whatever we decide shall be carried out to the last detail. I must know where I stand. I am no longer prepared to endure a situation where I cannot be sure that you will deliver what you promise."

O'Donnell struck the table angrily with his fist. "I have done as I promised. I made war and peace, as you dictated but I will not surrender, as long as I have breath in my body. If you make peace, you will do so on your own," he said in a raised voice.

"And for the three months? Do you pledge that we will be bound by our agreements, that we will abide by what we both decide is the better course?" O'Neill asked.

O'Donnell walked over to the fire and stared into it. O'Neill could see the clenched hands, the tensed shoulders and knew his difficulty in reining in his emotions. After a few moments, he turned back to O'Neill.

"I will abide by our agreements, provided that you do likewise," he answered. "But you cannot speak true when you say that you will make peace with the English. We have travelled too far down this road for us to change direction now."

O'Neill looked at him, weariness and sadness engulfing him. He felt sure that they would be forced to come to terms with the English, sooner rather than later. He wondered how he would bring O'Donnell to accept it.

Suddenly, his thoughts were interrupted by a huge roar from the bank opposite them. O'Neill seized his sword and he and O'Donnell rushed outside, drawn swords in hands. O'Neill's bodyguards spilled out of the other dwellings and they all raced to the shore. O'Neill and O'Donnell, upon reaching it, looked across the water and saw a boat, rowed by his sentries, advancing towards the island. Their excited cheers carried across the water to him and he listened in astonishment, doubting that he was hearing properly.

"The Spanish! The Spanish have landed! They have landed!" they shouted.

O'Neill looked at O'Donnell who returned his gaze in wonder and disbelief. They turned back to observe the approaching boat, no words having passed between them. Then he saw a black clothed figure stand up in its prow. Even at the distance that still remained between them and the boat, they both recognised him. His jet-black hair, beard cut in the Spanish fashion and Jesuit garb, made him unmistakable. It was McDermott, O'Neill's agent in Spain. The previous summer, he had guaranteed Hugh that the following year would not pass without a Spanish army landing on Irish soil. He had also promised Hugh a solid silver, red plumed Spanish helmet, which he could wear at the head of the new army of Spanish and Irish soldiers. The figure produced such a helmet and held it over his head. O'Neill immediately recognised its significance. The Spanish had indeed landed.

He turned again to O'Donnell and read his face. For a moment they simply looked at each other and then O'Donnell's face broke into a wide grin, his eyes dancing with delight. "Oh you of little faith," he said laughing and throwing his arms around O'Neill, their argument now totally forgotten. "All is changed, changed utterly."

O'Neill returned the embrace. He struggled to believe that it had finally happened. Elation washed over him. He had never experienced anything like this before. The murder of his father and brother when he was only a child, the long, tortuous path to the Earldom and thereafter to the O'Neillship, had taught him to guard his feelings and always keep them in check. All his achievements he had accepted with equanimity, quietly content to reach his goals. Now, he found himself overcome by a wave of exhilaration. All around him, soldiers were shouting with enthusiasm. Tears came to his eyes. He looked at O'Donnell and saw that his cheeks were wet.

Now, one single event had changed everything. The Queen would now finally pay the full cost for her appalling misgovernment. He watched as the boat ran up on the gravel shore and he stepped forward, helping McDermott alight from it. He disembarked athletically, the silver helmet still held aloft. The rain had stopped and the sun appeared from behind the clouds, reflecting upon the polished helmet, which gleamed and glistened in its light. McDermott placed it on Hugh's head, then both men embraced fondly.

"They really have landed?" Hugh asked eagerly.

"Yes," McDermott answered.

"But where? And how many?" O'Neill asked.

"Four and a half thousand troops with extra munitions for their Irish allies sailed from Spain, but only three thousand eight hundred and fourteen made it safely here. The flagship and eight other ships were separated from the others in a storm and have not arrived safely yet. It is to be hoped that they still will, or at worst, that they will return safely to Spain," he answered.

Four thousand trained Spanish veterans and fully equipped!

"But where have they landed, Sligo? Donegal?" O'Neill asked impatiently.

"Kinsale," McDermott replied.

O'Neill was dumbfounded. Kinsale! That was in the extreme southern tip of Munster, of Ireland! The whole country lay between them and the Spanish and most of that was, once again, in hostile control. How could they ever join forces, he wondered.

"But did you not get our most recent communication?" O'Neill asked, suddenly deflated. "Have you not heard of how the rebellion in Munster has collapsed?"

A look of consternation crossed the Jesuit's face.

"We always said that an army of four thousand or less should land no further south than Galway," O'Donnell added, equally devastated. "They must take ship again and come north."

O'Neill was aware of his men gathered around them, still jubilant, as yet, ignorant of the problem. McDermott was about to reply and he motioned him to be quiet. "Come inside," he said, "where we may talk in privacy."

The three men entered the dwelling in silence and once inside, Hugh shut the door behind them. McDermott was troubled, his former confidence having deserted him.

"They cannot take ship again," he said limply. "The vessels have been ordered to return to Spain. Before long the English navy will blockade the port. They have arms and powder for the Irish rebels who, you promised, would flock to their cause and they await them eagerly. Here, I bear a letter from their leader, Don Juan del Aguila. He requests that you join with his army as soon as possible," he said, passing the document to O'Neill.

At least a good commander, Hugh thought, somewhat mollified.

They had requested del Aguila who had proved himself an excellent leader in Brittany, adept at operating behind enemy lines. He would not be easily displaced from Kinsale. Now that His Majesty had finally sent his army, he could not allow it fail for lack of supplies or reinforcements. He would not be able to take the field with such a number, but if he was reinforced from Spain, anything was possible.

"He will be reinforced?" he asked.

"Yes. But he is anxious that your army joins with him. He wants to take the field before the English have time to build up their forces in the country," McDermott replied.

"We cannot march the length of the entire island," O'Neill answered. "We are besieged on all sides. If we leave our lands, who will defend them from the vultures that are on our borders? If we split our forces, we will not be strong enough for both tasks."

"But you must march to join with him," McDermott answered. "You promised His Majesty that you would support his army if he should send it here. You cannot renege upon your word."

"I will not revoke mine," O'Donnell responded. "I will not be found wanting."

"This changes everything," McDermott said. "Do you not see, those who have deserted will flock back to join with you once again?"

O'Neill turned to O'Donnell. "Tell Niall Garve of this development," he suggested. "He might reconsider and join with you again. If you leave him to your back, you will have no country to return to."

O'Donnell retorted contemptuously. "Niall Garve is currently under siege in Donegal Abbey. His luck is running out. There was a fire, which demolished most of the building. They will have to surrender before long and when they do, then I'll be avenged upon that bastard!"

O'Neill shook his head. "There will be time for revenge when we've won the war. It's worth the approach. It will save you time and resources."

O'Donnell flushed in anger. "How can you dare suggest such a thing. Niall Garve killed my brother, Manus, outside Lifford. He handed over my sister's son to Mountjoy. It is a blood feud now and there can be only one outcome, Niall Garve's death."

O'Neill recognised that it was useless pursuing the topic. He shrugged his shoulders. McDermott addressed him. "And you, Hugh? What will you do?" he asked.

"I do not know. First, I will try and win back those who have deserted me. Then, depending on what the English do with their garrisons, which ring Ulster, I will decide whether or not it is safe to march south. At the moment I can promise nothing," he answered.

McDermott was crest-fallen. O'Donnell rose. "I must depart," he said. "I will organise my forces for the march south. I expect you, Hugh, to choose the same path. If you do not, Irishmen will forever curse your name," he said, looking steadily at O'Neill. Without another word, he left. O'Neill followed him, eager not to part in such a manner, but as he and McDermott left the dwelling, O'Neill's bodyguard pressed around them, lifting both him and the Jesuit onto their shoulders. They marched around the tiny island to the shouts of 'O'Neill abú.' From his position on their shoulders, Hugh watched O'Donnell being swiftly rowed back to the mainland.

Chapter 21

Don Juan del Aguila stood at the casement of the Great Hall. Desmond Castle had been used by the English as their headquarters in Kinsale. Now, it was in Spanish hands and the Spanish flag flew from its battlements. Del Aguila seethed with angry resentment as he looked out at the dark rain clouds, which seemed to be impaled on the surrounding hills. Rain, rain, and yet more rain! Would it never cease, he wondered. It had not stopped raining since their arrival at Kinsale, ten days previously. He resented everything about this posting. He had not volunteered for it, indeed he had no choice in the matter. To make matters worse, he had to have the opinionated, arrogant Archbishop Oveido foisted upon him. He should have chosen to stay in gaol. All he had done was exchange one prison for another and in his Spanish prison he had the company of his wife and warmer weather to make the time pass more agreeably. He wondered how she was managing without him and, for the thousandth time, he felt the ache of loneliness in her absence.

She had stayed with him throughout his military career, travelling with him from Flanders to Italy, where he fought the Turks. For twenty-four years he had been exiled from Spain on military service, during which time he rose through the ranks until he reached the position of Colonel with command of his own regiment. Then, after a few short months at home, the previous King Philip had sent him to Brittany. By dint of a brilliant campaign there, he had managed to hold it against all potential rivals, for over seven years. His success was, in no small way, responsible for forcing the French King to make peace with Spain. Obviously, King Philip III thought that he could perform the same miracle in Ireland, thus forcing the Queen to agree a peace treaty, which would recognise Spanish rights in the New World.

However, del Aguila felt used. His wife had been prevented from travelling with him and was being held under house arrest in Spain. That was his reward for all his years of service in the Spanish cause! His success in Brittany had not been achieved without enormous personal sacrifices. He had demanded, indeed insisted on absolute discipline, drawing his soldiers to the limits of their endurance so that victory would be theirs. Time and time again, he brought them further than any other commander could, and what reward did he obtain for it? The ignominy of being arrested by his own men who rebelled and imprisoned both him and his officers! Even worse, when he returned to Spain, the King instigated a thorough investigation into the whole affair, the end result of which was that del Aguila, his wife and his paymaster were lodged in prison. The commission had found that they had benefited over much from the Royal treasury while it concluded that his men had suffered from a dearth of food and clothes. It had incensed him beyond measure. The mutineers had not even been punished. It was an absurd judgement. How could his army have achieved so much if it was underfed and lacked clothing? He had never asked his men to endure anything that he would not himself.

He knew in his heart, however, where he had gone wrong. In Brittany he had spent the King's money as he saw fit, bribing people when the need arose. There were many items that required purchase, civilian labour, food and accommodation. He could have taken what he wanted, but if he had, he would have turned the local populace against him and, without their acceptance and aid, he could not have survived there for as long as he had. His mistake had been in not keeping the necessary records to justify his expenditure. He had simply been too busy in winning the war to undertake the necessary book keeping. Of course, that was what the state servants wanted, a full reckoning for every ducat spent. He would be more careful this time. No one would be able to accuse him of mis-spending a single coin, as he would only spend what was absolutely necessary and account for it down to the last detail.

He was also angry about the location in which he found himself. He had been totally opposed to landing in the south and, though he had been backed by Alonso del Campo, he had been over ruled by Oviedo and Don Diego de Brocherio, the naval commander of the expedition. Oviedo had swayed de Brocherio and as he was in charge of all matters while the fleet was at sea, del Aguila had found himself forced to land in Kinsale. Oviedo, in his pompous manner, would not listen to any of the arguments that he had made, insisting that he had been in contact with the northern Lords and that he alone knew their minds. If they had gone north, they could already be in the field. He was absolutely determined not to spend another seven years operating behind enemy lines. This time, he would fight until the matter was resolved. He did not intend being under siege again with all the hard ships, which that would entail. If he could win this campaign, he might be finally allowed retire and live out the rest of his life in some quiet Spanish backwater, a prospect, in which he found considerable solace.

Shortly after they had made their decision to take Cork, the largest town in the south of the country, the inevitable storms struck the Armada, splitting it in three. Zubiaur and del Campo, with nine ships and six hundred and fifty soldiers, had been last seen, being blown back towards Spain. The remainder of the soldiers, some three thousand eight hundred men, had been swept further along the coast to Kinsale.

Kinsale was not as defensible a position as Cork would have been. Its harbour ran in a northerly direction, straight from its entrance for about a mile and a half, before turning sharply westwards to where the River Bandon flowed into the sea. The town was built on the northern side of this bend and lay almost on an island, as its whole eastern side was bounded by the sea, while a creek from the Bandon River ran along the town's western and northern sides. On the eastern side of the harbour, about a mile from the entrance, stood Rincorran Castle. It commanded the harbour in two directions, southwards towards the entrance and westwards towards the town. Another fortification, Castle Park, stood on a little promontory, half a mile across the bay from the town, just where the harbour turned from north to west. Castle Park commanded the town and its anchorage. Backing the settlement, was a great, wide, circular sweep of high hills. Only to the east of the town, was the land a little more level. From the start, del Aguila had worried about those hills. It would be possible for an enemy to use them to rain shot down upon the town. Rincorran Castle and its twin, Castle Park, were also very important in Kinsale's defence. If they fell into enemy hands, it would make the Spanish position in the town less tenable.

Del Aguila thought how fickle life could be at times and how random events could affect that life, leading to a particular challenge. This expedition would never have been sent had not France and Savoy made peace. The Archduke Albert's army, decimated in the Battle of the Dunes, had lost over six thousand Spanish soldiers and a hundred companies of infantry. He had appealed to his brother-in-law for replacements and the King had not allowed that appeal go unanswered. Del Aguila's present army had been assembled in Lisbon and would have been dispatched to the Archduke, only for the peace treaty between the French and Savoy. And the King, finding himself with an army without a cause, decided, finally, to send the long promised aid to Ireland.

At least it was a force of which he could be confident, del Aguila thought. The recommended total of six thousand men had not been marshalled and when the ships had finally sailed, only four and a half thousand soldiers were aboard. However, they were all veterans, the very best soldiers of which the Spanish Empire could boast. There were men from many parts of its far-flung empire, Spain, Italy, Portugal, the Azores and North Africa.

Finally, del Aguila saw the figures, which he was awaiting. They approached along the narrow street that led to the castle. Oviedo, dressed in his clerical purple, waddled like a well nourished duck whereas Brocherio's erect, tall figure sauntered easily beside him. He watched them enter the doorway, thinking what an odd couple they made. Within minutes, there was a knock at the door and he called out to them to enter.

Oveido swept into the chamber first, his purple cloak swinging behind him and stood dour-faced before del Aguila. In had been a mistake and a gross one at that, to appoint him Archbishop of Dublin, del Aguila reflected. The promotion had gone to his head and now, because of that and the fact that he had been to Ireland on a number of missions previously, he imagined that he could meddle in military affairs. As for Brocherio, he also had an inflated view of his own ability and del Aguila was glad that now that they were finally on dry land, he, himself, was in charge of matters. He motioned to both men to take their seats around the large oak table, which commanded the middle of the room. Once they were seated, he opened the proceedings.

"Well, Don Diego, do you still propose to return to Spain and abandon us here?" he asked.

Brocherio nodded. "You know my orders. As you are safely put ashore, I am to return to Spain with the King's ships. The other vessels can go back to their rightful owners. My task here is completed. I intend taking the next tide," he answered.

Del Aguila shook his head angrily, clenching his hands into fists, until his knuckles showed white beneath his tanned skin.

"You have landed the men but not all the provisions. There are still 5,000 quintals of biscuits to be unloaded from the supply ships and the León Dorado has another 600 still aboard. Even when that is unloaded, we will be dangerously low in stores, especially in powder and match. The food that has already been unloaded has suffered from the grossest carelessness of your men. It was thrown so roughly onto the shore that the boxes were broken and the food contained within is now damp and unusable," he said, with more than a touch of spleen.

"I have retained only twenty one days' rations for our journey home. It took us thirty-five days to make landfall here, which means that I shall have to put my men on half rations. There will be no more unloaded. The eight supply ships that were separated from us in the storm, carried most of the match. There is nothing that I can do about these matters except return to Spain and ensure that more supplies are sent to you," Brocherio answered evenly but del Aguila could see that his eyes remained cold, betraying the dislike that he harboured for him.

"If you leave, the English ships which hide outside the harbour will take your place and my men will be exposed to fire from their vessels. There is much work that has yet to be done on the town's walls to make them strong enough to withstand an onslaught of artillery," Del Aguila said anxiously.

Brocherio lost patience and answered with a sneer. "You fail to see any other person's problems. How could you feed us if we wintered here? Do you know that I am more afraid of my own men than those of the enemy? The English galley slaves naturally have no stomach for this type of work. If they get the opportunity, they will swim for shore and take their chances. The crews of the French and Germans ships, which were commandeered for this expedition, are unhappy also. I have had to keep an armed guard of Spanish soldiers on each vessel to ensure that it remains loyal. Until Spaniards begin returning to service at sea, Spain will never again be great."

Del Aguila scowled. "I am not interested in excuses or in your diagnosis of the woes of the Empire. Things have changed drastically since we arrived here. Your sailors' lack of discipline should not be an issue in this matter."

Brocherio snarled. "Well I do not intend being imprisoned by my men. It is enough that one of us had that experience."

Del Aguila felt rage surge through his blood. He would not have anyone taunt him on that subject; it had been too painful and demeaning. He drew his dagger and, in fury, drove it deep into the oak table, jarring his wrist as he did so.

"How dare you speak to me like that," he shouted angrily. "I have done my utmost for my country and given over forty years service in the army. When you have done as much, then perhaps you might be in a position to criticise me."

Brocherio smiled ironically. "I have had to keep the supply ships anchored half a league from the town, owing to the problems, which I have just outlined. I have transported all the stores from them to the quay in small boats and it was your responsibility to take the supplies from there into the town and store them in a safe dry place. You have nearly four thousand men under your command and control all the town's citizens. If your food is wet, you have no one to blame but yourself. If I had waited for your help, I would have been here until the spring. Perhaps that was your intention?"

Del Aguila looked at Brocherio's taunting face and something gave inside of him. He had suffered enough indignity in the last few years without having to put up with more from a man half his age. Men like Brocherio had dared to judge him and find him guilty. During the planning of this expedition, Brocherio and he had clashed often and he had repeatedly asked to be allowed return to prison with his wife. It would have been preferable to working with such a man. This was the face of the Spain he had spent his life serving, ungrateful, arrogant, judgmental. He had enough of it all, he thought, as he drew his sword from its scabbard. He would no longer suffer himself to be mocked.

Suddenly, the Archbishop, who had observed both men silently up until this, moved with an alacrity that belied his age and girth and del Aguila found his fleshy hand firmly upon his sword arm, preventing him from withdrawing it any further.

"Come, come, Don Juan," he entreated. "Put your sword away. Why, it is treasonable for brother officers to duel when they are on active service. There are plenty of enemies upon whom you can both use your energies. The King had specifically asked the two of you..." here Oviedo paused and cast Brocherio an accusatory glance, "ordered the two of you," he continued, "to put aside your personal animosities and to work instead to enhance Spain's greatness."

For a few moments no-one moved, del Aguila standing stock still, his sword half drawn with Oviedo's hand still on his. He struggled to regain composure. He wanted to strike out at someone or something and the fat Archbishop's clammy hand made him recoil inwardly from such physical contact. Finally, common sense won out and he replaced his sword in its scabbard.

"I will not be treated with so little respect," he said angrily. "I will be making a full report to the Council in Madrid."

Brocherio nodded. "And I also will be making mine," he replied.

Oviedo returned to his seat at the table. Del Aguila followed him with his eyes. His hand was damp from the Archbishop's touch. He wished with all his heart that the fat cleric would return to Spain with Brocherio. Del Aguila thought of how he was responsible for their present predicament and snarled at him. "You have done Spain a great disservice with the advice that you furnished, regarding a suitable landing place. What do I find when we yield to that counsel? That the two allies you promised me, MacCarthy and Desmond are imprisoned in the Tower. I find a province totally at peace and no one rises to drive the English into the sea, as I was promised. O'Neill and O'Donnell are over three hundred miles away, hemmed in by a ring of forts with over fifteen thousand enemy troops between them and us. If we had acted, as I wanted, we would, by now, be in a position to take the field with the Irish at our side. As it is, we are confined here with the mountains surrounding us, in a town whose walls are mere slate, a bare two and a half feet wide, without a moat or traverse."

Oviedo snorted impatiently and, placing his index finger on his small one, began counting. "I will not listen to such complaints. One, you complain about lack of allies. Did not one of the neighbouring chiefs, Daniel O'Sullivan Beare, come and make an offer on behalf of himself and his fellow Chiefs to provide you with two thousand men, one thousand armed and the other thousand to be armed by you? He offered to block Mountjoy's march south and prevent a siege until the northern Lords and their allies join with you. Two, did not the Admiral offer to take you off by ship again and land your army further north? Three, did not the Admiral also offer you artillery from his ships to fortify Castle Park, which would secure control of the harbour, and did you not reject his offer?"

Del Aguila slapped the table with his open palm. Why was this cantankerous religious man sent to hound him? "Why should I trust this O'Sullivan Beare person? His name appears no where on the list of possible allies that I might secure in Munster. Why should I arm a thousand of his men when those same arms might be used against us? I told him, by all means, he could attempt to delay Mountjoy and he would earn King Philip's gratitude, but we had no surplus arms to give."

Here del Aguila ceased speaking and ran his hand through his greying hair. The storms at sea had been the most frightening experience of his life. It was the helplessness of it that had terrified him. He had lain in his cabin, listening to the creaking, straining timbers and the shouts of the crew as they battled to keep them afloat. The ship had plunged and heaved like a bucking horse, and the vessel, at any moment could have floundered or capsized, spilling him and his soldiers into the freezing fierce Atlantic water. He knew it would be difficult to get his men to embark again, now that they had safely reached dry land and had obtained good dry quarters for the winter that was fast approaching.

"Regarding the offer of transporting us to a better port, there are now too many risks associated with such a venture. The element of surprise is now lost to us. The English would have ample time to prepare for us and block our landing. We might even encounter the enemy fleet at sea and a maritime battle would be disastrous. Finally, the weather is now against us. Should we meet another storm, we might be further scattered and then a landing might not be possible."

Oviedo's face betrayed an annoying smirk and del Aguila felt his anger rising again. He forced himself to remain calm and continued. "As for the offer of artillery, I agree with the Admiral that Castle Park is the key to Kinsale and that by fortifying it, I could keep the harbour mouth open for ships from Spain and help secure the town. The problem is, however, that the castle is too weak as it stands. We need a proper fort there, enclosed within a strong four-walled stockade, on which I could mount the artillery. For that I need lime and men, I also need to erect extra fortifications on the landward side of Kinsale. I have no horse for moving heavy artillery around and even if I had, I'm so short of powder that I must keep what I have for my soldiers' muskets. If I send men to defend Castle Park, that will weaken my defence of Kinsale."

Oviedo shook his head. "You have money, 170,000 escudos! You can hire the labour to build your fortifications. You, yourself, have said that the Irish make good infantrymen. You saw what they could do in Brittany when they were properly trained. Take a few thousand in your pay and train them. Buy horses so that you can mount your calvary. Such men are never happy acting as infantry. You can use some of the horses to transport your heavy guns. You must open your purse strings. There is no point in husbanding your allocation. Remember the parable of the talents? The one who buried his talent and returned it unspent, earned his master's displeasure. Spend, buy victory."

Now it was del Aguila's turn to smile ironically. He had spent the King's money freely before, achieved the desired result, but still that had not saved him. He would not be caught a second time. "Considering the type of campaign that I am expected to wage, far from our own country, one hundred and seventy thousand escudos is not a lot of money. I cannot be sure when I will receive another payment, so I must ensure that it lasts as long as possible. Until O'Neill and his allies arrive, I intend keeping it intact. It will be time enough to take on men and horses when we take the field. How otherwise are we to feed them? And I am not taking the field until we receive reinforcements from Spain or the Irish come south to join with us," he said defiantly.

Brochero stood up from the table, pushing his chair backwards, making an ugly, grating noise as he did. "There is no more to be said. I must go and prepare my ships for sailing. I will endeavour to return with the extra supplics and required men, as soon as possible."

Del Aguila went to a side table and took a letter, which he handed to Brocherio. "See that the King and his Council receive this," he demanded.

Brocherio turned it over in his hand. "Is this the report you talked of earlier?" he asked.

Del Aguila shook his head impatiently. "There is a war to be won yet before any such reports are made and it will not be won, unless the Council furnishes me with all that is requested therein. I need men and materials to fortify Castle Park and to build a fort at the entrance to Cork Harbour so that I may starve it into submission. Kinsale and Cork would be excellent bases for an invasion of England, if the necessary men were sent from Spain. You must press this case strongly. You see that our needs are great," he said.

"I will see that it reaches the Council," Brocherio said curtly and made for the door.

Oviedo, surprised at the suddenness of his departure, jumped to his feet and hurried after him. "Wait, Admiral," he shouted. "I must come with you and bless the fleet to ensure its safe return."

The door banged shut. Del Aguila fell heavily into a chair beside the large fire that blazed in the open hearth. The constant dampness was beginning to affect his joints, so he allowed the heat warm his knees, which had been giving him trouble of late. Yes, he thought, as an involuntary shiver ran through his body. This was going to be a difficult assignment.

Sir George Carew, President of Munster, rode through the gates of Kilkenny Castle. This was one of the strongest in the land and home of the Earl of Ormonde who was one of the most loyal supporters of English rule in the country. The sentries on the gates had delayed in opening them. No one could be trusted, in this most turbulent and dangerous time for the colony. Carew cast the nervous sentries a contemptuous look. It was the same throughout the Kingdom. The colony was suffering from an extreme case of fearfulness. The Irish, on their own, had caused them sufficient trouble but with the Spanish to aid them, matters had become extremely grim. Carew, himself, was not a man to lose his nerve; there was part of him that even welcomed the opportunity to test himself against the newly arrived army. It would also be a change to be at the centre of things again. Everyone in Europe would watch this fight develop. Up until this, no matter how many battles he had won, no one beyond these shores paid much attention to his efforts.

Once in the inner courtyard, he dismounted quickly and raced up the steps of the north turret, making for the council chamber. Upon reaching it, he barged in, without knocking. Mountjoy and Wingfield had already arrived and were deep in conversation with the elderly Earl. Mountjoy had instinctively gone for his sword when the door was thrown open.

"Well, Charles," Carew said, "don't tell me that you are suffering from nervousness over a few foreign yokels?"

"Sir George," Mountjoy greeted him warmly, delighted to see him. "It is good to see you in these troubled times."

Carew stood in the middle of the chamber, rain water dripping from his clothes. His hair was plastered to his head but his manner was undeniably confident. Wingfield was also relieved to see him. His loss would have been a sore blow at this time.

Carew bowed to all present and Mountjoy went over and clasped his hand in his.

"Any news of any defections thus far?" he asked anxiously.

"None, so far Charles," he said proudly. "Our good work over the last year has paid off, for the moment, at least. Munster is as quiet as Leicestershire. All the Chiefs who might have wavered are safely in custody and I have taken pledges from those of whom I have any suspicion. The garrisons, which we have installed throughout the province, should help to dissuade the Irish from rebelling. But what of Leinster?"

Wingfield knew that Carew was being diplomatic in sharing the credit for the peaceful state of Munster with them. They all knew that it was due to his efforts on the Queen's behalf, which had, until now, cowed the province into obedience.

Mountjoy replied. "So far, all goes well there also. All the rebellious Chiefs are either dead or in custody. I have garrisons in the lands of the O'Moores, O'Connors and the O'Byrnes, the danger points. Yet, in spite of our work, I feel that the whole country is watching us with bated breath. If the Spanish take to the field, there will be defections and probably important Chiefs among them. If they win a victory, then all may be lost."

"So, what do you plan?" Carew enquired.

Mountjoy turned to the Earl who had listened attentively to the proceedings.

"Perhaps you could leave us now as we wish to discuss different options?" he said gently to him. Wingfield saw Ormonde flush with embarrassment and felt sorry for the grey haired man. The Earl had spent his life in the service of the Queen. He was related to her through the Boylens and he and the Queen had been playmates while children. Nevertheless, in spite of all that service, Mountjoy's implication was clear. Ormonde and O'Neill had always been close and there was no point in taking risks. Part of Mountjoy's success, so far, had been that he had successfully kept his plans secret from O'Neill and his allies and they must not jeopardise that secrecy at this dangerous juncture.

Wingfield continued after Ormonde's departure. "But what of the Old English in the towns? Their loyalty will be essential if we are to have any hope of overcoming this invasion. Will they join with their co-religionists or will they remain loyal to the Queen? Has the Pope granted O'Neill's demand that any Catholic who would not support him, be excommunicated automatically?" He asked anxiously.

"The townspeople in Kinsale opened the gates to the Spanish and welcomed them as their deliverers from heresy. They found the invaders their billets, with more solicitude than if they had been the Queen's troops," Carew said, disgusted at such behaviour.

Mountjoy smiled. "At least, on the score of religion, there is some good news. The townspeople petitioned the Pope to allow them acknowledge the Queen as their temporal leader, while acknowledging him as their spiritual one. They left him in no doubt that they did not wish to be associated with the northern rebellion. The Pope did not wish to choose between two Catholic factions, so he turned down O'Neill's requests. He seeks to keep his influence over both camps and recognised the settlers' right to acknowledge the Queen as their temporal ruler," he said with satisfaction.

"These are glad tidings," Carew said, greatly relived. "The Queen is indeed wise to tolerate their superstitious religion until the danger is past."

"We should issue a proclamation that the Irish have no just cause to take up arms against their lawful Sovereign and that this war is unjustly maintained by the Spanish King," Wingfield said.

"Let it be done," Mountjoy answered. "Will you draw something up for me to peruse?" he asked.

"Yes, I will do so as soon as we have concluded," Wingfield answered.

"And what action do you intend taking?" Carew asked Mountjoy for a second time.

"I am considering withdrawing to Dublin to await reinforcements. We are short of men and supplies," Mountjoy answered.

"You must not do so," Carew said vehemently. "You must go forward. If the Irish see the Lord Deputy turn his back upon the enemy, they will be emboldened and flock to the Spanish. The country is on a knife-edge. Take the wrong step now and all is lost."

"I am in agreement with Sir George. The Spanish must not be allowed fan out into the countryside," Wingfield added.

"And with what will I feed my men? Food is in short supply in Dublin. That is a greater problem than the shortness of men," Mountjoy said despondently. "As you know, a large portion of our harvest has been destroyed by the Irish. The Pale's agriculture had been ruined and is only now beginning to recover. It will not be capable of supplying an army of the size that we shall employ. As a consequence, we must be supplied with the necessary provisions from England before we can take the field."

"We cannot wait," Carew said. "We risk losing not only Ireland but England itself. We must march immediately and with all possible speed for Cork. I have prepared for this day in more ways than just pacifying Munster. The peace that we have brought to Munster has allowed us gather a good harvest there this autumn. I have had my troops billeted within the province for the last six months and have managed to build up large stocks of food. We will not be lacking in supplies."

Mountjoy sprang from his chair, and shook Carew's hand in gratitude for such foresight. " The Queen is fortunate to have a man such as you in her service and I will see that she hears of your excellent work. I will heed your counsel and we will hasten to Cork. I look forward to beating the great Spanish breeches as well as we have ever beaten the Irish trews," he said.

"I'll drink to that," Carew said, taking a pitcher of whiskey, which Ormonde had left for them.

Mountjoy continued, now suddenly animated at the prospect of taking action. "Outside of the Waterford garrison in Munster, which must at all costs stand fast, every other garrison must be cut in half and must march to Cork to join with me. I also want to strip the forts on Tyrone's borders of all the men whom they can safely spare. Sir Thomas," he said as he turned to him, "you must march north and bring the forces from the Pale and Armagh south to Cork. I want fourteen hundred men from the forts on Tyrone's borders. Leave enough men to guard the forts but there are to be no more attacks on Tyrone. We must concentrate on keeping O'Neill inside his borders."

"But what of the northern Irish? What will they do?" Carew asked Wingfield. "You know O'Neill's mind better than most."

Wingfield nodded. "He will not come south. He never fights unless he is guaranteed success. Look how difficult it has been to bring him to battle thus far. If it had been a year ago, when he still had support outside his own lands, he might have risked such a course, but even that is far from certain. Now, even in Ulster, his support has waned considerably. On no account must we move Chichester or deplete his garrison. O'Neill would never dare leave his territory, knowing that Chichester would destroy it in his absence."

Mountjoy nodded in agreement. "I have never come across a single case where a general deserted his own country and people, leaving them defenceless against their foes. Even if he wishes to come south, the soonest that he can possibly do so, is in the spring or early summer," Mountjoy agreed.

"And you are sure he will not act, given these altered conditions?" Carew asked Wingfield.

"Three hundred miles from remote Dungannon to remote Kinsale, in mid winter, across flooded rivers in full spate, with our troops waiting to ambush him in every county! Rest assured. I know his mind. He is as incapable of undertaking such a march as you are of kissing the Pope's fat arse," Wingfield answered.

Mountjoy was convulsed in laughter at such an image. Carew grimaced and shuddered in its contemplation. "His whole military strategy is based on fighting a defensive war. He is incapable of going on the offensive. He is incapable of taking the risk and coming south. The Spanish have miscalculated badly, if they thought that they would join with him, by landing where they did," Wingfield continued.

"That, or they have other plans, perhaps the attack upon the English mainland from Kinsale," Mountjoy said gravely, his merriment suddenly deserting him.

The others were silent a moment as they gravely pondered such a possibility. This was indeed a strategy, which the enemy might embrace.

"There is also another issue that worries me," Wingfield said. "If you reduce the garrisons, might that not lead to what we most fear? A general rebellion once more in the North."

Mountjoy sank back into his chair. He was not a gambling man and yet he was undertaking one of the biggest wagers that any subject could ever take. The prize was a kingdom and he fully realised the enormity of the risk. Yet, he feared inaction above all else. "It is a risk, which we must take," he answered after a pause. If we make a show of authority and are fearless, perhaps we can cover over our weakness."

"Yes," Carew said confidently. "Permission to return to Munster and muster my forces?" he asked.

"Absolutely," Mountjoy answered, "but you will wait and stay the night with us?"

Carew hesitated before agreeing. "Another day will not matter either way. It might be one of our last chances to sleep in a warm bed. Let us avail of Ormonde's hospitality, he keeps a very good cellar."

"You two go ahead, I will join you anon. I must prepare a report for Her Majesty," Mountjoy replied and turned to the table, strewn with parchments and writing materials.

Both men bowed and left the chamber. Mountjoy picked up a quill. He would write to Cecil and not the Queen. He had been courting him over the last few months in an effort to win his backing and good will. He knew that there were still questions that he could be asked and some of his actions might still have to be accounted for. It was imperative that he be allowed join Cecil's faction. Essex was no more.

He sketched a first draft. "Owing to the delay in the arrival of rein-forcements, I have been compelled to weaken the northern garrisons more than is desirable, but the Spanish must represent the main objective. If we beat them, you shall have them all return to obedience before long with halters about their necks. I face a world of difficulties comforted by the fact that I now have an opportunity to show how prodigal I will be of my life in any adventure that I shall undertake in the service of my dear Mistress," he wrote.

He stopped and reread the letter. Yes, it was a good beginning, he thought. He would finish it later. He would have to get just the right blend of humility, confidence, reliability and good humour. He was under no illusions. He might be forgiven, but only if he was successful in Ireland. This was his one great chance to redeem himself with the woman who controlled his destiny. Elizabeth could end his life like she did Essex's.

Chapter 22

Over a month had passed since the Spanish had landed in Kinsale and, finally, Mountjoy was on the last leg of his journey there. He had left Cork the previous day, his departure having been delayed by three whole days, owing to the extremely heavy rain that had been falling for over a week. He had wearied of waiting for it to cease, anxious to invest Kinsale before there were any more developments in the province. His men had grumbled but he had decided that he could not safely delay any longer and his forces had marched defiantly into the falling rain and muddy tracks for their ultimate destination.

He had ridden to Cork, as agreed with Carew and Wingfield, some four weeks earlier. They had had a meagre escort of just a hundred horse and he had set about assembling his present army, which now amounted to six thousand nine hundred foot and six hundred and eleven horse, no mean force. He had camped the previous night at a point five miles distant from Kinsale and now, in the late morning, he was finally approaching the town. They had already caught a glimpse of the Spanish scouts through the trees but they had disappeared quickly and hurried back to the town on seeing the number of his troops. Mountjoy was pleased that, at last, he was in the field and about to confront the Spanish. He had done all that he could in preparation. Carew had supplied him with enough victuals and munitions for three months. He had bombarded the Queen with pleas for more supplies and men and he had warned Cecil that the Kingdom would be lost if they were not immediately forthcoming. Cecil had taken his pleas seriously and had already dispatched two thousand men, who were now with him, and had promised him another four thousand, as soon as they could be recruited.

A proclamation was issued by del Aguila, acting as a counter to Mountjoy's earlier one. In it, del Aguila had said that he would never seek to draw any man from his allegiance to his lawful Prince, but that Elizabeth had been deposed by the Pope, thus every Irishman who aided the Spaniards was not failing in due obedience, but rather obeying God's word, as uttered by His Holiness, His representative on earth. They had come to Ireland, he continued, as a result of an appeal from the Catholic Irish for aid against the English who had treated them most cruelly. He finished by calling on all Irishmen to take up arms in defence of the Catholic faith. The proclamation was signed by del Aguila and Oviedo and had been broadcast widely in Munster. Mountjoy was relieved to see that there was no notion within the proclamation of Ireland as an independent kingdom. Instead, there was simply an attempt to prove that Elizabeth was not its lawful Sovereign. It was now obvious to all that the Spanish King simply meant to add the country to his own empire.

He had immediately begun a campaign to persuade both the Irish and Old English to ignore the call of religion and remain loyal to their rightful monarch. He had dispatched Carew, who had spent the month travelling up and down the province speaking to the Irish Chiefs and the Old English townspeople, doing his utmost to ensure that they held allegiance to the Queen. He continuously referred to Pope Gregory's declaration that allowed Catholics to accept the Queen as their leader in temporal matters. He was loud in his praise of the Old English for the manner in which they had always distinguished between their spiritual and temporal allegiances. Equally, he lauded the Queen, who had always accepted that distinction, allowing them the freedom to pursue their private beliefs as long as they did not renege on the loyalty due to her on all other matters. Mountjoy knew that her tolerance on the matter was owing to the possibility of an invasion such as this, and that she had been wise in her forbearance upon the matter. Carew had now assumed the guise of reason, charm and fairness. Mountjoy had waited anxiously to see which of them would win the hearts and minds of the Catholics, but luckily del Aguila's proclamation had fallen on deaf ears. So far, all had gone well for the government in Ireland. Even none of the Irish, who had submitted to Carew, had relapsed.

He had been delighted when he had heard that the priests, who ministered in the towns to the Old English, were preaching that the Munster Irish and Old English should make common cause and take up arms against the Spanish and their northern allies. Mountjoy was now content to rely upon the Old English but he did not feel the same about the Irish natives. He knew that there were Spanish Jesuits roaming the lands, preaching the reverse of what these urban priests proclaimed and his spies had told him that some of the Irish Chieftains were beginning to waver. He knew the majority of the Munster Irish were content to wait. That was what had forced him to take the field now, rather than later.

He and his army found themselves climbing Knockrobin Hill, one of the many hills, which encircled Kinsale. Their progress had been slower than he would have liked and even though they had been on the march for only a few hours, the newly arrived raw recruits from England were already beginning to falter. Carew, who rode beside him, halted his horse again to wait for the infantry to catch up with them.

"I suppose," he said harshly, "Cecil couldn't have found us any real soldiers."

Mountjoy looked at the men labouring up the hill. His veterans were hardened to this type of campaigning but the new arrivals worried him. Carew was right. They were not up to standard but they were not to blame. They had been plucked from their homes and sent across the sea to fight this war with only the most rudimentary of training. The sea journey, undertaken in the worst of weather, had not encouraged them either and they were not inured to marching. The wet weather and muddy tracks made for treacherous footing and their heavy boots chafed their feet. Their clothes were inadequate for the weather they now faced and each of them carried his equipment, food and whatever else was needed for the upcoming siege, upon his back. They would need a lot of training before they could call themselves soldiers.

He was too anxious to see what lay before them, to await them any longer. He turned to Carew. "Come with me," he ordered and spurred his horse up the hill at a gallop. Carew immediately dug his spurs into his horse's side and raced after Mountjoy, also eager to have his first view of Kinsale. He had caught up with him by the time they reached the summit. They reined in their horses and, on the crest of the hill, looked down on the town far below them. They were sheltered from the rain by one of the great oak trees, which grew there and they looked at the zig zag line of the wall, protecting the buildings, which were densely packed behind it. The Spanish flags flew proudly over the houses' shiny, wet, slate roofs and he also noticed them, flying from the two forts further out in the bay. Mountjoy felt his heart quicken at the sight and the muscles in his stomach tighten. He was going to take on the might of the Spanish Empire here in this lonely spot. He noticed that del Aguila had entrenched his outposts on one of the hills just outside the town in an effort to command, to some extent, the approach to it. He turned to Carew. "Well, George, where will we set up our camp?" he asked.

Carew shrugged. "It all looks pretty inhospitable to me," he answered. "That was the one thing that appealed to me about serving in Ireland, the fact that I would, so I was told by everyone, never have to lay siege to any town as the Irish refuse to allow themselves be trapped. I hate sieges more than anything else. They are the most miserable of affairs."

Mountjoy nodded. "Damn those Spanish!" he said angrily. "One more summer and I would have defeated O'Neill, once and for all. But I am glad that they have chosen a weak port for their headquarters. I would, however, be happier if they had a less experienced leader than del Aguila," he said as he pointed out the two castles on either side of the harbour. "Rincorran Castle and Castle Park control the sea approach and harbour. Our first task must be to take them. They were not particularly strong and I am surprised that del Aguila has not done more to add to their defences. As for the walls of the town, they are weak and if we place our cannon properly, we will force a breach.

Carew nodded. "So, let us decide on the site for our camp and start to get organised. We must prepare shelter for our men before nightfall."

Mountjoy stood silently looking down at the town and surrounding countryside, deep in thought. From his vantagepoint on Knockrobin Hill, he was half a mile from the town. Southwest of him was Camphill and west again of Camphill were two other hills, Ballinaboy and Kippagh, which stretched out into the sea. However, it was to the east that he looked. Parallel to Kinsale harbour, separated from it by a promontory a mile or more wide, lay Oyster Haven. This inlet reached inland and Knockrobin Hill was formed at its head.

"We will make our camp down there," he said to Carew. "The inlet will protect our left flank and our rear. Also, and more importantly, I know that at high tide it is navigable right up to the site I propose for our camp. That will give us direct access to a waterway along which supplies can be ferried and so avoid the necessity of using Kinsale Harbour at all. We can land the heavy guns, which will be necessary for taking Castle Park and Rincorran. Once those strong points are in our hands, the navy can bombard Kinsale from the sea, while we can continue the attack from the land. Another advantage of situating our camp there, is that we should be able to prevent any victuals from reaching the Spanish."

Carew chuckled. "That's a master plan," he said admiringly. If we had to haul our heavy guns and supplies over those accursed hills, we would not be in a position to begin hostilities for weeks. I almost feel sorry for those Spanish bastards! They have come so far and have chosen such a weak position, in which to defend themselves. They need not expect their brave allies to rescue them either as they will never dare leave their northern strongholds."

Mountjoy shook his head gravely, unwilling to join in with Carew's levity. "Do not for a minute pity those Spanish. Del Aguila is like the plague. Once he gets a grip on the countryside, he is every bit as difficult to get rid of. You must always remember that we are not facing Irish troops here, these men will know how to conduct themselves over a long siege. Mark you well," he said earnestly, "the Kingdom has never been in more danger."

He stopped, aware that he was sounding almost hopeless and the last thing that he wanted anyone to think was that he was unduly worried by the arrival of the Spanish.

"But come, enough talk. There is much work to be done before dark. We do not want the men sleeping in the open, at this time of year. The entrenchment tools have not yet arrived, so we must be on our guard tonight. Doubtless, the Spanish will sally out and attempt to dislodge us when they see what we plan to do. No matter what, we must hold our position."

Carew gave one last look at the town wall below them. Even at this distance, they could see it fill with Spanish soldiers who were looking in their direction. Their scouts must have reached the town and informed them of the army's approach.

"Before long, I will make sure that they dare not look over those walls," he said grimly.

But will we be able to look in, Mountjoy wondered, but he kept his thoughts to himself.

"Will I give the orders to the regiments and move them up?" Carew asked.

"Yes, let us get started," Mountjoy replied.

They turned their horses and thundered back down the escarpment through the still falling rain and rejoined their men. Mountjoy struggled to wrap his cloak around himself. The weather is always the same, he thought, wet and foul. This was going to be the most disagreeable engagement that I have to undertake so far, he thought darkly. He would have to try and keep warm and healthy throughout the siege. He had worried often about his health in the past, before coming to Ireland, and he had, as a consequence, done everything possible to guard against illness and infection. He would only have to hope that it would not let him down now.

Del Aguila heard the drum beat and hastened from his headquarters to the town's gate, which was being opened by the guards on sentry duty. His scouting party entered and its captain, on seeing him, hurried over to him and saluted.

"Well, Captain?" Del Aguila asked.

"The English are approaching, as we were warned, and their army is large, well over five thousand. They are just over the hill," he answered.

Del Aguila nodded, turned and walked briskly towards the nearest steps, which led to the ramparts. He quickly mounted them and stood on the walls of Kinsale, anxiously scouring the hills, which overlooked its harbour. He sought his first glimpse of the enemy that would oppose him here in this outpost of Europe. He had received warnings from the Irish of the preparations, which Mountjoy had undertaken at Cork and had been told of his departure from there the previous day, by local Irish people, friendly to his cause. He had been expecting such a development for over a month now and he had done all in his power, in the interim, to prepare for their arrival. Now the siege would close in and, for the foreseeable future, they were stranded here.

The wind was rising, blowing the rain in sheets of water from the Atlantic. It lashed fiercely over the ramparts, dying at times to a drizzle before gusting again in a fearsome frenzy. The waters of the harbour, normally too enclosed to be stirred by anything other than the moving tides, were now whipped into bucking white horses, which raced speedily towards the shore. Two more supply ships had reached Kinsale since the departure of the rest of the fleet. Their business executed, these vessels were now struggling through the towering, wind-lashed waves, which kept them imprisoned in the harbour. It was unwise to start their return journey to Spain in weather like this, but their captains had preferred to take their chances with the elements rather than await the arrival of an English fleet. They would not have been able to defend themselves against any English warship, as they were unarmed and had relied on the Spanish Men-o-War for protection.

All the supplies that had come on the ships, including some of the missing match, was now safely stored deep in the town's cellars. There, the powder and other consumables would be safe from the English artillery. The only good thing about all this rain, del Aguila thought, was that the town would hardly go on fire. The whole place was too wet and they could use seawater to extinguish any fire, should one somehow break out in the town. They would not be short of fresh water either, as they had been able to fill every possible receptacle with rainwater.

He turned back from the sea and looked down at the town's square, distracted by the terrified lowing of the cattle below him. Two soldiers, who had been butchers prior to conscription, were busy dispatching the cattle with their long knives, while another three were swiftly and expertly cutting the still warm carcasses into bloody cuts of meat, which they pickled with salt and crammed into barrels. He watched as the animals' blood mixed with the rainwater and ran down the streets, out the gate, a red, bloody torrent of water. He hoped that it was not a premonition of defeat but then reassured himself that it would be rivers of English blood that would run before this battle was out.

He had opened his purse strings a little, after all, but only on the provision that every single transaction would be recorded in full. He had paid for what he had taken. He had determined that he could not afford to antagonise the local Irish, as he would have to rely on their good will in the future. Already, their help had been considerable. Some of the local Chiefs had also sent him cows and grain as gifts, and he had been delighted to accept them, even though he would have been happier if they had joined him openly in the struggle. He had fed the cows on the sparse grass that was still available around the town but now, as he had no fodder for them, he had given the orders to have them butchered.

He had sent his men out into the surrounding countryside to get what they could in the way of food, powder, match and firewood. The firewood had been the easiest to acquire. A company of men had felled tree after tree and he had them dragged back to the town where they were chopped up into more manageable sizes. It was good to keep the men busy and all of them were set tasks, which ensured that they were fully employed and out of trouble. The largest amount of men were involved in work on the walls and fortifications, reinforcing them and constructing new defences where his engineers judged it necessary to enable them to withstand the enemy's large guns. He had dug trenches outside the town, which would be manned by his soldiers. Their function would be to keep the English from bringing their large guns too near the town's walls.

He had sent his quartermaster and Oviedo out into the countryside with some local scouts to those Irish who might be friendly, and he had given them permission to buy the extra powder and match, which he desperately needed. He had been surprised at the amount that they had managed to amass. It seemed that every Irishman wanted to keep his own weapons and was able to get ready supplies.

He had no scarcity of shot and he knew that he could always melt down the lead roof from the town's two churches should he run out of bullets for his muskets. So, he was as prepared as he could be. He saw Oviedo approaching him along the ramparts, some hundred and fifty paces from him. The cleric was still angry that del Aguila had not purchased horses for his cavalry, but the town was already too crowded with townspeople and soldiers, without having to find space for animals and their fodder. In any event, he could not locate suitable horses for his men. He would rely on the defensive squares, which his infantry could draw up, to face the enemy's horse. His muskets could now pierce the thickest armour and the pike could ward off even the heavy horses, which they rode. He could not expect Oviedo to understand the complexities of modern warfare. He would run the campaign and not that meddlesome cleric.

He turned and hurried to the steps, leading back down into the town in the opposite direction to the approaching cleric. He heard him call his name but the wind had almost whipped it away from him and he pretended not to hear. He had no desire to stand in the rain and listen to him talking about matters, of which he knew nothing. He would postpone the pleasure of seeing his enemy for another while yet. He was certain that he would be sick of the sight of them before long.

Deep in the dark, vast wood, which covered most of Maguire's country of Fermanagh, Cuconnaught Maguire had established his headquarters. He was Hugh O'Neill's man, set up in opposition to his cousin, Connor Roe. Most of the clan gave their allegiance to Cuconnaught. He was recognised as the legitimate successor to Hugh Maguire who had died so tragically the previous year outside Cork. Hugh O'Neill had called a meeting, which was to take place in Cuconnaught's headquarters, as it was centrally located for many of the leaders of the rebellion. Most of those who had been summoned had arrived and Hugh O'Neill looked around the makeshift cabin at the assembled leaders who were chatting quietly among themselves.

A large log fire blazed fiercely in the centre of the building and the smoke curled upwards and exited through a hole in the roof. The rain, which fell through the aperture, hissed fiercely as it splashed onto the fire. The space was lit by the fire and tallow torches, suspended from the walls. There were no windows and Hugh looked out the open door at the rain as it continued to pour down from the heavens, which, though only three o'clock in the afternoon, made it seem as if dusk had already fallen. No one could remember a wetter winter.

All the Chiefs sat facing each other at two tables, which ran along the length of the cabin. Hugh could see the steam rising from the clothes of some of the newly arrived Chiefs. He was gratified that so many of them had returned once more to his side. A month had passed since the arrival of the Spanish and in that time he had achieved much. It had been made easier for him by the fact that within days, Wingfield had begun drawing off the northern garrisons with many of the English soldiers marching south. That had allowed him break through the weakened forts and he began raiding Monaghan, the Fews, Breffni and the Pale. He had hoped that his activities would have forced Mountjoy to send some of his soldiers back to defend Dublin, but he had been bitterly disappointed. Mountjoy had just said that if the Palesmen would not defend themselves, then they could suffer the consequences.

He had also set about winning back the defectors among the bor-

der lords and, as most of them had been forced by their own vulner-
ability to change sides, they now readily changed back again on
learning of the Spanish landing. He had worked ceaselessly since
receiving the news of the landing, spending long days in the saddle,
riding and fighting, destroying villages and crops every day, while his
nights were spent meeting people in an effort to persuade them to his
side. Hugh was now in his fifty-first year and, of late, had felt his age.
His hair was more grey than black and his forehead was scored by the
wrinkles, which time had wrought upon it.

As well as Cuconnaught Maguire, Brian McMahon of Monaghan,
Ever McCooley, Tirlagh Mac Henry of the Fews, Hugh Magennis,
O'Reilly of Cavan, Sir Oghy O'Hanlon, Henry Hovendon, and his
brother Cormac were present. They could deliver many men to his
cause and it meant that he could, once again, put a considerable force
in the field. They were waiting for just one more arrival, one who,
they could not be certain would arrive, Hugh Roe O'Donnell.

"Late as usual," Maguire said.

O'Neill nodded. He expected that O'Donnell would come. He could
not afford to allow the opportunity of persuading them to join him
pass.

"He'll come," he said, even though he could not be sure of it.

"Perhaps, he did not receive your summons. We cannot wait forever. If you like I can send someone to fetch him. I have a good man
here who knows O'Donnell's country and is well known and liked by
his people. If we set a new date, perhaps a week's time, we might..."

O'Neill held up his hand. "No, we will wait a little longer. He
received our message. My messenger returned after delivering it into
his very hand."

Cuconnaught nodded in agreement and refilled Hugh's goblet with
wine. He then turned to the Chief on his other side and did the same.
A week would be too late, Hugh thought. It might even be too late
already. He knew O'Donnell had given the order that all forces loyal
to him should assemble at Ballymote in Sligo by today's date, with
provisions for a march south to Kinsale. He might not choose to delay
their departure to confer with this gathering. Hugh had not seen him
since the day that they had received news of the arrival of the
Spanish. He was distracted from his thoughts by the sounds of horsemen arriving and he listened acutely, anxious to establish if it was
friend or foe. He heard the amicable greetings of the sentries and
relaxed. He should have known that enemy forces would not have
been able to penetrate this far. Maguire had stationed sentries in well-
camouflaged hiding places in the forest, where they were dry and
sheltered from the elements, but yet able to guard all the approaches

to his camp.

He peered out into the falling rain and saw four men ride into the stockade and over towards the cabin. There was no mistaking the figures, even though they wore long dark sodden cloaks and had their hoods pulled over their faces. The leading horseman galloped over to the open door and leaped energetically from his horse. His movements betrayed his identity as surely as if he had shouted out his name. It had to be O'Donnell, O'Donnell who never walked when he could run, who attacked everything with an excessive energy and enthusiasm. The three large, bearded men with him, their chain mail visible underneath their cloaks, which had flapped open, were the leaders of O'Donnell's Gallowglasses, Mac Sweeney na dTuadh, MacSweeney Fanad and MacSweeney Banagh. They also alighted from their horses but in a more leisurely fashion, and all four animals were led away by the sentries to be fed and rested. The four men strode purposefully to the door of the cabin and entered, nodding to the assembled gathering.

Cuconnaught got to his feet and as host, welcomed them to his headquarters with an apology for its humbleness. "Perhaps when this war comes to a conclusion and I rebuild Enniskillen Castle, I will be able to entertain you all in a more fitting manner, which you all deserve," he finished and sat down again once his four guests had been shown to their seats.

O'Donnell, however, chose not to sit and the MacSweeneys followed suit. He moved to the centre of the cabin, in front of the fire, threw back his hood and removed his rain sodden cloak, throwing it onto a stool. The rain had penetrated through it and his clothes underneath were wet. His eyes were wide and he looked around the gathering of people, acknowledging each, in turn. If he was glad to see them, which he must have been, he did not allow it show in his face, which was immobile.

"Well there is only one question, which must be answered at this gathering, and that is what you intend doing?" he demanded brusquely. "I know how you should proceed. You should join with me in my march south. We cannot disappoint the King of Spain, now that he has finally sent an army to aid us. The only question is, when will you be ready to move?"

Before O'Neill could answer, Hugh Magennis leaped to his feet, and stormed angrily.

"O'Donnell, will you not have a bit of sense and think things out? You expect us to act like simpletons and desert our lands, leaving them to the Queen's impostors whom the English have set up against us. Do you ever think of the consequences before you act?" he demanded wrathfully.

O'Neill knew that many, if not all of those present, were strongly opposed to the idea of leaving their lands and marching off to the far distant south. O'Donnell cast a scornful glance in Magennis's direction, before addressing everyone present.

"Now, the time has come when you must decide, once and for all, which side you are on. Some of you left our cause and took pardons from the English. That can be forgiven once, but never a second time," he said with iron in his voice, looking Magennis straight in the eye. "There are those among us who prefer the safe course and who are not prepared to risk anything, but risk is an imperative. It will not save you when the day of reckoning comes if you have not wagered, because not having wagered is worse than wagering and losing all. There will be no forgiveness for cowards who would not help when help was needed. You are either with us or against us. No man can serve two masters."

Magennis, bristling with anger, pointed a finger at O'Donnell. "I will have no-one call me a coward," he said in a voice, tremulous with rage. "It is not cowardly to put one's family and people before some foreigners who have foolishly chosen to land in such a remote location."

Hugh now rose to his feet, judging that proceedings were already getting out of hand. He held up his hands and spoke, "Enough."

Both men turned to look at him and a hush fell on the gathering. Hugh could feel his face flush with anger. He took a moment, as he attempted to regain his composure.

"The Devil take the two of you," he said angrily. "Isn't it bad enough that the clans cannot unite together, without we also fighting among ourselves? What sort of accursed race am I dealing with that I cannot forge it into some sort of unity? No decision has being made yet and we are gathered here to discuss our options," he said forcefully.

"I do not know about the rest of you, but I have made my decision and the men of Tirconnell and Connaught are backing me. I want the rest of you to do likewise. That is why I delayed my departure to Kinsale," O'Donnell answered.

Cuconnaught nodded sympathetically. "I can see both sides of the argument," he said gently. "What concerns me also, like The Magennis, is our own people, our womenfolk, our children and our elderly. What will the English garrisons do to them when we are far away, fighting a war many miles from home? Why, they will hunt them like wild animals through the forests, for sport. I say we should not leave our strongholds. Let the Spanish come to us or, if they are not strong enough to do so, let them send for reinforcements from Spain to aid them. You, of all people, should be the last person to leave your lands, Hugh Roe. Dowcra has three very strong garrisons along Lough Foyle, right in the middle of your domains. And Niall Garve still holds Donegal Abbey. We have heard that you have raised your siege of it, leaving him in possession. By the rood, Hugh Roe, how could you leave your country at the mercy of a man like him?"

"And, why did you raise the siege?" Magennis persisted.

"All I have done for the last few years is engage in one siege after another. If it's not the English whom I am trying to starve out, it's that hoor's son, Niall Garve. When Niall Garve heard of the Spanish landing, he said that he would never forsake his rightful monarch no matter what promises King Philip would make him. What a jest! When we have use of the heavy guns that the Spanish have brought with them, then we will see how long he can hold out against us."

O'Neill interrupted sternly. "I have learnt that the Queen has raised extra troops, which are to be sent to Dowcra and to Chichester. Imagine what they both will do with extra soldiers to call upon. If we are not here to oppose them, they will have a free rein to do as they wish."

O'Donnell's face lost some of its sneering confidence and he finally took his place at the table. The MacSweeneys sat also.

"As it is, I don't know how to defeat Niall Garve," he said wearily. "My men have no stomach for sieges and, even if we win this one, we then have three more before we remove the English garrisons from my lands. I see the best, perhaps the only chance, for victory in this war, lies with the Spanish. They would make short work of Dowcra's forts and Niall Garve would sing a different tune if a Spanish army arrived in Ulster. This is it. Our last chance. Either we stay in the North and face a slow, lingering, but sure defeat, or we can gamble on the Spanish. No doubt, we could hold out another few years, but what then? If we succeed, why the whole country will be ours, whereas if we fail, I for one might have nothing to come home to. That is the size of the wager. Nevertheless, it is one that I think we must take." O'Donnell fell silent and looked around the gathering. Everyone present turned to O'Neill. O'Donnell's gaze also alighted upon him.

O'Neill felt anger rising inside him. Immediate decisions, that is what O'Donnell always pushes for, ignoring the effort necessary to bring people with him. He looked at the eager faces turned expectantly towards him and he recognised the responsibility that he carried. He was aware that it would take a mammoth effort in diplomacy to convince the northern Chiefs present, to turn their backs upon their lands. He knew, in his heart of hearts, that O'Donnell was right.

They would have to travel south but the others present were not yet ready to commit to that course.

"I can see the merit in both sides of the argument," he said at length and heard O'Donnell snort in exasperation. He continued, ignoring him as best he could. "I agree with Maguire and Magennis that we cannot abandon our people to the mercies of the English. There is much more to be done yet before we can consider leaving our lands behind. Yet, I admit, we have a moral obligation to the Spanish who have travelled from their country at our request. Never forget that it was our appeal for aid that has brought them here. They also are wagering all in this venture. We know the revenge the English will take upon them should they fail. I was present at the massacre in Smerwick Bay and saw what happened the last foreign troops to land here."

O'Donnell could hold his peace no longer. "So, Hugh, speak plainly and to the point." he demanded impatiently.

"I have worked ceaselessly since I received the news of their arrival" Hugh answered. "There are others who can be won to our side yet. We must attack the Pale and force Mountjoy to send some of his men north to protect Dublin." O'Neill answered.

O'Donnell laughed mirthlessly. "You should know the man you are dealing with by now. When Tyrell and O'Moore burnt the Pale to the gates of Dublin last year, did he disengage from Ulster and rush to defend it? No, he let it burn and mark my words were we to burn Dublin itself, Mountjoy would not leave the Spaniards."

"We must attempt it and destroy what grain they have. Mountjoy must not be able to call on it for any supplies. There are still many more clans whom we can rouse. I agree with O'Donnell, those who are not with us are against us and an example must be made of them. Time is on our side. We must be sure that if we travel, we will be able to leave behind a force sufficient to defend our lands," O'Neill said evenly.

"How can you say time is on our side?" O'Donnell asked incredulously. "The English will continue to build up reinforcements here."

"And so must the Spanish," O'Neill answered. "Now that they have finally committed troops, they must reinforce them also."

"Only if they hold out. And how can you be sure that they will hold out without our help? You saw del Aguila's letter," O'Donnell demanded impatiently.

"Yes, but we all know of his experience in withstanding a siege. The Spaniards are in a good position. They are safe and secure within a walled town. It is the English who will bear the worst of the siege. It is a fact that during the winter the besiegers are in a much worse position than the besieged, in every respect, except for food. They will be exposed to the worst that winter weather can unleash, while the Spaniards will be living in good, dry houses, warm and sheltered, absolutely the reverse of the English whose trenches will fill with water, leaving them wet and miserable. Eventually, they will begin to die of cold, disease and exposure and their morale will weaken. Even food will be a problem for them, as the task of feeding such an army will be a mammoth one. The victuals will have to be brought in from England, which will create further problems for them. Additionally, the besiegers must be constantly on the alert, as the besieged can sally out at any time and attack them, without warning. The besieged, however, can relax until they are called upon to take part in such a sally or to repair the breaches that the enemy cannon will make, from time to time. Believe me, the Spanish are in no danger. They are the experts in resisting such a siege," Hugh said, trying to win O'Donnell to his way of thinking.

"That is true," Hovendon said, anxious to support Hugh. "Did not Sir John Norreys lose fifteen hundred men while besieging one of del Aguila's forts in Brittany, held by only two hundred Spanish? Think of how many four thousand Spanish soldiers could kill."

"And surely they would have brought sufficient provisions with them to withstand a siege?" Maguire said.

"And they've had over a month to acquire more locally," Magennis added.

"So time is on our side," O'Reilly concluded. "I think we should plan for a spring campaign. Let the English die in front of Kinsale. If we travel south, we will have to endure the same conditions as they."

O'Donnell stood up, his eyes aflame. "No," he said addressing his comments to Hugh. "I have gone along with you up until this. I have allowed time, sickness, famine, and penury take their course. The only drawback to using such weapons is that they are double-edged. They can also damage us. Let us suppose the Spanish can hold out, but who gains most from our inaction? The English. Perhaps King Philip will not reinforce his men until he sees how we second them. Why should he waste any more resources on us if we are not generous enough to aid his soldiers? The Queen's ministers are labouring through the night to raise more and more men to send here. If Dowcra and Chichester are already being reinforced, the garrisons on our borders will be brought up to full strength again and, come next Spring, we might not be able to break out to march on Kinsale. The longer we wait, the stronger the English forces in Ireland will become. Now, at this moment, we have the possibility of swelling their numbers and if we do, there is every likelihood that together we can defeat Mountjoy.

Then it will be all over for the English. The whole country will join with us and sweep them from our shores. Elizabeth will have no one here to reinforce, there will be no point in sending an army to Ireland. Two thousand men at a time would no longer be of any use. She would have to raise an army of invasion, perhaps twenty thousand strong, and they would be entering a foreign country where they could expect no help. The Spanish would further reinforce us once we had achieved that measure of success. It would be far more likely that the invading force would travel in the opposite direction, from Ireland to England. Just think of it for a minute," O'Donnell implored, looking from one of the gathered Chiefs to another.

They all avoided his gaze. He turned back to O'Neill again.

"I know, I feel it in my bones, Hugh. This is not the time for delay. Now at last, the time for action has arrived, for immediate action. Our destiny calls us, the destiny of our race and country. This is the chance that we have waited for, the chance to guarantee the survival of our country, our way of life, our religion, laws, customs and language. We cannot turn our backs on this opportunity, our descendants would never forgive us. We must respond to del Aguila's pleas and we must respond now."

O'Donnell paused for breath, flushed and breathless. O'Neill mused, considering his words and finally spoke. "Let us presume that we march tomorrow. We would have to march lightly if we were to avoid the English. We could bring no carriages or wagons, as they could not travel the paths at this time of year. Do you realise how many rivers in full flood we would have to cross? And what happens when we arrive at Kinsale? What can we achieve? We will be confronted by Mountjoy's and Carew's armies on open ground. We have never dared to fight such an army in open field before and we would be totally without the advantages that we have always sought, advantages of cover and mobility. There will be no vanishing into thin air, if the battle is not proceeding as we wish. We will be in a foreign terrain, unable even to rely upon the locals for support. It is likely that we shall have to besiege the English, so if you are already weary of sieges, prepare for more. We will be lying in the open with little to eat when our scant supplies run out. We will be far from home, without any reinforcements. My whole being shrinks from such a vista."

"Obstacles are there to be overcome," O'Donnell replied, running his hand nervously through his dishevelled hair. "Yes, there are problems but I and my men will make the march. Each man must carry his own weapons, food, powder, shot and a spare pair of brogues. Each horseman must do likewise. As for facing the English in open battle, we have prepared for that now for over five years. We knew that if we were ever to win this war, we would have to do so. Why have we drilled our men in such warfare for many years now? Why have we given our men colours and drummers and had them recognise the drum commands so that they could react as one body and face the assault of the English cavalry? We must trust that our good work will pay off. In any event, King Philip has ordered us, through del Aguila, to come south, and south we must go. I will obey his summons. Most of my forces are already assembled at Ballymote. As you see, the MacSweeneys are with me. McDermott has mobilised his men and many of the northern Connaught men have already joined with me. The rest will flock to my army as we march through the province."

O'Neill rose from his seat and approached O'Donnell. He noticed his flushed cheeks, his rapid, shallow breathing. His nerves were stretched to the limit. He was eager for action, indeed, desperate for it. Without any hope of changing his mind, Hugh urged. "Hugh Roe, all I ask of you is that you wait a little longer. There are still Chiefs whom we can win back to our cause. The Leinster men have yet to be roused. Wait another few weeks and then we will make our plans together."

O'Donnell shook his head decisively. "No, Hugh, on this occasion I must follow my own instincts. I will return to Ballymote and we will march the day after tomorrow. I hope that the rest of you will follow after me, if you cannot join with me now. I intend marching through Galway and Roscommon and will cross the Shannon at Shannon Harbour. Then we will travel through the gap between the Devil's Bit and Slieve Bloom Mountains and will wait for you at the ford on the River Suir, five miles south of Roscrea. If you do decide to march, you should take an alternative route. March through Leinster, gathering support as you travel. Then we can join together and march on Kinsale. I'll wait a week for you, no longer."

It was now O'Neill's turn to shake his head. He saw that it was useless to pursue the matter further. O'Donnell would not be delayed. He would march. Hugh knew that he would not be ready to do so for some time yet. He did not have the control over his adherents that O'Donnell seemed to possess They would have to be persuaded that it was the proper course and that their lands would be protected in their absence, no easy task, but one that he would have to accomplish.

"I will make you no promises. I cannot see myself ready to march for another two weeks, at the earliest. I will fix the twelfth of November for a conference with all my adherents at Lough Ramor, on the borders of Cavan and Meath, to decide, to decide mark you, whether we should march south or not. Perhaps, we will send a division of our army under Cormac. I am not going to prejudge the outcome of the meeting," Hugh said, honestly admitting that he had considered the possibility of sending his brother, in his stead.

O'Donnell flushed even more deeply. "I came here today, only on the understanding that it was to decide this matter. Instead, what do I find? That the decision is, once again, deferred for another fortnight. Such delay is folly. Is there no-one here who believes that we should march south immediately?" he asked impatiently, his eyes scanning the assembled Chiefs. No one answered and the three MacSweeneys rose from their seats and took up positions behind him. O'Neill went to him. He knew that the Chiefs would not be harassed into doing what they were still uncertain of and that O'Donnell's approach would lose them.

"We will make our decision on the twelfth," he said gently. "I only wish that hot blood of yours would allow you to delay your march awhile yet, but if your decision is made, I wish you good speed."

O'Neill held his hand out to his son-in-law but O'Donnell would not take it. Instead he looked deeply into O'Neill's troubled eyes.

"You had better come south, O'Neill. We have suffered too much in the past, to cast it all away now. Together we can achieve victory. On my own, the outcome is less certain. But I have delayed too long, I must be off, " he said in conclusion.

Maguire now stood up, anxious that his hospitality would not be seen to be lacking. "Take your ease Hugh Roe. Change out of your wet clothes and have something to eat. Stay overnight, it will be dark shortly and the night will be foul."

O'Donnell laughed bitterly. "There will be time for such indulgences when the English are defeated and driven from our country. I expect to see you, Maguire, at Roscrea," and then turning to the rest of the gathering, "I expect to see you all at Roscrea," he said and then departed.

Maguire followed him. "Take some fresh horses with you. One of my men will show you where they are stabled."

Hugh watched, as they stepped out into the rain. A general murmur of conversation resumed in the cabin as the Chiefs began discussing among themselves the outcome of the meeting. Hugh watched O'Donnell's retreating form, flanked and dwarfed by his three Gallowglasses. Henry Hovendon came and stood by his side.

"Well Hugh," he asked in a low voice, "where to now?"

"I am not sure, Henry," he answered wearily. "He is right on this matter but I cannot force the issue, at this time."

"You have acted wisely," Hovendon answered. "If you forced a decision here today, you would have marched without many of these present."

Maguire returned. "Well, Hugh," he said loudly. "You and the rest of my guests, will stay the night?" he asked eagerly.

O'Neill nodded. "Yes," he answered. A good night's company, followed by a sound sleep, is just what I need."

Maguire beamed. "Good. I will call on my harpers and the seanacoy and we will enjoy the night. We need some cheer."

O'Neill replied. "That we do." He would use the night to talk with each of the Chieftains in turn and win them to his way of thinking.

Chapter 23

Mountjoy, Carew and Wingfield stood listening to the Spanish ensign who, standing on the walls of Rincorran Castle, shouted down at them. When he had finished, Wingfield, proficient in Spanish after serving in Her Majesty's army on the Continent, translated for the other two men. "He offers to yield up the castle, provided the garrison is allowed retire to the town with its arms."

Wingfield waited for Mountjoy to make his decision. This was the third day that they had kept up a continuous bombardment on the castle. Three large cannons had arrived at Oyster Haven. They had used them and the guns from the pinnacle "Moon", anchored in Kinsale Bay, to attack the castle. This ship had also prevented del Aguila from sending reinforcements by water to the besieged castle. The Spanish in the town, however, had not stood idly by. They had dragged a demi-cannon outside the town's gates and had, in turn, started to bombard the English camp in an effort to draw English fire. Mountjoy, however, was not to be distracted from the matter in hand. The Spanish had also sortied on both nights but Mountjoy had his main force wisely positioned to frustrate such an attack. They had eventually managed to beat them back into the town, even though they lost many more men than the Spanish in the effort. If the castle still holds out tonight, Wingfield thought, it is certain that the Spanish will sortie in force again. Mountjoy was desperate to take the fortification and get his campaign off to a good start but, hopefully, Wingfield thought, he will not accept the ensign's offer.

"Tell him no, I will accept nothing less than a conditionless surrender," Mountjoy said coldly.

Wingfield approved of Mountjoy's decision. So far, they were making progress and nothing should be allowed jeopardise that or their reputation as a determined force. Within ten days of arriving at Kinsale, they had forced the Spanish to abandon the defensive trenches, which they had constructed in front of the town. That had allowed them advance their camp to Spital Hill, overlooking the town from where they had commenced a damaging bombardment on both it and Rincorran Castle.

He translated quickly for the Spanish ensign and withdrew speedily. It would have been folly to allow the defeated Spanish escape into Kinsale. It would give the enemy there great heart, as they would presume that the English had not the courage to force the siege. So, they would just have to prepare for the inevitable Spanish attack later in the night and be sure that they could repel it. They would not follow the enemy back to the gates of the town again tonight. They had learnt their lesson the previous night. Once they were within range of the town, the Spanish on Kinsale's walls had murderously raked them with fire, killing many of their number.

They had only agreed to the parley, which the Spanish ensign had requested, as it had given them the opportunity to go forward and take a closer look at the breach, which they had opened in the west wall of the castle.

"Well, can we force it yet?" Mountjoy asked as he looked at both Carew and Wingfield.

Both men shook their heads.

"It's too narrow," Carew said, "and our troops would have to use ladders and climb twelve feet to reach it. The defenders can quite easily concentrate their fire to protect such a small breach."

"We need to make it larger, and ideally, we should attempt to open a second one," Wingfield said. "It's a bloody business taking such a fort. Our men would have to carry the ladders to the castle, which would slow them down, then climb them to reach the collapsed wall and then scurry like ants up the fallen masonry. If we attempt it too early and lose a lot of men in the process, we run the risk of damaging the army's morale. We must give our men every opportunity of success. We must continue our artillery attack until the whole wall comes down, rendering the slope of the fallen masonry more suitable for such an assault."

"But they will mend the breach under the cover of darkness again, as they did the last two nights," Mountjoy said despondently while they trudged back to their camp. "When morning comes, we will have to start the whole process all over again."

"We could get more out of our guns," Carew said authoritatively. "I began my career in Her Majesty's forces in charge of artillery on the Continent and gained much experience in such matters. It is possible to keep the guns firing through the night."

"But how can we be sure that our aim is true?" Mountjoy asked eagerly.

"If you give me leave, I will lay the pieces myself. With my quadrant, I will take a level for all three guns and then the bombardment can be maintained at night, as well as day. I guarantee that we shall not lose any accuracy either," Carew said.

"Very well, do so," Mountjoy answered, pleased at the news. "We will see to it that the garrison will not get any sleep tonight. Tomorrow, we will force the breach."

Carew saluted and withdrew to get his sextant.

The bombardment was kept up all night. At two in the morning, the Spanish drums beat again for a parley but Mountjoy ignored them. All night the guns rang out across the bay, the sound carrying to the Spanish in the town. They sortied in force again and this time the fighting was even fiercer than before. Hand to hand combat swept north and south alternatively, as first one side and then the other gained the advantage. The Spanish managed to get within a hundred paces of the guns, but Mountjoy had concentrated his main force there in order to guarantee that the weapons would remain safe. The Spanish then turned suddenly and made for the castle, nearly reaching it before they were driven back. Some of its garrison, however, escaped down the rocks behind it and, joining their countrymen, they were brought safely back to the town.

As dawn broke, Mountjoy was pleased to see that the breach was still open and, indeed, had been widened. The remaining Spanish again beat the drum for a parley but he continued to ignore it. The rain started to fall, making it more difficult for the gunners to continue their work, but by covering the weapons and powder from the downpour and by priming them carefully, they managed to keep them firing. All morning they kept their onslaught up until Mountjoy's ears were ringing from the noise. Then at two-o clock in the afternoon, they heard the Spanish drums, once again, beating a request for parley.

"Well," Mountjoy said, "Let us get a closer look at the breach. I think the time might have come for decisive action."

Wingfield nodded and gave the orders for the guns to cease. Then he, Carew and Mountjoy walked out towards the castle. Again, they found themselves underneath its walls and the same ensign appeared above them. There were fewer men with him this time.

The ensign addressed them and when he finished, Wingfield translated once again. "He offers to yield the castle and their arms, provided they are allowed retire within the shelter of the town's walls."

Mountjoy shook his head. "They are in a weaker position than yesterday. There are not as many of them and the breach is larger. We could storm it now with a reasonable expectation of success. Tell him that only an unconditional surrender will stay us from attacking the fort and killing everyone inside. If they chose to surrender, mind that you give them no guarantee of their lives. I do not want my hands tied on this matter."

Wingfield translated and the ensign shook his head, angrily replying to Wingfield who turned to the other two men. "He swears that he would rather be buried in the ruins, than surrender on such terms," Wingfield translated.

"We must see that his wish is fulfilled," Carew said darkly.

"Let us return and prepare the assault," Mountjoy said and both he and Carew turned to leave.

"Wait," Wingfield said as he watched a disturbance on the castle's battlements. Angry voices carried down to him and he was surprised to see that two of the garrison had taken hold of the ensign and were holding him over the breach.

"What is going on?" Mountjoy asked.

Wingfield laughed. "The garrison does not possess the courage of the ensign and they say that they will throw him from the breach, if he does not yield to us."

They saw the man's captors release him and, after smoothing his clothes, he came to the edge of the wall and called out to them. Wingfield explained. "He is now prepared to yield the castle provided that he is allowed to keep his sword."

Mountjoy nodded. "That will save lives. Tell him we accept but that they must leave the castle immediately. Sir Thomas, send for men to garrison it."

Wingfield saluted and went to carry out his task.

"We should hang the lot of them in front of the town," Carew said bitterly. "Invaders should not be allowed live."

"That would only strengthen the resolve of the remaining Spanish in resisting us, if they knew that they would receive no mercy from us. When they have all surrendered, then we shall be free to deal with them as we see fit," Mountjoy answered.

Minutes later, the gates of the castle opened and the Spanish garrison marched out, their drums beating funereally, with their colours, the ragged red cross of St. Andrew and Burgundy, dipped. The ensign marched up to Mountjoy and bowed low. He stood abjectly before him as his men deposited their weapons at his feet.

"Once they have handed over their weapons, take them away and make them secure," Mountjoy said to Captain Cooper, ignoring the ensign. "See to it that these prisoners are transported to Cork and jailed there. How many of them are there?" he asked Sergeant Smith who was busy counting them.

"Sixty-five, my Lord," he answered, "but look at this one, if he's Spanish, then I'm a Moor."

Smith pulled one of the prisoners from the rear of the Spanish column. He was dressed in similar fashion to the other musketeers. He wore a plumed morion, a peascod doublet, trunk hose and canions. Around his neck he had tied a scarf over his small collar but what had caught Smith's attention was the bright, red hair and pale skin, which stood out from the sallow skins and dark hair of the rest of the prisoners. The prisoner was armed with the standard Spanish musket, which Smith quickly took from him. He then pointed to the bandoleer, which the prisoner wore over his right shoulder that carried the main charges for his musket in wooden boxes, which hung from it.

"Take it off," he ordered and the prisoner quickly removed it. Smith took the bandoleer and then he quickly plucked the small flask of priming powder from the prisoner's waist.

"An Irish rebel, My Lord," Smith said.

"Separate him out," Mountjoy ordered.

Smith and two other English soldiers grabbed the Irishman and pulled him from the ranks of the other prisoners. Immediately, the Spanish ensign began protesting vehemently. Mountjoy held up his hand and the Spaniard fell silent. Wingfield translated. "He says that the man that you have separated from the rest is a soldier in the Spanish army, like all the others, and deserves to be treated in the same fashion as the rest of them. He calls him Don Dermuchio."

"Bring him here," Mountjoy ordered. "Ask him his real name."

One of the Irish born soldiers in his army addressed the prisoner in Gaelic and translated his answer. "He says he is Dermot McCarthy from West Cork, a musketeer in the Spanish army."

"Take him and hang him in full view of the town," Mountjoy ordered. "He is in rebellion against his lawful Queen, a crime that cannot be ignored. His crime is greater than that of the others. At least, the Spanish soldiers are remaining loyal to their lawful ruler. We must make an example of any Irish rebel who falls into our hands, as a warning to others of what will happen to them, should they be tempted to join with the Spanish. The townspeople of Kinsale must see what their fate will be if they openly support the invaders."

Half an hour later, two divisions of the English army were drawn up just outside of the musket range of the town's defenders. The carpenters had quickly assembled a makeshift gallows, consisting of two vertical and one horizontal planks, from which a rope, ending in a noose, swung in the strong, rain sodden wind. The prisoners were marched out to the open ground in the middle of the two divisions. The captured Spanish flags were waved tauntingly by some of the English army and a great cheer of victory rose from their assembled ranks. McCarthy was then dragged forward, his hands bound behind his back. The drummers began the death roll and Carew, mounted on his horse, addressed the waiting soldiers.

"This is what is in store for all Irish rebels. Such base ingratitude to their lawful, sacred Queen, deserves no less."

"That heretic, cursed Queen is not mine ..." MacCarthy shouted but he was cut off in mid sentence by one of his guards who rammed the hilt of his sword into his stomach, causing him to collapse, doubled over in pain.

The drummers took up the death roll again and two of the soldiers seized McCarthy. Between them, they lifted his kicking, squirming body up to the noose. A third soldier quickly slipped it over his head and then they released him. His curses were abruptly cut short and Carew watched his encounter with death. As a sizeable portion of his army consisted of Irish born soldiers, it was important that they knew the consequences of desertion. He never fully trusted them, never knowing when they might decide to head for home or worse still, desert to the enemy.

He saw a messenger ride up, head straight for Mountjoy and hand him a dispatch. He watched Mountjoy read it, trying to decode from his face if there were good or bad tidings. Mountjoy finished reading and put the dispatch away. Carew tried to catch his eye but Mountjoy chose to look steadfastly at McCarthy who was in the final stages of his horrible ordeal. Finally his struggles were over and one of the captains hurried to Carew.

"Will we cut him down?" he asked.

"No, leave him up as a warning," he answered. "Dismiss the men."

The captain hastened to carry out his orders and Carew went to join Mountjoy. When he reached him, he found that Wingfield was already with him.

"What news?" he asked anxiously.

"We will discuss it in my tent," Mountjoy answered as he turned and marched briskly towards it.

Carew threw Wingfield a quizzical look, raising his eyebrows, but Wingfield just shrugged his shoulders. They continued in silence until they reached the sanctuary of the tent.

Mountjoy turned to them. "O'Donnell is on the march south. It has been confirmed," he said, obviously shaken. He addressed Wingfield. "I thought you guaranteed me that he would not dare undertake such a journey," he said accusingly.

Wingfield was at a loss for words. "I am surprised ..." he began, before breaking off.

"What concerns me even more is that O'Neill will, most likely, join him," Mountjoy said angrily.

"That does not follow," Carew interrupted. "O'Donnell was always fanatical and he shows it, once again, by abandoning his people and country. O'Neill is a far shrewder man, he will not make such a mistake."

"I can no longer be sure of that," Mountjoy said. "Both of you assured me that neither of them would march, You were wrong once, you could be again. O'Donnell's arrival in Munster could alter everything. If the Munster Irish join with him, then we have lost this war."

"They will not," Carew said. "I have beaten the fight out of them."

"Even if they do not and O'Donnell and his army arrive at Kinsale, all will be altered here and altered for the worse" Mountjoy said impatiently.

"We can reinforce the north side of our camp, as we have done with the south side," Wingfield said.

"Yes," Mountjoy answered. "I have already decided to do that, but I do not want O'Donnell reaching Kinsale. I do not even want him entering Munster. I have decided that you both must go north and destroy his army. I will give you two thousand-foot and three hundred and twenty horse. That will leave me enough men to continue the siege here and you can pick up reinforcements on your march north."

"We should not split our forces," Carew said anxiously. "If the Spanish learn of such a move, they will attack again and with more vigour. You have seen what they can do already and they only used five hundred of their men in the sortie last night."

"Yes, I have seen it and that is why they must not be reinforced. We must keep the Irish and the Spanish apart, at all costs. Let me worry about the Spanish, you take care of O'Donnell," Mountjoy said forcibly.

"When I took my present position with your army, you said that I could speak freely, whenever I felt the need," Wingfield said, "and I feel the need now. I am in agreement with Sir George. The Irish have always proven too quick-footed for the Royal troops. I can see the same thing happening again. I think it would be foolish to split your forces on, what more than likely will be, a wasted effort."

"Then it is time that we remedied that shortcoming in our army," Mountjoy answered decisively. "Sir George is well acquainted with the country. You both have much experience of Irish warfare. There has never been greater need for success and I have faith in the two of you. My mind is made up. You must get your forces together and march to intercept O'Donnell. I want you on the march today."

Carew and Wingfield nodded.

"I will go and prepare the foot," Carew said with a bow. "Sir Thomas, you prepare the horse."

Wingfield bowed. "Yes, Sir George."

Mountjoy watched them as they left his tent. He knew that he was acting correctly in ordering them north. So much depended upon it. But he would have to do something to take his mind off them, otherwise, he would not rest, wondering what had become of them and whether or not they were successful. He would concentrate on taking Castle Park, he decided. That would further weaken the Spanish. But first, he must go and fortify the north side of his camp.

There was little sleep to be had that night for either the English soldiers or their officers. The night was cold, bitter cold, the sky totally clear, littered with a multitude of stars which cast an eerie glow on the surrounding countryside. Carew huddled by the large campfire, which burned fiercely in front of him. The rains had finally ceased but the weather had changed from what had been mild and wet to one of extreme cold and dryness. He looked around at the trees and saw that the heavy frost had blanketed them in a veil of white rime. This weather was unusual, he thought. Normally such harsh conditions do not set in until January or February. As a consequence of the numbing cold, which penetrated deep into his joints, it had been impossible for him to sleep in his tent and, so he had risen and joined his men around one of the campfires.

In spite of the misery in which he found himself, he smiled at the thought of O'Donnell, a bare mile away, stalled many miles from home and from his ultimate destination, Kinsale. They had learned that he was marching through Connaught, attacking those in that province that remained loyal to the English cause, men like Clanrickard and Thomond, whose lands he wasted. They also knew that O'Donnell would reach the River Suir and would have to choose to continue south either on its western or eastern bank. Whichever side he picked, Carew knew that O'Donnell would be forced by the tributaries to the east and the bogs and Slieve Feilim Mountains to his west, to pass through Holycross. That was one advantage to all the rain that they had had over the last few months, he thought. The rivers would be impossible to ford and the bogs and mountains to his west had become an impassable quagmire.

His reasoning had proven accurate and two days previously, his scouts had made contact with those of O'Donnell. He had then fallen back to his present position, which he had chosen carefully for its ease of defence.

He was confident of victory. If O'Donnell wished to advance any further south, he would have to defeat his army and that, he would never do. The English army would, for once, be on the defensive. It was O'Donnell who would have to advance and take Carew's position. Carew thought that would be impossible for him as he had just been reinforced by newly arrived troops from England under the command of Sir Christopher St. Lawerence. Carew's army was now at least equal in number to O'Donnell's. Even better, O'Donnell was caught in an impossible situation. If he retreated he would be caught between Carew's forces and the combined forces of Clanricarde and Thomond, which Carew had summoned. If he remained where he was, he would still, in a matter of days, be caught in the same vice. Carew was content to sit and wait. For once, time was on his side and he was confident of his army. His own troops were experienced and seasoned. They would smash the rebels who would have no familiar countryside in which to vanish, no woods and bogs from which they could shoot his men in craven fashion. He closed his eyes and tried to get some sleep, He allowed his mind settle on the reassuring thought that now, at long last, O'Donnell would pay for all his treachery.

He found it impossible to slumber, however, as his knee joints were paining him and his back was numb with cold. He rose and stretched himself wearily. He moved closer to the fire, turning his back to it, allowing the heat penetrate the heavy cloak, which he wore and which had become damp from the dew. Most of his men were gathered around the campfires and he noticed how some of them slept with their arms still wrapped around their weapons, as if for reassurance. Three men who were sitting at the next fire to his, nodded a greeting, which he did not bother acknowledging. Their task was to keep the fires stoked so that they would burn fiercely throughout the freezing night. They had to stay awake until they were relieved. Their duty was as important as that of the sentries on the outskirts of the camp. He knew that the Irish would not surprise them. He had plenty of time to organise hiding places for his sentries before the arrival of the enemy and some of them were even lodged high up in the surrounding trees, keeping an eye out for any Irish that might be heading their way.

He discerned a movement at the edge of the camp, in the gloom of the trees, just outside the rim of light thrown by the campfires. He grew tense. It was probably an animal or one of his sentries, he thought, squinting into the darkness. He then saw a form take shape and his hand rested on his sword's hilt as he considered calling out an alarm. Careful, he said to himself, the last thing you want is to appear nervous in front of the men, and then was relieved to see that it was Wingfield.

Wingfield walked briskly over to him. "Good, you're awake," he said quietly. "There's something amiss and I have a bad feeling about it."

Carew felt a sudden knot of apprehension in the pit of his stomach. He had learned by now that Wingfield's judgement was uncannily accurate.

"What is it?" he asked anxiously, afraid that the Irish might be on the march to attack them.

"I went forward to the top of the hill to look at the Irish camp in the distance. It gives me a great sense of contentment to see them so near and to know that we have out guessed them for once," Wingfield replied.

"That we have," Carew said. "So what concerns you now?"

"Their campfires," Wingfield answered simply. "I could not sleep, no more than yourself. I've been up on that hill for the last hour keeping one of the sentries company. I brought some whiskey with me and we stood under a tree looking across at the fires, envying them the heat, while we froze with nothing but the whiskey to warm us."

"Let them enjoy their heat for now. Before long, we will be sending them to a much warmer place, God willing," Carew said with relish.

"But that's just it," Wingfield said earnestly. "They weren't enjoying the heat or, at least, that's how it appears. As we were watching, the sentry, a man from Devon, said to me, 'The Irish are too lazy to keep their fires stoked.' I looked and saw that he was right. Their fires were dying down, not one of them, but all of them, at the same time and at the same rate."

"Do you think that they are on the march to attack us?" Carew asked anxiously.

"I do not know. If they are, they should be here by now. I sent some of our sentries further forward and I warned them to be alert. The Irish could also be retreating, which is more likely," Wingfield suggested.

"Or they could be trying to make us think that, so that we would rush after them and fall straight into an ambush prepared for us," Carew said pensively as he weighed up the different options.

"There's only one way to find out. That is to go forward and see. I returned to warn you, just in case they are approaching, and now I'm going forward to find out for myself," Wingfield said decisively. "All I need are Ensign Cooper and Sergeant Smith."

He marched over to one of the campfires and kicked the boots of one of the sleeping men. The man woke with a start and automatically grabbed his musket, which lay by his side. He stared, wide eyed at Wingfield, then recognised him, and smiled, baring a mouthful of black, rotten teeth. He was a man in his late thirties but he could be mistaken for a man fifteen years older, small and lean, but Wingfield knew, from experience, that he had more stamina and strength in him than many a man twice his height and weight.

"Are the bastards attacking?" he asked hopefully.

"I don't think so," Wingfield answered. "Go wake Sergeant Smith," he ordered, "we three have some scouting to do."

"Four of us," Carew said, as he joined the two men.

Ensign Cooper saluted and hurried away to do as he was bid. Wingfield turned to Carew. "You should stay here," he suggested. "We do not know what might happen out there and the army needs its leader."

Carew shook his head. He was curious and he definitely would not sleep now. He would find it much more difficult to remain behind while the others went forward. He was confident that he could look after himself, having always led a charmed existence. What was it Essex had said about him? 'The Devil looks after his own.' He saw Wingfield's disapproving countenance but decided to ignore it. That was one of the privileges of command.

"I'll wake Sir Lawerence and acquaint him with our plan," Carew said. "He can take over command while I'm absent. Meet me here in five minutes. Bring your pistols and see that the others bring cavaliers. The muskets that they are so fond of, are too heavy and awkward for this type of work."

Twenty minutes later, the four men were struggling up the hill, which blocked their view of the Irish camp. The hard frost had transformed the ground conditions and they slipped and slid as they attempted to reach the summit, sometimes reduced to scrambling along on their hands and knees. Yet, they made little noise, even Carew, despite his girth and age, who managed to move as lightly as the others did. When they reached the top, they stopped, breathless from the effort. The sentry from Devon stepped out from the shadows.

"Sir Thomas," he said in a hushed tone. "Did you bring any more whiskey?" he asked optimistically.

"Drinking on duty is a hanging offence," Carew said angrily. He resented Wingfield's familiarity with the men but he had to admit that they were very attached to him and would probably do more for him in an emergency, than they would do for himself. Nevertheless, he preferred that his soldiers should fear him rather than like him. It was the natural order of things.

"Yes, Sir," the sentry said smartly as he snapped to attention and saluted Carew, shocked to see him so far forward.

"Anything to report?" Wingfield asked.

"No, nothing, Sir," the scout replied.

"Very well," Wingfield answered. "Get back to your post. We are going to go forward to see for ourselves. Keep your eyes open."

"Yes, Sir," he answered enthusiastically, before disappearing hurriedly back into the gloom.

The men turned to look in the direction of the Irish camp. The campfires were now mere dull, red glows that were barely discernible on the distant plain.

"They're much dimmer than earlier," Wingfield said as he turned to Carew. "I'm positive that there's something amiss."

"We will discover soon enough," Carew answered as he set off down the other side of the hill.

Though the camps were only a mile apart, it took the four men nearly an hour to cover the distance in the dark, slippery conditions. They had to be constantly alert for any of the enemy who might be lurking unseen behind any tree or bush. As they approached the site, they moved more slowly and carefully, climbing the small incline, behind which the camp was located. They crept on their stomachs until they reached the crest and looked into the camp.

"Where have they gone?" Carew asked, as he scanned it for any sign of life. All he saw were the dying embers of the campfires, which glowed dimly in the darkness. He stood up and walked briskly into the camp.

Wingfield and the other two men followed him and Smith and Cooper went to opposite ends of the camp, searching for tracks that might help explain the mystery.

"We should get back to the army," Carew said angrily as he kicked at one of the dying fires, sending vermilion embers and sparks across the frozen whiteness of the grass. "They've obviously withdrawn. We must rouse the camp and follow them immediately."

"We must make sure that they have withdrawn," Wingfield said as he walked briskly towards the camp's western side.

"What else could they have done," Carew asked impatiently, "vanished into thin air?"

A disembodied voice hailed them. They approached the western edge of the camp where Smith was already searching the ground with the aid of star and moonlight. They looked in his direction and were amazed to see him walk out onto the boggy land, which rose gently towards the Sliabh Feilim Mountains. He strode across it, like a man walking on water, the pools beneath his feet, reflecting the stars and moon above.

"How does he do it?" Carew asked perplexed and slightly in awe. "Is this place bewitched?"

"The frost," Wingfield answered, suddenly aware of the ruse behind the disappearance of the Irish. "Don't you see? It's been a bitterly cold night, one of the worst I have ever experienced. It has frozen the bogs and made them passable," he said as he hurried to join Smith.

"But it cannot be so!" Carew said, incapable of believing that the Irish army might have eluded them. "Their horses, their wagons, it would not be possible."

"You know the Irish can travel lightly when they wish and they have not brought any wagons with them," he said. He had reached the edge of the bog and hesitantly placed a foot on the frozen ground. The ice under his foot crunched but it did not yield.

"Over here," Smith shouted and beckoned to him.

Wingfield waited no longer but trusted both his feet to the frozen bog and walked swiftly over to Smith. As he walked on its surface, he was awed at nature's power that could, in such a short space of time, so totally transform the ground's condition. He reached Smith who pointed down excitedly. "See, they went this way," he said.

Wingfield looked at the ground. There was a strip of land twenty feet wide, which was marked by the hooves of horses and he could also make out the imprints of the brogues, which the Irish soldiers wore. He looked towards the Slieve Pheilim Mountains in the distance and, as far as he could make out, the track made in a straight line for it. He looked again at the depressions that the horses' hooves had created. They had only sunk a few inches into the bog and they must have been fully laden with stores.

"They've gone over the mountains," Smith said needlessly.

Carew joined them and looked in the direction of the distant uplands. "In the dark?" he asked incredulously.

"Yes," Wingfield answered. "They must have set the campfires and left immediately afterwards. They have a good head start on us," he said, scanning the distant countryside in an effort to get a glimpse of them, but could see nothing.

"Their escape is as miraculous as that of the Jews when the Lord parted the waters," Smith said in wonder.

"I have no doubt that O'Donnell is in league with the Devil rather than the Lord," Carew responded irefully.

"We might yet catch him," Wingfield said without any great conviction. "O'Donnell had to climb the mountains and then come down the other side. It is worth the effort to pursue him."

"How?" Carew asked. "By the time we rouse the army and have them march back here, the Irish will be even further gone. It is probably too late already," he added despondently.

"O'Donnell aims to travel through Limerick on his way south. To do so, he will have to cross the Mulkear River at Cappamore. There is still a chance that we might reach it before him. We will have the easier route. He will have the mountains to contend with and will not expect to be discovered before morning. His men are bound to tire during the night and will need rest. If we rouse the camp and march through the night, we should make Cappamore before morning.

Imagine his surprise if we reach it before him," Wingfield said eagerly, anxious to win Carew to his way of thinking.

"You're right," Carew said. "Let us attempt it. We too can march lightly. Leave our camp unstruck and have the men carry their weapons only. Just think of the glory, should we manage to catch him. Come, let us hasten back to the camp."

Carew turned and strode purposely back the way he had come. Wingfield, Smith and Cooper followed after him.

"The men will dislike being roused at this hour," Cooper said to Wingfield.

"That is of no consequence," Wingfield answered abruptly. "You two must see to it that the orders are passed on. I want the men ready to march within ten minutes of our return. Speed will be essential."

He saw Cooper cast him a doubtful glance but he answered without hesitation. "Yes, Sir, ten minutes it will be, Sir."

Wingfield nodded and hastened his step so that he might catch up with Carew who was already disappearing into the trees on the edge of the camp.

Chapter 24

"After an overnight, forced march, we reached Cappamore at eleven o'clock the following morning," Carew said, "but there was no sight of O'Donnell. He had passed through it earlier that morning and continued marching. I was told that he had already reached Croom, a further twenty miles into Limerick."

Mountjoy did not comment but looked into the distance, deep in thought.

"It is the greatest feat of marching of which I ever heard," Carew continued, "over forty miles in a single advance, in bad country! And we did not hear of any stragglers from his army, which has been estimated at over three thousand."

Carew paused again but Mountjoy remained pensive, seemingly unaware of the latter's words. Carew looked at Wingfield for support.

"We decided to march back here with all possible haste," Wingfield said, "as we were anxious that the Irish army should not reach Kinsale before us."

Mountjoy started, as if coming out of a trance. "Well, there is nothing that we can do about it now," he said resignedly. "It is good to have you safely back with us."

"And how fared you in our absence?" Carew asked.

"We managed," Mountjoy said. "Del Aguila learned of your departure and sallied out but, luckily, he was not prepared to risk a general engagement and, by concentrating our forces, he never realised how weakened our position was. Fortunately, I received further reinforcements soon after your departure. Two thousand men who had been levied in Bristol, arrived from Waterford, where they disembarked."

"And we presume that it is our fleet that is riding in the harbour. We saw the lights bobbing in the distance, as we rode into the camp," Carew said.

"Yes, it is under the leadership of Sir Richard Levison who brought another two thousand men with him," Mountjoy answered.

"Thank God for its safe arrival," Wingfield said with feeling. "We can now be certain that the Spaniards will not receive any reinforcements or supplies by sea. Is it a strong force?"

Mountjoy nodded. "The Spanish will need a formidable Armada to win back control of the harbour. The Warspite, Garland, Defiance, Swiftsure, Crane and Merlyn, together with several smaller ships, will guarantee our control of the inlet. I look forward to the day when the

Spanish attempt to gain entry to it."

"We noticed too that our cannons are firing on the town from Castle Park. It was well to gain control of such a position," Wingfield said.

"It was not a very strong position," Mountjoy replied. "Once the fleet arrived, I decided that the time was right to attack it. For six days we bombarded it from land and sea. The Spanish replied with repeated sallies from the town. During one of those sallies, they managed to cut their way through our men and reach the castle, taking off most of the garrison. The following day, the fort surrendered, but there were only sixteen fit men left inside. So, on the same night, we both experienced victory and loss, I over del Aguila, you to O'Donnell."

Carew bristled at the comment. "I would not call it a loss," he said in pique. "He ran away from us. Let me meet O'Donnell in open battle and I will give you another victory."

"The gain of Castle Park will facilitate the bombardment of the town, as our ships can now draw close to it," Wingfield said in an effort to defuse the tension that he felt building between both men. He knew that Carew could not abide criticism.

"Yes, we have kept it under a sustained barrage since then," Mountjoy answered. "We had to allow the townspeople to pass from it. Del Aguila had appealed, that for their own protection, they be allowed leave."

Carew, still stung by Mountjoy's comment, reacted testily. "You should not have done so," he said. "The Spanish would have had to keep them fed and that would have depleted their food supplies. We owe the townspeople nothing. They opened the gates to the Spanish and provided them with ready billets."

"You must not forget that the Queen's garrison, put there to defend them, ran away without firing a shot. What were the townspeople to do? They are not soldiers. What choice had they? I refused his request but he turned them out the gate, nonetheless. I could not shoot the Queen's subjects in cold blood. I decided to retaliate as best I could. I commissioned four more large cannon, which Leviston had brought with him and adding them to the demicannon, which have been bombarding the town from the east. I mounted three other culverins in Castle Park and with those and the ships in the harbour, I have kept up an incessant attack on the town."

"And is there any sign of a weakening of their resolve?" Wingfield asked hopefully.

"Unfortunately not," Mountjoy replied. "Earlier today, I sent a trumpeter to summon the town to surrender. Don Juan, himself, answered the call. He said that he held the town first for Christ, second for the King of Spain and would defend it contra tutti. His soldiers are in no way disheartened either. They stood on the wall, jeering and swearing at us. I am afraid that they have a lot of fight left in them yet."

Carew shook his head. "So, what do we do?" he asked. "O'Donnell is out there, somewhere close by. I fully expected to find him here before me. And what of O'Neill? Is there any news of him?"

Mountjoy nodded gravely. "There, the news is not good. He is also on the march. Our last reports place him in the midlands. He is still trying to win as many as he can to his side. He, too, is carrying out his share of destruction, razing the property of those who will not join with him, which, the Lord be praised, are many."

"These are indeed ill tidings," Carew said, attempting to come to terms with the fact that he had, once again, been wrong in his judgement of O'Neill.

"There is, however, some good news on the northern front," Mountjoy added. "For once, the Queen and her advisers are listening to our needs and supplying us with our requests. We are the centre of their thinking at the moment. Men have arrived from England to reinforce the northern forts and they are at full strength once again. Chichester will see to it that Tyrone burns in O'Neill's absence and Niall Garve has proved invaluable since he has joined our cause. He has done what we could not do for the last eight years. He has taken Ballyshannon."

Carew laughed outright in delight. "At long last, the gate to Ulster from Connaught is ours! O'Donnell will be furious. We can lock him out now. He will not be able to return home."

"It is good news and we also have some that we omitted to tell you," Wingfield said. "We have brought some reinforcements, Lord Clanrickarde and his men, but more importantly, Donough O'Brien, Earl of Thomond. He has brought one thousand-foot and a hundred horse. That he is a descendant of Brian Boru, gives our cause greater weight. It signals to the rest of the Munster Irish that they should join with us, rather than with the Ulster warlords. It makes this a civil war rather than the war of liberation, which O'Neill tries to paint it."

"So, what is our present muster?" Carew asked.

"Twelve thousand foot and nine hundred horse," he answered. "So, the question now is, what do we do? We know that the Spanish have somewhere between three and a half and four thousand men in Kinsale. That is a considerable number, especially when they have the protection of a town's walls to hide behind. It would be an exceedingly bloody business to storm it."

Carew nodded. "I must agree with you but what other choice do we have? O'Neill and O'Donnell will bring at least another five thousand men with them. If they are successful in gaining support in the countryside, there is no limit to the number with which, they might ultimately come. There is also the possibility that more Spanish soldiers could arrive. King Philip is not going to allow his army to go unaided. It would be an unbearable slight to Spanish prestige. The longer we wait, the more dangerous the situation becomes. We must hasten to finish this business."

"I must agree with Sir George," Wingfield said.

Mountjoy, once again, stared into the distance. Carew and Wingfield watched him intently. Finally, he took stock of both men. "Unfortunately, I see no other option either. We simply cannot afford the time it will take to starve them out. Time is of the essence. We must discourage the King of Spain from sending any more men to Ireland, and the only way we can achieve that is by forcing the Spanish in Kinsale to surrender or to annihilate them. I have moved some of our artillery and trained it on the western gate and I have been battering it all day. Just as dark was falling, a breach was noticed to the right of it. We are continuing our bombardment and I have a company of shot who are endeavouring to halt the Spanish that are working continuously in an effort to repair it. Come daylight, if it seems possible to force the breach, we will attempt it."

"I request your permission to lead the attack," Wingfield asked.

"No, I cannot accede to that," Mountjoy replied. "It will be a bloody business and I cannot afford to lose you. Sir John Barkley will lead the attack and the newly arrived recruits from England will be his force. We will follow them up with more experienced troops."

"Good," Carew said and yawned. "We have made our decision. And now, if you do not mind, I will attempt to get something to eat and get some sleep. What I wouldn't do for a nice warm bed and a willing wench, even an Irish one!" he said with a laugh.

"Yes, let the two of you get some rest," Mountjoy agreed.

"And so should you. We did not expect to see you still awake at this time," Wingfield observed.

Mountjoy returned. "Sleep eludes me. My mind is filled with endless questions and possibilities. I do not feel as if I shall ever need sleep again."

"When this is all over and the Spanish are defeated, you will sleep like a babe," Wingfield replied.

"If you had been on the march with us, you'd have no problem sleeping tonight," Carew said as he made for the door of Mountjoy's hut. "Until tomorrow then, Sir Charles."

"Good night, Sir Charles," Wingfield added, before also withdrawing.

Mountjoy watched them leave. He had found himself isolated in their absence, there being no one else whom he could consult. A wave of gratitude swept over him for their safe return.

Bread, cold meat and a pitcher of wine had been distributed to the Spanish soldiers, but most men found the food difficult to swallow and so contented themselves with the wine. As the English troops came closer, their drums becoming louder, the wine was hurriedly downed and the food was placed carefully on the ground beside their musket rests.

A shell passed over the heads of the defenders on the wall, landing well behind them in the town. Don Pedro Morejón, the officer-in-charge of the detachment on the walls, looked back into the town where Spanish soldiers were busy extinguishing some fires that had broken out as a result of the bombardment, which had been at its fiercest for the last twenty four hours. They seemed to be getting the better of the flames, he noticed with relief. His men would just have to concentrate on repulsing the vast English column that was marching ever closer to the town.

He looked down at the two hundred Spanish soldiers who manned the trench, dug outside the town, in front of the breach. The breach itself had been protected by the construction of an earthen embankment. It was up to the men below and his men on the walls to halt the English before they could reach it. If they failed, a thousand Spanish soldiers in full armour waited in the protection of the streets below him, ready to repulse any English soldiers who made it over the earthen bank. They would charge into the advancing English soldiers, driving them from the town. Hopefully, it would not come to that, he thought. Such hand to hand fighting was dangerous and disorganised and to be avoided by the defenders of a breach, at all costs.

The musketeer, Navarra, for the twentieth time, lifted the pan lid to check that his musket was primed. Morejón shouted angrily at him, "Keep your match away from the priming."

It was the most basic of mistakes, one that the drillmaster always warned against. A soldier should never hold his burning match in the same hand as he holds his musket, a stray spark could easily set off the priming and fire the weapon accidentally. It was a sign of Navarra's nervousness. This was to be his first battle.

By now, the English drums sounded clearly throughout the whole town, punctuated only by the fire of their big guns. Between the rattled passages of drumbeats, there was a pause filled by thousands of voices, "For the Queen."

Morejón saw Navarra shiver and took pity on him. "They're only words," he said dismissively. "We will show them who is master when the fighting commences." He looked at the column, a great mass of men, which advanced implacably over the sodden green fields. It seemed to be invincible, over two thousand men, marching in perfect formation, all making for the town. On the distant hills, he could see more drawn up, no doubt, waiting to see how the first column would fare. Morejón knew that formations were designed to contain half-trained troops. Such troops could be intimidated into defeat. English skirmishers were deploying in the fields in front of the main advancing body of men and one of them shot a Spaniard through the temple, in the trench below them. A musket cracked beside him and he saw the Englishman fall under the cloud of his own musket smoke. He turned and saw Navarra grinning happily. He had killed his first Englishman.

"Well done," Morejón said, "now you'd better reload. There are many more upon whom you can practise your aim." He watched and waited until the enemy was less than one hundred paces away, then filling his lungs, he shouted. "Musketeers! Fire!"

The soldiers, below him in the trenches, fired in unison with those on the walls, over seven hundred muskets spitting fire and death simultaneously.

Almost a hundred men in the leading ranks of the English column keeled over. Immediately and without hesitation, the column stepped over the bodies. A slow ripple seemed to move along it, as the succeeding ranks negotiated the dead and wounded.

The musketeers concentrated on reloading, working with fast, practised hands, ramming ball, wad and powder down the barrels. The powder for the main charge came from the wooden, bottle-shaped containers, which hung suspended from the bandoleers, around their shoulders. Each bottle contained exactly the right amount of powder for one shot, doing away with the possibility of overcharging the barrel, which would cause it to explode or, undercharging the weapon, which would cause the bullet to fall short. This was a coarser powder than what they used for priming, and they poured it down the barrels of their guns. Next, came the ball and wadding and they rammed all three home with their metal ramrods. Then they took the finer powder from a flask at their waists and this, they carefully placed on the priming pan.

When Morejón had completed reloading his musket he looked around at his men. Most of them were replacing their muskets on their rests. He waited a moment, then shouted again. "Fire!"

Another wave of musket balls cut huge swathes in the English ranks. The line shuddered and paused for a moment, but kept advancing. Once again, he ordered his men to reload. He saw one of them, hit by a skirmisher's musket ball, spin backwards, totter on the edge of the battlements and then fall in a bloodied mass onto the cobblestone street behind him. Next, he saw the skirmisher take a musket ball right between the eyes and fall backwards.

"Fire!" he shouted again as the shells flew over their heads into the town. Morejón took careful aim at an English officer on a horse, barely fifty yards away, who was urging his men onwards. He fired and saw the officer slump forward in his saddle and then slowly slide off the horse's back. The horse, frightened by the smell of blood, turned and galloped towards the column's rear, dragging its dead master after it.

The musketeers, knowing that victory depended on the speed of their labour, worked rapidly and faultlessly. Musket balls ripped into the enemy but still the formation advanced towards the town. Morejón was amazed at the amount of punishment that it could take. The shape of the attack was now becoming clear to him. At the front of the column, the English had put raw recruits, men whose loss would not weaken their army too severely. They were being propelled to slaughter by the men behind them who looked older and more experienced. Unless the defenders could destroy the remnants of those conscripts and get to the men behind, they would not halt the advance. The veterans behind carried the ladders that would be needed to scale the earthen banks. Morejón gave two shrill blows of his whistle and the gates of the town were thrown open. Three demiculverins were lined up, pointing out at the advancing enemy.

"Fire!" he shouted and the large guns spouted fire, cutting three large paths through the advancing men. He saw the column falter, a bare twenty paces from the trench below him, from where the Spanish soldiers still fought on relentlessly. He had held the big guns back until the last moment and now he wondered if he had waited too long.

"Fire!" he shouted again at his musketeers and he saw the Englishman whom he had aimed at, spin completely around, as his musket ball caught him on the side of the face. Another fusillade erupted from the three large guns and the air hissed with shot, musket fire and the rattle of ramrods.

Morejón saw the column finally halt in its advance, as the men in front attempted to turn and run, but those behind continued to press forward.

"We've got them beaten," Morejón shouted to his men. "Now see the bastards off. Kill as many of them as you can."

His men loaded as fast as their tired hands could manage, and musket ball after ball tore through the English formation, which had stopped but, which had not yet broken, owing to the men at the rear who arrested the reverse motion within the column.

Morejón fired his musket once again into the massed ranks. He saw Navarra take a musket ball in his chest and he slumped backwards, astonishment etched on his face and blood on his bandoleer. "I'm shot," he said in surprise as he put his hand to his chest, took it away and looked at the bright, scarlet stain that had covered it. He gasped for breath, each exhalation a terrible, pitiable moan. A look of sheer terror crossed his face.

"Leave him," Morejón bellowed at one of the musketeers who had gone to comfort him. This was no time to give solace to dying men. This was a time to fight.

Morejón, himself, was then shot in the left arm, the ball ripping cleanly through the muscle of his upper arm, luckily avoiding the bone. It felt like someone had passed a red-hot poker through his limb, but he forced himself to ignore the pain and continued loading his musket. He must not show his discomfort before his men.

The field in front of the trench was full of flames, smoke and musket balls dispensing death. Men dying, men wounded and screaming in agony, men panic-stricken and dead, filled the space.

"Fire!" Morejón shouted again and once more the musket balls tore into the flesh of the men below, blood erupting from the bodies, men falling in their scores. Finally, the column broke totally, the men at the rear, no longer able to contain the pressure, which had built up from the front.

The Spanish continued to pour musket balls into the backs of the retreating enemy, working as diligently as they had at the battle's outset.

"Keep firing!" Morejón shouted, continuing to shoot after the retreating men. He was elated by the victory, revelling in it, ignoring that the men he was killing were men just like himself, pressed into the service of their country, who, if matters had been otherwise, might have been his comrades.

"Fire!" he shouted again and English conscripts, who a bare four weeks previously, had never been beyond the village where they had been raised, bled to death on green fields not unlike the pastures that they had farmed all their lives.

His men saw that victory was theirs and they cheered, in spite of their throats, which were raw from the acrid gunpowder smoke that engulfed them.

Morejón looked proudly at his troops. Their faces were black and their teeth showed brilliant white in their powder-darkened faces.

There was, at this moment, nothing else in the universe for them but the smoky fields, the pungent, rotten smell from the powder and the view of the retreating enemy. His men loaded and rammed, fired and killed, rammed and loaded, fired and killed again. The musket balls continued to slam into the backs of the retreating enemy until Morejón observed that the English had passed out of range. "Cease firing!" he shouted. "Cease firing!" There was no point in wasting powder that they would yet need. He would have relished ordering the men, waiting below, to follow after the retreating enemy, as he could see that they were severely shaken, but del Aguila had been very definite on that score. They were to defend the town but were not, on any account, to leave it to pursue the English. He felt better now than he ever had since his arrival in the country. After the disappointment of the enemy's capture of Rincorran and Castle Park, it was good to have tasted victory at last.

Carew and Wingfield watched their men retreat in total disorder. "It's a complete disaster," Wingfield said despondently.
"It couldn't be worse," Carew said. "We've lost hundreds of men and such a total failure will undermine the army's morale. It will be harder to mount the next attack, the men will know what is in store for them."
"It is worse!" Mountjoy said as he approached both men. Carew and Wingfield spun around to face him. Wingfield had noted Mountjoy's disappearance earlier but in the heat of battle, had not investigated it. Now, as he looked at his ashen face, he wondered what could possibly be worse than what they had just witnessed. Perhaps, Mountjoy was not aware of how truly disastrous the attack had been.
"What news have you received?" Carew asked anxiously.
Mountjoy looked around apprehensively. When he was sure that he could not be overheard, he replied. "Bad news, George, very bad."
Wingfield suddenly knew. "More Spaniards?" he asked.
Mountjoy nodded despondently.
"But where have they landed? We have had no reports of ships," Carew asked urgently.
"Castlehaven, three thousand more Spanish soldiers," Mountjoy answered. "I have just received word."
Carew whistled. "The stakes have indeed been raised," he said.
Mountjoy added, "Even worse, Don Pedro Zubiaur is in overall command and he has brought the secretary to the Adelantado, Pedro de Soto, with him. De Soto is to command the infantry."
Carew shook his head in disbelief. "Those two here in Ireland, just a matter of miles across the country. Just think of the fame that will

befall us should we capture or kill them."

"That will be no easy task," Wingfield said. He was dismayed that two such veterans should have reached Irish shores. "They have the experience of many years' warfare and are feared all over the Continent."

"There are even more bad tidings," Mountjoy continued. "O'Neill has finally joined with O'Donnell and they have both been seen heading towards Castlehaven. Tyrell is with them also. Our spies inform us that O'Donnell and his Connaught men amount to approximately two thousand foot and three hundred horse, O'Neill, four thousand foot and seven hundred horse and Tyrell, five hundred foot and fifty horse."

"A sizeable force," Carew said. "Why, that's over seven thousand men."

"Yes," Mountjoy said, "and you must remember that they are also veterans of seven years' continuous warfare."

"But not this type of warfare," Carew rebutted. "Let us see how they fare in open field."

Wingfield knew that the situation had changed totally and they would have to face up to the fact. As it was, he could see no way of avoiding defeat if they were confronting such an army with three thousand Spanish veterans to bolster them. There was no knowing what they could achieve and they must not forget the four thousand in Kinsale, under del Aguila. Then another concern sprang to mind. "And what of the Munster Irish now?" he asked. "Such a large force in their midst is bound to cause unrest."

"Unfortunately," Mountjoy said, his face graver than before, "there have been defections already and defections by men against whom there was never, until now, any suspicions of disloyalty."

Carew thundered. "Who? What knaves?"

Mountjoy shook his head. "The news of their defections is perhaps the worst news of all. Sir Finnian O'Driscoll More of Baltimore who handed his castles at Donneboy and Donneshed to the Spanish..."

Carew swore violently. "Damn that Irish bastard to hell. Why, I almost considered him an Englishman".

Mountjoy nodded. "Daniel O'Sullivan Beare handed over Doneboy and Berehaven castles to them also. He and O'Driscoll swore oaths of loyalty to King Philip."

Carew shook his head in disbelief. "If men like those desert us, what hope have we? Are we going to see this disloyalty spread through the land, like a plague? Their desertion of our cause means that the Spaniards have now control of three fine harbours, Baltimore, Bantry and Castlehaven through which they can receive supplies and reinforcements."

"So what do you suggest?" Mountjoy asked. "There is now a Spanish army, free to move wherever it sees fit and it is almost as strong as that which we have besieged here. If we march to deal with it, del Aguila will follow us and we will be caught between both forces. If we remain here, the second Spanish army will arrive and we will find ourselves in the same position. Should we split our army, we risk defeat by one or other of the Spanish companies. Perhaps the wisest course would be to withdraw to Dublin and await further reinforcements."

"No, that would be disastrous," Wingfield said vehemently.

"Yes," Carew agreed. "That is the last thing we can consider. Do that and you will go down in the annals of history as the man who lost this kingdom."

"So, what do you recommend?" Mountjoy asked, almost humbly.

"There is only one course of action open to us," Carew answered belligerently. "We must mount a general assault on Kinsale and take it before the Irish and their Spanish allies arrive. Then we will be free to deal with their combined army."

Mountjoy shook his head. "You saw how they fought. They are in fine form and have much spirit left in them."

"That may be so," Wingfield said, "but do it, we must. I agree wholeheartedly with Sir George. We must take Kinsale. We must move our big guns nearer to the town's walls so that they can inflict more damage on them. We should open more and larger breaches in so many places, that the Spanish will not be able to repair them.

"The Spanish will realise what we plan to do. They will know that if they allow us come any closer with our guns, they are lost," Mountjoy said.

"We have rushed the matter here today without preparing properly," Carew said. "We under-estimated our enemy. Before we mount another attack, we must establish a new fort nearer the town. Tonight, under the cover of darkness, we must commence its construction. It should be located within half a culliver's shot distance from the walls. We will man it with seven companies from the main camp and leave some of Thomond's men on guard outside. We can mount artillery there and we must also raise some platforms on the eastern side, in front of the gates. Our men must dig trenches and erect gabions to protect the gun emplacements."

"Yes," Wingfield said animatedly. "Once that is accomplished, the Spanish will be in an untenable position. They will no longer be able to communicate with the outside world and, hopefully, they will not receive any word of the arrival of their countrymen. We will destroy the walls and take the town if they do not surrender."

Mountjoy looked at both men for a moment and then, infected by their optimism, asked, "Well, why are you waiting? Go and organise the work."

Wingfield and Carew both saluted, before turning to hurry back to the camp.

"Wait," he shouted after them in afterthought. "See that the wounded are looked after first. Sir Thomas, have a temporary hospital set up, away from the main camp, perhaps down at Oyster Haven. It is always bad for the men if they are forced to listen to the surgeons go about their bloody work."

"And even worse, when they see how many they kill," Carew said grimly.

"Seek a parley with the Spanish and ask for a truce so that we can rescue any wounded that still lie out there and bury our dead," Mountjoy added. "We will have a day's mourning tomorrow and then, the day after, we will start the work on our new positions. Oh yes, Sir Thomas, see to it that the fleet leaves for Castlehaven. They might yet catch the Spanish ships there and destroy them. We must attempt to win back control of the harbours they hold before they become too entrenched."

Both men saluted again and left to carry out their tasks.

At last, the combined Irish army approached Castlehaven, tired and weary from their long journey south. O'Neill and O'Donnell rode side by side in front of their men, watching a small detachment of Spanish soldiers, led by a mounted officer, approaching them. They had already made contact with the Spanish scouts outside Castlehaven. Then the scouts had galloped off, eager, to relay the news of their approach to their countrymen, in the town. The sound of distant cannons echoed over the fields to them. The scouts had told them of a naval battle that was being fiercely fought in Castlehaven Harbour.

"It's Cobos," O'Donnell said excitedly and, beckoning to Pedro Blanco, he spurred his horse and galloped towards the approaching body of men. O'Neill followed.

On reaching the Spanish soldiers, O'Donnell and Cobos leaped from their respective horses and embraced fondly.

"Don Alonso, it is good to see you again," O'Donnell said as Blanco began the task of translation.

Cobos laughed. "At last, I bring the help that has been promised for so long," he said. "My only regret is that it is not more, but I promise you, the King shall send further reinforcements. He will not let his army be squandered now that it is committed. I always knew that getting that commitment would be the difficult part. Now that the decision to send it here has been made, the rest will be easy."

O'Neill, who had by now reached them, dismounted and greeted Cobos warmly. "We are glad to see you again," he interjected. "You do yourself an injustice, though," he continued, "the help that you have brought already is most welcome. When we heard of the extra three thousand men you brought, we were overjoyed."

Cobos shook his head and looked embarrassed. "There are no three thousand soldiers," he confessed. "Zubiaur gave out that story as he wanted to win the local Irish to our cause. As you are probably aware, it worked. Two local nobles have joined us and yielded up their castles to us."

"How many of you are there?" O'Donnell asked.

"Seven hundred," Cobos answered.

"Only seven hundred?" O'Donnell echoed in dismay.

"Yes," Cobos answered. "However, the local Lords brought three thousand men to us to use as we saw fit. At the moment, we have only arms for a thousand of them. O'Sullivan Beare raised another thousand men, whom he equipped from his own resources and O'Driscoll supplied a company of horse. They have already proven useful, as they were successful in preventing the English Admiral from retaking Castlehaven."

O'Neill was satisfied that, at last, the influx of support from the native Lords had begun to materialise. He could not understand what had delayed it until now. Hopefully, this was the start of a major desertion from the English cause, which they could use to their advantage.

"And the naval engagement? How goes it?" O'Neill asked.

"Well," Cobos answered. "But come, you might see its conclusion."

He mounted his horse, O'Neill, O'Donnell and Pedro Blanco doing likewise. They set off at a gallop towards the cliffs, which overlooked the bay. Right at the top, the Spanish had mounted six cannons on the barbican at the foot of a tower, which covered the entrance to the harbour. Contrary winds had stopped the Spanish and English ships from coming to close quarters and the battle was being fought with artillery. The men at the cannons were working tirelessly, firing and then hurriedly reloading their guns. O'Neill and O'Donnell dismounted and went to look down into the bay below them. They had never before seen anything like the sight that greeted them.

Four large English Men-o-War, a merchant vessel and caravel were in battle with six Spanish merchant ships. O'Neill saw the dirty white blossom of gun smoke rise, as the English flagship traded broadsides with one of the smaller boats. It seemed an unequal battle but the six cannons on the cliff side gave the advantage to the Spanish. The English vessels were being battered by both the guns on the cliff and those on the Spanish ships, their sails being shot to ribbons and large holes appearing in their hulls.

As they watched, the cannons on the hillside erupted into noise and flame. They witnessed cannon balls striking into another English ship below them. A triumphant cheer went up from the Spanish gunners, cut short by their commander who urged them to reload swiftly.

"The English fleet sailed into the harbour at first light two days since, full of confidence," Cobos confided to the two northern Lords, "but their confidence was misplaced. They did not expect the reception, which they received from us and now, the wind has changed, and they cannot escape from the harbour. We have hit the flagship over three hundred times already!"

"And the ship that has sunk?" O'Donnell asked.

"One of ours," Cobos answered. "It was but a merchant vessel, lightly armed. They must have expected to sink the others as easily but they have come off the worse. But come, you must meet with Don Pedro de Zubiaur."

They walked over to the commander of the artillery.

"Don Pedro," Cobos said, "the Irish Lords have arrived."

Zubiaur swung around. His helmet, a Spanish morion, was lavishly engraved with gold and plumage. His peascod breastplate and remaining armour were similarly decorated and polished.

"The O'Neill, Prince of Tyrone and The O'Donnell, Prince of Tirconnell," Cobos said, introducing both men at once.

Zubiaur embraced them both. "I am delighted to see you at last after all I heard about you and my thanks for having made the dangerous journey south to join with us in our fight," Pedro translated.

Zubiaur brought both men to the edge of the cliff and pointed at one of the warships below him. "That ship below us is the Swiftsure. I crossed paths with it before, during the first Armada in '88. It gives me great pleasure to have a second attempt at it, as I came off second best the last time."

O'Neill looked at the ship. It was in an even worse condition than the much larger flagship. As he observed the naval battle, he felt a sense of excitement grow inside of him. The Spanish, with four small ships and five land-based cannons, were defeating six of the Queen's most powerful vessels. He had heard tell of naval battles before, but had never imagined that he would ever witness one. The Irish confederacy, which he had built up, would never have dared imagine that they could contest the control of the seas with England. It was obvious, however, that their newly arrived allies could. He admired their professionalism. The Spanish gunners worked efficiently, firing their cannons as soon as they had reloaded. The cannons' barrels were red hot and the putrid smell of rotten eggs hung heavily in the air.

Below them, they saw the flagship lower one of its small boats into the water and its crew start rowing towards a small island near the entrance to the harbour, a rope trailing behind them in the water. Zubiaur ran back to the guncrew and they began attempting to realign the cannon, aiming it at the little craft.

"What are the English attempting?" O'Donnell asked Cobos.

"They have taken enough punishment and are anxious to be gone. It means the victory is with us and the harbour will be kept open for the reinforcements and stores, which will follow us from Spain. They will tie the rope to a suitable tree on the island and will attempt to warp out of the harbour," Cobos answered.

"Warp?" O'Donnell asked.

"They will haul the ship out once the rope is attached to a suitable fixed point," Cobos explained.

O'Neill saw Zubiaur returning. "I want you to join with us for a celebratory Mass and a feast tonight. We must thank God for our safe deliverance to these shores. Then, tomorrow, you must march for Kinsale. I will give you two hundred of our troops, commanded by Cobos. He has especially requested the honour," Zubiaur said, as Cobos looked on with a proud smile.

Both O'Neill and O'Donnell were aghast. Only two hundred Spanish! That would be totally insufficient.

" It is not the time to split our forces. We need every man we can call on to be with us at Kinsale. The future of the whole rebellion, of Gaelic Ireland, will depend on the outcome of that battle," Hugh said anxiously.

"Don Pedro will also send seven hundred Irish under O'Sullivan Beare and another five hundred under O'Sullivan's brother. Zubiaur is determined to hold for King Philip the three harbours that he has been given, and as such, needs the bulk of his men himself," Cobos explained hurriedly, anxious to avert any disagreement.

O'Neill was bitterly disappointed. Two hundred men instead of the three thousand he had assumed only a few hours earlier. Two hundred men would not be enough to give his army the backbone that it would need to stand in open battle. O'Sullivan and his men were untrained and would be impossible to rely upon.

"Could you not allow O'Sullivan hold the harbours and all your forces come with us?" he asked desperately.

Zubiaur answered, "We must have the harbours, through which we can be reinforced. O'Sullivan Beare could never have repulsed the English fleet. Once the expected reinforcements arrive, we will join with you in Kinsale. You forget that del Aguila is a very able commander. You will bring many more men to him. Trust in him and trust in us. Together, we will triumph."

"Do not translate," O'Neill ordered Pedro, "I must speak privately to O'Donnell." He turned to O'Donnell who had, uncharacteristically, remained silent throughout the exchange. "Well, what do you think?" O'Neill asked.

"We do not seem to have a choice," he replied. "We must not seem to be afraid. We have prepared for a long time for this day. Zubiaur is right, we must trust in ourselves."

Zubiaur, curious as to their conversation, interrupted them. "You must join us for dinner. We should feed your men also."

O'Neill nodded and Zubiaur went to recover his horse from where he had tethered it to a tree.

The English siege works advanced steadily, in spite of the Spanish guns and the heavy, unremitting rainfall, which fell continuously for forty-eight hours. It lashed and ricocheted off the town's walls, running from the ramparts and the roofs of the houses, creating a stream which, owing to the town's topography, ran through the streets, flowing rapidly from the northern to the southern wall. It seemed impossible that rain could be so savagely incessant but, hour after hour, it continued until everything and everyone was wet through. It drummed on the defenders' helmets, it flooded all the low low-lying areas and its noise kept men awake at night. The Spanish soldiers compared it to the rains before the great flood, a deluge of Biblical proportions, and cursed the luck that had brought them to the edge of Europe, to such an inhospitable land.

Their only consolation was that, however bad it was for them, it was immeasurably worse for the English. The rain had doused their campfires, leaving them without heat or a method of cooking. It had flooded the tents, in which they had to sleep and it had made the digging of their trenches infinitely more difficult. They worked day and night, inching forward, shoring up the sides of the trenches with timber in an effort to stop them from caving in. The bottom of the trenches filled with water and they had to wade through it each morning, to reach the mud face where they would shovel the muddy water out of their way.

The Spanish continually harassed them with their large cannon, in spite of the atrocious weather, which slowed enormously the rate of fire from both sides. It turned the powder in the musket pan to a gritty, inflammable mud within seconds, making the use of muskets well nigh impossible. To keep their cannon firing, it was necessary for the Spanish soldiers to protect each barrel of powder from the rain and each vent had to be covered until the last second, before the touch-hole was fired.

Meanwhile, the English guns continued their unremitting attack upon the town's slate wall. At first, they had little effect on the breaches but then, almost unexpectedly, the fractured slate cascaded down into the river, which ran beside its walls. By night, however, the Spanish had worked to repair the damage. The English guns continued to play on the breaches, thanks to Carew's sextant, but by morning the stonework had been repaired and an earthen defence, had been erected before the walls. So, each morning the English gunners had to start anew. They reckoned that once they relocated the weapons to the new positions that were to be constructed, they would finally be able to complete the demolition of the wall and draw this siege to a conclusion.

Finally, the English had reached the point, towards which they had laboured for so long. They had begun the construction of the fort at one end of a trench, which ran parallel with the northern wall, while at the other end the platforms for the gun emplacements began to emerge. As darkness fell, the Spanish army began preparing for an attack on the newly constructed earthworks, knowing if they were not destroyed, then all was well and truly over for them.

Don Pedro Morejón stood inside the town's gates as the rain drummed down on him and his men who were lined up behind him. The rain would help them, he thought. There was not a single star to warn the English of their approach. He looked up at the sentries on the town's walls above him, wondering if they could see any sign of the enemy. They knew that the new fort was garrisoned at night and that the trenches were also manned. His men had gathered at the gate, without any sound. The English were so close that any noise might betray their plans. He listened carefully but the only sound from outside was that of shovels digging into the mud. They were aware that the English worked on through the night, by torchlight, employing fresh sappers and that companies of soldiers kept guard over them. The fact that they were still digging was a good sign, he reasoned. He hoped that their attack would be a surprise, even though the enemy would be foolish not to expect such an assault from them. He hoped that the English were duped by their inaction so far and that they were dispirited by the weather and the conditions under which they laboured.

This would be their largest sortie so far. Over two thousand men in full armour stood lined in the streets, awaiting the word that they were free to advance. Morejón hated this time before battle, when all one had to do was wait and imagine the worst. He always pondered his own mortality and he loathed being prey to such morbid imaginings. Finally, an hour after darkness had fallen, he saw del Aguila walk towards the gate and nod to the men beside it. A silent ripple of anticipation ran through the massed men and the gates creaked open.

Immediately, Morejón raced out through them, at the head of his men. They raced west towards the partially built fort but once they heard the gate creaking closed behind them, they changed direction in the dark and made for the trenches.

The English soldiers shouted the alarm and their drums beat it out urgently. The Spanish had decided that they would first attack the men in the trenches before most of them could exchange their shovels for weapons. There would be no use for muskets, the weather being too wet to allow their matches to remain lit and the powder would be too sodden for use. No, it would be hand to hand fighting, and Morejón could already hear the screams and the clash of steel as the battle started to rage. Earlier, he had spent an hour sharpening his sword for this night's work. He had concentrated on its tip as the enemy's wet clothes would offer greater resistance to slashing strokes and it would be easier to stab his foe instead.

He drew his sword, glad to feel its familiar form in his hand. The men behind pushed at him in their anxiety to come to blows with the enemy and he found himself being shoved into the trench, which had suddenly appeared in front of him. He tumbled down into it, landing awkwardly and off balance. This was the moment of death but his fear deserted him as he saw an English soldier raise his shovel over his head to strike him. He regained his balance with his left arm by grabbing the shoring timber, while his right hand moved rapidly, thrusting his sword point into the man's face, just underneath the jaw. He pushed as hard as he could, driving the blade through the man's mouth and deep into his brain. He ignored the blood, which ran down his sword's blade and saw the man crumple on top of him, dropping the shovel behind him. Morejón pushed the man from him and pulled his sword free, as the dead man fell backwards.

The trench was crowded with soldiers and he fought his way along it, calling out in Spanish so that his fellow countrymen would not confuse him with one of the enemy. He heard his men jumping into the trench and he swung his sword ahead of him, clearing a path. Already he was wading in dead bodies, slipping on gore as he sought out more victims for his sword.

Hands clutched at him, trying to pull his down, and out of the darkness, a shovel swung at him, catching him in the hollow of his back. He turned and saw a man rear up in front of him, clawing at him with his bare hands. Morejón hammered down with his sword hilt upon the man's head. The latter stumbled and Morejón stepped backwards, giving himself room to swing his sword again, slicing the man's neck and opening an angry red fissure along it. He then stood over him as he lay on the ground and, taking the sword in both hands, he drove its point through the man's neck, pinning him to the sodden earth. He placed his foot on the victim's head and withdrew his weapon, then turned and hurried along the trench. All he could find were other Spanish soldiers, those of the enemy who were not dead, having deserted their position. He came to the gabions and the large guns that were lying beside them, ready to be mounted the following day. "Where are the sappers?" he shouted as all along the length of the trench, his men used the abandoned shovels to remove the timber shoring and fill it in. Morejón looked towards the English main camp but, as yet, there was no sign of reinforcements.

"We are here, Don Pedro," replied the sappers' ensign, as his men hurried up to join him.

"See to the guns and be quick about it," Morejón ordered. "We have yet to destroy the fort. We will attack that and you must follow us when your work here is completed."

"Yes, Don Pedro," he answered and turned to his men.

"You heard our orders," he shouted. "Now get to it."

The men rushed forward, mallets in hand, while others of them began demolishing the platforms that had been constructed for the guns. The men hammered metal spikes into the touchholes of the large guns, in order to cloy them. When they had driven them as far as they could, the spikes were sawn through and filed flat so that no pincers would gain sufficient purchase to draw them clear.

"Make haste," the ensign shouted, aware that they had only a certain amount of time to carry out their task and that they were now on their own, the rest of the army having made for the new fort. "We must catch up with the others."

Morejón and his men raced for the dark outline of the partly built fort. As they waded through the mud, Morejón was, for the first time since he arrived in Ireland, glad of the rain. He could see no lit matches, they would not have to face a fuselage of musket balls. Once again, it would be hand to hand combat and that always favoured the attacker. Suddenly, they were at the edge of the fort and they spilled into the trench surrounding it. Morejón knocked a pike out of the way and fell on top of an Englishman. He pinned him down, his sword arm across the man's head, while he drew his dagger and ripped his stomach open. He scrambled to his feet, slipping on the fleshy innards. His men were all around him and the screams of the dying and wounded rang in his ears.

He looked at the earthworks in front of him, which delineated the outline of the fort. He could see the English soldiers massed on top of it, waiting for their assault and for a moment he considered remaining in the relative safety of the trench. Immediately, his sense of honour got the better of him, and his feet were on the slope, leading to the peak of the earthworks. He scrambled up the wet, muddy bank, slipping as he went, desperately trying to make headway. "To me," he shouted urgently, "to me!"

He heard a new sound from the trench behind him and he turned, his sword dark and wet from gore. His men were scrambling out of the trenches, shouting like men possessed. "Death to the heretics," they shouted in unison and the slogan rang out over the damp, sodden field, back to the town and down to the main English camp.

The Englishmen on the top of the earthworks heard the chant but could not understand it. All they could see was that the trench was taken, the Spanish were spilling out of it and the side of their earthworks was already alive with men, angry bloodthirsty soldiers who seemed to know no fear.

The madness of battle had taken possession of Morejón's soul and he did not stop to calculate the odds as he scrambled up the last few feet and finally reached the summit. He chopped down on an enemy soldier who faced him, knocking his sword easily out of the way, before running him through. He ran on, snarling at the defenders, and killing without mercy or remorse.

A boot kicked at Morejón's groin and he moved, just in time, to avoid it. He drove his sword forward with both his hands so that its point skewered his assailant's throat. A pike was directed at Morejón from the second rank of English soldiers but one of his men, seeing the danger, deflected it away from him.

There were men grunting, kicking and slashing all around him. He could smell their sweat, their breath, and even their fear. He needed more space to use his sword effectively, but the sheer weight of Spanish soldiers behind him was pushing him forwards. With an enormous effort, he pushed rearward and got the yard of space he needed and screaming his war cry, swung his sword in a fearsome, sideways swipe. The English soldier in front of him ducked and with a twist of his wrist, Morejón lunged with his sword and the English soldier moaned as the blade gouged out his stomach.

Immediately, he stepped over the body and he felt the push of his men behind him as they were anxious to continue the fight. This was gutter fighting, something learned in a hard childhood and never taught by drillmasters. Here men clawed and kicked, slashed and thrust and smelt the flesh and blood of the men they killed. This was what his men excelled at. They had been specially picked from all over the Spanish Empire because of their blood lust.

The dead bodies of the English soldiers were like a barricade now, but the Spanish clambered over them, thrusting their wet blades forward, seeking out more victims. Morejón was using his sword to press the enemy further back. He watched their eyes, smiling cruelly at them, showing them that he had nothing but contempt for them as fighting men and that he would kill them, one by one. He lunged, parried, stamped forward, and lunged again, every action, a reflex. A lifetime in the service of his country had created the perfect killing instrument. He again experienced the strange sensation that he had noticed before in battle, everyone else about him seemed to be slowing down while he was the only one who moved at a normal pace.

An English officer, blood on his hands and jacket, rammed his sword at his chest. Morejón easily knocked it aside and thrust his own blade into the man's face, penetrating his right eye, driving it deep into his brain.

"To me, to me!" he shouted and his men rallied to his side, attacking the English with a ferocity and confidence that put terror into the English, left fighting. And Morejón knew that terror was the first and chief weapon of war. The English began to yield before their ferocious attack, unable to bear its brunt. The soldiers behind their front rank, seeing what was happening their comrades, turned to flee and suddenly, the English were abandoning the fort, realising that the fight was lost.

His men followed them, still killing brutally, even though their hands were now tired from such work, and soaked in rain and blood. Morejón ran after them, calling them back. Del Aguila had been definite on the matter. They were to take the fort and trench, destroy the guns and return to the town. On no account were they to become involved in a general engagement. Morejón bitterly regretted that imperative. He sensed that they could take the English if they followed up their attack. He was unimpressed at the defence, which they had mounted and the soldiers who had run away were in a state of absolute panic, a panic that would be communicated to the others in the main camp. Reluctantly, his men returned.

"Destroy the fortification," he ordered and his troops immediately took the shovels, which they had strapped to their backs and began dismantling the walls. Morejón stood between the fort and the main English camp, straining to see if there was any sign yet of a force making its way towards them.

Where are the sappers, he wondered, looking back in the direction of the trench, which they had taken earlier. He saw movement. Yes, they were on the way. He went to meet them. "Quickly, he shouted. "There are three more guns, which you must take care of, in there."

The ensign nodded and hurried inside. The noise from the English camp reached him, as their officers attempted to assemble a force. They were still not organised, Morejón noticed, frustrated that he had not been free to force home his advantage. The enemy's reaction time was too slow. He looked at his men, working ceaselessly behind him. The earthen walls, which the English had built so painstakingly and with considerable loss of life, were coming down quickly and easily. Two thousand men could accomplish quite a lot when they put their minds to it. Another ten minutes passed and he thought he saw movement from the English main camp. He retreated towards the fort and went to the guns.

"Are you done?" he asked, as he watched the men filing off the last steel spike, which projected beyond its touchhole.

"Last one, done," the ensign said, as he peered at the surface of the weapon.

"Good," Morejón replied, looking around at his men's work. They had done all that they had set out to do.

"Back to the town," he ordered and his men began retreating in an orderly fashion towards its gates. It's a pity that we had not some horses," Morejón thought. Then we could have dragged the weapons back with us. Still, tonight's work will give the English something to think about.

The following morning, Carew, Mountjoy and Wingfield went forward on foot to investigate the result of the previous night's battle. An unofficial truce existed so that they could collect their dead and wounded on the proviso that any Spanish wounded should be left near the gates of the town.

"It's a disaster," Carew said despondently. "A total disaster."

"Have you yet any numbers of casualties?" Mountjoy asked Wingfield.

"Four hundred and thirty dead, eleven hundred wounded and you know how few of them we can expect to survive. Both garrisons wiped out and all our hard work destroyed. Worst of all is the destruction of our guns," Wingfield answered.

They stopped and looked in shock at the battlefield around them. As they observed the trenches to their east, they could see the remnants of a fierce and bloody contest. The English and Spanish soldiers lay side by side, united in death, but the English soldiers far outnumbered their enemy. They looked for the trenches but there was no sign of them. Then they turned and walked towards the site of the fort. They still found it difficult to believe that all traces of it could have been wiped out so totally. All around it, however, bodies lay strewn in various postures of death.

"How many Spanish dead?" Mountjoy asked.

"Fifty," Wingfield replied. "There are two officers among the dead and, from their personal effects, it appears that one is Bernarado de Soto, son of Pedro Lopez, our enemy at Castlehaven."

"At least, that is some good news," Carew said vindictively. "That should cause him some pain."

They reached the site of the fort and walked over to the cannons, which still lay on their sides where the Spanish had left them. Carew bent down and looked at them, carefully running his index finger along the touchhole.

"Can it be repaired?" Mountjoy asked.

Carew grunted. "You are fortunate to have me with you. This is a rushed job. I think I will be able to mend it," he said. He went to the next one. "They made a better job of this one but there still is a way that we might free it. In France, I uncloyed some guns by pointing them upwards, loading three times the normal charge into them, placing a fuse down the barrel and loading stone ballast on top of the charge. If the explosion does not rupture the barrel, it will force the steel spike back out the touch-hole."

"Good," Mountjoy said. "These guns are vital to our success."

"So what do we do next?" Carew asked "Re-dig the trenches and re-establish the fort?"

"I am afraid that we will have to give up the idea of taking the town by force. They are still too powerful and their morale is too high. We must attempt to starve them out instead," Mountjoy answered.

Carew disagreed. "But what of O'Neill and the other Spanish? We will become the besieged, caught in the middle between two hostile armies, like a nail in a vice. Why, that goes against all the rules of warfare. We will be fighting front and rear. It should not be attempted."

"What other choice have we?" Mountjoy asked impatiently. "You, yourself, counselled against disengaging. We will never defeat del Aguila unless we meet him in open battle and he is not going to risk that unless he has the aid of the Irish and the Castlehaven Spanish. It seems that the enemy in Castlehaven is not as numerous as was first reported. I have again sent a request to London for urgent aid. We must hold out and see what transpires."

Carew looked closely at Mountjoy. "This is the first time that I have seen you so worried, Sir Charles," he observed. "All is by no means lost yet."

Mountjoy nodded. "I know that, Sir George. If, however, the Irish and Spanish march over that hill, then I am afraid, that this kingdom is lost to Her Majesty. However, come what may, we must fight and make sure that our men never realise how perilous our situation really is. We must, at all times, keep up a brave face. We should take immediate steps to reinforce further the northern side of our main camp, and we must draw all our artillery back into it."

"And what of the horse?" Wingfield asked.

"Yes, those also. The wind does not often blow from the east in this season, so we might have to wait for some time until we receive the reinforcements, which we so badly need. At least, the westerly winds will bring our dispatches quickly to England and the Privy Council can begin the process of levying the necessary men. Hopefully, Leviston will return from Castlehaven shortly with good news, and will have dislodged the Spanish there."

"And what of Thomond's camp?" Carew asked.

I intend reinforcing that. Wilmot's regiment will be posted there and we will have the camp move a little closer to the southern gate. We will erect two small forts between Thomond's camp and the water to the south. I want trenches dug to link those two forts together. Those trenches should continue on to Thomond's camp and from there to our main one. The town will then be totally invested from Scilly Point, north eastwards to Camphill and thence westward to the Bandon River. Thus, we should be able to stop the Spanish receiving any messages or food from the Irish. We must start immediately, as the work will take us some time to complete. All the trenches and fortifications will be out of musket range of the town. I want the earthworks on either side of the trenches to be high enough that they cannot be scaled, except by ladders."

"It is not the Spanish stomachs that I am worried about, but our own," Carew cautioned. "We must lay in food ourselves."

"It shall be done," Mountjoy answered. "There is also one other precaution, which we must undertake. Our soldiers behaved in a cowardly fashion last night and brought dishonour to Her Majesty and to us. Our men were also too slow in reacting to what could have been a disastrous situation. I want to set up a flying column of eleven hundred men to answer any alarms, which we might encounter. They are to be constantly ready for action, in full armour, their weapons to hand. They must even sleep in their armour. In return, they are to be relieved of all other duties, even watch duties. Give the command to

Sir Henry Power and tell him to pick only the very best men. He is to be allowed have whomsoever he wishes. They are to have double rations and to be given the best quarters."

"We better get started," Wingfield said, "there is much to be done before the Irish and their allies arrive. Permission to return to the main camp?"

"Granted," Mountjoy answered. "Sir George, will you do what you can with the guns?" he asked.

"Yes, Sir Charles," Carew answered and turning, hurried away.

Mountjoy watched both men go. Carew had been right, he thought. He was worried. Fate had brought him here and in so doing, had saved him from a direct involvement in Essex's rebellion. He still had Essex's confession hanging over him but he knew that was immaterial in comparison to the threat that now hung over the Realm.

He tried not to dwell too much on what was at stake. Work, he must lose himself in work and in preparation for the trial that was almost upon him. He must trust his intuition when the time came for decisive action. Its timing would be of utmost import; too soon and the Kingdom would be lost, too late and the Irish rebels, backed with the might of Spain, could possibly prosecute the wars beyond these shores, even to the soil of his most beloved England. But the Lord had been on their side so far and He would not forsake them now. He would cleave to that thought when troubled by doubts, but he would try and banish any misgivings. He decided to follow the others. As he went, he cast an anxious glance northward as if expecting to detect the first grim presence of the Irish.

Chapter 25

Don Juan del Aguila paced angrily from one end of his council chamber to the other. He still kept Desmond Castle as his head-quarters, even though he had insisted on housing all his men in the many cellars beneath the Kinsale houses. They were, thus, safe from the English bombardment of the town, which continued night and day. He wondered where the Archbishop was, being already over an hour late for their meeting. Finally, just as del Aguila was about to stride to the door and order the cleric's arrest, it opened and the Archbishop entered the chamber. Without so much as a glance at Don Juan, he strode over to the table and sat down heavily at it. Del Aguila was surprised at the ferocity of distaste and anger that welled up in him upon seeing him.

It was typical of him, he thought, to enter in such uncivil fashion. He looked with revulsion at the grossly over weight body, the heavy jowls and the balding white pate, which glinted in the candlelight. A moment's gratification filled him on recalling that he had insisted that all, from the lowest private to himself, should suffer equal privations while under siege. It had been good for morale among the common soldiers, even though it did not find favour with the officers. He was sure that Oveido loathed living on biscuits, rice and water. He was obviously used to much better fare. Granted, he though, Oveido had enough reserves of fat to survive a siege of years. But such a man, who obviously consumed far more than his needs, would find it more difficult than soldiers, accustomed to surviving on meagre army rations.

"I have heard that you have held meetings in your lodgings with some of my officers. Is that true?" Del Aguila asked provocatively.

Oveido's eyes narrowed and he contemptuously shrugged his shoulders. "I might have had some visitors from time to time," he answered evasively. "Surely you do not expect me to remain friend-less and alone?"

"I am not referring to social calls," del Aguila replied heatedly. "I have heard that you are fermenting revolt among my men. In the pri-vacy of your lodgings, you have traded criticisms of my conduct in this war with my captains, Muneza, Cuellar, Cardenosá, Jaén, Millo, and de Tezada. You have gone so far as to question my competence."

Oveido snorted disdainfully. "You did not mention Morejón. I doubt not but that he is your informer."

"It matters little who my source is," del Aguila replied. "What is of utmost importance is whether or not there is any truth in the allegations?"

Del Aguila paused as he observed the Archbishop closely. Oveido hesitated, considering his reply. "What occurred in my lodgings is my concern. I am not going to confirm or deny whether any or all of those men visited my chamber, or give you details of my conversation with them," he replied intractably.

Anger engulfed del Aguila. He drew his dagger and brandished it menacingly. "I must warn you, if I ever get the least proof of any treacherous talk, I will act immediately. I will have you, and any others who conspire with you, hanged from the town's walls. I promise you that any man who tries to undermine my authority, will pay for it with his life!"

Del Aguila glared at the Archbishop, who sat immobile and expressionless, returning his gaze unflinchingly. The former privately cursed his luck, for the thousandth time, at having been sent to this backwater on the edge of Europe with its accursed climate. Oviedo spoke. "If this was all you required of me, I will take my leave. I have important matters to attend to."

Del Aguila could not credit the man's insolence. Oviedo attempted to rise from the table but he angrily motioned him to remain seated. "Remember what I have told you," he threatened. "I will not warn you again! And as for your Irish friends, O'Neill and O'Donnell," he continued venomously, "two weeks have now passed since their arrival at Kinsale and yet, though I daily entreat them, they refuse to engage the English. I have sent them Ensign Bustamante to conduct them to a rendezvous. I have repeatedly informed them that we would immediately sally from the town, with all our forces, on hearing them give battle. I have informed him of how short we are of food. And what occurs?" he asked rhetorically. "Nothing! Are these Irish cowards that they refuse to take this last step when that is all, which stands between them and victory?"

Oviedo became apoplectic. "Cowards! Cowards!" he raged. "I can hold my peace no longer. How can you call men who have forsaken their lands to march through three hundred miles of hostile territory to aid you, cowards? Men who have held out successfully against the English Queen for over seven years, defeating her best generals! Men who were offered good terms by the English but who preferred to abide by their principles and defend the one true faith! How dare you call them cowards!" he shouted.

Del Aguila scowled. "Their epic march would have been unnecessary had I not been badly counselled and ordered to make landfall here. Your advice was half-witted. As for the Irish, they must now realise that the time for action has arrived. Their destiny stares them in the face. They must seize it with both hands before it slips away. Victory can be ours if they find the courage for decisive action."

Oviedo rose from the table, his great bulk shaking. He was incensed that del Aguila should once again taunt him over the landfall. His remaining self-control deserted him. "You talk of the Irish lacking courage," he countered ironically. "Ever since we landed here, you have made one error after another. You refused to take O'Sullivan Beare as your ally and he has since proven his worth. You refused to strengthen the fortifications at Castle Park and Rincorran, in spite of the pleadings of Brocherio and myself. If we still controlled those castles, it would be much easier to rendezvous with the Irish. Even worse, you did not erect any other defences and you, shamefully, let them be taken. In craven fashion, you allowed yourself be invested by sea and by land. The money, which you were given, you husband with miserly frugality. You could have bought plenty of provisions locally with it. The only possible reasons for your behaviour so far, is either cowardice or outright sabotage. Perhaps you hope to enter the service of the Queen!"

Del Aguila stood speechless, rooted to the spot. He looked in disbelief at Oviedo. How could he speak thus to a man like himself who had spent his whole life in the service of his King and country? He was not going to undergo an inquisition, again accounting for everything he spent. For a moment, he considered ordering Oveido's execution. He had the power under his commission to exert marshal law but he knew that it would be subject to investigation. If he had proof of treachery, then it might be different, but without it, he was powerless to act. When the campaign ended, then there would be time for recriminations. If he arrested Oviedo, he would split his officers, as quite a few of them would support the Archbishop. Once Mountjoy was beaten, then he would deal with the troublesome cleric.

"I must remind you that to undermine the authority of the King's Commander in the field, is the greatest act of treason, which a subject can commit. The King can judge between us when this campaign is over. In the interim, I order you to desist from making allegations against me, which are pernicious and false. If you disobey my orders, I will have no choice but to place you under house arrest."

Del Aguila paused, awaiting a reaction, but there was none forthcoming. He proceeded. "I am assigning the deacon, Pedro de Colmenares to accompany you from this day forth, on all your dealings with any of my men."

Oviedo snorted in disgust. "Why not put me under house arrest?" he queried sarcastically. "I would much prefer that than having to endure Colmenares. I can only think of one other who would be worse!"

Del Aguila ignored the implication of Oviedo's words. He had utter faith in Colmenares and knew that he would report accurately, any transgressions that Oveido would commit. It was an added boon that both men disliked each other.

"I am going to send another letter to the Irish, informing them of the dire circumstances to which we have been reduced, ordering them to come up and fight or be forever dammed in the sight of King Philip and their own countrymen. This will be my third such letter," del Aguila said contemptuously.

"May I go now?" Oveido asked insolently, disregarding this further slight.

"You may, but remember what I said," del Aguila warned. "Take care, Archbishop, you are not beyond my grasp."

Oveido rose clumsily, pulling his great girth upwards and without replying, made for the door. As he opened it, del Aguila called after him.

"And just so that you are forewarned, if I hear of my officers echoing any of your sentiments, I will hang them forthwith. I am only longing to be able to make an example of someone."

Oviedo proceeded out the door, without responding, banging it behind him. Del Aguila spent a few moments looking at the quaking door, wondering if he had taken decisive enough action. Any hint of mutiny severely distressed him and awoke in him very painful memories. With a struggle, he dismissed the thought and walked back to his table and took up his quill. Now, he thought, he must word this communication as strongly as possible. He dipped the quill in the ink and began writing.

To the Prince O'Neill and Lord O'Donnell,

I thought Your Excellencies would have come at Don Richardo's request since you had promised that, on receiving aid from the Castlehaven Spanish, you would do me that favour. And so, I beseech you now that you do it for me and come as speedily as you can. I assure you that our enemies are very tired and few and cannot guard the third part of their trenches. Once we overcome their initial resistance, then all is ended for them.

Del Aguila paused, looked at the letter and, after a few moments, crumpled it. He threw it on the fire, which blazed in the hearth. Too weak, too imploring, he thought. I must start again. He procured a fresh sheet of parchment and began anew.

Dusk was falling as Carew strode through the main English camp, making for Mountjoy's headquarters. The men whom he passed were all dispirited and downcast. He was wrapped up against the rain and cold, but was wet through and smelled of dirt and damp, like all the rest of the soldiers. He had not removed his clothes in over a month, even for sleeping. Washing was a luxury, long forgotten, as were hot meals, the Irish having cut off their supplies of fuel and food.

On reaching Mountjoy's headquarters, a solidly constructed wooden building, he knocked and entered. It was dark inside and he smiled to himself when he saw Mountjoy by the light of the solitary candle on the table, at which he sat. He was wrapped in even more clothes than usual. It looked like he had doubled his weight since the siege had commenced. Like Carew, he had also grown a beard.

"Our scouts allowed one of del Aguila's messengers get through our lines. He passed between both our camps and our men aimed over his head," Carew said.

Mountjoy heaved a sigh of relief. "Good work, George," he said. "Hopefully he carries the same message to O'Neill as the last courier whom we captured. With any luck, O'Neill will obey del Aguila's summons to attack us. That is probably our last chance of avoiding defeat here and is but a slim one at that. Did you call the muster?"

Carew nodded. "The result is disheartening and becomes more and more so each day," he said. "We have barely six thousand fit men left. Sickness is now epidemic in the camps. We are losing over sixty a day. Men continue to desert and the Irish allow them pass through their lines unmolested, once they yield up their weapons. The threat of instant execution, which is carried out when any are caught, does not seem to discourage them. Over two hundred deserters were arrested on the road between Cork and Waterford. We cannot even leave the camp to bury our dead, as the Irish shoot our men in droves. Our camp has become most unhealthy and the conditions in which we live, unbearable."

Mountjoy shook his head disappointedly. "The numbers are bad, much worse that I imagined. We know that O'Neill has at least seven thousand men and the Spanish, over three thousand. Our only hope must be to force a decisive battle now, the sooner the better, because as each day passes, our strength ebbs away. We cannot rely on the wind changing to favour us, as it might not do so for many more days or weeks. If it continues to blow from the west much longer, George, I fear that we will be undone."

Carew had long known the importance of cultivating hope, in spite of ever ebbing expectation. They had all endured their black moods when success seemed unattainable, even Wingfield, but fortunately, as yet, they had not all succumbed to such thoughts together. "I do not intend allowing any Spanish Dons or Irish rabble to best me," he said. "We hold a very strong position here. Let the Irish come and we shall beat them. All is not lost yet. O'Neill cannot continue to procrastinate for ever, eventually, he must do as del Aguila commands."

Mountjoy replied. "There is no such thing as 'must', where O'Neill is concerned. He will do as he pleases and, unfortunately for us, his natural inclination is towards caution. My wager is that he shall wait and refuse to attack. If he does, we are lost, as if we leave our trenches to attack his camp, we shall employ most of our men in such an undertaking. The Spanish could not fail to notice such a move and would follow us and attack us from the rear. We would be caught in the open between two armies, an indefensible position. If our strength declines much further, we shall have to be taken off by water. Another week or two without a wind from England and all is lost."

Carew frowned. "The horses will not survive another few days. The forage has completely given out and they are starving. Another day, two at the very most, and we shall have to order the cavalry to break out and make for Cork. If we leave it any longer, they shall not have the energy to attempt it."

Mountjoy nodded despondently. "I am aware of the problem and it worries me deeply," he replied. "Three more days and if, by then, we have not forced a confrontation, we shall allow them go, even though it shall leave our position severely weakened. We shall soon run out of food, if we do not receive more supplies."

"At least there is one thing that we have in plentiful supply that the Irish envy," Carew said. "Whiskey! You will never believe it. Brian McMahon, the McMahon Chieftain, sent one of his men to me, requesting some. His eldest son was a page in my London household. He now calls upon my bounty again."

Mountjoy shook his head in disbelief. "And what did you do?" he asked.

"I sent him some, of course. You have to admire his cheek, but that's the Irish, they'd cut your throat, but there would be nothing personal in it!" Carew replied.

"We must make sure neither he nor any of his allies get to cut ours," Mountjoy returned. "We should intensify our bombardment of Kinsale and we must attempt to force their hand. I do not worry about the Irish, but the Spanish have experience in forcing trenches and we saw already what they can accomplish. Our men are weary and the enemy is very efficient at keeping them on their feet. The Spanish, with their nightly sorties, and the Irish, sniping at our men during the day, ensure that they have little rest. We must do something to restore morale. Spread it around among the men that an end is in sight, that the Irish will attack in days and that I expect every man to do his best. Is the emergency squadron still up to strength and ready for action?"

Carew nodded. "We replace men as they die or fall sick and have, in spite of the lack of supplies, kept those men on double rations, as you ordered. They are not as weary as the rest and are eager for action. When it comes, it will be a relief to them, as it will be for everyone else."

"Good," Mountjoy said. "But come, we must concentrate our artillery. Let us pray the Irish are pressed into action before our cavalry is forced to leave. The horse is our mainstay, the Spanish have none and the Irish horse is no match for ours. If it comes to a battle, the cavalry will swing the day in our favour. If it is a battle between our respective infantrymen, well then, the victory would be with our enemy," Mountjoy conceded reluctantly. "But let us not be melancholy. Perhaps the wind will change tomorrow. O'Neill would then be forced into action, knowing that it would be only a matter of days before aid could arrive from England. Let us mingle with our men and show them that we are not faint-hearted."

O'Neill sat huddled over a fire in one of the temporary cabins, which the Irish had built inside a circular earthen wall, topped by a wooden stockade, surrounding their camp. He was feeling weary and the prospect of the impending conference filled him with disquiet. There would be yet another bruising encounter with O'Donnell. Relations between the two men had deteriorated drastically since they had arrived at Kinsale. O'Donnell was eager for battle, unable to stand the inaction of the siege or to ignore the pressing letters from del Aguila. O'Neill had constantly counselled caution, urging him and the others to bide their time. If he had more than the two hundred Spanish soldiers under Cobos with him, his sentiment might be different.

He was keenly aware of the passage of time and that the decisive moment was almost upon them. He had long prepared for this day but, now that it was at hand, he feared its outcome. He had tirelessly persisted in training and preparing his men. He was confident of them but was fretful about the Connaught and Munster men. They were entirely without discipline and, even though he had tried to have them trained over the last few weeks, they had proven themselves unwilling to learn, lazy and dissolute. He now regretted leaving his own heavy horse back in Tyrone. They were the only force, which could stand up to Chichester and his cavalry. Cormac had insisted on having them to defend their territories. They would be a loss, he reflected ruefully, as the Irish horse, drawn from O'Donnell's ranks, had vehemently refused all attempts at modernisation and still rode without proper saddles, placing them at a great disadvantage to the English cavalry.

His thoughts were interrupted by a clipped English voice. "Hugh," he heard and looking up, saw Tyrell standing over him. He and Ownie O'Moore had served him well but sadly O'Moore had not survived to see this day. He thought of the many others who had been lost, but of all of these, the greatest loss had been that of Hugh Maguire. He missed him now not only for his military skills but also for the good cheer and humour he had brought with him. Hopefully, Tyrell would come into his reward soon, Hugh thought. He had promised him the Lordship of Westmeath when victory was theirs. He had brought six hundred men with him to Kinsale, six hundred of the best troops in Ireland. They had endured great privation and hardship and won through it all, tempered and strengthened by their experience. It was said that the English hated meeting his soldiers above all others.

"Yes, Richard, is it time?" he asked.

Tyrell nodded. "The Lords await us in the council tent," he said.

O'Neill rose slowly, cold and damp penetrating his joints. He felt the weight of his years upon him. As he walked to the door, he asked Tyrell. "And O'Donnell? How fares he?"

Tyrell laughed. "As bad as ever. If he does not get to fight the English soon, I reckon that he will turn and fight the rest of us."

O'Neill sighed and they continued to walk in silence, Hugh marshalling his thoughts for the impending encounter. On reaching the tent, Tyrell held back the flap, allowing O'Neill enter. O'Donnell was sitting at the makeshift table, idly toying with a dagger, while McMahon supped deeply from a flagon of whiskey. He rose unsteadily and crossed to Hugh. "Here, O'Neill have some of this, it will warm you up," he said.

Hugh took a draught and passed it to Tyrell. "You never lost it McMahon," he said. "You'd find whiskey in a nunnery."

McMahon grinned. "It's not the best, mind you, but in the present circumstances, 'twill suffice."

Tyrell, having taken a draught, passed it back to McMahon and he and O'Neill took their places at the table.

"Let us begin," Tyrell said. "Hugh Roe called this meeting and is anxious that we attack the English immediately."

Hugh nodded. "You all are impatient, no doubt, with this prolonged absence from your lands. I would appeal to you, however, not to yield. The English grow weaker by the day, so why hasten matters?" he asked.

Hugh Roe shook his head. "We have all seen del Aguila's letter. He implores us to attack and promises that victory will be ours. I trust his judgement. He will join with us and together we will defeat Mountjoy. At last, he is within our power and must not be allowed to escape."

O'Neill replied, choosing his words with deliberate caution. "Every day, the English die in their hundreds from disease and cold. Let time, ague, hunger and the weather do our work for us. The winds still blow from the west. Everything is in our favour. It is Mountjoy who must act, either to attack us or to leave the field. His is the more calamitous predicament. He is surrounded and cut off from all aid."

O'Donnell sneered in exasperation. "Now is the time to make his misery absolute. We must destroy him. We cannot wait longer. It is not only the English who die, our men die too. They have marched the length of Ireland and what do they find when they reach Kinsale? That they must live in the direst conditions and endure the ravages of this most bitter winter. They brought what supplies they could carry upon their backs and they are now all gone. You know our difficulties in procuring more provisions. We are no better than dogs, living off scraps. We sleep in wet huts, our clothes sodden from the ceaseless rain. There must be an end to this siege and it must be now," he finished in defiance.

O'Donnell paused and O'Neill returned his gaze unflinchingly. He was aware that all eyes in the tent were upon him. After a few moments, he replied. "I acknowledge the hardships our men are enduring and that some of them have died, but that number is slight when compared with the losses that Mountjoy endures. We can bear such losses because those of the enemy are so much greater. Their strength is wasting away, their army haemorrhaging to death. Can you not suffer your discomfort a while yet, knowing that the English affliction is far more grievous than ours?" he urged.

O'Donnell sighed. "Our men were content to fight in Ulster, secure in the knowledge that the people there supported them, but that same support has not been forthcoming here. They have no stomach for a prolonged siege. There are murmurs of discontent within the camp. While we sit here inactive, Dowcra and Chichester are destroying our lands at home. Our men want action. The Munster men, whose homes are close at hand, have started to desert. If the north was not so far away and had we not made so many enemies on our march south, I fear our men might also be tempted to leave. All west Munster has declared for us and once we have defeated Mountjoy, the rest of the country will join us too. As for the wind that blows from the west, with God's grace, it will continue to do so for another month or more. We should achieve as much as possible before English reinforcements can arrive. The longer we remain inactive here, the more we lose our advantage. Our first step must be Mountjoy's defeat. Then, we can organise ourselves and prepare for the English soldiers who, doubt-less, are being readied to sail. I propose we attack tomorrow. We can-not wait any longer." He finished speaking, his eyes appealing to all those present.

No one spoke, all gazes firmly fixed upon O'Neill. His thoughts flew back to Tyrone. It had been with a heavy heart that he had left the North and, before leaving, had appointed as his heir, his first born son, Hugh Óg, leaving Cormac to hold the province. It had been a most difficult decision but one he knew he could not shun. Now it seemed as if the fateful moment was almost upon him. He turned to Cuconnaught Maguire. "Well, Cuconnaught, what is your opinion?" he asked.

"I must agree with Hugh Roe," he answered uncomfortably. "We never expected delays such as these, each one, exposing our families to greater peril."

"And you Brian?" O'Neill enquired of McMahon.

"Attack, seize the moment," he replied unwaveringly.

Hugh turned to O'Sullivan Beare. "And you Donnell?" he asked.

"For God's sake, let us attack and be done with it," he cried impa-tiently.

Hugh nodded, still unable to bring himself to the final decision. He turned to Tyrell. Above all others present, he valued his opinion most. "And you, Richard?" he asked.

Tyrell hesitated. "I do as I am ordered," he said.

"Yes," O'Neill replied, "but, on this occasion, I desire you to give us your opinion."

"We have waited long enough for this day. I also think we should attack," he answered without further reluctance.

"Is there anyone here who thinks we should hold off?" Hugh asked. No one answered.

O'Neill nodded resignedly. He could not over-rule them all. Much of their argument could not be denied. And yet, his whole intuition shrank from ordering this attack. Their entire strategy of warfare had required forbearance and trust that time would be their best ally. Why change now when victory was within their grasp? But the argument was already lost. He had endeavoured to hold off this day as long as he possibly could but, finally, they had ordained that the time had come for action. He privately acknowledged that it would be a relief, even for him.

"Well, it has been decided," he said reluctantly. "Tomorrow night, we will attack."

A murmur of approval ran through the gathering.

"Richard," O'Neill said addressing Tyrell, "you inform Cobos. We must plan our attack carefully and get word to his countrymen in Kinsale."

Tyrell nodded.

O'Donnell then addressed O'Neill. "As your heart is not fully behind this onslaught, I should command our forces tomorrow night. It would be disastrous were we to fail because our commander lacked the stomach for this venture," he said in bold unconcern for the older man.

O'Neill was confounded at such brazen effrontery. He had always commanded when they fought together. His army had always been the numerically superior and better trained. It was he who had been responsible for the planning, which had brought them all their victories so far. He wondered how much support O'Donnell had from the other Chieftains present. He had been unable to ignore how strained their relationship had become of late, but he had never anticipated this. "I have never lacked courage," O'Neill answered angrily. "Let any man here furnish me with one example," he challenged them. His fury with O'Donnell knew no bounds. This dissension was what they needed least on the eve of this most decisive battle.

"I will command our forces as I have always commanded them," he continued irefully. "I have brought the majority of soldiers with me and Tyrell is answerable only to me. I refuse to yield up command. The idea is pure folly."

"And I refuse to be subordinate," O'Donnell answered implacably.

An embarrassed silence descended upon the gathering as the two men glared at one another.

"Perhaps," Maguire said, "Cobos should take command. He has experienced wars on the Continent."

"That would not be acceptable to me," O'Neill retorted balefully.

"Nor me," O'Donnell added with virulence.

"Well then," McMahon said, "you must share the command."

"Hugh Roe can take command of the horse and Hugh the infantry," Maguire intervened.

"O'Donnell has always been under my command," O'Neill rebutted in outrage. "In battle there can only be one leader."

"And tomorrow, I will be under my own command," O'Donnell retorted. "You can have the foot. I will not have it said that O'Neill commanded and that it was he who won the day. That is my final word upon this matter."

With that, O'Donnell rose to his feet and swept out of the tent. The others sat in mortified silence. O'Neill looked into their faces, which were turned towards him, awaiting his guidance. "We will leave things as they are for tonight," he said wearily. "Tomorrow at noon, meet me here and we will plan our attack."

With that, he departed. He did not return directly to his hut, as he knew he would not sleep. Instead, he made for the edge of the camp and stood there, looking upward. Above, the firmament was stippled with brilliant stars, which glistened in the cold, clear night. That same sky would be visible from Dungannon. He wondered if Catherine might also be looking at it, at this very moment. He considered what the morrow's sky would bring. Would it be as bright? He hoped not. There was a hint of a change in the air. The die was now cast and soon all would be decided. But he doubted the decision taken. Try as he might, he could not banish the feeling that the time was not yet meet. But reasoned argument had won. If they should win tomorrow night, England's claim over Ireland would be vanquished for evermore. But if they should lose, he could not even bear to contemplate the implications.

Chapter 26 - Christmas Eve, 1601

The skies over Kinsale were dark, the worst winter storm of the season having disgorged a continuous deluge on the town and its surrounding landscape. From time to time, the scene was brilliantly illuminated, as incandescent lighting flashed through the blackened skies, followed by peals of thunder, which caused the very buildings themselves to quake. The English bombardment, even at its worst, could not have competed with this display, which nature was providing.

It was Christmas Eve, but there was no sign of festivities in Kinsale, itself as quiet as death. The streets were deserted, the only sign of life being the sentries who stood at their posts on the town's walls, keeping a watchful eye on the English emplacements. In the centre of the town, however, light issued forth from the church of St. Multose, into the dark streets and market place surrounding it. St. Multose had established this church in the middle of the sixth century. The present stone building dated from 1195, when a local Norman Lord built the edifice, with the combined aim of providing a structure that would serve both as a place of worship and a centre for the town's commerce. A screen separated the sacred from the temporal areas, neither of which had pews, thus providing a large covered area.

It was the only building in the town that could facilitate all two and a half thousand Spanish soldiers who had assembled there, and it had been necessary to remove the screen to achieve that purpose. Don Juan del Aguila knelt with his men, listening to Oviedo drone through the final prayers of the Latin Mass. Every soldier present had received the Blessed Eucharist. It had been a lengthy process, which had been hastened thanks to the priests from the Carmelite Abbey, just outside the town's walls. They, poor friars, had been obliged to witness the destruction of their abbey, stone by stone, as English guns had concentrated on it until it was completely demolished. Del Aguila could not understand Mountjoy's decision to waste valuable time and powder in flattening a structure, which posed no threat, but was personally gratified that it had saved the town's walls some damage.

Within, the tallow candles cast only a murky glow on the assembled soldiers. A brilliant flash of lighting drew del Aguila's eyes to the vertical slits in the five-feet-thick walls. He counted. He had just reached five, when the thunder boomed out, causing Oviedo to pause, yet again, unable to compete with the storm's voice. Del Aguila smiled as he saw the look of frustration upon the cleric's face. Any discomfort that Oviedo suffered, he enjoyed.

He fixed his attention upon the crucifix that hung over the main altar. It was unworthy of him to entertain such thoughts in the Lord's house, he reflected. He tried to pray for success but found it difficult to concentrate. All through his long military career, he had always believed that right was on his side, and that he fought in support of the one true religion. Nevertheless, bitter experience had taught him that the justness of Spain's cause was not enough to guarantee them victory. The defeat of the first glorious Armada had been proof of that. No, God expected his followers to do their duty by him, but the powers of the Evil One were potent and victory would be gained by whosoever had most desire to win. He prayed silently for a few minutes that he might be worthy of the task allotted him and then returned his attention to his preparations.

He looked around him and the highly polished armour of his soldiers, reflecting the glimmer of candles, suspended along the walls, reassured him. He had no doubt about his men's abilities. He would prefer to have command over them than over any other soldiers who drew God's breath. He could see it in their faces. They were confident and eager for battle. It would be a resolution to their current predicament and their morale was high. In all their previous sallies, they had proven themselves to be the better soldiers. Indeed, his problem had been to restrain them this long, anxious, as they were to test the English fully. Now that the Irish were finally committed to attack, and that their combined forces outnumbered the English by three to two, all reason suggested that there could only be one outcome.

But then, he thought to himself, reason wasn't always proved right. He thought of the Irish. He still did not know just how reliable they would turn out to be. He would willingly trade the seven thousand Irish soldiers for two thousand Spanish veterans, given the choice. Again, he stopped himself. He was being churlish once more. The Irish, who had fought in Archduke Albert's army in Flanders, had proven themselves to be excellent soldiers, once they had been properly trained. The Archduke had been asked to allow any of them who wished to return home to aid the rebellion in Ireland, to do so, but he had absolutely refused. They had proved too useful to him and he had expressly forbidden them, on threat of execution, to set sail for Irish shores.

Tomorrow would be Christmas Eve, del Aguila thought, the eve of Our Lord's birthday. It should not be a day when Christians fight, but perhaps that very notion would put the English off their guard. He contemplated the celebrations that Christmas Day would bring, with the English defeated. It would herald a new beginning for Spain, for Ireland, and for Europe. Again Iberia would hold the balance of power upon the Continent, flanking the heretic nation to its west. Ireland would be freed and would carry the torch of true faith high up on the ancient Continent's northern edge. This would be but the first step in the realisation of Spain's ultimate ambition. How easy it would be to cow the English Realm from the vantagepoint of this western satellite - how meet was its location, history and ancient grudge. Ireland could not have proved a more valuable resource for the great might of Catholic Spain.

"In Nomine Patris, Filius et Spiritus Sanctus," intoned Oviedo and the congregation replied in one voice, "Amen." With a jolt, Aguila realised that this wearyingly protracted Mass was over. He blessed himself quickly, rose to his feet and went to the altar, candle light reflecting from his burnished, gold-embossed armour.

Oviedo addressed the men. "May the Lord go with each and every one of you this night," he said earnestly, "because you are going forth upon His work. Do not be afraid. God willing, you will all return safely and victorious here tomorrow morning, but do not fear dying for His cause. Remember that any of you who fall will sup at the Lord's right hand this very night. A place of honour is already set for you. Go with God and remember the great responsibility that you carry."

Once again, the Archbishop blessed the men and bowing to del Aguila, vacated the centre of the altar. Del Aguila stepped into the space and stood looking at his men for a minute. They had been ordered to assemble in full armour but the night's ultimate details would not be confirmed to them until now, far too late for the English to gain any hint of them.

"Tonight, we finally show the English exactly what the Spanish infantry can do when it commits itself fully to an attack," he said loudly.

A murmur of approval ran around the church and he held up his hands for silence. "I wonder did any of you notice the statue over the western door, on your way in tonight?" He paused briefly, the question lingering in the air. He was using the moment to reinforce further the message that was to come. He continued. "It is of the saint who founded this church and it commemorates a curse, which he put on the natives. It was that only strangers will ever prosper in Kinsale. He placed that curse on the inhabitants because they refused to help him construct this shrine. Are we not strangers to Kinsale where the English have been residing for over four hundred years now? We will prosper here, we will be the victorious ones - it has been decreed in this sacred place" he said, his voice rising to a crescendo.

Again, a murmur rippled through the church. "The Irish have decided to unite with us tonight, in a joint attack on the English position," del Aguila continued. "We have been in contact with them over the last number of weeks and we know that the enemy's army is much weakened and that we now outnumber it considerably. The plan we have agreed is very simple and leaves little room for misunderstanding."

Here he paused, as he looked around the church, picking out the officers in particular. They were most anxious to come to grips with the enemy and he would have to ensure that they waited until the correct time to start their attack. Too early, and they would forewarn the English before the Irish could get into position and thereby destroy their whole stratagem.

"The Irish are to march tonight under the cover of darkness," he continued. "They will march to the west and outflank the English main camp on Ardmartin Ridge, which is located between them and us. They will then march towards the town and the much weaker English trenches, which guard the western approach to it. Once the Irish are in position and ready to attack those defences, they are to loose a volley of shots and then we will sally forth and attack the English from the other side. Once we join forces, we will sweep away the English main camp. We must await the signal from our Irish allies and they shall be in position well before dawn. Then we shall do the rest."

A growl of excitement went up from his men. They sensed blood and were eager.

"Remember, you fight for Spain's honour tonight," del Aguila said earnestly. "You fight for much more than a local cause here. By just being here, the balance of power in Europe has switched once again in Spain's favour. Victory here tonight will guarantee Spain's triumph in her long war with the English and their heretic Queen. With a Spanish led Ireland on her western coast, think of how weakened the Queen's position will be. But there is even more at stake than that tonight. The whole honour of Spain's military power stands in the balance. I know you will not be found wanting."

A massive affirmation greeted his words.

"Our navy has disappointed Spain's honour in the past," he continued, "but never her infantrymen. The Spanish soldier is the best in the world, of that I have no doubt. You have already shown your superiority over our enemy on a night such as this. It will be hand to hand fighting that shall win this battle and after their last experience of Spanish steel, the English will not relish such a prospect."

Laughter greeted his comments.

"Let us go down in history as the first invading army, since William the Conqueror, to defeat the English on their own territory," he said grandly, knowing intuitively that their vanity as men of arms was finally what he must evoke. He looked around the church and saw that all the faces turned towards him, betrayed neither fear nor doubt.

"Get to your stations," he said. "May God go with you and tomorrow night, when we say Midnight Mass in honour of Christmas Day, may it be a truly joyous occasion."

He watched as his men began to stream slowly from the church, through the double doors at the rear, talking of the plunder that would be theirs on the morrow. This was what they had come for, this was why they had enlisted. They would never get rich on what the King paid them but who knew how much plunder they could win in this country? For the first time since he landed in Kinsale, del Aguila felt something approaching gratification. Tomorrow, his army would fight and win and the stain on his character would be erased forever. He might yet be remembered as Spain's foremost general, more revered than even Archduke Albert. With that comforting thought, he turned and left the church through the sacristy. He would not be partaking in the nighttime assault, but would be at the gates, ensuring that his forces did not leave the town too early.

Mountjoy rose from his table, walked to the flap of his tent and looked eastwards. He had, of late, adopted the habit of staying up all-night and sleeping during the day, as it was at night that the Spanish had proven most difficult. He coughed a long, hard racking cough, and worry assailed him about his health. So many of his men had died. It never ceased to amaze him that he had still not contracted some disease. Yet, he had no doubt but that his health would be irrevocably damaged from this most difficult of campaigns.

It was a half an hour before dawn, the darkest part of the night before the faint rays of light would appear over the eastern hills. There was no sign yet of any glow in the sky. He was gravely disappointed. Another night had passed and no attack. His hopes had been raised. Carew had received a communication from McMahon, warning him to lie low as the Irish and Spanish were to mount a joint attack before morning. He knew that it was a lot to hope that a man would betray his cause in gratitude for a few flagons of whiskey, but nothing about the Irish would surprise him.

He had taken all due precautions, doubling his guards and placing his army in readiness. He had also directed that the flying squadron, under the command of Sir Henry Power, should take up station west of the camp, close to the main guard of the cavalry, where they had been led to expect the Irish attack. After that, all they could to do was wait and it had been a long night. He looked south in the direction of the town but there was no sign of any activity.

He was about to re-enter his tent when he heard horsemen riding towards him. He watched them approach, his hand on his sword's hilt and was relieved to recognise Carew and Wingfield. They reined in their horses and dismounted quickly. Carew addressed Mountjoy. "Sir Charles, it is time to arm. The Irish are almost upon us," he said urgently.

Mountjoy felt a surge of elation. So the night was not over after all, he thought. Perhaps they stood a chance of turning things around. "How many? Who saw them?" he asked eagerly.

"One of our scouts spotted the full Irish army on the move, some time ago. They separated. O'Donnell and his men seem to be taking a more westerly approach to the town, whereas O'Neill and the rest of the Irish army are directly approaching our western defences. O'Neill has well over three and a half thousand men with him and only a handful of our men face him," Carew said in haste.

Just then another horseman rode up. He reined in his horse. "My Lord," he said. "Sir Richard Graeme of the horse guard, bade me find you and inform you that he has seen the glow of Irish musketeer matches. His men are severely outnumbered and he seeks reinforcements immediately."

Mountjoy nodded. Now that the action had finally begun, he no longer felt any fear.

"Sir Power's flying column is located nearby, just to the west of Thomond's camp. Ride as fast as you can and tell them to join your master," he said, before turning to one of his sentries.

"Get my horse, quickly," he ordered, then turned back to Wingfield and Carew. He addressed them. "Well, we will soon see if I have learned enough of military matters to win this battle. I must thank you for all the help you both have given me since I arrived here. Should I not survive this night, I wish you to know that I am deeply grateful to you both." A faintly discernible hoarseness blurred Mountjoy's words.

"Nonsense," Carew boomed, "we will all survive this night and must see to it that neither O'Neill nor O'Donnell do."

"Sir George," Mountjoy said, "it pains me to part with you, but part with you I must. I must ride to confront the Irish. I cannot do so unless I leave a commander to face the Spanish and repulse them when they attack. I can think of no other, more suited to such a task, than you. Will you take the command?"

"Willingly," Carew answered, "and you need have no worries regarding the Spanish. They will not win through."

A ghost of a smile played upon Mountjoy's lips. It was no more than he had expected. "You shall have five regiments with which to hold the main camp," he continued, "mine, yours, Lord Clanrickarde's, Lord Audley's and Sir Richard Moryson's. You will also have another four to hold Thomond's camp, Thomond's own, Percy's, Wilmot's and St Lawerence's." He turned to Wingfield. "Due to the distance between the camps, I wish you, Sir Thomas, to take command of Thomond's."

Wingfield's face fell. He stood silently for a few moments and Mountjoy could not fail to read the look of utter disappointment on his face. "You are unhappy, Sir Thomas?" he asked gently.

"I have never asked you for any special favours in all the time I have spent in your service, nor shirked my duty in any fashion," he said.

"No," Mountjoy answered, "you have been beyond reproach and I am much in your debt."

"There is one favour that I must ask of you. Should you refuse it, I will bide by your command," Wingfield said stiffly.

"Ask it," Mountjoy invited him.

"For over ten years," Wingfield said, his voice betraying his emotion, "I have been driven by one desire, to avenge myself upon O'Neill; to avenge a lady, whom he did most foully abuse, to avenge my comrade, Henry Bagenal and all the rest that fell at Clontibret, the Yellow Ford and elsewhere. I wish to confront him. I swear that he shall not break through our defence and that I shall follow him to the gates of hell itself, should fate so require it."

Wingfield ceased speaking and stood to attention, eyes fixed straight ahead, awaiting Mountjoy's decision. It can do no harm to have such a man along with me who bears such a personal interest in the outcome of the morning's battle, Mountjoy thought. Carew and Thomond, between them, could be relied upon to face the Spanish.

"So be it," Mountjoy said. "You accompany me and we shall rely upon Thomond and his Irish royal blood to hold the other camp. He boasts how his ancestor, Brian Boru, defeated the Vikings. There is no great difference between the Spanish and them. Both are marauding pirates, so he should be up to the task."

Wingfield smiled.

"But come," Mountjoy exhorted, mounting the horse, which his sentry had brought him, "we must not waste any more time. To our stations."

"But Sir Charles," Carew said, "You will have too few men. You leave Thomond and me four thousand, while your combined force will be just eleven hundred men, against five thousand Irish."

Mountjoy replied. "There must be no general alarm. The Spanish must not see us drawing off any forces. Should they do so, they would attack immediately. I shall have enough men. Do not forget that I shall have the horse with me. That shall help to even the odds and I do not intend attacking the Irish. We have already fortified the best defensive position we have in that area, between both bogs. We shall hold it. Let the Irish come and we shall see how they like to attack a secured position for a change. I fear that it is you who shall have the more difficult job tonight, but send for me should you have need."

Carew nodded. "I'll manage, never fear. May God go with you, Sir Charles and you too, Sir Thomas," he said, saluting both men. They returned his salute and then turned and rode away quickly westwards. Carew approached the sentry. "Go speedily and spread the word. The Irish are on the move," he said urgently. "Make sure that the men you send to carry the news, do so quietly. On no account must the Spanish think we are in a state of emergency. Tell our men to keep their eyes on the town's gates, but especially the western one. Go man, get about your task."

He watched as the sentry hurried off. He tethered his horse to the tree near Mountjoy's tent. He would have no need of it awhile yet. He looked anxiously to the east and saw the sky lightening over the mountaintop. Good, he thought, relieved that the darkest hour had passed. It was Christmas Eve and before day would close, this time of uncertainty would be over.

"Why have you ordered us to halt?" Cobos asked of O'Neill, through his interpreter. "We are barely a mile from the town. We must press on immediately. We have lost so much time already, marching hither and thither all night, that we are late for our rendezvous. Look to the east, my Lord, dawn is upon us. We were to have launched our attack before now."

O'Neill turned to face his interlocutor who stood before him, his armour dripping, his beard and clothing, one sodden mass.

"You should have stayed with the van and your men," O'Neill answered brusquely, affronted that his decision should be questioned in this manner. "Tyrell stayed with his men to await my orders, you should have done likewise?"

Cobos ignored the reprimand. "Now is not the time to hesitate, the rain has just ceased." Cobos countered urgently. "From the display of the enemy's matches, there are no more than four or five hundred men before us. Why our van alone outnumbers them. My two hundred Spanish soldiers, Tyrell's five hundred and the five hundred Munster men can sweep them aside. Tyrell is as confident as I. Give us leave to attack. You and your Tyrone men can follow on our heels. Once we're through, we will be in sight of the town's walls and can signal del Aguila and the battle proper can begin."

"No," O'Neill said decisively. "There is no sign of O'Donnell. We must await him and his Donegal men. An army cannot attack without its rearward to second it. Where is he, God damn him," O'Neill swore angrily.

He was furious with O'Donnell. This whole night was turning into a disaster. They had set out six hours previously, in the pitch dark and torrential rain, to travel a mere five miles and yet had managed to lose their bearings completely. Their flanking movement necessitated their travelling over rough paths, through a dense wood. This, coupled with the atrocious weather, had resulted in their present impasse. They had to fight their way through the branches of the trees and the densely packed undergrowth and somehow, somewhere, he still did not know exactly when, O'Donnell and the rear had become separated from the rest of the army. O'Neill was appalled at such incompetence. None too privately, he cursed his son-in-law.

Prior to setting out, they had still not resolved their disagreement regarding the leadership. O'Donnell tenaciously fought to take sole command of the Donegal and Connaught men. O'Neill had heatedly resisted such a stratagem, accusing the younger man of sabotaging the entire plan of campaign. Tempers had become short as accusations and counter accusations mounted. Nightfall had cut short their mutual recriminations, without allowing sufficient time to reach a compromise. Not for the first time this night, did O'Neill wonder if O'Donnell had purposely given him the slip to ensure the necessity of both men assuming independent commands. O'Neill knew that the exertions of the night, the foul weather and the obvious disharmony amongst the leadership must have left his men exhausted and robbed of confidence.

"O'Donnell will catch up with us," Cobos said reassuringly. "We must press on," he begged, "To do otherwise, is to risk failure."

"We are not sure of our exact location," O'Neill said, turning to the bodyguard of horse, which surrounded him.

"Let six of you go and seek O'Donnell out and bring him here to us. Two of you return the way we came, two go west and two east. Return, post haste, with news when you make contact with him. The rest of you, follow me to the summit of that ridge ahead. From there, we will be able to observe the English lines and the town and then I shall decide what is the best course to follow."

He rode away. Cobos paused for a few moments and then, with an oath, spurred on his horse and raced after them.

The intense darkness of the sky had abated and the rain clouds had begun to move eastwards. "See," O'Neill said, "there is no sign of any activity from the town." Dawn had slowly gathered strength, brightness and pale shafts of sunlight, reflecting up at them from the wild stormy sea far below. They could make out the town and the English camp, a mile distant from them, both quiet and unstirring."

"But of course they will not have sallied yet," Cobos said. "They are awaiting our arrival at the agreed location and our signal."

O'Neill was stationed at the top of the ridge, surrounded by his bodyguard and translator. "Look over there," he said. Cobos cast his gaze in the direction of O'Neill's outstretched arm. Immediately to the west, he noticed one regiment barring their path. Coming from Thomond's camp, two miles distant, two entire regiments were moving towards the ridge, upon which they stood. More worrying by far was the large detachment of horse, which was quickly closing the intervening distance.

"How many horsemen are there?" O'Neill asked Cobos.

"Four, five hundred," he said. "We have as many with us."

"Yes," O'Neill said, "but they are no match for such heavy cavalry."

He turned and looked behind him. Still there was no sign of O'Donnell. Why hadn't the Spanish sortied, he wondered. They must have seen the English troop movements and gauged their chance to attack. He saw that the English had prepared their defences well, having dug trenches and erected embankments to halt their advance. He would have to fight the English if he advanced in that direction, but fight them on ground of their choosing, he was not prepared to do. If he had O'Donnell with him, he might possibly consider it. Where was he, he wondered. Why now could he not be where he was most needed? Taking on the English in open ground here in Kinsale had been his idea. Damn him, O'Neill thought. He racked his brains for an alternative. There was no other course open to him. He would have to withdraw, even though that would carry its own perils. There would be another day. He turned to Cobos.

"We must retreat while we can. If we wait, the English might outflank us and cut us off from O'Donnell when he eventually decides to turn up. Our men are tired. We will delay events for another night," he said decisively.

"No, I beg you," Cobos said, vigorously shaking his head. "You must not retreat. That would be madness. Draw up your men in battle formation and we will cut our way through to del Aguila. There are not many English barring our way, we outnumber them greatly. Do not be afraid of their horse. The disposition of our forces will stand up to them and defeat them. I have often done so on the Continent before. The Spanish tercio formation has proved its worth many times in the past and will do so again today. Once del Aguila hears the noise, he will issue from Kinsale and attack the rear of the English army. Now is the time for action. Trust in your men, in your cause," he urged.

O'Neill had remained impassive throughout Cobos's impassioned plea. As he listened to his translator, he measured their distance from the town. They were still too far away. The English had prepared the intervening ground well. Even if the Spanish were alerted by the noise, O'Neill's present position was still too far distant from that agreed by them, for the Spanish to join them.

"We will retreat," he said and turned to go.

Cobos leaned over and grabbed the reins of his horse. "But the further we go from Kinsale, the harder it will be for del Aguila to aid us. We must, at the very least, hold our ground."

O'Neill pulled his reins free. "Get back to your station with the vanguard," he commanded bluntly, "and prepare your men to retreat." He turned his horse and rode swiftly back to join his men in the main guard.

"Well, Sir Thomas," Mountjoy said to Wingfield as he observed the Irish army in the distance. "Why have they stopped? What do you make of it?"

"They can hardly expect del Aguila to come to them there. They are much too far from the town. They seem to be missing one section of their army. I see but two. Tyrell's, O'Neill's and the Spanish standards are much in evidence, but there is no sign of O'Donnell's. Perhaps we should attack them now before he comes up?" Wingfield suggested eagerly.

"No," Mountjoy answered quickly. Wingfield could be too impetuous. "We are already vastly outnumbered. All we must achieve here is to stop them from approaching any nearer to the town."

"But look," Wingfield said in amazement, "they are withdrawing."

Mountjoy looked and was surprised to see that Wingfield was correct. The Irish army was withdrawing towards a stream that ran across the plain behind them.

"So what do we do now?" Mountjoy asked Wingfield. "Is it a ploy? Are they trying to draw us from our defensive position so that they can destroy us? The land before us is certainly marshy."

Wingfield looked pensively after the Irish. They had reached the stream and were crossing it. "The further we drive them from the town, the better," he said at length. "If we do engage them, the Spanish will not hear the battle. They are not retreating in good order.

Allow us to attack," he implored.

Mountjoy watched as the Irish army reached the boggy ground beyond the stream. Should he attack or not, he wondered. They vastly outnumbered him but Wingfield was right. They were not retreating in good order and they were travelling further and further from the town. Yet, he was worried as to what surprises might lie in wait for him out of sight. Where was O'Donnell? Was he waiting to ambush him, he pondered.

"Beyond the bog, what is the land like underfoot?" he asked Wingfield, who had been responsible for a full reconnaissance of the terrain surrounding Kinsale.

"As fair a champaign as you did ever see," Wingfield replied. "The Irish could not ambush us there."

"Then send the cavalry forward immediately," Mountjoy ordered. "Tell Power to bring his men on as quickly as possible."

Moments later, Mountjoy watched his horse thunder across the plain towards the stream. He saw that O'Neill had left a company of musketeers to contest the ford against the approaching horse. They formed up in two ranks. The first rank discharged their weapons and ten horses collapsed under the volley. The horses veered off the attack and retreated towards the advancing foot. They could not put the lives of any more of their horses in danger. They were too valuable.

The sound of the discharge of Irish muskets carried faintly over the hills to the Spanish, waiting in full armour in the streets, near the town's western gate. The men were tired and wet through from the night spent awaiting the call to action. Immediately, they rushed into the houses on either side to recover their muskets and powder where they had left them to keep them dry. At last, their time had come. Some of them looked up at the sun, slung low in the sky, cursing its presence. It would rob them of the possibility of surprise.

"Quickly, quickly," Morejón shouted at his men. Speed would be of the essence. He rushed towards the gates of the town, relieved to see that his men were already congregating there. .

"Open the gates," he shouted, and the men on the gate raced to carry out his instructions.

Suddenly, a loud voice boomed out and he looked up to see del Aguila on the town's walls.

"No, do not open them," he shouted as he ran to the stone steps and hurried down to the gate. He placed himself in front of the soldiers. "There is no sign of the Irish and no movement of English troops in their trenches. The Irish are not where they should be. No one is to leave the town," he ordered.

"But the gunfire," Morejón insisted eagerly. "It is obvious that they are attacking and have been intercepted by the English. We must keep our part of the bargain."

A growl of support went up from the men behind him. They were ready for action, they had been promised it and they would not be denied.

"Silence," del Aguila roared. "Any man who disobeys my orders shall be hung from the town's walls."

He stopped and glared at the men before him, daring them to disobey. Morejón seethed internally, but kept his peace. He knew how important army discipline was and an officer undermined it at his peril. After a few moments, the sound of the gunfire became more distant and faint, gradually dying away.

"It is an English ploy," del Aguila said. "The gunfire is much too far away. The English attempt to draw us prematurely."

"We are already far past the appointed hour," Morejón said. "Can our men stand down?" he asked, angry that they were not to be allowed forward. There was no point in standing idly by.

"No," del Aguila said wrathfully. "We will wait until we are sure the Irish are not coming."

Meanwhile, Sir Henry Power had sent forward two hundred of his best skirmishers towards Millwater Creek. He was backed by the newly arrived regiments of Ffolliot and St John. Shots rang out and the Irish skirmished as they fell back, but made no serious effort to deny passage of the stream to the advancing English. They now passed over it and followed the Irish into the broad flat fields beyond. Mountjoy and Wingfield rode with the horse. "Look, they are deploying," Wingfield said excitedly.

Mountjoy looked and was agreeably surprised. The Irish army had ceased retreating and was, indeed, deploying for battle. At last he would meet O'Neill in open battle, no trenches, no bear pits, no ambushes. A fair fight and one that he must win. They were now at least two miles from the town. The noise of the battle should not carry to it. He looked off into the distance and saw the enemy's rear guard approaching rapidly. It was still well over a mile away. O'Donnell, after his brilliant march from Ulster, has botched the easiest march of all, he thought with delight. Once again, luck was with him. This is what he had hoped for. A chance to face the Irish in open battle, away from the Spanish. And good fortune had sent O'Donnell astray, for good measure.

O'Neill watched the English advance towards him while he shouted to his men to deploy. He could not continue his retreat as the English horse would decimate his men, if they caught up with them, unde-ployed in such open country.

His scouts had located O'Donnell who had taken the wrong direc-tion during the night, continuing to march west, instead of turning south to approach the town. Now, he was hurrying to join them. O'Neill cursed his luck. He must place his forces between the English and O'Donnell until he had time to deploy. In the mounting confusion and loss of precious time, O'Neill discovered his forces spontaneously deploying on the right wing, with Tyrell taking up the centre, a rever-sal of what he had ordered. The formation was totally misplaced. He wondered how long it would take O'Donnell to discover the mistake and attempt to rectify it by protecting the left wing, when he eventu-ally arrived. It was a disastrously misbegotten deployment. His force, being the largest, should have been in the centre, but there was noth-ing that he could do but attempt to hold the ground where he found himself.

It had been decided that when the inevitable battle against the English would occur, they would employ the tercio formation that had ensured numerous Spanish victories. His pikemen quickly formed a large square, at the corners of which stood smaller squares of muske-teers, while other men with firearms formed fringes around its side. His own tercio would number almost three thousand, the recom-mended number for such a formation. O'Donnell would have well over two thousand and Tyrell, twelve hundred. O'Neill looked over his shoulder. O'Donnell was nowhere near enough yet to deploy. They must, at all costs, defend him until he was in a stronger position, he thought. He ordered the five hundred horse fronting his army, to harass the English foot, should they draw in.

O'Neill watched the English three hundred paces from them. His soldiers completed their deployment and both armies stood facing each other. A silence fell upon the battlefield as both armies took stock of one another. Overhead, the steel grey clouds scudded across the sky and a freshening wind broke from the west. Dawn's glacial light now scarred the firmament. The tramp of marching feet was stilled and even the impatient neighing and whinnying of horses had ceased.

In the silence, O'Neill's mind was inundated with thoughts, thoughts of Ulster, thoughts of his father and grandfather, thoughts of his youth in the Pale, with the Hovendons, thoughts of Sidney and Leicester, thoughts of Essex and Elizabeth and finally of Catherine and his sons. It was he who was responsible for this battle. He could have accepted what was offered, like Thomond or Clanrickarde and countless others. For a moment, he was assailed by doubts but they did not last. Thomond and Clanrickarde were traitors to their country. They had changed religion, language, laws, customs and way of life in order to hold onto what they had. The material gain with which they had been rewarded, was not worth the loss of all those other things. They had lost the respect of their own people. They would have to rely on England's military strength to retain what was allowed them. His lot was other, his calling higher. This war was a noble one – one which his whole nature urged him to uphold. With a supreme effort, he marshalled his thoughts. Before him lay his enemy, its horse and its relentless leader, Mountjoy, whom his reason, distracted by recollection, could not afford to ignore.

Why had it to be Mountjoy, he wondered. If only it had been Fitzwilliam or Burgh or, indeed, any of the other deputies he had encountered. He had learnt to respect this man as an opponent. He remembered the battles he had fought over the years, many of them on the English side. He had been young then, just like Clanrickarde and Thomond. They might come to regret their choice too. He thought of Aoife and her father and his own part in the Ratlin Island massacre. This present battle would be a retribution for past wrongs, a final erasure of a stain on his soul, a stain upon his country's history.

"Why do they not attack," Mountjoy asked Wingfield. "They outnumber us vastly."

"They are waiting for O'Donnell to come up," Wingfield answered. "We know that they are not used to such a formation. Perhaps they do not trust themselves to charge us," he added as Clanrickarde rode up.

"What are you doing here?" Mountjoy demanded. "You were told to remain with Thomond."

"Thomond says he can spare me. We both have much reason to avenge ourselves upon O'Donnell so, I pray you, grant me that pleasure for us both," Clanrickarde implored.

"And the Spanish?" Mountjoy asked anxiously. "Is there any movement from the town?"

"No," Clanrickarde answered. "But do I have your permission to stay?" he pressed.

Mountjoy looked at him for a few moments before making his decision. There was no point in sending him back now. He might prove useful. "Yes," he replied. "But do exactly as I shall command." But what to do now, he mused to himself, contemplating closely the assembled Irish ranks, trying to decode from their formation what lay within their minds.

Wingfield, somewhat timidly, interjected, "Let me take the horse and charge them," he suggested. "They are not used to that formation. Five hundred heavy horses charging across the plain towards you is a frightening spectacle. Who knows, they might even break."

"It's too hazardous," Mountjoy replied. "Let them make the first move."

"But," Wingfield countered, "if we wait, we give O'Donnell time to arrive and deploy. Let me attack," he pleaded.

"Sir Thomas is right," Clanrickarde said. "Attack now."

Mountjoy looked across the plain at the massed Irish army. He felt intuitively that he should no longer defer his decision. It was time to act.

"We shall attack. You, Sir Thomas, take charge of the cavalry. I can guess which section of the Irish army you wish to engage," he said with a wry smile.

"O'Neill's," Wingfield answered unhesitatingly.

"I will second you with Power's and Ffolliot's regiments and St John's regiment can attack Tyrell," Mountjoy ordered. "You, Clanrickarde, go now and prepare to attack with Wingfield."

O'Neill's thoughts were shattered by the loud, bloodthirsty cheer of the English horse, which thundered across the field towards him. He, himself, was located a hundred paces behind his main battle, on a small incline where he had a better view of the battlefield. He looked anxiously at his formation but could see no nervousness in his men. The musketeers at both ends of the square, facing the charging cavalry, shot a volley at the approaching enemy. About thirty horses went down but the rest kept charging straight at the tercio. O'Neill watched anxiously and then, at the very last moment, when the English horse was almost touching the massed pikes of the Irish square, they wheeled away and rode towards O'Neill's flank. A massive cheer went up from the Irish ranks and O'Neill felt a moment's exhilaration.

He watched as his horse charged after the retreating English cavalry, cheering wildly. Cuconnaught Maguire had taken command of the cavalry and all the Irish Chieftains were with him. This was where he would miss Cuconnaught's cousin, Hugh Maguire, he thought, as he noticed that Cuconnaught was leading from behind. That had never been his cousin's way, he reflected, watching the English horse wheel as one body and return the charge of the Irish horse.

The manoeuvre was so elegantly simple as to be completely unanticipated. With renewed vigour, the English horse charged again. The leading Irish horsemen never stood a chance. The English cavalry impaled them with their lances, shot at them with their pistols and ran them through with their swords, knocking such light Irish horse contemptuously out of their way. The rest of the Irish cavalry was thrown into total disarray.

O'Neill watched horror stricken. He could scarcely believe what was happening. His horse had turned and was now beating a panic stricken retreat into the home ranks, heading straight for his main battle.

"Go round!" he shouted desperately, "Go round!" but his words were swallowed up in the gusting winds, which raged around the battlefield, above the din of the English war cries. Even if they had heard, his command would have made no difference. He watched, hoping that the Irish horse would veer left or right. "Stand firm!" he shouted despairingly, but the square parted and the Irish horse ploughed through it. Men hurried to get out of the way as they galloped through, knocking over their own comrades and trampling them underfoot. O'Neill watched, tears of frustration coursing down his cheeks, while the English horse followed into the very centre of the formation.

The men in the centre were packed solid with barely enough room to raise their arms to defend themselves. They were there to replace the men who would be shot on the square's exterior. That was the rule of the tercio, to stand firm, to be fired into, to be shot down - and the men in the centre, to fill the gaps - but always and ever to stand. Now that it had broken, it would mean death for those caught in the middle.

He saw the English infantry follow its horse into the channel that had been carved through the square and, before his eyes it broke, fractured beyond repair. He saw his men flee, a disordered rabble, some of them throwing their weapons from them in their efforts to get away more quickly. The Irish horse, still retreating, thundered past him. "Turn and fight!" he shouted at them, but they galloped on heedlessly, leaving the battlefield, heading north as speedily as they could.

One of them reined in his horse and he saw that it was McMahon. His side was soaked in blood and he was barely able to remain mounted.

"Come away, Hugh," he gasped urgently. "The day is lost."

"It cannot be," O'Neill said in disbelief.

"See with your own eyes," McMahon said. "Let some of us survive to fight another day. I think the bastards have done for me," he added and sure enough, Hugh noticed the pallor of death upon his brow. Ignoring McMahon's injunction, he watched distraught, unable to effect any change. He saw Tyrell order the vanguard into motion in an effort to place himself between the English and the remnants of the main battle. Immediately, Sir John Roe's regiment charged Tyrell's flank as he passed in front of him. Tyrell men's deployed and easily beat them off, but they were unable to give any further aid to the main battle.

O'Neill's bodyguard circled him and McMahon again begged him to come away. Hugh watched the English cavalry following his men, their swords red with their blood as they hacked and killed them effortlessly, cutting them down from behind, trampling them under-foot. McMahon was right, it was all over. He could not believe that it had happened so quickly. Why, O'Donnell had not even deployed yet! How long had it taken, he asked himself. Less than an hour. In less than an hour, a lifetime's planning and a nation's future had been undone. His mind was disorientated, his heart filled with shame, shame at how little opposition they had put up when it had mattered most.

"Come away, Hugh. McMahon is right. All is lost here. Deny them the ultimate victory, you in chains," O'Reilly, the captain of his body-guard, pleaded earnestly.

Hugh looked one last time at the battlefield. Already, his men were streaming past him, anxious to get away from the English horse, which was cutting its way through the field in their direction. Tyrell and the vanguard were now surrounded and cut off from the rest of them. He saw that they had separated out from the Castlehaven Spanish and were retreating in good order towards the west, in the opposite direction to his own men, who were streaming northwards. The two hundred Spanish under Cobos were standing rock solid in the middle of the battlefield, completely surrounded by the English foot, with whom they were trading volley after volley of musket fire. There was no more to be done. He nodded to O'Reilly, wordlessly turned his horse and together they withdrew from the battlefield, overtaking their fleeing foot.

As he rode away, he met O'Donnell, advancing on horseback from the other direction, his sword drawn. He raged at O'Neill's men, order-ing them to turn and fight. Fury and resentment seemed to possess his very soul. He swiped wrathfully with his sword at them when they ignored him and as O'Neill drew abreast of him, he swore at him. "So, this is how the mighty Tyrone men, with all their training and prepa-ration, perform; this is how the great general, O'Neill, wins battles," he vociferated, his voice almost incoherent with rage.

O'Neill reined in his horse momentarily. "And I see the Donegal men are winning the race," he answered bitterly. "They will not have played any part in this day's disaster, neither good nor bad. That is the real shame."

He spurred his horse again and continued his flight. O'Donnell turned and looked behind him and saw that he was right. His own men, unnerved by what had happened to O'Neill's troops, had turned and were fleeing too. He howled in frustration, unable to believe his eyes. His own men were leaving, without having fired a single shot or having struck a single blow. He turned back again to the scene of utter heartbreak in front of him. He saw the English horse drawing ever closer to him. One of his Gallowglass leaders, Mac Sweeney na dTuadh, seized him by the arm.

"Come away, the day is lost," he said urgently, "we must save our men if we can."

He hesitated for a moment, looking at the scene in front of him. The Spanish, under Cobos, were still holding their ground, two hundred desperate men surrounded by hundreds of English, while Tyrell's force had managed to reach a hill on the west of the battlefield. There were, perhaps, three hundred of the main battle who had managed to reform, holding the centre of the field, but they were also surrounded by English foot and horse. Elsewhere, all was mayhem; the English horsemen were riding freely over the field in pursuit of the fleeing Irish, cutting them down as they ran, as easily as if they were swatting flies. He felt the scene before him being etched, deep into his memory and as long as he lived, he would not forget it. Despair seized him. It could not end like this, he thought. He could not endure it. There was nothing left for him if they failed. He would prefer to die rather than live with this defeat. Everything was lost. He had wagered all and all was gone. With a mighty roar, he rode to face the English.

Almost immediately, he was surrounded by his own horsemen. "No, Hugh Roe, it would be certain death," Mac Sweeney na dTuadh said to him as he caught hold of his horse's reins. "It would be an empty gesture and will not change anything. The battle is lost. It would be the coward's way out," he said forcibly.

"The coward's way!" O'Donnell asked in amazement. "To die facing one's enemies on the battlefield?"

"Yes," Mac Sweeney countered with spirit, "when the future is so uncertain and when your people have dire need of you. You cannot forsake them, they need you, now more than ever."

They remained motionless for a few moments, Mac Sweeney still holding the reins of O'Donnell's horse. Finally, Hugh Roe nodded limply to him. Mac Sweeney released his grip of the reins. Hugh Roe turned away from the battlefield, tears of misery running down his cheeks and then rode after the fleeing men into the cruel harshness of this new day.

Just before noon, Mountjoy's three regiments marched triumphantly back to the main English camp outside Kinsale. Mountjoy, Wingfield and Clanrickarde sought Carew out. On seeing them approach, he rushed to them.

"Well?" Carew he asked anxiously. "How went it? Had you much difficulty in holding them off?"

Mountjoy smiled broadly. "Better than we could have ever hoped," he replied. "The Irish are defeated. We need only concern ourselves with the Spanish from now on."

"Defeated?" Carew asked in disbelief. "But how can that be? You were so few in comparison to them."

"A miracle," Mountjoy answered. "A miracle, aided by the horse, led by Sir Thomas. Their forces are routed. I'm sure that they're half way back to Ulster by now, given the haste in which they ran away."

"O'Neill and O'Donnell seem to have escaped, damn their souls," Wingfield said disappointedly. "They were not found among the dead."

"And are there many casualties?" Carew asked.

"Very few on our side. We lost more horses than men. We have counted twelve hundred Irish dead on the battlefield. Our horse followed them as far as it could. As the animals are half starved, we had to abandon the pursuit after a mile. Otherwise, we would have killed many more," Mountjoy answered.

"It truly is a miraculous day," Carew said looking at the prisoners whom they had brought with them. He was pleased to see Spanish soldiers among the Irish captives. "The Spanish?" he asked. "You destroyed them?"

"Yes," Mountjoy answered. "However, they acquitted themselves with honour. They fought until three quarters of their number were dead and the rest wounded." He turned to one of his officers. "Pick out three who can walk and send them into the town to tell their countrymen of how poorly their allies fought today and of how they have run away," he ordered. "Put the rest of the Spanish under guard and start hanging the Irish. I want every one of them hanged, all three hundred. They deserve no less."

The officer nodded and went about his task.

"But how can you be sure that they will not regroup and return?" Carew asked in concern.

"Because we defeated them utterly," Clanrickarde answered in buoyant mood.

"They threw their guns away, so anxious were they to escape," Mountjoy said. "We collected over two thousand arms from the battlefield."

"We've also taken control of their camp, all their baggage and food. We'll have a feast to celebrate tonight," Wingfield added.

"Yes," Mountjoy said, "a celebration is very much in order. Have the musketeers fire a feu-de-joie."

The musketeers were lined up and they discharged their weapons into the skies, while the rest of the army shouted triumphantly, relieved at last that they would be free to receive food and stores once more and that they would no longer be confined to their camps and trenches.

Inside the town, the musket fire echoed loudly through the streets. The Spanish soldiers were still waiting, even though most of them were, by now, seated in an attempt to sleep after their night of vigil. Morejón leaped to his feet, coming quickly out of the shallow slumber, into which he had fallen.

"To arms!" he shouted. "To arms!"

He rushed towards the gates and he saw del Aguila stumble out of a house beside it, looking dishevelled and half-asleep. He stood near the gate as the men assembled, shaking themselves as they attempted to prepare for the upcoming battle. Morejón looked at del Aguila, half expecting him to find some other reason not to attack, but he was wrong.

"Open the gate!" del Aguila shouted at the guards and slowly the large gates creaked open.

"May God go with you," del Aguila called out as his men streamed out into the green fields beyond. Morejón was one of the first through the gates and he took up his position to its right. As it was now day, almost noon, they had decided to form the Spanish tercio to attack the English, but the sight that greeted him caused him to halt in shock. His men continued to pour out the gates and soon all two and a half thousand stood lined up, under the town's walls, looking at the enemy's position.

The English were flaunting the standards, which they had captured from the Castlehaven Spanish, waving them triumphantly in their direction. They could see no sign of the Irish, except for the wretches who were being hanged in front of their very eyes. They saw three men approaching them, all Spanish, and each one wounded.

"It's all over," the leading one shouted at them. "The Irish ran away and left us alone on the battlefield. There will be no aid from them."

Morejón looked at the English army and horse, drawn up to face them. He cursed viciously. That had been the battle earlier. Once again, del Aguila's caution had cost them dear. There was nothing for it now. They would have to retreat within the town. With a heavy heart, he gave the order. A loud, mocking cheer rang out from the English ranks as they saw them returning to safety behind the walls.

The fleeing Irish did not stop until they reached Inishshannon, eight miles to the northwest of the Bandon River. There, O'Neill stopped to confer with what was left of his allies. They met under a large oak tree, while their army rested nearby, huddled together in dispirited groups in the freezing cold of the winter evening. O'Neill had only eight hundred of his men with him; the rest were either dead, scattered or captured. O'Donnell's forces had survived, almost unscathed, being too quick off the mark for the English to inflict much damage upon them. Tyrell was missing. He had withdrawn in a different direction and they had been unable to make contact with him.

All of those present were still shocked, desperately trying to comprehend what had gone awry.

"Why did your men not stand for longer?" O'Donnell asked angrily, his eyes ablaze.

"If you had been there on time, you'd have seen it yourself and would not need to ask," O'Neill answered dourly. "It is over. Appropriating blame now will gain us nothing. The important question is what should we do next?"

One of the Connaught men, O'Rourke, stood up. "We must go back. We still have an army. We can surround them once again, follow your plan and starve them out."

Many of the Connaught and Donegal men nodded in agreement as they looked at Hugh Roe. O'Donnell grasped at this possible straw of comfort. He could not face the prospect of failure. Anything, but that. Perhaps O'Neill was right after all. Starve them out, yes, they could try that.

"It seems to be the only alternative left," he said.

O'Neill looked at them all in disbelief. How could they be so wilfully blind? Did they not realise that everything, which they had fought for over the last eight years was lost irrevocably? Their epic march to Kinsale, against the odds, through floods, snow and hostile territory, had been for naught. And when the odds had swung in their favour, they had thwarted them and handed Mountjoy a glorious victory against all probability. He could not blind himself to the facts. He had tried, and God knew that he had tried his best, to drag his people forward to embrace a better vision of themselves, but he had failed. Now, in the face of the failure that these countrymen ordained in refusing to follow his counsel, they had the temerity to suggest adopting the tactic that he had vainly urged them to embrace. The irony of such a gesture cut him to the quick.

Divisions, always divisions. If the country had risen, then victory would have been undeniable. It has always been the same story, he thought, the English united, the Irish in discord. Their refusal to recognise any central authority was the problem, curse and cause of failure. Try as he had, he could not instil in them loyalty like that which the English felt for England. Yes, there was an Irish people, but there was not an Irish kingdom. Even at Kinsale, there had been many Irish prepared to fight with the enemy, he reflected broodingly. Aware that they were still awaiting his reply, he answered. "It is over. One brief interlude has decided our future and the future of this island forever. The best we can hope for now is that the English give us fair terms. How can we go back to Kinsale without an army, without a camp, without a reputation, without the support of the people, without adequate weapons, our morale destroyed? The future now lies in our coming to some sort of accommodation with the English."

O'Donnell leaped to his feet. He could not believe that O'Neill could speak thus. "It's not over, we must fight on," he railed dementedly. "More Spanish aid will arrive, we can yet win, we must fight on."

O'Neill shook his head. "The world does not owe us a living. The Spanish can fight on or not, as they see fit," he said. "Now, I must try and guide my people to accept English ways and laws. It will be the only way to survive into the future. Perhaps I should have done that at the start and saved all this carnage. Our reputation is gone. All the uncommitted Chiefs now know which side they should back. They are, even now as we speak, rushing in to congratulate Mountjoy. Worse still, our own allies will be scrambling to change sides. When the news reaches Ulster, many of them will hasten to seek terms from Dowcra."

O'Donnell shook his head wildly. "You exaggerate! It is only one battle, the first we have lost since we started this war!" he cried desperately.

"But this was the only one that counted," O'Neill countered brutally." In losing it, we have lost the war and had you followed my counsel, our destiny could have been different."

He realised, as he said it, that he was not being fully honest. He had always known that no war was ever won without taking the offensive. While all the Continent of Europe stood watching and when Ireland was fighting for its life, he had failed to ensure that his men stayed on the field until the last blow was struck. All their former success was now erased.

"I have done as much as I can," he said wearily to O'Donnell. "I fought on, even though the English had offered us good terms, because I believed that we could win our freedom with Spanish help.

That dream died here today. Unless we return to our lands with all possible haste, we will not be able to cross the country safely. Remember the destruction we inflicted on our march south? The clans, whom we attacked, are not going to allow us pass, unmolested. Let us move quickly northwards and salvage what we can."

A murmur of agreement passed through the gathered nobles. O'Donnell looked aghast. Then one of his priests, a Jesuit, Fr. MacDuff spoke. "And what terms will you accept from the English heretics?" he demanded indignantly. "The outlawing of the one true faith?"

Hugh's anger spilled over and with it, all the gall and spleen, which he had long struggled to hold back. "And where was your God today?" he asked bitterly. "Why did He allow the heretics to win?"

The priest crossed himself. "Look into your soul and the darkness that must reside therein," he said ominously. "The victory of the few over the many could not have occurred without His intercession. It is His judgement of you. Mend your ways, heed His warning."

"Remove that priest from my sight before I acquaint him with his maker," O'Neill thundered.

"You need not give yourself the trouble," the priest retorted, shaking off the hands of O'Neill's bodyguards who had rushed to remove him. "I will travel to Castlehaven and request a passage to Spain, where religion is held in proper reverence."

O'Donnell spoke. "All my strongholds are in English hands. I will not be reduced to the status of a mere outlaw, without a bed to call my own. I cannot accept it, I will not accept it. I too will cross to Spain and will persuade King Philip to send more aid, but to Donegal."

O'Neill looked closely at O'Donnell. His fanaticism had often disturbed him and he wondered now if defeat had finally unhinged his mind. "You are needed here," he said gruffly. "If the King sends more men, it will be to Munster, but I doubt that del Aguila will hold out much longer. He said he would have to surrender, if we did not relieve him by today. Now that we are defeated, he can seek terms with a clear conscience. It will be all over before you reach Spain."

O'Donnell looked at him but appeared not to register either his presence or his words. He then turned to his brother, Rory. "You must lead our men back to Donegal and do what you can to hold our position there. I will take twenty men with me," he said and then turned and walked away.

O'Neill watched him leave, feeling that this would be the last time that he would ever lay eyes upon him. He understood his need to believe the dream. Reality's bleakness was too bitter a cup for him to sup. But O'Neill knew too that they had not kept their promise to the

King. He would never trust them again. O'Donnell's journey would be an exercise in futility. He looked around at his own dishevelled band of men. They would need to get on the march immediately and try to outstrip the news on its journey northwards. He would give it out that Mountjoy was defeated and that del Aguila and O'Donnell had moved their army to invest Cork. It might just work.

There was one last thing that he must do before departing. He would have to communicate his intentions to del Aguila. This one, simple task now exercised his whole being. How? What words could ever evoke the magnitude of their failure? How could syntax bear the burden of such a loss? Where would he begin and how would he conclude? Heartache and despair assailed him with blows more trenchant than any he had ever endured upon the field of battle or, indeed, of life. His breath came fast in short, sharp, piercing stabs. This burden seemed to crush his very spirit. The spectre of defeat reared up again and desolation swept the very corners of his soul. Perhaps, those most at ease were the supine figures upon the plains outside Kinsale, he thought. For a moment he yearned for death. He could feel history's judgement upon him and he shuddered involuntarily. He would have to face Catherine, his sons, his people, but most of all his broken, bruised and beaten self. How could one live without hope or pride or heritage? How could he live, his dream destroyed, interred in vaults forever sealed by history?

He looked up and saw the grey landscape stretching out before him, grey skies, grey mountains, dissolving into steel grey bitter sea. He turned to one of his officers.

"Get the men ready to march," he said. "We are going home. And fetch me my scribe. I must send a message to del Aguila."

Epilogue

Del Aguila continued hostilities for another week, making daily sorties, to no avail. He then surrendered to Mountjoy on very generous terms. Del Aguila and three thousand six hundred Spanish troops were repatriated safely to Spain, without ransom or massacre. When he reached Spain, he was put under house arrest and died there before he could be brought to trial.

O'Donnell travelled to Spain and died there, eight months later without securing any further aid from Spain. In Ireland, after Kinsale, the fighting did not end. In the year following, Ireland sank into a state of darkness and ruin and famine spread across the land. One by one, O'Neill's allies made peace with the Queen until O'Neill was left fighting on his own. Eventually, O'Neill was persuaded to surrender to Mountjoy, which he did on March 30th.1603

O'Neill and Mountjoy became good friends and under the peace agreement, O'Neill became the custodian of law and order in Ulster. Rory O'Donnell inherited his brother, Hugh Roe's lands and was awarded an Earldom. Niall Garve received nothing for his services. Both O'Neill and O'Donnell increased their personal estates but lost all political power.

In March 1605, Sir Arthur Chichester became Deputy Viceroy and immediately set about undermining O'Neill and making his position untenable. As a result, he and Rory O'Donnell decided to flee the country. On Friday, September 14th 1607, they sailed away from their country forever, along with ninety-seven of their followers. The English effectively prevented them from receiving asylum in any country other than the Vatican, where the Pope welcomed them and gave them a large house for their use. It had been their wish to settle in Spain but King Philip would not permit them to do so, as he was still at peace with England. O'Neill spent the rest of his lifetime plotting an invasion of Ireland but he died on July 20th 1616, his dream unrealised. The English used his absence to confiscate his lands and the lands of the other nobles who had fled to Europe and their territories were given to Protestant settlers from Scotland in what became known as the Plantation of Ulster in 1609.

Mountjoy returned to England in 1603 and married Penelope Devereux. He died two years later. Cormac O'Neill did not depart the country during the Flight of the Earls and petitioned the English for his brother's lands. He was sent to the Tower of London for his audacity and never returned to Ireland.

In 1609, The O'Doherty, who had fought with the English throughout the Nine Years War, rebelled and was defeated. Ineen Dubh had her revenge on Niall Garve by implicating him in O'Doherty's rebellion. He and his son, Neachtan were sent to the Tower of London. Twenty years later, Niall Garve died there. Neachtan was never released.